OUT AT KEATON

by

H. B. Bowen

MKA

Makall Publishing

Permissions and acknowledgements at the end of the book.

Printed in the United States of America

Library of Congress Cataloging-in-Publication Data
Names: Bowen, Harry, author.
Title: Out at Keaton: a novel / by Harry Bowen
Description: First edition. Tifton, GA: Makall Publishing, 2020
ISBN 9781735305509 (ebook)
ISBN 9781735305516 (pbk)
ISBN 9781735305523 (hbk)

Cover design by Mitch Green
Editing and Layout by Joshua Clements and Shelby Evans
Executive Editing by Coni Holt

DEDICATION

It took thirty years for me to complete this novel. I'm dedicating this work to the memory of the fight in my cousin Ray, for the gratitude of perseverance in my wife Kay, and to the challenge I give Macy, Allie, Bowen and Baylor to never give up. No matter how tough it gets—never quit. Keep moving forward. Never give up on yourself or your dreams.

Love you, Harry

PROLOGUE

It is strange how human beings relate. Sometimes it's out of fear. Sometimes it's out of love, guilt, greed, jealousy, compassion, or kindness, but most often it's a sense just beneath our knowing. It is in our subconscious mind, our instinct, our personality, our genetic code, and in the way our brain tells us how to view the world. And in this vein, it is also how the circumstances we have experienced are viewed as positive or negative.

All of these factors a person must deal with and react to, and these reactions form the flow charts of our lives. But this is the human experience of self-interest. What about the other? That side of life which is indescribable—the soul. The part of being human that loves in spite of itself. That is unconditional in being able to give to all and accept each of life's creations for what they are. No more no less.

Blended into all this is a drive called survival, and the jigsaw puzzle is not quite complete without it. But survival for what purpose? There is but one reason to live, and everyone intuitively knows what this is. Yet most spend our entire lives searching for that which stares us directly in the face each day.

The idea for *Out At Keaton* came to me in the late 80s. At thirty-six, I found myself sitting in front of a computer. I had not been writing in years. Working as a pharmacist and raising children was challenging, and for me, it takes time and a quiet setting to do my best work. As I sat there staring at the blank screen, I wondered if I could still do it.

The first chapter involving the squirrel was an actual event in which I took part. After writing and retelling that story, I knew that this had to be the first chapter of a book. I had wanted to write one for many years but would get only so far before my desire would evaporate with an adulterated plot. Some paths I went down even in this book had me going in the wrong direction. When I'd see this happening, I would read back over the first chapter and realize what it was that I wanted my book to say.

For some reason the title *Out At Keaton* kept coming to mind. I knew it had something to do with what I was writing, so I pursued that trail. I had fished from Keaton Beach, Florida, with friends on many occasions. I love the Gulf of Mexico in shore and off. I love its wildlife, its purity, and its serenity. I endured many of the storms and rough weather that I write about in the book while on these fishing adventures. Whether it was fishing, camping, scuba diving, or dancing at the Governor's Ball, the one thing I wanted to remain consistent in the novel was its honesty. The story and characters may be fiction, but the uniqueness of the settings and the complexity of the individuals are very real.

As I have stated, the book is written from my recollections concerning similar events. Remarkably to me, the characters of the book almost wrote the plot themselves. I knew the general direction I wanted to go, but if a scene didn't look right, my characters would make sure that it was obvious.

Out At Keaton is a book about the lives of three men growing up as best friends. It starts out in South Georgia in the 1960s and follows their triumphs and tribulations until they eventually go their separate ways. Reaching adulthood in their mid-thirties, they decide to have a reunion by going on a fishing trip offshore from

Keaton Beach, Florida. Unwittingly, this reunion tests their mettle concerning the reality of who they are as individuals and friends.

Out At Keaton

"The wind blows where it wishes, and you hear the sound of it, but cannot tell where it comes from and where it goes. So is everyone who is born of the Spirit."

(*New King James Version*, John 3.8)

CHAPTER 1

South Georgia August 1961

(Summer in Grammar School)

"Come on, he's gettin' away. Wade! Wade! Don't let him jump over there to that other tree! Start shootin' fast!" Karl screamed anxiously.

Wade grabbed a handful of rocks from the stale alley, and slipping one at a time into the leather hold of his slingshot, he fired at the panicked squirrel as fast as he could. The squirrel reeled and turned as the volley of shots cut off its plan of escape. Quickly it scampered, jumping and hopping from limb to limb, back up higher and higher into the tree.

The creature was being assaulted on three fronts. Wade was in the clay-rocked alley on the southwest side. Karl, who kept calling orders to keep everyone positioned, was on the north side just behind Wade's parents' musty-smelling garbage can rack. And Lester, who never could get to where he was supposed to be, was in Wade's backyard to the east. He had fallen twice as he cut through the azalea bushes to get from the alley to the back yard.

"Can you see him, Wade?" Karl queried.

Three heads were cocked back as the boys strained their eyes scanning limb to limb with the anticipation of finding the squirrel in the top of the tree

"He must've got away, Karl," Lester hoped. He didn't have the stomach for this sort of thing anyway.

Karl paused to look at Lester in sour disgust. "He's up there all right. Keep looking!" he ordered. "Do you see anything, Wade?"

"Naw, I can't see 'em, Karl."

"All right, everybody. Just start shootin'. He'll move."

Each of them shot, paused to look, and shot again. Leaf-covered twigs fell from the oak. Rocks ricocheted with a crack from trunk to branch.

"How 'bout it, Wade?" Karl called over to him.

"Still don't see nothin'."

"I think I see him, Karl," said an unsure Lester.

"Where at, Lester?" Karl demanded.

"Well, I thought I saw something move up in that fork toward the top."

All three started launching a barrage of shots in that direction, and sure enough, the squirrel nervously dashed for the treetop. But there was no cover as it scrambled up as high as it could go. In this higher perch, the small tender branches swayed precariously with each flinch the critter made from the volley of rocks zipping past.

Frantically, it shot down the branch back to the main trunk and headed for the connecting limbs of the adjacent tree. If it could get to that one, it would be on its way to the telephone wire that crossed 8th street. The boys' mothers wouldn't let them cross this busy street; therefore, the squirrel almost certainly could make good his escape.

The boys met this challenge by rapidly firing at their prey. Twice they turned the squirrel back away from the connecting branch. But on its last try, the city trash truck that they hadn't noticed came down the alley at the most opportune moment for the squirrel, which jumped into the next tree.

The boys paid no attention to the trash truck except for Karl's disgusted look during its interruption. They were too busy keeping the squirrel from getting to the telephone line. Once again, the small animal took cover in the high limbs of the second tree catching a quick breather before its final attempt at freedom.

The boys held their fire momentarily. Wade and Lester looked nervously at the ground for more rocks to fill their pockets, as Karl, with his slingshot half drawn and ready to fire, searched the limbs for the squirrel.

"Come on, y'all! Get over here! Y'all are going to let him get away!"

The other two boys rushed to his side. He then directed them to their stations.

"Lester, get back by the other tree! Don't let 'em go back over there! Wade, get over on the other side by the little pear trees!"

"Do you see him, Karl?" Wade yelled running in the direction of the pears.

"No. Look up on your side."

"Here he comes!" Wade called out excitedly.

The squirrel dashed down the tree limb connecting the telephone wire.

The move was a suicide mission, and the squirrel quickly found it had made the wrong decision.

Karl stretched his slingshot fully, aimed, and let fire with a zinging whoosh. The squirrel screamed clucking as an excruciating pain nearly slapped its hindquarters from the limb. Quickly it regained enough balance to head back in the other direction. But the feeling in its right rear leg was gone, and it was obvious to the boys below by the squirrel's slower limping pace that they had it on the ropes.

"I got 'em!" Karl shouted out with pride. "He's coming toward you, Wade!"

Wade opened up with a barrage of rocks, but the squirrel didn't seem to even notice. Methodically it ran to the branches connecting to the pear tree.

"Hold your fire!" yelled Karl. "Let 'em get into the pear tree! Let 'em get into the pear tree! We'll surround him!"

Shouting, he berated the ever-dragging Lester to hurry and get on the other side of the tree.

The circle now complete, the squirrel crouched in the highest fork of the smaller tree.

"Open fire!" Karl commanded. The rocks bore down on the squirrel unmercifully. One grazed its back causing it to panic and run terrified back and forth down the short limb it was on. It was amazing that more rocks didn't hit the animal, but when one did, the creature would shriek loudly and then frantically go back and forth as before.

A steady parade of leaves and limbs spiraled to the ground during the onslaught. At last, the crippled squirrel tried climbing down out of the tree.

"All right, everybody! Back up, he's comin' down!" yelled Karl.

The boys were frightened that in this state the squirrel might try to attack them, even though none would ever admit it, save maybe Lester. About halfway down the tree, the desperate squirrel was hit just as it jumped to the ground sending it screaming and soaring in Wade's direction.

A panicked Wade turned and ran the other way as the squirrel hit the lawn. Karl, hot on their quarry's trail, fired relentlessly at the small crawling creature.

Blood ran from the animal's nose as the little gray squirrel drug its paralyzed back legs across the green summer grass. Most of the fur had come out of its tail and the once shiny gray coat was disheveled and blood stained.

Within two feet of the squirrel, Karl drew back and fired the largest rock he had in his possession. The rock struck the nape of the animal's neck causing the squirrel to jump two feet off the ground in epileptic convulsions.

The boys backed up in hidden terror and stopped firing until they saw what was going to happen. After a long minute of screaming and clonic jerking, the squirrel lay still.

Karl beamed proudly. "We got 'em, Wade! We got him!" he yelled out as he shook his buddy's hand.

With all this shaking going on, Wade looked down at the squirrel with a nervous smile. "Yeah we got 'em, didn't we?"

As the two boys recounted how they had made the kill, Lester stood over the fallen squirrel in awe. He hadn't really been in on the actual killing but felt just as responsible for this little animal's death as the other two. As he stood there looking down at the tortured creature, he saw its tiny paws start to move and its eye flicker. Could he help this small animal survive? He thought only as a naive little boy could think. Fearfully he looked up toward his friends hoping they would not see the life left in the squirrel.

As the other two boys walked away, Les bent over the stricken animal. Sadly, he looked at its crumpled body—the blood and bruises. In his little boy's mind, he thought what the squirrel might be doing right now if it weren't for him and his buddies. Guilt surged through his big heart.

Then he heard his buddies returning. Quickly he looked up and knowing they would be angry with him if he didn't shoot the squirrel, he yelled, "It's moving; he's still alive!"

Wade and Karl ran to where Les was, their slingshots drawn full. They shot the pathetic little creature six or seven more times. When they stopped, the squirrel lay limp.

"I bet we put 'em out of his misery that time," Karl said smiling at Lester. He and Wade then darted off to the alley in search of their next victim.

Lester stayed behind looking down sadly at the dead squirrel. *If I just hadn't said nothin'*, he thought to himself.

"Come on, Lester!" Karl yelled from the alley. "We got us another 'un!"

CHAPTER 2

Days of Dreaming

The hot gnat-ridden days of August were fast coming to an end, and the rock alley hunts for squirrels were all but finished for now. It had been a splendid summer. Swimming, playing baseball, carefree lying on their backs in the thick green centipede grass on sunny afternoons watching the billowing clouds float by like lions and elephants against the deep blue sky—nothing much mattered in their young lives. Why should it? There was no knowledge that suggested a need to worry. Only adventure and discovery, and the utter amazement of things never before seen.

Just before school started back, the boys took another interest in their home away from home—the creek. It was located behind Wade's house at the base of the same alley where the boys had hunted squirrels. It was here that the city had carved one of its many large drainage ditches. Running east and west, it and the other ditches in low-lying areas ran parallel almost the entire width of the city finally merging and emptying into a river on the other side of the county.

The creek was a magical place. It was often referred to as the "woods" by the neighborhood kids because it was as close as they could physically get to the uninhabited wilderness of the great outdoors. More importantly, it was a sanctuary from adults—especially parents—and every child's imagination once he entered the thick concealment of the canopied creek sprung open and free.

It was a place for dreams and for dreamers. In their minds, Tarzan and Cheetah could live here, but certainly not Jane. Girls were not allowed in these protected confines save by a miracle only that they might even want to enter this hot, sweaty, bug crawling pile of bushes that their brothers seemed to love so much. So it could be said, and without hesitation, that this indeed was paradise to the young boys of Ridge Avenue. Only later in their youth would they venture out of this oasis of freedom, but for short periods only, to pursue that other enticement in life—the opposite sex.

As the three lads met behind Wade's house next to his parents' dilapidated rack of pungent garbage cans, they each carried at least one sharp instrument. Karl had a bow in one hand, a machete in the other, and a quiver full of arrows flung over his left shoulder. Wade had a sharpened Barlow pocketknife in the front pocket of his blue jeans, a hatchet in a case hanging from the right side of his belt, and a knife-sharpened wooden spear made from the soft wood of a willow tree in his right hand. Les, as usual, was less armored. He only had a dull Boy Scout knife that his cousin had given him in his front pocket and a set of binoculars.

After admiring each other's equipment, save Lester's, the three of them strode down the dirt road heading for the creek. The closer they got, the quieter they grew. The slower they walked, the warier they became. The transition from young boy to Indian brave neared completion as the boys moved closer and closer to the woods. Every noise was a threat, every movement of a bush, a danger. Their eyes cut back and forth to each sound and each movement.

"Did ya hear that?" Wade whispered to Karl who was quietly walking in the lead.

Karl looked back with a frown as he brought his index finger to his lips signaling silence.

The other two boys stopped in their tracks as Karl indicated for them to get down. Squatting, they eagerly looked to their older buddy to see what to do next.

Intently, Karl scanned the woods just on the west side of the roadway to their left. The other two boys, their imaginations running wild, did likewise listening, watching, and waiting. Lester had his binoculars out, but seeing through the thickness of the dense creek foliage was impossible.

"See anything, Les?" Karl whispered back past Wade.

"Naw, too many bushes," Les answered quietly as he continually tried focusing his binoculars on any opening in the thicket.

Motioning his arm for the others to follow, Karl slipped quietly into the woods and headed down the well-worn path leading into the creek's interior. Without this trail, which extended all the way to the very edge of the alley itself, a wall of vegetation would have met them. It was an impenetrable mix of blackberry and bamboo briars, ferns, palmettos, elephant ear, small scrub oaks, and large willow trees. It made a great hiding place for the boys to spy on others who were outside its premises, or to be spied on by their foes that were hidden deep inside.

To make it even more inaccessible, a deep-cut ditch running parallel to the road emptied into the larger drainage ditch below. It lay about four steps into the thicket, and the athletic Karl easily glided his lanky frame across its width. Wade had a bit more trouble with the jump, and Les wouldn't have made it at all if Wade hadn't reached back and grabbed his smaller friend's hand.

Standing in the dappled shade of the creek, the boys marveled at what they found all around them. Tall pines and oaks canopied the area. A little lower were the tops of large willows, then bamboo. These tall cane poles walled the area off making secret chambers and rooms in which they could hide. At the base of it all was the creek providing moisture and nourishment to their secret jungle, which ran half the width of the city's block.

Stealthily they stole their way to a small clearing, their heads turning, and scanning to see if they were being watched. After squatting for several minutes in furtive silence, Karl stood up. Content that they had not been seen he hung his bow and arrows on a nearby tree limb and flung his machete deep into the ripe moist soil of the leaf-straw covered forest floor.

The other boys, now relaxed, gathered around him. It was always their ambition to build something in the woods. Sometimes it was a secret trail. Other times it was a trap for animals or enemies, but more often than not it was a fort, a command center, a secret hideaway, a creation they could call their own. Until now, they had not successfully constructed one. Either the weather, an enemy, or hasty workmanship would destroy any attempt.

This time they told each other it would be different. This was their mission for the day. Now confident there was no one to mess with them, they could concentrate fully on the task at hand.

"All right, look for four good trees," Karl yelled over his shoulder. He turned and headed through the thick brush away from his pals.

"Four trees?" Les looked questioningly at Wade.

Karl, overhearing Les, turned to face the two. "For the corner posts, you morons." Exasperated, he turned to look for such a configuration.

Les frowned toward Karl until his bigger buddy had walked back into the woods. Then, rolling his eyes, he looked at Wade and grinned. Wade grinned back shaking his head. The two of them drifted apart looking for the perfect spot for their hut.

Across the trail, down by the creek, and into the bamboo thickets, they made their way. Each boy viewed the area through his own mind's eye, seeing something different.

"Hey, y'all come here," Les soon hollered from the middle of the woods.

The other two boys quickly made it to where he was. Karl, seeing what Les had found, roared sourly, "Naw, Les, those trees are too big."

"It looks pretty good to me," Wade said timidly.

"There's no limbs on 'em. How ya' gonna lay the walls with no limbs, you fools. That's the dumbest thing I ever heard of."

He paused staring up at the treetops. With a sigh, he looked back at the other two shaking his head and then walking away.

Karl, as usual, had made his point, and his smaller, younger friends, having been beaten up and backed down by him on more than one occasion, let him have his way. There was a limit, however, to what his buddies would take. Especially Les, who had gotten mad and left the other two boys to play by themselves more than once.

Again the boys drifted off in separate directions searching for the "just right" spot, and finally, without much surprise, Karl found it.

"Hey, look! Here it is!" Karl yelled with glee.

Les and Wade ran up to see what he had found. When they got there, Karl continued sarcastically, "See. These got limbs!" He pointed to the branches with a stick he was holding. "All we got to do is lay some sticks across 'em and we got us a wall," he said with pride.

The other two boys surveyed the scene, but knew Karl was not looking for their approval. No matter, the idea of their fort becoming a reality was almost more than the boys could contain. Excitedly, they rattled off how they wanted it built.

"Yeah, and we'll have a door right here!" Beaming, Les stood at the spot where he wanted the door.

"And we'll have a trap door back here," Wade exclaimed from the back of the structure. "And hey! How 'bout a secret tunnel? It'll go all the way out to the alley! We can sneak out without nobody seeing us," his eyes sparkled.

The boys' imaginations were whetted with delight. Now they could create whatever their imaginations could impart. They tore through the woods bringing back branches and bamboo for walls, straw for the floor, and ferns and tender leafy limbs for the roof. Vines would be used to tie parts together. Forks in the trees would be used to lay long boughs across to connect to other trees for support.

Karl was in charge of gathering the larger wood with his machete, and the constant chopping of young soft wood saplings sounded throughout the early morning air. The leafy tops of the trees being hacked trembled and shook as each blow carved closer and closer to cutting it half in two. Then, with Karl yelling, "Timber!" the tree would start to fall, and everyone nearby would run for his life. In reality even if one of these small trees had hit one of them square in the head, it wouldn't have done any damage. To the boys, however, in this frenzied and imaginative state, this was as dangerous as a redwood falling down a mountainside in California.

Slowly the fort was taking shape. The walls were made of long limbs with their branches stripped off or limbless saplings with their tops cut out. These boughs were laid parallel to the ground resting on the branches of the four corner trees. To add strength and rigidity, they were interlaced with thin green bamboo shoots in a binding fashion. The roof was made of a grid of crisscrossed dead bamboo poles covered with ferns, green straw, and bamboo leaves.

Wade was concentrating on his trap door which led to a secret tunnel he had cleared out through the thick briars and weeds concealing the back of the hut. Les was laying green pine straw on the floor, and Karl was adding bamboo poles to the roof for support. All the boys were working hard, but through the humidity and sweat, and the strain and pain of an occasional cut or splinter or bump, no one complained. They were doing what they enjoyed, what they truly loved and believed in.

Each had his own way of working. Karl was the architect. He liked building the frame, making it solid by searching and correcting points of weakness. Wade liked anything novel such as designing the trap door or placing a window in a certain spot to capture the afternoon sun. And as for Les, well, he liked the details. Trimming individual limbs so they would thatch together aesthetically, arranging the straw on the floor to be smooth and clean, blending everything together as a whole where nothing looked out of place was his forte. And unlike his pals, he could do ten tasks at once. Nothing ever seemed to distract him.

Dusk finally settled, and the boys frantically worked to utilize each last ray of sunlight before leaving. At last a whistle came from the back porch of Wade's house. It was the signal his mother used to tell him to come home. Wade sprang up, grabbed his spear, and started out of the hut.

Karl looked up at Wade from where he was tying two limbs together with a vine.

"Where ya' going?" Karl asked antagonistically knowing full well what the whistle meant.

"Gotta go home," Wade said meekly.

Karl stared into his buddy's eyes with an intimidating glare.

"Home? Come on, Wade!" Karl paused menacingly. "What? Ya' afraid ya mama's goin' to give you a spankin' if ya' don't run home right this minute?"

Wade snickered nervously through his nose as he smiled down in embarrassment.

Again Karl started in on him as he looked back at the window on which Wade had been working.

"That window still ain't right. You could at least finish that before ya' go home to ya' mama."

Wade stood frozen, his eyes dancing in the agony of indecision. First, he looked wincingly at the glaring Karl, and then his eyes fell on the warm look of his smaller more compassionate friend.

The whistle sounded again from the back porch of his home. Half-heartedly, he smiled at both of his friends then turned with spear in hand and quickly disappeared down the trail.

Karl and Les watched him leave and then heard him jump the ditch and scamper up the road toward his house.

Karl turned to Les with an attitude of disgust and dismay.

"That Wade beats all. He's so scared of his mama and daddy, it stinks. I bet if they told him he couldn't use the bathroom at night, he'd crap in his pants trying to hold it in."

Les listened, but said nothing as he spread more pine straw on the fort's floor. When he finished and as Karl was bracing a weak spot in the hut's roof with a vine, Les spoke. "Wade's mama and daddy are strict. You do what your parents say, don't ya'?" he asked in his friend's defense.

"My parents are neat. Geez, they never get on to me the way his do."

Les asked defiantly, "You get a spankin' when you do something wrong, don't ya?"

"Heck no. I hadn't gotten a whippin' in years."

"Shoot. You're lucky," Les responded incredulously. "Hey, I don't get many, only if I really do something bad. Like when I was at my uncle's farm and I hit the horse my cousin was riding with my baseball 'cause she was bragging that I couldn't ride . . . and it bucked her off. I got one then."

Karl doubled over laughing. When he righted himself, he smiled gleefully back at his buddy.

"I didn't think you had it in ya', little Les. Way to go, boy. But just think, if your parents had been Wade's, they'd have pulled your pants down and whipped you right on the spot. Right in front of your girl cousin."

Les grinned at the thought of Wade's bare butt shining in front of the girl, and then asked, "So I guess you don't never do nothin' bad, huh, Karl?"

"Bad—ha! I'm the nicest kid my parents know. They better be damn glad they had me."

Karl smiled impishly.

Les stared back, half smiling and shaking his head in disbelief.

Each minute brought more shadows and darkness. Soon they wouldn't be able to see what they were doing.

Fifteen more minutes passed as the two feverishly worked to complete a few more tasks they wanted finished before leaving for the day. At last, it was too dark to continue. Only the warm glow of pale-yellow light from the curtained windows of surrounding houses could be seen through the clutter of foliage now enveloping them.

Everything had grown quiet and still. As if on cue, the frogs and crickets sounded their chorus. Softly at first, then growing louder and louder as the nocturnal music crescendoed through the creek bed. Echoes of the wilderness chilled the boys' bones as the first stars of the damp cool evening spotted the darkening sky.

The twosome sat at the entrance to their nearly completed hut. A feeling of solitude and pleasure overwhelmed the boys as they silently watched and felt the woods transform into the unfamiliar eeriness of the night.

They had witnessed this event from their backyards while playing hide and seek with their friends on late summer evenings, but they had never been in the depths of the woods after darkness had fallen.

Dogs started barking down at the other end of the creek. The hollow they were in and the quietness of the early evening caused the howls to echo sinisterly throughout the woods. The boys looked at each other in alarm as the barking got closer.

"Wild dogs!" Karl shouted. "Let's get out of here!"

They sprang forth, Karl leaving his bow and arrows and Les his binoculars. Tearing down the trail and making a few new ones, the boys charged to the little ditch. In one quick leap Karl was over it, but Lester, who was right behind him, landed short and slid on his stomach back down into the gully. Only by chance did he grab a small sapling to break his slide.

Dangling precariously, he was stuck and at the mercy of the oncoming ravenous dogs. Karl was halfway up the road before he realized his friend wasn't with him.

"Help," came the feeble call from the edge of the woods where Les was hanging on with all of his might.

Karl stopped and tormented his poor friend.

"What's the matter, Les?"

"I'm stuck!" Les struggled to say with his last bit of energy.

The barks sounded again, and in a flash of blinding speed, Karl was at his friend's side lending him a hand. The pair ran up the alleyway together, and neither stopped until they reached the safety of their homes.

Back at the alley hopping easily over the ditch came the two hideous canines wagging their tails. It was Wade's dog Beau, a collie, and Flugie, a neighborhood terrier, both of which had just treed a possum and neither of which would harm a flea.

II

The next morning couldn't come soon enough for the boys. They hardly slept from the excitement about their hut. All sorts of dreams ran through their minds as they lay awake in bed. Surviving the wilderness of the creek for months at a time with no contact with civilization, living off squirrels and birds, and the wild animals of their secret jungle, or even staying dry and warm in their fortress during the most torrential rainstorm. These thoughts and more ran rampantly through their minds in ecstatic bliss.

At their age, the boys didn't know worry. For them, everything was focused on the present. They were not preoccupied with the faults of their past or concerned with what the future might hold. Their minds were free and boundless. They were creative and imaginative. There were few things that could not be done or done with adventure and fun. To them, impossible was just a hard word to spell.

The three boys were up at the crack of dawn and found themselves in the alley gathered at the edge of the woods. Karl squatted down pointing to the wild dog tracks with a stick.

"Here's where they crossed," he mused while rubbing his chin. "If I hadn't come back for Les . . ." He paused for effect. "They'd probably torn him apart!"

The other two boys' eyes grew wide with terror.

"Y'all were lucky all right!" Wade blurted out as he looked at Karl. "Why didn't you shoot 'em with your bow and arrow?"

"They were on us too quick," Karl said. He crept down the sandy lane following the tracks.

The other two boys were close on his heels looking for more signs.

"There must have been a bunch of 'em," Les suggested as he looked at the many prints torn through the sand and dirt.

"Looks like ten or twelve!" Wade remarked.

"Well, they stop right here," Karl concluded at a grassy empty lot running adjacent to the other side of the ditch.

"They're gone," Karl said about the dogs. "Probably on the other side of town by now."

Relieved, the boys quickly ran back up the rocky path and hopped the ditch heading toward the fort. When they entered the woods, it was with quiet respect. Not just for the beauty of the place or that someone could be out there hiding and watching them, but today, just behind a palmetto or fern, a clump of brush, or a tree, there might be a bobcat, or a cougar, or maybe even a wild dog.

With this in mind, they stealthily crept to their fortress. Wade's trap door escape route seemed especially needed at this point, and the boys tried it out over and over testing its effectiveness. Wade beamed with pride as the other two boys bragged on its design and usefulness.

"Hey, Karl," Wade said as the boys finished the last bit of thatching on the hut's walls. "I got a great idea."

Karl looked at his friend as he worked.

"We need a lookout post," Wade noted. "You know, like up in the top of a tree. That way we can see anything that comes in here. Those dogs wouldn't have got close to y'all last night if you'd had one."

Wade hoped this tidbit of usefulness would win his point with Karl. After all, creating and building the unique was Wade's desire, and he needed Karl's approval and help to get the project done. A negative response from Karl and there was no hope for the plan.

Karl and Les both beamed with eagerness at the idea.

"Yeah, we could even connect it to the fort!" Karl exclaimed.

"I know where some boards are," hollered Les. "Mr. Allen's got a pile of 'em out in that grassy spot next to the trash cans behind his house."

"All right," Karl grinned. "This is what we'll do. Y'all go get the boards, some hammers, and some nails. I'll be picking out which tree to put it in."

Les and Wade started discussing who was going to do what between themselves when Karl roared, "Y'all hurry up and get the stuff. Get going!"

Like darts, the boys took off, and they were so full of their great plan that even Les made it across the ditch in a single bound.

"Get something to eat too," came the far away echo of Karl's voice as the boys dashed up the narrow backstreet almost out of breath.

The morning stretched past dinner as the friends labored on their new project. Back and forth down the rocky road, Wade and Les made their way bringing back hammers, nails, and boards. Their mothers even sent them sack lunches and drinks as they smiled watching their sons' joy at working on such a secretive mission.

At last, the project was completed. Boards of all sizes and lengths made a ladder up a small pine that stood next to the hut. Standing on the highest rung, they could lean over to a long oak limb and gain access to this taller tree. About three-fourths of the way up the oak, the top branches and limbs started forking out. A couple of two-by-fours strategically positioned formed a bracing network to lean on as they could peer in almost any direction.

The lookout they had constructed was wonderful indeed. From it, the boys could see almost everything on both sides of the creek bed below and part way across the entire width of the city's block. Except for a few blind spots caused by walls of bamboo or a house here or there, they would easily see their enemies before their enemies would be able to see them.

Each boy had his turn observing the area as the tree stand was made for only one person. The others had to wait on the big branches below until the lookout finished checking it out.

Satisfied with their workmanship, hunger and thirst brought them down to earth to eat and rest. It was mid-afternoon as they gathered in the hut. This was great, they thought out loud. "Just like Indians or Daniel Boone," Les suggested.

"Daniel Boone didn't live in a grass hut, Les," Karl scoffed. "Tarzan and Boy lived like this."

"Except their hut was in a tree," Wade remarked flippantly.

"Well, Indians did, Karl," Les shot back in his own defense.

"Indians lived in teepees, you fool," Karl countered cynically.

"Whatever," Les replied, not to be out done.

The argument was soon lost to the peanut butter and jelly sandwiches their mothers had sent. They took turns slurping down water from a canteen Les had brought with him.

"I bet Tarzan didn't eat this good," Les smiled at Karl as he wiped his mouth with the napkin his mother had put in his paper sack.

"Tarzan didn't eat like this. He ate crocodile meat," Karl said confidently.

"Would you eat crocodile meat, Karl?" Les asked with a disgusted look on his face.

"Of course," Karl said with pride. "It's supposed to be the best meat you can eat. My Dad says it tastes just like fried chicken."

"Your dad's eaten crocodile?" Wade asked in amazement.

"My dad's eaten about everything. He's even eaten rattlesnake."

"How did it taste?" Wade asked.

"He said it tasted like chicken too," Karl said.

"You reckon all wild animals taste like chicken?" Wade queried.

"I don't know. They might," Karl replied.

As Karl and Les lounged inside the hut, full from dinner, Wade suddenly got up and walked outside starting down the trail in the direction of the ditch.

"Where ya' goin', Wade?" Les called out.

"I'll be right back . . ." Wade's voice echoed.

Les and Karl looked at each other. If he had to use the bathroom, he would have just stepped out the front door. That was unless he had to do a number two. But a number one? Well, boys love doing a number one in the great outdoors. There was a therapeutic value in it for them. Call it a mixture of freedom and adventure. And better yet, to boys at this age, it was something girls cannot do. And girls despised them for being able to do it when they couldn't.

Wade returned, but it wasn't the bathroom he sought. It was a sack full of fat ripe blackberries he had picked from the briars by the edge of the alley. As he sat down next to his comrades, he ripped the sack half open and shared his bounty to his friends' delight.

"Hey, Wade?" Les asked as he leaned back on an elbow resting and reflecting, "What you gonna be when you grow up?"

Wade thought a second as he rolled a berry from his palm to his fingers, then to his mouth. "I'm gonna be the President of the United States," he said.

"Yeah," Les grumbled, "but besides being President what do you want to be?"

"Well," Wade said squinting his eyes and thinking hard, "maybe a Park Ranger."

"A Park Ranger," Karl goaded him.

"Yeah, you know, out in California where they have those fire towers and all, and they watch for fires way back out in the woods. And there's nobody back there for miles and miles. No houses. No nothin' but woods and lakes and rivers. And bears and mooses." Wade's eyes sparkled.

"You wouldn't be scared out there, Wade?" Les asked curiously.

"Naw," Wade exclaimed. "I'd have a gun and a knife. Nobody'd mess with me out there."

Karl, who had been whittling a sharp point onto a cut sapling they hadn't used, laughed.

"Nobody, but ya' mama, you moron. She'd whistle and make you come home."

Wade glanced at Karl then quickly looked down at the straw floor in embarrassment.

Les asked with a tinge of anger as he came to Wade's defense, "What you going to be, Karl?"

"A doctor like my dad," Karl said. "That's so I can see girls naked."

All three boys rolled in the straw laughing. Then all decided they wanted to be a doctor too.

Like a shot, a loud voice came from outside the hut down by the creek.

"Hey! What y'all doing over there you guys?"

A stony silence fell over the hut as the three boys looked at each other startled. Karl jumped up and ran out the front door with his spear drawn to his shoulder ready to throw.

Across the big drainage ditch that divided the city block stood a pale-skinned redheaded boy in prissy yellow shorts and a matching blue and yellow shirt.

Karl's charge came to a sliding stop at the sandy edge of the huge ditch below.

"What are you doing down here?" Karl lashed out.

"I'm visiting my grandmother, and she told me to come down here and play," the smiling youngster explained.

"Well, this is our neighborhood, and strangers aren't welcome around here, you got that," Karl blasted back.

Lester and Wade had made it to Karl's side. Lester tried to calm Karl down as Wade stood in the background away from the confrontation.

The redheaded boy was undaunted by Karl's efforts of intimidation.

"I can play here if I want to. You can't make me leave."

Karl's jaws tightened as he glared back at the boy, incensed that this little sissy would dare try challenging him.

"Karl, leave him alone," Les admonished. "He's not bothering us."

Karl ignored Les and called out, "Hey, kid! I'm gonna' give you one chance to get lost before I jump this ditch and beat your butt."

Karl gritted his teeth at the boy as he fake pumped throwing the spear at him. The kid flinched as Karl did this, but once he figured out that this big goon on the other side wasn't going to throw it, he grinned back mockingly.

Infuriated, Karl could stand it no more. There was no way he could jump the width of the huge ditch before him. Instead, he slung his spear into the ground and made a mad dash for the alley. From there, he could easily circle to the other side where he could get to the little prick.

The boy wasn't stupid. Once he saw what was happening, he bolted for home yelling back over his shoulder, "I'm gettin' my big brother! He'll get you—you turd head!"

Karl made it to the other side as the youngster made good his getaway. The little rascal ran hard as he tore through the hedge bordering the creek. If Karl caught the boy out in the open on the other side of the barrier where a parent or other adult could see him, they would surely intervene on the smaller boy's behalf, and Karl would get in trouble.

Karl stopped just as he made it across the hedgerow and into the adjoining neighbor's yard where he shouted, "Go ahead and get him, carrot head! I'll take on the two of ya'!"

With that, the smaller boy disappeared around the neighbor's house and out of sight. Disgusted, Karl retreated up the roadway, jumped the little ditch, and made it back to where his two buddies stood waiting. He plucked his spear from the sandy bank and made his way back into the hut. The other two boys followed him inside where they all took a seat.

"What we going to do?" Wade whispered nervously to Karl.

Karl looked into Wade's wide eyes. "We ain't going to do nothin' but wait."

"How old do ya' reckon his brother is?" Wade asked again worriedly.

"What, Wade? You scared ya' gonna' get hurt? Ya' chicken?" Karl goaded his smaller friend.

"Nah, uh-uh. I'm not chicken," Wade responded, but without much confidence.

"Listen," Karl commanded, appalled by Wade's obvious lack of guts. "You climb up the lookout. I'll take care of big brother if big brother shows his butt down here."

Handing Wade his spear, he signaled for his younger friend to get into the tree.

"Les, you hide out in the bushes at the other end of the creek. You know where Wade can't see for the bamboo down there."

Before Les left, Karl hollered to Wade, "Give the Indian whistle if you guys see 'em coming." He paused looking at his pals. "You two got that now?"

With Wade already in the tree and Les heading out the door, both stopped and turned toward Karl. They nodded in affirmation.

The Indian whistle Karl was referring to was high pitched and shrill. Blowing air into clasped hands where the thumbs came together and formed a small opening made the whistling sound. It took months of practice for the boys to get their hands situated correctly and their mouthful of air blown properly through the opening to make it work. It was loud and effective, and would easily carry the length of the woods.

As Wade and Les got to their positions, Karl readied himself for what he hoped would be the upcoming battle. Taking some of the blackberries left over from lunch, he smeared purple stripes across his face. Then he took off his t-shirt and rolled it up rope-like and tied it into a bandana around his head. A large bird feather he had found earlier in the day went on the side of his headdress. Then, with his bow and quiver of arrows strapped across his shoulder, he took to his hiding place in a thicket of bamboo about halfway down the creek.

After all of the excitement and adrenaline created by the event, the boys were ready. Karl ready for a fight, and Wade and Les ready for this to be over with or better yet, never to start. The sense of urgency to get to their stations seemed all for naught. The smaller boy and his brother were nowhere to be seen.

Fifteen minutes passed, then thirty. The boys were too far apart to consult each other about what to do. So they waited and watched, looking as much for each other to walk up and discuss this matter as they were to signal the warning that the other boys were coming back.

Forty-five minutes passed then from behind the houses across the street at the far end of the block, Wade could see the redhead and his hulking brother approaching. A long, loud whistle echoed from the top of the lookout. As the boys got to the end of the creek where Les was, another whistle sounded from Les. At last, Karl could see his two opponents marching down the other side of the massive creek. Finally, they stopped at the same spot Red had been earlier.

No one moved on Karl's side of the ditch. No one wanted to give away his position. In camouflaged silence, Karl spied on his enemy, observing his strengths and measuring his weaknesses.

The two boys on the other side of the ditch carefully scanned the bushes on the opposite side for a sign of the threesome. The three buddies blended into the underbrush like trees and leaves.

The redheaded boy shouted, "Hey, you chickens! You too scared to come out now that I got my brother with me?" He laughed and smiled at his brother as he started throwing rocks into the bushes on the opposite side of the bank.

Les carefully made his way behind layers of bamboo and elephant ear until at last, he chanced upon Karl. The larger boy, noticing his presence, let him slide up next to him.

"Hey, Karl," Les whispered emphatically. "Look how big his brother is. He must be thirteen or fourteen."

Karl was the oldest of their group and he hadn't even turned twelve yet. As Karl heard Red keep mocking him and his unseen buddies, Karl just smiled. But this was no regular smile, and that's what bothered Les. It was more of a sneer, a sinister grin, cold and calculating.

"I knew you guys were cowards!" the pale-skinned boy continued yelling from the other side. "I knew y'all'd run when we came back down here!"

With that, he and his brother started throwing a barrage of sticks and rocks at anything that moved on the other side of the creek. Then suddenly from high above a spear dropped into the bank about ten feet in front of the two rock-throwing boys.

Karl and Les were stunned. Wade had been the first to engage the enemy. Almost immediately, the boy and his brother found and attacked Wade with an onslaught of pinecones, sticks, and rocks. Karl, who was a little put out with Wade for ruining the timing of his charge, dashed to the creek's edge for the confrontation.

Like a Mexican standoff, everything stopped as the two sides paused to take stock of each other. Les was the first to talk.

"Hey, come on fellows, there's no need for all of this," he pleaded to both sides.

The redhead, full of confidence with his brother standing next to him, exclaimed, "He started it," pointing at Karl.

"You been messing with my little brother," the older boy growled in Karl's direction.

Karl stared at the bigger boy defiantly, feeling no pressure to respond until he wanted to.

The big brother continued chastising Karl. "You ever give my brother any lip again, and I'll whip your tail, you little punk! You got that?"

Karl's eyes never left the older boy's as he listened, then spoke, "I'll tell that little redheaded turd whatever I want to, you big fat queer!"

Like a shot fired from the enraged older brother's hand came a huge clay rock, which went whizzing just inches by Karl's head, but Karl did not flinch. In a single motion, he drew a feathered arrow from his quiver directly into the string of his outstretched bow. Lester watched in horror as everything including his pleas of "No! Don't!" seemed in still-framed slow motion.

As Les desperately reached out to stop the shot, Karl easily nudged his lunging unbalanced friend to the ground. He aimed again.

"Karl! No!" Lester yelled again as he looked back up from the ground. It was too late. Helplessly he watched as Karl released the arrow. Unable to see it score from his awkward position, he heard the zinging swoosh and horrible thud of the arrow making contact with its target.

Closing his eyes in pain and shock, he then rolled over. Slowly opening them, he saw what had happened—the arrow was just two inches from the older brother's head.

The small boy and his brother took flight, never once looking back as they ran as hard and fast as they could go.

Wade helped Les to his feet. Running to the other end of the creek pursuing his vanquished enemy, Karl hurled insults at them as far and as loud as he could.

Wade smiled at Les nervously, "I guess we showed them, didn't we?" Blood trickled from a small cut on Wade's ear made by a thrown stick.

Les looked across the creek at the arrow buried deep into the trunk of a pine. Then he stared back at Wade and said nothing.

CHAPTER 3

The Struggle Unrealized

(*School* 1969 - 1972)

Life did not tarry for the boys growing up in South Georgia. It never does for young people anywhere. Just ask their parents whose deeds never seem to catch up with their good intentions of doing this or that for their children. Yet most survive; it appears. Even though appearances can sometimes be deceiving.

From the early sixties until the time the boys graduated at the beginning of the seventies many things happened. On a historical note, two cataclysmic events occurred that shook their way of life to the very core: the civil rights movement and the Vietnam War.

It is an understatement to say everyone is a product of his or her time. People in the 1960s thought their world was turned upside down by these two episodes of strife and turmoil. All one has to do, however, is to look back a hundred years to the 1860s and the Civil War to see that those people found themselves trapped in time by circumstances as well

Unlike Les and Wade, Karl had been relatively unfazed by the events of their time. Karl could handle almost anything and could survive anywhere. His pronounced "me first, you last" attitude would allow him to live at the South Pole and prosper.

Karl was a member of the Beta Club and made straight A's throughout his school career except for one B, which cost him the coveted position of valedictorian of his class. That went to a scrawny bookworm named Marion, and Karl was incensed over this.

Unlike Karl, Marion had not lettered in two separate sports for four straight years. Nor had he attained the status of All-State linebacker his senior year. No, Marion sat home every night burning the midnight oil just so he could knock the strong, handsome Karl out of the top dog spot of academics and accept the glory all for himself. At least that's how Karl viewed it, and he scoffed and scowled every time Marion came in contact with him, torturing the poor frail boy for beating him.

Even with all the accomplishments Karl had compiled, he still had to deal with the times in which he lived. Unlike others who got sucked along by whatever was happening, Karl usually dealt with life on his own terms.

It was the first year of integration at the high school, and Black students were marching through the school to show White students they demanded respect. Karl was leaning against the hallway wall next to his English classroom reviewing notes for a test that he would soon have to take when he heard the loud commotion coming his way. Unperturbed he kept reading his notes.

Karl had no concern with racial issues. His goal today was to beat Marion's score on this test. Unfortunately for those involved as they passed by yelling and chanting, someone reached out and slapped the burly White boy in the face. Flushed with anger, Karl punched the student to the floor as everyone in the vicinity quickly got out of his way. The six-foot-three-inch two-hundred-and-twenty-pound All-State linebacker showed no animosity to any African Americans after the fray. But whether students were Black or White, no one ever tried crossing him again while he was in high school.

Finishing his senior year, Karl enrolled in the University of Georgia where he turned down a full football scholarship accepting an academic one instead. He had no trouble making this decision. At the start of Fall Quarter, the handsome, blonde, blue-eyed young man entered college as a pre-med student determined to become a surgeon. Les and Wade still had another year of high school to get through, but unlike their older friend who set and accomplished personal goals ambitiously, these two boys seemingly lacked direction.

Like the teenagers they were, they too often got caught up in the events of the day and were forced into taking sides on issues such as the Vietnam War, race, and drugs. Les, who was thoughtful and laid back by nature, let most of the controversy slide off him like water off of a duck's back. Wade was a different story.

Wade was fairly strait-laced. He fell into the conservative element of school society and was pro on the issue of Vietnam. He, like most conservatives, hated change, and unfortunately for him during this period of time, he became less and less of a risk taker.

Wade came from an upper middle-class family. His father, more than his mother, could at times be a harsh disciplinarian leaving Wade little room to express his thoughts or opinions. This took its toll on the young boy's heart and mind in serious ways. Most of his friends were allowed to listen to the music of their choice and dress as they wanted, while he had no such luxury.

Unfortunately, this mindset of conduct was forced on him rather subtly by his parents. Using positive reinforcement for his "good behavior"—short hair, conservative dress, "yes man" attitude, they also resorted to guilt trips and anger when he didn't conform.

Wade was one of those wonderfully innocent people. He saw only the good in those around him. Even though he learned to be more cautious as he grew older, he was still an easy target for a manipulative friend.

On the whole, however, Wade was waiting in life, waiting to be discovered. He was an exceptional athlete, but when he played a sport, he wouldn't fight for the position he wanted. In football, he was a born receiver with great moves and soft hands, yet he was placed in another position to shore up a weak spot on the team's defense. Rather than confront the coach asking him for a change to the spot he wanted, Wade waited. Waited for the coach to discover his talent and move him to that spot. It never happened. Even though he was touted at the position he was stuck in, he always dreamed of what might have been.

Not only was Wade a good athlete, but he also enjoyed success as an artist and as an above average student. He had the dark haired, brown eyed, good looks of his mother as well as many other positive attributes but coming from an affluent family gave him a false sense of security concerning his future. As a consequence, his drive and ambition suffered. He always felt he would go off to college, get a degree, and then come home to work with his Dad. He gave little thought to the insecurity he felt in his father's presence, an insecurity that transferred to anyone he confronted in a position of authority.

Les, on the other hand, could get along with anybody. He had friends in every group from red necks and hippies to Blacks and even drug users. Unlike Karl and Wade, he had not grown up being the athletic type. He was still a small guy and took a lot of friendly ribbing for being such. It was ironic that even the powerful Karl could not intimidate him even though there was no other person around that his larger friend could not humble. The reason was unknown, except to say that Les was one of those special people whose virtue always seemed to protect him.

So it was that both Les and Wade made their way through the final year of school. Neither gained the fame that Karl had attained, but both achieved a sense of success in their endeavors. Wade had been a solid performer in track and football lettering his junior and senior years, and Les had become an articulate member of the school's Debate Club and a much-liked trainer on the football team.

In the fall of 1972, they enrolled in their community's college. Whereas racial problems dominated high school life, the mood at the college was strongly influenced by anti-war and anti-establishment sentiment and by the break-in at the Watergate Building by Republican operatives. These were all liberal causes that flew in the face of Wade's upbringing.

Any transition was tough for Wade. Getting acclimated to his new surroundings at college was challenging enough without political turmoil quickly destroying his conservative way of life. Even some of his best friends dressed and acted hip trying to gain the acceptance of their new more liberal peers.

For Wade, it had taken years to establish himself in high school. He had attained a comfortable level of status and respect from his classmates over time. They all knew who he was and what he could do. Now all of that achievement was gone. He was back to ground zero at a place where most did not know who he was. The few that did were so busy trying to fit in that Wade was all but lost.

Les, on the other hand, was making friends left and right. Just as he had done in high school, he networked his way into every group. The liberal, conservative issue that caused Wade to struggle was not a concern for Les, and his blend of sincerity and diplomacy made people feel comfortable in his presence. So, everyone ended up liking the unassuming young man.

Taking the same courses, the boys shared only one class. Both arrived at the school for an 8 o'clock morning class and left after their 2 p.m. class ended.

In the college's parking lot, Wade, who had just finished for the day, heard a thumping sound coming from his car's passenger-side window.

"Hey, Les," he said noticing who it was. "Get in."

Les crawled into the car's front seat carrying a pile of books.

Wade looked at him. "What you been up to? I've only seen you in our English class, and you seem to get out of there pretty fast every day."

Les smiled, "Well, I met someone at the Baptist Student Union a couple of weeks ago."

School had been in session for almost two months, and Wade and Les had been hanging out together up until recently.

"A girl?" Wade questioned him grinning.

Les had not been as adept as Wade at dating in high school. He wasn't as handsome, lacking the dark features of his artistic friend.

"Yeah, I met a pretty nice girl over there. You ought to come with me sometime. Might find one yourself."

Wade had been downhearted lately feeling like the invisible guy on campus when it came to girls. The sexual dynamics of college life as opposed to that of high school confused him. Trying to look a little more mod and hip, he now sported a Fu Manchu mustache and longer hair. He didn't realize his problem was his introversion and not his looks.

"Yeah, I might take you up on that. I haven't had too much luck lately. It's different out here than back in high school. All these girls around here seem to go for the hippies or some of those guys who've made it back from 'Nam."

Les agreed. "It's a little different, I guess. Girls always seem to go for the older guys. Even in high school, they did."

Les was well aware of how depressed his friend was. He knew him well and knew, though Wade would never admit it, that his friend was insecure around new people in general, not just females.

Wade interrupted Les thoughts. "All right, boy, tell me about this girl of yours."

"Well, her name is Louisa, Louisa Wess."

"Louisa Wess! Are you kidding me?" Wade was shocked.

Louisa was the best-looking coed on campus by far. She was taller than most other girls standing five feet eight inches. She had shimmering black hair, sparkling blue eyes, and a radiant olive complexion. With a set of long legs and a well-proportioned body, she had the affection of every male on campus. The boldest of these guys tried hitting on her, but she would turn them down with an enchanting smile. Their efforts were to no avail. They couldn't have her, and they couldn't hate her.

In disbelief Wade asked, "How on earth did my best pal end up with that creature? She might be the best-looking woman I've ever seen, Les. Every guy on this campus would love to go out with her."

"I don't know," Les said a little embarrassed. "We just kind of hit it off for some reason."

"Well, I guess you know you've got all the jocks out here jealous. She's all I hear them talk about when I'm at the student center and they're shooting pool."

"I don't know about all that, Wade. She's a pretty girl., I suppose." He tried to downplay her looks. "She lives in Meigs west of here. You know, toward Cairo. She's got three brothers, and she's the youngest one. Her daddy farms."

Wade listened intently.

"She's kind of special—different," Les asserted.

"What do you mean by that?" Wade asked puzzled.

"Well, she's already been voted in as the president of the B.S.U., which is unusual for starters. It usually goes to a guy and usually an upperclassman at that, not a freshman. But she has this kind of . . ." Les struggled for words. "Maybe it's magnetism?"

"That's for sure," Wade gave his buddy a grin.

"Nooo, I'm not talking about her looks, Wade. People are drawn to her personality too. She has this really big heart, and it's not just the guys who notice. The girls also see it in her. She's very thoughtful, and everybody just seems to like her."

"Well, Les. I think that special, different thing you're talking about—I think it's you're in love, son," Wade chuckled. "And who wouldn't be with her?"

Les shook his head with a grin.

II

With Fall mid-quarter approaching, Wade was working at a clothing store after school to pay for the used car he was driving. Les had gotten a job at the school's library.

The boys had not spent much time with each other after the first few weeks of college, especially since Les had discovered Louisa. Other than the banter after English class each day concerning tests, professors, and their other classes, the two didn't cross paths much. But when they did get to sit down for a long talk, Les could tell by his buddy's attitude that Wade's social life had not changed.

At the end of October, Les saw an opportunity to change all of this for Wade. There was going to be a B.S.U. fish fry as a getting to know each other event for the new students. Everyone on campus was invited, and Les and Louisa were going to be in charge. Needing help with the preparations, the two decided it would be a good time for Wade to meet Angie, Louisa's roommate.

Angie was from Broxton, Georgia. Neither she nor Louisa knew each other before college, but when they were thrown together as roommates, they hit it off well.

Angie was not as devout spiritually as was her new friend, but she attended church regularly. This gave the two something in common. Angie was turning out to be one of those late bloomers in life. In high school, her friends had viewed her as a skinny, cute girl. As a budding adult, she was becoming more attractive with each passing year, and her once boyish figure had blossomed into that of a curvaceous, young woman.

Growing up in Broxton, Angie often helped her father run their dry goods store. Her mother, a housewife, took care of Angie's younger sister. Theirs was a middle-class family who lived a simple life.

Angie was not completely content having lived all her life in a small town in a rural agricultural setting. A trip for her and her family was to go a few miles down the road to the somewhat larger city of Douglas to visit her grandparents. At the age of eighteen, she was more than ready for the change that a college experience would hopefully bring.

Being a small-town country girl, Angie was ready to see the bright lights of a big city. And though the small South Georgia municipality where the junior college was located was far from this, it didn't seem to matter. The lure of the unique, and the excitement of the different were almost more than she could stand.

Les approached Wade, and Louisa asked Angie about helping them set up and prepare for the upcoming fish fry. Neither Wade nor Angie knew this was a matchmaking event, and both innocently and eagerly volunteered their services to help their friends.

Unlike Wade, who was having difficulty finding a date, Angie was turning guys down left and right. Almost all the guys who asked her out were either geeks or party animals, but none had suited her fancy.

For apparently very different reasons the two were uniquely ready to meet. Two nights before at an event planning session, Angie was introduced to Wade and afterward, with some sly questioning, Louisa and Les, found the two unattached students mutually attracted to each other. It was with this knowledge that Les and Louisa decided to put them on the same work detail for the gathering so they could get to know one another better.

It was Fall and a gorgeous afternoon on the South Georgia campus. The sky was blue—a deeper blue than at any other time of the year. There was not a cloud in sight. Looking upward, the only contrast interrupting this view was the shingled rooftops of the old faded red brick buildings, which gave the college its antebellum character, and a plethora of green pine needles topping the school's many stately, old longleaf pine trees.

Ambling along students strolled the sidewalks through the crisp, clean air of autumn's wind. Classes were over for the day as many of these young people headed back to their dorms, back to their sanctuaries of rest and security.

Thankfully it was not too cold this evening Les thought as he drove his Ford Pinto down the two-rut road heading for the shelter at the base of the college's lake. Had the weather not cooperated, the event would have been taken indoors to the college's loud, echoing cafeteria. No one wanted that, especially Les, who sought the intimacy that only an outdoor environment could provide.

As Les parked his car and got out, he noticed Angie and Wade were already there putting out tables and chairs. Les smiled as he watched the two laughing and chatting as they worked together.

Walking to where they were under the metal roofed building, Wade looked up and after unfolding another chair grinned at him.

"Glad to see that you finally decided to make it out, Les. What'd you do? Get me and Angie out here early to do all the dirty work for you?"

Hearing this, Les chuckled along with Angie at Wade's accusation.

"Yep, that's how I had it figured," Les replied with a grin. "Have y'all seen Louisa?"

"Yeah," Angie replied. "I think she had to run back to the cafeteria for more paper plates."

"Well, folks, I guess everything's going okay?" Les questioned.

Wade and Angie looked at each other with a shrug.

"I guess so," Wade ventured. "We've about got all these tables and chairs put out. I don't know how it's going over there where they're frying the fish."

"Smells like it's going pretty good to me," Les smiled as he headed in that direction. "How about you two guys lighting the candles and torches for us," he called over his shoulder.

Wade retorted, "Is that all? Or have you got something else up your sleeve, Bud?"

"Check with me later," Les shouted back with a grin.

Smiling, Angie looked at Wade. "We better hurry up with these," she said referring to the remaining chairs and tables, "if we plan on getting all those candles lit before everyone gets here."

For another fifteen minutes, the two worked until they had set up all the folded tables and chairs. Finished, they spread red-checkered tablecloths over each table and centered an unlit candle on each. These were the same red glass cup types used for every special occasion and especially for Christmas events.

Once they finished, Wade stood under the center of the shed looking around puzzled.

"What ya looking for?" Angie asked.

"We need something to light the torches and candles with. You don't smoke do you?"

"Uh-uh," Angie responded looking around too.

As both scanned the growing crowd for anyone smoking or carrying cigarettes, a tall blond headed boy who was helping fry fish smiled and waved at Angie. With a half-smile, Angie waved back cutting her eyes at Wade as she did this. Turning to him, she abruptly said, "I'll be back in just a minute."

Wade watched as she walked over to the guy hoping she would quickly return with matches or a lighter. Talking animatedly to the young man, however, she seemed neither in a hurry nor interested in getting something to light the candles.

Soon Wade saw the two of them looking back in his direction as they laughed and shook their heads. After another few minutes passed with just the two of them standing there, some more girls and boys joined them who were dressed a little freakier than met Wade's approval. From time to time, each one of these students would seem to look in Wade's direction with a noticeable smirk.

Wade had taken a seat at one of the tables hoping Angie would report back soon with some matches, but after this last display of seeming rebuke from her and her friends, he'd had about enough. He fumed that he must not have been hip enough for them. He decided as he sat there that surely she wasn't coming back to help him finish.

As he was just about to get up and find a way to light the torches himself, he felt someone's hand gently straightening his collar from behind. In the next instant, hands were softly touching his head patting down a hair that must have been sticking up.

Startled, Wade looked back over his shoulder to see who it was. With a sigh of relief, he found the most pleasant surprise staring down at him. It was his cousin Ann, who was a year older than he.

"What are you doing here, Kitten?" This was a nickname she allowed only family members or very close friends to use.

"Taking care of my little cousin who can't seem to take care of himself," Ann declared with a loving smile. Ann, since childhood, had always been Wade's foremost confidant. When Wade could not talk to his parents or other friends about his problems, Ann had always been there for him.

She was attractive. To other boys, she had an exotic, sensual look, but to Wade, having grown up with her, she was more like a sister. He knew she was good looking with her long blond hair and hazel eyes, but he just couldn't see her as sexy at all.

As a second quarter sophomore, she would be graduating at the end of winter quarter because she was going straight through, summers included. From that point, she planned to go to the University of Georgia where she would finish with a degree in education.

She would make a fine teacher no doubt. She had all the capabilities needed: smarts, patience, tenacity, and compassion. She was the complete picture.

As Wade stood up from the table, she reached over and warmly held his hands.

"So little cousin, what are you up to tonight?"

"Well, I'm supposed to be helping Les out with this . . ." Wade stammered, as he looked about the place confused.

"Me and Angie," looking around, he still couldn't find her, "are supposed to be lighting all these candles and torches."

Wade's disappointment showed as only Ann could tell. "Ahhh, a new flame, Wade?" she said dramatically.

Wade laughed back. "Not hardly, we just met two days ago. We were put on the same committee to help get the tables done and torches lit tonight. It's no date."

"What then? She didn't show up to help you out?"

"No. We've both been out here over an hour putting up all these tables and chairs." Wade sighed. "She must've got tied up with this fellow she was talking to. Anyway, she's not where she was a few minutes ago."

"Well, you better get going with those torches," Ann said as she noticed more people coming up.

"Yeah, you're right. You mind giving me a hand?" Wade asked gesturing for help.

"Not at all. I'll do the candles and you do the torches."

"It's a deal," Wade exclaimed relieved, "but we got to find some matches first."

Looking across the floor at Les and Louisa, Wade called back to Ann, "I'll be right back."

Les and Louisa were dipping coleslaw onto plates as Wade walked up. Looking up to notice him, Louisa called out over the roar of the fish fryers and the chattering of the growing crowd. "Where's Angie?"

From the other side of the assembly line of lunchroom tables filled with paper plates and coleslaw, Wade shrugged.

"Do you guys know where I can find some matches?" he asked.

Louisa looked around at a boy frying fish. Knowing what she wanted, the student shook his head indicating he didn't have any and didn't know where any were.

Her brow furrowed deep in thought, Louisa brought her index finger up to her lips. Remembering, she broke into a big smile as she signaled Wade with the same finger, "I got some in my car. Hang on."

Louisa came from behind the long line of tables and catching Wade's arm in hers, she escorted Les' handsome dark-haired friend out to her car.

Wade was a little taken back by her behavior. After all, he didn't know Louisa that well, but it sure felt good to be arm in arm with the most gorgeous girl on campus. When they got there, she let go of him long enough to retrieve a large box of kitchen matches.

"Here you go, Wade," she smiled handing them to him as she clasped his shoulder with her other hand.

Wade looked deep into her smiling face still bewildered. "Thanks, Louisa," he exclaimed as his ego turned from the mush Angie had created into the mighty that Louisa now inspired. "I guess I better get going getting these torches lit," he said lifting his eyebrows and tightening his lips into a smile.

Before releasing him, Louisa looked toward the shelter with concern. "Where's Angie? I thought she was helping you?"

"Oh, I think she found some friends she wanted to talk to or something."

"Hey," Louisa called out just as Wade had turned to leave. "Les says you're quite an artist. You mind if I see some of your work sometime?"

Wade flushed as he looked back over his shoulder to where she was standing. "Not at all. Anytime you'd like, Louisa."

Wade was almost glowing as he quickly made his way back to the shelter where Ann was standing and watching.

"Who was that?" Ann asked in amazement.

"Oh, that's Les' girlfriend, Louisa Wess. Attractive, isn't she?"

"I'll say," his cousin exclaimed. "And she's dating Les? Our little Les that used to live across the street from you?

"The one and only," Wade said confidently. "She's crazy about him."

"It looked like she was pretty crazy about you too." Ann said plainly.

"Nooo. She's like that with everybody. You know, as pretty as she is, she's really a genuine person. Besides, even if she wasn't, Les wouldn't have to worry about me."

Ann looked at her cousin fully realizing that what he was telling her was the truth. He was as honest and trusting as they came. A virtue she was afraid would come back to haunt him some day. In any regard, she knew girls, and she knew that look well.

Interrupting Ann's trance with a wink, Wade said, "Hey, we better get going. Here, take some of these matches."

As soon as they divided up the matchsticks, they both feverishly went to work, Ann on the candles and Wade lighting the torches. To their dismay they found that lighting the luminaries was more time consuming and difficult than they had anticipated.

More and more people were making their way to the lake and the shed. Several boys who were in Wade's classes helped him light the wicks to the kerosene vessels atop the metal poles surrounding the lake. Once lit, the torches set off the large pond in a glimmering and festive display of light.

As Wade and his new gang of friends made their way back to the main gathering, they discussed football and found out that they had all played against each other in high school. It was a good feeling for Wade to find students with whom he had something in common.

The guys arrived back at the shelter and located Les and Louisa. They asked if there was anything else that needed to be done. Louisa sent his friends to the cafeteria for more silverware while she put Wade into the assembly line next to Angie. As Louisa's roommate was working, Wade found that it was their job to pour iced tea into paper cups and pass them out to the long line of students and faculty who were arriving.

Getting to Angie's side, Wade noticed that when she finished pouring a cup, she would smile and hand the person across the table from her a drink. She didn't look up or speak to Wade until she needed for him to pour more tea from a large jug into her pitcher or to fill her bowl with more crushed ice.

Wade took the indifference he was being subjected to in stride. He was no nerd who had not dated, and he had been put down by the opposite sex before. Such an occurrence, however, had been years ago. After all, this was not a date they were on. They were simply working together as volunteers at a B.S.U. function for heaven's sake. But it was a put down all the same, and he knew it. He felt he had to have missed out on some clue. He despised a girl who could laugh and cut up with him one minute, then care less if he dropped dead the next.

As the college's coeds came by, Wade uncharacteristically chatted with them all and focused even more on the better-looking ones. This was unusual behavior for Wade who was normally a bit shy, but he was mad about his awkward circumstance and wanted to do something about it. As he flirted with each of the girls, to his utter amazement and surprise, he found many of these girls showed an interest in him likewise. Their telling eyes and inviting smiles gave them away. Oh, how good this did his ailing ego. He hoped the jerk next to him noticed.

After everyone had been served, the workers went and sat together. Wade was one of the last to get a plate. As he grabbed a tea, Louisa called for him to sit next to them and Angie, but Wade had other ideas. He had already seen an empty chair next to his newfound football buddies at the back of the shed. With his cup of tea held between his teeth and his hands full of silverware and a plate of food, he motioned with his finger and eyes that he was going to sit elsewhere.

Angie hung her head in silence, then looked away with a sigh. The seat next to her would remain empty throughout the meal. Louisa looked at her friend sympathetically and tried carrying on an uplifting conversation with little success. Angie sat stoically, talking and smiling little as she ate.

When the meal was over, everyone started drifting away to dorms or homes. Not all the students lived on campus, and only a few of those who lived in town participated in after school functions such as this.

Wade and his friends helped Les round up trash, chairs, and tables for the college's maintenance crews to finish relocating the next morning. Angie helped Louisa clean up leftover food and gather silverware and tablecloths.

The cleanup was taken care of in short order without Wade and Angie having to cross paths. The event was over as was the weekend, rather quickly, and everyone was soon back in the grind of school once more.

III

Neither Wade nor Les were impressing their teachers with good grades. In Wade's case, he was trying but it was difficult. The initial phase of integration had occurred during their high school years. A lack of discipline in the school setting and a lack of motivation among students to excel academically were an unfortunate consequence of this period of time. In high school, Wade had been one of those hated students ruining the curve because, unlike about ninety percent of his classmates, he cracked a book ever so often. Now he had to compete with kids with good study habits who were serious about their majors. In light of this newfound competition, Wade wasn't faring too well.

Les was doing better than Wade, but only by a little. His preoccupation with Louisa was his downfall at first, but as the quarter progressed, her disciplined study habits were starting to benefit him as well.

Angie and Louisa, like most girls in college, had an enormous hormonal advantage over the boys on campus. While their male counterparts had turned into testosterone-laden sex-seeking maniacs who couldn't concentrate on brushing their teeth in the morning without picturing a naked coed, the girls remained calm and resourceful. The overpowering urge to have sex processed through their brains rather than through their glandular regions. With little trouble, both roommates maintained A or B averages in all of their courses.

The next week was grucling as Les and Wade studied and took tests. Though they had not mastered the art of studying, at least they were dedicating more time to it. Their test scores were finally starting to reward this newfound effort.

The last test the boys had to take during this period was in English. This was the only class the two shared the entire quarter, and both had managed a mid C average. The final exam was long and tedious as the two friends poured over page after page of faulty grammar and punctuation that had to be corrected. At last and with a sigh, Les finished his work.

Wade looked up at his buddy watching him make his way to hand in his test. Worried, Wade looked down at his exam. What he saw before him was five more questions, one which involved writing a small essay. Several more people got up and walked to the teacher's desk to turn in their work. A shiver of anxiety raced down Wade's spine as he tried to concentrate on the remaining questions. Would he have time to finish, he wondered.

It wasn't long before Wade and only two other people found themselves sitting in the almost abandoned room. Empty desks where other test takers had sat only moments before were all that remained between Wade and his female professor sitting at her desk in front of him. In stoic silence, the teacher kept looking down at her watch, then back up toward her remaining students.

At last, the silence was broken.

"Time," Dr. Barnes exclaimed. "Turn in your work."

Wade quickly put the finishing touches on his essay as Dr. Barnes commanded, "Turn in your test now."

She stood at her desk where the three remaining students scrambled in her direction straightening their rattling papers as they went. With a look of disgust, she took each one of their exams, and in a chastising tone, she said, "If you spent more time with your lessons, you'd spend less time taking these tests."

All three pupils stopped to listen. Then, like whipped dogs, they humbly left the room, Wade bringing up the rear.

This was the last class of the day, and all of the other students had left the building. As Wade made his way down the second-floor hallway, the echoing clips and clops of his steps were all that broke the silence to the solace he sought after such a grueling ordeal.

Down the darkened hollow stairwell, he descended. At the bottom, he hit the squeaking push bar to the ground floor's metal exit door. Out into the brightly lit sky of fresh air and freedom, he squinted his eyes and breathed a huge sigh of relief.

Across the yard on the steps of the administration building, he could barely make out Louisa talking to her girlfriends. Noticing him, she smiled and waved. Then she yelled, "Ya' looking for Les?"

"Yes!" Wade responded coming to a stop. His eyes adjusted so he could observe the stunning young woman standing across the lawn from him.

"He's over at the student center!"

"Thanks!" Wade shouted back smiling and waving at her. He immediately became self-conscious noticing the other students in the area staring at him.

He tried to get his mind off the torturous test he'd just taken; even Louisa's glowing beauty couldn't keep the exam from polluting his mind.

Continuing to walk across the campus, Wade headed up the steps to the entrance of the center. Opening its glass door, he was instantly exposed to an environment of pounding reverberating music, smoke, and chatter. The smell of hamburgers and fries permeated the place, as did the cracking sound of pool balls being hit.

In the far corner of the room, he saw Les sitting in a booth with, of all people, Angie. Wade acted as if he didn't notice them, but seeing Wade, Les called out. "Hey, Wade. Come on over."

Apprehensively, he approached the small table and sat next to Les. Angie stood up.

"I got to be going," she said in Les' direction. Looking at Wade with a tentative smile, she asked, "How you been doing, Wade?"

"Doin' fine, Angie," he responded in kind. "How 'bout yourself?"

"Doing just fine," she confirmed. She stared momentarily into his eyes. Catching herself, she looked to the side and said, "See y'all around."

With that, she picked up her books and strolled to the front door disappearing outside. Both boys watched her in silence as she went. Wade slid into the seat across the table from Les.

"I think she likes you, Wade." Les smiled once the girl was gone.

"Bull," Wade countered.

Les looked puzzled. "I thought y'all hit it off pretty good the other night?"

"Well, we did at first—then she went off with some of her hippie friends when we were supposed to be lighting those candles, and she just didn't bother to come back. I had to get Ann to help me out," he said shaking his head.

Someone across the room called out Les' name and waved. Acknowledging the person with a wave and friendly smile, Les turned back to Wade. "Yeah, but I thought y'all got back together later on?"

"Yep, we poured tea together—what can I say," Wade said. "But that was about it—hey it wasn't like we were on a date. I don't know what her problem was."

"Well, she's been telling Louisa how cute you are," Les mused with a smile. He grinned, and while shaking his head, he asked, "Who understands women anyway?"

"That girl's got snakes in her head. You can count on that, Les."

Wade's attention returned to the exam they had just finished taking.

"How 'bout that test?" he asked discouraged.

"I think I did okay," Les said.

"Man, I thought it was a killer."

With a smirking grin and a sigh, Les tried appeasing him.

"You did all right, Wade. You always do. So quit worrying sport."

Wade sat pondering the plethora of possibilities if he failed. His expression grew dour as these thoughts cycled through his mind.

Les could sense his buddy's agony. He asked, "Hey, Wade? We got a trip lined up to go to the Georgia-Florida game. You interested?"

Wade came out of his doldrums. "Sure, if I can get off work. Who all's going?"

"Well, we'll be staying at Karl's and Laney James' family beach houses at Fernandina. Me, you, Karl and Laney are going to be staying at Laney's and the girls at Karl's.

"What girls? Does everybody have a date?"

"No. Only me and Karl. There might be some other girls down there, but no one has to be together or anything like that."

Wade looked sternly at Les, "As long as Angie's not one of 'em. I'm not interested if she's gonna be down there."

Les raised his shoulders with a smile.

"I'm telling you, Les, I'm not going if she is."

"Whatever, Wade. I mean, I don't know."

Wade looked carefully back at Les, trying to read his friend's eyes. Unable to discern the truth, he quit. He looked across the room then back toward Les.

"Is Karl still dating Terrie?"

"Yep," Les paused. "Since the 11th grade. Looks like she'd wise up, huh?"

"Hey," Wade shot back. "Terrie's a good girl. Karl doesn't know a good thing when he's got it."

Karl and Terrie had numerous spats over the years they'd been dating, and being fond of Wade, she would often come to him afterward for consoling.

Apologizing for his remarks, Les affirmed, "Yeah, you're right. I just think he uses her, that's all. I guess I'd just like to see her with someone else. Wouldn't you?"

Wade raised his eyebrows as he nodded his head slowly in agreement.

"You know it was kind of strange the way this trip came about," Les continued.

"How's that?" Wade asked.

"Well, Karl came home last weekend and called me up to meet him at the Pizza Hut for supper."

"Terrie wasn't with him?"

"No. She was still in Athens."

Les paused and gave Wade a puzzled look.

"It was odd the way he was acting. I mean something was eating at 'em."

"Something's always eatin' at Karl, Les," Wade said.

"Nah, I think he wanted to talk to me about something important. I've never seen him so fidgety and nervous. Almost depressed. Just when we started talking about more serious things, Louisa came in. I had told her to meet us out there to eat so she could meet Karl. When she sat down—Karl acted as though he's doing just fine. No more somber looks or attitude."

"What kind of serious things were you talking about?" Wade mused.

"Well—we started off talking about how each of us was doing at school and all. He's still making straight A's, of course. I told him what I was up to, and he actually listened for once. He's always been such a 'me' person. Likes to talk about what he's been doing and couldn't care less about you. You know what I'm mean."

"That's a fact."

"That was odd for starters, then he told me what a great guy I was and said he wished that he was more like me—more thoughtful, I guess? I don't know if that's really so true about me or not."

"Yeah," Wade confirmed. "That's pretty true, and you're right. That's strange coming from him."

Les continued emphatically. "I'm telling you, Wade, he was really being sincere. I mean, this ain't the Karl we know."

"What else did he say?"

"That was it. That's when Louisa came in."

"Who knows with Karl, Lester. There's no telling what's going on with him. But you're right. That's not like him. Not like him at all."

"Well anyway, he came up with this beach trip while we were eating, and it sounds pretty good to me. I think we all need to get away from the grind around here. How 'bout you?"

Lost deep in thought, Wade scanned the smoke-filled room of the loud and jabbering student center. Everything grew quiet as he saw the boys had stopped shooting pool across the wide spread of tables surrounding them. All stood looking at the front door. From the entrance to the building, in walked two girls. One was the glowing Louisa Wess, the other cousin Ann.

Smiling the girls walked to where the two boys were sitting. Watching them approach, Wade responded. "Yeah, I think you're right."

CHAPTER 4

The Fork In The Road

(The Destiny of Decisions)

Outside it was cold and wet. The mixture of sprinkling rain and fog blurred the driver's view as it turned everything in sight into the dull blended grays of shadow and light. Like so many situations in life, most things are not colored black or white, but in that range somewhere in between. Somewhere between needs and wants—between what's in the heart and what's not—and ultimately between life and death itself.

The redundant bump and scrape of the windshield wipers were all that was heard as the sleek red Corvette cut through the wet, foggy drizzle of this early morning hour. Hardly another car passed by and the driver, isolated by time and space, was lost in the moment. He settled into his seat before reaching into his shirt pocket to retrieve an open pack of Winston cigarettes. Shaking it with his right hand, he thumbed one up between his waiting lips. Fumbling momentarily, he pulled out his lighter, lit the tobacco, and inhaled a deep lung full of refreshing smoke.

Exhaling, he reached over and vented his window to draw out the fumes. The ride was quiet and relaxing as he inhaled and exhaled each enjoyable puff. When he was finished, he opened the ashtray and stubbed out the butt. Looking up as he did, he turned the rear-view mirror onto himself to check out the haircut he had gotten the day before.

It was perfect, he thought and smiled to himself admiringly. He looked down in deep thought, and when he glanced back into the mirror, a shadow of darkness covered his face. He reached up and rearranged the mirror.

For several minutes, he stared into the fog and drizzle ahead, his eyes paling into the grayness themselves forlornly, but only for a moment. He reached into a black alligator skin box and pulled out an eight-track tape. Without emotion, he inserted it into the stereo tape deck. A wave of sonic sound blasted the car's interior with Steppenwolf's "Born to Be Wild."

Get your motor runnin'/ head out on the highway/ Lookin' for adventure/ and whatever comes our way./ Yeah, darlin' go make it hap-pen/ Take the world in a love embrace./ Fire all of your guns at once and explode into space."

Like a shot of electricity, the pulsating music entered the young man's mind vibrating him free from the temporary depression he felt. Goosing the motor, he kicked in the four-barrel carburetor causing the supercharged engine to roar as the needle on the speedometer read 60, 70, 90, 115, 125, 130.

Into the mist and fog, the red car sped. Like a warrior charging up a hill to meet the enemy, the driver's face radiated an expression of controlled wrath. His teeth gritted into a menacing smile. His eyes blazed with excitement.

In a couple of hours, he would be at the beach. He could hardly wait. The only problem he could foresee was the State Patrol. A sinful smile radiated from across his face as he pushed the pedal even harder to the floor.

Trees whizzed by in a blur as the '*Vette* traveled at top speed. Rounding corners, he straddled the two-lane road. Daringly, he blasted his way through the dimness of the gray fog ahead where an unexpected car could kill him in an instant. The adrenaline, the high, was what he lived for and thrived on. It was his life's blood. And he loved it—every second of it.

He was on the outskirts of Waycross before he slowed down: 100, 90, 80, 70, 60—just in time. As he topped the next hill, he saw posed on the right-hand side of the road aiming his radar gun, a Georgia State Patrolman. Passing the patrol, the driver waved and acknowledged the trooper. He came to a stop about a mile down the road at the town's first red light.

The glare from the streetlights and red light cast an eerie reflection of the driver across the inside of his windshield. A mood of darkness enveloped the young man as he waited for the light to turn from red to green. As the light changed, the red Corvette slowly rolled ahead.

II

It was close to 8:00 on Saturday morning when Wade awoke. Rolling over in the bunk, he gazed at the clock on the dresser instantly alarmed.

"Hey, Les! Get up!" he yelled, kicking the top bunk where his buddy slept. The boys were staying at Laney's beach house, and they were supposed to get up at 7:30, so they could head to Jacksonville by 9:00 for the game. Too much partying the night before kept them up late, and forgetting to set the alarm clock did them in.

"What time is it?" Les muttered as he rolled over groggily.

"Eight. We got to get rollin'," Wade shouted as he staggered to the bathroom.

"Hurry up in there," Les hollered. "I need to go real bad."

Laney James, who was sleeping on one of the single beds in the room, yelled up at Les, "You can't possibly need to use the bathroom, boy. I bet you went ten times last night, and you woke me up every time, you little turd."

"So I got a tee-nee little bladder. Hey, what can I say?" Les yelled down as his bare feet dangled over the side of the top bunk.

Laney looked up at his friend. "I see it still doesn't take much to get him all wired up does it?"

Les shook his head as he uttered back, "No, not really."

On this trip down, the boys were staying at Laney's family beachfront house. The white concrete block structure had been built in the early sixties, and Laney and his family had spent almost every summer there since he was six or seven years old.

Laney was from Jacksonville where he lived with his father who was an attorney and his mother who was a housewife. They were good Christian people who valued their family above everything else. Only rarely would his parents allow Laney to invite friends over without being chaperoned, and this was one such occasion.

Les and Wade had met Laney through Karl when they vacationed with Karl's family at their beach house in Fernandina. Karl's house was only a quarter of a mile down the road from Laney's. Over the years, Laney started inviting Wade and Les to spend some weekends and holidays with his family as well.

The boys, from Georgia and Florida, had grown close over the many years they spent with each other at the coast. The white sandy beach of the foaming Atlantic was like their second home, even better than the woods behind Wade's house.

It was a great place to be as the youngsters rode the waves of the rolling Atlantic surf or relaxed while floating on giant inner tubes just beyond the breakers for hours at a time in the hot summer sun.

When they were younger, it was fishing from the surf, the pier, or the jetties that captured their attention. Sometimes it was crabbing at the toll bridge. It was all about who caught the most or the biggest, and there was always a fabulous seafood dinner that Laney's parents would cook to celebrate the boys' catch. This feast usually occurred at the end of each summer just before Wade and Les would have to return home to get ready for a new school year.

As they grew older, it was looking—looking at girls as the boys swam, fished, sat on the beach, or walked on the shoreline. Finding females was one thing, but doing something about it once they found them was something else entirely. Only Karl seemed adept at this challenge.

"The girls are going to kill us," Wade yelled from the bathroom. Angie and Ann were staying at Karl's parent's beach house just down the road, and the boys were supposed to be picking them up at any minute. Louisa was coming down later in the day, and Karl and Terrie were going to bring her over to the game when they came in from Athens.

"Ahh—they probably aren't even up yet," Laney moaned as he drug himself out of bed.

"You don't know Ann like I do," Wade tried hollering above the roaring faucet from inside the bathroom. "She's got a temper and a half, and I'll tell you one thing, she'll sure let us know—ouch," Wade yelled cutting himself with his razor.

Sarcastically, Les called back, "Why don't you watch what you're doing in there, you moron! I'll take care of cousin Ann when we get there." He slumped back on one elbow as he waited.

Sticking his head out of the doorway from the steaming bathroom just long enough to shake his head, Wade grinned up at his smaller pal, "Wrong, Les. She'll kick your butt."

"Come on. Hurry up in there, Wade. I gotta take a leak." Les scolded him.

"I'm not stopping you; there's room for two in here, you little dipstick."

Laney, meanwhile, got his shaving kit and clean underwear from his overnight bag. Stretching and yawning, he sat on the edge of his bed waiting his turn for the bathroom also.

"Hey, Les," he said rubbing his hands across his face and scalp trying to wake up. "I think I had one too many last night."

"I think you had about five or six too many, big guy."

Laney had the same build and power as their older buddy, Karl. The only differences between them involved their looks and personality. Karl appeared more handsome and Laney more sociable and laid back.

"Hey, I'll tell ya' one thing—I won't be drinking today," he exclaimed. "I'll be like you, a teetotaler, Les."

"Yeah, right," Les said sarcastically. "You'll be a teetotaler till twelve o'clock. Then you'll be funneling 'em down again."

"Nah. I really don't think so, Les. You see, I'm not like a Bulldog. I'm not used to drinking this much."

Hearing the shower running and knowing Wade couldn't hear them, Laney whispered up to Les, "Talking about having a few, you reckon ol' Wade enjoyed himself just a little bit last night?"

"Yeah," Les laughed lowly. "He came down here saying he hated Angie. Boy, ya' sure couldn't tell it last night the way those two carried on."

"If that's hate, I'd hate to see love," Laney chuckled back.

The shower stopped, and Les and Laney grew quiet.

"All right. Next," Wade called out as he emerged from the bathroom with a towel wrapped around his waist.

"Go ahead, Les," Laney responded. "I don't want you to have to wait. You might wet your little panties."

Les cackled at Laney disgustedly. "I hear ya', dimwit."

Steam floated off Wade like a baked potato as he stood in the cooler bedroom. Walking to the closet, he retrieved a hanger containing his gray trousers, white shirt, and red sweater.

Laney got up stretching his arms and walked into the kitchen, his bare feet freezing on the floor's cold tiles as he made his way. "Hey, Wade. You want some orange juice or something?"

"Yeah," Wade called back.

Wade heard glasses tinkling and cabinet doors slamming as he too entered the kitchen area. "What we got to eat?" he asked opening the refrigerator door.

"Not a whole lot," Laney retorted. "Get that milk out, and if it's not sour there's some cereal up in the cabinet over the sink."

The two boys sat silently, Wade draped in a towel and Laney in his underwear, as they crunched down a bowl of tasteless cornflakes. Both of them were still in a hung-over fog from the extensive partying they had done at the Palace Bar Saloon the night before. They were on their second bowl of cereal, when a very sober and vibrant Les walked into the room.

Fully aware of how bad his buddies were feeling from a night of drinking, he taunted them loudly, "Man, isn't this a great day to be alive, fellows?" He took a seat at the table wearing only his trousers and an unbuttoned shirt.

Upbeat, smiling, and still obnoxious, he called out, "Boys, there's half a can of beer in the bathroom. Someone last night must have left it in there by mistake. Y'all sure one of you hearty drinkers don't want to suck it on down for good measure."

The two boys, suffering headaches, winced at Les' loudness. Thinking of that hot, flat beer made them almost want to puke. Laney, knowing what his smaller friend was doing, shouted back even louder, "Hey! If you see a 'boy' in here son, pay him a dollar."

"Waste not. Want not." Les sang back. "Y'all shouldn't have opened that can if you weren't going to finish it."

Laney turned to Wade. "Is he always this sickening in the morning?"

"'Fraid so. A real morning person. I think we ought to start calling him sunshine! How 'bout you?"

"Yeah. Sunshine. That's perfect." Laney echoed back sarcastically.

"Sticks and stones, boys! Sticks and stones." Les beamed at his two friends.

"I told you, son. If you saw a boy in here to give him a dollar." Laney chided him again.

"Okay then. Men." Les chuckled, still being loud.

"That's more like it. Right, Wade?" Laney cracked.

Wade responded with a little smirk as he slurped down his last bite of cereal.

About this time Laney slid a spoon and bowl down to Les at the other end of the table. "Milk's in the fridge—Boy."

"Did I hear you say 'Roy'? My name's not Roy, boy," Les sang out as he headed for the refrigerator. "Hey, Wade." he said pulling the jug out. "How 'bout that Annnnngie?"

Laney and Les died snickering and laughing as soon as Les got the words out of his mouth.

Wade frowned, embarrassed. "I was drunk, man."

"Drunk, hell. You were in love, son," Laney shouted.

Grimacing, Wade tried to explain himself. "Maaannn, you know how it is! A couple of drinks—then any woman starts looking good."

"Bull," Laney declared. "Angie's damn good looking stone sober, you fool."

Wade smiled an expression of sheer contentment. "Eat your hearts out, boys."

Recounting what Wade had told him at the student center, Les mocked Wade by making his voice sound like a whining cry baby. "She's got snakes in her head. I'm neverrr talking to her again."

Trying not to act embarrassed, Wade could only smile as his two friends burst out laughing.

It was now Laney's turn to carry on the whining routine.

"I'm not going to be sitting by her at the game! No matter what!" Laney cackled. "Isn't that what he said, Les?" He and Les bent over double again. Through their choking sobs of laughter and snickering, Laney shouted, "That's because she's going to be sitting in his lap!"

Wade had taken this ribbing with good humor, but his patience was growing thin. "Hey, fellows, enough. Enough already. Let's talk about something else. Like how bad Georgia's goin' to put a whippin' on those scrawny orange lizards from Florida. How 'bout that?" he shouted.

Trying to regain their composure, Laney and Les sat up wiping the tears from their eyes and catching their breath, but each time they looked at each other they burst out laughing.

Wade was done with their antics. Jumping up with his glass, he headed for the sink and started filling it with icy cold tap water. The other boys, realizing their peril, ran for the bedroom, but it was too late. A spray of freezing liquid filled the air soaking a screaming Laney as he dashed for the doorway.

"Ahhh! You bastard!" Laney cried out as the cold air and ice water froze his spine. "I'll get you, you asshole!" The bedroom door slammed shut. Wham!

As Wade stood on the other side of the door, he realized that the room inside had grown strangely quiet. The other two boys were up to something, but what? He knew he would have to find a way to retaliate. Feverishly, he scanned the room for anything, but found nothing—it would have to be water. Quickly, he filled two glasses then waited at the right-hand side of the closed bedroom door.

Several minutes passed before he heard Laney's crybaby whining voice singing out. "Oh, Wade, you better come get your clothes on. Ann's gonna be mad if you don't hurry up, and Angie might not let you sit with her at the game."

Things grew quiet again except for the two boys snickering from inside.

Les now had his turn, and in the same mock voice, called out, "It's almost nine o'clock. We're supposed to be there already. Angie might be mad and not let you sit by her on the way to Jacksonville."

Making his move, Wade feigned an attack. Rushing the door, he rattled the handle vigorously and hid. It worked. Immediately from inside Les came charging out spraying a can of shaving cream only to be doused right in the face by a cold glass of water held by Wade. Les quickly retreated.

Wade, thinking he had them on the run, dashed into the room to soak Laney. Just as he made it through the doorway, a torrential cascade of water soaked him from head to foot.

Wade let out a bone-chilling shriek. Laney danced on his knees from the top bunk holding the now empty trash can from whence the water came.

"Yes! Yes! We got 'em, Les! We got 'em!" Laney cried out.

Les danced in celebration too, as if he'd made the winning touchdown in a tight football game. Wade stood frozen, looking stunned. Realizing he'd just been had, he playfully tackled Les onto Laney's bed. Laney dove on top of them both in a wild free for all.

Suddenly, something didn't seem right. The boys stopped. Who was clearing their throat? There it went again. In embarrassed unison the three looked wincingly toward the doorway. Standing before them utterly disgusted was Ann.

No one said a word for a long moment.

Wade muttered under his breath, "What was it you were going to tell her, Les?"

A quiet, humbled Les uttered not a word.

Ann spoke up. "Well, my, my, my, if it isn't the three little pigs in here."

Angie's face appeared from just behind her shoulder.

Ann continued in an understated voice. "Can you believe it? One's halfway in his clothes, one's in his underwear, and one almost has a towel wrapped around his waist. And my, my, they're all wet and in a pile." She paused for effect then asked, "Fellows, exactly what are y'all doing in here?"

The boys eyed each other in humiliation as Les bravely spoke up, "Uh, well, we overslept, girls."

"You overslept? You lazy slugs! And that's why you're all three in here wet and groveling all over each other in one bed half naked this morning when you are supposed to be down at Karl's house picking us up." Ann's stinging words indicated both girls' total outrage.

"Well, not exactly," Les tried explaining. "We just—"

"Listen, you guys. We really don't want to know what's going on in here. Just put some clothes on, will you? Let's try not looking like we're all from Florida while we're down here, okay?" She turned and spoke to Angie, so the boys could hear her too. "Would you look at this place? Water all over the floor. Dirty dishes all over the table. It's a pig sty."

She stuck her head back into the doorway to the bedroom. "How 'bout hurrying it up, fellows. We'll clean up out here for you. You pigs! Where's the mop, Laney?"

Sheepishly Laney spoke up, "It's in the broom closet by the back door, Ann."

Shutting the door to the bedroom, the two girls silently died laughing. "Can you believe those guys?" Ann snickered. "They'll never live this one down, not if I can help it."

As the girls laughed on one side of the door, the boys remained shaken on the other.

"How the hell did she get in here?" Laney asked Les.

"I think Wade gave her your extra key before we left last night. I think she was concerned that we might not get up this morning. If you can remember, Wade was feeling no pain down at the Palace."

"Hey, don't blame it on me, boys," Wade spoke up. "I told you she'd be mad if we weren't there on time."

Les chimed in, "Hey. Listen, guys. This is nothing. Laney, just think if that had been your dad standing there."

All three boys blanched at the thought of Mr. James in the doorway.

They busted out laughing that it was only Ann.

"I'll tell you one thing," Les said dryly. "If that'd been him—with all the empty beer cans sitting around this place, I don't think we'd be going to any ball game today."

Wade chimed in from the bathroom where he was putting on his clothes and combing his hair, "Yeah, I don't think so either. Speaking of beer, guys, how much do we have left?"

"Not much. You must have drank it all," Laney said acting miffed.

"Me? I didn't drink all that beer," Wade chuckled. "You've got me mixed up with your Florida buds."

"Well, we know it wasn't Les," Laney replied sarcastically.

"Yeah, that's what I know. Look in the mirror. I think it was you, pal," Wade shot back.

Smiling over at Wade, Laney buckled his pants belt, "I don't suppose you'd make a run to the Quickie Store for us?"

"What?" Wade protested. "We can get beer and liquor on the way."

"No," Laney responded. "We'll get this place cleaned up while you're gone. That way we can leave here quickly when you get back."

"Whatever," Wade replied halfheartedly. "What do you want?"

Laney held out some cash. "Some beer and maybe a bottle of bourbon. Surprise us."

Les grinned at his wisecracking friends. He then handed Wade his keys. "Here, take my car. The store is over by …"

"I know where the store is, Les. I'll be right back. Y'all get a move on. We're not running too late yet."

Wade left the house while his friends cleaned and straightened up. Soon they were done and sitting in rocking chairs on Laney's front porch. From there they could see the sand dunes, the beach, and then the Atlantic Ocean just beyond.

Wade made it back from the liquor store where he stacked two cases of beer and a bottle of bourbon on the kitchen table. Seeing his friends sitting on the screen porch, he called out, "All right, guys! We got the beer, we got the liquor, how 'bout let's go skin us some Florida Gators!"

Not a sound came from the porch. The door exiting the den to the porch was wide open. Certainly, they could hear him.

Bemused, he again called out, "Okay, folks. We got to get going. Come on or we're going to be late to the game, now."

Still not a peep. Nothing.

Wade walked out onto the front screened in porch where his friends were seated. Taking note, he could see they all seemed downcast.

"Okay," he said carefully. "What seems to be the problem here?"

Ann looked up into her cousin's eyes. "Well, nothing if you've got them on you."

"What am I supposed to have on me? Are you talking about the game tickets?"

Ann smiled relieved. "So, you have them in your pocket, right?"

"No, I haven't seen them. So, who is it that's supposed to have them?"

"Don't you remember? I got worried and gave them all to you last night at the bar. When you got home, you guys were supposed to split them up and keep them in your wallets. You don't remember us talking about that."

"No, Ann. You never gave me any tickets. That's something I would have remembered for sure."

"Yes, she did, Wade," Laney spoke up. "We were at the Palace. I was there when she gave them to you." Laney hung his head. "I told Ann you were too drunk and to keep them herself. No telling what happened to the things.

Perturbed, Wade shot back, "I wasn't drunk last night, and Ann never gave me those tickets. Did everyone look through their things to see where they might be?"

"Yes," Laney said," Nobody found anything. I guess we need to go back through the house at least one more time. But I honestly think, they're gone."

Wade was pissed. "Listen up. I didn't lose those tickets.

Laney fired back, "Well you were the last one to hold them. Maybe they're somewhere in your stuff. Why don't you at least go look?

"I've never touched or seen those tickets, Laney. How could I lose them?"

"I don't know, Wade, but I think that's a moot point now. Our best plan would probably be to just go on over to the game. At least we could entertain ourselves with the fans outside the stadium."

Wade opened the door to the screen porch and headed down the steps for the beach. This ticket mess was B.S. and he knew it was B.S. Angrily, he spouted over his shoulder, "Y'all knock yourself out over there. Have a great time. But I won't be going with you."

Watching what happened, Ann desperately called out, "All right. The jig's up, guys. Somebody stop him!"

Laney scrambled to the front doorsteps yelling, "Come on, Wade! It was just a joke, man! Ann has everybody's tickets! Come on back!"

But the defiant Wade kept walking.

Les spoke up. "I told y'all doing that was a bad idea. You just can't mess with him like that. He's too high strung."

"I'll say," Laney responded a bit dejected. "I didn't think he'd walk off like that before he found the tickets."

"You've known him most of your life, Laney. You know how he is," Les scolded the larger boy in Wade's defense.

"Yeah, you're right, but he'll get over it." He paused with a look of frustration. "Well, I guess somebody better go get him."

Volunteering as she walked for the door downhearted, Ann said, "I'll go. It was my idea and probably more my fault than anybody else's."

To the other's surprise, Angie spoke up. "Let me! Y'all wait here! I'll be right back!"

Down on the beach, Wade kicked off his shoes and started walking the edge of the water. The wind blew in gusts as a cloudy front came through causing the ocean to white cap and send huge rough breakers pounding the shoreline.

Distressed with what had just happened, Wade made his way slowly down the beach deep in thought. *What a great day this could have been. I probably should have just stopped and turned around when they said they were joking, and I wouldn't be down here feeling like an idiot.* A surge of guilt ran through him for making them run late to the game.

How many times in his past had this same sort of thing happened? But why, he kept thinking, did he always have to overreact? Why did he always make a big deal out of nothing? So what if he had lost those tickets and had to take the blame. Punishing himself even more, he kept ruminating why he didn't handle the episode differently.

Suddenly, shaken from the doldrums of his thoughts, he heard the sweet voice of a girl calling his name from far behind him. Slowly turning his head, he could see coming toward him the loveliest sight—Angie. Walking quickly, she made her way stopping a few yards away as they faced one another.

Standing with her hands clasped behind her back as she hung her head, she toed the sand with her foot. Looking up through her windblown bangs and with her beautiful green eyes and an impish grin, she softly asked, "Pretty bad joke, huh?"

Wade gave her a subtle smile, glad to see her radiant face in front of his. He was embarrassed for losing control and storming off in such an immature manner.

"Ahhh, that Laney can carry things a bit too far, sometimes," he scoffed but with a grin.

"Well, it wasn't just Laney, it was Ann too. Les and I were just silent witnesses. What do you call that, legally? Oh yeah, that made us accessories to the crime. So, what was supposed to happen was they were going to search the room and find the tickets rubber banded to an empty beer can. That was their big plan for a good laugh.

"Pretty elaborate, for sure," Wade beamed back as he shook his head.

"Yeah, Les and I told them it was a bad idea, and it wasn't going to work. But Ann and Laney were beside themselves about trying it."

"Real practical jokers those two, huh?"

"Yep. They're real cards all right."

"Did they send you down here to get me?"

"Nope. I wanted to come myself." She paused. "In case you haven't noticed—I kinda like you." She smiled seductively into his deep brown eyes.

Wade smiled back as Angie reached out and took his hand. "I'm glad," he said.

"You 'bout ready to go back?" she asked.

"Yeah. Let's get going."

As they neared the first sand dune before going on up to the house, Angie abruptly stopped. "You know, they've had their fun with you today, Wade. And they were mean doing it. I think it's time for a little payback. What about you?"

"What are you talking about?" Wade asked puzzled.

"Listen. Just do what I tell you. No questions, okay?"

"Okay." he said, glad to do whatever the attractive girl wanted.

"What you need to do is to hide down behind that curve in that sand dune over there until I get back down here. I don't want you to come out from behind it until you see me and I give you a signal, okay?"

"All right."

"You'll see the others come down first, but don't come out until I motion for you. You got it?"

"What on earth are you pulling here?" Wade chuckled.

"Trust me." With a quick kiss, she turned and headed up the first dune.

Wade grinned and headed for his hiding place.

That kiss was worth being down here after all, he thought to himself

Angie charged through the sand her hands flailing in the air as she made it up and down each large dune on her dash toward the house.

The group inside was milling around the front porch waiting for her to return with Wade when they saw her coming.

"Something's wrong," Ann shouted alarmed.

The rest of the group looked on anxiously as Angie headed toward them. By the time she arrived, Laney was standing in the front yard and Les and Ann were on the steps and in the doorway.

"What's the matter?" Laney asked as she approached.

Out of breath, Angie grabbed Laney's shoulder and held her other hand over her chest. Gasping for air, she spat out, "It's Wade! I found his clothes on the beach! He must have swum out too far!"

Laney started for the surf dropping the beer can he was holding as he went. Grabbing him by the arm, Angie yelled, "No, you need something to swim with. That surf's too rough out there."

Pulling away from Angie, a shaken Laney called back to Les to get the surfboard. Then the three dashed for the shore, Les trailing the other two retrieved and carried the large board.

Following the panicked friends, Angie watched as they made it over the last dune heading for the shoreline. Wade waited for her signal then strolled over to her side out of sight from the others who were far in front of them. She let him in on the stunt.

Ann was in tears, as she, Les, and Laney frantically scanned the white-capped horizon for any sign of their friend. Angie and Wade crept up just behind their panic-stricken friends.

In a loud voice, Wade yelled, "What y'all doing, you fools!"

The trio turned around stunned but glad to see their pal alive.

"We've been had! Get 'em!" Laney roared with a menacing grin.

Laughing Wade and Angie turned and ran for the beach house as hard as they could go; the other three friends charged from behind in hot pursuit.

III

The rain stopped as the driver of the Corvette made it to Yulee. On his journey, he paused once in Waycross to eat breakfast in order to slow his pace. *Timing is everything*, he thought to himself as he looked at his watch. It read 9:30 a.m.

As the sleek car glided down the two-lane road, the pavement finally became dry. Leaving the rain behind him, the young man rocked to the soulful beat of Santana's "Black Magic Woman." At ease, the driver coasted down the highway in rhythmic ecstasy.

Soon he topped the A1A Bridge to Amelia Island. From this high perch, the towering smokestacks of the paper mills could easily be seen down the intra-coastal waterway north toward Cumberland Sound. Through Five Points, he made his way. Up ahead, the gray-green turbulence of the Atlantic Ocean on an overcast Saturday morning appeared before him. Turning south, he passed Laney's beach house where only Les' brown Pinto sat in the oyster shell driveway. He continued until he reached his own house.

Turning into the driveway, he saw an unfamiliar green Chevrolet Vega with a Georgia license plate. *It has to be hers*, he thought.

Parking alongside it, he came to a stop. He turned the rearview mirror onto his face as he primped his hair. Straightening the mirror, he climbed out of his vehicle shutting its door. Stretching his cramped muscles and smiling in anticipation, he headed for the house.

The door was unlocked and partially opened. He pushed it gently and peered inside. It took a moment for his eyes to adjust to the darkness. He made out the silhouette of someone standing in front of the fireplace. Wearing black polyester slacks, a white blouse, and a matching black vest, a young woman lost deep in thought stared into the red-hot coals of the den's massive hearth. Hearing the door open, she spun around surprised, her jet-black hair flowing as she did so.

"Gosh, Karl!" She placed her hand on her chest. "I wasn't expecting y'all so soon."

Karl entered the room and stood before her. "Sorry, Louisa, I didn't mean to scare you," he smiled back.

Louisa glanced back toward the door in anticipation. "Where's Terrie?"

Karl hung his head. Looking up pitifully, he remarked, "She didn't come." He paused staring at the floor once more.

"We broke up last night." His voice cracked and his crystal blue eyes grew teary as he spoke. He tried smiling bravely.

"Karl, I'm sorry," Louisa said not knowing what else to say.

Shrugging in a pathetic 'what can I say' display, Karl stood, staring downward. Raising his head and making eye contact with the concerned girl, he softly spoke, "I had an idea something was wrong, Louisa. She'd been kind of acting funny lately. She wouldn't ever really say it, but I think there's somebody else."

He paused with a sigh as his head drooped once more. Stumbling with his words, he went on, "I was a little upset, to say the least, and uh, I forgot my tickets and about half my stuff."

As if asking for forgiveness, he continued, "I can still carry you to the game now. Don't worry about that. I doubt I'll be able to find a ticket, uh, but I can drop you off and you can ride back with your friends if that'll be all right?"

Louisa's heart broke as she saw the sadness in Karl's eyes.

"It's okay, Karl," she said. "I got here a lot earlier than I thought I would. I really wasn't expecting to make it to the game anyway. Maybe you can just show me around Fernandina until they get back. Would that be okay with you?"

Karl shrugged with a sorrowful expression, "Whatever you want, Louisa, but I won't mind carrying you to the game one bit now."

"No," she said firmly as she placed a comforting hand on his shoulder.

Karl gazed deeply into her eyes then looked down at his watch. Nervously, he said, "Hey, it's ten o'clock. Have you had anything to eat?"

"Nope, not yet," Louisa replied.

"You hungry?"

"Yeah. A little bit."

"Well, I know a quaint little diner downtown. They serve bacon and eggs," he grinned.

"Something that exotic! Ooo—I can hardly wait," Louisa giggled.

Heading for the back door, Karl, in every way an apparent gentleman, opened it letting Louisa walk out first. He exited, turned around, locked the door and followed her to the driveway.

"Nice car, Karl," Louisa said as she opened the door to the red Corvette. After she slid down into the low riding bucket seat, Karl, continuing his solicitous attention, closed her door.

Heading to the driver's side and climbing in, he said, "Ahh, It's nothing special. I've already got sixty thousand miles on it. Going to trade it in pretty soon."

"Still looks brand new to me," Louisa observed as Karl backed out of the driveway. Shifting gears, he headed north in the direction of town.

Karl fumbled for a tape in the alligator skin box resting between the two of them. "Hey, why don't you see if there's something in here you want to listen to," he grinned. Pushing the clutch and down shifting to second, he rolled to a stop at the red light at Sadler road.

Louisa fingered her way through his music collection. She found a recording she liked and pulled it out of the box.

"Here's one," she exclaimed handing the tape to Karl. Its label read, "Cornelius Brothers and Sister Rose."

Taking the cartridge from her, Karl pushed it into the slot of his tape deck where the sounds of the Black soul group blasted the car's interior. Karl turned it down. "I guess I had the volume turned up a little driving down here," he laughed.

"I'd say," Louisa winced and smiled back as she rolled her eyes. "You know they came to Valdosta State at the first of this quarter, and Les and a group of us went down to see them. They were great."

"Yeah, they're pretty good. We had Cheech and Chong up in Athens this past quarter," Karl said with a grin.

Louisa stiffened. "They're a little too vulgar for me."

"What do you expect with a couple of pot smoking comedians?" Karl asked as he paused to read her thoughts. "You're right though. Hey, I tell you who you would have enjoyed—Elton John came to the Coliseum last spring."

"Really?" Louisa grinned at him enthusiastically.

"Yes! You wouldn't have believed it! I mean the place was jam packed and rocking out, man! I don't think you could've squeezed another body in there if you had wanted to. All kinds of people showed up to see ol' Elton. Hippies. Rednecks. Blacks. Mostly students, I think." Excitedly, he looked at her. "I even met a couple of dudes that came all the way down from Kentucky for the concert. Can you believe that? From Kentucky!" he shook his head in disbelief.

Louisa gave him a look of amazement.

"Did he play, 'Goodbye Yellow Brick Road'?"

"Let me tell you. It was the first song he played when he came on stage, and the place went absolutely bonkers. You couldn't even hear yourself think. And when he broke into 'Benny and the Jets,' they went totally ballistic, man. I mean, you really had to be there to experience how crazy it was."

Louisa's eyes lit up as Karl described the event.

"Everywhere you looked, people were either so stoned on weed or so tanked up on liquor that half of them probably didn't even know where they were. A lot of the girls down in front of the stage rode their boyfriends' shoulders. And some of 'em even took off their tops and threw them up on the stage for Elton. You wouldn't have believed how wild it was."

Louisa grew disapprovingly quiet. "You mean the police weren't there to stop all of that sort of stuff?"

"The 'Pigs'? Man, they didn't have a chance. There were about a hundred drunks and stoned freaks for every one cop. I mean what could they do? Arrest everybody?"

As Karl continued, he noticed a tinge of disapproval still lingering on Louisa's face. Quickly changing his tune, he said, "Me and Terrie just kind of sat there in awe of all this hell raising going on around us. You know, being from South Georgia and our parents bringing us up with values, going to Sunday School and Church and all, well, all I can say is that it was country come to town. We'd never seen anything quite like that in our lives."

Karl paused for a moment. Then, in a depressed tone, he spoke softly, "Me and Terrie." He shook his head as they had made it to town and pulled into a parking place in front of the diner. Turning off the car, he glanced at Louisa who solemnly peered into his sad eyes.

"You ready for some grub?" he tried sounding cheery.

Silently smiling, Louisa pulled herself up from the bucket seat as she made her way out of the car. As she headed for the entrance to the restaurant, Karl briskly made it ahead of her and opened the door to the rustic eating establishment.

They found the typically busy eatery almost deserted. It appeared they were among the few people remaining in Fernandina. Everyone else had gone to watch the big game in Jacksonville with friends. They made their way to one of the restaurant's empty booths. Once seated, a waitress appeared at their table with ice water and a set of silverware.

"What will y'all have?" she asked smiling and pulling out her pencil and order book.

Karl looked at Louisa, "It's my treat. Get whatever you want."

"Well, thank you, Karl," Louisa responded. Looking up kindly at the waitress, she said, "I think I'll have some French toast and orange juice."

"Anything else?" Karl asked.

Louisa shook her head no.

"Okay," Karl continued as he scanned the menu.

"I'll have some ham and eggs and a strawberry crepe. You ought to try a strawberry crepe, Louisa; they're really delicious."

"No, but thanks anyway," she answered.

"Well, you can try some of mine," he suggested as he noticed her smiling at him.

"How would you like those eggs, sir?"

"Fried and well done."

"Anything else?" the young waitress asked as she stared blissfully down into Karl's alluring eyes.

Dismissing her, Karl responded smugly, "No. That will be all."

As the waitress turned to leave, Louisa noticed the look the appealing young woman had given him.

"I think that girl found you quite interesting," she told him trying to lift his spirits.

"Humph," Karl rolled his eyes in disgust. "I bet when she's not working here, she's helping her dad head shrimp down at the docks."

Rationalizing that Karl probably felt hurt and bitter from Terrie dumping him, Louisa took no offense at the cruel remark. Quietly she leaned back in her seat and began looking around the restaurant at the mounted fish, paintings of ocean scenes and relics from boats covering the green block walls.

With unusual clarity, she was capable with just a glance of seeing the joy or pain in other people. She smiled to herself. The place had a happy atmosphere.

After a few moments of checking the place out, she turned to Karl as he leaned back in his chair admiring her. She asked, "Well, Karl, when do you think our gang will get back?"

Raising his eyebrows and his shoulders simultaneously, Karl declared, "Gee, Louisa. Probably pretty late. Maybe around seven or eight tonight."

Louisa cringed when she heard this. Karl, seeing her wince, asked if she was getting tired of his company.

"No, of course not. I just thought they'd make it back a little sooner than that," she smiled.

"Well," Karl sighed. "It's the traffic over there. Coming back through that mess will be awful. Terrie and I went to the game the last two years in a row, and it took us about an hour just to get out of sight of the stadium. It's a nightmare."

The waitress came back to the table with their plates full of food.

"Okay, you had the ham and eggs and a strawberry crepe." The girl sat Karl's plate of food before him first. "And you had the French toast, right?"

"That's right. Thank you," Louisa said as the waitress stood ready to wait on them further.

"Can I get you anything else?" she asked Karl with a kind look.

"No. That will be all," he responded, but this time without expression.

As Karl started to dig in, he looked up and froze as he saw that Louisa was saying grace. Embarrassed that she had caught him with a mouthful of food, he hastily gestured with his face and hands a sign of an apology. With a twinkle in her eye and quick little smile, Louisa forgave him as both began to eat.

When they finished, Karl took her on a walk down to the docks to see his family's cabin cruiser, but because of repairs being made to the wharf's walkway, they were unable to get to it. Instead, they turned and went up to where the shrimp boats were docked. *The Miss Frances*, *The Amelia Queen*, *Lady's Luck*: most all of the boats in Fernandina's shrimping fleet were in port due to the rough weather badgering the coast.

After viewing all they could down at the landing, they headed back to the restaurant and Karl's car. Karl poured his heart out to Louisa concerning his breakup with Terrie. He appeared obviously distraught as Louisa listened, but spoke little as they headed back.

IV

By 12:00 they returned to Karl's house. The house, Karl's dad had built, was something to behold. It had taken over two years to construct from blueprints to the final board being laid.

He had created a tan, stucco, two-story villa with a large wooden sun deck overlooking the ocean from the second floor. A boardwalk centered on the home's ground floor connected to the stairs of the upper deck and ran out through the dunes to the beach.

Two bedrooms upstairs and one master bedroom downstairs made up the back or roadside of the building. This allowed the neatest part of the structure, the den in the front part of the home, to hold a huge exposed wood beam cathedral ceiling. A banister railed walkway surrounding the inside of the second floor allowed one to look down into the den from up above. This walkway also exited to a stairwell out to the second-floor balcony.

A massive fireplace located on the downstairs wall facing the beach set the place off. Along with charcoal slate floors and oak hardwood on the walls and ceilings, the place reeked of the expensive. Angie, who had spent the previous night upstairs, fell in love with the place. But Ann, growing up with Karl and knowing his father's shortcomings, remained unimpressed.

Karl took Louisa's suitcase upstairs to the bedroom she would be sharing with the other two girls. He gave Louisa a tour of the house ending up on the upper deck overlooking the beach and the Atlantic Ocean in the distance.

Both leaned casually against the rail of the veranda's high perch. The sky started to show patches of blue as the clouds gathered into great cumulus cotton balls drifting briskly eastward.

Watching this spectacle, Karl and Louisa saw everything succumb to the intensity of the wind. They could see it in the dipping sea oats and the churning sea. They could see it as the flag on its backyard pole whipped and flapped its chain clinking rhythmically to its authority. Everything appeared to bow to this overpowering force. There was nothing it did not touch; nothing it did not affect.

As it blew, Louisa kept pushing her flowing hair back from across her face. She was enthralled with the sound of the pounding surf and the fresh clean smell of the ocean's salty air.

Surveying every nuance of the stunning young woman, Karl said, "It's beautiful out here, isn't it?"

"It's gorgeous," Louisa confirmed as she shivered from the coolness of the late autumn air. "No problems, no worries, no hurry, it just takes it all away doesn't it?" As she said this, she peered far out into the deep churning Atlantic.

Karl stood silently watching every feature of the beautiful girl. His eyes filled with the glow surrounding her. Mesmerized he kept staring, but she was unaware as she watched the gulls course with the wind overhead.

As she turned his way, Karl asked, "You want to go for a walk on the beach?"

"I'll have to change clothes," she said, cocking her head to one side as the wind blew her hair once more across her face.

"Okay," Karl said. "I'll meet you at the end of the boardwalk when you're ready."

Louisa disappeared into the house as Karl made his way to the beach. At the end of the walkway, he took off his shoes and rolled up his jeans to his knees. Soon Louisa, wearing a pair of white jeans and matching sweatshirt, made her way to his side. Getting to the end of the walkover and noticing Karl's bare feet, she kicked off her shoes too.

Unlike earlier this morning when Wade and the others were on the beach, the wind had become more severe causing the waves to pound the surf with a roaring intensity.

"Which way you want to go?" Louisa shouted trying to be heard above the loudness of the wind and sea.

"Let's go down to the old pier," Karl shouted back.

Loose sand from the lower dunes came blasting across the upper beach in torrents covering them and getting in their eyes.

"This stuff stings, Karl," Louisa commented as she squinted her eyes. She brought her hands to her face for extra protection.

"Follow me," Karl cried back.

In a slow sprint so as not to leave Louisa behind, Karl headed for the surf. At the water's edge, the sand remained wet and packed, or it at least had finely crushed shells mixed with it that the wind couldn't pick up.

As they had made it out of harm's way, they were able to dust off the sand covering them. They turned to walk up the beach. Louisa came up behind Karl and dusted off the back of his shirt.

"Thanks. You turn around," he called over to her still having difficulty being heard over the howling wind and crashing waves.

When she did, he graciously dusted her off, but included her pants as well.

"That stuff's worse than sandpaper if it gets under your clothes," he yelled. "And to beat everything, we got to go through it all over again when we go back to the house."

"Maybe the wind will die down by then."

"I doubt it," Karl said with a squint-eyed frown.

The two strolled down the beach toward the pier picking up shells and looking at a dead fish or two that had washed ashore. The tide had reached its low point and was starting to come back in. Up ahead of them was a shallow run-out crossing the beach and pouring into a long tidal pool that ran parallel to the ocean for about a quarter of a mile.

"Louisa, you better roll up your jeans. We got to cross this little run-out up here."

"It doesn't look very deep to me."

"It's not, but you don't want to get your pants wet, do you?"

Anticipating the depth, Louisa rolled her jeans up to her calves and headed for the crossing.

"Woo. It's cold," she said shivering as she stepped ankle deep into the water.

"You'll get used to it. Come on," Karl called back to her.

Louisa made it through the small ditch with Karl slowly leading the way. For the next thirty minutes, the duo walked the shallows looking for shells and talking about school. They made it to the pier where Karl showed her the small fish and periwinkles that were trapped at low tide by the washouts surrounding the barnacled pilings.

The tide turning by now had come rushing inland, and the distance between the adjacent baby pools and the surf was growing narrower. Oblivious to this circumstance, the pair made their way back, sometimes walking on the sand and sometimes at the edge of the surf.

As they ambled along, Louisa caught sight of a huge conch shell being pushed and pulled by the tides in the shallows up ahead. She ran to where it had been, but could not locate it. As the next wave broke and its breaker rushed heading for shore, she saw it again.

Karl appeared at her side, as she had gotten deeper in her effort to retrieve the shell. A massive wave broke sending a large foaming breaker in their direction catching them off guard. Louisa saw it first and quickly grabbed Karl's hand as they rushed back to the safety of the beach.

Winded, they both bent over resting their hands on their knees as they laughed between each gasp of air.

"I sure wanted that shell," Louisa laughed as she watched the water to see if it had resurfaced.

"Yep, you sure did. You almost drowned us trying to get it!" Karl said looking back to a spot where he thought it might have washed up, but it wasn't there.

"I think it's a goner, Louisa," he said as they both stood upright.

"Yep, I think you're right."

Continuing on their way, Louisa skipped up onto the beach and started drawing sea creatures in the sand with her big toe.

"Hey, you know, Karl? Les says Wade is quite an artist."

She grinned as the outline started to take shape.

"He's all right, I guess," Karl remarked indifferently. He had seen Wade's exceptional work, but didn't want to admit it.

"Les says he's not just average; he's really, really good," she exclaimed as she finished cutting the shape of a starfish in the sand.

"You got to realize, Louisa, that Les is Wade's best friend. So he's a little biased, wouldn't you think?" Karl shouted toward Louisa, who was scooting down the beach outlining a giant whale.

"I thought you were Wade's best friend too," she hollered back.

"We grew up together. What can I say?"

Louisa stopped drawing the whale and stared intently at Karl, but said nothing.

"What?" Karl grinned nervously. Without responding, Louisa went back to her sketch.

"I like Wade. I just haven't seen him in a year—that's all. And besides, I don't know that much about art anyway." As he said this, he scrambled to catch up with the girl.

Louisa had finished her picture of the whale and was writing 'Louisa loves Les' in the sand as Karl pretended not to notice.

"What's your opinion of Les, Karl?" Louisa asked.

"What is this, the Spanish Inquisition?" Karl shouted. "Les and Wade are both friends of mine! I'd do anything for them! And they know it!"

Louisa stopped her writing and glanced up amazed by Karl's outburst.

"I'm sorry Louisa, I'm just not myself today," Karl apologized.

He took his big toe and wrote in the sand 'Terrie loves Karl.' When Louisa saw what he had written, he put an enormous 'X' on it. He gazed watery eyed into Louisa's face.

Louisa reached out and took Karl's hand.

"I'm sorry, Karl. Today hasn't been a good day for you has it?" She turned his hand loose as they started walking back to the cottage.

The wind had not let up and the small patches of blue sky, which had previously been above them, had turned gray and overcast. As they continued to walk, the breeze in gusts flapped at the folds in their clothes and kept their hair tousled and disheveled.

As the tide poured back in, the area of beach between the ever-enlarging tidal pools and surf grew narrower. This had gone unnoticed by the two until they made it back to the shallow run-out they had crossed earlier.

"Good gosh that's gotten deep, Karl," Louisa said to him.

"Yeah it sure has, but those baby pools up there are deeper than this." Pointing to the tidal pools, he indicated they were trapped. "I think we can jump it. Hang on. I'll go first."

Jogging back about five yards, Karl turned around and sprinted to the edge of the run-out. With one long leap, he barely made it across.

"I don't think I can make it jumping," Louisa shouted at him.

"Try wading out into the surf. It might be shallow enough to make it over out there! Can you pull your jeans up any higher?"

Quickly but calmly, Louisa rolled her jeans up over her knees, but they would go no further. She waded the surf to go out and around the run-out.

The waves were coming in constantly. At first, she didn't realize she had to time them and she had to run back for shore before getting soaked. After standing at the water's edge and measuring the time it took each wave to come through, she decided to make her move.

Pulling her legs through the ever-deepening water became slow and difficult. As the next wave grew closer, she tried moving faster. To her surprise, she hit a hole and stumbled just as the wave crashed.

Down and under she went. Soaked from head to toe, sputtering and cold, she rushed out of the water to the other side. Her clothes clung to her body in an icy grip.

Karl charged up to her side, a huge grin affixed to his face.

"That's one way to do it," he yelled. "Let's get you to the house!"

Taking her hand, they ran the last quarter of a mile for home. Through the stinging sand of the dunes and up the boardwalk, they ran until they entered the cottage.

Louisa was shivering. She could hardly move as Karl escorted her upstairs to her room. He opened a closet and pulled out a terry cloth bathrobe. He then went into the room's bathroom and turned on the hot water faucet.

He sighed disgruntled. "Dad must have mis-set the timer on the hot water heater. I told him we'd be using the place for the whole weekend. I hope the girls had some hot water last night. I'll get it going for you though.

He picked up the robe and gently tossed it on the bed.

"Here, get out of those clothes and get into this. I'll get the fire going downstairs to warm you up."

Getting out of the wet garments proved harder than Louisa had anticipated. They were heavy, cold, and sticky. Distracted by her agony, she didn't realize Karl had left the door to her room slightly ajar.

As he stoked the hot coals and piled on more wood, he chanced to turn and glance back upstairs. With Louisa's back to the doorway, she was unaware that he watched as she took off each article of clothing and stood momentarily naked before putting on the robe.

Once finished, she wrapped a towel around her wet hair and made her way downstairs to get next to the fire. Nearing the den and hearth, she noted Karl wasn't in the room. Looking at the wood that he had just piled into the fireplace, she saw mostly smoke. Little heat radiated in her direction.

Her teeth still chattering, she stood in front of the fire pit as the burning logs toyed with producing flames. The phone on the table adjacent the fireplace started to ring. On the fourth ring, Louisa decided that Karl must have been indisposed, so she picked up the receiver to answer it. Her timing was imperfect as Karl simultaneously picked up the receiver in the back room.

Louisa heard the voice of a crying, frightened female.

"I did it, Karl!" the voice burst into sobs. "Why weren't you here! I needed you!" she cried. "It was your idea to do it!"

Louisa gently hung up the receiver so no one would notice. She heard an angry muffled voice coming from the back room, "Don't call back down here again. I'll be back tomorrow."

Louisa's mind churned as the hurt from the female's voice echoed through her heart.

The door opened from the downstairs' master bedroom. Nonchalantly and smiling, Karl re-entered the room as if nothing had happened.

"Is the fire starting to heat you up, yet?" he asked as he made it to her side.

"It's getting a little warmer," Louisa said coolly.

Karl pulled back the fire screen and with the poker, busted open the glowing coals coming from the wood he'd placed on it earlier. The dry oak logs, responding to his prodding, became engulfed in flames causing them to crackle and pop.

"Is that better?" he asked replacing the screen.

"Well, I'm about dry anyway," Louisa said. "I think I'll go upstairs and get dressed."

"Well, your hair's still wet," Karl said noticing her towel draped around her shoulders. Catching her off guard, he took the towel and started lightly drying her hair with it.

Louisa began to feel uncomfortable.

Was that Terrie on the phone? she thought to herself. *What had Karl made her do?*

Casually talking and smiling, Karl made his way around to the front of Louisa as he kept stroking her hair with the towel. Drying the back of her head as he stood facing her, he gently pulled her forward. Swiftly and unexpectedly, he kissed her lips.

"I think that's enough!" Louisa stated pulling back.

Using the towel to restrain her, Karl spoke softly, "Come on, Louisa. We're all alone. No one will ever know."

As he pulled her face closer to his, the once panicked girl suddenly grew calm and controlled.

"That was Terrie on the phone wasn't it, Karl?"

"Who cares," he continued pressing his lips closer to hers.

"What did you make her do, Karl? You want to talk about that?"

"I don't want to talk about anything. What are you fighting me for?" he asked, as she tasted his hot breath across her face.

"I'm not fighting you, Karl. You're fighting me. Why don't you turn me loose?"

Releasing her, Karl smiled victoriously. "Let's go in here," his eyes implying the bedroom.

"No!"

"Every girl I've ever been with always said no when she really meant yes," he laughed as he grabbed her hand pulling her to the doorway.

With one roundhouse swipe of her free hand, Louisa slapped his face as hard as she could. The towering Karl lunged at her with a menacing scowl. But there was no fear in Louisa's eyes as she stared him down.

As hard as he tried to regain his composure, Karl could not. His nostrils flared and his chest heaved as he glared menacingly at her. Without a word, he turned and retreated to the master bedroom slinging the door open, rattling it as he went. Angrily, he flung his belongings into his suitcase, smashing something breakable on the floor as he did so. Kicking the door to the bedroom open, he exited through the kitchen and stopped at the back door.

"You'll regret the day you ever met me, you little bitch!" With that, he slammed the door as hard as he could.

Louisa's eyes never left his until he was gone. Her composure was still intact even as she sighed a deep breath of relief upon his leaving. Outside a car door slammed, an engine roared, and tires squealed as Karl's 'Vette left the driveway.

CHAPTER 5

Junior College

(*Winter* 1973)

For the college crew, the trip back to Georgia proved uneventful. When questioned, Louisa never mentioned the episode she had endured with Karl to anyone. She told the group that he and Terrie must have decided not to come. Soon all were busy going about the mundane rituals of winter quarter: buying books, reacquainting themselves with old friends they had not seen since the Christmas break, and trying to figure out the weather.

Winter in South Georgia was a mixed bag. One day it could be eighty degrees outside while the next it could be twenty-five. It was the perfect recipe for a cold or bronchitis, and poor Les seemed to have one or the other if not both. Louisa doted on him between classes as Angie and Wade also took time off to be alone.

Unlike fall quarter when he was single, Wade, now with Angie on his arm, started to feel more accepted on campus. Without her presence, he felt tentative and insecure around others. What made him feel this way, he did not fully understand, but painfully he realized it all the same.

Angie had fallen in love with the handsome brown-eyed boy, enamored with his glowing olive complexion, thick jet-black hair, and kind heart. Even though she wanted to let Wade know how much she loved him, she held back. The tension that separated the sexes was still there, so Angie waited for Wade to give her a sign. That sign was universal to females the world over. It was just three little words.

By the end of the first month of the quarter, an unusual weather pattern was forming over southern Georgia and northern Florida. A strong cold front was making its way into the area from the northwest. At the same time, a tropical depression, abnormal for this season, moved north from the Gulf of Mexico pushing upward through Tallahassee.

Snow, something that hardly ever occurred in this area, was in the forecast. The region was buzzing with excitement.

It was Thursday afternoon, and classes were canceled for Friday. Laney James was supposed to be coming up from Jacksonville to take advantage of this long weekend for a visit. It seemed he and Ann had hit it off well at the Georgia-Florida game and had been in close contact ever since. She had even gone down to see him twice already.

The news on the local television station said it was already snowing in the Floridian Panhandle and would soon be covering an area clear across to the Atlantic. It was peculiar that the snow was starting in Florida and moving up toward Georgia instead of vice versa.

Laney, shortly after leaving Jacksonville, encountered the first snow flurries of the evening. What was usually a three-hour drive lengthened as the white stuff started accumulating along the roadsides, then onto the road itself. By two hours into the trip, traffic had slowed to a crawl, and Laney hadn't even made it halfway to his destination.

People in South Georgia maybe get to see snow three times in their entire lives. Expecting them to drive in the white mess, however, was more than improbable as Laney passed collision after collision along the roadside. Several travelers had pulled off on the emergency lane or along the center median to get out of harm's way, but Laney, laid back and confident, would have none of this as he made his way onward.

Laney's pals had started gathering at the Interstate 75 Holiday Inn bar waiting for him to arrive. A television set above the bar kept them posted on current weather conditions as snow had started falling outside the motel.

Ann, Wade, and Angie were the only ones in the place when they first arrived, but as travel conditions worsened, more motorists were pulling off the Interstate to take refuge, and the bar was becoming packed. Laney was supposed to meet them there at 6:00, but it was now 7:30. Composed, Ann seemed to take it all in stride even though the news bulletins kept reporting more accidents occurring along the highway.

"Another round of beer over here," Wade called out signaling a nearby waitress.

The buzz of the incoming crowd, made up primarily of traveling salesmen, grew louder. By 8:00, with the jukebox blaring, the mob inside the bar celebrated the beginning of an excusable long weekend off from meetings and appointments.

The three friends sipped their beers as they watched the hilarious commotion going on around them. The blue fog and stench of cigarette smoke filled the air, as did laughter and music. It was a carnival atmosphere of merriment and for the driven salesmen—relaxation.

One gregarious guy gained Wade's attention over the loudness of the music and mayhem.

"Hey, buddy! You know how to play the spoons?" The man beamed as he asked.

Slightly inebriated, Wade yelled back, "No. What are spoons?"

The man grabbed up two of the utensils from his table and began playing them on his legs, feet, and about any other part of his body. He clicked the spoons to the beat of the jukebox's music.

Angie and Ann clapped for the guy when the music stopped, then laughed as Wade gave it a shot. He dropped the spoons to the floor on his first attempt. With some coaching from the laughing salesman, he finally caught on. As "Dead Skunk in the Middle of the Road" played all three at the table spooned and stomped to its cornball beat. When the song was over, the entire crowd gave the spoon players a standing ovation. Wade and Angie couldn't stop laughing as they raised their beer and toasted the others in the room. But Ann remained quiet as the thought of Laney driving in the storm began to worry her.

"Hold on, everybody," the guy with the spoons shouted. He asked the waitress to turn the volume down on the jukebox and the sound up on the TV. He caught a special weather bulletin coming on and wanted to hear it, making those around him feel that he was doing them a favor too.

The weatherman appeared on the screen and said Interstate 75 was officially closed south of Valdosta, and would likely remain closed through Monday. A huge cheer went up from the crowd as they heard this, realizing this could mean an extra day off from work.

Noticeably lit, Wade eyed Ann. "Where the hell do you reckon Laney is, Cuz?"

"Wade!" Angie scolded.

"It's all right, Angie. He's probably past Valdosta by now, and if not, I guess we'll see him tomorrow."

Angie tried sounding calm. "The news did say a lot of phone lines were down—that's probably why he hasn't been able to get in touch with us yet."

With a smile, Ann remarked, "He's a big boy; he can take care of himself."

As the weather announcement ended, the jukebox was turned back up and the partying continued. Once again the noise level became deafening as the trio tried to talk. The crowd at the entrance to the bar suddenly grew quiet as a small gap opened up in that area.

"Hey, baby! Will you marry me?" came the drunken slur of a middle-aged reveler propped up at a table in the corner of the room.

Wade, Angie, and Ann turned toward the doorway to see the cause of the commotion. It was Les and Louisa. Smiling, the duo escaped the throng and made it to their table.

"Hey, don't you want to marry that guy?" Ann laughed at her friend.

Ignoring Ann's comment, Louisa politely took a seat. As Les sat beside her, almost every man in the bar stopped to stare at his gorgeous dark-haired date. Les leaned over the table toward Ann and said, "Laney called from Valdosta and said he'll be here in about an hour. He said that I-75 has been closed and he is going to take Highway 41 instead. For some reason, they left it open."

"How long ago did you talk to him?" Wade asked.

Les turned to Louisa for confirmation. "What—about forty-five minutes ago?" Louisa nodded in agreement. Catching herself staring at Wade, she glanced awkwardly at her other friends.

"How long have y'all been out here?" she asked.

Feeling mellow, Wade responded, "Since before six thirty." A clock on the wall read 9:00.

"Looks like you've been enjoying yourself, Wade ol' buddy." Les patted his friend firmly on the shoulder.

"I'm driving us home tonight. You can count on that," Angie said cutting her eyes at her boyfriend.

"I'm fine," Wade stammered as he reached into a bowl of salty yellow popcorn. "I've driven after drinking more beer than this, and I've never had a wreck yet."

"When's the last time you've driven in snow, hot shot?" Ann quipped back.

Glaring at his cousin, Wade sipped his beer before turning his attention to the crowded bar.

"How much longer are y'all gonna stay?" Les asked as he leaned back in his chair.

Angie, not wanting to show her nervousness, glanced at her roommate.

But Ann seemed not to notice as she stared across the buzzing room filled with revelers. An impish smile crept across her face, and everyone at her table turned to see who was receiving it.

"Laney! My main man." Les shouted as he saw his Floridian buddy making his way through the ever-tightening crowd, heading for their table. Les stood up, and the two friends shook hands. Laney saluted the rest of the group.

"Didn't think I'd make it, did ya'?" he asked gazing into Ann's eyes as he took a seat.

"I never had any doubt," Ann said. "After all, you were coming to see me, weren't you?"

The rest of the group laughed as Laney and Ann mirrored each other's glee upon seeing one another. Breaking up the celebration of Laney's arrival, a drunk from the bar came up and introduced himself as Bob. Mystified by his appearance, everyone at the table grew quiet.

Loud and obnoxious, he began to slur his words. "You ladies are the best-looking women in this bar. Matter of fact in this crummy little town—matter a fact in this whole damn state." Trying but not succeeding in acting more subdued, he asked, "Now which one of you young lovelies wants to dance with me?"

Each person at the table eyed each other laughing under their breath.

"Well, ladies does anybody want to dance with this fine gentleman?" Les asked in jest.

No one said a word as the drunk, a sizable older man, staggered while inspecting each girl.

"Well, it looks like there's no takers," Les smiled up at the guy.

"Shut up, you little damn shrimp! Give 'em time to make up their minds!" he shouted.

Wade stiffened nervously as Les responded. "You need to get on back to the bar, friend. We're out here just for some fun.

Again, the salesman told Les to shut his damn mouth, but as soon as he did, Laney grabbed the man by his tie. Jerking it hard, he yanked the drunk's head down to eye level. "Pal, didn't you hear what my friend here just said?"

Laney, his jaw tightening, glared into the drunk's shifting eyes.

Pulling away meekly his arms outstretched and spilling his beer, the man apologized for his behavior. He slurred, "I'm sorry. I think I might a' had just a little too much to drink maybe."

"You damn right you had!" Laney scolded him. "Now get on back to that bar over there and mind your manners."

The drunk obliged continually apologizing as he staggered back to his seat.

Wade and Angie had turned white as a sheet. Ann and Les laughed during the whole episode, and Louisa watched with sympathy as the drunk went back to where he'd been sitting.

Laney shook his head as he glanced at Ann with a smirk.

"Typical redneck Thursday night in South Georgia I see."

Ann retorted, "The only difference is if this had happened in Jacksonville, some dumb Florida girl would have gotten up and danced with him."

Everyone at the table laughed, Wade and Angie still nervously.

"Well, have you eaten supper yet?" Ann asked.

"Yep, back in Valdosta before I called," Laney responded.

"Tired?" she continued.

"Very," Laney yawned.

"We're about shot too," Ann said. "We've been here since about six o'clock waiting on you." Looking around the table at everyone, she asked, "Aren't y'all about ready to call it a night, guys?"

It took little prompting from the girls to get the boys up and heading for home. Each couple took a separate car. Les and Louisa picked Angie up at Wade's house after she drove him home. Les then dropped the girls off at the dorm.

Laney, who was staying with Wade for the weekend, didn't make it back to his pal's house from Ann's until after midnight. It seemed Ann wasn't quite as tired as she had proclaimed to be.

The next morning came late as the friends slept in. This was unusual for Wade as his dad usually had something for him to do on Wade's day off, but with Laney here, he was going easy on his son. Wade's little eight-year-old sister Kelli came bounding into the room and pounced onto Wade's bed to wake them up.

"Wake up, Wade!" the jubilant little girl sang out. "It's snowing outside! Come on. Get up. Mamma won't let me go outside without you."

Wade moaned as he pulled the covers over his head.

"Wa-ade," the little girl whined in her best southern drawl.

"K-ell'," Wade moaned, muffled by blankets. "It's going to be here till Monday."

Laney sat in his bed, too embarrassed to get out from under the sheets in front of Kelli wearing only his underwear.

"Kelli. How have you been doing," he roared with a grin.

"Fi-ine," Kelli said sheepishly trying to hide her immense smile.

"Well, I'll tell you what we'll do this morning. We'll build a snowman, a ginormous one, and we'll get your snow sled and slide down some hills. How about that?"

Kelli's eyes lit up until the part about the snow sled. Confused, she scrunched her little nose in puzzlement. "I don't have a sled, Laney."

"Sure you do," he bellowed. "Every little girl in South Georgia has one."

Kelli eyed Wade questioningly for the truth. He asked, "A sled? Come on, Kell', has Laney ever lied to you before?"

The little girl turned and faced her brother's big friend. Scolding him, she said, "Yes, he has."

Laney made his voice sound small and squeaky, "So I fib a little bit. But it's just every now and then, Kelli. I guess I got carried away talking. You know how it is."

Kelli gave him a mean don't-do-it-again look. Then, as hard as she tried not to, her eyes sparkled and a grin crept across her face.

"Well," Laney asserted, "if you want us to hurry up, you got to let us get up and get dressed, all right?"

"Okay," she said. She continued to sit on Wade's bed not moving an inch.

Wade propped himself up on one elbow and took aim at his little sister. "Beat it, Kell'. Laney's telling you he'd like to get dressed."

Puzzled, Kelli didn't understand. After all, she never had to leave the room when Wade got dressed. "Scat, girl," Wade grinned as he playfully popped her on the behind sending her on her way.

Laney laughed, "She's a doll, Wade. She's going to break some hearts one day."

"Nah, she's going to aggravate someone to death," Wade shot back.

Having missed breakfast, the aroma of home cooking coming from Wade's mother's kitchen aroused the boys' appetites. Hard at work, she had been preparing lunch all morning. Roast cooked with carrots and potatoes, fresh baked buttered biscuits, steaming gravy from the delicious roast ready to be poured over a bounty of rice, steamed broccoli with hollandaise sauce, and finally, a giant pitcher of sweetened iced tea Southern style with the smell of a refreshing mint leaf mounted on each glass.

Showered and dressed, the boys followed the wonderful scent of food straight to the kitchen like bears to honey. When they walked in, Wade's mom was standing over the sink, grinning. She was glad to see them, especially Wade's weekend guest.

"Well, Laney, how have you been doing?" she asked.

"Doing just great," Laney beamed as he walked over to give her a huge hug.

"We were sure worried about you last night driving up in that snowstorm and all."

"Oh, it wasn't nearly as bad as everybody made it out to be," Laney said. "A couple of minor wrecks and I guess the highway patrol just panicked. I finally got off of I-75 and took Highway 41. Couldn't believe that there was hardly a soul using it."

"Well, we sure are glad you made it here in one piece," Wade's mom said placing a pot into the sink.

Taking note of the spread on the kitchen table, Laney roared so everyone could hear, "Holy mackerel! Can you believe this Wade? People where I'm from just don't eat like this every day. Y'all are spoiled up here in Georgia!"

Wade's mother, who was eating up every patronizing word Laney was laying on her, tried sounding modest.

"Oh, it's really nothing Laney."

"Shoot," he responded. "If I lived up here I'd weigh another fifty pounds. You could count on that."

Kelli entered the room and giggled.

"What? You think I'm already big enough, Kell'?" Laney chuckled reaching over and poking her in the ribs.

The little girl just laughed as Wade's mom motioned for them to all take a seat at the table.

"Where's Dad?" Wade asked tentatively looking toward his mother.

"Oh, he called and said he wouldn't be able to make it. He's tied up with some of his business doings. Wade, would you mind saying the blessing for us please?"

Wade bowed his head obediently and started returning thanks.

"Lord, bless this food to the nourishment of our bodies, and our bodies to thy service. Amen."

"Amen," Laney echoed as he and Wade's family cheerfully began filling their plates.

The small talk at the dinner table centered on Laney, what he'd been doing, his plans for college, and his trip up in the snow.

When they finished eating, Laney helped the family clear the table and put the dishes in the dishwasher. Laney kept crowing about the wonderful meal he'd just eaten. When all the work in the kitchen was done, Laney again gave Wade's mom a big hug as a final show of thanks.

Wade retreated to the other side of the kitchen's bar where he used the phone to call Angie. The girls had planned to go shopping in Albany at the mall while the boys had intended to go quail hunting. But the rare presence of snow had put all such plans on hold.

Laney and Kelli meandered to his side of the counter to see what was going on.

"They want us to come to the dorm," Wade said. "Ann's already out there. They want us to bring some pans to sled down some hills."

Wade's mother turned and faced her son.

"Look in that drawer under the stove there," she pointed at the spot. "There should be quite a few old pans in there. Y'all will probably need some big flat ones like pizza pans or cookie sheets. Don't you think?"

"You must think I can't get my big derriere in a little pan. One with sides on it, huh?" Laney shot back.

Wade's mother laughed and said, "Now, Laney, I wasn't going to say that."

Laney chuckled and looked at Kelli who had a hurt look on her face.

"What's the matter Kelli?"

Wade knew exactly what her problem was. "You want to go with us?" He asked with a teasing little smile.

"Yeess," she said meekly, her head hung down and her big eyes peeping up. She was trying hard to see if he was being serious or not.

"Mom," Wade called to his mother who had left the room. "Is it okay if Kelli goes with us?"

"Kelli, let the boys alone. I'm sure they want to be with their girlfriends today."

"It's all right," Wade remarked still watching his little sister.

Laney chimed in agreeing as he picked her up and hung her over one of his big shoulders.

Wade's mom quickly stepped back into the room.

"You boys sure?" She watched the boys as each nodded his head in affirmation.

"Well, all right. But y'all be careful."

The boys gathered the cookie sheets and pizza pans from the drawer and after getting their heavy coats and gloves rounded up, they headed out the door with Kelli tagging along.

In Laney's car, they pulled out of the driveway, down the alley, and past the creek's woods. *It's now like a winter wonderland, covered in ice and snow*, Wade thought. Only he seemed to notice.

Making their way to the college, they drove past several snowmen in people's yards. Each one of them, large or small, was built with varying degrees of sophistication and success. Good workmanship or poor, it mattered little to Kelli as she was enthralled and delighted by any such sight involving snow.

A sparse crowd of students mulled across the snow-blanketed campus as they arrived. Signs that a larger crowd had been there earlier in the morning were evident everywhere. The day's date was scrawled on car windshields, along with snowmen, snowballs, and snow angels littering the once powdery lawn.

Leaving the car, they walked down the snow-covered sidewalk and up the slippery steps to the entrance of the girls' dorm. Wade held Kelli's hand as they walked inside to the warmth and chatter of the residence. They found Louisa, Ann, and Angie all waiting for them.

"Kelli!" the girls beamed as they had expected only the boys. "How are you doing?" Surrounding her, they thought she was precious all bundled up in her little pink-hooded coat.

"Would you like to come up and see our room?" Louisa asked.

Being in a women's only dorm was a grand experience for Kelli and getting to go upstairs where even Wade and Laney couldn't go was icing on the cake. Louisa took Kelli's hand, and along with Angie, they left the dorm's large sitting area and headed upstairs to show her around.

Groups of girls and boys were returning to the dormitory's lobby for a rest after playing out in the snow for most of the morning. Watching them pour in, Ann and Laney made their way to a secluded corner of the room for a little privacy, leaving Wade amid the throng.

Wade started to feel insecure. Not one to start a conversation, he acknowledged people with a "hi" and a smile. As more and more unfamiliar students entered the building, the more uncomfortable the dark-haired boy became. Quietly in an attempt to escape his anxiety, he found an isolated chair at the far end of the room and took a seat.

After about ten minutes, and much to Wade's relief, the girls came back downstairs with Kelli beaming and jabbering to Wade about all she had seen and heard. As if she were a coed herself, she defiantly finished by saying, "and Wade you can't go up there either."

Louisa and Angie laughed at the little girl's attitude.

"Well, I guess she told you," Angie snickered.

"She always tells me," Wade retorted. "Isn't that what girls were born to do?"

The door to the lobby opened suddenly and in walked Les. Everyone turned in his direction when he entered. People from across the room greeted him enthusiastically. When he finished shaking hands and hugging coeds, the always-affable Les, joined his friends. Laney and Ann had gotten up from where they'd been talking and joined the others.

"Hey, folks, what's going on?" Les boomed out happily. Noticing Wade's little sister, he exclaimed, "Well, Kelli, I can see that Wade and Laney needed a chaperone today."

Puzzled by his comment, she said boldly, "Les, you can't go upstairs. Did you know that?"

"Yep. But you sure can, and I bet you have, haven't ya'?"

A wide-eyed Kelli nodded, "Angie and Louisa carried me up there, and it was really neat."

"I bet it was," Les said as he rubbed her head.

Les asked Wade, "Did y'all bring the pans with you?"

"Yeah. They're out in the car," Wade confirmed.

"Well then, let's get going, gang," Les sang out as he started toward the doorway.

"Wait a minute, Les," Angie stopped him. "Where are we going to go? Are there any good hills around here?"

The group fell quiet for a moment. After all, South Georgia was not exactly noted for its looming hills. One of Les' friends shouted from across the room, "Go over to the lake. That's where everybody's at. There are some pretty good ones over there."

Les thanked the guy with a wave and pointed the rest of the group to the door.

As they exited, Laney said in a falsetto voice, "Where we gonna go?" He poked the ticklish Angie in the ribs. "What difference does it make? There's snow everywhere. We're not going out there trying to find Mount Everest, girl."

Jumping from being poked, Angie smiled at Wade's taller friend giving him the evil eye. It was on now, she thought, and sure enough, as they made their way down the steps of the dorm, all bedlam broke loose. Angie made a large snowball and blasted Laney with it.

"Is this some of that snow you were talking about, Laney?" she laughed.

Laney made a snowball, as did everyone else. Angie ran behind Wade for protection.

"Don't get behind me," Wade shouted, but it was too late. Laney plastered them both with a huge freezing ball of the white powdery snow.

It was everybody for himself as they all joined in the melee. Little Kelli crouched beside the steps of the dorm to hide from the onslaught when suddenly Laney ran by and swept her up.

Laney, armed with a handful of snowballs, used Kelli as a shield. Everyone scattered in all directions, as he became the unconditional winner of the skirmish.

"Truce. Truce," Angie yelled as she and Wade were the first ones to come back into the area.

"All right. Everyone, drop your ammunition," Laney commanded as the rest returned. Satisfied that no one would hit him, he dropped his and put a dazed Kelli down.

The boys got the cookie sheets and pizza pans out of Laney's car. The girls along with Kelli started making angels in the snow. When they finished admiring their heavenly creations, they returned to the boys who had patiently waited on them.

The group strolled through the three-inch accumulation toward the lake, everyone marveling at the majestic scenery surrounding them. Whether it was ice or snow, the frozen substance covered everything. From the glint and sparkle of ice-covered limbs and telephone lines to the powdery whiteness of yards and fields, everything they saw astonished them.

As they made their way between the dorms and department buildings that made up the college, Louisa and Les fell behind. The rest of the group stopped to wait, as they saw Les struggling.

"You okay?" Wade asked.

Panting, Les responded that he was fine. He was just suffering from a slight cold.

Wade considered his pal cautiously, then slowly walked onward with the rest of the group. Soon, they found themselves at the apex of the lake's steepest incline.

"All right, gang! Let's get going!" Laney yelled as he jumped on his pan to slide down the slope. It appeared that several icy slicks had been created in the hill from people sliding down it earlier. Finding one, Laney literally flew down the embankment.

"Woohoo!" he yelled as he came to a skidding stop at the bottom.

The rest of the group joined in as they raced each other to get to the first of the several remaining slicks. The girls were much more tentative as they made their first trip down the slope. Laney and Les tried spinning themselves in circles as they headed down.

On her first sled ride, Kelli sat in Louisa's lap as Les' girlfriend carefully guided the pan down the lane's center. Laney retrieved the little tyke at the bottom and threw her over his shoulders for a piggyback ride back up the hill. She rode alone on her next trip down with Laney at the top giving her a push and Wade at the bottom making sure she had a safe landing.

After about thirty minutes, the girls grew tired of the sledding and decided to build a snowman. The snow started to fall once more, appearing as light flurries. As the clouds grew darker, it began pouring down in heavy gusts.

The boys, tired of this one hill, were off in search of steeper and faster runs. They found some on the back side of the campus a long way off and out of sight of the lake.

No one else had been to this spot, and the snow was still light and fluffy and a good three inches thick. The first run the boys made was a little slow because of the friction, but each subsequent one became icier and faster.

"You ready for a race?" Wade called up to Laney who was just starting his next slide down.

"You bet. Dufus," Laney shouted back laughing and trying to stay on track as he whizzed past Wade. When he skidded to a stop at the bottom, he yelled at Wade who was climbing the hill.

"What's the bet, retard?"

"Retard? How 'bout a six-pack, Goober?"

"Les doesn't drink, you fool," Laney said as he climbed back to the top.

"Hey, Les? Laney's starting to sound more and more like his twin Karl, isn't he?"

"You mean Laney's idol," Les chimed.

"Yeah, right," Laney responded. "Where is that butthole anyway?"

Unlike the other guys, Karl's demeanor did not intimidate Laney.

"Did y'all ever find out why he and his girlfriend didn't show up for the Florida-Georgia game?" he asked.

The other two boys shrugged.

Wade spouted sarcastically, "Nice call he made telling us he wasn't going to make it. Geez, how thoughtful."

Les and Laney shook their heads disgusted.

"So what ya' gonna bet me, fart head?" Wade asked.

"Fart head? You calling me a fart head? Retard," Laney shouted, marching his way through the snow to the top of the hill.

"Just me and you, turd knocker. A case of beer. How 'bout that?"

"You're on, pal!"

Wade turned to his smaller friend, "Hey, Les? How about going to the bottom? You be the referee. All right?"

Les agreed as he got on his pan and slid to the bottom of the hill. He signaled to the other two boys who were sitting on their pans.

"Y'all ready to go?"

Both raised their hands giving him a thumbs-up.

"Okay, I'm going to say ready-set-go and the first one to pass me is the wiener, wiener-heads," Les chuckled.

Both boys at the top rocked their pans back and forth on their icy lanes hoping to get less friction and the advantage of a good push.

Les yelled loudly, "Okay, guys. Ready! Set! Go!"

Both boys had strong starts as they leaned back on their pans to make themselves more aerodynamic. Being smaller, Wade was more capable of keeping his pan on track. Just as they passed the midway point, Laney ran off course and crashed sending him tumbling down to the bottom.

"And the winner is Wade," Les hollered as Wade shot past him.

When Laney stopped rolling and sprawling, all three boys busted out laughing.

"A case of beer for me, loser," Wade roared with delight.

Laney, covered in snow, jumped up. Grabbing his pan and heading back up the hill, he yelled, "Double or nothing. We'll see who the loser is going to be, fool."

Panting and laughing, Wade rushed up the hill after him. When the two boys reached the top, they stopped momentarily to catch their breaths. Holding their hands on their knees, they sucked in the thick cold air into their burning lungs.

Getting back into the seated position on their pans, they signaled for Les to restart the race.

Laughing, Les raised both his arms once more, gazed up at his two good friends, and collapsed face down into the snow.

The other two boys at the top laughed.

"Come on, Les! Let's go! I gotta win my beer back," Laney shouted, but Les did not move.

Wade grew concerned, "Something ain't right, Laney. He's been acting sick all afternoon, and he hasn't moved yet."

The two boys glided their pans down the hill to see what was wrong. Les was still lying face down in the snow.

"Let's get him turned over," Laney spoke softly.

The boys grabbed him by the legs and torso and turned him upright. Wade gently wiped the snow from his pale face.

"Look at his eyes, Wade," Laney remarked.

At first, Les' eyes were closed. Then they started flittering. When they stopped blinking, they would partially open. The boys could not see his pupils, but only the eyes' white sclera.

Wade became panicked. "What da' you think, Laney?"

Laney remained calm. "I don't know. He might be having an epileptic seizure the way he's acting. Give me your coat."

Removing his and putting it over Les' torso, he took Wade's and placed it over Les' legs. "We'll give him a minute to come out of it."

Wade hovered over his pal nervously.

"Hey, Les," he said trying to get his friend to come out of his stupor. "Can you hear me?"

Les did not respond. He only moaned smacking his lips, slobber drooling from the corners of his mouth.

Waiting several more minutes with no improvement, Wade nervously asked Laney what he thought they needed to do, but before Laney could respond, Wade blurted out, "Why don't we carry him out of here?"

Laney thought for a second and countered, "I can carry him by myself. Why don't you run back and send for help? You know, get an ambulance. They can meet us halfway."

"Okay. I'm gone."

Wade took off like a shot. Now and then, he would stagger and almost fall, as he would hit a submerged limb or a deeper drift where a ditch or crevice lay hidden from sight.

Laney kept speaking softly to his friend trying to wake him as he shielded the snow from hitting Les' face, but Les showed no reaction. A good five minutes after Wade left, he gently took Les in his arms and, as fast as he could go, made his way back toward the school.

The girls had headed back to the dorm. They had grown tired of the snow and cold, and they worried that Kelli might get sick if they kept her out in it for too long.

As Wade made his way across the field by the lake and back to their first sliding spot, a group of people sledding there could tell something was wrong. Noticing Wade's sense of urgency, one boy called out asking him what the problem was.

Breathing hard, Wade shouted back between breaths, "It's Les—he's having a seizure or something—back of the lake. We need to get some help." Everyone there headed for the site as Wade continued seeking emergency assistance. Making it back to the main campus, he flagged down one of the school's security guards making his afternoon rounds.

When the students Wade had met reached Laney on the other side of the lake, they found him rapidly moving across the field with Les in his arms. They tried to stop him so they could carry Les the rest of the way, but Laney would have none of it. Onward he drove himself quickly outpacing even those who had come to help. By the time he reached the lake's sledding hill, Wade and the security guard were there waiting with an ambulance that had just arrived.

Retrieving a stretcher, two of the medical attendants headed to meet Laney as he made his way up the last portion of the hill. Putting the gurney down at Laney's feet, they took Les from his exhausted arms and loaded the still-unconscious young man onto their cot. Laney fell to his knees gasping for air.

As one E.M.T. wrapped Les in a blanket, another asked Laney what happened as he started checking Les' vital signs. Laney still breathing hard couldn't respond.

Wade spoke for him. "Just like I told you before. He just passed out. He wasn't doing anything."

The medic nodded as he continued to take Les' pulse. He looked up at his partner and said, "Tachycardia. Heart's really racing here. Looks like his pupils are dilated too. Let's get him in the van out of this weather and see about his blood pressure. Call the ER and tell them we got him coming."

Picking up the gurney, the two men carried Les up the remainder of the hill headed for their ambulance. The vehicle's red lights were still flashing, as were rumors of an accident involving Les on a hill down by the lake.

Wade accompanied the paramedics back to their van. Turning back toward Laney, he called out, "Get the girls and get Kelli to the house. I'm gonna ride over with Les."

Word traveled fast, and the news that something had happened to Les made it to Louisa before Laney could get to her. Meeting Laney halfway back to the lake, the girls were frantic.

"What's happened?" Louisa asked anxiously.

"I don't know. He just collapsed out there," Laney said between breaths.

The ambulance silently appeared between two campus buildings heading down the front road of the school. Tears streamed down Louisa's face as Laney put his arm around her shoulder. They all headed for his car to drive to the local hospital.

"Listen, Louisa, Wade's with him. He'll be okay," Laney tried consoling her as he helped her into the vehicle.

A crowd of students gathered in the Emergency Room waiting area. Angie carried Kelli home before coming herself. Kelli cried the whole way, frightened by the unusual experience and worried about her buddy Les. Only after climbing into her mother's arms did she stop. As Wade's mom comforted her daughter telling her Les would be all right, in a more serious tone, she whispered to Angie to call them as soon as they found out something.

Back at the lobby of the Emergency Room, the gathering crowd anxiously awaited word. Louisa finally composed herself and took a seat to wait. From the looks in the waiting room, she might have been the only girl there who had gathered her wits as most were sniffling and crying into tattered hand-wrung tissues. Most of the guys who had come along with them had either gathered into groups or were walking around alone trying to look stoic.

Minutes turned into hours as those who could take a seat did so. The rest stood around quietly whispering as the intercom went off from time to time calling a family in to see one of the patients residing in the back.

When the group arrived, everyone speculated about what happened. Everything from Les drowning in the frozen lake to him running into a tree and being paralyzed was suggested. As time progressed, it seemed that almost everyone had run out of things to say.

Now their minds had begun to slow enough to notice the mundane things. Like the way the bell to the nearby elevator sounded, or the smell of the place, or even what the many signs surrounding them said.

At long last, a nurse appeared about the same time Les' parents arrived. She asked for the family to come with her. Immediately recognizing Louisa and Laney, who stood up, Les' mother motioned for them to come too. Everyone else stayed behind.

"How's he doing?" Les' mom asked the nurse.

"He's going to be fine. I'll take you to him," the woman said as she walked them back to a small waiting area where Dr. Jackson, Karl's dad, and Wade were standing.

"Robert. Grace," Dr. Jackson greeted them.

"Bill," Les' father, returned the greeting shaking his former neighbor's hand. It was amazing how calm Les' parents were, only knowing what Angie and Kelli had told Wade's mom. Les' whole family seemed to share this unflappable trait.

"Les is doing well," Dr. Jackson said. "Looks like you've just gotten yourselves a diabetic in the family and he went a little hypoglycemic is all. Are either one of you diabetic?"

"No," they shook their heads responding to the doctor in unison. "But his grandmother, my mother, was," Les' mom commented.

"Well, it does appear to run in families, Grace. You should get that checked yourself the next chance you get."

Les' mom nodded indicating that she would.

He paused as he gathered his thoughts.

"Uh," he stammered as he began. "Concerning Lester, his sugar level got too low, and he basically just passed out. I happened to be out here when they brought him in, so I went back with him to see what was going on. Right now, they've got him hooked up on an IV to rehydrate him and get his sugar level back up to normal. It would be my guess that he'll probably be ready to go home in the morning, and he should be fine. You might want to thank these two guys especially," he gestured at Wade then shook Laney's hand since he hadn't seen him in a while. "Had they not gotten him here as fast as they did—things could have gotten bad quickly."

The intercom went off calling Dr. Jackson to a code. Immediately becoming more serious, he quickly walked away. Over his shoulder, he hurriedly said, "I'll check on you guys and Les later. Gotta run." Through a set of swinging doors, he disappeared.

Standing outside Les' curtained-off room, Les' mom and dad thanked Laney and Wade, giving each of them a hug. Smiling at Wade, Les' mother said, "I heard you rode in the ambulance all the way over here with him."

Wade nodded his head, "Yes, ma'am."

Mrs. Ellis leaned over and whispered into his ear, "Les has always thought of you as a brother, and we do too."

She patted Wade on the cheek then turned and pulled the curtain to Les' room revealing numerous monitoring devices and an I.V. hooked up to her son

Pulling a thermometer from Les' mouth, a nurse spoke softly into Les' still glazed eyes, "Hey, Les. You've got visitors. Recognize any of these people?"

Les looked up at his parents and friends in the room. Feebly, he said, "Hi, Mom."

"Hi, hon'," she replied. She took his hand and, kissing him on the cheek, whispered, "I love you."

Les mumbled, "I love you too, Mom."

His dad reached over and kissed him on the forehead. Then he knelt beside him, gently holding his other hand. Les smiled when he saw who it was.

Still groggy, he stared at the end of the bed. He saw Louisa, calm and serene smiling, down at him.

"Hey, Louis'," he tried calling out.

"Hey, Les," she said softly mouthing the words, "I love you."

Les smiled back. Wade and Laney exited the room, aware that this was a private moment for Les and his family. As they walked down the hallway of the busy Emergency Room, Laney told Wade it would probably be best if they let the crowd in the lobby know that Les was going to be all right.

They broke the good news concerning Les' condition to a few of the girls standing nearby who had been at the hospital from the beginning of the event. Word of Les' recovery quickly spread to the rest of the gathering. The crowd dispersed slowly from the building.

The next day Les was amazed at the number of visitors and flowers he received for just a one-night stay in the hospital. Alert and back to normal, he took his own phone calls and let anyone come in for a visit at any time except when the nurses came in to check on him.

Late that afternoon, he was released with a prescription for glucose tablets. He was also informed that he should get some test strips to monitor his daily sugar and ketone levels. Other than that, he was told to make sure he ate many in-between meal snacks throughout the day.

Strangely unlike most other peoples' diagnoses of diabetes, Les' problem involved not being able to keep his glucose level consistently high enough. He was directed to manage this problem primarily through diet. In case of an emergency drop in his sugar level, he was given an injectable product called Glucagon, which could rapidly return his blood glucose level to normal.

Earlier in the day, Laney and Wade had come by to check on Les. Finding him doing so well, they left the hospital to enjoy the rest of their day. Of course, all the girls went by to see Les, even Kelli and her mom. Only Louisa stayed by his side.

With the plans for the weekend in total disarray, Wade and Laney found Angie and Ann, and they all decided to go to a local pizza parlor. As they sat eating and talking, finally the four started to relax.

"Man, I didn't know how tired and hungry I was," Laney said as he sipped his drink. The others agreed as they all leaned back into their seats.

Laney said to his pal, "Do me a favor, Wade. Don't call me to come back up here quail hunting anytime soon. Okay?"

"Bud—that isn't what brought you up here." Wade gave his cousin a little wink.

Coolly, Laney gazed into his girlfriend's eyes, "Well, I thought I might as well see her while I was up here. You know, to make sure she was doing all right and all."

Ann gave him the evil eye as she took another bite of her pizza.

Laney smiled back and turned his attention to Wade. "Well, folks," he proclaimed. "You guys probably already know this, but we've got a star in our midst."

"What are you talking about?"

"I'm talking about you, Wade. Have y'all ever seen any of this guy's paintings?" Laney asked, referring to several pictures Wade had either finished or was working on.

Wade hung his head embarrassed.

"I've seen 'em," Ann said admiringly. "They're unbelievable."

Angie turned to her boyfriend bemused. "I haven't seen any of them. He's never even mentioned to me that he is an artist."

Wade mumbled timidly in her direction, "You can see them whenever you'd like, Angie. I just didn't think you'd be interested, that's all."

"Get him to show you the one he's just finished," Laney said. "It's a picture of this beautiful woman standing where you can partially see her in the front doorway to her house. There's a little boy feeding some squirrels on a picnic table in the side yard. It's the expression that this woman has on her face. I couldn't figure out if it's the look of desire or desperation. It's almost like she's looking right into your heart."

"What's it mean, Wade?" Angie eagerly asked.

"I don't know. Nothing really, I guess."

Ann scolded him. "Wade, you had to come up with an idea to paint something like that. Come on, tell us your thoughts about it."

"I'm being honest," Wade said in his defense. "I mean, I just start painting, and the ideas come as I paint. I mean, it's really no big deal."

All three were staring at him in silent frustration at his humility. All knew it was sincere, and it would be pointless to try to get him to open up any further. It was the uniqueness, that kind of strangeness that any good artist has. Though they knew this, they couldn't understand it, but for that matter neither could he.

After the pizza, they spent the rest of the day playing in the snow with Kelli at Wade's house. The snowstorm had ended Saturday night, and by late Sunday afternoon, the blanket of white was melting away. Laney decided it was time to head home to Jacksonville much to Ann's sorrow and left just before nightfall.

As winter quarter came to an end, it proved a more successful venture for both Wade and Les academically as they both were starting to figure out the system and what it took to excel. Les ended up with an A and two B's and Wade with three B's. The girls made all A's as usual.

Spring quarter quickly passed ending the boy's first full year of school. Les continued to work at the college where he had nailed down a summer job, and Wade continued working at the clothing store.

During his first year, Les had won several awards at the college including a good citizenship award. He'd also won several debating contests against other area colleges, and he won the "Best Fan" award for supporting the school's basketball team.

As for Wade's first year, he worked, fell deeply in love with Angie, and painted. Until this point, his painting had been the love of his life. With Angie around, it was starting to place a distant second.

CHAPTER 6

Athens

(Fall Quarter)

Most young people happy to be graduating from high school have only fleeting flashes of the future and the responsibility it will bring. Usually, they learn quickly the "right" thing to say when someone asks what they plan to do with their lives. Sometimes it's parroting back what their parents have told them they should be doing. Sometimes it's saying something that sounds cool. Most of the time it's a mistake . . . but mistakes, fortunately, can be overcome.

In deciding these issues, the girls had an advantage over the boys during the seventies. The social norm of marrying a breadwinner and raising children still existed. For the young women, salary and advancement, though important, didn't seem as crucial as opposed to their boyfriends. This circumstance allowed the girls to major in what they enjoyed and kept the boys focused more on what they could earn.

The second year of school at the Junior College went by as before with one exception. When it ended, everyone would have to decide either to continue his education or enter the world as a working adult. If they planned to further their education, they also had to decide where their academic record would allow them to go.

Wade's father pushed him hard toward accounting. As for Les, though his father didn't drive him like Wade's, he still desired a job that could offer him and his future family a good living. During the last year of school, he took a few electives in finance and was leaning toward a degree in that area. Both friends, especially Wade, were nervous about the choices they had to make. They wanted to get this part of the process over with fast. After all, when boys became a certain age, living at home with their parents was unacceptable.

Angie decided on a degree in secondary education and Louisa in psychology specializing in adolescent behavior. After graduating from junior college, they, along with Les and Wade, elected to finish their four-year degrees at the University of Georgia in Athens.

With the help of his father, Wade landed a job at a textile factory for the remainder of the summer of 1973. He earned a good wage and shared in the interactions with his new workmates.

By mid-summer, Les used his extensive network of friends to find a job at a local bank, a great position for a finance major. He started out as a teller and quickly worked his way into serving as an assistant for a loan officer. As the summer ended, and with the blessing of their parents, all four friends prepared for their next great adventure: going off to The University of Georgia for their final two years in Athens.

Ann had gone the year before, so Louisa and Angie would be her roommates. As for Les and Wade, they would have shared an apartment with Karl had he not transferred to Duke in Durham, North Carolina, where he planned to enter medical school.

The two boys found a reasonably priced trailer park out on Atlanta Highway, not too close to the school's main campus. For them, the only accommodations they needed were a roof over their heads, a refrigerator, and for good measure, a shower and toilet.

The girls needed a little more like style, amenities, and status. Security appealed to their parents, so they got them what they wanted, especially since the price tag tended to keep the riff-raff away. Ending up at Sussex, the crème de la crème of the Athens apartment scene, they made their home while their boyfriends lived just down the road.

II

The trip to the University had been a long one. When Louisa and Angie arrived at their destination, the girls, with help from their boyfriends, unloaded their cars. They made their way up the steep steps and stairs and into Ann's second story suite. Back and forth, again and again, they marched carrying luggage and containers until they had emptied their vehicles.

The boys were sent away more than glad to be finished unloading all their girlfriends' stuff. With them gone, the roommates began to work methodically folding clothes and placing them in drawers, hanging up dresses and suits, unloading box after box of pots and pans, dishes and plates, silverware and appliances. It was all there. Too much of it as a matter of fact. Some of it would have to go back on their next trip home.

With everything in its place, the new coeds decided to get a feel for their new city. For girls, there appeared no better way of doing this than to go shopping. From Milledge Avenue, Lumpkin, and Baxter Streets over to Prince and North Avenue, they made their way. As Ann drove, she showed them the location of every neat store, shop, pub, and restaurant.

At the end of their shopping and sightseeing tour, she drove them across the school's campus. She pointed out the psychology department to Louisa. Heading to the southeast corner of the school, she drove them past Aderhold Hall, the main building housing the school's education department. Both Louisa and Angie were eager to discover this site. Aderhold was where most of their classes would be held.

After a couple of days of exploration, the day for class enrollment arrived. The school's large coliseum on the south end of campus hosted registration for new students. A frantic ordeal for most, it proved no different for the junior college transfers.

Standing in long lines to sign up for classes they wanted, the four friends finally completed this task. Catching a University bus, they proceeded across campus to the school's bookstore. With the materials they needed, they headed home ready for classes to begin, or so they thought.

After only a matter of days in classes, the newcomers realized that their experience at UGA would be vastly different from the one they had at their smaller two-year school. Their classes now were sometimes three to four times larger. Asking the teacher who taught using an overhead projector in a large auditorium a question looked to be, for all practical purposes, out of the question. The workload each of their professors gave seemed overwhelming if not insane.

Wade found the totality of this change unnerving. Finding his way around campus via the bus system had been difficult enough. With his teachers piling on all the work at such an accelerated pace, he found himself being left behind quickly.

III

Wade left the Journalism building from his accounting class. The long sleeve shirt he wore had protected him earlier, but now a biting chill enveloped him. The climate in Athens caught the boy completely off guard. He made his way onto the expanse of the second story patio. Down a set of stairs leading to a sidewalk, he crossed the street and headed for North Campus. Up a set of concrete stairs, he continued. Terraced into the side of a hill running past the English department, these steps and accompanying sidewalk ended on a plateau in front of the Terry School of Business. Up and down. Up and down. The school's setting with its field of cascading hills surrounded and elevated the university in almost every direction. But even the drudgery of having to overcome these inclines carrying a twenty-pound stack of books, could not overpower the spectacular scenery, especially this time of year. Leaves from hardwoods plastered the concrete sidewalks and courtyards in bright colors of purple, yellow, and red. The grass, once green from summer's growth was fading in spots. Deep orange stains appeared where the red Georgia clay leeched into each withered blade.

Wade noticed none of this as he climbed the hill huffing and puffing. A warm, wet fog blew from his mouth and nose, and immediately frosted, smoke-like, from the near freezing atmosphere surrounding him. Briskly he walked, shivering with each frozen step. Past the English department, past the Business school, taking a left at the Law Library, he cut down the road passing the school's infirmary and headed across Lumpkin Street in the direction of the Kappa Omega house.

Karl had been a member of this fraternity his first two years of college before transferring to Duke. It had been over a year since he left the University, but his near godlike reputation and stories about his wild escapades remained well intact. Countless times his old fraternity buddies recounted these stories to Wade immortalizing Karl in the process.

Hurriedly walking wanting to get out of the cold, Wade headed for the fraternity house. The brotherhood, thinking Wade would be the next "Karl" of the house, doted on him trying hard to get him to join. Wade had use of their parking lot, which proved very convenient. Other new students were forced to park on the other side of the campus where they had to catch buses to get to their north campus classes.

As Wade got to the Kappa O parking lot, he rushed to his car hoping no one at the house had seen him. Meeting and hanging around strangers still proved difficult for him. Quietly and quickly, he disappeared as he exited the area heading for the safety of his trailer and Les.

IV

At the girl's apartment, glasses tinkled as Louisa dropped ice cubes into each one. She set them on the table for their evening meal. In her bedroom, Angie labored over homework as Ann, in the kitchen, carved a ham she baked earlier. All three girls had been in Athens for over a month. Surprising and unusual for finicky females, they all seemed to get along. Ann, comfortable with Athens, proved to be a fun, outgoing personality.

After 'going steady' for nearly two years, Ann and Laney had decided to date other people. The couple found it produced more pain than either had anticipated.

Uncharacteristically, Ann's mood became more somber as the quarter progressed. Angie and Louisa trekked right along with their lives as nothing had changed with their itineraries except their new and more exciting location.

As Louisa finished setting the table, the doorbell rang.

Hearing Les identify himself, Ann opened the door for him to enter

"Have you eaten yet?" Louisa called from the kitchen.

"Yeah," Les replied. "I ate at Arby's a little while ago."

He glanced at Ann. "You won't believe who I ate with."

Ann looked at him questioningly.

"Terrie Brooks," Les continued. "She looked terrible."

"I'm not surprised," Ann quipped. "She's still dating Karl if you can believe that. And from what I'm hearing, he's still running around on her like crazy. Why she puts up with him and all his crap is beyond me."

Les nodded agreeing. "I was over at the KO house with Wade about a week ago. Wade went off somewhere with some of the 'brothers' and the guy I was left with filled me in on what Karl had been doing the last couple of years. You can only imagine what I heard. Anyway, it came up that about two years ago he had gotten someone pregnant, but he had it taken care of. The guy says this with a grin now. Like no big deal, Karl is really cool; he can take care of anything." Lester shook his head disappointed.

"An abortion?" Ann scoffed. "You think it was Terrie?"

Les shrugged, but the look he gave Ann agreed with her suggestion. "What's really interesting is that according to this guy who seemed to know him quite well, Karl's dad was the one who made all the arrangements." Les' eyes never left Ann's as he spoke.

"Hmmp," Ann smirked. "I'm not surprised. Karl's only doing what he's seen his daddy do for years. His mother knows he's running around on her too. I don't know if it's the money or if she just feels too helpless to do anything about it. Either way, she ought to give the sorry jerk the boot."

"I wouldn't go that far," Les said. He sat on the sofa and picked up the day's paper to read. "We don't know if any of this is true about Karl or his father. It's all third hand. Just speculation."

Louisa said nothing during the conversation. She kept to herself in the kitchen taking in what she expected all along.

"When's the last time you've seen brother Karl?" Ann questioned Les sarcastically.

"What?" he said, momentarily glancing from behind the newspaper. "Oh, this past summer. He was working up at a hospital in Raleigh, and he came home for a few days to visit his parents. I found out he was in town and went over to see him."

"Why do you waste your time? I bet he wouldn't have come over and see you."

"Maybe he would. Maybe not," Les responded, puzzled by Ann's continuing negativity. "Karl's Karl. He's got a huge ego. We all know that. But underneath it all, I think he's okay."

Louisa called from the kitchen, "Okay, gang, supper's ready."

Ann looked back at Les and with a steely stare said, "You'd have to have a sharp knife to get down that far, Les."

V

After an hour or so of talking with the girls, Les left their apartment and made his way back to the trailer finding Wade eating a large bologna sandwich and watching T.V.

"What's going on?" Les asked as he sat his books on the kitchen counter.

"Nothin' much. Got tired of studying and decided to take a break. What are the girls up to tonight?"

"Ahh, the usual." Les opened the refrigerator and pulled out a pitcher of ice-cold lemonade. "Studying. By the way, you got a call from some of your buddies over at the frat this morning. They wanted to know where you were last night."

Wade gave Les a frustrated look. "Those guys are driving me crazy. They want us over there to eat. Over there to clean up. Over there to put on skits and take pledge tests. Man, I haven't got time for all that stuff. I don't even have time to study. If my dad wasn't so gung-ho on me doing this . . ."

Les stood in the kitchen sipping his lemonade. "Hey, don't blame it on your good ol' pappy, boy. You're the one who kept bragging about all the partying you were going to be doing when you got here. Remember all that stuff Karl told us about, 'life at the great fraternity house?'"

"Yeah." Wade looked down at a test paper in his hand. Disgusted, he held it for Les to see. "I made a sixty-nine on this accounting test. Got it back today. Dad's gonna' kill me if I don't do better than this."

Les smiled sympathetically. "Made a seventy-two on my first finance test. So, don't feel like the 'Lone Ranger,' son. We just got to get into the swing of things here, that's all." Having finished his drink, Les came into the den where he propped himself on the sofa across from Wade. With his statistics class notebook in hand, he started going over the day's notes.

"Well," Wade continued, "I'm going to give this fraternity thing a little longer. But I think the you-know-what's gonna hit the fan' when we have our first 'Social' with the Tri Delts. All hell is going to break loose when Angie finds out that's happening."

"When's that supposed to be?" Les asked looking up from his notes.

"Not this coming weekend, but the next." Wade shook his head.

"Well, before you get too worried about all that, I better let you in on a little secret. One that I'm not supposed to tell you."

Wade's neck and shoulders tightened as he cut his eyes at his friend.

"Angie told me tonight that she might join the Zeta's."

Squinting his eyes, Wade moaned loudly, "You're kidding me, right?"

"'Fraid not, ol' buddy. They've been after her for weeks to pledge."

Sitting in angst, Wade could only imagine Angie leaving him for some wealthy, handsome guy. "I can't believe after all she's seen me go through with the KOs that she'd want anything to do with all that. Man, I didn't even know they were talking to her." Wade was dismayed he had been clueless as all this was going on behind his back.

Les tried calming his pal down. "Look, Wade, she's just like you. She just wants to meet some new friends and have a little fun. That's all."

"Meet guys! They have socials too, you know," Wade's temper increased the more he thought about the situation.

"Give me a break, Wade," Les chided. "You were planning on going to socials. Right?"

Wade glared at him. "How would you like it if Louisa joined a sorority and went to parties by herself?"

"I'm sure they'll let you go with her, Wade," Les exclaimed still chastising him.

"No, you didn't answer my question, Les. How would you like for Louisa to be at a party with a bunch of drunk guys without you?"

"Louisa's a big girl, Wade. She can take care of herself. But if in your worst-case scenario, she found another guy and I think that's what you're worried about here—well then, I'd rather find out now than after I married her. Wouldn't you?"

That would have made perfect sense to Wade had he not been totally in love and revved up at the thought of losing his girlfriend. He gave no verbal response to Les' remark. He fumed at his friend momentarily and sighed heavily at the thought of it all.

Les smiled at him as he shook his head. Rising from the couch, he said, "I'm pretty tired. Think I'm going to call it a night, Wade. I'll go over my notes in the morning." He paused a second to look down at his friend. "You need to lighten up, pal. Don't make this molehill into a mountain, boy."

Wade nodded, but said nothing. They exchanged good nights as Les made his way to the back bedroom where he closed the door to get some sleep.

Wade remained in his recliner trying to focus on his studies, but couldn't. Sitting in silence, the same horrible thoughts kept circulating in his mind. Even the sounds and scenes coming from the television couldn't distract him from his apprehension. What would he do? How would he handle this situation with Angie? But nothing—not one positive thought came to mind.

The days passed with no more of a solution to his problems than the day before. Everything compounded in his mind. From dealing with school, worrying about his girlfriend, or trying to do what he perceived his dad wanted him to do, his grades suffered. He tried catching Angie talking to other boys between classes, and the fraternity called him constantly to come over and get involved.

As Wade struggled with the Kappa Omegas, Angie did likewise with her sorority. She kept putting them off for Wade's sake. But the idea of meeting new and exciting people, going and doing and having wondrous new adventures, was tantalizing to her. After all, she was young and away at college. This time, she realized, would never come her way again.

After much consternation, she decided she'd had enough of her moping jealous boyfriend. One Wednesday afternoon when classes were done for the day, she asked Wade to meet her at a park west of town by the Oconee River. The meeting was down the road from Wade's trailer park. Ann had carried Wade, Les, and all her roommates to this spot for a picnic when they first arrived in Athens.

Angie purposefully beat Wade to the spot giving her time to collect her thoughts, burning thoughts of Wade's possessiveness and jealousy. Sitting on the hood of her car at the river's edge, she watched the white-water rolling over the jagged rocks in the channel before her. Upriver and still in full view, she could see outcroppings of stones as they caused the river to narrow into tight, fast-moving currents before the water spread back out and slowed again further downstream.

The rushing water was hypnotic as was the scenery. Fall in the Piedmont of Georgia. Slow rolling hills filled with hardwoods along the river's bank. Leaves of yellow and orange and purple scattered across the forest floor, and those not yet fallen being whipped to and fro by the limbs of the deciduous trees as they danced to a hard-north wind.

The sky was blue and cloudless. Wade came driving down a steep embankment, which led to the clay-sand parking area below where Angie's Chevrolet was parked. As he got out, he looked at the silhouetted figure of his girlfriend as she sat on the hood of her vehicle. How beautiful she was, he thought. Her long sandy blonde hair was blowing in the breeze as she leaned back on her hands looking skyward.

She wore a pair of faded denim jeans and matching jacket with a red flannel shirt underneath, the perfect picture of laid-back Athens in the early seventies. How lucky he was to have her, he thought as he admired her long legs and curvaceous figure.

Sauntering, he made it to the side of her vehicle. "Hey," he called out gaining her attention. Looking out over the rapids and forest beyond, he remarked, "This really is something, isn't it?"

"It's pretty, all right," she said with a disarming sense of confidence and directness in her voice.

Wade stared at her puzzled as he detected this. "Why did you want to—"

"Wade," she hesitated. "I think we ought to start seeing other people." She glanced at him hard turning her head.

Wade stood speechless as his heart began to race.

Angie continued rapidly, not wanting to give him a chance to respond. "We've just kinda gotten in a rut," she said coldly.

"Is it the fraternity?" Wade exclaimed. "I've already decided to quit."

"No. It's not that. It's just us. You know, you keep getting mad if I talk to other guys. Remember the fight last week? You were yelling, accusing me of flirting with that boy over at the journalism building. You won't let me pledge Zeta. I think you'd be happier if I wasn't around."

"No, come on. You know better than that. It's just that . . ." Wade sighed heavily agonizing over what was happening.

"It's what, Wade?" Angie asked angrily.

Wade looked down at the ground searching for words, then back at her with his sad brown eyes. Dark circles stained them from all the worrying he had done lately. "It's just that I love you so much. I'm afraid of losing you." He paused gazing back down. "I'm sorry. I didn't realize I was doing all that."

"Well, you were," she said defiantly. She knew she was in total control of the situation. She attained a certain evil satisfaction in knowing that he knew it too.

"Well . . . I'm sorry," he said again in atonement. "Will you forgive me?" Wade's will was broken. Had she not known him as well as she did, she would have sneered at this display of pathetic submission. With an unkind word or look, she could render him helpless if she wanted and the temptation was great. Why did she want to be stuck in this sort of love affair limiting her ability to meet new people and see what the greater world was all about? In her heart, she knew the flame still burned, but in her mind, which now overpowered her, she saw other possibilities.

"I don't know," she responded stoically. "I'll have to think about it. Just give me some time."

Wade gently squeezed her hand saying okay, but she did not squeeze his back. Rather she pulled away from him like sliding away from a leper and opened the door to her car. Looking back once more at his hollowed, desperate face, she paused momentarily then slipped down into her seat. Cranking her automobile, she backed out of her parking spot then drove away without a word or a look in his direction.

Wade stood watching as her vehicle went up the steep clay stoned ramp toward the highway, the tires crunching through the rocks as it pulled its way to the top of the hillside. Turning onto the hard pavement of the road, it suddenly disappeared.

Stunned and confused, Wade remained frozen, a despondent gaze etched hard into his face. After taking several painful minutes to regain his composure, he slowly made his way down to the river's edge. He found an isolated grassy spot along its bank. Taking a seat, he leaned against the massive girth of a maple's trunk. A large lump swelled in his throat as he fought back tears. Nothing appeared the same. He could find no solace in the magnificence of his surroundings. His heart, his body, his soul ached from losing his girl.

There was no concept of time for the pitiful boy as he sat staring in a trance of grief. The afternoon soon stretched its shadows with the setting of the sun. In the almost colorless haze of twilight, Wade made it back to his car and headed home. How devastated he felt by this sudden turn of events. As the days and weeks went by, everything started falling apart. His grades went from bad to worse. He couldn't sleep. Every time he tried calling or seeing Angie, she would put him off or grow short with him.

Wade heard that Angie had found a new man. Some guy at her apartment complex started seeing her regularly. Wade was furious when he first heard about it then heartbroken as he realized there was probably no hope getting her back.

Ann had discerned her roommate's treachery toward Wade even before the quarter began. She witnessed nothing overt at first but became aware of it intuitively like a bad impression. She knew Wade couldn't read people like she could. He was too good of a guy. He certainly had his share of faults, but when it came to the big issues like truth, loyalty, and friendship, he could be counted on, and he did not understand why others could not be. Angie was taking advantage of this.

Wade had been blindsided by his girlfriend dumping him. Ann had seen it coming a mile away. Ticked off, Ann was mad as fire at the way her roommate had been treating her cousin.

Angie had been more than precocious and flirty with the boys since arriving in Athens. Ann knew she couldn't stop her roommate from doing this. If the girl didn't care for her cousin anymore, Ann certainly couldn't make her. However, she was furious with the way Wade was reacting to what Angie had done. After watching this soap opera of Wade trying to beg his way back into Angie's life, she had seen enough. One afternoon at his trailer, she scolded him for the way he had been carrying on.

"Listen, Wade!" she shouted as he sat mouse-like in his recliner. "You've got to get a grip, bud. I've never seen any girl get to you like this. You're one of the best-looking, smartest guys I know. Any girl would be glad to go out with you." She grew more adamant as she paced the floor stopping only to fire off another expressive volley. "What are you doing?" she asked in disgust. "Sitting out here like a moping crybaby? Calling her up? Begging her to take you back? Are you that damn worthless, Wade?"

Wade glared at her angry and insulted, but Ann didn't let up.

"Is she really that special? I say screw the bitch! Forget her!"

Wade snapped back retaliating, "Yeah, like you've done with Laney, right!"

"That's different," Ann cried back. "He still cares about me. He hasn't given me my walking papers."

"Right. That's why he's been up here to see you about a thousand times."

Ann intimated a smile. A sobering one as she glared at her dark-eyed cousin. Like a Mexican standoff, Ann blinked first going into the kitchen and the refrigerator for something to wet her thirst.

"Want something to drink?" she coolly asked as she opened the door to the icebox.

"No thanks," Wade responded as he climbed out of his recliner, walked into the kitchen, and sat down at his small kitchen table. He was rattled by the chewing out he'd just received.

Ann came and sat down across from him with a glass of ice water. "Well, buddy, I guess I'm coming down on ya' a little hard, huh?" she asked but not too apologetically.

"Not really," he sighed. "You're right. I've never acted like this before in my entire life, but I've never felt this way about anyone either."

Ann reached over and put her hand on his, which were folded and resting on the table in front of him. "You got to let her go, boy," she said warmly. She looked into his eyes firmly.

"I know. And I am," he responded.

Ann stood and went over to the sink. Pouring out her ice, she washed and dried the glass and put it into the cabinet. She turned around and, leaning her back against the counter, faced Wade. "I've got this neat friend," she chose her words carefully while looking down at the floor. "From Macon. My last year's roommate."

Wade rolled his eyes and shook his head. "I don't think I want to meet anybody just yet. Give me a little time."

"Well, if you change your mind . . ."

Wade studied Ann thoughtfully. "Thanks, Kitten, I'll remember that."

"Okay. Just think about it now." With that said, the two of them parted ways.

Wade put more effort into studying as he attended school. Painfully his feelings for his former girlfriend still plagued him. For Ann, things weren't going much better. Laney, her love, remained far away.

VI

This was the most difficult time in Wade's life. His once predictable mundane world was turned upside down, and unforeseen pressures were coming at him from every direction. His expectations concerning Angie, the fraternity, and school had fallen apart. What could he do now? What were his goals? His self-confidence was low as was his morale, but time marched on, stopping at nothing and for no one.

The bell sounded as Wade finished jotting his last notes for Dr. Cobb's insurance class. Closing his notebook, he got up with the rest of his classmates, put his books together, and headed for the doorway.

Many students collected in groups outside in the hallway to chat about the course or to gossip about school in general. Not Wade. He marched through the crowd on a mission: a mission of getting away from the strangers who surrounded him.

He didn't see it that way. He was blind to what he was doing. Wade could do the small talk and chitchat thing, but he felt awkward and out of place doing it. It was like he didn't belong there. His excuse for feeling this way was he needed to be doing something else, something planned or constructive.

Out of the journalism building and across the street, he headed to the bookstore. He needed another notebook and pens because the ones he had been using were starting to skip and let him down. Really, he was going there just to do something different even if it was just seeing the latest technology in hand-held calculators or the neat bulldog paraphernalia stamped and plastered on every conceivable object in the room.

Browsing his way through the place, he found a much-needed workbook for his accounting class. Lifting it from the counter, he continued down the aisle of the upstairs loft. He scanned the booklet's table of contents deep in thought. Rounding the end of the book-laden gondola as he read, he bumped into someone. It was a girl. The collision caused her to drop the armload of books she was carrying.

Wade bent down to help her retrieve them apologizing as he did so for his clumsiness. Looking at the young woman as he picked up some of her notebooks to hand them back, his eyes met those of an attractive blue-eyed blonde. As Wade kept apologizing, the girl's face blushed with a hint of shyness. She was embarrassed, but even so, the smile she gave him was warm and forgiving.

Standing back up, Wade apologized one last time. "Sorry about that—I should have been watching where I was going."

"That's all right. I should have too," she smiled timidly. Pausing, she hoped he would talk to her more.

An uncomfortable silence ensued as the two nervously stood staring at one another. Grinning, Wade looked down at one of her books.

"So, I see you're taking accounting. I am too and I hate it."

Laughing at the way he said this, the pretty young girl asked, "It's not that bad, now is it?"

"Yeah. That's why I'm buying this workbook," he said holding the booklet for her to see.

"Mind if I look?"

"Not at all."

Resting her handful of books on a nearby table, she took the workbook from Wade's hand and methodically scanned it. "Yeah," she said with a bit of an accent. It wasn't quite Southern. It had a little something else in it Wade couldn't make out.

"It's pretty similar to the one I've been using. It's been helpful to me," she said giving the book back to him.

Wade watched as she gathered her books and turned to face him.

"Well, I got to get going," she said. "My friends are waiting for me down at the checkout counter."

She paused for a second. As she started to turn, Wade called out, "What was your name again?"

"Mimi," she smiled stopping as she turned around.

"Mine's Wade," he grinned back. "Maybe I'll see you over at the business school sometime?"

The girl nodded with a shy smile, turned, and headed down the stairs to the ground floor.

VII

As school continued, not much occurred in the way of excitement for Wade. Pitifully, the big event in each day for him had become eating. At the first of the quarter, he and Les would buy groceries together, and they still did to some extent. Les was eating more often with Louisa and her roommates leaving Wade, for the most part, eating alone.

When Wade had money, his cupboard was only barely full and almost empty when he did not. This depended on the stage of the quarter. His father gave him a certain amount of cash for each school term. It was a tight but sufficient budget that Wade set. Tuition, books, and school-related items took the bulk of his money when the quarter first started, and if he wasn't careful with his spending, things could get pretty sparse before the next quarter got underway.

Wade developed a new routine. It was Spartan and frugal, and far too lonely, but in it, he found a sense of security. His life was sinking slowly and further into the depths.

By midterm, Wade didn't see or hear from Angie. Enthralled with her new man, she had even turned down the Zeta's offer to join their sorority. Wade wasn't seeing or hearing much out of Les and Louisa either. They had joined the Baptist Student Union and were participants in several class clubs involving their respective majors. They appeared even more preoccupied with each other than they had been back at junior college. Wade had to fend for himself.

On a blustery, overcast morning, Wade stood alone among a mass of people at one of the school bus stops. The jacket he wore did little to protect him from the frigid air. Shifting back and forth from one foot to the other, he shivered and rubbed his arms trying to stay warm.

In the distance, he could make out two buses heading his way as they climbed the hill from south campus. The one he wanted to get on coming from the direction of the pharmacy school was the north-south bus. The other coming from Aderholt was known as the east-west. Anxiously, he awaited their arrival hoping he could quickly get inside and get warm. Students in the area were starting to congest the place trying to squeeze through the crowd to get closer to the curb. Those at the front hoped they would be picked up; those at the back feared they would be left behind.

As all of this positioning was going on, a yell from the other side of the throng caught Wade's ear. Someone was calling his name. Glancing over his shoulder where people were getting in line for the east-west bus, he saw Ann waving at him excitedly. Standing next to her was Mimi. A bit bedazzled upon seeing him, she smiled and waved, then said something to Ann. Eyeing the two girls, Wade wondered if they knew each other.

As both buses arrived, people started squirming and pushing for position to get onto the large transports. Wade, distracted by the onrushing crowd, glanced away momentarily then looked directly back at his cousin who waved and yelled, "Steverino's at eight o'clock."

Wade nodded and gave a thumb up affirming he got the message. With the other hurried students, he made his way onto his crowded bus. Wade checked his watch as he sat and took notes in each boring class. *What was Ann up to*, he thought. *Did she know Mimi? Was Mimi coming to eat with them?* When his last class of the day was over, he rushed home on a mission. He made sure he had something cool to wear just in case Mimi might come, then he started studying his day's notes and reading the required material for his next day's classes. Uncharacteristically he finished all this work in record time.

He showered and shaved and put on a pair of blue jeans, a blue and white Denham shirt, his suede ankle-high hush puppies and a matching belt. Slipping on his short, tan fur-lined jacket with its fur collar, he went back into the bathroom to check his appearance. Combing his hair first, he splashed on some cologne, glanced in the mirror one more time, and left for Steverino's.

He hoped the girls would be there when he got to the sub sandwich and pizza shop at Five Points, but they weren't. He took a seat at a table by a window and watched other students come into and go out of the place. Some gave their orders, received their meals, and left. Others took a seat to eat.

Curiously Wade watched a group of three guys and two girls seated at a nearby table. Why, he always wondered, were the best-looking girls with the ugliest boys? Amused, he overheard the fellows brag about the great party they had just attended at a popular countryside venue. The girls they were with seemed impressed.

After a good fifteen minutes, Wade began to wonder if he had gotten Ann's message right. Maybe he was here at the wrong time or something. Twiddling his thumbs, he emerged from his chair and went to the counter at the entrance of the place and ordered a draft beer. After what seemed like an eternity, he heard the door to the establishment open and in walked Ann. Wade waved at his cousin; when he did not see Mimi behind her, his hopes sank.

Ann came up and took a seat at the table. "You didn't order me one?" she said referring to his beer.

Wade shook his head. "I didn't think you were going to show."

"Well, I got a little sidetracked. I had to borrow some notes from a girl over at Oglethorpe dorm. She wanted to talk. You know how it is with us girls." Ann looked around the room searching then back at Wade.

Curiously he asked, "Looking for someone?"

"Nope," she responded. "Think I'll go get a beer. You want another?"

"Yeah," Wade said as he started to stand, but Ann stopped him.

"Keep your seat. We need to save this table. It's starting to get crowded in here."

Wade reached for his wallet, but Ann stopped him. "It's on me, Cuz. You can get the next ones."

Wade watched as she made her way to the counter to order. Several people surrounded the pick-up area waiting for the cooks to finish preparing their food. She retrieved two frosted mugs of cold draft beer and an order of fried mushrooms.

"Is this all you're gonna eat tonight?" Wade queried.

"What's the hurry, boy? You starving?" she fired back.

Wade smirked and popped a mushroom into his mouth. "Man! Those are good!" he remarked as he finished eating the tasty morsel.

Ann grinned back, "They always are. It's their specialty."

Looking over Wade's shoulder, she waived at someone and smiled. Soon, the person appeared at their table. Wade glanced up, surprised to see it was Mimi. He stood to greet her.

"Hello," she smiled shyly at him.

"Hello again," Wade responded.

Ann chimed in as Mimi took a seat next to her and across from Wade. "Mimi told me she met you on campus a while back."

"Yeah," Wade grinned. "We had a little run-in at the bookstore a couple of weeks ago."

Mimi blushed as Ann continued. "Well, Wade, this is Mimi Brightlow, my last year's roommate. Remember the girl I—"

"Yeah, I remember," Wade interrupted.

"Can I get you a beer or something?" he asked Mimi.

"I'll have a coke if you don't mind," she responded with a grin.

"Sure, I'll be right back." With that Wade left the table to get her a soda.

Looking at the pub's menu, they discussed what they thought the sub shop's best foods were. Agreeing to each try something different, they placed their orders.

With Ann acting covertly as a catalyst for a conversation, Wade and Mimi began to talk. The discussion centered on the accustomed icebreaker topics when meeting someone new at college. What's your major? Where are you from? Did you go to the latest rock concert or football game? This feeling out process lasted only a short time as the two subconsciously searched for what they had in common. One thing seemed certain; both found the other attractive.

As they ate and talked, they decided they would all go to T.K Hardy's bar the following Saturday night. T.K.'s was a bar on the edge of town that had once been an old train depot. T.K. Hardy, a local entrepreneur, renovated most of the old buildings that occupied the site. Renting out all the extra space not needed to accommodate his drinking establishment, he lured other business owners into his complex making 'The Station' a diverse and interesting gathering spot, especially for college kids.

The evening at Steverino's had been wonderful. Not only for Wade, but also for Ann, who quietly longed for Laney, and for Mimi, who was a little timid and unattached. The plans for T.K.'s gave them all a new sense of excitement for the future.

Things were slowly falling back into place for Wade. He had decided against joining the fraternity offering an excuse that they were too heavy into the drug scene. Wade's insecurity, however, was what stifled the proposition. Now he had one less problem to worry about even though he had to park far away from his classes at the Coliseum's south parking lot as a consequence. With his growing interest in Mimi, his angst over Angie had subsided. He no longer thought about calling or going to see her at Ann's apartment. With someone else to look forward to seeing, his hope and aspirations revived. Except for worrying about his father's displeasure concerning the fraternity and his grades, Wade was on the rebound.

After a long week of school drudgery, Saturday night finally arrived. Ann and Mimi went out to Wade's trailer to pick him up. Ann knew her cousin probably didn't want to come to their apartment where he might find Angie with her new boyfriend. A knock shook the metal trailer door as the two girls waited outside in the cold night air.

Hearing someone at his door, Les opened it. "Hello, Kitten," he greeted them as Wade appeared behind his shoulder. "Come on in, girls."

As they entered the trailer's den, Ann introduced Les to Mimi.

"Hey, Mimi," he grinned at the smiling blue-eyed girl.

"Hello," she responded. The two coeds were at this point standing next to his sofa.

"Have a seat. Have a seat," Les continued obviously interested in their plans.

Both girls sat as Les asked if he could get them anything.

"No thanks," Ann said. "We're heading to T.K.'s for the evening. Would you like to come along?"

Louisa was finishing a term paper, and Les had nothing to do over the weekend. Ann had already clued him in on what was going on with Wade and Mimi.

"Sure," he exclaimed. "I thought you'd never ask."

"Uh huh," Ann said sarcastically. "All right everybody. Let's get going."

Grabbing his coat, Les got into Ann's new Mercury Cougar leaving Wade and Mimi to sit in the back. Wheeling out of the parking area, Ann sped down the Atlanta Highway as she headed for 'The Station'.

Vehicles crowded the parking lot at T.K.'s. Taking note, Ann drove down an adjacent street to park. Exiting the car, the group headed for the bar. As they climbed the steps to the tavern's wooden walkway, muffled music and chatter could be heard coming from inside. When they opened the door, the atmosphere was alive and blaring. Smoke filled the room as did loud laughter, shouting, and the pulsating rhythm of a live band. With the electric guitars, drums, bongos and brass sections, the mood was surreal.

Ann and Les started to playfully dance as the group made their way to a table near the bandstand. As soon as they were seated, a waitress appeared and the two couples ordered drinks. Sodas for Les and Mimi, and bottled beer for Ann and Wade. Ann whispered into Wade's ear that Mimi didn't drink. Wade signaled with his eyes that he got the message, and once the drinks arrived, they sat back casually listening to the music except for Ann. Gazing into the eyes of the lead singer, she kept rocking to the rhythm of the beat.

Trying to carry on a verbal conversation in this festive environment, especially with someone as soft-spoken as Mimi, proved difficult. Unable to hear what the other person said, the couple mostly smiled at one another. Les chuckled at Ann as she too took note of the situation.

When the music stopped for an intermission, Ann and Mimi went to the restroom as did most other girls, leaving the place looking less full and much quieter. Angie and her date entered the building. Wade bristled as he noticed the long-haired boy with her.

Seeing them also, Les remarked, "Lighten up, ol' buddy. You're with someone, too."

Angie did not see the two boys as she and her new flame walked past and took a seat on the other side of the room.

Wade glanced at his pal. "Is this 'the guy'?" he uttered in disgust.

"Yep. That's him," Les noticed the couple engaged in an animated conversation.

"Nice haircut," Wade smirked. "She always went for those hippie-biker looking types."

Not responding to his friend's remark, Les smiled. "Here come our girls!"

He noticed Angie as she saw Ann walking across the room. Angie tried signaling for her roommate to come over to her and her new boyfriend's table. But Ann either didn't see her gesturing or just plain ignored Angie.

Both Ann and Mimi took a seat, as Les grinned at them, "Well, y'all haven't missed much."

Ann looked over to where Angie was sitting and coolly retorted in her deep Southern drawl, "Rightttt."

Wade had become tense since his ex-girlfriend's arrival. Mimi, feeling something was wrong, sat quietly and peered around the room.

"Hey! What do y'all think about this band?" Les asked trying to liven the mood.

"I like them," Mimi grinned back.

"I do too," Wade responded trying to focus on his table of friends.

As the awkward silence returned, Les gleefully announced, "You guys know Hall and Oats are coming to the Coliseum this winter. Tickets are going on sale this week."

"Yeah," Ann replied enthusiastically, "You better get 'em quick. It'll be a sellout, don't you think?"

"Probably so," Les exclaimed. "Louisa loves them. So, I'm sure we're going to go. You want to go with us?"

"Sure," she said. She cut her eyes at Wade and Mimi who showed little response. Exasperated, Ann looked back at Les who also acknowledged the direness of the situation.

The members of the band finished their break and made their way back to their instruments. They were very good and had to be to please the young music critics surrounding them. Having listened to an extensive portion of their repertoire before the break, the four friends marveled at the diversity of the group's sets. They could play just about anything from the current popular hits of Chicago with its upbeat brass sound all the way over to the heavy bongo and guitar solos of Carlos Santana. Even the light and airy melodies of Three Dog Night were played with ease.

During the 60's and 70's, students in college towns reveled in the music of soul bands. The Tams, The Temptations, Junior Walker, and The Supremes played music with a vibrant, contagious beat. Songs like Carole King and Gerry Goffin's "Up on the Roof" performed by the Drifters or the Isley Brothers pulsating hit "Shout" could instantly bring people up out of their chairs and onto the dance floor.

As the musicians chatted for a moment and finished their drinks, the lead singer took to the microphone and asked in a deep, gravelly voice, "Well, are you guys ready to get down and jam?"

The crowd, back at their seats, responded with a few here and there shouts of, "Yeah, yeah."

"Man, we might as well pack our things and leave if 'you all' don't want it more than that." The group's leader, from New Jersey, enjoyed kidding his audience about their southern accent. Looking back at the other musicians, he shrugged to suggest if the crowd couldn't respond better than this, they might as well split. The others in the band pretended to start packing their gear to go.

Stepping back to the microphone, he shouted, "Do you want us to leave or do you really want it?"

"Yeah!! came a huge cheer from the crowd.

"I mean, DO YOU REALLY WANT IT, MAN?" he shouted even louder.

A more booming roar came from the revelers, "YEAHHH!!!"

"Hey, I wish my ol' lady would say it like that," the singer laughed back toward his group as the drummer hit the drums vaudeville style pa-dump-bump. With a quick hand signal, the band charged into a popular soul song by The Tams. Going crazy the crowd headed for the dance floor.

Be Young, Be Foolish, But Be Happy oo-oo, oo-oo-oo-oo / Be Young, Be Foolish, But Be Happy oo-oo, oo-oo-oo-oo / Don't Let The Rain Get You Down, It's A Waste Of Time …

Couples crowded the small floor in front of the band as they began to dance.

"Hey, you want to dance, Les?" Ann asked jumping out of her chair.

"Sure," he exclaimed.

As Les and Ann headed to the floor, Wade signaled to Mimi asking if she too wanted to dance. Smiling, she indicated she did. Taking her hand, they made their way to Les and Ann who were dancing at full throttle.

As they laughed at the clowning Ann, Wade took note that Mimi could dance as good as she looked. She followed Wade's lead as he broke into the Shag. One and two. Three and Four. Five Six. She could follow, pivot, and turn as smooth as silk following his every move with effortless ease. Wade loved it as the band played on:

Same Old Story All Over The World / Girl Meets Boy And Boy Meets Girl /

So Be Young, Be Foolish, But Be Happy oo-oo, oo-oo-oo-oo

When the song finally ended, Les and Ann went back to their table for a quick break. Sitting down they realized they had been successful. Wade and Mimi were alone and enjoying each other.

With the first song of their session completed, the versatile band performed a hauntingly soulful song by The Chi-Lites, "Oh Girl":

Oh Girl / I'd be in trouble if you left me now / 'Cause I don't know where to look for love / I just don't know how.

Before Wade knew it, Mimi reached over and crossed her delicate wrists around his neck and rested her arms on his broad shoulders. Dancing slowly and rhythmically with her body close to his, she stared into his alluring eyes as hers, pale blue, radiated a sense of excitement. A sensual smile parted her lips as he beamed back at her.

Inhaling her delicate, alluring perfume, Wade sighed with comfort as he gently grasped the girl's soft slim hips. Swaying slightly to and fro the two young romantics gazed into each other's eyes mesmerized by one another and the haunting melody of the music that was playing. *How nice*, Wade thought.

Angie watched in shock as her ex and Mimi held each other close. Wade was right. Angie's new boyfriend had hippie tendencies, and one predilection was he didn't care much for slow dancing. Matter of fact, he didn't care much for dancing at all. Hearing several more songs and watching Wade and Mimi dancing their way into Nirvana, Angie and her date, who didn't have a clue what had occurred, left the building.

When Ann came back to the apartment later that night, Angie confronted her angrily.

"Who was that girl Wade was with tonight?" she bellowed.

"Oh, that was my friend Mimi," Ann responded, taken back by Angie's indignation.

"Did you line him up with her?" she asked in an accusatory tone.

"Well, yes. I did sort of," Ann remarked closely watching her roommate's reaction.

Angie sat down on the sofa with her feet curled under her, her expression sullen and agitated.

"Hey! What's the big deal?" Ann fired. "You had a date tonight. What do you care what Wade does?"

"I just didn't think you'd do this to me!" Angie pouted.

"Do what?" Ann responded sharply. "Wade's my cousin. You quit dating him. I got him a date. What's the problem?"

Angie stormed out of the den and headed for her bedroom slamming the door behind her. Ann smiled to herself on a job well done.

VIII

As the weeks passed, the quarter came to a subdued end for Wade. Even though his life now bore some semblance of order, and though he had scored well on his remaining test, these results proved insufficient. He ended the quarter with two D's and a B, nothing he was proud to bring home to dear ol' Dad.

A worrisome prospect for sure, this didn't bother him, yet. Mimi was just the tonic he needed, as he spent more and more time with her. Her personality matched Wade's well, but she was a comforter not a worrier. Having the ability to stabilize the emotions of the dark-haired boy, she rapidly fell in love with him.

Angie, on the other hand, made a 3.2 for the quarter. Not bad considering what happened to her since dumping Wade. It didn't take long hanging out with her new cool boyfriend for Angie to realize she just didn't have much in common with him. He liked heavy metal music; she didn't. He was an intellectual talking head, and she was the let's have-some-fun type. The flame of the new and different soon wore off. It could have gone on for quite some time, but she heard about Wade's relationship with Mimi blossoming. As long as Wade acted like a whipped dog and begged for her return, she had the best of both worlds. With the scene at T.K.'s burned into her mind, she started to see the light. She became aware of what she hadn't realized before. She truly was in love with Wade. How she could get him back, she didn't know.

CHAPTER 7

The Return

Fall quarter at an end, most students headed back to their homes for Christmas break. Wade stayed in Athens, close to Mimi, for as long as he possibly could. When she left, there was no reason to remain.

He arrived at his parent's house around dusk and parked his car under one of the huge laurel oaks that lined each side of the street. Up the sidewalk he strode, stepping on and crunching an occasionally fallen acorn as he made his way. Brown lifeless oak leaves blanketed the ground as did straw that had fallen from several large pines standing in his front yard. Stopping momentarily, Wade looked back toward the alley and the great woods of his youth. How secure he had felt in those days, he thought. But now, all he could see was the stark, leafless silhouettes of thick, round tree trunks and naked gray limbs barren from winter's calling. Up the steps to the front porch he observed thankfully that his father's car was not in the driveway. This eased his mind a little as he opened the front door to his house.

Kelli was playing with her Barbie dolls on the living room floor when she saw her brother walk in. She exclaimed exuberantly, "Mom! Mom! Wade's home!" The little girl sprang into her big brother's arms with a clinging hug as he playfully spun her around singing her name.

Wade's mother rushed from the kitchen into the living room. "Waaade!" she sang out and hurried over to kiss and hug him. He had only been home once this quarter and both his mother and sister were elated to see him.

"Hi, Mom," Wade said as he tried hugging her with Kelli still in his arms. "Where's Dad?"

"Oh, he's still at work," his mother smiled at him. "He's running a little late tonight."

Wade was relieved. He wouldn't have to confront his father with his grades just yet.

"Well," Wade glanced back at his vehicle through the still opened front door. "Y'all mind giving me a hand?"

Before he got the question out of his mouth, Kelli managed to slip out of his arms and zipped down the sidewalk toward his car.

"Doesn't she need a jacket, Mom? It's cold out there."

"No, she's too excited Wade. She'll be all right."

The little girl had made it into the car's back seat where she wrestled a large, full duffle bag out onto the sidewalk. Wade's mother, who had followed Wade out to the car, reached over and took the heavy, green bag from her struggling daughter.

"Dirty clothes, Wade?" his mom asked her son with a chuckle.

"No, ma'am. They're all clean," he proudly smiled back.

"Hmmmm," she responded, unbelieving. She knew this wasn't the same boy she had sent off to Athens. Maybe being away from home and out on his own had done him some good after all, she thought. "How's Miss Angie doing?" she asked as she headed back to the house with her arms full.

Wade hesitated.

"Well, we aren't seeing each other anymore," he said. He reached into the back seat for his hanging clothes.

His mom stopped and turned around. She was shocked at this news, but more so with his demeanor. Wade seemed quite composed. "Sorry," she said, then more emphatically, "but there's other fish in the sea." She didn't pry into why they had broken up.

"Yeah, I know." Wade paused as he adjusted his grip on the rack of clothes he'd just grabbed. "I've already found someone."

His mother wore a funny expression wondering if he had been the one to dump Angie.

Wade instantly read her thoughts.

"No. I didn't break up with her. She broke up with me."

"Then good for you," his mother declared proudly.

After several trips to the car, they had retrieved all of Wade's luggage. Suitcases, hanging racks, and bags of clothes were stacked all over his bedroom floor and bed. They started putting his things away.

Kelli looked up at her brother with a concerned look and said, "I liked Angie, Wade."

"I did too, Kell'. But I guess she got tired of liking me. You know what she did?"

Kelli's eyes grew wide with anticipation.

"She left me for a hippie. Can you believe that?"

A scowl crossed Kelli's face.

"A hippie?" she asked in disbelief. Her father had ridiculed these long-haired weirdos on many occasions especially when they showed up on the evening news. The thought of Angie leaving her brother for one was unfathomable.

Wade continued. "But guess what? I found myself a new girlfriend! You want to know what her name is?"

"Louisa!" she shouted with delight.

"No. That's Les' girlfriend," Wade said in frustration. "Mimi. How about that for a girl's name?"

Kelli shrugged and grinned. "What's she like, Wade?"

"Well, she's beautiful, of course. You know I don't date anyone that's not real, real, pretty," he teased his little sister. Watching her roll her eyes, he continued. "She has blonde hair and pretty blue eyes and a really pretty smile. And she has a little brother about your age. Would you like to meet him?"

"No," Kelli said defiantly. Boys were disgusting creatures.

Wade's mother sat on the edge of Wade's bed and smiled to herself at Kelli's response. She got up and left the room to prepare the evening meal. How wonderful to be young and romantic, she thought.

With Kelli's help, Wade finished putting away his things. She started asking her brother what he'd been doing at college. Listening to Wade talk about going to the huge crowded stadium to watch the Georgia Bulldogs play football, or riding the big buses across the campus, or sitting in a classroom with over a hundred people in it thrilled her beyond belief.

When Kelli finally finished asking him everything she could think of concerning school, the two of them went into the den. Wade's mom had finished preparing supper and was sitting in the room watching TV as they entered.

Sitting and talking to each other, they heard a car drive up outside. Expecting it to be her husband, Wade's mom got up and went into the kitchen to greet him. Anxiously and with a large lump in his throat, Wade sat motionlessly in his chair fearing the encounter he knew would soon be coming his way.

Kelli, oblivious to her brother's dilemma, ambled into the eating area behind her mother as the door to the side porch opened. Through it walked a sturdily built man of medium height in his late forties with dark hair and piercing brown eyes. With an armful of turnips, he quickly headed for the kitchen sink.

Wade made it into the room and stood next to his little sister in humbled silence.

"Wade," his dad ordered. "How about getting the rest of those turnips out of my trunk?"

"Yes, sir," Wade responded instantly.

As his father washed his hands, he remarked to his wife, "Bill Tomlinson gave me these. He must've had a pickup load. Aren't they beautiful?"

"They sure are," she said enthusiastically as she stacked them on the counter.

"Yep, ol' Bill has always liked me. He said he's got some half and half venison and pork sausage he and his sons made that they want to give me too. You know they have their own slaughtering house out on the farm there. I think they feed out the whole family with that meat."

Wade returned with the rest of the greens.

"Just put those out by the back door," his father commanded.

"Yes, sir."

As Wade went outside to take care of the turnips, his mother started taking up the evening meal. Pots and pans rested all over the stove and in the oven where she had kept the meal simmering. The meals at Wade's house had always centered on his dad's schedule. No one ate until he did.

His father, mother, and little sister all had taken a seat at the kitchen table, when Wade reentered the room. "Wade," his dad snapped, "Go wash your hands. There's sand and probably chemicals all over those plants." He said this as though Wade couldn't figure it out for himself.

"Yes, sir," Wade responded timidly.

After cleaning up, Wade joined the rest of his family for supper. Kelli said the blessing and they all silently served their plates and began to eat. For Wade, this meal was a far cry from the spam and green beans he survived on in Athens. There were steaming baked sweet potatoes all orange and wrapped in aluminum foil split down the middle with a couple of big lumps of yellow butter melting into them. Country fried steak lightly covered with flour and seasoned before being dropped into a large skillet of hot vegetable oil and deep fried until crispy brown. Butter beans seasoned with salt pork and boiled until soft, wrinkled, and light green in appearance. Homemade buttermilk biscuits slathered with gravy made from the fried steak drippings. And all of this was topped with a gorgeous red slice of glazed strawberry pie capped with a creamy white curl of whipped cream and a large glass of sweet iced tea.

What a feast, Wade thought as he surveyed the delicious food before him. Even so and with his appetite primed, it was going to be a hard meal to swallow as he painfully knew, sooner or later, the subject of his grades would surely come up. Fortunately for Wade, his father didn't seem to be in a talkative mood. Everyone at the table sensed that something was out of sorts with him and fearfully remained quiet. This was nothing new for the family. Problems he was having at work would usually filter their way back home, often in intractable ways.

Wade's mother, perturbed by her husband not even acknowledging his son's return home from college, affably tried cajoling him. "So, how was work today, Hon?" she asked cheerily.

Wade's father glared at his wife in anger, but only momentarily. "A rough day. The farmers are getting too much rain and can't get into their fields. It's the usual," he started to sound angrier as he thought about it. "I got three empty semis sitting at the office! I probably won't have them back on the road for another week!"

Wade's mother bowed her head meekly as did her two children. Any further comments or questions directed at Wade's dad at this point would probably be met with the same hostile reaction. No matter how cheery and light-hearted they wanted to be for Wade's sake, his mother and sister didn't dare take the chance of crossing the head of the house again. It wasn't worth the risk. The tension in the room was palpable. Each member of the family except Wade's dad stared at their plate as they ate. No one dared to look in his direction. His father wasn't even aware that he had a problem. As far as the rest of the family was concerned, however, they had to learn to deal with it as part of life.

"How's school going?" Wade's dad asked gazing at his boy.

Wade was terrified. The last thing he wanted to discuss now was his grades.

"It's been real hard up there," Wade's neck tightened as he spoke. "Nothing like it was down here."

"Yeah. I can remember how it was when I was at Tech. Now that was a real school, pal. You played around over there, buddy, and they'd kick your butt to the curb pronto. I can well remember when I went up. I had a brand-new Ford coupe that I had bought and paid for with my own money. The money I'd earned helping my dad with his cows. Pop and Mr. Silas McGhee were partners in a cattle deal when

I was a teenager back in the forties. And as a learning experience, I suppose, Pop gave me five steers that I could sell if I'd take care of the entire herd for him and Mr. Silas for one year. Ol' Si' had a big farming operation, around two thousand acres of farmland and timber from what I remember. He was as rich as two feet up a bull's butt. I recall Pop telling me that the old man had several hundred thousand in silver dollars hid in different locations all over his farm. You know after the Crash wealthy people were a little reluctant to put all their cash back in a bank. That's hard to picture today, isn't it? Can you imagine what all those solid silver coins would be worth in today's dollars?" Wade's father's eyes sparkled.

He continued. "This was just a little something for Mr. Silas to piddle with, but Pop could make some good money on the deal. And Mr. Silas liked daddy; that's probably the only reason that he even did it. Anyway, I tended the herd that year—which was pretty simple. I had a slew of colored hands helping me. All I did was mostly supervise. It finally came time to carry a portion of the cows to market. But two days before the sale the market went bust and cattle prices dropped almost in half." At this point, he smiled to himself. "I'll never forget it. I drove Mama's new Buick out to Mr. McGhee's farm like I always did each morning to help feed the cows, and when I got up to the pack house and corral where we were going to herd our steers the next day, Mr. Silas and Pop were there leaning on the fence talking."

"When I walked up, I could hear Mr. Silas laughing and could see my dad about to have a nervous breakdown. Mr. Silas kept saying 'it'll bounce back up, Jim. We don't have to sell yet. Hell, we got plenty of feed here for 'em'. But Pop was about to bust. Anyway, to make a long story short, with some money I had inherited from my Uncle Bill, Mama's uncle who died several years earlier, I talked my father into letting me use some of the money to buy a couple dozen more steers at the next sale. He thought I'd gone crazy. But he thought, all and all, that I couldn't lose much more, so he let me do it. The market for beef on the hoof doubled a month later when the war got going, and I made a bundle," Wade's dad gleefully remarked. Suddenly, his expression turned down. "I think Pop was proud of what I did, but he never did let on."

Wade watched his father's every nuance as he told the story. How much he wanted his father's love and approval too. Then his grades came to mind. *What a disaster,* Wade thought and wondered how he was going to survive the tongue-lashing he was sure to get.

Kelli yelled from across the table. "Tell him about Angie, Wade." This bothered her badly as she had become significantly attached to his former girlfriend.

"Ahhh," Wade sighed in embarrassment, but glad the conversation was being steered away from school and his grades. "We broke up, that's all."

Wade's father looked at him, but showed no sympathy.

An awkward moment of silence befell the table. Wade's mother became excited, "Yes, but he's got a new girl, and her name is Mimi."

Wade's father asked, "Who's Mimi? What's she studying to be?"

"Oh, she's just one of Ann's friends. She's majoring in home economics and getting a minor in accounting."

Wade's dad groaned sarcastically. "Yeah, we had a few of those up at Tech too, but not too many. It took real brains to get into that school I'm telling you, and most of those types who made it in were just going after their M.R.S. degree anyway."

"Y'all better not be making fun of wives who work at home," Wade's mom chimed in trying to take some of the sting out of her husband's remarks concerning Wade's girlfriend.

Cynically her husband shot back, "We're not talking about housewives here, Mama. We're talking about degrees. If you'd finished college instead of quitting after two years, you might understand what I'm saying."

"Well, I only quit to marry you," she smiled back trying to humor him.

"You quit because you got what you went for—a husband! Besides, you'd probably have flunked out in another quarter or two."

"That's not true," his wife said defiantly.

"Yeah, well, if you remember back," he remarked condescendingly, "you were making C's over there at the ol' community college and that's pretty awful, wouldn't you say?"

"That's not true either. I made mostly A's and B's. I only made a few C's, I'll have you know." She glared at him for a long moment and pretended to eat again.

Wade sat tensely throughout this exchange as he watched his little sister nonchalantly twiddle with her food. Kelli had heard this carrying on between her parents more than she had wanted. She'd become a pro at hiding the hurt she was feeling when they did this.

Wade's dad caught on that he might have been digging at his son and wife a little too hard. But he didn't apologize. Rather, he tried to redeem himself by acting more interested in Mimi. "So, Son, where is this new girlfriend of yours from?"

"She's from Macon," Wade said stoically not wanting to discuss the matter any further.

"What's her folks do?" his father asked as he forked a piece of meat into his mouth.

"Her dad's a pilot."

Wade was trying hard not to act testy at his father's criticism of Mimi. He knew it would only set him off again if he did. He also knew that if he did get into an argument with his dad, he couldn't stand up to him. Years of being put in his place by the man made the sensitive boy as fragile as glass. Sitting in silence, he waited for the next slam his dad was going to deliver.

"Delta?" his father asked.

"No, sir. Air Force."

"I bet she's seen the world!"

"Yes, sir," Wade said with excitement thinking that his dad was impressed. "They've lived in Germany, Japan, California, and Texas before moving here to Georgia."

"Yeah, they move you around a lot all right. It can be a hard life being in the military. I had a lot of buddies that, when the war was over, got college degrees with the G. I. Bill. There were some pretty smart guys that did that and became quite successful businessmen. Some that were not so smart stayed in the service though. They liked someone telling them every move to make and liked drawing a check once a month," his dad scoffed.

"Her dad's a fighter pilot," Wade shot back, angered by the analogy. "He's seen a lot of action in Vietnam."

"Yeah, uh-huh," his father said. Dismissing his son's response, he stood up from the table ending the conversation. "Well, I think I'm going to take a shower and hit the sack everybody. I'm tired," he said. As he started to leave the room, he reached down and kissed his wife on the top of her head. "That was a good supper, Mama." Nodding tentatively, Wade's mother stared down at the table as her husband left the room.

Disheartened, Wade sat miffed at what just transpired. He should have told his father his grades and gotten it over with, he thought. He couldn't have been hurt any worse.

Wade's mom stood up and started removing the dishes from the table.

"Come on, Kelli," she said. "Let's get the table cleared off, Honey."

Wade got up too and helped his mother clean and sweep the kitchen. He worked quietly and, though his mother tried prying into his life at college, he said little except finally telling her his grades and how upset he was with himself for not doing better. His motivation for doing this was practical. He decided it would probably be better to let her tell his father about his grades. This would give his dad time to simmer down before they talked. With the kitchen cleaned, he excused himself and went to his room.

Wade's bedroom, at least at night, had always been his place of refuge. With everyone asleep, and the house still and quiet, he had time to think, and time not to think. His father wouldn't burst into his room at such late hours asking him why the yard wasn't raked or why he wasn't doing something constructive. The sense of urgency to please his dad by being productive wasn't evident either at this time.

Depressed, Wade picked up his sketchpad and charcoal pencil, and after shifting some of his empty luggage around on the bed, he stretched out to draw. At first, his thoughts were of his father and the barbs his dad poked at him at supper. As he continued to draw, he thought of how he should have responded to his dad. Stroke by stroke, the lines and shading grew. In his mind, he wasn't sure what he wanted to draw as thoughts of his father faded and a new sense of focus replaced them.

As he lay there half-seated with the sketchpad across his lap, his hands and eyes became one, and soon a young woman's face appeared on the sheet before him. Time filtered everything away leaving only a concentrated effort. With each fluid movement of his hand and arm, the etching became more precise. At first, he thought he might extract Angie. Then Mimi. But much to his surprise, the stunning and compassionate face of Louisa appeared. He made the final touches of shadow and light to emphasize her eyes, as the digital clock clicked to 3:00 a.m., temporarily breaking his concentration. At last, it was done, and he signed it.

Why did his thoughts keep returning to her, he wondered? He would never in a million years try to seduce her and break her and Les up. But she captivated him in some other way. Not that he couldn't visualize himself having sex with her. What man in his right mind could avoid that? No there was something else about her. Something that continually intrigued and compelled him. Silently, with her face still glowing in his mind, he drifted off to sleep.

The next morning, his mother gently awakened him. It was Sunday and she quietly asked him to get ready for church. Wade had attended Sunday school and church for as long as he could remember or at least up until he started college and his parents no longer forced him to go. He had been saved and become a member of the Rose Avenue Baptist Church when he was eleven years old, probably more from his dad forcefully implying that he do so one Sunday morning than really understanding what it meant. But he did love and understand God, though it was in his own unique way when he was hunting, fishing or painting, or in the solitude of the outdoors.

Together this Sunday morning, he and his family piled into his mother's four-door sedan and headed out to the midday service with his father at the wheel. Once there, many friends greeted them, and they all took a seat.

The service unfolded as it had since Wade could first remember. Starting off, everyone gossiped busily with one another while the organist played a quiet but beautiful religious arrangement by Bach. Then the choir entered the choir loft as the pastor, assistant pastor, and minister of music walked in and stood on the platform. The congregation grew quiet as these three gentlemen and the choir simultaneously took a seat behind the elevated pulpit. The minister of music led the choir and congregation in a couple of well-known hymns. The assistant pastor then led a prayer for everyone who was sick or who had recently died. After the collection plate was passed, the preacher started his sermon. The sermon, to Wade's relief, lasted about thirty minutes and then everyone stood up and sang a hymn of invitation as the pastor beckoned those who wanted to be saved to come down front. Everything up until this point of the service had gone on as usual. Several young people and one older person openly professed their faith as they came forward for salvation. Then, to Wade's astonishment, down the aisle came Les.

Greatly puzzled, Wade watched him walk to the front. Knowing Les had been baptized before, Wade wondered what his friend was thinking. When the church's pastor finished acknowledging and introducing the other post-service participants, he turned his attention to Les. Reintroducing the young man to the membership, the pastor told the congregation that Les had rededicated his life to Christ and wanted to become a preaching missionary.

Wade was immediately taken aback by this revelation. The two of them planned on completing the next two years at Georgia with Wade obtaining a degree in accounting and Les in finance. *What the heck is going on,* Wade thought. They'd never kept any secrets.

The preacher handed the microphone to Les, and the young man gave a poignant, heartfelt talk on how and why he came to his decision. He ended his speech by telling the congregation that he was immediately transferring to Southwestern Seminary School in Houston, Texas for winter quarter.

Wade sat stunned. Why hadn't Les let him in on this monumental development? Certainly, he was pleased Les was doing this, but at the same time, he felt left out to dry.

As the service ended, the entire congregation, so inspired by what Les had said and so pleased that one of their own had been called to take this course in life, flocked to the front of the sanctuary to congratulate him. Wade's family followed suit, but Wade, not wanting to gain only a handshake from his friend, chose to wait and go to Les' house later in the day to see what this was all about. Church ended with Wade standing on the front steps of the building waiting for his family to return from the altar.

After the throngs of well-wishers exited the heavy wooden doors of the church's entrance, Wade's parents and little sister finally emerged. His dad was noticeably mad as he made his way toward his son. "Why didn't you go down and wish Les good luck?" he asked, glaring.

"There were too many people down there. I thought I'd go over and see him this afternoon and find out what's going on. He didn't tell me that he was going to be doing this."

In stony silence Wade's father walked his family to the car. His mind burned. It was the proper thing to do to go and congratulate Les as everyone else had done. It was the right thing to do, and his son, Les' best friend and roommate at school, had not done so. Instead, his son had stood noticeably outside during the whole affair. As they got into the car and headed for home, Wade's dad repeatedly said how great a guy Les was; how any father would love to have a son like that; how mature Les had become, and what guts it took for Les to make that decision. In reality, all Wade's dad was doing was belittling his own son as he had done so many times before.

Wade sat in the back seat of the car saying nothing as his mother unwittingly joined his father in singing the praises of Les. Kelli peered at her big brother with a look of sadness and compassion intuitively realizing something was wrong. When they got home, Wade quickly changed clothes and told his parents he had made plans to eat with friends, though this wasn't really true. In reality, he wanted to get as far away from his oppressive father as fast as he could.

When he left, he had no idea where he might go—he didn't care. Most of his former friends were either married, had moved away, or faded into the background. Even Ann, whom he usually went to for comfort and advice, had gone to Jacksonville to see Laney. As he despondently drove around town avoiding his house, he stopped and ate a hamburger at one of the burger joints lining the interstate. Taking as long as he could to eat, he got back into his car and continued to drive around. Memories of how things used to be filled his mind as he passed the high school, an old friend's house, and at last ended up at the shed by the lake where he had first met Angie.

For quite some time, he sat alone staring out at the lake and remembering the crazy night that he and Angie had almost had a date for the fish fry. *What on earth had happened that strange evening*, he wondered. Her dumping him in Athens, how much stranger could it get? *Good riddance*, he thought. He didn't need someone that uncaring and fickle around anyway.

Mimi—he smiled at the thought of her. She was the elixir that had revived his spirit. How much he desired to be with her. How much he missed the warmth of her touch and the compassion and caring he saw in her eyes. But he knew thoughts of seeing her were just an illusion. He knew full well that his father would have him doing something productive starting the next morning. There would be no rest for the weary and this would be especially the case when his dad found out his grades. Beyond this one circumstance involving school, Wade wondered, how could a father give his son such little dignity and show him such little respect? Wade knew his dad loved him, but he could not comprehend what would make a father treat his son in such a way.

Sitting there, Wade pondered his dad's cruel remarks and reflected on the shocking news that his best friend was heading out to Texas to seminary. Over and over these thoughts circulated in his mind. He stared out toward the lake until, at last, the wind whipping through the pines on this unusually warm winter day caught Wade's attention. The water began to ripple coming alive as each small wave lapped the shoreline. Out across the lake, he saw a Kingfisher dip down and catch an unwary minnow. Perching on the limb of a pine, the bird swallowed his catch and began scanning the waters for more. A sense of peace came over Wade. The same feeling he got when he walked alone on the sandy beaches of Fernandina. How he wished he could bottle the stuff. How fleeting he knew it was. After several more grand views of the lake and its surroundings, he got up and reluctantly left. He made his way across town, this time heading for Les' parent's new house on the edge of the city. He had gone by the home several times earlier, but on each trip, he noticed one or two strange cars parked there and fearing company was present, he did not stop.

Only Les' car was in the driveway this time. Not even Les' parents were around. Parking his car, he walked to the front door and knocked. Waiting for a half-minute or so, he knocked again. Finally, he heard a rumbling coming from inside.

Les opened the door. "I called your house around lunch, but your mom said you had gone out to eat with some friends."

"Nah," Wade said. "I just had to get out of there and you know exactly what I mean."

"Yeah, your dad, right?"

Wade nodded in confirmation as Les motioned for him to come in.

Sitting across from Wade in his living room, Les became solemn. "I saw you in church today, and I'm sorry I couldn't let you in on this news a little sooner."

Wade listened intently.

"This issue, me becoming a missionary, has been on my mind for over a year now, but I didn't want to trouble you trying to make my decision. I mean, one day I thought it was the thing to do. The next, I wasn't so sure. And with all you had going on with school and Angie and all, I didn't want you to be concerned about what your roommate might or might not be up to. Does that make sense?"

"Yeah, I understand," Wade tried easing Les' mind. "So, did Louisa know you were going to do this?"

"Well, she knew it was on my mind and we'd talked about it a lot, especially over the last few months. But both of us knew that it ultimately was my decision to make." Les went on, "You know, I've been home for about five days and this is all I've thought about. I kind of came to an impasse, so finally I brought it up with my parents."

"What did they have to say?" Wade asked curiously.

"Not much. Basically, they told me to think it through carefully, then to trust my heart."

"Sounds to me like they gave you some really good advice," Wade responded.

"Yeah. It was because I couldn't totally think it out. I had to trust my gut and my heart."

"So I suppose you and Louisa have all this planned out now?"

"No, I didn't tell her until after church today just like I'm telling you."

Surprised, Wade asked, "Really? She had no idea?"

"None. She had no clue that I would do this today."

Wade chuckled and shook his head.

Puzzled by the response, Les asked what was so funny.

"It's you, Les. You've always been so organized and punctual. Procrastinating and making decisions at the last minute, that sounds like something I would do. Not you."

"Hey. What can I say?" Les laughed. "But if this is how you have to make all of your important decisions, boy do I feel sorry for you."

"Well, welcome to my world, Les. You might want to start counting your blessings because this is exactly how I do it. It's either fight or flight for me. I have to have a little adrenalin circulating in my bloodstream to get me going in one direction or the other."

Les grinned shaking his head in disbelief. Then, leaning back in his chair he became more serious. "There's a few things I'd like to go over with you if you got a minute?"

"Sure. I've got all the time in the world, Les. What's on your mind?"

"The first thing I want you to know is that I'm not going to bail and leave you with a bunch of rent to pay. I signed that lease agreement with you for nine months and I'll pay my fair share until you either find another roommate or until the year ends."

"Come on, Les. You're going to have to pay a lot of money to get moved to Texas and all. Don't worry about paying our rent up here. If I don't find a roommate, that'd mean you'd have to pay two rents."

"Well, you'd have to pay two rents if I didn't pay, and you didn't find another roommate. What's the difference?"

"I can handle all that. It's not a problem."

"It is to me, Wade, so I'm paying whether you like it or not. Case closed."

Wade frowned but knew full well that once his friend made up his mind, it was next to impossible to make him change it. "Okay," Wade conceded. "If that's the way you want it."

Les nodded confirming that it was.

"All right. You ready for our next issue?"

Not being particularly happy with the last one, Wade shrugged, "I guess so."

"I'm going to tell you something you probably don't want to hear and because I know how you are, you'll probably even deny this."

Wade cringed wondering what on earth Les was about to tell him.

"Bud," Les said looking at his friend. "You might be the most talented artist I've ever met. In Athens, I've got some artists that are friends of mine and I've gone to some exhibits with them. Nothing I've ever seen at one of those shows comes even close to what I've seen you do."

Wade hung his head embarrassed. "I appreciate that," he mumbled.

"Well," Les continued more firmly. "I want you to do something about it. Personally, I think that you ought to be majoring in art."

Wade kept his head bowed as Les spoke.

"Go to the art school and look around. Talk to some of the teachers or the department head. There's a lot you can do with your skills as an artist."

Wade nodded his head that he would. "You got anything else on your mind?" Wade asked apprehensively.

"Matter of fact, I do. I have one last thing. It's a favor I want you to do for me."

"And what might that be?" Wade asked sounding more optimistic.

"I want you to take care of Louisa for me while I'm away."

"Not a problem there, Les—I can definitely handle that. Uh, how long do you suppose you guys will be apart?"

"Probably for the rest of this year. After that, we'll kind of see where we are.

"Y'all planning on getting married, engaged, or anything like that?"

Les momentarily grew pensive. "I don't know. We've talked about it a few times. Maybe this will kind of be a test to see if we're really serious about doing it. I guess time will only tell, won't it?"

"I guess so," Wade responded thoughtfully. "But you know I've got you covered in Athens. I'll make sure she's okay while you're gone."

"I know you will, Wade. You're my most trusted friend." With an expression of gratitude, Les stood up. "Wade, I hate to run you off so quickly, but the preacher and his wife are due here in about fifteen minutes or so. I don't want you to get stuck and have to hang around for all that. I've still got your back, ol' buddy," Les winked at his pal.

"Thanks." Wade grinned. "Hey, I have to admit, I was a little surprised by what you did at church today. But I certainly understand the reason you did it like that though. You know I'm proud of you, right?"

Les nodded smiling, then escorted him to the door. As Wade headed down the steps, Les blurted out, stopping him, "Remember, I've got the rent taken care of for you. You've got Louisa taken care of for me. Just don't forget about that other thing we talked about. Think long and hard about it. Do something about it," Les coaxed Wade vigorously.

Looking toward the top step where Les was standing, Wade smiled. He nodded that he would, then turned around and headed for his car.

II

Wade hated the thought of going home as he drove back across town, but there was nowhere else he could go. Sooner or later, he realized, he would have to face the inevitable. But as he made his way, he was not resolute. When he got to his house and went inside, Wade found his dad sitting in the den watching the Falcons play and reading the Sunday paper.

Noticing Wade's presence but without looking up from his reading, he uttered, "That new girlfriend of yours called."

"When?" Wade asked trying not to sound too excited.

Glancing up at the clock on the wall, he said, "About an hour ago." Pausing he gave his son a steely stare. With that look, Wade felt sure his mother had told him about his grades.

"Thanks. I need to tell her what's going on with Les," Wade said anxiously.

Seemingly uninterested, his dad returned to his reading as Wade immediately left the den for the kitchen and the phone. Entering the room, he saw his mother standing at the sink washing the turnip greens her husband had brought in the night before. "Did your dad tell you that Mimi called?"

"Yes, ma'am. I thought I'd try and call her back."

Understanding his need for privacy, his mother joined her husband in the den.

Wade opened his wallet and extracted a folded piece of paper with Mimi's parent's number on it. Fumbling with the receiver, he held it to his ear with his shoulder and dialed. Waiting for the connection after several rings, he heard the soft voice of an older woman answer. Realizing this was probably her mother, Wade kindly asked to speak to Mimi.

"This must be Wade?" Mimi's mother asked cheerfully.

"Yes, ma'am."

"I've heard a lot about you and everything I hear seems to be real good," Wade visualized the charming woman as she spoke.

"Thank you, ma'am," Wade responded.

"Hold on just a minute. I'll get Mimi for you." There was a pause then he heard her calling to her daughter in the background. Wade heard another receiver pick up.

"Hello?" came the excited voice of the girl. Her mother then hung up the other phone.

"Hey there," Wade said softly. "What's going on?"

After a pause, Mimi spoke. "Well, quite a lot really. My dad's been called back to active duty."

Nothing was said for a long moment.

"I thought he was through with all of that?"

"Well, we did too, but when you're in the Air Force you go when and where they need you," she said trying hard to sound calm. Wade could hear in her voice that she was not.

"Vietnam again?" he asked.

"Yeah. Something big must be going on over there. They won't tell us, of course." She paused again. "But that's normal."

Wade wondered what she was trying to say.

"So—, when is he leaving?"

"Tonight," she said, her voice growing weak. "You think you could come up sometime this week to see us?" There was an underlying tone of desperation in her voice.

"Yeah. Let me see what I can do. Uh—my dad's got some things, maybe a job lined up for me, but I think I can work it out, okay?"

"Okay," she said again with that same fragile tone of anxiety in her voice.

Wade realized that all he had wanted to tell her about Les becoming a missionary was irrelevant. She was worried about her daddy.

"Let me see what I've got going, and I'll call you back either tonight or tomorrow. All right?"

"Okay," she said. "Goodbye, Wade."

"Goodbye, Mimi."

Wade softly hung up the phone. Mimi was scared, and he knew it. Somehow he had to get up there to see her, to help comfort her.

As he left the kitchen, he entered the den and took a seat across from his mom and dad who were both watching the ball game.

"How's Mimi doing?" his mom asked.

Concerned, Wade said, "Not so good. Her dad's been called back to Vietnam."

His mother, realizing what the poor girl must be feeling, was sympathetic, "Oh, I'm so sorry Wade. That's got to be hard on her and her family. And right here at Christmas. Sometimes I wonder if that war over there will ever end."

"Dad?" Wade asked as he carefully interrupted his father watching the game. He expected a blast about his grades coming from the older man at any second.

Looking at Wade as a commercial came on, his father spoke directly and to the point. "Yeah, I told you about that military life being tough, didn't I? Tough on her family and tough on her dad."

Wade acquiesced and nodded.

"Say, Dad," he paused not knowing how to ask a favor of his father. "Mimi wants me to come up there sometime this week because of all this going on. You reckon that'll be all right?"

Stiffening, his father stared into Wade's eyes and spoke plainly.

"Wade, I've already asked Walt Cole if he'd let you work for him down at the plant again. They're expecting you tomorrow morning at eight a.m. sharp."

"You reckon there's any way I could start Tuesday. I could tell Mimi was really upset about this. And she really wants me to—"

Blisteringly his father cut him short. "Listen, Wade. Her family's been through this sort of thing plenty of times before. And without any help from you. So I'm sure they'll do just fine this time around too. Now, if you want to go on up there, that's up to you! But I'll tell you one thing, son. Don't count on me for helping you out with any more of your gas money or car or insurance payments. That will be all yours from now on. You understand what I'm saying?" Almost shouting, Wade's father didn't give his son a chance to respond. "You know what, Wade? I'm tired of doing everything for you! It takes money to do all the things you want to do. I pay for your clothes, your food, your room and board, and your tuition. None of this stuff is free. I work hard for the money I make. And you come home all smiles talking about wanting to go see your new girlfriend after making a B and two damn D's this past quarter! You've got to be damn kidding me!"

Scared of her father's shouting, Kelli called for her mother to come see about her back in her bedroom. With pursed lips, his mom stoically exited the den.

The berating continued, "Look at your friends, boy! They're going to do something and be somebody when they get out of school. Karl's going to be a doctor. Les—he's going to preach. And then look at you! Two D's and a B. Are you proud of that, son? Hell, I always knew you wouldn't amount to anything."

Wade hung his head in almost tearful silence as his father's harsh words rang through him like a bell. Even though he had bought and paid for his car with his own money and never had asked his dad to pay the insurance on it, he could not muster the wherewithal to defend himself.

"So you can't say anything, huh? Just hang your head in shame like you always do. You think somebody's always gonna be around to take care of you? Well, no one's going to take care of your butt but yourself. You understand that? Nobody out there gives a damn about you. I've told your mother a hundred times that if you don't change your ways, you won't amount to a hill of beans. You're pitiful. You've been to college for over two years now. And either you aren't trying hard enough or you just plain can't cut it. You'll probably end up like your mama. Quitting. I guess you can start flipping burgers somewhere for a living."

He paused glaring at his son who was seated humbly before him. Angrily, he rose from his seat. "If you can't cut it in accounting, then what is it you think you can make it in, Wade? What is it you want to do, son?" his father shouted down at him.

Slowly a glassy-eyed Wade raised his head hoping against all the odds that this was the break that he'd been looking for. Hoping that after all the years of being a beaten down yes-man, he could claim the chance to pursue the dream he really wanted. With tears in his eyes and a cracking voice, he stammered out what was locked inside his heart so tightly. "I'd like to be an artist, Dad." The words he had wanted to say his whole life were finally set free. But before he sighed in relief, his dad roared at him in disgust.

"An artist? You can't make a living being an artist! That's something you can piddle around with as a hobby, but you're going to have to support a family. How do you think you're going to put food on the table and kids through college drawing pictures? Artists are a dime a dozen, boy. Go anywhere. You'll see them standing in line waiting to find a job."

Stunned, Wade had allowed himself to reveal his deepest secret and, unbeknownst to him, to his most ardent adversary. He had laid all his cards on the table, and his dad had crammed the full deck straight down his throat.

Frustrated at what he viewed as an almost pitiful lost cause, his father continued. "I think you can make a decent living as an accountant, Wade, feed a family at least." His father paused and gave a depressed sigh. "I've got some good friends who can get you a job with their firm. They've already told me so. All you've got to do is pass your classes. You don't have to make A's or B's or anything hard like that. C's will do just fine." Even more disgusted, his father demanded, "Now, do you think you can handle that, Wade? I mean, you don't have to become a CPA or anything that difficult. Just graduate with an accounting degree. That's all you've got to do."

Any wind in Wade's sails was gone. "Yes, sir," he mumbled half dazed. Like a fine crystal bowl being dropped to the floor, his dream was shattered into a million pieces. In his mind, Wade kept hearing his father speak.

"Well, I'm not going to keep sending you to school with grades like that. You understand?"

"Yes, sir," Wade muttered.

"What's that, son?" his father was sickened by Wade's pitiful response.

"Yes, sir," Wade spoke up trying to hold himself upright but just barely.

Disgusted with his son's frailty, Wade's dad marched out of the room.

Hanging his head, Wade drifted into a stupor. Finally, he got up despondently and drug himself off to his room. Confused and hurt by all that had transpired in the last few days, he could hardly think. Silently he lay on his still-made bed fully dressed staring at the ceiling with the lights off. Slowly, as he lay there, his mind began to reel like an old movie projector. His life had started off so happy. He could remember the good times he had with his dad when he was a little boy. Wrestling, playing, hugging, and teasing with him, going fishing and hunting and learning how to play all the sports with him. But somewhere along the way, maybe when his dad got serious about making a living, things changed. *Why?* Wade thought. How had he lost his father's acceptance?

His desire to call Mimi back was gone. There was no use. There was no use in even being alive, he thought. A pall of despondency came over him as thick and dark as a storm cloud. His desire to even breathe was gone. Slowly and in a state of numbness, sleep finally overcame him.

He awoke early the next morning, and by not eating breakfast, he made it to the mill by 7:30. Knowing exactly the routine of this job from doing it so many times before, he made his way to the back corner of the plant. There, using a box blade, he would cut the remainder of spent cord from giant spools, which had been used in the process of spinning twine. The loud rhythmic drone of the spinning machines surrounding him was appropriate for his state of mind. Wade did not want to think about anything. Not his father, not his situation at school, not Les, not even Mimi. In the roaring vibrations of the plant, he found a certain solace, a refuge from these issues that kept trying to bubble up in his mind. Issues he'd like to resolve, but lacking self-confidence, felt powerless to handle.

When the day ended at 5:00, he stopped by a pay-phone and called Mimi to tell her he couldn't make it up to see her right away, that he was stuck in a job with rotating shifts and didn't know when he'd get a break. Disappointed, she told him that she understood, and said to call back when he had a chance. The conversation, though brief, had been painful for them both. When Wade left the phone booth, he went home. Feigning the actions of a 'good' son, it was work-home supper and bed. The routine only changing as it revolved around which shift he worked. Except for Kelli, he tried his best to avoid his family at all cost, especially his father, the man who kept his mind reeling each night with suppressed anger and fear.

Two weeks of work came to an end on Christmas Eve. If Wade had his way, he would have gone back to school at this point to avoid exchanging gifts with anyone the next day. Christmas fell on a Saturday, and according to Wade's parents, Les was scheduled to preach his first sermon the next day at church. But Wade would not be attending. He made plans to leave for Athens early Sunday morning instead. He claimed he wanted to get a head start on his next accounting class. In reality, he wanted to get as far away from his father as he could.

Before he left, Kelli, dressed in her Christmas outfit for Sunday school, cornered her brother in his bedroom. "Are you sure you've got to go back today?" she said with sad brown eyes looking up at him.

Wade reached out and gently held her small shoulder. "Yep. And probably you're the only person in this house who really knows why. Right?"

"Yeah," she said tears flooding down her cheeks. "Are you ever gonna come back to see us, Wade?"

"Sure, Kell'," Wade said softly as he held her tight in his strong muscular arms. "I'll never leave you. You can count on that."

"Mama cried last night in her bedroom after you told us at supper that you were going to leave today," She murmured with her face buried in his chest.

"I know," Wade responded. "Everything will be okay though. You hear me?"

"No it won't," she muttered, her voice muffled from hugging him so tight. "He hates us."

"He doesn't hate us. He loves us. He just has a hard time showing it."

"No, he doesn't. He says mean things to you. He doesn't love anybody," Kelli said crying uncontrollably.

"Shhh—Shhh," Wade whispered as he sat on the side of the bed gently rocking her and patting her back. "You know, when you were a baby, I used to rock you all the time. I loved to rock my Kelli. I'd check on you every night when I'd come home from a date too and make sure that you were tucked in your bed and all covered up before I'd go to sleep. And lots of times I'd come get in the bed with you when you were scared. Do you remember that?" Her head still pressed against his shoulder, she nodded yes.

"And remember all those times we camped out in the backyard together? And how I taught you to fish and carried you hunting with me? You're like my own little girl. I'll always be here to take care of you, Kelli. So don't you worry. Dad's not mad at you. He's upset with me. I can handle that. I always have before, haven't I?"

"I know, but it makes me cry."

"It's okay to cry when you're sad," Wade said wiping the tears from her eyes, and tenderly stroking her head. "Do you feel better now?"

"A little bit," she said again pressing her head against Wade's chest.

After another big hug, she straightened up. Wade looked compassionately into her watery eyes. "Okay now?"

She nodded her head okay.

"All right, scoot to the bathroom and wash your face. Don't let Mama see you crying."

After she left the room, Wade continued packing. His mother came into the room. She tried putting on a smiling front, but both knew better.

"Well, are you about ready to go?" she asked.

"Yes ma'am," Wade responded.

She hung her head and fiddled with a string on his bedspread, then took a seat by Wade.

"I'm sorry about the way your dad snapped at you over the holidays."

"That's all right, Mom. With grades like that, I deserved it. I understand."

"No, I don't think you do." She paused searching for words that wouldn't sound disloyal to her husband. "You know that story about the cows your father told you and your grandfather being a nervous wreck?"

Wade looked at his mother intently.

"Well, your dad's just like him. He just doesn't want anyone to know it."

Wade gazed back at her questioningly.

She tried to show as little negativity toward Wade's father as was possible. "I think that tension comes to a head sometimes. He lets it out. He just can't help it, but he loves you. He wants the best for you."

Wade comforted his mother with a hug even though what she had told him did little to ease his pain. How could a parent show love through cruelty? By being condescending and arrogant? By being competitive rather than nurturing? It made no sense. He pretended that it did for his mother's sake.

"I think I know what you mean, Mom."

He said goodbye to his mother and sister giving each a hug and kiss. His dad had already headed to the church in a separate vehicle. He left word with his wife to tell Wade goodbye. That was fitting, Wade thought to himself as his mother told him this. Wade made his way to the car. Cranking it up, he drove down the alley and past the woods which looked so much smaller and more insignificant to him now. Going out past the high school and on to I-75, he headed back toward Athens and an uncertain future.

CHAPTER 8

Alone

Wade arrived in Athens to no one. The trailer was cold, icy, and barren, just like his life. He made his way to the thermostat to turn on the furnace. The click from the heater sounded with a purring noise as the propane lit. The fan switched on blowing warm air through the vents into the cold rooms surrounding him. Lifting the back of his heavy corduroy coat, he plucked his wallet from his back pocket and plopped down into the biting chill of the den's vinyl recliner. The phone's receiver was uncomfortably cold as he pinched it between his shoulder and ear. He stared at Mimi's parent's number on the faded yellow paper he retrieved from his billfold. He dialed and waited. The phone rang—and rang—and rang. There was no answer from the other end as he waited in anticipation. But nothing. Finally, he hung up and methodically went through the motions of putting his clothes away.

The heater worked well. Quickly, the place began to warm up. With his father far away, Wade took a deep breath and let out a long sigh of relief as he once again fell into the recliner. He rubbed his tired eyes and face. Pinching the inside corners where his eyes and nose met, he gently massaged the area releasing the tension residing there. Downhearted he realized there was no one. That was all he could think about as he sat there looking around the place. Les was gone and would not be back. Mimi, he couldn't get in touch with her. And neither Ann, Louisa, nor Mimi would be back up until after the first of the year. Depression settled over him. Loneliness and insecurity sprang up inside him, worse than any he had experienced before. He had to get out of this place, he told himself. He had to shake this feeling.

It was almost dark when he decided to leave the trailer. Down the clanking metal steps, he made his way observing the emptiness of the park complex. He noticed a few stars were peeping through the early evening haze as he climbed into his car and headed for town.

Cast against the darkness of the night, the orange neon lights of Arby's shone brightly. He drove slowly, noticing even more than on his drive back how empty this side of the city was. Only a handful of people were at the sandwich shop when he arrived. Usually at this time of night on a Sunday, the place would be packed. That was when school was in session. Now, hardly a soul.

He placed his order. Not wanting to go back to the emptiness of his trailer, he got his food and took a seat. A tall somewhat attractive redhead sat across the room from him at another table. Something didn't seem quite right about the girl, he thought. She appeared a little ragged around the edges. He wondered what she was doing back at school so early. Had she not gone home for the holidays or were they just two lonely people on this normally gleeful night? He chuckled to himself shaking his head. Finishing his meal more rapidly than anticipated, he put his leftover trash on the tray he had brought to his table and stood up. Heading toward the garbage bin on the young woman's side of the diner, he pushed in the lid to the bin with his tray and emptied it, catching the girl's eyes as he did so. She gave him a friendly but fragile smile. Smiling warmly back at her, he paused for a long second then turned and walked out of the restaurant.

Wade made his way back to the trailer, back to its emptiness and isolation. Entering his home once again, he picked up the phone's receiver and dialed Mimi's number one more time, but again no answer. His only feeling now was the disappointment he felt after each unanswered ring. The night ended as the day had started, in agony. And just like this one, each successive day passed slowly by. One by one, they progressed with the same tired ritual as the day before. He had no desire to sketch or paint. Even the pseudo-urgency of the daily television news broadcasts or the sitcoms' escapism could not distract him.

Many times, he thought about calling Ann to find out if she knew where Mimi and her family had gone. Wade gave little consideration to actually making contact with anyone from back home, however. The chance of hearing something negative that his father might have said could easily send him over the edge and he knew it.

If only he could reach Mimi. With her warm personality and calming demeanor, she had lifted Wade's spirits from the quagmire of the previous quarter. Wade had fallen for the attractive girl, and likewise, she seemed infatuated with him.

Six lonesome days passed before he found himself sitting in his den on New Year's Day. The night before he had watched the giant ball fall at One Times Square in New York on television. For him, the occasion was bittersweet. The crowds on T.V. emanated fun and excitement, but Wade with no friends around to celebrate, felt downhearted. Tired of cloistering himself away in his self-made prison, he decided to leave his trailer for an early evening meal. A buffet-diner that he and Les and some of their pals had eaten at several times the previous quarter was just down Broad Street.

Going through the line and filling his tray with an assortment of fresh vegetables, prime rib, and desserts proved a much-needed reprieve from the Spartan meals he'd been living on at his trailer. His appetite satiated, he was now ready to make a night of it. Rather than going straight home, Wade stopped at Jack's Liquor store where he purchased a six-pack of beer and a bottle of Cold Duck Champagne. "By God I'll find a way to enjoy this evening," he said aloud as thoughts of Mimi danced in his head.

Getting back to the trailer, he had already popped open a beer and was sipping on it as he entered the place. Putting the rest of the beer and the bottle of champagne in the fridge, he went and turned the television on and searched the channels for a bowl game to watch.

After flipping through several, he found a good one. It was the Sugar Bowl at the Dome in New Orleans, Alabama versus Notre Dame. For a young man from the vanquished South who had grown up listening to and reliving stories of famous Confederate battles, nothing could be more satisfying than watching a famed team from the Southeastern Conference knocking off the best the North had to offer. This season Alabama came into the game with a perfect 11-0 record and was ranked by the Associated Press as #1 in the nation. Notre Dame likewise came in with a perfect record of 10-0, beating Pittsburg, USC, and Michigan State along the way.

The stage was set for a tremendous battle as the two best teams in the country faced off to see who would earn the coveted title of National Champion. Although Wade was alone and would have preferred watching the game with a group of friends, he became absorbed in the contest. When the ref made a bad call, Wade jumped to his feet protesting. When an Alabama player missed a tackle, he moaned and groaned. From the score that gave Alabama the lead, much to Wade's delight, to Notre Dame regaining it, causing him much despair, the game was a barnburner.

The combined scoring drives between each team totaled eight. Notre Dame was in the lead with only two minutes and twelve seconds of play remaining and holding the ball deep in their own territory on 3rd down and long: the stadium and Wade were rocking at a fever pitch. It was an obvious running situation as Notre Dame certainly wouldn't chance putting the ball in the air this close to their own goal line. Cunningly the Notre Dame coach had other plans. With only a one-point difference as Notre Dame led 24-23, the Fighting Irish broke the huddle to run the play for 3rd down. As the ball was snapped, the massive Alabama defensive line charged across the line of scrimmage to stop the running play, but they were duped. The Notre Dame quarterback made a quick pass resulting in a first down. The game was over just like that. In Wade's mind, another loss to his Southern heritage had been dealt. Painfully, he watched as the remaining seconds ticked off the clock ending the contest. Tonight, there would be no gleeful popping the top to his champagne bottle. He leaned back in his chair, shocked and despondent, one more blow to his severely damaged ego.

II

As the Christmas holidays and quarter break ended, Ann made her way back to her apartment where she found Angie and Louisa. The next day would be the start of winter quarter. Busily, the girls went about organizing their clothes. Some, new from Christmas, were put into almost empty dressers and closets from the previous year.

Ann and Angie weren't as close as they had been before Angie's break up with Wade, but they were getting along. Angie knew her ticket back to her old boyfriend would be through her roommates, so she tried hard not to show any antagonism when Mimi's name was mentioned, even though it ate holes in her whenever it was brought up.

Intrigued by Les' call to the ministry, Louisa's roommates excitedly listened as Louisa told them about it. When she finished her story, they asked her if she was planning to move down to Texas and if she and Les had talked about or made any plans to get married. Purposely, Louisa remained vague on such details, telling them she planned to finish the year at the University before deciding on anything further. As was her nature, Louisa turned the tables on her two friends by showing more interest in their activities over the Christmas break than hers.

As the girls engaged each other with what they had been doing and what their next quarter's classes were looking like, Ann's thoughts suddenly shifted to her cousin. She knew by a telephone call from Mimi that there had been problems and for some reason, Wade had come back to Athens unusually early for winter quarter. Wanting to find out what was going on with him, she excused herself from the other girls' conversation and sat down on the sofa to give him a call.

Hearing Ann say his name over the phone, Angie made it a point to find a nearby chair and pretend to read a magazine. Quickly into the conversation, Ann realized Wade had no idea what was going on with Mimi. She knew Mimi had tried calling Wade's parents' home on Sunday, the day after Christmas, but nobody was there. That's when she decided to call Ann. Giving Ann her new address, she told her she would be unable to communicate with them for a short time. Wade was not privy to any of this information.

After talking to Wade for several minutes and realizing that Angie was eavesdropping, Ann told him goodbye and said she would be out to see him shortly. She put down the phone and told her roommates where she was heading.

Angie asked if everything was okay with Wade and said she hoped there was nothing wrong.

"Nothing that I know of," Ann responded. "I just want to see how things are going out there without Les. That's all."

Still quizzing her, Angie asked, "I thought his girlfriend would be back out there by now with school starting tomorrow?"

"She might be." Ann said stoically. "I didn't ask."

Louisa re-entered the den where her two friends were talking. Hearing Ann say she was going out to the trailer, she told her roommate to tell Wade she would come by sometime soon to get some of Les' things that he had forgotten, but she'd call him first.

Driving down the four-lane road to Wade's trailer, Ann wondered, *What on earth is going on here? Why hadn't he and Mimi been talking with each other over the holidays?* She unfortunately would have to be the one to break the bad news to her cousin. Arriving at the mobile home, she found Wade sitting on his front door's metal steps. Wondering himself why he hadn't been able to contact Mimi, he was eager to find out what Ann knew.

Glancing around the place as Wade invited her inside, Ann noticed how junky and unkempt his living quarters had become. The sink was full of dirty dishes. Newspapers and magazines were lying all over the place. Wade looked rough. His hair was disheveled and his shirttail hung sideways out of his jeans. He wore only socks as he sat cross-legged on his sofa.

Dismayed by what she saw, but trying not to let on, Ann took a seat in his vinyl recliner. "What ya' been doing, Cuz?" Ann asked with a smile. She knew he had been in Athens a week already and, knowing this fact plus observing how bad the boy appeared, she could tell something was wrong—really wrong.

"Oh, nothing. Just getting ready for this quarter. That's all. So, I guess you know what's going on with Mimi?"

Ann peered questioningly into Wade's eyes. "When's the last time you two talked?"

"A few days after I got home for Christmas break," Wade reflected as he watched his cousin with concern.

Ann sighed as she gazed downward. Looking back up at him, she carefully chose her words. "I hate to have to be the one to tell you this, Wade, but Mimi and her family have had to move to California."

Wade was in total shock. He couldn't believe what he was hearing. A sincere, heartfelt expression of loss and sadness covered his face. He had blocked out of his mind what he'd already known. He knew that with her dad being called back to active duty and with no one answering the phone, it had to be something bad like this.

"For good?" he asked solemnly, not wanting to hear the answer.

"For now," Ann affirmed. "You know about her dad having to go back in and all?"

Wade nodded his head slowly confirming that he did know.

"Well," Ann continued. "When you didn't go to Macon to see her, she thought you didn't care about her as much as you had seemed to, and . . ."

Wade rubbed his face and eyes and sighed heavily.

"I'm so sorry, Wade," Ann continued. "Mimi was really upset. Her parents had given her the okay to continue school here if she wanted. But that's a long way for her to be away from them especially with no one . . ."

"Around to count on," Wade finished her sentence solemnly. His eyes grew pale, his voice weak. "You know. If I'd just gone up to see her, Ann—she'd be here tonight." The thought of her not being with him, not ever seeing the girl again who had gotten his life turned back around, and who he was so in love with, was almost unbearable.

Ann watched with deep compassion as her cousin continued to rub his face and brow in agony. Blankly, he stopped and stared across the room gazing at nothing. Ann wished she could comfort him somehow, but there was nothing she could do. Nothing at all except be there for him.

"It was Dad," he softly spoke as he regained his focus and glanced back at her. A painful expression was drawn across his face. "He wouldn't let me go and see her."

"He what?" Ann asked incredulously.

"You know my grades weren't so hot last quarter. I made two D's, and a B." He paused thinking back to the one-sided conversation he had with his father. "I had it coming, I guess. He chewed me out pretty good. You know how he can be. Anyway, he had that job at the mill arranged for me again during the Christmas break. There was no way I was going to get out of it especially after he found out what my grades were."

Ann understood what had happened. She well knew the hell Wade's dad at times could lay on his son. The two cousins had discussed it on many occasions, or at least almost every time his father had gone overboard.

"So that's what you were doing back here so early?" she asked sympathetically.

"Yeah. Besides, after I told him about Mimi and her family, I don't think he was too impressed. He seems to think that people in the military are basically a bunch of bums."

Ann frowned.

"So, he wouldn't let you even call her?" Ann asked taken aback.

"No. He didn't stop me from calling her. After I told her that I was tied up with a job and all, and that I wouldn't be able to make it up there anytime soon, I guess I just gave up." Hanging his head as he thought about this, his anger toward his father began to grow. "If it wasn't for that jerk! All of this wouldn't have happened! I guess I should have just gone up to see her anyway. I don't think things could have turned out any worse. I've lost my girl. Lost the chance to do what I really want to do with my life. I've pretty much lost just about everything because of *him* and the way *he* wants things done."

Confused, Ann asked, "I understand about losing Mimi, but what you want to do? What are you talking about, Wade?"

Wade sneered. "You would think that you could trust your father with your most precious dreams, right? But that's not always the way things work out—now is it?"

Perplexed Ann listened quietly.

"Dreams," Wade scoffed sarcastically. "He yelled at me, Ann. Said 'if business and accounting aren't what you want to do, then tell me what is it that you want to do, son?'" Wade paused again, his spiteful glare still lingering from the wound his father had thrust deep into his soul. "Mistake of mistakes, Ann. I finally got up the courage to tell him the truth for once. Told him that I wanted to be an artist. But boy, oh boy that was the wrong thing to say. He blasted that idea right out of the water," Wade exclaimed shaking his head, madder than ever.

Cunningly Ann laughed out loud catching Wade completely off guard. "What the hell does your sorry dad know about art, Wade? You're not going to let that ignorant moron get you down over that, now are you?"

"He pays the bills, Ann. So, I'm pretty much stuck doing what he wants me to do."

Ann interceded cynically, "And just what's that supposed to be, Wade?"

"He wants me to be an accountant."

"An accountant?" Ann questioned as she shook her head in disbelief. "Has he ever even seen any of the drawings and paintings you've done, Wade?"

"Oh, yeah, he's seen them, but he shows no interest in them one way or the other. Gives me no opinion whatsoever for whatever reason."

Angrily Ann blew up. "Well, I'll give you the reason, Wade! It's because you're his main competition! Bad parents compete against their children. It happens all the time. He couldn't care less about your fantastic ability to draw and paint because it's something that he can't do and he can't stand the fact that you are better than he is at anything. He's a pitiful piece of crap for treating you like that."

"Well," Wade responded, "as much as he's pissed me off, I think he just wants to make sure that I can make a living at what I do when I get out."

"Bull crap!" Ann retorted. "You can make all the excuses you want for him. All he is is just a self-centered, egotistical jackass who wants to control your life and keep you in your place. To keep you beneath him. What father would deny his son's talent to the point that his son wouldn't even believe in his own ability? You wouldn't do that to your boy now would you, Wade? You'd back him up one-hundred percent, and I know you would."

"Yeah, I suppose you're right."

"No. There's no supposing to it. I know you definitely would. But getting away from your sorry ass father, Wade, let's talk here about someone who really does care about you and who really does love you. And I'm talking about the girl who's really, really in love with you—Mimi." Ann reached into her purse and withdrew a folded piece of yellow notebook paper. "This is the address of the base where Mimi and her family are in California. She wants you to write her. She said they might have to make several moves before they get a permanent phone, so no need to call. Write her. She says they have a central processing center out there and your letter will get to her that way. Okay?"

Wade smiled an appreciative grin then stood and took the paper from her hand. He knew his dear cousin had saved him once again, and he was thankful.

As Ann got out of the recliner to leave, she looked around the place and said, "Pretty messy in here, wouldn't you say?"

"Yeah, I know. I need to get this place and myself cleaned up. Start the new quarter off on the right foot and all, right?"

Ann smiled at him. "I'll see you sometime tomorrow. Maybe we can eat supper together tomorrow night somewhere—oh, I almost forgot, Louisa says she's gonna come over sometime this week to get some of Les' stuff. Said that she'd call you first, though."

"I'll be listening out for her, and supper sounds great, Ann."

As Ann left, Wade noticed she was right. The place was a mess. Relieved from the uncertainty of what was going on with Mimi and knowing she still had deep feelings for him, Wade happily took on the task of cleaning his residence. As far as his father was concerned and all the angst the older man had put him through, well, Ann had helped free his mind from that issue too.

III

School started the next day, and Wade made his way across campus to his new classes, Economics 102, Accounting 102, and Marketing 304. It was a heavy load for one quarter, he thought. He sighed knowing he would have to get a jump on this quarter or else. The thought of his father staring down at him loomed large in his mind. As he opened his first book—the phone rang. "Hello?"

It was Ann. She had a surprise for him and wanted to meet him at the Western Sizzlin steakhouse on Baxter Street.

"Sure," Wade responded. "Seven-thirty would be fine. I'll see you then."

It was 6:00 as Wade poured over his marketing homework finishing it by seven. He took a quick shower and made it to the steakhouse right on time.

Standing at the entrance was not only Ann but also Louisa. Maybe she was the surprise, he thought. Glad that they were all together, the three casually made their way through the line and placed their orders. Putting their tea and silverware on a single tray, they found a corner booth where they could talk and eat their meal in private. They were extremely happy to see each other and it was the first time Wade was able to get Louisa's take on Les going to seminary in Texas.

Looking across the table, Wade gave Louisa a little smile. "Les tells me that you'll be in Athens for the rest of this year. Is that right?"

"That's kind of our plan right now. Imagine we'll run up quite a long-distance phone bill, you think?"

"Probably so," Wade grinned back. "All I can tell you is that it's mighty quiet out at the trailer without him, and that's a fact."

"Yeah," Louisa said, as her eyes seemed to dim. "I'm already missing him too."

Catching on that he had brought up a bad subject, Wade tried to redeem himself. "But it's like you say—he's only a phone call away, Louisa. And you'll be fine. Ann and I will see to that. Right, Ann?"

Thoughtfully Ann looked at Louisa. "She'll be okay, Wade. The time will fly by faster than she thinks." Ann paused for a second and gave Wade a funny look. "Okay, ol' buddy!" she suddenly exclaimed.

Wade noticed Louisa's sad countenance replaced with an excited radiant smile. Taken aback by the girl's sudden change in mood, he was perplexed.

Ann spoke up, "All right, Louisa, what was that guy's name again?"

Louisa spoke softly, intently watching as Ann jotted down what she was saying on a small note pad. "Dr. Owen. Fredrick Owen. Art 322."

Wade watched them curiously as Ann finished writing then slid the paper in front of him.

"This is the course we want you to take over in the art department. You know, over behind where I had that sociology class where you met me one time last quarter."

Wade glanced down at the paper, then up at her. "What?" he asked puzzled.

"This is the professor's name, and this is the art class you need to take this quarter," she said matter of fact.

"What are you guys talking about?" Wade grinned. "I've got a full load already."

Both girls were smiling intently at him. Louisa started to bite her bottom lip as Ann began to speak. "Well, Wade, I hope you're not mad, but Les and Louisa carried that picture of the older man hugging the young boy down by the dock. You know, the one you let Les hang in his room—to this guy here." She pointed to Dr. Owen's name. "He said that you really need to be taking his class. He was very, very impressed and was insistent that he meet you."

Wade sighed looking at Louisa who was scrunching her nose and making a facial expression like please, don't kill me. "When did you two clowns do this?" he asked with a disbelieving grin.

"Last quarter," Louisa winced, not knowing how Wade was going to react.

Wade scanned the room as the girls sat watching him in earnest. He looked back at them. "Guys, I'm loaded. I've got three tough courses already. There's no way I can do that this quarter. If I have to read one more thing, I'll explode," he exclaimed in exasperation.

"No, Cuz, you've got it all wrong. This is strictly a painting class. No real homework."

Wade laughed. "That's a good one. This guy will probably want to go over tools, brushes, and techniques. There will be tests all right. You can count on that." His eyes blazed as he spoke.

"Yeah, but you know all that stuff already, Wade," Ann scoffed. "You're a fool if you don't do it." She immediately had second thoughts about challenging him. "At least go talk to the guy and find out," she pleaded.

Wade gave a half smile to the two schemers. "I don't know girls—Ann, you know the problems I'll have with my dad if I don't do well this quarter."

"He'll never have to know, Wade," she said still trying to encourage him. "Besides, you'll ace this course and it can't do anything but improve your grade point average."

Wade paused as Ann finished stating her case. He gazed in Louisa's direction as she gave him an unusually serious look.

"You owe this to yourself, Wade," she asserted.

Looking back once more at Ann, he half-heartedly relented. "Okay, I'll go talk to him. But I won't promise you guys that I'll take his course. Is that a deal?"

Both girls nodded with big heartfelt smiles. Their meals were delivered to the table where they ate in relative peace. Before they left, Louisa asked if she could come to Wade's Friday evening to gather a few things that Les had forgotten.

"Of course," Wade responded. "I'll see you then."

CHAPTER 9

Art Class

(January 1974)

The next day Wade found himself in the lobby of the art department trying to figure out where to find Dr. Fredrick Owen. He had an hour to kill before his course in marketing started at the business school.

It was the last day of drop-add, and if he were going to pick up another elective, it would have to be today. Still, he couldn't see how he could squeeze another course into his busy itinerary. But he told the girls he would talk to this guy; so here he was, lost as a possum on a city street.

Wandering helplessly around the building, he finally saw a room that he guessed was the administrator's office. Asking the art department secretaries sitting leisurely at their desks, he was told nonchalantly where the teacher might be.

Their directions sent him to an empty classroom on the other end of the building. Asking a guy standing outside this room if he knew the professor's whereabouts, Wade was sent to another distant location. Here he found a class in progress, but the person teaching it was not Owen.

Wade had had enough. As usual it didn't take much to set the temperamental boy off, especially in a strange place with such weird, somewhat freakish looking characters surrounding him. Heading through the building's lobby for the front door, he was ready to forget the whole idea and move on. As luck would have it, he was rescued.

A guy with long hair wearing a buckskin jacket, bell-bottom jeans, and tennis shoes was sitting cross-legged inside the entrance to the building reading a book. The title to the paperback he was holding read *The Spaceships of Ezekiel* by Josef Blumrich, a chief program developer at NASA. Using the principles of physics, the author analyzed the supposed sighting of an extraterrestrial spacecraft by the prophet Ezekiel as described in the Bible. Leaning against the wall, this intellectual hippie looking student noticed Wade marching back and forth through the building appearing completely lost. As he saw Wade heading toward the exit, the friendly young man called out to him.

"Hey! You there! Can I help you find something, man?"

Wade stopped. Shaking his head, he smirked. "I've been trying to find this professor—Dr. Owen. You know him?"

"Sure do," the student glanced at the clock on the atrium's wall. "Look in room 206. He usually takes a break about now between classes every day. Cool, dude."

"Room 206?"

"Yeah. Down the hall to the left," the student pointed in the direction Wade was to take.

"Thanks," Wade replied gratefully.

"Anytime, man."

Wade strolled back down the hallway heading for the room. Noticing the door ajar, he found himself peering in at a small man he presumed was the professor. Dr. Owen appeared to be in his sixties and had a short crop of wavy silver-gray hair with a widow's peak and no sign of a receding hairline or bald spot. Wade thought this was odd for an art teacher. Most instructors had long hair, even the older ones. The guy's attire was even more shocking. No bell-bottoms. No tie-dyed shirt. No sandals. Of course, it would be too cold for sandals this time of year even as odd as art teachers and students were. The professor wore only a simple white short sleeve shirt and a pair of black woolen slacks and wingtip shoes. *Interesting looking fellow*, Wade thought.

Sipping coffee as he looked over class materials, the man must have felt a presence in the doorway. Lifting his head slightly, he smiled warmly at the young artist. "Please come in," he said peering through his fragile wire rim glasses. "Can I help you?"

Wade ambled over to the desk where the older man was sitting and wondered what he should say. Stammering, Wade started to speak, "You're . . . Dr. Owen?"

"Yes," the man nodded.

"Well, a girl named Louisa Wess and—uh—another friend of mine named Les brought a picture for you to . . ."

"Louisa Wess," he interrupted. "Oh yes, a lovely girl. And an excellent student too, by the way. Yes, she said you'd be dropping by to see me." A wide grin stretched across the teacher's face. "You're the young fellow who painted that wonderful composition of the people on the dock, I presume?"

"Yes, sir," Wade tentatively responded.

Dr. Owen leaned back in his chair and reflected on the painting.

"Very complex piece indeed. Very intriguing. Yes, I remember them bringing it over for me to see. Sure do."

The doctor leaned forward in his chair and propped his arms on the desk. "Your name's Wade, I believe, isn't it?"

Wade nodded surprised that the instructor would remember such a small detail.

"Well, Wade," he stood and reached out to shake the young man's hand, "it is truly a pleasure to meet you, son."

After shaking hands, the professor went to the door of the room and closed it. He walked back to his desk where the curious student was still standing. Leaning on the table top in a half sitting posture, the professor looked directly into Wade's eyes.

"You may not know it, friend, but you've got a fabulous talent."

He paused a moment to think about what he had just said then gazed over at Wade.

"You probably do know it."

He paused again placing a bent index finger under his bottom lip resting his thumb under his chin in a pensive mood.

"Louisa tells me you're majoring in something else. Why aren't you majoring in art, Wade?"

Wade placed his books on one of the seats in front of the teacher's desk. Cocking his head, he began to rub his neck slowly with his right hand. "Well, to make a long story short, sir, I just didn't feel like I could make a living at it."

Dr. Owen smiled back. "What's your major, son?"

"Accounting."

"I see," the professor responded. "Let me be frank. I don't just take people aside and tell them that they have some wonderful ability, Wade. Matter of fact, I usually do just the opposite. Most of the students coming through here are quite good at what they do. They observe and they copy. Quite well actually. And because all of their lives they have been praised for what they have done by their families and friends, they come in here thinking that they are going to be the next Rembrandt or Picasso." He stopped to chuckle as he shook his head. "But you, my friend, are different. You don't capture the feeling that was in that picture by luck. That's the difference," he hesitated, "that's the difference between a picture and art."

Wade listened intently to every word Dr. Owen told him. Honored by the compliments the teacher was giving him, Wade still showed more embarrassment than pride. "Thank you," he responded finally accepting the compliment.

"From what I remember, your friends wanted to see if I thought you had the makings of an artist. You're lucky you have such good friends. They're rare these days with everyone looking out for *numero uno*." Nodding, the instructor said, "Absolutely you have the ability. The question is, do you have the desire? The heart for it?" Curiously he peered into Wade's eyes and waited for a response.

For the first time, Wade spoke plainly. "Art is and has always been my first love, sir. It's just that I don't know if I can put groceries on the table doing it."

With a twinkle in his eye, the older man asserted, "Follow your passion, son. The rest will come in time. Don't squander the talent the good Lord gave you on groceries for heaven's sake."

Wade chuckled at the remark, as did the professor.

"Take my course, Wade," Dr. Owen insisted. "Give it a chance. It would be my honor entirely."

Wade knew no way to refuse the shining eyes and impish grin. He had never met a teacher as optimistic and interested in his welfare.

The two of them examined Wade's schedule and found a way to get the young artist into the class. It took a couple of calls by the instructor to the registrar's office to pull the strings needed to get it done. Wade would start class the very next day.

When Wade got home that afternoon, he called Ann and Louisa to tell them about his meeting with the professor. They were delighted that he had gone through with it and praised him for taking the chance on the class. When he got off the phone, he wrote a letter to Mimi telling her what was happening. He related the big screw up at Christmas with him and his father, and how he had called and called her to no avail. He included that he was taking an art class knowing she would be proud of him. He told her how much he loved and missed her and told her to call or write him back.

The letter was signed, sealed, and sent the next morning. As he dropped the envelope down the chute of the large red and blue mailbox near the corner of Baxter and Milledge, he had no idea how long the letter would take to get to her or even if it would make it to her at all. With thousands upon thousands of people at the busy military complex, it was a risk he'd have to accept. All he could do now was wait hoping she would call or write him soon. The thought of getting a response, hearing her voice, or reading her words gave Wade a warm fuzzy feeling. Only a beautiful, radiant woman, completely enthralled with him could produce such a sensation.

After weeks of uncertainty, Wade was excited about life once more. Finding his relationship with Mimi still intact, and his business classes going well, Wade felt a new day was dawning. The advanced art course was invigorating, and there was no struggle to keep pace, even on his first day. Art came as natural to him as waking up each morning.

By Friday, Wade was physically weary but not tired. Painting under supervision and learning new and interesting techniques bolstered his already incredible skill level. With this accentuation, his newfound sense of joy and inspiration made his other courses easier. Not that it made him more relaxed, but he had an outlet to express his true self, something that had been hidden for a long time.

On Friday afternoon, he decided to finish his lessons early before the weekend started—just in case something he wanted to do might occur on Saturday or Sunday. In actuality, it was more evidence of his new thrill for life. Completing the last of his accounting problems for Monday's class, he heard the phone ring. He scrambled to answer it hoping it was Mimi, but it was Louisa.

"Sure, you can come over." Pausing momentarily to listen, he continued. "No, I haven't eaten. We'll order a pizza. How 'bout that?" He paused listening again. "Okay, I'll see you when you get here."

He put his books aside and flew into his bathroom for a shave and shower. As he lathered his hair with an herbal shampoo thinking of what clothes he might wear, he stopped for a moment to reflect. *What the hell am I doing,* he thought. *I'm acting like this is a date or something.* Trying to rationalize the situation, he thought what girl wanted to be around an unclean smelly guy? He laughed about his concern. Les would have no worries about him being alone with Louisa, and Wade knew it.

He washed his dirty dishes piled in the sink and vacuumed the floor. Something still didn't seem right. Wade concluded that what was missing was Les. The trailer felt empty since his friend had left. Soon Wade heard Louisa arrive followed by a gentle knock at the door. He called for her to enter. Louisa opened the door and walked inside. She gave Wade a warm smile. Her brilliant blue eyes sparkled.

"Good evening, Wade," she spoke softly.

"Hey, Louisa," Wade greeted her, happy he wouldn't have to spend another evening alone.

Looking around the room and noticing how barren the place appeared, she took a seat on the edge of the sofa. Wade sat down in his recliner watching the girl as each one of them waited for the other to say something. There was a strangeness to the situation. Neither knew what to say, especially not Wade. He didn't want to seem uncomfortable and run her off. He wanted company—someone to be with.

Louisa broke the ice. "It seems a little different without Les here, doesn't it?" she asked sadly. Wade had seen this sad expression before when they had eaten out with Ann recently, the look a girl gets right before she starts to cry.

Sensing this, Wade leaned forward in his chair. "Yeah, a little bit. I miss him, all right. But he's doing fine and doing the right thing too. He'll make a great preacher, don't you think?"

Louisa nodded with misty eyes. The tears started to come. Wade waited anxiously wanting to comfort her, but he felt too awkward to do it. As the tears began to pour, she stood up and reached out for him. Wade held her in his arms.

"It's okay, Louisa. It's okay," he said softly, wanting to kiss her dark hair to ease her pain. He was taken aback that the cool-headed girl had lost her composure especially in front of him. But he knew how she felt. He felt the same way about Mimi.

After shedding tears for a few moments, Louisa stopped. Wade gently pushed her back while holding her shoulders and looked deep into her red eyes. "There—there—now," he consoled. Taking the wrung Kleenex she held in her hand, he gently wiped the teardrops away from her cheeks. "I got a great idea," he whispered. "Why don't we call Les and see how he's doing?"

"That'll cost too much, Wade," she sighed appearing fractious.

"Naw, not for one call. It'll be on me," he said cheerfully. "I got his number right here." He picked up the phone book resting on a table next to him and turned to a page full of handwritten notes. Dialing the phone number, he soon had Les on the other end of the line. As was usual his pal was in great spirits. Wade talked to him first. "Hey, Les. It's me, Wade."

"Hey, boy! What you up to?" came the gleeful response from his buddy.

"Nothing much. Hey, I got one of your pals over here with me. You want to guess who it is?"

Les took a wild guess, "Who? Karl?"

"Are you kidding me?" Wade laughed. "Someone a lot nicer and a whole lot prettier!"

Les chuckled. "Louisa?"

"Yep, that's right. She wants to talk to ya'. Here she is." He handed the phone to Louisa and went off into Les' old bedroom to give them some privacy. After ten long minutes of conversation, she ended the call then walked to the room and timidly tapped on the door.

Wade was sprawled out on Les' bed reading an old Reader's Digest he'd found on one of Les' bookshelves. Hearing the knock, he got up and opened the door. "All done?" Wade asked.

Louisa looked down nodding her head affirmatively as Wade observed her. Then, reaching over, she tightly wrapped her arms around him and buried her head in his shoulder. "Thank you, Wade," she said gratefully.

Holding her, he compassionately responded, "Feel better now?"

"Yes, much better," she replied more calmly.

Mutually they broke free from each other's grasp and went back into the den.

"How 'bout that pizza now?" Wade asked with a grin. "Regained your appetite yet?"

Now more cheerful, Louisa told him that she had.

After ordering their meal from Domino's, Louisa gathered a few books and pots and pans Les had forgotten when he moved out heading for Texas. Wade helped her put them in the back seat of her car. The pizza arrived just afterward, and the two of them spent the rest of the evening eating and watching old movies on the TBS channel. When it came time to go, Louisa asked Wade if it would be all right if she came over every now and then. This was the only place it seemed that she could get away from it all and relax.

"Sure," Wade replied. "You can come out anytime you please. Don't wait for an invite but do give me a few minutes notice. I'm not a neat nick like Les. I'm much more of a pig especially since I've started back painting. Give me a minute or two to get the place presentable."

Grinning, Louisa headed for the door then suddenly stopped. Turning around, she walked back to Wade and gave him another big hug. "Thanks again for letting me talk to Les. I needed that."

"I know you did. I'd love to be able to give Mimi a call myself."

As he walked her to her car, Louisa tried lifting his spirits. "Things will work out for the best for you and Mimi."

With a half-smile, Wade replied, "I hope so." Then he said, "I really did enjoy tonight, Louisa. You're good company, and I do hope you'll come back over soon. We can commiserate together." Chuckling, he watched Louisa get into her car.

Louisa left, and the weekend went by as usual. Nothing special happened around the town or over at the college. Even if something was going on, Wade had no one to go with to enjoy it. Bored, Wade threw himself into his artwork and his other coursework. But all was not as bad as it appeared. For now, he had a sense of purpose, and other than being lonesome at times, he was excelling in almost all other areas of his life. On Sunday he got a surprise call, but once again, not the one he wanted—Mimi. It was Angie this time. She asked what he was up to and how things were going. More unexpectedly, she wanted to come out to see him.

"Sure," he said cautiously. Even though he had found a new love, Mimi was far away, and getting tangled back into a web spun by his ex-girlfriend was something he didn't want to do. Being hurt by Angie on more than one occasion, he hoped he had the girl out of his system entirely.

Just as she said she would, Angie arrived at his trailer that afternoon. The day was slightly overcast and cold. Wearing a heavy parka with a hood covering her head, she made her way up his steps and knocked on the door. From inside, Wade called for her to enter. He did not meet her cheerfully in the doorway as she had hoped. Instead, he stood in his kitchen where an eating bar with floor level cabinets separated him from her as she walked into his den. "You been doing all right?" she asked with a friendly smile pulling off the hood of her jacket.

"Doing okay, I guess," Wade replied with little enthusiasm. Saying this, he placed a dish he was drying into a cabinet above the sink. *Why was she here*, he wondered? *Had she and her longhaired boyfriend parted ways?*

Taken aback by his demeanor, Angie asked if she could sit down.

"Sure. Have a seat," he replied with obvious detachment. Then, as he finished drying the last of the dishes, he came around to his recliner, took a seat, and leaned back. "What do you want, Angie?" he asked coolly.

"Oh, nothing," she replied flippantly. She wasn't prepared for this new hardened attitude. She had found out about Mimi being in California and thought with Mimi out of the way, Wade would be glad to see her. He didn't appear to be. Seeing this, she became nervous. "I guess I was just missing you and wanted to make sure you were doing okay without Les and all," she tried sounding upbeat.

"I'm doing fine, Angie," Wade responded, but without a smile.

"Well, I heard you were taking art now. I was glad to hear that. Are you enjoying it?"

"Yep, it's been a lot of fun," he said.

Suddenly the room grew quiet. At first, Angie glanced around wanting to find something else to discuss to lighten up the situation. There was not much else to say. Looking back at him, she could not help but relish his good looks, his penetrating soft brown eyes, his dark olive complexion and gorgeous jet-black hair. He was so physical yet so tender and passionate, she thought. But in her mind and in her heart what she missed was more than this. Much, much, more. She wanted to sit by him and for him to reach out and hold her. For him to tell her that he still loved her as she loved him. But in those mesmerizing eyes, she saw a stranger—like an animal wondering whether to run or to fight. She realized she had hurt him much worse than she'd ever imagined. All of these reflections flashed through her mind in an instant. "I'm sorry I did what I did breaking up with you, Wade. I was so wrong for doing that," she said weakly.

Wade said nothing—just looked back at her with an icy stare.

"I didn't realize how much I missed you until you weren't there. I don't blame you for not wanting to . . ." She stopped unable to utter the words.

There was a long pause of silence as Wade watched her carefully. Then, as she dropped her eyes, he felt sorry for her. Without Mimi in his life and the fact that he'd moved on, he doubted he could have found himself being so compassionate.

"Angie, I don't hate you anymore. I did for a while though. But looking back, I think I didn't act my best when we first got up here either."

Pitifully, she asked, not knowing whether he had completely excluded her from his life or not, "Can we still be friends?"

Wade's expression was empathetic. "Of course," he said kindly.

At this point, Angie stood not wanting to press him too hard on their relationship for now. She thought this might turn him off and just as quickly as he had started to open up to her somewhat, he might end it.

Wade followed her as she walked to the door. Spinning around, she gave him a quick kiss on the cheek, then with an uncertain smile, she left.

CHAPTER 10

Angie Baby

Dr. Owen's art class was giving Wade a renewed sense of purpose. The metamorphosis in his life was evident to all who knew him. The phone rang and rang as Wade arrived home from a long day of classes. Hearing the rings as he exited his car, he hurriedly gathered his books and bolted up the steps to the front door. He fumbled with his keys and couldn't get the door unlocked in time. "Damn it," he shouted. *That could have been her*, he thought. Frustrated Wade poured his books across his kitchen table. He retrieved a cola from the refrigerator and took a huge burning gulp. Pausing, deep in thought, he conjured Mimi's image in his mind. How badly he missed her. He momentarily closed his eyes. He took another large sip of his drink, sighed deeply, and put the half empty can back into the door of the cooler.

Wade had put an easel up in his den and was painting in his spare time. Spare time—that phrase, until now, had been foreign in the young man's mind. With Mimi and Les gone, and Angie and the frat scene fading somewhere into the past, he wasn't as distracted by life and was able to concentrate on things at hand. Even his ability to study had greatly improved.

Straightening up his books and washing a few dishes he'd left in his sink earlier, Wade found himself sitting on the stool contemplating an unmarked canvas resting on his easel. An improvised table held his water-based paints and brushes on one end and his acrylics and oils on the other. Music reverberated from his stereo, pouring out melodies from his favorite radio station. Seldom did he waste his time on inciting television talk shows or sentimental sitcoms from the past. His frame of mind was much more subdued as he put more emphasis on becoming productive as well as creative.

The telephone suddenly rang shaking him from this trance-like state. Wade lunged off his stool desperately. "Hello?" he yelled almost knocking the phone off its setting.

"Wade? Is that you?"

"Yeah," he responded, embarrassed by the way he sounded. "I thought you might be Mimi."

"Sorry, it's just me," Ann replied apologetically. "Haven't heard from her I guess?"

"Not yet."

"Well, Cuz, do I have a surprise for you. It might even help you get your mind off things maybe. Why don't you meet me over at the IHOP on Baxter tonight for supper, and I'll tell you what I'm talking about?"

Wade scoffed. "Another surprise, Kitten? I can hardly wait. Let me guess. You want me to take a course in astrology this time, huh?"

"Listen up, fool. Be there at seven-thirty. You got it?"

"Seven-thirty and this better be good!" Shaking his head, he hung up the phone and went back to his stool refocusing on the canvas. Thoughts of what Ann was up to soon faded as he began choosing and mixing the colors he would be using for his composition. With a framework in mind, he laid out the basic features of his work. His brushstrokes became more deft and precise as he brought out the finer details of his creation. Time sped by as he concentrated on the varying aspects of his task. The clock resting on the television set read 7 p.m. He had started at 5. Shocked by how much time had elapsed, he hurriedly cleaned up and headed out the door for the restaurant.

Miraculously he arrived at the pancake house right on time. The clock in his car read 7:31 p.m. Noticing Ann's car parked out front, he entered the building and began searching for her. Hungry customers sitting in the partially-filled restaurant obscured his view, but eventually, he spotted her. Sitting in a back-corner booth, Ann waved directing his attention to her table. Cautiously approaching, he wondered what on earth she had up her sleeve this time. Sliding down into the booth, he asked, "Okay, girl. What ya' got for me this go 'round? A coupon for some free waffles, maybe?"

Trying to respond subtly, her eyes sparkling, she slid an envelope that she had held concealed in her lap onto the table.

Wade gave her a questioning stare, then gazed back down at the letter. Lifting it, the return address read, *Mimi Brightlow, Vandenberg Air Force Base, Vandenberg AFB.* Beaming back at his cousin, he eagerly opened it.

Ann watched as his eyes raced excitedly over each line of each page. Sometimes he would seem to swallow hard and grow pensive. In the next instant, his demeanor would become warm and radiate with affection. When he finished it, he gazed back at Ann who was ready and waiting to hear what Mimi had to say.

An irrepressible sense of relief and joy showed in Wade's face. "Well, she got my letter," he beamed. "But she couldn't read my return address because it somehow got smeared in the mail. That's why she wrote to you." Pausing, he handed the pages to his smiling cousin. He continued, "She said she now understands about my dad and wishes that I had told her what was going on earlier."

The two cousins were leaning in close to one another as Ann started reading the letter aloud. "Says here that she tried calling you and me, but they will possibly have to move to the Philippines, and she is so involved helping her family that she hasn't had the time to get through."

Ann read further. "Good. Good. They're staying in California. Still loves you, Wade."

They shared a moment of happiness before Ann continued. "Says she'll write to you again and call." Impetuously, Ann reached over and gave her cousin a hard push. Shockingly, in her exhilaration, it was more of a shove as it caused Wade's whole body to slam loudly into the back of his cushioned seat. She laughed out loud. Only a girl can get away treating a boy so rough then laugh in his face after doing it.

Stunned, Wade righted himself in his seat embarrassed that almost all of the people surrounding them had turned in his direction. Seeing only the humor in the situation, Ann never stopped cackling. "Well, Wade, what do you think?" she beamed back over at him.

Noticing that most of the people had turned back to what they were doing, he whispered, "I'll tell you one thing. It's damn good to hear from her. I just hope that we can somehow get back together."

"According to the letter, it sounds like it's just a matter of time, Wade," Ann replied cheerfully.

Suddenly the waitress that Ann had sent away before Wade's arrival appeared at their booth to take their orders. The happiness of the moment seemed contagious as the young girl laughed and joked with the two while jotting down their order. When she left, Ann turned her attention back to Wade. "Oh, by the way," she said with glint in her eyes. "Louisa needs you to do her a little favor."

Wade peered back at his cousin inquisitively. "I knew there had to be a catch to all of this. What's she need?"

"Well, she's been given the 'honor' of attending the Governor's Ball in Atlanta next month. Last quarter, the Dean of the Psychology Department had gotten some tickets. He decided that he didn't want to go and made them a prize to be given to one of his students based on grades or merit or something." Ann rolled her eyes.

"Sounds like looks might be involved to me," Wade chuckled.

"Probably so. Anyway, she's stuck with 'em."

"Why doesn't she just give them to someone else?"

"Well, it's been made into a big to do. It's being touted as a big 'privilege,'" Ann said. "Louisa is supposed to not only represent the University of Georgia Psychology Department at this thing but the rest of the school as well. She can't get out of it according to her."

"Sounds like a crock to me."

Ann nodded in agreement.

"I actually think that what they're trying to do is to impress some large contributors who'll be there. Politics—you know how that goes. At any rate, Louisa needs a date. You know, an escort."

"And?"

"And that's where you come in."

"No way," Wade exclaimed fidgeting nervously in his seat. "I'm not cut out for doing that kind of thing, Ann. You know me. I'd be like a fish out of water at a stuffed shirt affair like that. I don't think you really want me involved in this at all."

"Sure we do," Ann said assertively. "There'll be nothing to it. Just go over, be seen, dance a little, and come home."

"Dance a little. What on earth are you talking about? I don't know anything about dancing at some big formal event like that. You two girls must have lost your minds," he said incredulously.

Ann tried to calm the boy down, "Listen, Wade. They've got all that taken care of."

"Who's they?" Wade asked cynically.

"Well, I suppose the Dean. They've got y'all all lined up for some dance classes."

"Y'all! Now, wait a minute. I haven't volunteered for anything yet."

"I know. I already volunteered for you."

Wade glared across the table into Ann's defiant eyes. "You did what?"

"Listen, you little jerk. Louisa's counting on you. Do you want someone else carrying her over there? You think Les wants someone else?"

Wade nervously scanned the room groping for a way to get out of this mess. Nothing came to mind. With a deep sigh of desperation, he asked once more, "You sure there's no other way?"

"None," Ann replied firmly. "Louisa's tried everything."

Vacantly staring down at the table for a long moment, he peeked back over at his cousin with a painful wince then yielded with a sigh of resignation, "Okay. What do I got to do?"

Even though Wade dreaded the hoopla he was going to have to endure in Atlanta, he still had a smile on his face as he left the place. At last, he had heard from his love. Ann too was smiling, even if it was just to herself concerning her poor cousin and her roommate's plight.

II

The following Friday Wade got two tests back, one in accounting and one in marketing. He made an A and B respectively and was obviously pleased with himself. His classes couldn't be going better.

What was happening with Angie was a different story. Ann came back to the apartment the night she had eaten supper with Wade spouting happily about the letter he had received from Mimi. Angie was crushed, but despite being heartbroken, she kept in mind that Mimi was clear across the country. The odds were that Mimi and Wade would never get back together. Angie would bide her time waiting and would take her shot when opportunities arose.

On Saturday after lunch, Louisa was getting ready for the first dance class that she and Wade would take later in the afternoon. Humming to herself, she ironed her slacks and blouse then sat at her dresser carefully putting on her makeup. An hour before leaving, she brushed her shimmering black hair and read the next day's Sunday school lesson. Since arriving in Athens, she and Les had been attending this class each Sunday morning at the school's Baptist Student Union.

As Louisa studied her assignment, Angie came into the room and sprawled out on the bed next to Louisa's dresser wearing an oversized "Go Dogs" T-shirt, a pair of faded jeans, and red woolen socks.

"Where are y'all taking this dance class, Louisa?"

"Myers Dance Studio. It's over at the Homewood Shopping Center," Louisa responded.

Angie snickered as she stretched out on the bed, her hands folded behind her head. "I can hardly see Wade fox-trotting around a dance floor in a tux." Angie actually could think of nothing more wonderful than to be dancing with him herself.

"We'll see," Louisa chuckled wryly. "I think it's going to be me having problems doing it, not him. He's so athletic and all."

Angie hastily changed the subject. Thinking of Wade that way hurt her to the very core. "Say, have you heard from Les lately?"

"Yeah. He's doing fine," Louisa sighed. "We talk to each other about twice a week."

"Do you miss him?" Angie asked.

Louisa stopped brushing her hair and stared at her roommate. Defensively she countered, "Of course I do, Angie."

"Oh, I didn't mean it in a bad way." Angie fought for words. "I just meant you know how you get in a routine with someone. I just wondered . . ."

She couldn't find her way out from what she'd just asked. "I'm sorry, Louisa. I hope I didn't upset you?"

Louisa paused secretly realizing what Angie had meant, understanding her roommate's comment had nothing to do with her relationship with Les at all. Smiling, she peered down at her friend. "I think I know what you mean. It's kind of like you've been around someone so much that when you turn around to say something to them and they aren't there, it's almost like they've died." She stopped momentarily, appearing forlorn. Bouncing back with a grin, she added, "But you can take comfort knowing that you'll be back together soon. It's not forever."

"Yeah, that's what I meant," Angie agreed. "It's kind of like Wade and me. You get away from somebody for a long time and sometimes it makes the heart grow fonder. But sometimes you get out from under their spell and other people take their place."

Louisa lowered her head as she sat quietly and pensively for a moment.

Angie continued, "I'm not talking about you and Les now."

Louisa spoke candidly, "Which way do you feel about Wade, Angie?"

Angie was caught off guard. "Well, I still like Wade." She stopped abruptly. "I've talked to him. We've made up as friends and all, but that's about it. It's no relationship that I'm trying to get back into."

Louisa rose still intently observing her friend. "Well, I better finish getting dressed. I'm supposed to meet him shortly."

Angie stood abruptly, realizing Louisa was politely asking her to leave the room. Trying not to show her agitation about exposing her feelings for Wade, she excused herself and headed to the den.

III

At 3 p.m. Wade entered the Myers Dance Studio. Inside, he found a group of young girls roaming the floor in leotards. Some stretched their legs on a banister rail that ran around the giant room while others stretched on the floor.

A moderately attractive but stern looking woman wearing a navy-blue sweat suit and black tennis shoes walked out of an adjoining office and made her way to the center of the floor. She was middle aged, roughly in her forties, and had a hint of a scowl drawn across her face. In a foreign accent, possibly Russian, she called out, "Okay, girls. Gather a-round." All the girls came running. It was obvious she was in complete command as the chattering group of youngsters grew completely quiet as they encircled her.

Examining a clipboard in her hand, she looked up and loudly proclaimed, "Next practice, Tuesday at four-thirty sharp. We will have our vinter ballet recital in two weeks, young ladies. I have calendars for dis month's events printed up for you at de front door. Make sure you get one as you leave please. Those of you who need new slippers, please sign de sheet in de office on de vay out. Mrs. Billie will help size you for your recital costumes. We have a lot of hard vurk to do before de recital. Be here on time." She paused gazing down more amicably at her small wards. "Any questions, ladies?" She glanced around at the entire group. "No questions? Okay, I will see you on Tuesday."

The young girls scattered about the place chattering as they gathered up their things to leave. With mothers connecting with their children in the lobby, they all left the building hurriedly.

Someone poked Wade from behind calling his name. Shaken from his trance, Wade jumped. He turned his head around to see who it was. "Good grief. You scared me half to death," he scolded a beaming Louisa. Overcoming his embarrassment, he questioned, "How long have you been standing there?"

"Long enough to see that you might be interested in ballet."

"Riiiight," Wade exclaimed in his most southern drawl.

With an implausible smile, he said, "You talkin' about feeling out of place. I'd hug a guy if I saw one in here right now."

Louisa snickered noticing the place inundated with females, no other men in sight.

Still perplexed, Wade asked, "By the way, where is the rest of our class?"

"You're looking at it," Louisa smiled coyly.

"You've got to be kiddin' me. Just me and you?"

"You got it."

Miss K, the instructor, suddenly appeared in front of the pair. With the hard edge of a drill sergeant, she asked, "I presume you are my students from University?"

Louisa and Wade faced each other shrugging their shoulders. A graduate student who worked for the Dean of the Psychology Department had arranged these lessons, and all he had told Louisa to do was to meet here at this time with her partner.

"Dr. Horton sent you, yes?"

"Yes," Louisa said cautiously.

Wade gaped at Louisa wondering what in the Sam Hill she had gotten him into.

"Okay," the teacher said seemingly in a more cheerful mood. "My name is Kelinivitra. Kelinivitra Staline." Her accent highlighted the pride of her heritage.

"You're not kin to the 'Stalin,'" Wade asked impishly.

Louisa burst into a snicker.

"No, I am not, young man." she responded sternly, "My name ends in an 'e'."

She said this without cracking a smile. "But I will tell you that my name caused great pain for me and my fam-i-l-y back in the motherland. Now, young man, I will cause you great pain in teaching you how to dance. Yes, like the Russian." Her jovial expression turned sinister.

Louisa and Wade gulped simultaneously as her voice echoed throughout the empty studio.

"First, I will teach you the foxtrot, then I will teach you the waltz, then the polka, so on and so forth. Your teachers have given me complete instructions on what you should know. I intend to see to it that their contract is upheld. Now!" she clapped her hands twice, "let's get started."

Later that evening, the two made their way to Wade's trailer. Wade arrived first and got the heater going and the place straightened. When Louisa arrived and made it inside, the two exhausted dancers acknowledged each other grimacing. Wade spoke first. "Two hours?" he said in disbelief. "How many lessons do we have left?"

Louisa, laughing, doubled over. "Nine," she said trying to hold up nine fingers as she laughed uncontrollably.

"Nine! My God! I'd be in good enough shape to run a marathon with that many. I haven't worked and sweated that hard since I trained for the regionals in track back in high school."

Louisa couldn't stop laughing as she sprawled on the sofa as if she were dead one arm thrown across her forehead and the other dangling lifelessly to the floor. Wade came and sat down on the carpet next to her. A huge grin spread across his face. When Louisa finally calmed down, he looked down into her teary eyes.

"I could kill you for getting me into this. You know that?"

Playfully he acted as if he would choke her. Giggling, she fought him off then rolled on top of him from the sofa pinning his arms to the floor. In a mock voice of desperation, she yelled, "You've got to go through with this! You can't abandon me."

Wade peered into her wide radiant smile. "Uncle. Uncle. I surrender. I'll do it," he beamed.

She stared back down more soberly. Wade reciprocated, mesmerized as he looked into her alluring eyes. Her smile returned, and she rolled over. Lying on their backs side by side, they were completely worn out.

"Pizza again tonight?" she asked unenthused as she lay there. They had eaten pasta at least four times together already. Wade propped on one arm.

"Sounds like you're ready for something different, huh?"

Looking up at him from the floor, she said, "*Dr. Zhivago* is on tonight over at the Beechwood Cinema. Do you want to go see it? Maybe we could grab a quick bite somewhere on the way."

"That sounds good to me," Wade responded with delight. He was tired of hanging around the trailer each time she came over anyway.

Both sat up leaning their backs against the sofa. "What time does it start?" Wade asked.

"I'm not sure. I'll call and find out." Louisa found the number to the theater and gave them a call. "Starts at eight p.m. It lasts over three hours though."

Wade shrugged. "That's okay with me. I don't have anything else to do tonight." He was in the kitchen fixing himself a drink.

"Care for a coke or anything?" he asked.

"No thanks."

Realizing what he just said, Louisa responded, "So, that's the only reason you're going to go with me? Nothing to do! Gee thanks!"

In a mock kid's voice, Wade retorted, "Hey. What can I say? You're just a stranded little kitty with nobody to take care of ya'. I've just got this great big ol' soft spot in my heart for lost little kitties, that's all."

Louisa cut her eyes at him not exactly sure how to take his remark. "Listen, you don't have to go unless you want to," she replied defensively.

"No. No. I 'tink' 'dis' movie about 'de' motherland will help us in our ability to understand our teacher—no?"

Louisa smiled back with unsure eyes. "Can you pick me up at seven-thirty?"

Wade responded warmly, "Sure, but that won't leave us much time to eat."

"Maybe we can get something to eat afterward?"

"That works for me."

"Okay then," she said. With their plans made, she was out the door and into her car. Wade stood on his steps and waved as she backed her car away from the trailer.

Time was in short supply as he hurriedly shaved, showered, and got ready. Checking his appearance in the mirror, he told himself, *remember, this is not a date. Just an evening out with a special friend.* Throwing on his jacket, he was on his way.

As Wade arrived at the Sussex apartment, Angie opened the door and greeted him cordially. She wondered what he was up to. At first, she thought he'd come to see her. When she found out he and Louisa were going to the show, she hinted that she hadn't seen the movie either. She tried hard to get invited, but her efforts failed.

Neither Wade nor Louisa seemed particularly interested in sharing company with anyone else. They dashed out to Wade's car and got to the theater in just enough time to grab drinks and popcorn entering the darkened room.

The movie, *Dr. Zhivago*, centered around a doctor, his beloved wife, and the circumstances that tenderly, yet tragically kept him and his mistress together and apart. With stunning scenes of Russia's spectacularly colored falls and frozen winters, the time period involved the downfall of the Russian Czar. Several times during the feature length film, Louisa reached over and grabbed Wade's hand as tears ran down her cheeks. When the movie ended, Louisa remained quiet.

"Girl," Wade whispered as he wrapped his jacket around her shoulders to beat back the cold night air as they walked outside, "I never knew you could cry so much."

Louisa gave no response. They made it to the car and headed for Sussex. Wade thought the whole ordeal of the day plus the movie had been too much on Louisa with Les so far away. Maybe all those feelings of sadness she had been repressing as she carried on gallantly were getting the best of her. Whatever the case, Wade made no further mention of her emotional state as he drove back to her apartment in silence. When they arrived, he started to get out, but she stopped him.

"No. I can make it up okay." As she slid out of her seat, she glanced back into the car and smiled. "Thanks for a great day, Wade."

Wade acknowledged her with a nod. Watching her climb the steps and go inside, he slowly headed back to his trailer.

IV

The dance classes came and went. Only the first class was a two-hour ordeal. The rest were just one and a half hours, but they were hardly less tiring. The psychology department must have paid Miss K well, because their instructor was unrelenting. Louisa, since going to Wade's trailer to gather Les' things, had started going over occasionally to study. But with the dance lessons, she was becoming more and more a familiar presence.

Two weeks before the big "Ball," Ann made plans for her roommates, including Angie, to eat spareribs out at Wade's house, a kind of fun get together that they hadn't had since Les had left town. At the last minute, Laney called Ann to come down to Gainesville. The relationship for the couple had not been going well for a long time and lingering problems had dramatically come to a head. Ann offered no excuse as she left for Florida.

Even without her presence, the rest of the group decided the cook-out was still on. It would be set for Saturday evening after Wade and Louisa returned from their final dance lesson. Angie would get the fire going on the old cast iron grill Les had left for Wade. Wade would barbecue the ribs when the two dancers got back to the trailer.

By lunchtime Saturday, Louisa was informed that their afternoon class had been pushed back two hours to 5 p.m. With this unforeseen circumstance jumbling their evening's plans, the pair left for their lesson, leaving Angie in charge at the trailer.

Alone, there was not much for her to do. Her duties, according to their plan, was to start the charcoal fire at about 6:00 and somewhere in between she would make iced tea and get the pork and beans ready to cook.

Except for starting the fire, Angie finished doing her other chores. With nothing else to do for an hour or so, she opened a can of beer she retrieved from Wade's refrigerator and stood in the middle of his kitchen looking around. How she wished she were here under other circumstances. She walked to a canvas resting on an easel where Wade was working on a painting. It was a picture of three boys standing on a set of rocks gazing out at a sunset. It was nowhere near completion, but it did look to her as though it might be an ocean scene.

She sat down in Wade's recliner where she thumbed through some of his current and old notebooks. *Was there some other girl?* The notes she saw only involved annotations referring to accounting, marketing, and economics. Continuing to snoop, she found one of his sketchpads and started going through it.

Wade never showed Angie much of his artwork since most of it was at his parent's house. From what she had seen, she had been impressed, but what she saw now was mind-boggling. He made sketches of the human body; the detail and realness of which were astonishing. She grew excited as she flipped each page, even to the point of talking out loud with admiration. She got to the last page of his sketches. Nothing. Only blank pages.

She went into his bedroom and began browsing around. All of his clothes were neatly arranged. She knew this wasn't his style. He was trying to be tidy for the girls. Sipping on her second can of beer, she sat on Wade's bed leaning against one of the walls of the small room. Glancing at the end of his bed, she saw hanging on the paneling, the picture of the people on the dock, the one Les and Louisa had carried over to the art department for Dr. Owen to see. There was a sense of tragedy in it. An older man hugging a younger man. Another man and his family walking and holding each other—forlorn expressions cast across their faces. A little boy ran to meet them. A tremendous feeling of loss was there, but much love too.

As Angie sipped her beer, she wondered where or how Wade could come up with such an idea. How could he draw with such feeling? Why on earth would he even want this disturbing picture hanging on his wall in the first place?

The phone rang. It rang again and again. Angie stared at the receiver wondering whether to pick it up. It rang again, again, then it stopped. Quietly she went back to the refrigerator, opened it, and took out another can of beer. If Wade and Louisa didn't get back soon, she thought, she was going to be wasted. Checking the time, she whispered, "Damn, I need to go light that fire." It was already 6:30 p.m. and the two would return before long. She went outside into the cold dark air and realized the back-porch light was not on. Stepping back inside, she hit the switch.

With the single bulb fixture hardly lighting the area, she found the grill and poured the charcoals into it. After stacking the coals, she soaked them with lighter fluid and waited. She had done this many times for her father and was quite capable of grilling the meat herself. With the flick of a match, the fire roared causing the surrounding area to grow almost completely dark. Trees and bushes and objects just out of proximity to the flames were lost to the brightness of its light. Over the roar of the fire and the popping of the flames as they burned into the charcoal, Angie thought she heard something. There it was again. It was the phone. This time, Angie ran up the back door's metal steps into the trailer. She thought it might be Wade. Maybe he was having car trouble or needed something. She was a little unbalanced as she made it to the den. Probably the beer, she thought. "Hello?" she answered. "Oh, hi, Mimi. No, this is Angie."

CHAPTER 11

The Governor's Ball

Louisa and Wade made it back to the trailer. They came in laughing and joking more than usual. Both thanked the good Lord that this had been their final class with the fastidious, Russian Bolshevik, Kelenivitra. Seldom did they ever get a "Da," from their headmistress. Instead, it was almost always a "Nyet. Nyet. Nyet." At which point she would stop the music and show them what they were doing wrong. Once the problem was corrected, she would give a loud double-hand clap which echoed off the hollow studio walls and floor followed by her shouting, "Over. Start-tover." And again, the music began.

The drill sergeant of dance! The madam of the malcontents! But even in their happiness to be through with her, they realized she had done exactly what had been expected of her. They had arrived at her class complete novices to the established forms of ballroom dancing. Through her regimented practices highlighting discipline and perfection, they became convincingly proficient, the finished product even more artistic and finessed than even she, of the Bolshoi Ballet, could have ever imagined.

As Wade walked from the front door to the kitchen, he could see the table already set. Angie just finished peeping into the oven to check on the barbecue pork and beans simmering and bubbling inside a large Pyrex dish. Their aroma saturated the entire room with the sweet smell of baking brown sugar, onions, and sauce.

"Oh man, that smells good," Wade exclaimed as Angie carefully closed the oven door. "Those ready yet?"

Angie smiled and nodded, "Just about."

"How 'bout the charcoal? Did you get the fire going?"

Wade hurried to the refrigerator. He opened its door and searched for the packages of pork ribs he'd purchased the night before.

"Slow down there, Fred Astaire," Angie interrupted as he searched the cooler's shelves in earnest. "The fire's going, and the meat's already cooking."

"Super," Wade was impressed. "Let's go outside and see how they're doing. I'll bring the barbecue sauce with me. How about finding a pan we can put them on." Wade went out the back door toward the grill with Angie following close behind. Pulling up the lid, he flipped the ribs over with a fork. "These look great, Angie." Taking a basting brush from the sauce bowl, he began painting each rib with his homemade concoction. Almost immediately the grill rack became engulfed in flames as the sauce sizzled hitting the glowing red charcoal briquettes below.

"Is that the only pan you could find?" he asked pointing to the thin cookie sheet.

"I left the one I brought them out here on in the sink. You want me to go get another one?"

"No. Here," Wade said as he gave her the fork and took the flimsy pan from her. "You flip the ribs over to me. I'll manage with this pan."

Angie forked the hot ribs onto the sheet, and Wade's hands instantly began to burn. Grimacing, he raced to his trailer's steps. "Open the door, Louisa! Open the door—quick!" he shouted in pain. He rushed through the entryway dashing over to the stove and dropped the hot pan onto the appliance with a loud metallic clank. "Geeze, damn that was hot!" Gritting his teeth, he began waving his hands and fingers in the air as he gave Louisa an agonizing grin.

Hurrying in behind him, Angie begged for his forgiveness. "You were right, Wade. I should have gotten you something better to put them on. Are you okay?"

"I'll be fine," he grunted, unable to hide his pain.

Heading to the kitchen sink, Angie turned on the spigot. "Come here," she told him. "This might help." She watched as he placed his hands under the cold running water. "That feel better?"

"Yeah, a little bit."

Louisa tried not to laugh but couldn't help it. With her hand over her mouth, she attempted to turn away, but the first snort of a snickering laugh got out anyway.

Wade and Angie peered at her.

"What's so dadburn funny?" Wade asked.

Facing him, Louisa burst out laughing.

"You are such an idiot, Wade. Anybody with any sense would know that holding a thin hot pan like that without a cloth would burn their stupid hands. What were you thinking?"

Wade watched as both girls began to giggle. "I can't believe you guys," he grimaced as he confronted them. "That pan was too little. I almost dropped it, and …" He could tell that neither one was listening to him. They were too tickled. "Geez," Wade protested loudly. "I'm sure glad I didn't blow myself up with a gas can out there. Now, that'd really be funny, wouldn't it?"

Louisa laughed so hard that she had to sit down to catch her breath. Taking a few moments to compose herself and feeling a bit guilty, she got out of her chair, walked over, and gave Wade a big hug. "I'm really sorry, Wade," she said. Pulling away, a short snort came out of her nose. Embarrassed, she quickly placed her hand across her mouth.

"Nice try, Louisa," Wade retorted cynically.

Angie placed their meal on the table.

As Wade watched her, he said, "Okay ladies, now that you've had your little fun for tonight, I guess it's about time to eat." With tongue in cheek, Wade spoke plainly, "All right, Miss Louisa, in light of your lack of sympathy for your fellow man, I think that you should be the one to return thanks tonight."

With an impish grin, she replied, "Okay. Let's all hold hands."

"Still trying to hurt me, I see," Wade muttered.

"Be nice," Louisa declared as she bowed her head.

Angie held Wade's less burned hand while Louisa gently clasped his more wounded one. "Father," Louisa began to pray. "Look down on all of us with Your benevolent mercy, forgiveness, and unconditional love. Open our hearts and give us the wisdom to follow Your path of righteousness. Bless Les down in Texas and watch over him and thank You for this wonderful food we're about to eat. Amen."

Tired and hungry, the three friends soon dug into their delicious meal. They gave it their best to show some measure of formality; however; their hunger soon overcame their etiquette. A festive mess of eating barbecue and joking ensued. When they were done, Angie instructed her two companions to go sit in the den insisting she was the one in charge of clean up.

Rising from the table, Wade countered. "No way. There's a good movie coming on. Let's knock this out right quick so we won't miss it."

"What movie are you talking about?" Louisa asked excitedly as she made it to the sink and began helping Angie clean and put away the dishes.

"*Play Misty For Me.* Y'all remember that Clint Eastwood movie, don't ya?"

Wryly the girls eyed each other. As if on cue, they both started singing the romantic theme song to the movie. Softly at first then growing louder, they began to harmonize. Angie held the saltshaker for her microphone. A glass was Louisa's. Wade stood by in slack-jawed bewilderment.

"I don't know if watching this movie with you two is such a good idea after all," he said.

Laughing and giggling at successfully embarrassing Wade, they entered his small den. Still beaming, both girls sat next to each other on his sofa as he found the movie. Though it was halfway through, it didn't matter. It was fun having friends over even though Wade still had his doubts about Angie.

II

The following Monday, Ann made it home from Florida. It appeared her relationship with Laney was over for good this time. She went out to Wade's trailer to talk things over with him. Trying to justify what had happened in Gainesville, she seemed truly heartbroken even though it was she who did the breaking up. "He was just too far away. I couldn't handle it anymore," she said. There were no tears. She claimed she cried them all out on her trip back to Athens.

Changing the subject to get her mind off Laney, Wade told Ann about his and Louisa's dancing class drudgery. It took a while for him to accomplish this feat. Nevertheless, he finally got Ann to laugh as he made their teacher out to be a secret Soviet KGB agent in charge of ruining the way Americans danced.

"Your roommates told you about our cookout, didn't they?"

"Yeah, I wish I had been here," Ann said soberly.

Wade realized he shouldn't have brought this up.

"Mimi is supposed to be calling me any day now. I'm kinda concerned that I haven't heard from her already."

Ann shook her head surprised but didn't respond. She was too preoccupied with her own problems to be concerned with his. She stood up from her seat.

"Well, I better get going. I've got a lot of classwork to catch up on."

"Okay, keep in touch. Call me if you need me."

Watching her drive away, Wade went back inside and climbed into his recliner. Soon Mimi would call, he thought, and all of the heartache and uncertainty of these many weeks apart would be over. How he had gone from being so despondent when he had returned from Christmas break to feeling so confident and upbeat now, he did not know. Was it that his grades had improved dramatically at this point? Was it that he was taking the art class and painting again? Maybe it was the thought of reconnecting with Mimi? Or maybe, just maybe, it was something else entirely. Delving deeper into his thoughts, he could not figure out this conundrum. The one thing he did realize was this feeling of security was somehow incomplete. That gnawing feeling of tension and despair could befall him at any time. He knew it was there always just one step one episode from getting to him.

A week passed, then another, but the phone call Wade had been counting on from Mimi never occurred. Even though he sent her three more letters, he received no response by phone or mail. Puzzled and confused by this disheartening turn of events, Wade knew that any hope of them ever reuniting was rapidly diminishing. Caught in what seemed to be a never-ending dilemma with Mimi, Wade had no choice but to be optimistic.

III

Following weeks of endless practice and preparation, the climax of all the hard work for the dancers finally arrived. This night would reveal if Miss K's rigorous training would pay off. Regardless of whether or not the lessons proved successful, the couple felt physically prepared for the challenge. Nerves and emotions aside, neither of them could recall ever being so ready.

Wade had been given instructions, hand-delivered in fact, on where to purchase his attire for the evening. He had already visited the men's shop and was sized for the outfit twice over the preceding weeks. He was expected to pick up his tuxedo several days in advance. When he had not done so, the tuxedo shop owners called to remind him.

Wade drove to the shop shortly after speaking to the owner and was amazed to find that his bill had already been paid. He started putting it all together. When someone else pays, there's usually a purpose, he thought as he drove home. Until now, he hadn't given much credence to what Ann told him about large contributors and politicians being behind this command performance.

Back at his place, the tux hung on the top molding of the open door to his bedroom. Still in its cellophane cover, it swayed gently rocking from the breeze Wade made as he walked back and forth cleaning up his den. Unkempt textbooks filled almost every chair as did spiral notebooks and piles of stapled handouts. He briskly went about the business of organizing the room.

The Ball would start later in the evening. He had hours to go before he had to dress. With time on his side, he laid out his paints and brushes, adjusted his easel, and placed a new palate on the table along with solvent. Reaching down below the lip of his kitchen counter, he flipped through several canvases and retrieved a partially used composition.

Standing, he carefully rested the frame on the stand and climbed onto his stool. Relaxed and confident, he leaned back contemplating the colors he would use to bring forth his ideas into shapes and forms, images expressing his innermost feelings. Hauntingly these seemed to emerge intuitively in flashes of enlightenment and strokes of despair.

Each brush. Each stroke. The angles of shadow and light came forth to him in a timeless concentrated effort. The blending of the paint, the tricks of the brushes, the techniques he used—all gifts he received. All knacks that he had. But it was the desire to do it that was his most compelling gift. Even with the hundreds upon hundreds of mistakes and start over's that he had been through, he still felt an almost spiritual obligation to continue. There was no reward he desired save for the passion of doing it.

As Wade worked, Louisa spent her morning studying. She really had no time for this "gala event." She had a test in adolescent psychology first thing Monday morning, and she didn't feel as prepared as normal. She had spent a great deal of her time at Wade's trailer thus far, time she would usually spend studying. She was not upset that she had done this, just a little guilty that she was enjoying his company so much.

The morning passed for each of them. Wade absorbed in his efforts perfecting his canvas; Louisa drinking in the knowledge from her books that she would need to do well on her test. Both subconsciously longed for an evening together away from the doldrums of their college lives. Both blocked out that they were becoming far too reliant on and affectionate with one another.

At 5:00 p.m. Wade observed himself in the mirror as he brushed his teeth. He had gotten a haircut from his favorite barber on Baxter the day before. The guy had done a good job, he thought. He even allowed the barber to talk him into cutting the corners of his Fu Manchu off. Now his mustache appeared neatly trimmed and classic. *Nice*, Wade thought.

He slipped the white Marcella cummerbund over his white shirt and suspenders. It fit snug and classy. A much better fit now than the first time he had tried it on at the men's shop. Both cufflinks were in as were the similar silver-colored studs with white mother of pearl facings he had used to button his shirt. Straightening his bowtie once more, he slipped on his black tailcoat. He had never worn one before.

The owner of the men's shop had insisted that with this outfit he also wear their black patent leather shoes and white cotton gloves. They looked good but neither were particularly comfortable. Removing his coat and gloves, he discovered his fancy tux pants with their black satin stripes had no pockets. Searching he found the only place to put his wallet was in his tailcoat's inside pocket. Shaking his head, he left the trailer.

Ann was at the apartment helping Louisa get into her dress. Louisa had spent over an hour painting her nails, fixing her hair, and putting on her makeup. She hated getting dolled up like this even though she certainly had the body and looks for it.

Staying back in her bedroom, Angie had kept to herself most of the afternoon. She only came out reluctantly when Ann called her to come see Louisa. They were in the den when Angie walked out. Unsmiling when she saw her glamorous friend, she made her best effort to act upbeat, but it was not wholehearted as she told her roommate how nice she looked.

Louisa was ready at last. She had just put on her new full-length wool coat. It was a beautiful thing in itself. The jet-black, front swing tuxedo coat had slash pockets, turned back cuffs, and full lining. It hid the features of her dress except around her lower legs and ankles.

Hearing a knock at the door, Ann smiled at Louisa. Opening it, Ann's eyes met Wade's. "Wow! Look at you, Cuz," Ann paused for effect. "For a South Georgia redneck, you're almost presentable. Hey. I like that 'stache too."

Wade glanced back at Ann with a friendly scowl as he entered the room. After all, she had gotten him into this mess, monkey suit and all. "Ladies," he said bowing toward Louisa and Angie. "Good evening."

Gleefully impressed, Louisa and Angie acknowledged him with a nod.

"I hope this goes well and fast," he joked.

Louisa rolled her eyes laughing, "You and me both."

Silent until now, Angie gazed at Wade from head to toe. "You look nice, Wade." She paused staring at him. Catching herself, she said, "You both look nice." Leaving the room, she called back down the hallway, "Y'all have fun."

"Thanks," Louisa responded eyeing her escort. "Wade … I guess we better get going."

Ann walked them to the door calling from behind, "Y'all be careful in all that get up. Someone over there might mistake you guys for somebody important." Giggling, she closed the door.

Outside, it was a dark, very dark February night. The air was cold and clear. The stars sparkled in the heavens like diamonds on black velvet. Louisa, not being able to help herself, stared up at them as Wade opened the car door for her to enter.

"Oh, it's such a gorgeous night, isn't it, Wade?" she asked gazing wistfully. A frosted steam rose from her breath as she spoke.

"Yes. It's very beautiful," Wade answered as he too stopped to view the shimmering Milky Way.

Louisa grew solemn for a moment. With a spark of delight, she caught his eye. Pausing serenely, she stared into his eyes then slid down into her seat. Remaining quiet as they left the Athens perimeter and its businesses, the two drove out into the remote countryside. Louisa peered through her window at the cloistered light coming from an occasional country house where the weary residents had come in from a hard day of work. *How ironic*, she thought. Here she was all adorned heading over to this lavish Ball. There they were, at home, comfortable and warm. Deep in her mind, she knew these thoughts were mere distractions, methods of keeping her mind away from the pleasure she was feeling being with him.

At first, the silence didn't bother Wade. As only his mind could do, in the quietness, his thoughts slowly started to reel. *Maybe she doesn't want to be with me tonight. She was just being nice asking me in the first place or maybe she just felt sorry for me because I was alone and had nobody. Why am I thinking all this crazy stuff,* Wade chided himself. *Damn, we've been together for weeks. We've had a great time. What the hell's going on here?* If there was one thing the passionate young artist could do and do quite well, it was feel. The tension he felt in the air was palpable, more than palpable.

Finally, Louisa turned toward him. As she did so, Wade realized that in the darkness he couldn't read her face.

"Wade," she said struggling for words, "I don't know how to thank you for all you've done. I don't mean just taking those classes and what you're doing for me tonight. I mean—everything you've done. Do you understand what I'm …?"

Wade tried glimpsing Louisa's face through the darkness. Before he could answer, she continued.

"You are a very, very special person, Wade, and very special to me. I just always want you to know how much I . . ."

Listening intently as her words trailed off, Wade responded warmly.

"Louisa, it's been my pleasure entirely. Having someone to eat with and talk to. Go to the movies with. Even learning to dance for the communist with you was a trip for me," he chuckled.

Louisa smiled back at him, still vexed, uncertain of her feelings and how she should react to them.

With an inaudible sigh, Wade was relieved that the silence had been broken, and she was seemingly still happy and glad to be in his company.

The trip to Atlanta didn't take long. Unlike their elders who worried about missing turns and having wrecks, the young couple sped through the city's outer expressways in total control. Swerving to get into the correct lanes and cutting people off to catch an exit, the duo took the traffic in stride. They found themselves in the heart of the city. The lighted, gold dome of the State Capitol building glistened in the cool, clear air of Atlanta's nightscape of huge office buildings and towering skyscrapers.

Turning off I-85 and heading east on Memorial Drive, there it was, the Regency Hotel, the site of this administration's Governor's Ball. The right lane had already been cordoned off with orange reflective cones as uniformed Atlanta City police officers directed traffic. Georgia State Patrol cars were parked in strategic locations, blue lights flashing, warning motorist to slow down as the troopers directed the party's guests to special parking lots and garages surrounding the building complex.

After the couple drove up a parking deck, a traffic detail with flashlights pointing got them parked. Wade cut the engine and peered at Louisa. "You ready?"

Louisa seemed nervous but nodded. Wade got out, put on his coat, and walked around to the other side of the car. Opening the door, he reached in and took Louisa by her now gloved hand.

It appeared that most of the partygoers were heading for the stairwells or elevators of the parking garage en masse. As Wade and Louisa joined the parade of people, Wade couldn't help but feel as though he was walking into the stadium of an exciting college football game, one that was being held at night, except that the attendees at this event were dressed to the max. Most guests seemed to travel in groups or cliques, some boisterous, some quiet. Almost all instinctively knew where to go—like migrating birds. Those who didn't know just followed the crowd. The elevators were full, so Wade and Louisa took the stairs. Traversing a skywalk to the adjoining hotel, they took an elevator to the ground floor. Entering the Regency's lavish lobby, they found themselves in a huge reception area that was resplendently decorated. Floral arrangements, ferns, and ivy adorned almost every aspect of the grand atrium. Select portraits of past governors and busts of famous Georgians were strategically placed around an immense cascading water fountain at the room's center. Just past this marvelous fountain, a tremendous Georgia State flag covered the wall. Majestically, this enormous emblem tightly draped the back wall of the room where large mahogany doors created entranceways into the grand ballroom.

Going into this room, containing massive, cut glass chandeliers, guests could see a seated orchestra in the far corner. An array of tables fitted with white-linen, floor-length tablecloths sat along the room's perimeter. These were used as staging platforms for varying delicacies, drinks, and floral arrangements. In the main ballroom was an area of hardwood floor designated for the main events dance floor. As guests made their way through the decorated hall, they couldn't help but notice the magnificent aroma of delicious foods now surrounding them. All of these were arranged and displayed on the finest silver settings. In three of the four corners of the room, wet bars had been set up. Several coatless bartenders wearing white tux shirts, red bowties, and black silk vests staffed each of these stations and rapidly mixed and poured drinks for the Governor's many patrons.

Giving their tickets to the doormen, Louisa and Wade toured the extravaganza in awe. Nothing struck them as ordinary. Neither of them had seen such grandeur in their lives and were bewildered that such a large sum of money had been spent for just a single night's event. It was insane, but they were glad to be there to enjoy it, even if their pleasure at being with each other remained concealed.

Vaguely understanding where to go, they made it to a table just to the left side of the grand ballroom orchestra and took a seat. They watched as the white coat, black tie, tuxedoed band members tuned their instruments and casually talked to one another. Turning away from the band and back to Louisa, Wade asked loudly, "How exactly is this thing supposed to come off?"

Louisa scanned the room. "There's supposed to be a woman—master of ceremonies—or something, meeting us here in front of the band somewhere."

"What's her name?" Wade asked. "Do you know what she looks like?"

Still searching the room, Louisa replied, "She's supposed to be wearing a red dress. A tall blonde. Her name's Alice—Alice Dupree."

Wade grinned nodding his head, but Louisa didn't notice. She kept scouring the room for her contact.

"There are dozens of tall blonde women wearing red dresses in this room, Louisa."

Louisa balked as she watched him shrug playfully. "You think this is funny, Wade?"

Trying to act indifferent, Wade watched as two tall blondes both wearing red dresses walked past their table.

Cutting her eyes at him, she noticed them too. "Not much to go on—huh?"

With his arms folded across his chest, Wade leaned back into his chair as he gazed over at his distressed date. "Listen up, sweetheart! I can guarantee you one thing one hundred percent. These people will definitely find you. So, stop worrying your pretty little head about that not happening."

Amazed by his confidence, Louisa couldn't believe this was the same shy guy who had kept her company over the last several weeks. Whispering anxiously, she asked, "You're not just a little bit nervous about all of this, Wade?"

Devilishly, he responded with a glint in his eye. "Why should I be nervous, Louisa? I'm here with the best-looking woman in the place."

Louisa blushed. Noting how rapidly the room was starting to fill, she whispered, "How can you kid around at a time like this?"

Wade stared back into the crystal blueness of his companion's eyes. "I'm not kidding you at all, Louisa."

Startled by his directness, Louisa wondered why he would pick now to start acting so bold.

Her heart was already beating fast enough from the anxiety of having to be introduced at this thing. She could feel her chest heaving inside her coat. Turning away, she tried to conceal the excitement she felt from his remark.

"Look. There's the Governor," she whispered discreetly pointing to a man shaking hands with well-wishers on the other side of the hall.

Slowly the Governor and his wife worked the crowd as they made their way across the ballroom floor to the end of the band's section where Wade and Louisa were seated. At a small podium adjacent to the orchestra stood a tall blonde. Wearing a red gown and holding a mic in the palm of one hand, she used her other hand to signal those in attendance to quiet down. A few of the spectators grew hushed as they watched and listened to her, but even so, there was still a buzz emanating from some of the Governor's patrons.

"Miss Dupree, I presume?" Wade whispered to Louisa who was observing the speaker and pretended not to hear him.

Again, the energized voice of the cheerful woman sang out as she tried to quell the crowd. "Ladies and gentlemen! May I have your attention please?" Raising her voice to a crescendo, she proclaimed, "Has the Regency outdone itself tonight?" The jam-packed assemblage burst into a wild, raucous round of cheering and applause. She continued, "Indeed they have, haven't they? But on to the real reason we're here tonight." She paused momentarily then vibrantly asked, "This is the time we've all been waiting for, am I correct?" Another reverberating round of applause erupted from the victorious mass with yelps and hollers of, "Here! Here!" Waiting for the cheering to subside as she smiled at those standing nearby, she sang out, "What we've all worked so hard and long for—right!" More intensity and more pandemonium filled the room as the spectators, mostly campaign volunteers and big financial donors, cheered and yelled with even more vigor.

The lights were subtly dimmed as the master of ceremonies regained the audience's vigilance. More calmly, she said, "So now, ladies and gentlemen, without further adieu." For effect she stopped, then shouting into the microphone, she exlaimed, "Let's all say hello to the new governor of the great State of Georgia!"

Just as the band struck the first notes to "Happy Days Are Here Again," a spotlight from the ceiling beamed down on the politician. Miss Dupree shouted his name with conviction over the audio system to no avail. The instantaneous roar of the screaming crowd combined with the loud music from the orchestra drowned her voice. Several minutes passed as everyone, now standing, chanted the newly elected official's name over and over again as they applauded him. The Governor and his wife waved and smiled enthusiastically to everyone they could see. Finally, after what seemed an eternity to Wade, the speaker once again regained control.

"Governor," she spoke as the applause and cheering slowly abated. "Governor," she said again. "Tonight, is your night! And speaking on behalf of all your wonderful supporters, most of whom are here ..." Another resounding response arose from the crowd as she said this followed by several more minutes of cheers from his boisterous fans. Finally, she was able to call out above them. "We are truly honored to be here with you and your lovely wife and to be a part of this marvelous victory." With an additional ovation from the multitude, chants of "Speech! Speech!" echoed around the great room. Hearing these shouts rapidly growing in unison and spreading across the hall, Miss Dupree quickly squelched the idea. "No! No! We aren't going to make him work tonight. No. Tonight, we are going to let him off the hook." Pausing she asked, "Governor, are you ready for the fun to begin?" This was his cue to get ready for the festivities, which primarily meant the dance. Smiling, he saluted the moderator to get things started.

Taking note, the announcer sang out, "If everyone would clear the center of the room, please! We'll let our new governor take his glamorous wife on a waltz to our state's favorite song." The orchestra behind Wade and Louisa broke into Hoagy Carmichael and Stuart Gorrell's famous melody, "Georgia On My Mind." It was an awkward start to the event as the Governor and his wife seemed not to know exactly how or when to start dancing. Escaping their entourage, they made their way onto the floor. As they began their dance, it became apparent they weren't going to be the most elegant performers this evening. Even so, they did seem to relish basking in the spotlight of victory. When the Governor and the First Lady finished their single loop around the Grand Hall, the speaker asked the audience for an ovation.

"Ladies and gentlemen, what a lovely couple and a lovely dance! What a wonderful team to now preside over the fine citizens of the State of Georgia! Let us all give our new First Family another round of applause!" The crowd honored their newly elected official with a round of cheers and clapping. "Next, for your dancing entertainment, we have our new Lt. Governor—"

While the moderator began announcing the next set of dancers, Louisa looked up startled to see Dr. Horton, her psychology teacher and the dean of the Psychology department, heading straight for her. "Are you both ready?" he asked eagerly.

Puzzled, Louisa stood up. "I thought you weren't—"

"I know. I know," he interrupted. "I had to come over anyway," he laughed cheerily.

Louisa began to understand what Wade had already concluded about why they were there. It was all about making a statement and contributions. The University and its Board wanted to make sure that this thing went off without a hitch.

The doctor continued, "You know they'll be introducing you right after the Secretary of State, right?"

Louisa nodded. The professor pointed to the Secretary who was seated in front of Wade. "You see he's in a wheelchair. He won't be dancing, okay? So be ready." Louisa glanced at Wade just as the spotlight hit the older man. Introducing the dignitary, Miss Dupree sang out, "and our not so new Secretary of State—Ben Fortson!"

A tremendous ovation broke out as the entire crowd honored the venerable older gentlemen who had served through numerous administrations.

"Wade. We're next," Louisa whispered frantically. "My coat. What will we do with it?"

It was their turn as the speaker announced, "Now, ladies and gentlemen, we have some very special guests with us tonight."

Wade stood nonchalantly across the table from Louisa. *What was he doing way over there?* She worried. This could not be the same Wade she knew only hours before.

Miss Dupree kept speaking. "First, we have representing the University of Georgia—"

Immediately, a huge roar went up from the crowd due to the many loyal Bulldog fans in attendance. When the cheering finally subsided, the speaker excitedly called out, "Miss Louisa Wess!" A bright shaft of light hit Louisa from above. Everything else in the room stopped and grew dark; the radiant beam aloft illuminating only her. Still wrapped in her coat and trembling, she stood there alone—blinded. *Where was he?* She remained frozen and in shock as the crowd, on pins and needles, had grown very quiet, uncomfortably so. Suddenly, she felt his calming presence. Wade slowly opened her black wool coat and carefully helped her slip out of it. As he did so, a gasp of excitement sped through the spellbound crowd as though they had just witnessed the unveiling of a fine piece of art.

Before them stood a dazzling ethereal princess. Her dark olive complexion glowed in the brilliant white sleeveless gown which hugged her hips. Her camisole was adorned with a tasteful array of sparkling red and black crystals. Continuing downward and cascading, her ruffled skirt draped to her ankles. With her shimmering raven hair pulled back into an elegant chignon and her radiant blue eyes and curvaceous figure now more evident, every man and woman in the room stood mesmerized.

No one noticed what the announcer was saying as Wade moved into the spotlight. With his jet-black hair parted and slicked, the handsome young man wearing the black tailcoat and white bowtie placed his right arm behind his back. Bowing, he offered the bedazzled beauty his left hand. Louisa curtseyed. Wearing elegant elbow length white gloves, she slid her right hand into his and rested her left arm across the sleeve of Wade's black tuxedo. With her back arched appropriately and her head turned at an angle gazing just over his right shoulder, the couple stepped into several quick rotations of a spinning stationary fleckerl. Louisa's glimmering white dress and Wade's black coattails flared outward as they did so. To the rhythmic beat of "Moon River," Henry Mancini's and Johnny Mercer's haunting love song from the theme to the movie *Breakfast at Tiffany's*, the twosome took flight.

Moon River wider than a mile

I'm crossing you in style some day.

Like two regal swans gliding across a lake, they began whirling forward, rotating clockwise, deftly and silently, revolving their steps, sliding up to their toes, then back down on their heels. The pair's movements were seamless and effortless as they spun their way across the large expanse of the ballroom floor.

Two drifters off to see the world

There's such a lot of world to see.

Pausing but never stopping, Louisa turned her head rotating her gaze in the opposite direction then back. Counterclockwise, the two whirled around again and again. Their footwork was so nimble and amazingly fluid, it appeared to onlookers as if the dancers were floating on air. As the romantic music tugged at the audience's heartstrings and as the couple's performance quickly whirled them forward, a joyful unspeakable aura seemed to engulf the pair casting their audience into an almost hypnotic trance. Wade and Louisa boldly and gracefully danced. Their impassioned embrace aroused romance in even the coldest of souls. Every woman observed every nuance of the dashing Wade. Every man that of the stunningly beautiful Louisa.

The claps started slowly. As the couple progressed to halfway around the room, the applause began echoing resoundingly with cheers and bravos. The engaged patrons were enthralled. Like a prince with his princess, the pair completed their performance to a rousing ovation. Giving their audience an elegant bow, they continued to dance as the remainder of the guests were introduced. In defiance of Miss K's teachings, they had forsaken the more graceful form of the Viennese Waltz and regressed to simply staring into each other's eyes. Holding the soft and delicate beauty closely, Wade effortlessly guided his partner across the immensity of the dance floor. The music at last came to a stop, breaking both the couple's trance as well as their embrace. As Wade looked down into Louisa's enticing eyes still holding her hands, Dr. Horton appeared at their side. Taking Louisa by the arm, he gleefully said, "I finally found you. Come with me there are some people I want you to meet."

Wade, turning his partner free, had expected this intrusion to occur. Poor Louisa had thought after this dance, their obligation to the school would be over. Little did she know that her night with the politicos had only just begun. As her instructor drug her through the crowded dance floor, Louisa glanced over her shoulder toward her date, but he was nowhere to be seen.

Louisa was at the mercy of the school's administrators as she was shuttled back and forth from one end of the congested ballroom to the other. Meeting dignitaries, politicians, movers and shakers, and making small talk was grueling and time consuming, and Louisa desperately wanted to make it back to Wade's side.

The Dean wouldn't let up as he made sure that not one single contributor, not one political ally missed an audience with his beautiful young escort. Everyone who was anyone knew that the University of Georgia had been well represented in breathtaking style. Louisa was finally let off the hook when the professor introduced her to the Governor for a second time. Cheerfully, the newly elected official chastised the Dean for hogging the pretty girl all to himself and asked what had become of her handsome beau, her fabulous dancing partner. The professor, trying not to act embarrassed, got the point and graciously thanked Louisa for her time. With a grin, he told her to go join the party and have fun.

Relieved, Louisa thanked the two men and left the area amid the music and mayhem. She was gone from Wade for over an hour and had not seen him a single time on her duty-bound blitzkrieg around the room. *Where could he be?* she thought, desperately searching the area.

As she walked around trying to locate him, men continually interrupted her with a suave line while most of the women stopping her did so to compliment her dress or dancing skills. Most guests at the venue were University of Georgia Bulldog fans and would give her at least one good "GO DOGS" before she could escape them.

It took her another five minutes to find Wade. Spotting her handsome escort in a smoking room adjacent the atrium, she noticed him sitting on a sofa listening intently to an attractive slinky blonde wearing a black silk evening gown studded tastefully with a few dozen glittering rhinestones. Furtively, Louisa observed the two from a distance. Cordially, he was engaged in an animated conversation. Watching the pair, Louisa caught a glimpse of herself in the reflection of one of the massive entrance hall mirrors. What on earth was she doing, she thought. It wasn't as if he was cheating on her with another girl. She and Wade were just friends. Again, she peered back at him and her heart skipped a beat. Pensively biting her bottom lip, she watched as the two continued to talk. Unable to stand it any longer, she emerged breathlessly in front of them. Wade looked up surprised as she seemingly had appeared from nowhere.

"Louisa, are you all right?" He rose from his seat.

Bedazzled by Wade's stunning friend, the blonde sitting across from him stood up too.

"Yeah, I'm okay. I just got a little too hot, I'm afraid."

"Would you like some punch? Maybe sit down for a minute?"

"No. No. I'm okay, really."

Wade paused a moment. Glancing at his new friend, he said, "Louisa, I'd like to introduce you to Candace Perry." He paused.

"Candace, this is Louisa Wess."

Both girls smiled acknowledging each other.

"Candace is a law student at Emory."

"I'm impressed," Louisa said sincerely.

"Don't be," the girl said flatly. "I've got another year to go, then the bar exam. I just hope I can make it."

"I'm sure you will," Louisa smiled back.

An uncomfortable pause followed. Candace commented, "You two were the dancers everyone was talking about, the students from the University of Georgia. Okay, I see …" Candace was confused, not knowing if the pair was dating, engaged, or married. Feeling she might be imposing on Louisa's date, she backed away smiling. Telling Wade it had been nice talking to him, she excused herself and disappeared into the crowd.

Louisa paused as she solemnly stared into Wade's eyes. In an apologetic tone, she said, "I hope I didn't get in your way. She was quite pretty."

"I can assure you that you didn't, Miss Wess," Wade said with a wry grin. Taking her by the hand, he startled his partner by pulling her hurriedly through the throng of chattering people toward the dance floor in the next room. "Are you through with all that pageant stuff?"

"Pageant stuff? What are you talking about?"

Wade snickered as he veered through the openings of the crowded floor. Playfully, he kept dragging her with him. Suddenly, they stopped. Finding themselves in front of the orchestra, he turned to face her. An expression of bewilderment radiated from Louisa's face as she caught her breath and smiled up into his warm brown eyes.

The band had put on the pomp and ceremony the event's elite had desired. Now tired of the stilted compositions demanded of them earlier, the musicians regressed into the free spirits that they were and played current hits even if they had to select the more subdued ones. The sensual melody of Melissa Manchester's "Midnight Blue" enveloped the room. Wade devilishly pulled Louisa into his arms for an old-fashioned, no-lessons-involved, slow dance. Feigning anger at this uncharacteristic and forward behavior he was displaying, Louisa acted reluctant to follow. Starry-eyed, she melted into his warm embrace. Slowly and rhythmically, they moved to the beat of the song.

Wade chuckled as he held her. "They had you over here as a beauty contestant, a showgirl."

Louisa lifted her head from his shoulder and stared him in the eyes with an incensed look. Watching him grin, she coyly remarked, "Does that make you mad?"

Wade pulled her back to his chest. Once again, she rested her cheek on his shoulder. Whispering into her ear, he said, "Nothing that you could ever do could make me mad." Like the rare sighting of deer at the edge of a forest, they disappeared from view blending into the maze of dancing revelers. Lost to all but themselves.

CHAPTER 12

Wedding Bell Blues

With the Governor's Ball over and the final few weeks of the quarter upon them, Louisa and Wade began to distance themselves from one another. When they got together, it was only in the presence of others. If they went out to eat, her roommates or a friend would come along. If Louisa went to the trailer, she had Ann or Angie with her. They were never alone together; neither allowed the temptation to grow any further.

Between quarters, Ann and Wade carried Louisa to Hartsfield International Airport in Atlanta to catch a flight to Dallas. Les would pick Louisa up and take her back to Fort Worth where he attended classes at one of the region's Baptist seminaries. The trip to Texas would be short considering Louisa only had three days, from a Friday through Sunday. Even so, it was a trip she felt was necessary.

She found Les eagerly awaiting her at the gate. Tears streamed down her face as she disembarked. Running down the final portion of the ramp, she dove into Les' waiting arms. Hugging him tightly and kissing him, she told him over and over how much she loved him and how much she had missed him. Whether it was from the pain she had suffered from being apart from Les for so long or from the uneasy feelings of pleasure she had felt being with Wade over the previous quarter, she honestly could not tell. It was probably some of both, as that gray area in life sometimes seems to overshadow even the most virtuous of souls.

After showing Louisa the school's campus and a few of the more popular sights of the city, the couple spent most of the rest of their time together alone at Les' apartment. It didn't take them long in each other's company to pick up where they had left off back in Athens.

II

The following Monday when Louisa returned to Athens, she informed her roommates that she had important news she wanted to share. Getting her luggage situated in her room, she called Angie and Ann in and asked them to have a seat.

"So, how was your trip, girl?" Ann grinned. "I bet Les was glad to see you."

Louisa, who was sitting at her vanity, smiled and lifted her left hand displaying a diamond ring on her finger.

"Oh, my gosh!" Angie rejoiced at the revelation. Secretly she was beside herself that Louisa's relationship with Wade was definitely at an end.

"Wow!" Ann chimed in. "It took him long enough to ask you!"

"Well, we've been discussing doing this for a while. It was a lot harder being apart than we'd thought it would be."

Perplexed, Ann noticed a sense of resoluteness in her friend's voice.

"So, when is the big day?" Angie asked.

"We haven't set a date yet, but after talking to Les and my parents and after much soul searching, I've decided to move out to Texas to be with him at the start of this quarter."

Ann and Angie were excited to hear that their friends were getting married but slightly taken back by the short notice. It wasn't like Louisa to leave them in the lurch of having to find a new roommate so suddenly. Just as Les had done with Wade, Louisa quickly assured them that she would pay her share of the rent for the upcoming quarter reasoning it would cost her little to live with Les in Texas.

If the suddenness of this unexpected news shocked Louisa's roommates, it came as a complete surprise to Wade who found it devastating. He put up a good front, acting as if he could not be more pleased with Louisa's decision. How good it would be for Louisa and Les to be back together he told her. However, even as Wade put on a smiling face for Louisa's sake, his heart was breaking. Even though it first seemed to be a repetition of losing Mimi—it was more—much more. If there were such a thing in life as a soul mate or destiny, he felt Louisa was certainly his. There was a connection that he knew was there but couldn't understand—some sort of magic between them that he had never felt with another woman. It was something so inexplicable yet so obvious, Wade knew that even though she would probably never admit it, she realized this too. Wade suspected it was perhaps one of the reasons, if not the reason, she was leaving Athens. Trying hard not to think of Louisa this way proved difficult for him. Les was his closest friend, and he loved him. He wanted Les and Louisa to be happy together. Wade was torn. If there was only some other way, he anguished. Of all the girls he'd lost in his life, *please not this one*, he thought.

III

With the first week of the new quarter just ahead of him, now was the time to make an obligatory trip home. Armed with three A's and a B from last quarter's work, Wade was less fearful of his father. The older man softened his tone a bit hearing his son's grades, but when he found out Wade was thinking about taking an additional art course as an elective his dad's crass attitude resurfaced. He was mad that his boy was wasting his money and time on such a foolish endeavor.

Keeping his stay at his parents' house brief, Wade returned to school vowing to keep the negative feelings his father imposed on him at bay. However, what he found even more difficult to handle was preventing his mind from drifting back to the dance classes, the Governor's Ball, and the enchanting young woman who was no longer there. Art certainly helped; however, something else lifted his spirits as well. A wondrous, almost magical event was starting to unfold all around him. The greenness and freshness budding everywhere brought the dull, dead, gray city out of the bitter winter chill into the joyful life of spring. The girls on campus played a huge role in this process. As the blazing sun raged overhead, they sported shorts, tans, and bikinis and laid out by pools whenever they could. There was a feeling of mirth in the air. People talked and smiled and sang. They were no longer cooped up in little rooms and apartments trying to stay warm and dry. Outside beckoning them, the sun beamed bright through a brilliant blue sky.

One Saturday afternoon the phone rang at Wade's trailer. Ann was calling to ask if he wanted to go with her and Angie to an open-air concert at Legion Field.

"Sure. When does it get started?" Wade asked.

"Right now! Come on over and get us."

Wade quickly drove to the girl's Sussex apartment and to town they went, laughing and chatting and poking fun at one another. Turning off Broad Street and onto Hull, they soon found a parking place in a lot behind and across the street from the Chi Psi house. The parking area, which was normally empty on the weekends, was starting to fill up as off-campus students interested in the concert flocked to it.

Wade popped open the trunk exposing a cooler filled with iced-down beer that he'd quickly put together as he left his trailer. "Here. Stick some of these extra cans down in your pocketbooks, girls," he suggested. "If we carry this cooler down there with us, they'll all be gone in a matter of minutes."

After stuffing their bags with the ice-cold containers, Ann popped the top to a frosty Budweiser and took a long cool drink. "Athens in the springtime!" She cut her sparkling hazel eyes at Wade. "It doesn't get any better than this now does it, Cuz?"

Wade grinned back then looked over at Angie. "Uh-oh. I think we're going to have our hands full with her today."

"With her," Angie said taking a sip from her beer. "You might be having some trouble with me too, hot shot."

"Geez. Is that why you two invited me to come down here with y'all—to be your chaperone?"

"How about our body guardguard!" Ann grinned. She interlocked her right arm with his left. Angie came up on his other side taking his right arm.

"Yeah," she said squinting her eyes at him seductively. "You can protect us."

"Protect you, hell," Wade laughed out loud. "What you're making me out to be is your pimp!"

The three friends laughed joyfully as they headed down the steep sidewalk on Hull Street. Crossing busy Baxter Street, they headed up the hill from Lipscombe to Mell Hall. Following the trickle of students down Cloverhurst Avenue, Wade noted the steep drop off from the sidewalk they were walking on down to the bottom of the hill. "Wow. It wouldn't pay to be too drunk walking down here, would it?"

Ann chuckled. "Wade, if you were that drunk you wouldn't even know you fell. You'd just wake up wondering how the hell you got there."

Wade smiled peering over the side. "Yeah, but that'd only be *if* you woke up. I'm not so sure you would."

They walked under an oak and hickory canopy of new spring growth; the limbs covered in leaves of a dozen shades of green. The sound of the band, which had been barely audible over on Baxter, was coming into focus as was a river of students pouring down the hill toward them from the opposite direction. The confluence of students merged just past the Bolton Dining Commons where a steep, slick footpath of dirt, clay, and rock, cut its way through a hill of ivy. The students could see down to the mostly open-roofed dressing rooms of the college's colossal open-air pool complex called Legion Pool. Just behind this fenced in swimming area, surrounded by hills, was a natural geographical amphitheater—Legion Field.

"Watch your steps, girls," Wade called back up the hill to Ann and Angie who were turning sideways and sliding downhill after every few steps.

"Hey, fool!" Ann called down to Wade. "You know we got to come back up this thing, don't you?"

Wade shouted back up as he was sliding too. "After a few more beers, this'll be a breeze." Angie lost her footing and landed on her behind. She slid down the hill toward Wade feet first. Lunging back up the incline, Wade caught her in his arms. Stopping her skid, he found himself on top of his former girlfriend, eye to eye. Both had big grins on their faces.

"Not here," Ann said in mock disgust as she walked past them.

Rolling their eyes at her remark, they got to their feet, dusted themselves off, and with the rest of partygoers headed back down the hill a bit more carefully.

The shade of the massive oaks, maples, and hickory trees thinned as the threesome walked over an old stone bridge crossing a small creek at the base of the hill. From there, they made their way out into the open air of Legion Field. The fresh smell of spring mixed with the sweet scent of women cast even the most virtuous man attending into an almost implacable position. The nectar of love and sensuality was in the air, and all in attendance seemed more than willing to imbibe.

Entering the green freshly cut lawn of the park's midway, they soon found the band situated on an improvised platform—two unattached flatbed semi-trailers. The pulsating music blasting from the giant speakers was intense and electrifying as the platforms and everything nearby vibrated to the throbbing beat of the band's drums and bass guitar. Playing an unusual cross of pop and metal, the band covered anything from the Doobie Brothers "Listen to the Music," to ZZ Top, and even Bruce Springsteen's "Born to Run."

Leaving Ann and Wade dancing, Angie slipped off to a nearby fraternity's beer keg and retrieved three cups of golden draft for herself and her friends. "Cheers!" she said grinning as they all tipped their drinks together.

Taking a sip as she continued to dance, Ann declared, "Isn't this music great?"

Angie, holding her hands and cup aloft, only smiled. She had pressed her swaying body as close to Wade's as possible.

Suddenly, a voice called out through the crowd, "Hey, Ann?" A nice-looking guy walked up to her and gave her a hug.

"How did you find me?"

Laughing sarcastically, he responded, "It wasn't easy."

Having stopped dancing, Angie and Wade looked in their direction. Noting her friends' intrigue, Ann introduced him. "Guys, this is Charles. He's been in several of my classes before this quarter, and we're in English Class now."

Wade extended his hand. "I'm Wade, and this is Angie."

"Glad to meet you guys. This is quite a concert isn't it?"

"Yeah," Wade responded as Angie pulled him toward her as she danced to the rhythm.

Ann was delighted by Charles' presence. Soon, they disappeared into the madding crowd of partiers surrounding them, but not before Ann whispered to Angie that she'd find her own way home.

For the first time in over a year, Angie and Wade found themselves alone with one another for a sustained period. It was an unconscious and unobserved moment for them as they celebrated and enjoyed the concert with the rest of the fun-loving students. The two did crazy things like bumming cigarettes off people when neither of them smoked. The result was their coughing and choking as they tried inhaling a few puffs. The alcohol, of course, had a lot to do with their behavior. Several of the fraternities and a few of the boys' dorms had slipped kegs into the park which was standard procedure for such events. Being philanthropic these fellows were more than generous with their brew and especially with an attractive coed – a la Angie. Unlike most of the nearby partiers who had to stand in line trying to gain access to the keg's tap, Angie had no trouble keeping Wade and herself stockpiled with cups of the golden beverage.

Reveling to the beat of the music, the throng didn't take long to feel the full effect of the alcohol, especially in this environment of heat and physical activity. As usual, it took its toll on the weak and the strong alike. Some located the shade of a tree to rest under finding themselves in a head-ringing stupor. Some passed out right where they had their last swallow, whether it was in front of the band, on the lawn, or on a sidewalk. Some puked their guts out repeatedly grossing out anyone who was unfortunate enough to be near them.

A detail of campus police came forward apprehending some of the drunks and pot smokers. This was not an effort to bust them as in a Gestapo raid but more an attempt to get them back to their dorms or apartments in one piece and without anyone starting a fight. Only the most wasted were carried away leaving a more mellow crowd to enjoy the rest of the affair. With the music still blaring, Angie and Wade finally grew tired of the event and left. Climbing the treacherous hill they'd encountered earlier, Wade held his tipsy ex-girlfriend's hand guiding her back up the steep knoll to Clovehurst.

Making it to the top, Angie rested her hands on her knees. "Wow! I'm beat! How about you?" she asked slurring her words.

"Not so much," Wade responded. "Remember Louisa and I had some pretty good workouts at those dance classes." Noticing that Angie was still panting and acting a little unbalanced, he asked, "Caught your breath yet? Ready to go on?"

"Sure," Angie replied trying to right herself.

Walking through the dorm areas and topping the hill behind fraternity row, they found themselves at Wade's car. Climbing inside, Wade asked Angie if she wanted to go to a nearby pub for a pitcher of beer and something to eat.

"Nope. I think I've got my limit, Wade," she slurred.

Wade smiled. "Got your limit? Shouldn't that be 'had your limit', Angie?"

"Yes, I have . . . and damn well had a good time doing it too, I might add."

Her words came tumbling out as she gave Wade a wide-eyed impish grin. She was inebriated all right, but not to the extent Wade seemed to suspect. Chuckling, he shook his head. "Then where is it that you would like to go, my dear?"

Before the words left his mouth, she shot back. "To your place of course," she grinned at him.

Wade thought, *Oh brother, she looks so good, but where will this lead?* Putting the car in gear, he backed out and headed for the exit.

Angie slumped down in the passenger's seat taking from her purse a bottle of beer she had bummed off a guy back at the concert. Having drunk over half of it back at Legion Field, she quickly chugged the rest. As Wade pulled onto the street behind the Chi Psi frat house, she slung the empty container from the open car window where it landed smashing into pieces in the fraternity's parking lot. "Let's ride, Clyde!" she yelled.

"Damn, Angie!" He shifted his five-speed into second gear squealing the tires in the process. "Those guys over there on that balcony are gonna be pissed!" He looked back at the frat house again while he tried making good his escape. Sure enough, here they came, four or five of them yelling and running as fast as they could in Wade and Angie's direction. Pushing in his clutch and shifting into third, Wade shot down the road to the sound of shouts and taunts coming from the fraternity's members as they made it to the curb just behind his car. "Damn, that was a close call! You almost got us killed, girl!"

Half dazed she responded, "They were a bunch of wimps! You could've killed 'em, Wade—sons of bitches!"

"Right, Angie," Wade replied nervously as he peered into his rear-view mirror to see if any of the members had decided to jump into their cars to give chase. Wade's heart was still pounding as he crossed into the Athens downtown area. Circling a few blocks just to make sure the frat boys weren't tailing him, he finally turned back down Broad Street more relaxed. He glanced at Angie who seemed not the least bit concerned about their dilemma. Noticing this carefree attitude of hers, he absolutely didn't want this little foray he was on to conclude with her at his place. With this in mind, Wade asked, "So, you're still not interested in getting something to eat? Maybe we can go over to the B & L Warehouse or something?" In his weakened state, he thought that being anywhere but alone with her at her apartment or his might prove most prudent. Even though he felt he couldn't trust the girl and shouldn't give her another chance, a spark for her still burned deep inside.

"No," she answered gazing into his eyes. "Let's go to your trailer, Wade. I'm tired."

Considering the bottle-throwing incident and the look she had just given him, Wade thought his best plan might be to get her to sober up somehow. Confident that no one was following them, he pulled into a nearby Huddle House thinking that a cup of coffee and a little food might go a long way in getting him out of this potentially disastrous situation.

"What are we stopping here for?" Angie asked curiously.

"Uh, I want to get a quick bite to eat and use the bathroom. You need to go?" Falling for his deception, Angie got out of the car and followed him inside the restaurant. She was about to bust to use the bathroom. When she returned, Wade had two cups of coffee, a hamburger, and French fries sitting at the table for each of them.

Taking a seat in their booth, a glassy-eyed Angie stared down at her plate of food and drink. Stammering, she said, "I'm not too much for coffee, Wade." As she told him this, she started nibbling at her fries.

"Now—Ang'," Wade scoffed. "Put a little sugar in it. It's not that bad."

Trying to comply, she daintily began shaking a little packet of sugar spilling almost half of its contents while trying to pour it into her cup. She gave it a taste. "Damn, that's hot!" she moaned loudly. Angie wasn't one to do much cussing, but the level of alcohol she had in her system seemed to be doing most of the talking for her at this point.

Reaching in his glass of ice water with a spoon, Wade flipped some ice into the steaming cup of coffee. Stirring it, he said, "Try it now." As Angie took a sip, her face grew into a grimace. "That stuff's awful! I just don't think I can drink it, Wade."

Seeing that he was getting nowhere with the effort, Wade ordered a Coke to go for Angie. Paying the bill, they went to his car and headed back down the Atlanta Highway. Looking at Angie as he neared the turnoff to her Sussex residence, Wade timidly asked, "You sure you don't want me to drop you off at your place where you can sleep this thing off? We can get with Ann and maybe do something later on, you know."

"No, Wade. I want to go to your trailer where I can be with you."

Oh hell! he thought. Even though he had drunk two cups of coffee back at the Huddle House and considered himself relatively sober, he knew only too well what carrying her back to his place could turn into. He wasn't sure what she had on her mind if anything, but whether she did or didn't, he felt confident that getting sober meant he could remain in control. Especially remembering all the hell she had put him through with their breakup.

Pulling up to Wade's mobile home, they both went inside. Wade flicked on the lights as Angie reached down and picked up a novel resting on a table next to his recliner. "*The Battle of Anzio* by T. R. Fehrenbach," she read the title of the book out loud. Suddenly she was starting to sound more sober. "I wouldn't have thought you would have had the time to read something like this with all your schoolwork, art, dancing classes, and such." She gave Wade a puzzled look as he smiled back at her.

"You know I'm not the fastest reader in the world, so I decided it might help me to do a little extra reading on the side. Besides, it's something I'm interested in."

"I didn't know you were into war stories," Angie said.

"It's more of the battle's history than anything else. I don't know if you studied much about World War II, but this is the beach where the Allies got stuck for several months trying to take Italy from the Germans. It's quite a brutal and horrific story. Probably not much a girl would be interested in reading, I'd suspect."

"Wow, Wade. A whole different side of you I never knew about," Angie said, fascinated that he would attempt reading the book in the first place. Replacing it on the table, she walked over to the canvas resting on his easel. It was blank.

"No new ideas going on inside that head of yours?"

"There's always ideas, but nothing that I really want to paint right now," he responded. Wade grew curious watching Angie make her way around his apartment. Gone by this time were her foggy eyes and stammering speech. Inquisitively, she stood in front of the open door of his refrigerator. "You hungry?" Wade asked.

"No. Just browsing," she called out. She walked back across the den to where he was still standing. Wade, perplexed by her actions, asked, "Is there something you want? Something I can—"

Interrupting him in mid-speech, Angie reached over with both hands and grabbed him by the collar. She planted a passionate kiss on the stunned boy's mouth. Wade wanted to pull back from her as images poured into his mind of how she had mistreated him. She had emotionally burned and castigated him. She had shunned him and treated him with apathy. In the split second it took for all those thoughts to run their course urging him to escape her—he was helpless.

She took his hand and led him to the darkened back bedroom closing the door behind them.

Later that night, around 1:00 a.m., Ann made it back to her apartment to find it empty. Concerned, she made a quick call to Wade's trailer where Angie answered the phone groggily and told Ann that she would see her in the morning. Silently Angie replaced the phone's receiver and laid back down staring through the semi-darkness at Wade's sleeping face. She was back in his heart, and she knew it. No more Mimi or Louisa to get in her way. How stupid she had been to have almost lost him. How long it seemed that they were apart. As far as she was concerned, nothing would ever separate her from him again.

IV

As the weeks progressed into months, Angie became an almost permanent fixture at Wade's trailer, encouraging him to study and waiting on him hand and foot. They double dated often with Ann and her new man Charles. Everything in her eyes was looking up and starting to settle into a pleasant routine. It had taken time, a lot of time, but Wade's lingering thoughts of Louisa started to subside. It was becoming a pleasure for Wade to have Angie back in his life. How different she seemed from before, so much more settled and satisfied with him and herself.

By the end of spring quarter of their third year of college, wedding plans were being finalized by Louisa and Les in Texas. At the start of the summer break before anyone got jobs, the bride and the groom would return to Les' hometown to get married. The prolonged hubbub and hoopla of most weddings was not a problem. Had they lived nearby, there would have been bridal showers and wedding parties given by close friends and relatives of the family. They would have been wined, dined, and shown off to the community. But these events were dropped for expediency. Besides, it was neither Louisa's nor Les' style. The wedding would be a simple affair held in the Chapel of their local junior college. The shelter by the lake would hold the reception, weather permitting. If not, it would be moved to the school's dining hall.

The wedding party arrived at the Chapel on the Friday evening before the actual ceremony. A member of Les' church was coordinating the event. When she finished walking them through their parts and was satisfied that everyone knew what to do, she allowed the group to leave and go across town to the rehearsal dinner which was held in one of the private dining rooms at the Ramada Inn.

Most of the old group would be participating in the affair. Laney, Karl, Wade, and three of Louisa's brothers were the groomsmen. Ann, Angie, and some of Louisa and Les' cousins were the bridesmaids. Because Laney and Karl were the tallest men there, they and the taller girls they escorted would stand closest to the bride and groom. According to the height of the groomsmen, the rest would follow suit with the shortest on the outside. With so many tall men present, Wade ended up escorting one of Louisa's cousins, and Angie, who was helping with Louisa's veil, was escorted by Karl. The rehearsal went off without a hitch and the wedding party gathered in front of the Chapel ready to head to the hotel. It was then that Karl, who had been attending Duke's Medical School, came in contact with Louisa in private for the first time since their fiasco at Fernandina. Louisa was standing by herself to one side of the sanctuary waiting on Les when Karl walked up. Karl spoke humbly, "Louisa, I wanted to catch you alone so I could apologize for the way I treated you down at the beach way back when. I was a young fool and an idiot, and I hope you will please forgive me."

Louisa stared at him stoically. She had not wanted Karl in her wedding, but she couldn't tell Les why. "Yes, you were indeed an idiot. I hope you've learned your lesson, Karl." She paused pensively for a moment. Then she said, "I'm not one to hold a grudge."

"Hold a grudge. Who's holding a grudge?" Les grinned as he came walking out of the sanctuary.

Karl put his arm around the shoulders of his longtime friend. "No one, ol' man," he smiled down at Les. "You're looking great, bud, and I'm so proud of you. The two of you," he said smiling at both Les and Louisa. "A preacher. I can't believe one of my pals is going to be a preacher." Karl paused reflecting on what he had just said. With an unusual tone of sincerity, he remarked, "Well, if anyone that I've ever met in my life will make a good man of the cloth, it's you, Les."

"Thank you, Karl," Les responded. He knew that for once Karl's words truly came from the heart.

People were starting to get into their cars to ride over to the rehearsal dinner. Everything at the Ramada Inn had been prepared and was waiting for the wedding party's arrival. Slowly, carload after carload of attendees made it to the hotel's parking lot and into the building to the private dining area. Les, Louisa, and their parents sat at the head table. Everyone else sat at two adjoining side tables. About forty people were present. Louisa had forgotten to bring the bridesmaids' presents and was frantic. Angie and Karl, who were standing nearby when she realized this, volunteered to make a quick run to Les' house to retrieve them.

The room, full of talkative chatting people, slowly grew quiet as they watched a small, bespectacled man, partially bald in his early fifties, approach the podium. Patiently and methodically, he reached up and carefully bent the microphone down to his speaking level. He peered about the room with a radiant smile while he waited to gain everyone's attention. The words came forth deliberately and thoughtfully from Les' father. Warmly, he looked down kindly at each person to whom he directed his words as he spoke. It was easy to see the rebirth of his personality and soft charisma in his son who sat next to him at the podium hanging on every word the older man was saying. The same compassion, the same thoughtfulness, the same wisdom, the same patience could all be found in Les.

It was a magnificent speech detailing his son's life seen through the eyes of a loving father. How he cherished his son more than life itself. How proud he was of him. How the few goofs in life that Les had made were nothing to lose sleep over. How no matter what his son had ever done and no matter what he could ever do, his father would never stop loving him. He turned to Louisa and spoke of first meeting Les' fiancée. How much he loved and cared for her. The same guarantee of unconditional love was given to her as well. The last thing he said was the most intriguing. At most affairs when a respected elder is given the floor to speak, he takes full advantage of the once in a lifetime role of being the wise master and prophesizes on the pleasures and pitfalls that the couple will encounter using his lengthy life experiences in matrimony as a guide. Les' father didn't do this. He simply told them that every day is a different day, that the times had changed and would continue to change, and that nothing was fixed but God's love. Now was the time of discovery for their marriage and what all it would bring forth. With that, he wished them good luck then raised a glass of wine and gave a toast to Les and Louisa. "With hope, faith, and much love."

CHAPTER 13

The Dream

"Keep down, soldier; they're right on top of us! Use your head! Use your head, son! Stay down in that trench! You hear me?"

Salvos from German eighty-eights were going off everywhere. Blackness, gunfire, smoke, missiles firing off just like during the German counter-offensive of World War II at Anzio or the Battle of the Somme during World War I. It was night and flashes of artillery being fired were followed by the thunder of illuminating explosions. The ground rumbled and the earth shook with each deafening blast and counterblast.

Everywhere there was death and despair. The carnage of mutilated bodies littered the battlefield, and those lucky enough to make it back to their trench or foxhole were mostly maimed or shell-shocked. Greenhorn officers wearing shiny new uniforms went through the trenches trying to assess the situation, shouting encouragement to all the raw recruits, but turning ashen-faced when looking into the steely glare of a battle-hardened veteran.

The conflict seemed relentless. There was no way of discerning who had the advantage, who was winning, or who was losing. Hunkering down and surviving the moment was all-consuming. It was personal. The others, those whose headless bodies lay strewn about. Their time had come. Now each explosion came quicker than the last. Each detonation. That much closer. The sound and the vibration growing louder and stronger. More and more soldiers were falling and dying everywhere. It was blast followed by death. Another blast! Then death! Loudness! Then death! Chaos! Then death!

Suddenly, this scene faded into the distance. A low, slow rustling sound which daylight revealed to be a gentle stream trickling through a wooded mountain pass in the Appalachians of North Carolina. Birds were whistling. A cool wind blew. The air was fresh and clean. The smoke and noise of battle had passed. A green shiny spring maple leaf fell from the upper branches of a hardwood standing on a mild sloping bank at the river's edge. Almost in slow motion, it drifted down to and fro gently landing on the current below. The leaf floated around the rocks and the gentle rapids of the stream's clear shallow bed. Peering up from the waterway, a hill of luxurious Kentucky bluegrass, which at its apex stood a magnificent chestnut oak spreading its canopy of leaves shimmering in the breeze of an early April wind. Out in front of the tree . . . the figure of an enchantress. A siren. Flowing long black hair, a long white gossamer-like dress blowing in the cool morning breeze, one hand drawn to her brow as she shaded her eyes from the cloudless sunlit sky scanning intently for something or someone down toward the river's edge.

Stumbling up a stony path—slipping and falling but looking to see who she was. Struggling to make it up, now in slow motion. Desperate to see. But no, she was turning away. Heading back over the hill. Climbing harder. "Wait! Wait! Don't go!"

A voice was calling back from just over the hill, "Wade, Wade," it echoed hauntingly bouncing from one mountain wall to the next. Repeating his name again and again. Jerking himself into consciousness, Wade awoke startled. Angie, who had left the trailer earlier, was sitting on the side of his bed. Softly she stroked his hair and head as Wade struggled to come to his senses.

"You were moaning and groaning. What on earth were you dreaming about?"

"I don't really know. It was crazy. One minute I was fighting a major battle in one of the World Wars, the next some girl on top of a hill was calling out my name."

"That girl better have been me, sucker," Angie said feigning indignation.

"I don't know who she was," Wade said with a heavy sigh. "The whole thing was insane."

"You don't know? You better know, buster. If it wasn't me up on that hill, then you better kick her big fat butt out of your next dream. You got that?"

Wade chuckled at Angie's jealous nature. "Yeah. Yeah. What time is it anyway?"

"Almost eleven," Angie responded.

"Good gosh. You let me sleep this late." Sitting upright, he was surprised at how long he had been in bed this Saturday morning.

Playfully Angie climbed onto his lap and pushed his shoulders back down to the mattress. She smiled at him provocatively. "Are you so sure you want to get up just yet?"

Wade grinned in anticipation.

"What'd you have in mind?"

"You weren't teasing me when we talked about getting married last night, now were you?"

After months of practically living with one another and enjoying each other's company, Wade at Angie's request had discussed this possibility the prior evening. "Why would you think I was teasing you, Angie?"

"Then it's true?" She asked more seriously.

"Don't you want it to kind of be like a surprise maybe?"

"No," she cheerily replied. "But that probably would be a lot of fun."

Wade looked up into her alluring green eyes. Beaming, she smiled back down at him.

II

Across town, Ann spent her Saturday morning at the grocery store. Usually, she and Angie went together to do this chore, but since Angie hadn't arrived on time, she went by herself. Buying what was needed for the week, she drove over to Charles's apartment to see what he was doing.

The relationship that resulted from Ann going off with this classmate at the concert had been good for her. Charles was an English major and was going to start law school at Georgia in the fall. However, that was not why Ann was interested in him. He was thoughtful and fun-loving like Laney, but he was only two miles away from her apartment, a factor that made for a much better relationship or so it appeared. Around 11:00, Ann made it back home with her groceries. Standing outside her suite with two large sacks of food, she could hear the telephone inside ringing relentlessly. She tried unlocking the door quickly to answer it but failed to get to the phone before it stopped. If it was something important, they would call her back, she thought. She continued bringing her groceries into the kitchen to be put away.

Ann heard the phone ringing again; she crossed the room to answer it. It was Les' mom.

"Hello? Hey, Mrs. Ellis. How have you been doing? No, I hadn't heard. What's going on?" Stunned, Ann's face grew pale. "Oh my God. When did it happen? … Last night. I can hardly believe this." Tears started streaming down Ann's cheeks. "Yes, ma'am. Me too. Are there any more details? … I see. Okay, I'll do that. I'm so sorry this has happened, Mrs. Ellis. Thank you for calling me … I will."

Placing the phone gently back into its cradle, she paused sighing deeply in heartbroken silence. She stared into space lost deep in thought about what she had just heard. Picking up the receiver once more, she dialed the number to Wade's trailer. The phone rang several times before Angie answered it.

"Hello?"

"Angie, can I speak to Wade please?"

"Sure. Did you go to the grocery store this morning?" Angie was still bubbling and upbeat from Wade telling her in so many words that he would marry her. Now hyper and not waiting for Ann to reply, she asserted, "I went by the apartment on the way to wash clothes, but I must have missed you."

"Yeah," Ann responded impatiently.

Angie rattled on, "You've gotten them the last two times by yourself. I'm so sorry. Just let me know how much I owe you and I'll get them the next time myself, okay?"

"It was no problem, Angie," Ann said becoming more assertive. "Now let me speak to Wade, okay?"

Detecting a serious tone in her roommate's voice, Angie asked if everything was all right.

"No. Not really. I've got something that I need to talk to Wade about. Something he needs to know."

"Is it anything that I can help with?"

"Angie. Please." She paused. "Put Wade on the phone, will ya'?"

Miffed by Ann's attitude, Angie called across the den to where Wade was seated on the sofa reading the Saturday paper. "It's for you," she said, holding the receiver as far away from her body as possible.

Wade stood and reached for the phone. As Angie handed it to him, she left the room noticeably mad. Bemused at his girlfriend's attitude, Wade answered, "Hello? Oh, it's you, Ann. What's going on?" Ann began to speak and as Wade listened his entire being grew downcast. Despair showed instantly in his eyes and face. Forlorn and depressed, he was not one who could easily hide his emotions. "When did it happen?" he asked.

Ann told him that it must have happened last night.

"Damn," Wade said pausing in thought. "She was supposed to get in touch with me about a week ago. Actually, right before Les' wedding, she called me and said that she wanted to talk to me about something important. I asked her what was on her mind, but she told me she couldn't talk to me over the phone about it. She needed to see me in person."

"Did you get to talk to her?" Ann asked.

"No. I didn't get to see her. Something came up. Anyway, I called her back and told her we could get together at Les and Louisa's wedding, but she said she wasn't going to be able to make it. Obvious reasons if you know what I mean. Then we tried again to get together about a week ago, and damn if my finance professor didn't move our test up, and I had to call off our meeting again. Whatever it was that was upsetting her so must have been bad. Real bad. She still didn't want to tell me over the phone. I swore to her that we would get together after my test, but when I tried to call her back, I couldn't reach her."

Wade paused, guilt-ridden by the thought of missing the meeting with the girl. "Good Lord, Ann. Had I just got to hear her out maybe this wouldn't have happened. Damn it! I can't believe what you are telling me is true. Surely this couldn't have happened."

Ann responded to his comments assuring him that it was not his fault. She asked when Karl and Terrie quit seeing each other and if that might have caused the suicide.

"I don't know, Ann," Wade paused to think. "They had been broken up for maybe eight to ten months. I'm not really sure. If it was even close to a year, you'd have thought that she would have gotten over him by now. Did they say when the funeral would be?"

Ann told him it would be the following Friday. "Wow. That's almost a week away."

Ann told him it was so some relatives from out in California could make it over. She asked Wade if he wanted to ride home with her to attend it.

"Sure. I'll get with you later on about when we'll leave and all. Thanks for calling me, Kitten." He paused for a long moment.

"We just never know, do we?"

Wade hung up the phone and sat down in one of the big upholstered chairs in the room. Burying his face in his hands, he rubbed his eyes and thought of why he couldn't have managed to get together with Terrie in the months since she had first called him. Where had she been over the summer, and why hadn't she been able to contact him more often this quarter? It was almost as if destiny or someone had kept her from getting in touch with him.

Angie was sitting on Wade's bed pretending to read a book as Ann and Wade talked. Hearing every word Wade said, she still did not know what was happening. What she did know was that it was another girl and that she had obviously died. What she also knew was Wade was extremely upset concerning her death. Angie went into the small den area and sat down on the sofa across from where Wade was sitting. Silently she waited for Wade to tell her what had happened.

Wade, as if in a trance, looked up at her. Knowing she was waiting to hear what this call had been about, he said, "I'm sorry, Angie. A good friend of mine killed herself with an overdose of sleeping pills last night."

"Oh my God, Wade. I'm so sorry. Who was she?"

"You remember my friend Karl at Les and Louisa's wedding?"

"I think so," she paused reflecting.

"Didn't you and he leave the motel to go get something from Les' house at the dinner that night?"

"Oh, yeah, Karl. I remember him now," Angie said tentatively as she glanced at the ceiling. "Was it someone kin to him?"

"Karl's girlfriend, Terrie. Make that his former girlfriend. They quit dating a while back."

"What do you think made her do it? Do you think Karl breaking up with her did it?"

"I don't know," Wade responded dispirited. "It's been close to a year, so I doubt it. I guess I hadn't told you too much about Karl or Terrie, for that matter. You remember you and Ann stayed at his dad's beach house for the Georgia-Florida game that time down at Fernandina. He and Terrie were supposed to come down to the ballgame, but they didn't for some reason. I always thought that was strange. After all, it was his house." Wade rubbed his brow thinking of the couple and wondering what had transpired between the two. He continued. "They quit dating around then, got back together for a while, then broke it off for good, or so it seemed."

Angie listened intently as Wade spoke.

"At any rate, Karl grew up in our neighborhood. I mean, you've probably heard me tell stories of some of the crazy things he did, and all that, but since he's been at college, well, me and Les—we haven't had much contact with him. He just kind of went his way and we went ours. He was actually supposed to come to Athens this coming weekend for a frat party. I heard that from one of his former fraternity brothers who is in my accounting class. I imagine with Terrie dying that he'll head home to the funeral . . . Anyway, Karl, Terrie, and I and some of my girlfriends use to double date back in high school. Karl could be pretty mean to Terrie, and he was constantly breaking up with her. Any time they would have a fight, Terrie would come running to me to be consoled. She had been going to school up here with Karl until Karl went to Duke. Like I said, close to a year ago they stopped dating. But what was strange, well, maybe not so strange after all, is that she wanted to talk to me. I guess it was strange that she wanted to talk to me about something right before she did this. *Right before she killed herself*, he thought. He felt a great deal of blame. "She called me two or three times starting at the end of spring quarter. I don't know where she was this past summer. Her last call to me was about a week ago. You hadn't gotten any calls out here from some unknown girl while I was at class or anything have you?"

Angie rubbed her nose as she picked up a magazine lying on the sofa and started thumbing through it. "No. I've never had a call from another girl out here before. I would have let you know about it if I had, though."

Wade rubbed the back of his head stretching his neck and sighed. "She was such a special person, and such a good friend. It's hard to believe that someone like her could ever kill herself. She had so much to live for."

"I bet she was a pretty girl with a boyfriend like Karl," Angie remarked. Angie thought Karl was quite the hunk.

"She was a red-headed knockout. Very attractive. But maybe just a little fragile." As Wade responded, his eyes seemed to fog over as he thought of her and how he could have or should have done things differently. The following week went by with Terrie's death casting a sad pall over everything. Wade and Ann couldn't get together to leave Athens at the same time, so each took their own vehicle. Angie decided not to go as she had a major test first thing Monday morning.

In Texas, Les heard the bad news concerning Terrie too. At first, he was going to fly back for the funeral alone. Realizing Louisa didn't know Terrie that well, he thought she probably wouldn't be interested in going with him. When she found out that Angie wouldn't be going either and was staying in Athens, she decided to fly back with Les and give her old roommate a visit. On Thursday morning, Les and Louisa landed in Atlanta at the Hartsfield airport. After visiting with Les' parents for a short period, the couple showered, got dressed, and headed for the funeral home's chapel for the visitation. They found themselves in the slow, quiet procession of broken-hearted friends and relatives.

The line was long; many people came to pay their last respects. After twenty minutes, they were, at last, signing the funeral guest book and only moments away from seeing Terrie. Reverently, they walked into the room where she lay. The smell and sight of dozens of fresh-cut flower arrangements blanketed the chamber. Across the room, they saw Ann and Wade. Both had tears in their eyes as they hugged Terrie's parents.

With a lump in his throat, Les made it to the side of the casket and peered down at the face of his friend. How ravishing she was even in death. The long sandy red hair, and those lovely lips that had cast such mesmerizing smiles at so many people, her facial features were still exquisite. Les paused staring at her as Louisa courteously backed off to one side. *How could such a wonderful human being end her life this way*, he thought. Something surely had gotten to her, had made her feel that there was no hope, no other way out. If only he could have helped her. That was Les' business now: hope through love, forgiveness, and salvation. A tear slid down his cheek and fell onto Terrie's as he bent over to gaze at his beautiful friend one last time.

The next morning, they went to the funeral which lasted about an hour. There were many young people in attendance. Classmates and people whose lives she had touched came from near and far. The graveside service was short. Afterward, Ann, Les, Louisa, and Wade drifted through the tombstones and slab markers to Wade's car. The four left the cemetery and headed back across town to Les' home. They all gathered around the kitchen table.

Les started the conversation. "I saw Karl standing by himself at the graveside service. Did anyone else get a chance to see or talk to him?"

"I saw him," Wade remarked. "He nodded his head that he saw me, but I couldn't locate him after the service was over."

"I'm surprised the jerk even showed up," Ann quipped disgusted by Karl's poor treatment of Terrie.

"Well, you can't blame everything on Karl," Les replied. "They broke up a pretty good while back, didn't they?"

Wade glanced at Les, "Ann and I figured somewhere around ten months or so ago."

"Yeah," Ann interjected. "I also heard that she had an abortion a couple of years back when she first got to Athens to be with him. Les, don't you remember us talking about that over at my apartment way back when? You heard the same thing from one of his fraternity brothers. You remember how the guy had bragged that Karl's dad had arranged for an abortion for someone Karl had gotten pregnant?"

"Yeah, I remember that," Les said, sadly shaking his head.

Wade responded, "I don't know about any abortion. It's possible, I suppose. Her parents told me that she had stayed out in California with relatives this past summer. She had been depressed, and they thought it might do her some good to get away from here. All I know is that I wish I could have seen her and talked to her just one more time. Maybe I could have prevented this from happening. I don't know." The guilt from what had happened was killing Wade which no one except maybe Ann realized. The agony of not making that connection with his dear friend in time circulated over and over in his mind.

Louisa was unusually quiet as she listened to the others discussing the possible cause of Terrie's death. She couldn't help but think that what had happened at Fernandina may have been the precursor to this event.

The group came out of its funk when the discussion soon turned into the direction each of them would take going forward. Ann told them she was going to teach eleventh grade English in Jefferson which was just outside Athens, when she finished graduate school at the end of the year. Wade told them he would probably be marrying Angie. They had discussed the idea recently, and he would try finding a job in the Atlanta area once he graduated. As for Les and Louisa, they told their friends that they were going to be missionaries and would be going to Brazil for the next couple of years to a mission near Fonte Boa along the Amazon River.

III

Louisa planned to take Wade's car and head to Athens early the next morning. She prepared for the drive up to her old apartment to give her ex-roommate Angie a surprise visit. After hearing about Wade's plans to marry Angie, even though he hadn't given her a ring yet, Louisa was more than excited to get the chance to see her friend. Wade, meanwhile, would catch a ride with Ann and return the following day. *What a wonderful secret*, Louisa thought. To know about it and to keep it from her good pal would be fun. What a remarkable turn of events, she smiled, thinking that less than a year ago the couple wasn't even talking to each other.

The next morning at 6:00 a.m. sharp Louisa was packed and ready to go. With a kiss, she left Les behind and headed toward Interstate 75. It had been a while since she had taken this trip to Athens and the ride up proved both nostalgic and refreshing. As much as Louisa had learned to love Texas, Georgia was still her home. Once she made it to Forsyth, she got off the interstate and headed northeast on Highway 83, which eventually wove its way through the rolling hills and lowland creeks of the Oconee National Forest. Like a Van Gogh painting, the fall leaf colors of bright orange, yellow, and red permeated the shimmering forest surrounding her. Soon, she found herself at Monticello. She drove around the town's square and continued on to Madison noticing the beautiful antebellum homes surrounding the small municipality. Making her way to the outskirts of Athens, she took a hard left toward Five Points, a central landmark of the city.

Athens, for Louisa like other returning students, was a home away from home. It was a place without parental supervision where you made your own decisions. You made friends, made your own fun, and unfortunately, made your own mistakes. These thoughts and memories ran through Louisa's mind as she went through town and headed to her old Sussex apartment. Even though she was content, there was one intrusive thought that preoccupied her mind. A thought she did not want to harbor, but it was there all the same. As the turn to her apartment complex approached, she did not stop. Down the Atlanta Highway she continued. *Just once more*, she thought, *just one more trip out to see Wade's trailer.*

When she arrived and parked in the small driveway to his residence, thoughts and feelings of all the good times she had at the place and with Wade overcame her. Turning off her car, she sighed heavily. It all appeared the same. Nothing seemed to have changed. There had been many times in the past that she had stopped and looked at that door wondering whether she should go in or not. All the things that had happened here poured through her mind: the dancing classes, studying together, consoling one another. At first, she had a tremendous feeling of uncertainty about coming back to this place. Smiling it off, she knew without a doubt, she was now married and deeply in love with her husband. She thought of the sweetness of those times as she cranked her car and backed out of the driveway headed down the road for Sussex.

It was only a five-minute drive from Wade's place to her old apartment. How convenient for Angie and her soon-to-be husband. Pleased at the thought, Louisa hoped that marriage for Angie and Wade would be as wonderful as it was starting to be for Les and her. Going up to the door, she pushed the doorbell but realized it was not ringing inside. You could always hear the doorbell ringing from outside, so Louisa guessed it was broken. She knocked on the door, but Angie did not answer. Leaning backward she could see Angie's car in the parking lot, so she knew her old roommate had to be there. In a moment of enlightenment, Louisa thought to check her key ring. She didn't remember giving her old roommates her key back, and unbelievably it was still there. It was 10:00 a.m. Louisa slipped the key into the lock and opened the door. She figured Angie, for some reason, must have still been sleeping.

From the back of the apartment, as she entered the doorway, she could hear a shower running. Feeling nervous, she hoped that her friends hadn't moved and that she was in someone else's apartment. Relieved, she recognized some of Ann's and Angie's things and headed to the back bathroom to surprise her friend. As she approached the door to the room, she heard two people talking and laughing from inside. Startled, she thought it best to turn around and leave as she was uncertain what was going on. As she did so, the bathroom door swung open and to her astonishment and theirs, she saw the two of them standing before her. Grinning with a towel wrapped around his waist and in total shock with a towel tucked around her body stood Karl and Angie. There was a long awkward moment of silence as they stared at each other. Angie quickly hung her head in shame. As she did so, Louisa left the room and the building.

CHAPTER 14

The Mission Trip

1976

The next few years brought many new developments in the lives of the friends from Georgia. Les and Louisa headed to the Amazon basin of Brazil where they took the Word of God and the Message of Jesus' Salvation to the unknown tribes of the river's jungle. Ann started teaching English at Jefferson High School as she had planned and became engaged to Charles who had been accepted into the University of Georgia's School of Law. As for Wade and Angie, they got married after their graduation in the spring of 1976. No one knew about Angie's indiscretion except her roommate, and it was a relief for the girl that both Louisa and her husband were far, far away in South America and had not been able to attend the affair.

Les and his wife had started their mission work by crisscrossing through the Amazonas and Loreto regions of the Amazon River in Brazil and Peru, respectively. While there, they ministered to the needs of the territory's indigenous peoples. They were the area's health administrators in charge of providing food and medicine when needed. They were the teachers of the young and old at the schools they created. Most importantly, they were the spiritual leaders at the missions they built.

It was hot, tiring work. The humidity alone was excruciating with the average annual rainfall around eighty inches and the tropical temperatures ranging from the low seventies to one-hundred-and-five degrees Fahrenheit. There was no so-called "wet" season; it seemed to them that it was almost always raining with precipitation occurring on average two hundred and twenty days out of each year. There was a high-water season, December through May, and a low water season, June through November, which in the Southern Hemisphere correlated to its summer and winter periods, respectively.

The remoteness of their locale and the tri-canopied river basin along the long winding waterway made it sometimes difficult for them to receive supplies or to communicate with the outside world. Considering they kept a short-range wireless radio with them, they often discovered themselves out of range, cut off, and on their own.

Spanish, they found, was the most common language spoken in these regions. Though they were both proficient in its use, sometimes this form of communication was even lacking. Delving deep into the flooded rainforest in search of wary primitive tribes, they often encountered strange and unique languages known only to the natives of that region. Languages that, until such contact was made, had never been heard by Westerners.

The tallest indigenous man they had come upon in their travels stood merely five-feet-six-inches while most of the inhabitants were much smaller in stature. For once in Les' life, he wasn't the shortest man around. Both he and Louisa got a good kick out of this unexpected discovery.

Being isolated in the vast remoteness of a river jungle could be overwhelming at times for the two missionaries. The blessing that kept them encouraged was when a shipment of supplies arrived. These came either from an airplane or by a small mission riverboat both of which came from Manaus delivering their provisions alternating on a bi-weekly basis.

A Christian mission's program in the United States financed both the plane and vessel deliveries, the list of inventories needed and their destination being per Les' instructions. If his supplies came by river, he would send the next list of provisions and directions back to the home base in Manaus via the boat's captain. If it came by air, he would have his guides flag down a passing motorized boat to ferry them back to his headquarters. Supplying the missionaries in this manner was not foolproof. The method that worked best was when Les utilized the Amazon River itself or one of its primary tributaries as a drop off site. It became trickier when he and Louisa made their way deeper into the woods. The sheer vastness of the Amazon basin along with a plethora of logistical obstacles made such deliveries problematic.

Besides the issues of resupplying, the missionaries had other dangers to confront. Probably the most threatening of these were cultural misunderstandings. Many of the more uncivilized peoples they encountered had never before seen whites from the outside world. Making this circumstance even more perilous was those who had often witnessed their relatives and fellow tribesman being hurt or killed by such intruders. If not seen firsthand, they had at least heard stories.

There were also territorial disputes occurring between the tribes in these areas often resulting in death. Even missionaries had been killed doing religious work along the Amazon as recently as the past decade because they had crossed the border of a warrior-like tribe. The prospect of being harmed never deterred Les or Louisa from moving forward in their efforts to meet and help as many people as they could. They did, however, lose their naiveté concerning those they thought they could trust. On more than one occasion, a member of their flock would wander back into the wild to attack another tribe. As was the norm, the other group had harmed this individual's clan in some way. The tribe's warriors, in their need for support, would contact the individual living at the mission to help them carry out a raid of retaliation.

Les spent many sermons addressing this matter by preaching forgiveness and loving one another. It was a tough sell for most of these people at first; an eye for an eye and a tooth for a tooth had been their way of life for thousands of years. Through his example of administering to the sick, feeding the hungry, and giving shelter to those of any tribe, soon the people began to understand what Les was trying to teach them.

In light of the many hardships Les and Louisa faced, such work took extraordinary people of faith and courage. Unlike the citizens of a civilized society who sit in the safe comfort of their homes and watch from afar, the missionary's life often hangs in the balance. The balance of good versus evil, of having food or going hungry, of being sick or well, and ultimately of being alive or dead. The routine of their life can change in a moment. It demands they be up close and personal with every aspect of life imaginable. Circumstances for a missionary don't always work out, and sometimes, even for the most faithful, the ultimate price is paid.

II

It was May 1980 and getting close to the end of the high-water season although a thunderstorm always seemed to linger in the atmosphere. Les and Louisa had become more acclimated to the harshness of this environment while living along the river for almost four years. Over this period of time a number of missionaries and medical staff from all over the world had come to serve and help the pair with their mission work. One young man from Baltimore, Maryland, found out what Les and Louisa were doing along the Amazon from the pastor of his church. Like many seeking adventure and an enlightening experience, he volunteered to help the couple. Traveling first by jet to the Atlantic coastal city Fortaleza, Brazil, John hopped a smaller plane to Manaus, the largest of Brazil's cities on the Amazon. He was fascinated by the uniqueness of the people and the immensity of the tropical rainforest. It wasn't until he boarded the riverboat at Manaus for his trip upriver to Fonte Boa that he discovered some of his luggage was missing. It contained medications his physician sent with him to ward off various infections. The most important of these was his preventative against malaria. Distraught, John headed for the boat's bridge to find the captain. Locating him, he asked, "Señor, I have lost my anti-malarial drug. Would you happen to have some I could buy?"

The boat's owner spoke a little English. Grinning, he shook his head. "Look around tis boat, mi amigo. I have twice as many passenger on board as I suppose to allow. I most hardly can contain them. Cannot supply medicine, you know."

John noticed the congestion of people on each of the vessel's three decks. With their cluster of family members, pets, and baggage along with the boat's load of cargo, there was hardly room to turn around. "Yes, I see we're jam packed in here. Do you think anyone on board might have some of these medicines?"

The officer gave the young American a more serious look. "You can ask, mi amigo, but most here from local villages, sí? They not worry about such things." He continued, "We soon come Aquas Negras y Blancas! The black an white waters of de rivers meet, but no join. Nutting like dis anywhere in world. Come to rail where you can see. All de travelers come to see dis."

Discouraged by his circumstance but grateful for the officer's attempt at lifting his spirits, the young man nodded that he would look for whatever this was. Before leaving, he asked, "Say, how long will it take us to get to Fonte Boa?"

Steering, the boat owner replied, "About three, four days. Probably more to four, sí?"

The new missionary, trying to hide the fear concerning his exposure for this amount of time, acknowledged the man then turned and climbed back down the stairs to the second deck where he had placed his luggage. As the riverboat headed upstream, it crossed over one of the world's true aquatic anomalies: the confluence of the Rio Negro and Solimoes Rivers—Aguas Negras y Blancas—the black and white waters. Just as the Captain had said, the passengers could see a line of separation where the two mighty rivers met but did not mix. For newcomers to the Amazon, this was fascinating, but not for John. Just as his trip was getting started, he had become almost obsessed entirely, panic-ridden that he was going to catch malaria.

John was beginning to understand that he would have to tough out this perilous journey the best he could. Through the sweltering heat, the rain, the unsanitary accommodations onboard, and the constant buzzing and biting of mosquitoes and flies, all of the plagues of which he'd been forewarned; he realized this trip would entail all he could endure. After two unexpected and prolonged stops for the captain to work on the boat engines, the exhausted young man finally made it to Fonte Boa. He was almost certain he had contracted the dreaded disease.

Locating him on the dock sitting on his duffel bag slumped over, Louisa was shocked by his demeanor. "John?" she called out as he turned toward her staring blankly. "Are you all right?"

Speaking softly, he responded, "Miss Louisa?"

"Yes," she affirmed. "You look like you've had a rough trip down."

"I have. Some of my luggage was lost in Manaus, and it had my antimalarial drugs in it."

Louisa could easily see his anxiety. Checking his temperature, she placed her hand on his forehead then clasped her hands on each of his cheeks.

Smiling at him, she said, "Well, you don't have any fever." Pulling his cheeks down to examine the sclera of both eyes, she said, "No jaundice in your eyes or skin. You're okay." Louisa knew that such symptoms wouldn't surface for at least nine to fourteen days, but her new missionary needed peace of mind.

John perked up. "Are you sure? Are you a doctor?"

"No," Louisa responded, "but I've seen my share of cases living here for four years, and I definitely know the symptoms. When we get back to our base camp, we'll get you a supply of the preventative. Are you ready to go?" Nodding, he stood up, gathered his gear, and followed Louisa to the small, motorized rental boat where Les was waiting for them. When they arrived at the mission, Louisa immediately made her way to the nurse's tent. She found out that the camp had no drugs to spare. It seemed that for some reason they had been omitted from the last supply drop. Knowing John was concerned, she let him have her ration of pills. Louisa had done this before for other new arrivals. She knew an airdrop with more drugs was imminent and didn't give the decision a second thought.

The week passed, and the young Marylander became more adjusted to his new surroundings. Les took note of an unforeseen problem. From a nearby village's broadcast, he was told via his short-wave wireless that an ominous weather event was occurring west of their mission. Unusually heavy rains for this time of year in the Loreto region of Peru had resulted in widespread flooding upriver at Iquitos and floodwaters were now heading rapidly in their direction. Finding Louisa with a group of women cutting up tomatoes, onions, chilis, and fish to grill in banana leaves for their evening meal of patarashca, Les interrupted them. Signaling for Louisa to step aside, he spoke in a whisper to avoid alarming the others. "A bad flood's coming our way, Louis'. We've got to move inland as soon as possible and find higher ground for our camp."

"How much time do we have?" Louisa asked concerned.

"I'm afraid not much. They're telling me the river's already starting to rise just above Leticia. It'll be churning through Tonantins then down on to us by early morning, I suspect."

Noticing the couple talking, John walked up. "What can I do to help out tonight, guys?" he remarked.

Les finished telling Louisa what she and the women needed to do before turning his attention to the new mission worker. "We've got serious flood waters heading our way, John." Les started walking as his recruit followed. "I want you to get with Mico when I find him and help get everything and everybody loaded into the boats to head upstream to higher ground. This area will be several feet underwater by morning."

Sensing the urgency in Les' voice, John gave him an astonished look.

Smiling at his new acquaintance's reaction, Les continued talking as they walked.

"Things aren't always Kumbaya peaceful out here, bud. Sometimes things can change in an instant—just like right now." Spotting his native pal, Les said, "There's Mico breaking down tents over there. He knows what's going on. I want you to give him a hand. He speaks English poorly and is just a little bit better with Spanish, but you'll understand what he wants you to do."

For John, this rushed move upstream was unnerving, but for the river's natives and local villagers staying at the camp, it was standard protocol. Moving their entire mission further up the tributary from where it had been situated, they were able to find higher, safer ground to construct their new residence.

Everything seemed to be in place. It didn't take long though until Maria, a mission nun, found that they had lost one of their most precious assets. Somewhere along the river between encampments, the batteries for their shortwave radio disappeared.

This news was disconcerting to Les. The radio was the mission's only tie to the outside world and the only way they had to relay their messages downriver to their headquarters at Manaus. Their next shipment could be in jeopardy. With no radio signal for the pilot to home in on, they had no way of guiding the aircraft to their location. Their vague backup plan involved only the use of maps and visuals. With the oncoming floodwaters pouring down toward them from the world's mightiest river, locating them was going to be a difficult task, to say the least, even for the most seasoned pilot.

The following day, with the weather heading north and away from the proposed drop off site, the Cessna took off from the runway at Manaus right on schedule. The pilot, using a similar sectional aeronautical chart Les had plotted and sent to him earlier, picked the appropriate radial's direction and headed his plane toward his destination. Oblivious to the missionaries' plight, he had no way of knowing that this shipment's target was of little value to him now.

The plan was simple; it was the same one that they had used many times before. Knowing his bearing and the approximate distance of his trip, the pilot would arrive in the general area listening for Les' radio signal. Homing in on this transmission and using a visual as a point of reference, in this case, a large treeless island, he would then find the missionaries paddling below and make his drop.

The skies were clear and the weather conditions perfect for flying. When the plane got to its objective only the chaos of flooding water pouring through a green maze of trees could be seen from above. Unable to distinguish any significant landmarks that Les had described in his instructions and with no radio signal coming from the missionaries to guide him, the pilot headed south back to the primary run of the Amazon River. Looking at his aeronautical charts, noting distances and angles, he quickly calculated, once more, where Les had instructed him to make his drop. Flying back into the area again, the pilot called out via his short-wave radio. "Les Mission Base this is Cessna Papa Papa 769. Can you read me?" Nothing but static on the receiver. Again, the airman called out, "Les Mission Base this is Cessna Papa Papa 769 can you read me?" Still, no response. Noting this unusual circumstance, the pilot tried giving Les his course in the sky above them. "Les Mission Base. This is Papa Papa 769 at two thousand feet. Heading three one zero searching for island drop site. Can you read me?"

No communication was heard.

Looking at his copilot, the airman said, "We will circle a few more times and see if we can spot them. Okay?" Giving a concerned sigh, the copilot nodded in agreement. Considering the amount of fuel required for their return flight, the aviator and his navigator flew several passes over the region where they thought Les had designated their delivery. Seeing no sign of either the island below them or the missionaries paddling their canoes, they decided to try making their drop onto the closest dry land according to Les' shipment instructions. "Les Mission Base. This is Cessna Papa Papa 769. Heading zero eight five. Have ejected cargo via parachute at approximate drop site. Returning to Manaus." Even though the pilot tried as hard as he could to get the chute to float down onto an open area of dry land, he couldn't determine if it had. Knowing his load could easily snare itself in a treetop or sink into the waters' depths, he had made his best effort.

Les took a group of Ticunas traveling in dugouts to the proposed drop's location. They did not make it to the spot before the plane's arrival. At one point, Les and his men thought they heard the faint buzz of an aircraft in the distance, but it was only for a few seconds.

As they paddled around the jungle to the drop site, they found that the rapidly rising floodwaters obscured even their own ability to recognize the spot—the large treeless island. Finding it completely submerged, they saw how hard it would be for the pilot to locate. They hoped he had at least been able to land their shipment close to the vicinity. Splitting into separate groups, they searched the area rigorously for the better part of two days. Finding nothing, they headed back to their base camp.

Every delivery made was important not only for the missionaries themselves but also for the local people they served. There were common medical issues Les knew he would encounter at each new location. Most of these dealt with wound care when someone had been hurt or bitten. Sometimes they dealt with dental problems where they had to fill or extract a tooth. Less frequently, it would be an unexpected issue like a fever going through a village making many people sick. Children were hit especially hard when such illnesses occurred as they were much more prone to die as a consequence of such outbreaks.

Arriving back at the mission without their supplies, Les and his crewmates were disappointed and exhausted. It would be almost two more weeks before another shipment arrived. Les knew this next delivery was guaranteed. It would get to them via boat. After finally getting through to Manaus about their lost shipment, Les was certain that on their next delivery his team's much needed medical supplies would also be included. Being more confident in their re-supply and seeing everything was going well at his base camp, he decided to take an expedition north up an unknown river tributary. Going deeper into the jungle than normal, he was hoping to make contact with some of the more elusive nomadic tribes. He was looking for the Yuhups who were native to this region.

Accompanied by three Ticunas, one Yagua, and the young Marylander, Les set out from the base camp. Everyone else including Laura, the mission's nurse from Texas; Maria, a nun from Spain; two male missionaries from Brazil, and Louisa would stay behind to take care of the mission's thirty or so inhabitants.

For more than two weeks Les and his party traveled the waterways and sloughs of an unmapped region of rainforest close to where the foggy border of Brazil and Columbia intersected. However, the closest they ever came to making contact with the tribe was when they found a recently abandoned encampment complete with grass huts. Les, sure that they were under constant surveillance, left food and other gifts as peace offerings which might win the tribe over the next time they crossed paths. Without making any further contact with the natives of the area as he'd hoped, Les and his party discontinued their trek and headed back home.

It was late in the day when the expedition paddled around the final bend of their river journey. Spotted by a few of their members upstream, a small crowd began to gather on the tributary banks just below the mission's encampment to await their arrival. Unlike most other homecomings they had experienced in the past where the people cheered, waved palm fronds, and clapped upon seeing them—now a more somber group collected to meet them. Paddling their dugout canoes up and onto the silted shoreline, they disembarked. Les noticed Maria, the Spanish nun, signaling for him to come and follow her. Quickly the pair made their way across the small mission's compound of tents and thatched huts until they reached Laura in the nurse's tent.

Pulling back the fold to this hut's entrance, Maria motioned for Les to enter then followed him inside. The room's interior was almost black. After going from the light of the outdoors into the darkened room, it took several long seconds for Les' eyes to adjust. Lying on a grass pallet just inside the doorway was his groaning, struggling wife. Les knelt by Louisa's side. Placing the palm of his hand on her pitching forehead, he could feel she was burning up with a fever. Delirious, moaning, and continuously moving, she barely recognized her husband's presence as he took her hand and gently folded it between his. Trying to gain her attention by softly calling her name, he realized that she was in far too much pain and discomfort to respond. Alarmed, Les looked up toward the nun, "How long has she been like this, Maria?"

"Well, I noticed right after you left on your expedition, she started showing signs of fatigue. It's not like Louisa to be lacking energy, you know. A few days ago she started having a little fever. I saw her looking clammy and felt her head, but she shrugged it off as nothing to worry about. Last night she started this bad fever."

"Has she been taking her medication?" Les queried alluding to her anti-malarial drug.

"No," Laura, the mission's nurse, said. She adjusted the thin wool blanket covering Louisa's body. "She admitted to me a couple of days back before these symptoms started that she had given hers away to John, the new missionary, when he got here. She was probably counting on that airdrop for her re-supply."

Les' face grew tight as he winced at the thought of the lost cargo shipment.

"Has the boat from Manaus made it up here yet?"

"About five days ago. They left before Louisa started showing any signs of sickness." Pausing, Laura glanced up from covering Louisa with the blanket. "She told me that she did get a couple of days' worth of the drug in her after they came, but …" As her words faded, Les' worried look turned from the nurse back down toward his agonizing wife.

"You sure it's malaria, Laura?" Les was hoping to hear the possibility of it being something less serious.

"I don't think there's much doubt. You can look at her skin and eyes. She's pretty jaundiced."

He nodded his head in agreement.

"Her spleen is enlarged too. Those are the classic signs, Les. You've seen all this before." She paused looking up at him. "And besides, she's been throwing up a lot, sometimes with a little blood."

Les gave out a deep sigh. "Well, I know you've got her taking chloroquine, right? That should clear this up pretty quickly, wouldn't you think?"

"Yes. I would have thought that too. I got her started on it several days ago even before this fever broke out because of the way she was acting. We should be seeing some positive results by now, but as you can see, she's only getting worse."

"Well, then it's probably not malaria, Laura!" Les exclaimed speaking to the nurse more pointedly. "You've certainly got her on an antibiotic, I hope?"

Agitated by Les' outburst, Laura glared at him. "Matter of fact, I have, Les! She's taking doxycycline. But that's had no effect either. Maybe it's too soon to see any results. I don't know."

Les stared down at his suffering wife then back at the nurse once more. Puzzled and angry that the drugs weren't working quickly to solve the problem, he said in disbelief, "Chloroquine always works on malaria, Laura. I've never seen it not work. It's got to be something else that's mimicking those symptoms."

Laura paused a moment giving Les an even more serious look. In a more sobering tone, she said, "I think I might know what it is. I just hope I'm wrong."

Les' gaze weakened as he heard the nurse say this. Apprehensively he leaned away from her dreading to hear what she was about to say.

"I read an article in the *Lancet Medical Journal* right before I came down here last year that scientist discovered a more resistant form of malaria, one that's normally found in Africa or India. According to the World Health Organization, it's started showing up here—along the Amazon."

Les watched her cautiously as she continued.

"It's called p. falciparum, and it's almost totally resistant to chloroquine. It's a much more virulent species, Les. I think that's what we're dealing with here." Taking a dry cloth, she dipped it into a pan of cool, purified water by her side. Squeezing the excess liquid out, she wiped the perspiration from Louisa's tortured face and arms. She continued, "About all we can do for her is try to keep her fever under control and keep her hydrated. I'm going to start an I.V. containing some electrolytes on her in just a minute. I highly recommend that you figure a way to get her out of here and to a hospital as soon as possible." She paused momentarily to wring out the cloth once more. Gazing directly into Les' eyes, she said, "I would say that time is of the essence here, Les."

Les stared back at her startled knowing full well what she meant. Louisa would likely die if something wasn't done fast. Thanking Laura for tending to his wife, Les got up and left her tent. He made plans for Louisa's evacuation. Gathering up and talking to his best guides, it was quickly decided that four of the mission's strongest paddlers would take to the river immediately. Their plan to get help involved the use of two dugouts. After the boats made it down the tributary and out into the main channel of the Amazon, one pair of paddlers would head upstream toward Jara for a power boat while the men in the other canoe would head east and downstream in hopes of finding a river boat heading in their direction. In either case, the idea was to get Louisa upriver to the small port city of San Antonio de Ica, which was located thirty-five to forty miles west of Jara, the small community where Les, Louisa, and their crew would soon be heading. At Santo Antonio's small landing strip, they could fly her westward up to Iquitos where there was a larger plane. There they could continue their flight carrying her over the Andes Mountains and to the Peruvian coastal city of Lima to get her to a first-rate hospital.

The two Ticunas who went downstream were the first team to make contact with a rescue boat. Seeing a riverboat drifting in midstream, one of the mission's crew hailed the vessel as their canoe came alongside it. A village passenger onboard addressed the men.

"Hey, señors! What do you need?"

Carrying on the conversation in Spanish, the Ticuna replied, "We have very sick missionary lady. Need hospital. She dying right now! We must need boat to help carry."

The boat captain, a gruff and quite sizable man, appeared from below deck where he'd been working on the boat's stalled engine. Taking a large swig from a whiskey bottle he held in his hand, he called out loudly, drunkenly, "What do these shit-faced Indians say they want?" Staggering he gripped the boat's railing for support.

Fearful of the captain, the passenger on his boat tried gaining his sympathy. "They say there's a woman missionary sick and dying who needs to be taken to hospital—pronto."

Roaring with laughter the captain shouted, "She's probably as dead by now as my boat's engines, señors!"

The two Ticunas eyed each other as the captain railed on vociferously.

"I swear I would help you fellows! But I'm going nowhere! Just drifting back down the river! How about that, señors?"

He laughed as the two pushed away from the larger vessel. Fighting against time they had no use for the drunken man's foolishness. Into the darkness of the early evening, they paddled onward in hopes of intersecting another vessel. Little did they know that their search would become even more perilous. Two of the areas drug cartels were involved in a deadly battle that had dried up most of the traffic in this region. Normally, there would have been a multitude of vessels traveling the channel that could have given them help. When several dead bodies of men were found in their shot-up boat which had run aground close to the shore of a nearby village, the news of the horror spread rapidly.

As morning dawned, Les loaded Louisa and Laura into the center of their largest dugout canoe which was manned by two Indian guides. When the boat was supplied, the paddlers made their way down the slough toward the main run of the Amazon. Another dugout with an Indian in the front and Les in the stern had been filled with food, water, and supplies for their long journey. Les and his compatriot pushed off from the bank and began tailing the other boat. By midday and after laborious paddling, the two boats had yet to make it out of the winding tributary and into the main channel of the Amazon. The extra weight of Louisa, her nurse, and her supplies made the going much more difficult for the small but tenacious paddlers.

Les was confident that either his guides or a powerboat would meet their party by the end of the day. They finally made it to the primary run of the larger river as the sun started to set and sadly, neither of these two contingencies had occurred.

During the hard day's journey, the dugouts had pulled over to the bank only twice for bathroom breaks. On their second stop, Les, tired from paddling and fighting the current, stretched out his arms as he looked across the river that had grown to about two miles in width. Feeling like a helpless speck in the empty vastness surrounding him, he fell to his knees. "God!" he prayed aloud. "Guide us through this valley of death! Please don't forsake us, oh Lord! Keep us strong and faithful! Amen." As he meditated in prayer for a moment longer, all he could hear were moans coming from his writhing wife as she lay in the canoe only a few feet away.

At both stops, the nurse changed out her patient's IV bag as Louisa was almost incapable of swallowing anything given to her by mouth. Laura hoped she would not become dehydrated. As the two boats paddled onward with darkness fast approaching, Laura became even more alarmed at the rapid decline of Louisa's condition. She knew malaria was one of the more insidious infections one could contract. The culprit, a protozoan introduced from a mosquito bite, enters the liver and red blood cells. The result culminates in severe anemia, kidney failure, stroke, seizures, coma, or a combination of these maladies. In the case of p. falciparum, if not treated promptly and effectively it can ultimately result in death.

As Laura looked down at Louisa, she could see her patient's skin and eyes were becoming more yellow. Her fever was spiking, and her urine was dark red in color, a sign her kidneys were starting to shut down. This condition, above all the rest, had the nurse on edge. With each passing hour and with Louisa now losing her ability to communicate even in the slightest way, Laura felt sure that if she didn't make it to a hospital soon, they were certainly going to lose her.

No one even considered slowing down. In total darkness, Les and his team pulled their canoes over to the riverbank as they searched for suitable wood to make torches. Once they retrieved what they needed, they climbed back into their dugouts with their cressets lit and began paddling back upstream. It was unusual, Les thought as they paddled, to see the river so abandoned. There were no pequi-pequis, motorized canoes with extra-long drive shafts, no paddling dugouts, and no larger vessels like ferries or riverboats running up and down the river.

Hours passed as the group paddled onward in a methodical, determined rhythm. No one made a sound except for the moans coming from Louisa. Laura did what she could to comfort her as she went from freezing cold chills to burning hot sweats. Blankets and acetaminophen were all the nurse could use to reduce her patient's agony.

At about 10 p.m. the lead guide in Les' canoe stopped paddling and held his hand up for everyone to stop and listen. From farther up the river came the sound of a humming engine. Everyone heard it except for the tormented Louisa and a cheer went up from the group. Hopefully this was the boat from Jara or at least someone coming that could help. With newfound optimism, the group intensified their strokes picking up speed in the direction of what they hoped was the oncoming rescue craft. After fifteen more minutes of hard paddling, the lights of a motorized boat were seen making its way toward them through the moonless night.

The approaching boat had geared down to idling speed as it came floating nearby. On the bow of the open wooden outboard, Les could see through the darkness with his boat's flickering torches his most trusted friend Mico. Les had met this man, a Yagua native, several years before while traveling the river's upper tributaries just above Iquitos. Using antibiotics, Les and his group of missionaries had been able to save Mico's son from a bout of pneumonia. After this occurrence and with Mico understanding the reason for Les' presence on the Amazon, he converted to Christianity. From that point on this diminutive but powerfully built man, along with his wife and son, had followed Les and Louisa throughout their travels.

Mico, whose native language was difficult to understand, greeted the missionary rescuers using a mix of both Spanish and English. "Hey, Senior Les. I see Miss Louisa—she okay?"

"No, Mico. She's not. She's terribly ill. We must move quickly to get her to the airport and the hospital in Lima."

Mico's new friends from Jara boarded Louisa's boat as he continued to talk. "We find no help on river, Les. Fisherman tell us cocaina batalla happening all around our mission camp. Up and down river. Fisherman say people shot and killed. None of Jaras' know of batalla. We tell them of it. They are fearful. They come because it is you and Miss Louisa."

Les nodded and thanked the villagers who were making room for his wife in their boat. It was clear to Les why the waterway was barren. Death, he realized, could come to them in many ways. A drug smuggler's bullet could kill just as quickly as a terrible disease.

Mico broke Les' train of thought when he said they would have made it back sooner, but the village of Jara was in the middle of a small festival. Their catch of fish over the last several weeks, in spite of recent flooding, had been unusually large, and the town had taken this day off to celebrate their good fortune. According to Mico, it wasn't this festival that had slowed them down getting back to Louisa. As soon as Mico had made the townspeople aware of their dilemma and word spread concerning who was in distress, the entire village was eager to help regardless of being told about the drug-related killings. Les and Louisa were well known to those in this region of Brazil as they repeatedly had come to give aid when past disasters had struck.

Yet even as the town's inhabitants were more than ready to do whatever they could, they had one significant obstacle to confront. Due to the latest flood, they lost their only large gasoline tank. The village fishermen had nowhere to refuel their boats' outboard motors. All they had in the way of gas now was what was left in each of their boat's reservoirs.

Knowing Louisa and Les' approximate location from Mico's story, the Jara fishermen knew it was going to take a lot of fuel to retrieve the couple and get them back past their village and on up to the landing strip at San Antonio. Their new container tank and its re-supply of fuel coming from Manaus in the next couple of days would be of no consequence. All those involved were more than aware of the urgency of the missionary's plight and scrambled into action. The boat owners picked the largest, fastest, and most reliable boat they had for the job. They quickly started draining their boats' small gas tanks. Each boat owner poured his retrieved can of fuel into the larger boat's reservoir filling it.

The remaining vessel owners continued consolidating any fuel they had left into one large metal can. This gas would be needed by the craft in the second leg of its journey as the villagers carried the missionaries on up to San Antonio and its airstrip.

The large canoe's occupants helped place Louisa's near lifeless body into the rescue boat. Les and Laura climbed aboard. As soon as the outboard drifted clear of the other dugouts, the driver of the boat turned the gas handle to full throttle making the outboard engine growl into action. He maneuvered the boat clockwise as the craft spun back around from the direction they'd come leaving a churning, foaming, iridescent wake in its path.

Louisa's rescue vessel made only one stop before arriving at its destination. They stopped at Jara to refuel. At San Antonio de Ica, a small four-seat single engine aircraft waited to carry Les, his incapacitated wife, and Laura to the large city of Iquitos. From there Louisa was started on yet another I.V., this time one containing antibiotics. The remainder of the trip went off without a hitch. Soon Les and Louisa were heading high over the Andes Mountains via a DC-10.

Louisa was unresponsive and barely breathing when the plane arrived at the Peruvian capital of Lima. As they disembarked, Les and a medical team hurriedly got her into a waiting ambulance where she was rushed to the intensive care unit of Hospital Nacional Guillermo Almernara. Noting that Les was probably an American, the doctor in charge spoke in accented English. "Senõr? Is this your wife?"

"I can speak Spanish," Les responded. "Yes, she is my wife. We think she has malaria. We've had her on chloroquine and doxycycline for several days now."

A team of doctors and nurses drew blood and examined Louisa as the primary physician continued quizzing Les.

"I see she is jaundiced. How long has she been this way, and how long have you been in the country?"

"We've been traveling the Amazon for several years, Dr. … ?"

"Sanchez. Juan Sanchez."

"Dr. Sanchez, she has progressively gotten worse over the last several days. She ran out of her malaria preventative when we lost an airdrop a few weeks back. We are Christian missionaries. Our mission currently resides just west of Fonte Boa."

A medical resident interrupted Les and the doctor when she handed Dr. Sanchez a clipboard. The doctor became more serious.

"Your name, sir?"

"My name's Les."

"Les, your wife is very, very sick as you well know. We are going to take her immediately to I.C.U. and try to stabilize her. We will also run a test to decide treatment, and I will call you as soon as we find out. There are no waiting rooms near where she will be. There is a waiting room downstairs in the lobby. You can wait there if you would like."

Les gave the doctor an exhausted look.

Taking note, the physician said, "I promise I will call you as soon as we make an assessment. The nurse standing by the door will take your wife's information as well as yours."

Les nodded reluctantly. Sighing, he turned to the woman who was the medical attendant.

As had been previously recognized on the river by Laura, the doctors quickly surmised the gravity of Louisa's failing renal system. Working diligently trying to save Louisa's life, some of them began thinking like the mission's nurse that the culprit might well be the chloroquine-resistant strain p. falciparum, especially after hearing that the drug was unsuccessful in treating her. Having come to a consensus concerning the disease etiology, the team of doctors decided to try a new drug called Artemisinin. They knew little about the medication's safety or its efficacy, but all had heard of its use in such cases. They simply had no other choice but to try it.

As the second day progressed into night, little improvement seemed evident in Louisa's condition. As the third night approached, they had to awaken Les who was asleep on the floor down the hallway from the intensive care unit. Not having any sleep for almost three days and his hypoglycemia from diabetes kicking in, he had finally given in to fatigue.

Shaking him into consciousness, a nurse leaned over him.

"The doctors are calling for you at your wife's bedside, Mr. Ellis."

Vaguely realizing where he was, he looked into the nurse's eyes.

"Thank you. I'm on my way."

The worn-out young man slowly struggled to his feet. Regaining his balance and senses from a dreamlike state, he sluggishly made his way down the hallway toward Louisa's room. As he walked inside, hearing the loud beeping and whirring of the various machines attached to her, he could see the somber expressions on the faces of the physicians. Les looked down at his wife's face through the oxygen mask and the tube running down her nose. Seeing the yellowish pallor of Louisa's once beautiful olive complexion, he sighed heavily. With her eyes closed, the only fluctuation he saw on her swollen face was a faint erratic twitch, but there was nothing more.

Two doctors observed Les as he tenderly stroked his beloved wife's hair. The doctor who was most involved with Louisa's care, Dr. Sanchez, stepped forward and spoke softly. "Mr. Ellis … we're not giving her much hope now."

Les immediately looked back down at his wife. Through the stupor of fatigue gripping his body and mind, he tried hard to make sense of what he had just heard.

Again, seeing Les' confusion, the physician repeated himself.

"Mr. Ellis, do you understand? There is no hope for her now."

Suddenly from deep within the missionary an unanticipated spark ignited, the glow from it reaching out through every cell of his being. "Oh no, my friend," Les smiled at the doctor. "There's always hope." Holding his gaze for a moment more, he said, "No matter the outcome."

"We'll do all we can," the doctor said, bowing his head as both he and his partner turned to leave the room.

Les, still smiling, stepped forward and extended his hand toward the physician. Stopping the doctor unexpectedly, he said, "I know you will. You need a good night's rest." Patting the clinician on the shoulder, Les turned and went back to Louisa's bedside as the practitioner stood momentarily staring at him from the doorway. Amazed at the spirit emanating from the young husband, the doctor thought about what Les had just said, "no matter the outcome." Shaking his head, he and the other physician walked out into the hallway.

CHAPTER 15

Atlanta, Georgia

(*May* 1980)

Wade sat in the recliner of his den reading the *Atlanta Journal Constitution* when Angie came through the back door from a long day of teaching school. Hearing her place her book satchel on the kitchen table, Wade listened to her footsteps heading in his direction.

Lowering the paper, he saw her walking toward him with an already opened letter in one hand. Wade looked up at her curiously as she handed him the envelope which was addressed to him. A dour expression covered her face. Pulling the letter out, he could see it was a copy showing his most recent test scores from the C.P.A. exam. Once again and for the third time in three years, he barely failed the rigorous accounting test.

Without a word, Angie turned around, retrieved her satchel from the kitchen, and went to their bedroom closing the door behind her. Wade sighed in frustration as he heard the lock to the doorknob click and the large floor fan at the base of their bed start roaring. It was her way of drowning out his existence.

Moving to Atlanta after their wedding, Wade took a position at a small accounting firm. Angie insisted that he become a Certified Public Accountant. Like his father, she wanted Wade to earn a good living and wanted him to know that this was of the utmost importance now that they were married. His artwork, she obliquely alluded to, was just an aside, something he could do on weekends as a hobby if he had the time.

In the four years since their marriage, he had not once pulled out his art utensils. Not once had he set up his tripod or gone to a museum or an art shop to see the works of others or to buy paints or brushes for a special project. No, what he had done during this time was go to work each day and come home where he would continue studying hard for the next C.P.A. exam.

This wasn't his desire. He had even argued with his father concerning his aspirations of becoming an artist on his wedding night. Shock was an understatement when he found out his wife had this sort of businessman's lifestyle in mind for him as well. He thought, however, that with several attempts at taking the test that he could pull it off and do both. He justified his studying by thinking he would make enough money as a C.P.A. to one day have his own art studio. Unfortunately, he found himself in a mire. After his first failed test, Angie tried encouraging him. After the second, her cheers turned into admonishment. Following this last disappointment, it appeared that it would be the silent treatment she would give him.

With each exhausting all-out effort Wade had given to prepare for and take the exams and with each failure, a little more of his self-esteem and physical well-being was surrendered. He sat devastated by this latest result and paid little attention to the letter and newspaper he had been holding, letting them slip from his lap to the floor.

Frozen momentarily as the shock set in, he stared upward at the ceiling disillusioned. Acknowledging to himself that he had to get up and do something, he walked down the hallway that led to his and Angie's bedroom. Turning before he got there, he went into their guest's bathroom. He flipped on the lights and stared at the hollow-eyed, overweight figure of the man in the mirror. How pale and waxy he looked. His once dark complexion had an almost alabaster tone now.

Turning on the faucet and filling his hands to splash his face, he noticed he had spilled almost all of it before getting it halfway up from the sink. Looking down he could see the reason why. His hands were shaking uncontrollably. Concerned, he folded them tightly together as he glanced back into the mirror at the hyperventilating figure standing before him. He could only tolerate his reflection for a second. Trying to distract himself from the overwhelming anxiety he felt, his eyes danced back and forth to any object that might calm his nerves, but there was nothing. Nothing in the room, nothing in the house, nothing could save him from his angst except his wife. Getting into their bedroom and being with Angie was not going to happen. Reconciled as best he could to this fact, he slept on their sofa in the den.

The next morning, Angie was up and heading out of the house much earlier than usual. Getting little sleep as he battled his nerves all night, Wade rose from the couch just as she was leaving. He momentarily caught her stoic look. He was on his own now, and he knew it. Wade had no one to give him counsel. After his first visit home following his wedding, he had another argument with his father and severed all ties with him. Not once had he been back, not even to visit the rest of his family.

As far as his other friends were concerned, Les and Louisa were somewhere down in South America; Laney was somewhere in Florida; and Ann and Charles were living on the other side of the city from him where he lived in Atlanta. With no one to turn to for advice or help concerning his predicament, Wade had to endure more of the same tormenting treatment from his wife over the course of the next several days. After work on Friday afternoon, Wade came into the house only to find Angie packing her bags. Shaken by what he was seeing and thinking that she was going to leave him, he desperately asked, "Where are you going?"

Angie said nothing as she sullenly continued to pack.

Nervously watching her, he softly began to speak. "Hey, I'm sorry I didn't pass the test. I guess you saw that I did do better, though. Maybe I'll get it on the next try."

Pretending not to listen, she continued placing more of her clothes into her luggage.

Despondently, he continued, "You know I'm trying hard. It's not like I'm not trying, Angie."

Staring back at him, Angie responded, "You know that they'll probably let you go at the office, don't you?"

"They'd never—"Angie interrupted, "They've already hired two new college graduates in front of you who've recently passed their test. They're not going to keep you around, Wade. You get the picture."

Angie closed her suitcases and with one in each hand headed for the back door. Wade quickly followed her asking if he could help carry them.

"I'm quite capable of handling things myself, Wade!" Stopping at the back door, she suddenly set her two suitcases down and returned to the back of their house to retrieve her makeup case from the bathroom. She made it back to her luggage where Wade was still standing. Ironically, it was he at this point who tried to console her.

"Listen, don't worry, Angie, everything's gonna be all right. I'll make sure of it."

Ignoring him, Angie picked up her suitcases, opened the back door, and left. Wade watched as she backed out of their drive and drove away.

Broken, insecure, and uncertain what to do next, he slowly turned back into the loneliness and despair of an empty house.

CHAPTER 16

The Amazon

As Wade struggled with his job and marriage in Georgia, Les arrived back in Iquitos alone. Catching an overcrowded triple-decked riverboat, he spent his first night on its second deck sleeping in a hammock. His was just one of the many colorful hammocks dangling from almost every available space on the boat's ceilings.

Les knew the drill well. Stopping at ports or midstream for a smaller boat to bring out another passenger or waiting on a fisherman whose canoe was filled with exotic fish as the man bartered with the boat captain—something in the form of a delay or an interruption predictably slowed their progress. Considering Les' frame of mind, it didn't much matter now.

As the sun rose the next morning, he climbed out of his hanging bed and headed to the boat's upper deck. Looking over the vastness of the tropical rainforest, he was still amazed at how green it appeared as amazed as he had been the first time he'd ever seen it.

The boat continued its way downstream, and the sights were familiar. Little children laughing and splashing in the edge of the water would wave and shout at the vessel as it passed. Solitary or in small clusters, huts dotted the shoreline sporadically as people milled around them. Communities, villages, and towns where they would stop and where he'd done much work as a missionary held little interest for him now. Preferring instead to stay on board during the offloading and loading process, he spent most of this time either watching from the boat's upper deck or sleeping in his hammock.

By mid-morning of the third day, they were passing but not stopping at Jara. Les stood at the helm next to the riverboat captain. Back at the stop at Tabatinga, Les had relayed a wireless message to his base camp for Mico to meet him at the mouth of the tributary down from the mission.

As the riverboat approached, Les watched a single dugout canoe push off the adjacent bank. Its sole occupant paddled out to meet him. Getting the captain to slow the large vessel, Les grabbed his backpack, greeted Mico, and climbed aboard. Soon the riverboat moved onward out of sight as Les and Mico paddled their way up the river branch toward their mission's base camp. Unlike his previous trip down this waterway, they did not have extra people and supplies on board to slow them down. By late afternoon they were in sight of the mission. Normally during such a return, a few villagers would be close by to welcome back those who had been away but not this time. Being notified that the missionary's canoe would soon be arriving, almost all of the small village's inhabitants were lining the banks. Somberly, the crowd watched as the boat hit shore. Their beloved Louisa was not with them.

Stepping out of his dugout into the crowd that had gathered there, Les immediately saw the cautious, disheartened looks the people were giving him. It had been just over seven days since he had left them, and they had been unable to receive any news concerning what had happened. The pall cast over the group remained as he made his way up the bank toward his quarters. Les finally stopped. Turning around from this higher perch, he now faced the entire crowd of followers who had come out to greet him. Compassionately looking at the people's faces, he wanted to be the one to tell them about Louisa.

He spoke in Spanish.

"I guess you haven't heard the news yet, have you?"

Apprehensively the group standing before him gazed up into Les' eyes.

"She made it! Louisa lives!" Les shouted.

Instantly a huge cheer went up as everyone started hugging him as well as each other upon hearing this wonderful revelation. They celebrated until late into the night with bonfires, dancing, and singing, but Les could hold up no longer. Slipping off early as all of this merrymaking was going on, he made it back to his hut where he collapsed from fatigue.

II

The following day, Les relayed a new set of plans for their mission's work to the other missionaries. They would break camp and move upriver across the border of Brazil at Tabatinga past Leticia, Colombia and into the Peruvian controlled waters closer to Iquitos. Les told them he would have easier access to Louisa if the need arose. Everyone in attendance agreed with his proposal, but all of them knew the move to this particular area of Peru was a much dicier proposition than they were accustomed to. Unlike operating out of Brazil, civil unrest in this region was rampant.

It took over a week for them to pull up stakes and another week of work to get settled in on the banks of the Napo River just northeast of Iquitos. Les received a letter from Louisa telling him how much she missed him and giving him an update on her health. Nuns were keeping her at their local mission, and the only difficulty she experienced was fatigue. The doctors told her that this was not uncommon for recovering malarial patients. She did express disappointment that the doctors would like to monitor her for at least another week or two before she would be released to join him.

Glad to hear this news and confident of her recovery, Les began planning his next expedition in earnest. After receiving a shipment of supplies via riverboat from Iquitos and refurbishing the needs of his mission, he felt that this would be as good a time as any to start his journey inland.

Gathering what he thought he would need and loading food and gear into several boats, he and his guides took to the tributary. They made their way north in the direction of the Rio Putumayo, the river that formed the border of Colombia and Peru. In this region, Les hoped to find the peoples of either the Nukak, Yuri, or Passé tribes. His travels took him almost to the doorsteps of the natives he pursued. Many times, the villages he found were deserted. After a week of travel and with little success in their initial hunt, it was decided that the party consisting of Mico, four other natives, and himself would make a base camp. From there they could re-supply their boats with an abundance of fish and food found in the area. Dividing into three groups, they would then head in different directions attempting to cover more ground. Whether contact was made or not, in five days, they would all meet back at this spot and decide their next course of action. Les and Mico would go north-west where there would be a higher probability of finding the Yuri tribe, and the others would head north-east trying to locate the Nukak and Passés.

Three days into their travels and heading west up an uncharted tributary, Les and Mico finally made contact. Unfortunately, it was not with the tribes they were seeking. Instead, they were ambushed by a small splinter group of Shining Path Guerrillas, communist insurgents who were on the run from Lima's military. Normally, members of the Shining Path were not found in this area. They usually lived in the rugged regions of the Andes Mountains. However, after Peru's forces had overtaken that area, many of the disjointed rebel bands headed east, deep into the jungles of the Amazon River basin. They thought this was a place where the Peruvian army and its Rondas were least likely to find them.

The two missionaries hardly looked intimidating enough to warrant an ambush. To the rebels, however, any and all people unknown to them were fair game. Letting out a screaming burst of fire from their AK-47s, they blew holes in the water all around Les' boat. With the shock of gunfire and water spraying everywhere, Les and his guide dropped their paddles and threw their hands high into the air. A scar-faced man appeared from behind a tree. He signaled with his hand causing the others to cease firing. He then gestured for Les and Mico to pull their boat ashore.

The frightened missionaries did as they were shown and as soon as the boat's bow hit the bank, both were yanked from the craft and thrown to the ground. Two of the rebels took all the food from the dugout and stuffed it into their backpacks. The rest of the soldiers, all wearing camouflage clothing and black headbands, pointed their rifles at Les and his friend as the two missionaries lay on their backs. Neither captive knew what was to come next as they anxiously glanced at the small group of rebels standing over them.

A scowl drawn across his face, the leader of the unit began rummaging through their dugout. Picking up a handful of colorful necklaces and bracelets, he then turned to Les with a threatening glare and in accented Spanish, he exclaimed, "Going to buy some friends, I see, amigo!"

Smiling back at his adversary, Les began speaking to him in Spanish. "No. We are Christian missionaries trying to find the Yuri and Passé tribes living here." Les didn't want to say too much as it might antagonize his captors.

The rebel leader took the handful of jewelry and tossed it into the river. Glancing down, he saw one of about ten Bibles. Reaching down, he picked one up.

"Very good cover, Americano," he laughed. "Christian missionaries. Sí?"

"That's right," Les said.

"No, señor Americano!" the Asháninka admonished him. "How about Green Beret? Maybe slave trader—curacas?"

Les knew that the Green Berets used in Vietnam were now being used in Peru to help overthrow the communist. This group of American Special Forces would be placed in villages with a high-ranking citizen, and along with this person would organize Rondas, populist militias used to help fight the Maoist guerrillas. "No. I'm no Green Beret," Les said plainly. "I don't have the build of a soldier."

One of the rebels took the butt of his gun and smashed Les in the mouth knocking him sideways from where he had perched himself up on his elbows. With a mixture of dirt and blood dripping from his nose and mouth, a dazed Les struggled to push himself back up to face his intimidators.

The rebel leader moved closer to the fallen American. With his AK–47 hanging diagonally across his back, he looked every bit the picture of an imposing and angry warrior. Squatting down and resting his elbows on his knees, he picked up a leaf from the forest floor. Slowly, he began to shred it as he waited for the injured Les to right himself from the muddy ground. "Señor Americano," the Asháninka continued as Les looked back up into his face. Now at eye level with Les and only inches from the American's nose, he started talking in a soft but sinister tone. An evil smile stretched across his face. "My friends do not believe you, señor. They thinks you are 'Sinchi' spy. They want to kill you—right here. Right now."

The rest of the soldiers gathered close to their leader laughing and snickering at his remarks.

Trying to regain his composure, Les reached into his mouth and pulled out a tooth that had been knocked loose by the blow. Spitting the excess blood from his mouth onto the ground, he slowly began to talk. The scar-faced man rose and stood over him. "I dislike the Sinchi as much as you do," Les said showing no anger. "They interrogated our mission's group in Iquitos years ago—but at least they didn't beat us."

The leader snorted with indignation at Les and gave out a loud roaring laugh. "Ha! Can you believe this fool?"

"Look," Les said trying to remain calm. "We have no guns. No ammunition. All we want to do is to bring Jesus, some food and a little medical care to these people here. We are not Green Berets. We are not Sinchi police."

The Asháninka leader paid no attention to Les. His gaze turned to Mico, the strongly built Yagua native. "Stand him up!" he ordered. He looked at two Asháninkas in the patrol and asked them what should be done with this captive. Both of the soldiers walked over to Mico and gave him a menacing stare. "Curacas! Traidor!" they shouted into Mico's face. One, acting as if he was turning away, lunged back toward the Yagua burying the butt of his gun deep into Mico's gut.

Groaning, Mico hit the ground curling into the fetal position as the Asháninka warrior stood over him.

There would have been good cause for the Ashaninka's outrage if what they had accused Mico of being, had been true. Curacas meant a traitor to his people. Since the arrival of the Spanish, individuals had sold their fellow tribesman into slavery along with their land for power and wealth. The Ashaninka trusted no one.

"Bring him here!" the scar-faced leader called out.

Quickly his men did as they were told. Grabbing Mico up and dragging him over to a large tree, they tied him to its trunk, his arms wrapped around it in a hugging fashion.

Upon seeing what was about to happen, Les jumped to his feet and tried getting between the soldiers and Mico. "He has done no harm to anyone!" Les yelled out in Spanish. "He is not a traitor. He is one of my missionaries!"

The soldiers beat Les to the ground with the butts of their guns as he protested for them to leave Mico alone.

Raising his hand, the rebel leader called his fighters to back off from Les. He walked over to the bloodied missionary and stooped so Les could hear him plainly. "This Jesus of yours is shit! You come into our land and preach your sick religion to my brothers and sisters! Turn the other cheek you say so my people will stay in their place! Hungry and poor! So, they won't revolt against their oppressors! So, they will endure your God's will for them to be slaves to the rich! And you call this your Jesus' *Salvation*?"

Les' eyes never left the scar-faced man as he listened. "Jesus is Life!" Les said. "Not death! He is Hope! Not despair! He feeds the hungry and cares for the poor! He is Love! Not hate! You kill in the name of your people. We feed and care for all people in the name of God!"

The rebel leader backhanded Les sending him sprawling across the forest floor. "There is no God in this place! We are the God here!" the Asháninka shouted. "Whip him!" He pointed to Mico.

The soldiers stripped several palm branches down to their stalks creating flexible, sturdy whips. Taking turns, each one lined up and slapped Mico across the back as hard as they could.

Les staggered back to his feet and tried to intervene once more. His interdiction was met with a knockout blow from behind as he fell unconscious into the pile of freshly cut palm fronds.

The beating did not stop with Les' unsuccessful effort to save his friend. It took on a form of competition between the soldiers to see which rebel could inflict the most pain. At first, Mico only grimaced and groaned with each whipping crack. Around the thirtieth blow, he screamed out the name of Jesus and did so passionately with each subsequent hit. After three calls of Jesus name, all of the non-tribal Amazonians pulled back and would not strike Mico anymore. Their Catholic upbringing shamed even the toughest among them to rethink his actions. The two Asháninka Maoists were relentless as they swung with as much force as they could. A crack followed by a whack. They were coming so fast and intense that Mico could not even finish screaming the Lord's name before the next blow was laid across his back. The other soldiers, now more subdued, looked the other way as Mico's cries finally fell silent.

III

As all days do, this one finally ended. Time does not stop for the powerful or the weak. It ticks on into the eternal present. It is indifferent as to what has happened or what will happen.

For hours darkness permeated every breath of the primordial rainforest. No human could see his hand in front of his face as the tri-canopied woodlands shielded out even the slightest ambient light shining down from the heavens above.

Hours passed as the deep darkness lifted its hand from the eyes of the living forest and a pale gray light reflected the silhouettes of the surrounding tree trunks and branches. Through the early morning fog, birds and monkeys called back and forth across the vast stillness of the Peruvian jungle. Only the fluttering of a waterfowl leaving its previous evening roost for food broke the stillness of the place.

As the sky grew red through the eastern forest canopy, Les finally started to awaken. Opening his eyes, he couldn't figure out where he was or how he had gotten there. He felt as if his head was about to explode. The only thing he knew was that he was in excruciating pain. Shaking and weak, he tried to sit up but fell back down. The pain in his head and body was too intense. He decided to lay still to get his bearings. Taking a deep breath, he tried rising again. This time he tried to stand up, and just as he made it to an upright position, he lost his balance once more and fell head first against a tall capirona tree. The jolt sent shocks of pain radiating from his head to his spine and every nerve ending in his body. He passed out as he fell at the base of the large tree.

An hour passed as Les lay unconscious beneath the hardwood. A capybara came into the area. The noise of bushes rustling and leaves crackling awakened Les once more. Vaguely remembering his last fall, he lay still and tried assessing his injuries, but trying to comprehend what he was feeling and what had happened to him seemed impossible.

Les could see the large rodent grazing on plants near the river's edge. As he watched the animal through his blurry eyes, it ate its way down the river's bank, his dugout, floating in midstream, came into focus.

"Mico…" Les tried calling out, but his pitiful voice sounded just more than a whisper.

The previous day's horrors started coming back in spurts, the Shining Path Guerillas, the beatings.

"Mico!" Les yelled straining as he struggled to his feet. "Mico!" He called looking around the area and finding the tree where Mico had been tied. He fell to his knees where Mico had been beaten. Touching the ground at the base of the tree, Les' hands were colored with the soft, sticky redness of Mico's blood. Standing back up, the battered missionary staggered from tree to tree searching for his companion. His blackened eyes were so swollen that only the pupils could be seen through narrow slits. His right jaw and the whole side of his face were so puffed up that bones had to have been broken or cracked. Still he moved onward searching for his friend. The torturous pain he felt coming from all over his body was only secondary as he pressed ahead. "Mico!" he shouted over and over as he stumbled through the wooded area around the place where the beating had occurred.

He came across a trail. He could see that someone had been walking on it recently as he followed the footprints down the path. He saw blood smeared across leaves. More blood drops and congealed clumps of it covered the forest floor. A little farther along a white powdery substance had spilled onto the footpath. Kneeling down, he pinched some of the powder between his thumb and forefinger and tasted it. Just as he had thought, cocaine. Les knew well the havoc this incendiary extract could create. He stood back up and slowly made his way around the next turn in the path. "Noooo!"

He fell to his knees. Before him hanging by a short shank of rope from the bow of a small tree was Mico. A knife stuck in the trunk of the tree looked as if it held a note. Les, in shock at what he had hoped he would not find—his friend—dead, stood back up, then limped over to the tree where Mico hung. The knife did hold a message. It read:

LEAVE WITH YOUR SHIT EATING JESUS FROM OUR LANDS
WE KILL ALL CURACAS
ALL MISSIONARY SINCHIS
I MEET YOU AGAIN AMERICANO YOU DIE

Les took the knife from the tree letting the note fall indifferently to the forest floor. With the blade in hand, Les cut the cord holding Mico's lifeless body and slung him over his weak trembling shoulder.

In a state of numbness and struggling for balance, he headed for their dugout. Laying Mico's body on the bank, he waded into the shallow river to retrieve the boat. He put his friend in the boat's bow face up. Getting into the dugout, he headed back up the river paddling to a spot under a grouping of tall Taraputus palms where the two missionaries had eaten only the day before. Mico had told him that a mission should be put at this place because he thought the stately palms and abundant flowers were so beautiful there.

Les buried Mico adorning his gravesite with wild orchids, passion flowers, Amazon lilies, and hibiscus. The pink, red, and white flowers were piled high over his buried body. The sheer number of them took Les quite a while to collect. Vowing to honor his brave Yagua friend, Les decided he would build a mission at this spot before he left Peru. Despite the threat he had received from the rebels, he would make sure that this happened.

Fashioning a makeshift cross from bamboo, he tied together with fishing line, he planted the symbol down into the soft soil of the alluvial forest floor creating the head marker for Mico's grave. On his knees and bowing his head, he read aloud from the Bible.

Blessed are they which are persecuted for righteousness' sake: for theirs is the kingdom of heaven. Blessed are ye, when men shall revile you, and persecute you, and shall say all manner of evil against you falsely, for my sake. Rejoice, and be exceeding glad: for great is your reward in heaven: for so persecuted they the prophets which were before you.

Flipping the page, he continued his soulful recitation.

Ye have heard that it hath been said, Thou shalt love thy neighbour, and hate thine enemy. But I say unto you, Love your enemies, bless them that curse you, do good to them that hate you, and pray for them which despitefully use you, and persecute you; That ye may be the children of your Father which is in heaven: for he maketh his sun to rise on the evil and on the good, and sendeth rain on the just and on the unjust. For if ye love them which love you, what reward have ye? Do not even the publicans the same? And if ye salute your brethren only, what do ye more than others? Do not even the publicans so? Be ye therefore perfect, even as your Father which is in heaven is perfect.

When he finished reading the scripture, Les looked up through a clearing in the forest canopy above him into the sky.

In a mournful, heartfelt voice, he told Mico's spirit, "I am so sorry that this has happened to you, my Mico. I feel so responsible for your death. Please forgive me, my friend. You have been there for me so many times and for Louisa. I will not let you down. I will build a mission here as you wished. I will try my best not to hate these people who killed you. I will pray for them and try my best to forgive them for what they did to you. Your wife and your son, I will care for as I know that's what you would want me to do."

He gave a short prayer to God telling Him how wonderful a man Mico was and telling Him how much he loved and would miss his good Christian friend. Quietly, Les stood up and walked to the river's bank. Sliding into the dugout, he paddled downstream and vanished into the thick foliage surrounding the river's edge.

CHAPTER 17

Leaving the Wilderness

(*Stateside* 1985)

It took three days for Les to get back to the temporary base camp where he and the other missionaries had split up. Fortunately, the others returned only having been threatened by a hostile tribe whose ancestry was unknown to them. No one was hurt in their party, but these men were greatly upset after hearing what happened to their beloved brother Mico. Although Les wanted no part of it, they made him stop so they could attend to his wounds.

The men repacked their boats and started their long trip back to the other missionaries, men, women, and children. It took a hard ten days of paddling to get there. With one of the expedition's members missing, Les' bruised and battered face showing gruesomely, and the grim looks coming from the other explorers, their return would be no cause for celebration.

Once onshore and ignoring the gasps and winces of those seeing his wounds, Les solemnly marched directly to Mico's hut. There he found Mico's wife and child inside. With tears and prayers, he tried consoling the distraught mother and son. Though his effort was heartfelt and sincere, there was little he could say or do to assuage their grief; he could hardly contain his own. Leaving their hut, he started making plans for a trip upriver to Iquitos. Notifying the Peruvian authorities there of what had taken place, he hoped, would bring those responsible for this crime to justice.

After making this two-day journey along with two men from the ill-fated expedition, Les and the missionaries finally arrived at the large river city of Iquitos. Gone was the wealth of the area which had made Iquitos regal during the early nineteen hundreds in the heyday of the rubber boom. Far from its former glory, the municipality was now filled with the remains of its once elegant buildings and a society born more from poverty than wealth.

Making their way down the streets of the city, they spotted the building for the city's governmental police unit. Les, from experience, was more than aware of the bureaucratic ambivalence he was about to face. Trying to be patient, he listened as the office worker described how their matter would be handled.

The first order of business, he was told, would be to file a complaint. This appeared to be a straightforward and reasonable request. The process was lengthy involving the documentation of everything that had occurred to them in graphic detail from the beginning to end. The government required that Les strictly adhere to its protocol. After three hours, they were done with this part of the procedure. They were assigned another official to discuss their case.

The police lieutenant involved was a stout, partially bald, middle-aged man with dark features who would best be described as a mestizo, meaning of mixed descent, probably having lineage from both Spain and South America. Sweating profusely and with a handkerchief held in one hand, the stern-faced administrator showed little compassion for what had happened to Les' friend. He scoffed at the death of a single native. Wiping his brow, he flipped through the pages of the report. "The jungles of Peru are dangerous. People die out there every day," he told the missionary.

This was hardly news to Les. He tried being patient with the contemptuous officer, but the man kept denigrating those he thought were too inexperienced to journey out into the foreboding areas that he kept calling "the deep jungle." When he finished, Les was more than incensed by the official's callous attitude.

Striking back at the constable, Les demanded to see someone higher up the chain of command. His insistence on this riled the bureaucrat, but after seeing that this fair-skinned Caucasian missionary was going to have it no other way, the man acquiesced. Provoked, the official sent Les and his two compatriots to talk to someone from the military who he told them had more authority concerning the matter. The officer he was sent to meet was a colonel in the Peruvian army. Forewarned, the commander had been briefed about the dispute between Les and the Police Bureau administrator.

As Les entered the military headquarters, the serviceman rose from his desk and extended his hand. "Hello, Señor Ellis. I am Colonel Alfredo Gonzalez. I am sorry that you were treated so poorly by the police."

Les nodded.

"Yes, Colonel. They didn't give me much credit for living on this river for over four years."

Smiling, the colonel continued. "You must realize regarding this particular situation any action taken by the municipality would probably be limited. Logistically speaking, the city's police force is not equipped to go that far out into the jungles to try and catch such a band of desperados. However, Señor Ellis, I and the Peruvian military are more than capable of such an endeavor."

A broad grin crept across Les' face. "I think you and I are going to get along just fine, Colonel Gonzalez. You have my report?"

"Yes. It is all I will need. Go back to your mission, Señor. We will handle this, I assure you."

In the aftermath of this visit, it appeared to Les that the military's willingness to help probably had little to do with protecting missionaries and converts. It was about the cocaine trade between Columbia and the Maoist Shining Path Guerillas. Whether the colonel was sincerely trying to protect Les and his companions and trying to snuff out that area's cocaine trade and communist insurgency or whether the officer and military had a stake in this trade would never be known. All Les knew was that they patrolled the area throughout the six years Les and Louisa remained in South America. The colonel held true to his word. Les took particular relief in this fact as Mico's wife and son had taken up residence at the mission built in Mico's honor on the Isle of Palms.

II

Les, Louisa, and their son Mike, who was born eleven months after Mico's death and had been named for Les' most trusted friend on the Amazon, arrived at Jacksonville International Airport in July of 1985. Trying to re-acclimate to the civilized world was a little awkward for the plainly dressed missionary family. The years of traveling on the world's mightiest river and its tributaries and through its most desolate jungles had made the darkly tanned couple, though slightly gaunt, rugged and tough.

It took time getting used to the loud noises of a large, busy airport again: jets landing and taking off, small forklifts moving luggage, loudspeakers blaring out arrival times and boarding requests. This plethora of distraction kept Les and Louisa on their toes while their young son, who could only see the magic in it all, enjoyed soaking it up.

Making their way to the airport's curbside after gathering their meager luggage, Louisa and Les peered across the multi-lanes of incoming airport traffic for what they were told would be a silver Honda Accord. After ten years of living in the wilds of Peru and Brazil, the pair had no idea what a Honda looked like. They were trying to find a silver four-door sedan with Laney James driving it.

Laney had become a clinical psychologist. He lived in Jacksonville, was married, and had two small children, six and nine-year-old girls. Besides Les and Louisa's parents, Laney was one of the few people who was concerned enough to keep up with the whereabouts of his missionary friends.

Louisa spotted their tall pal as he waved at them from across several lanes of traffic. "There he is!" she called out to Les who was holding his suitcase in one hand and holding Mike's hand in the other.

"All right," Les shouted back energetically. "Watch out for the cars now!" They made their way through the stop-and-go lines of traffic toward Laney's vehicle.

After welcoming his friends and loading them and their luggage into his Honda, Laney drove out of the airport complex and headed for Jacksonville's Atlantic Beach where he lived only blocks away from the ocean. Les wanted to know how everybody was getting along. As he drove, Laney caught them up on what he knew about Ann and Karl, and sighed as he brought up Wade. Glancing at Les in the passenger seat, he said, "You remember that Wade and Angie got married after y'all left? Did you know they ended up in Atlanta?"

"Yeah," Les responded. "Mom sent us a letter about that when we first got to Brazil."

"Well, believe it or not," Laney exclaimed. "Wade didn't get a job as an artist like we all thought he would. He got one as an accountant. Angie, of course, became a teacher. I think an eighth grade English teacher." Grimacing, Laney continued. "Everything started out fine for them at first but went downhill pretty fast when Wade couldn't pass the CPA exam."

"I'm a little shocked that he'd go in that direction," Les said amazed.

"Yeah, me too. I think he spent at least three years trying to pass it. You know Angie's idea of success and Wade's were quite different.

"In what way?" Les asked.

"Angie wanted the big house, the fine car—those kinds of things. Wade, on the other hand, had a simpler view of life. He just wanted to paint, have some kids, and provide a decent living for his family." Laney checked his side and rearview mirrors for traffic. "Now I don't mean to paint such an ugly picture of Angie. I'm sure she loved Wade and probably still does. I just think she's a misguided soul, and what she did to Wade—well, it definitely hurt him."

Les and Louisa appeared puzzled at Laney's last remark. "What do you mean, hurt him?" Les asked.

"You guys remember that Wade ended up with an accounting degree, right? He only minored in art. Of course, we all thought, like I said, he would probably follow his artistic talent. Do something with that. But there was a big reason why he didn't." Laney paused as Les and Louisa listened intently. "Ya' see, it seemed Angie never really wanted Wade to become an artist in the first place. Or, for that matter, to be just a plain ol' accountant. She wanted to be married to a CPA."

Les turned and gave Louisa a disappointed look.

Laney continued. "So, in order to get to this place she had in mind, she kept insisting Wade take that blasted accounting exam over and over, again and again. She also made him take all kinds of study courses and classes when he didn't pass it. I think his inability to pass the thing finally caught up with the poor guy."

Shaking his head, Les asked, "Are they still together?"

"No," Laney commented. "About two years ago they split up. According to what Wade told me, Angie asked him to leave. Told him that she thought it best if they went their separate ways."

"Did they have any children?" Les questioned.

"Nope. I think, according to Ann, Angie had to have a hysterectomy. I imagine that may have added to their problems as well."

Louisa sat in the back seat quietly listening with Mike resting in her lap. She couldn't help but remember the burning image of Angie and Karl coming out of the bathroom together. Though angry and disheartened with the way Angie treated her friend, she kept her thoughts to herself.

"Now this isn't where the story ends, gang," Laney continued. Pondering for a moment, he said, "I guess I maybe should now tell you about Wade's dad."

"Wade's dad?" Les asked mystified.

"Yep," Laney replied. "Wade's good ol', overbearing, jack-of-a-you-know-what father."

Mike had fallen asleep in his mother's lap.

Les interjected sarcastically, "Now this ought to be interesting."

"Oh, yeah. It's pretty interesting all right," Laney sighed as he wheeled his way out onto I-95. He continued, "Let me begin when I went to Atlanta for a psychology seminar several years back. It was to be held on a Saturday morning, so I booked a room for Friday night. After it was over, rather than making the long drive back to Jacksonville that afternoon, I decided to stay over for another night and go home the next morning. I didn't have much to do on that particular Sunday, so on a lark, I decided to make a stop in Wade's hometown and drop by and see his folks. I wanted to find out what Wade was up to. Now all this happened around three years ago, so bear that in mind."

Les nodded.

"Well, when I got to their house and knocked on their door, Wade's mom greeted me. She must have known that I had become a practicing psychologist. I assumed that Wade, Ann, or somebody must have told her this. But this aside, I can still remember how overly grateful she was that I'd come by. At the time, I recalled this being a little bit odd. After giving me a big hug, she asked me to take a seat on their living room sofa and sat down right next to me. I was still puzzled by how nervous she was acting until she started filling me in on what was going on."

Les cut his eyes over at his buddy. "Yeah. What was going on?"

"Well, she began to tell me that her husband was having some problems. She said he was back in their bedroom in his bed. When I asked her what kind of problems he was having, she told me he was severely depressed and very anxious. It was so bad, she said, he couldn't even leave their house. This had been coming on for some time, but it really escalated when he started having some problems with his business. She kept describing it to me as a nervous breakdown. To make a very long story short, I went with her back into their bedroom where I had a long conversation with the both of them. When we were finished, I called and got him lined up with a psychiatrist that I knew was living and practicing in their area. Unfortunately, like most people I deal with, the person has to hit rock bottom before they ever seek help. Up until that point, they're usually in complete denial that they even have a problem."

Les and Louisa listened closely.

"So, weeks went by, then months. I kept checking on him by phone; when I could, you know. When we talked, he told me he'd wished he'd seen this doctor years before. He'd suffered through this issue most of his adult life just like his father had. He had no idea what he was dealing with and that there were medications and therapies to help him handle it. I was more than delighted by the progress I found he was making. It was truly miraculous."

"I bet," Les said. "The apple doesn't fall too far from the tree either, now does it?"

Laney glanced at Les. "I was about to get to that. So, as you both have probably figured out, when Wade got the boot from Angie, the timing of all this couldn't have been more perfect." Laney continued, "You know, I've gotten to the point in my life where I just don't believe in coincidences too much anymore. Have y'all come to that conclusion? I would imagine that with all you guys have seen down in South America, you probably know what I'm talking about."

Louisa, nodding, affirmed his comment as Laney caught her eyes in his rearview mirror.

"Well, with his dad having done something about his problem and understanding the pain his son was probably going through himself, he wanted to help him out. He offered him an olive branch, so to speak."

Les gave Laney a puzzled look. "An olive branch?"

Glancing at Les, he said dryly, "Yep. He was going to have to make peace with Wade first."

"Make peace? What are you talking about, Laney?"

"Come on, Les. You remember how bad Wade's dad treated him in the past."

Agreeing, he said, "Yeah, you're right about that, Laney. I do remember."

"Well, according to Wade, all of the lack of respect and belittling from his father didn't stop, and Wade finally just got fed up. Eventually, he just cut the old man off altogether. For years the only one in the family that he kept any contact with was his little sister, Kelli. In retrospect, you guys were probably long gone before all of this came to a head."

Laney suddenly turned off the main road onto a side street. As Laney maneuvered the car, Les noticed the neat rows of modestly built homes as they entered his pal's neighborhood. Turning his blinker on, Laney pulled into the driveway of a single-story house with a small yard. Coming to a stop, he glanced at his two companions and said, "Okay, folks. We're here."

On edge, Louisa straightened herself up in the back seat. "Laney. You can't just stop the story and leave us hanging now. You've got to finish it and tell us what happened."

"Later," Laney said with a big grin. "Let's get unpacked first. My wife and kids are dying to meet you."

III

Inside the front door in the living room, Elise, Laney's wife, and Laney's two daughters, Jennifer who was six and Ellen who was nine, greeted them.

Mike, who was five, was still in his mother's arms about half asleep as he was introduced to Laney's girls. Groggily, he gave the sisters a little wave as his mother took him back to the room where they would be staying.

After unloading their luggage and tucking Mike into bed, Louisa and Les found their way into Laney and Elise's great room which combined their kitchen and den. The Florida couple had soft drinks and a snack waiting for their weary travelers.

"Have a seat," Laney said indicating the couch. He then turned to his wife. "I was telling them on the ride over here about Wade."

Elise raised her eyebrows. "Very interesting story," she remarked.

Louisa nodded in agreement.

Elise and Laney seated themselves across from the two missionaries. The girls who followed their parents into the room, giggling and curious, were sent back to their rooms to play so Les and Louisa could relax.

Les spoke first. "Wow, it really feels great to stretch out and rest after all that traveling. I thought we were in pretty good shape physically, but we're definitely not used to this faster pace of life. After being down on the river for so long, I'd almost forgotten how quickly you can get from one place to another in a plane and on a superhighway."

"I bet," Laney said. "Speaking of the Amazon, I'm sure you guys got some good stories to tell us, eh?"

Inquisitively, Louisa smiled back. "After you finish telling us about Wade."

Laney grinned. "Okay. Where did I leave off? Was I to the part about Wade's dad trying to reach out to him?"

"Yes," Louisa responded.

"Okay. But remember I told you Wade wanted nothing to do with him. Right?" Laney noted they were all in agreement. "Okay. Now bear in mind, Wade's dad never gave up trying. So time rocked on, and Wade told me that his anxiety and depression became unbearable. He said he had no one else to turn to and finally gave in. He returned a call from his father. This happened just a few weeks before Angie split up with him. Fortunately, Wade's dad had gotten him in to see a therapist before this."

"Wow," Les said. "The timing of that was amazing."

"Yeah, wow's an understatement," Laney responded. "In any event, he got the help he needed and over time has been able to sort his life out. Now he and his dad are as close as they can be."

Shaking her head, Louisa asked, "So, where's Wade now?"

Laney marveled at what he was about to say. "Believe it or not he started off by moving back in with his parents."

Amused, Les shook his head as Laney chuckled.

"Yep, his dad got him a job working as a bookkeeper and aid for one of his old high school buddies. Get this, the fellow owns an arts and crafts shop. You know, where they make and rebuild furniture—tables, chairs, dressers—that sort of thing. But guess what? They also handle art supplies, all kinds. And they have a large room in the front of this building; it's really a converted house where they display all kinds of creations, especially paintings. It didn't take long for the owner to figure out that he had a real talent on his hands. He was so impressed with Wade's artistic abilities, especially his ability to paint, that he's put him up in a loft apartment in one of the buildings he owns downtown. The guy, I think his name's Ben, is worth a lot of money. Wade has no rent to pay and gets all of his art supplies at cost."

Les cackled, "From the outhouse to the White House, looks like ol' Wade's luck has surely changed. What an unbelievable story, Laney."

"Yep, it's pretty remarkable all right," Laney responded.

"This is probably a dumb question considering what you just told us," Les said, "but I take it that he's doing some painting now—not just bookkeeping?"

"Yeah, he's pretty much back at it." Hesitating, Laney said, "I think when he first got into this apartment and got his things set up, he just wanted to see if he could still do it. He told me that during all of those years of marriage, he only occasionally painted and toward the end of it, he never did."

Les shook his head and frowned. He thought of all the time that Wade had let slip by. A smile parted his lips. "Well, that's all in his past now, isn't it? So tell me is he just doing it as a hobby or is he . . .?"

Laney grew more pensive. "Well, when I would first stop by to visit him, he was just using his new studio to entertain himself. I guess more or less drawing as a leisurely pursuit. But with each subsequent trip, I could see him slowly transforming. You know, going from someone just dabbling like you said, just doing a little hobby, to someone becoming more and more intent. Let's say—more professional. It's been over a year of his doing this now, and I'd say he's developed quite a reputation as one of the finest artists in the area. In my meager opinion, I truly believe that once he gets some exposure things are really going to take off for him."

Smiling both Les and Louisa nodded.

Louisa said, "Anyone in their right mind can see the talent Wade has the first time they ever lay eyes on one of his pictures. It's hard for me to believe that he didn't pursue this after college like we all thought he would. You know, I think about all those wasted years." Reflecting, she said, "But maybe not really. Sometimes I think it's the suffering and tough times a person has to go through that bring out the best in their abilities."

Les' expression grew dour as he thought about the struggles his pal had to endure. "Yeah, I think you're probably right about that, Louis'." Looking at Laney, he asked, "Tell me, Laney, with all that's happened to him, how is he doing emotionally? Has he calmed down some since going through therapy and all?"

Laney mused. "Well, I can still detect a little bit of that insecurity when I visit him. All in all, though, it appears to me that not only have the meds and therapy benefited him, but I also think that just being an artist has given him some confidence as well. When you see him again, you'll notice what I'm talking about. He's a much more self-reliant person than that guy you left behind all those years ago."

Les happily sighed and said, "That's great news indeed. I can hardly wait to see him either. How about his love life, Laney? Has he gotten himself a new girlfriend or anything like that?"

Laney gave Les and Louisa a little uncertain smile and said, "Well, that's an interesting story."

Louisa said dryly, "Let me guess, Laney. Angie's not quite out of the picture just yet, now is she?"

Laney stared back at Louisa bemused. "How did you know that, Louisa?"

"Same story. Second or third verse," Louisa responded without cracking a smile.

"Yeah, I guess they did break up a couple of times back in college, didn't they? Well anyway, she spent about a year away from him up in Atlanta teaching then followed him on back home. Lives out back of the college. Remember where those apartments were back there?"

"Yeah," Les answered. "Kind of back behind the B.S.U., right?"

"Yep, she moved into a small house back in that area according to Wade."

Louisa, not being particularly fond of Angie since catching her roommate with Karl at their apartment, prodded Laney for more information.

"What's Wade said about her being back in town?"

"Not much. Up until then, he'd dated several different women, but no one seriously, I think. Anyway, he's been out with Angie a few times, and it seems she really wants to get back with him."

"Do you think he will?" Louisa asked.

"Like I said, he didn't tell me much, but he did say that he had his guard up. You know he'd been burned so bad in that relationship, and it's just my opinion, but I don't think he's gotten over that hurt even now." Laney paused facing his two friends across the room as they listened intently to his observations. "You know all of that bust up wasn't just her fault though." Looking more so in Louisa's direction as he spoke, he caught her wincing at what he was telling them. "Well, maybe most of it was, but I imagine that as anxious and depressed as Wade was at the time that he probably wasn't the most fun guy to be around either. It's never just one person's fault when you see a relationship break up like that. At least that's what I've gleaned from my practice."

"No one's perfect," Les chimed in sympathetically.

"Yep, you're right about that," Laney replied.

Louisa listened to what the two men said, but offered no response concerning Angie.

IV

Both Les and Louisa's parents came down from Georgia to Jacksonville for a couple of short visits while Les' family stayed with Laney. Delighted to see their children and grandson, they wished their stays could have been longer, but time would not permit it. Les and his family would soon have to leave for a city in another part of the state. There, Les would take over as the full-time pastor at a small church. Their leisurely stay with Laney and his family would be short.

Les and Louisa enjoyed being in Laney's home and with his family. It was the first time Mike had ever seen the ocean, which was only a couple of blocks away from where they were staying. Even though he had grown up along the waters of the tropical Amazon River, this larger body of water amazed him.

Mike especially loved the Atlantic's waves, and to his delight Laney would take him out on a surfboard to catch one and ride it ashore. Les, Louisa, and the rest of

Laney's family sat on the beach cheering whenever Mike rode one all the way in and laughed and clapped whenever the tandem surfers wiped out.

Les' son learned how to swim along the Amazon River even before he had learned how to walk. He appeared to be a smiling, tanned little fish that sprang back to the surface with each roll off the surfboard wanting to do it again and again. Laney never tired of taking the little tyke back out until Les finally called Mike back to the beach to give his old buddy a break.

As Laney and his little pal made it back to shore, Laney's two daughters, Jennifer and Ellen, met them. They invited Mike to come and help them build a sandcastle. The two girls already had a good start on the project, but the tide had turned and the ocean's water was pouring back in rapidly eroding what they'd just built. "We need to build a wall," Mike shouted as the water came pouring back in even harder. "Hey, Dad! Come help us!" the little fellow called out to Les.

Les gathered up two small sand shovels they had brought down to the beach and ran over to help the children with the barrier. Taking one of the shovels from his father, Mike said, "The ocean keeps knocking it down, Dad!"

"Okay," Les said, "how about we build a moat around the castle first?"

The girls instantly knew what Les was talking about, but Mike was confused. "A boat?" he asked puzzled.

"No, a moat," Les said as the girls giggled in the background. "A moat is like a giant ditch from back when they had castles and princesses," he said for the girl's sake, "and knights in shining armor," he added for Mike's benefit. "The moat would keep the Black Knight and all of his evil men from entering the castle."

Mike's eyes sparkled, "Yeah, let's build one of those around our castle, Dad."

Les, Mike, and the two girls worked hard digging the ditch as they encircled their fortress. The girls placed their barricade in front of the ditch until Les told them it would probably work better if they put the sand behind the ditch, which they did.

Les and Mike soon completed a deep trench and high seawall that separated the incoming tide from the front of the castle. Even so, the ocean continued climbing the shoreline faster and harder. The seawalls the two girls had built on each side were collapsing under the pressure of the incoming waves. "All right, girls! It looks like we're going to have to sacrifice the castle to keep the ocean out. Is that okay with y'all?"

"Yes!" The girls yelled seeing the fruitlessness of their efforts.

"Okay," Les called out. "Y'all get inside there and use the sand of the castle to reinforce those side walls." Both girls immediately jumped over the structure's embankments.

"Mike, start over on your end and we'll make our moat wider. Hurry now!"

Both guys shoveled hard, but as fast as they dug the ocean would refill their ditch with sand even faster.

"Dad, it keeps filling back up!"

As the next breaker hit, Les knew it was pointless to try and clear the ditches any further. Grabbing up Mike, he gently tossed him inside the fort. As he did this, he stepped inside with all three of the children. "Come on, girls! We've got to get more sand to the front!" Les encouraged them. The next wave hit and almost made it to the top of the wall. "All right, we've got to go higher with this sand. Keep digging! Don't stop!" Just as they thought they were victorious—a huge wave came in from their right sideswiping the structure. In one enveloping whop, it blasted over the northern sidewall filling their sandpit with seawater.

Frantically with hands and buckets, they tried to dump the water back out, but there was no stopping the onslaught of waves. The next one cut the northern barrier in half, which was followed by another large breaker leaving the wall a mere mound. Retreating in exhaustion, the four weary warriors headed back toward the sandy shoreline where the rest of the adults looked on with heartfelt sympathy. Gazing back at their fortress, all that was left of their hard work was the remnant of the front wall that the sea would soon obliterate. Much like life, all that's done is soon taken back.

After spending the majority of the morning at the beach, the midday sun, with not a breath of breeze, became almost unbearable for Laney and his family. Even though their girls were dark from staying out in the sun, their mother constantly poured sunscreen on them. The sun-tanned missionaries, on the other hand, had little trouble enduring the heat or the U.V. light as the sun had been a near constant for them. Only during the hard rains of the monsoon season would they escape it for short reprieves. As the decision was made to go back to the house, Les reached down and grabbed Mike's little hands. With a swing and a tug, he landed the happy little imp on his shoulders. With his arms free, he grabbed two folding chairs in one hand and Louisa's hand in the other. Both families gathered up their things for the walk back across the dunes as they headed for Laney's house.

V

Louisa and Les stayed only a few more days with Laney at the beach before they made preparations for their move to their new home in Bradford, Florida. This small town was just below the border of Georgia's most southwestern corner.

Les was to be the pastor of the Baptist church there. The church would provide all the provisions he would need, even a parsonage in which his family would live. For Les, Louisa, and Mike, all they owned were the clothes on their backs. They had received a stipend at Iquitos to cover their airfare and to buy provisions including something to wear when they got back to the States.

The ten days Les, Louisa, and Mike had spent with Laney's family in Jacksonville had been wonderful. It was good seeing their old pal and enjoying the company of his wife and children. Now it was time to move on.

Laney arranged for Les and his family to catch a ride to Bradford with one of Laney's older retired friends named Robert. This gentleman, in his early seventies, was heading to Tallahassee to visit his daughter for a long weekend. The trip up to Bradford would be only another forty minutes or so.

They left Laney's house in a Chevrolet Suburban on Friday morning. Driving through the coastal city of Jacksonville, they soon found themselves on I-10, which would carry them along for most of their trip.

After three hours, they exited the Interstate north onto a two-lane state road where it took them less than fifteen minutes to make it into Bradford. They arrived at their destination. Their home was situated in an area of the city appearing much like the houses where Les had lived in his hometown years earlier.

There were differences. Bradford was unusually hilly, and the telephone poles ran in people's front yards instead of their back alleys where they had been in Les' old neighborhood. There was a nice sidewalk running parallel down each side of the street bordering the front yards.

Robert stopped the car in front of Les' new home. He got out and started to unload the vehicle. Les did not want him to strain himself by helping them with their luggage, but the older fellow insisted. Reaching under the doormat to the front door, Les found the house key where he had been told it would be. After several trips back and forth to the car, everything was placed inside the front entrance of the fully furnished home.

Les tried to pay for Robert's gas a second time. He had tried paying for it in Jacksonville when they started the trip.

"No," the older man said smiling. "You were good company. I really enjoyed having someone to talk to. Thank you very much."

With Mike riding high on his dad's shoulders, Les shook Robert's hand bidding him farewell.

"Give me a call if I can give you folks a lift to or from," the older man called out as he made his way to his vehicle. "I'm always heading back and forth to Tallahassee, you know."

Les shouted back with a grin, "We might just take you up on that. Thanks again, Robert."

Hearing the car door slam and the engine crank, Les and his family waved as they watched the car head down the roadway and out of sight. Turning back to the house, Les glanced at his wife as they both smiled at one another. It wasn't like this was the first time they had ended up at a strange new location together.

Louisa was the first one to speak. "This is an awfully nice place here. What do you think, guys?"

Taking Mike off of his shoulders, Les set the young boy on the ground feet first. "Well," he said staring down at Mike, "let's get in here and see what we've got."

Mike bolted up the steps opening the front door and disappeared into the alluring novelty of their new abode.

Raising her eyebrows, Louisa turned toward Les. "I think we're going to find out the answer to that question in around—say less than a minute?"

They waited on Mike's reconnoiter, and just as Louisa had expected, the little tyke's head came flashing, jutting out of the front door as he yelled, "Come on! Come on! You guys aren't going to believe all the neat stuff in here!"

CHAPTER 18

Wade and Laney

It was noon on a Friday as Wade sipped a cup of coffee at his large wooden desk in the back room of Ben's shop. Spread across the countertop was the local paper. As usual, he realized there was not much that he could glean from it. The only article of interest did mention the Atlanta art show in December that he had registered to enter. The piece that he would submit was an oil painting he had been working on for a while. He had completely redone it more than once, which was unusual for him. Normally, he had an inspiration that would make his work unique, but Wade didn't go with his original gut feeling for his composition this time. He found himself looking for perfection, and the more he tried to attain this ideal the more elusive it became. A sickly aura of indecisiveness engulfed him. Nervously, he flipped the page of the newspaper to get his mind off his obsession. Hearing the front door jingle, Wade turned his attention in that direction. Ben and Wanda, the shop's owner and helper, were both out to lunch. Rising from his chair, he left his desk to see if he could find what the customer needed. Rounding the corner from the shop's backroom work area, Wade almost ran headlong into Laney James. "Holy cow, Laney! I was expecting to find some little ol' lady up here, not all six-feet-three-inches of you."

"Sorry, Wade. Thought I might catch you napping back here," Laney laughed.

"Righttttt," Wade said. It was not often that he and Ben had the luxury of downtime. Ordinarily, they were noisily running a lathe or a router or some other piece of equipment.

Laney continued, "Stopped by your place first, and since you weren't there, hoped you'd be here."

Puzzled, Wade asked, "What's going on?"

"Nothing much. Didn't know if you knew that Les and Louisa have made it back from their mission trip in South America?"

"No, I didn't. Are they in town?"

"Oh no. They're in Bradford. Bradford, Florida."

"Bradford? Where on earth is that?"

"It's a small town just north and west of Tallahassee right close to the Georgia-Florida line."

"You know I ran into Les' dad several months back," Wade said. "He told me that they were coming back soon. He wasn't exactly sure when though or where they'd end up. He did say they were heading to Florida or maybe Texas. I'm sure he and Mrs. Ellis are glad it's close by instead of way out there. How long have they been back?"

"Oh, probably around two months or so. His parents and Louisa's have been back and forth, a couple of times to help them get situated."

"Have you seen them?"

"Yeah, I picked them up at JAX, and they stayed for a few days at the beach with us until the church over in Bradford got the parsonage ready for them to move in."

"They're both doing okay, I guess?"

Wade was disappointed they hadn't contacted him yet.

"Yeah, they're doing really good. They made a point to ask me to stop by on my next trip this way to let you know that they'd be coming soon."

Wade was a little more satisfied.

Laney continued, "They have a little boy, you know?"

"No, I didn't."

"Name's Mike."

Laney retold the story that Les had told him about how Mike had gotten his name from Mico, Les' best friend from Peru. Laney described Les and Mico's wonderful friendship from its beginning to its tragic end when Mico was killed. Wade sat listening in spellbound silence.

"Good God, Laney. I knew that there was some danger in being a missionary down there, but I never thought they'd come anywhere close to losing their lives—at least not like that."

"Yeah, neither did I. I'd kept up with the areas they were in by keeping in touch with Les' parents. In the letters they sent home, they never detailed any hardships that they were experiencing. I guess they realized that there wasn't much their parents could really do except worry. I think most of their correspondence home was pretty upbeat."

"How old is their little boy?" Wade asked, still shaken by the story.

"Around five and he's a free spirit and a half. I mean wide open and all smiles."

Laney told Wade how much Mike enjoyed riding the surfboard with him on the waves of Jacksonville's beach, and how much of a rascal he was with Laney's daughters.

"My girls love him to death. He's so outgoing. You know neither Les nor Louisa are really super extroverts. To me, they're more laid-back and reserved. Mike's the kind of kid who's going to be a fighter pilot someday, daring and unafraid of anything. I told Les that he might want Mike's blood tested. One of those natives down there might have slipped into Louisa's tent one night when he was away."

Wade laughed out loud. "Right. Now that'd be a good one." Both men laughed at the thought of Louisa being anything but virtuous.

"Yeah, and let me tell you, that boy really loves his dad, too. Les totes him around on his shoulders everywhere they go. And they're always playing some game, like ball, every time I see them together. I've never seen so much laughing and carrying on between a father and a son in my life."

"That's great. Absolutely great. That's the way dads and sons are supposed to be."

"Yep, you're right about that," Laney responded. "So, tell me, Wade. How are things between you and your dad? How are y'all getting along these days?"

"Couldn't be better. We see each other at least two or three times a week. Mom cooks supper for me every Tuesday night, and I try to go to church with them most Sundays. Dad's even gotten back into fishing, and we go down to the Alapaha River when we both have some free time. Spend most of our day talking if the fish aren't biting. I only wish it could have been like this my whole life."

Laney smiled. "Be glad for what you've got now, Wade. Let bygones be bygones. There's no way to change all that. You've got to just keep moving forward, you know."

Wade nodded. "Yep, I agree with you one-hundred percent on that."

Laney's face suddenly brightened, "Oh, yeah. You won't believe who came by to visit us recently."

Wade paused puzzled. "Who?"

"Ann."

"Kitten?"

"Yes, in the flesh. She and her husband have a condo down at St. Augustine, and she'd been down to meet someone regarding some repairs to its roof. On the way back, she had some extra time on her hands and decided to look us up and stop by."

"How about that," Wade remarked. "I haven't seen her since before I left Atlanta. Where is she living now?"

"Milledgeville. You were in her wedding, weren't you?"

"Yeah. She married Charles, the lawyer, and they were living in Atlanta at that point. The last time I saw her, which must have been a couple of years back, I think she told me that they might be moving to Augusta. Maybe to be closer to his family? But yeah, since then, I remember Mom saying that they were moving to Milledgeville now that you mention it."

Laney interjected, "Yeah, I think the connection was that he had a good friend living in Milledgeville, and he was moving over there to join his friend's law firm. That may have been the tie-in. I'm not sure really, but in any respect, I think they've done quite well considering they have a condo in St. Augustine."

Wade gave Laney a grin. "She hasn't let all that wealth go to her head now has she?"

"Heavens no. You can remember as well as I can that she didn't like fat cats or people who thought they were special because they had money. Speaking of which, she did fill me in on our pal Karl and what he'd been up to. Do you ever hear from him?"

"Are you kidding me? Not a peep."

"Well, don't feel like the Lone Ranger, bud. I guess we just don't run in the same circles as he does," Laney chuckled sarcastically.

"So, what's he been doing?" Wade asked as he offered Laney a stool. "This ought to be good!"

"As you can only imagine …" Laney grinned raising his eyebrows.

"Hey. Nothing would surprise me about Karl."

"Couldn't agree with you more. So, like you said, you won't be surprised by much I'm going to tell you. Just remember that Ann was no fan of Karl or his family. So bear that in mind."

Nodding his head, Wade agreed. "Seems like ol' Karl is on wife number two. His first wife caught him running around on her with a twenty-three-year-old buxom blonde, a nurse at the hospital where he worked in Augusta. You know he finished medical school at Duke. When he finished his residency, I think down in Savannah, he moved to Augusta where he became quite a prominent surgeon, or so it seems."

"Anyway, he had one child from his first marriage who is just shy of ten years old according to Ann. His ex-wife got full custody of her. That tells you a little something, now doesn't it?"

Disgusted, Wade nodded in agreement. "So as Ann put it, Karl didn't want to be the bane of hospital jokes and gossip over at the Medical College. He and his new flame started anew by moving to Tallahassee where he quickly became a leading surgeon at Tallahassee Memorial. His divorce was finalized rather swiftly, and he immediately married the young nurse. Ann told me that it was really random how she met his second wife. She was visiting a relative at the hospital in Tallahassee a year or so ago, and as she rounded a turn in a hallway, she found Karl talking to a very attractive young woman with big brown eyes and very large tits. Ann threw that in, you know."

Wade chuckled.

"She told me that as she tried walking by unnoticed, Karl looked up and recognized her and called out trying to gain her attention. Reluctantly, Ann said she stopped and turned around to face him and his new wife who Ann likes to refer to as his number two."

Wade laughed out loud. "Sounds just like her. Still minces no words, I see."

"For sure. Anyway, number two gives Ann the evil eye. Now Ann's still quite the looker you know, and numero dos doesn't exactly know what to think of this friendly greeting that her husband is giving this very attractive unknown woman. Can you imagine that, Wade? Why on earth would she be so afraid of someone stealing her man?"

"You mean her meal ticket?" Wade croaked.

"No, more like her Mercedes ticket," Laney laughed back. "But you know Ann. She can't waste such a golden opportunity as this. As always, still the prankster, she tells me she leans over and gives Karl a quick kiss right on the lips. Then she tells him, 'So good to see you, Karl darling. I'm running late for an appointment.' Says Karl starts bumbling trying to introduce Ann to his new wife. Of course, your cousin doesn't give him a chance. Instead, she walks into the open door of a nearby elevator. Turning back toward the couple, she blows Karl another little kiss and waves telling him, 'I'll catch you later, dear.' Ann laughed telling me that right before the door to the elevator shut, she couldn't help but notice the stunned look on Karl's face and a laser glare coming from number two."

Grinning from ear to ear, Wade howled, "Too hilarious. I'd love to have been there to have seen that."

"Classic Ann, wouldn't you say?" Laney laughed.

"Absolutely. Is his wife still a nurse?"

"Are you kidding me? No way, Jose. Ann says that according to a friend of hers who lives in Tallahassee and knows them both, his wife is all about the money. The new Mercedes, Ralph Lauren, Gucci, the million-dollar house. You get the picture."

"Yeah," Wade sighed disappointed. "Do they have any children?"

"Yes, one little girl who Ann thinks is close to eight years old and a little boy."

"With parents like that, that little girl isn't going to have too much of a chance, is she?"

"Unless things change, she'll be high maintenance from the get-go, all right. By the way, according to Ann's friend, Karl's still up to his old tricks. Still chasing 'the skirts.' I think his second head's going to keep him in lots of trouble."

Wade snickered and responded, "You know, sometimes one of those heads gets cut off by a jealous wife or husband." Both friends burst out laughing. As their chuckles subsided, Wade refocused the conversation back to Les and Louisa. "So how are our missionaries doing at their new church in Bradford? Do they like being back?"

"I've only seen them a few times since they stayed with me. I went over to a Sunday morning service this past weekend with Elise, and let me tell you, he's some kind of preacher. His words are so deliberate and compelling that you could hear a pin drop from the time he started until the second he finished speaking. I knew he'd be good, Wade, but I was astonished by what I heard. You've got to go down there and hear him sometime. You won't believe it's our little friend."

Wade smiled back at Laney. "I'm not surprised at all that he can do that, Laney. He's always had that special … something. I've never been able to quite put my finger on it, but whatever it is, he's got it."

"Couldn't agree with you more, Wade, and when he's in that pulpit, it really shows. You can tell his congregation can sense it too. Some of the members told me this past weekend that the Sunday's attendance has already more than doubled. That's in less than two months. Can you believe that?"

Wade shook his head, "That's pretty amazing, all right."

Laney continued, "And with Louisa by his side, they've all fallen in love with her too. But then again who wouldn't? From what I hear, she's re-established the church's Royal Ambassadors and Girls Auxiliary for the boys and girls that until they arrived had been defunct. She's in charge of most of the meals served at the church and has gotten the local citizens involved in their charity drive for a Meals on Wheels-type program to help feed the shut-ins. She even drives the church van transporting people out in the countryside who don't have the means of making it to church functions. What more can I say, except yes. The church is glad that they are there, but not nearly as glad as the citizens of Bradford."

"So," Laney continued as he looked thoughtfully at Wade, "I think it's pretty obvious why they haven't been able to get here to see you just yet. They both wanted me to make sure you knew they weren't trying to neglect you. That's why I stopped by today. To let you know that they'd be heading this way as soon as they could get a chance."

Standing up, Laney said, "So that's the long story short, partner. I've got to be heading on to Atlanta. Another seminar to go to."

Wade rose from his seat and walked Laney to the front door as he heard Wanda making her way into the back of the building. "Laney, I appreciate you stopping by and letting me know what's been going on. It's good to hear that Les and Louisa are back and doing so well. It's also good to hear that Ann is still up to her old ways and maybe not so good that Karl is still up to his."

Laney grinned.

Wade paused and said, "You'll probably get to see Louisa and Les before I will, and if you do, tell them that I can't wait to get together with them."

"I'll do it," Laney responded. "Still seeing Angie, I suppose?"

Wade blushed. "She pops in here or over at the apartment every now and then. You know how it is—we're still talking and all. That's about all I'll say about that."

"Good. Take care of yourself," Laney said with a wink.

"You too. Drive careful."

Turning away, Laney glided his tall frame down the front steps to the sidewalk heading for his car. Watching his friend momentarily, Wade went back inside closing the door behind him.

CHAPTER 19

The Artist

It was less than a mile from the shop to Wade's downtown studio apartment. The building he lived in was only a block away from the county courthouse at the intersection of the town's two major thoroughfares. Ben had bought and renovated the old three-story building which was based on an architectural square form design called Palazzo. The outside edifice required little effort with what was an already dignified appearance. Just beneath the roof's large projected eave ran a grand, ornate, gray stone, Florentine cornice amplified with a band of darker oblong dentil blocks. Below this feature, Ben turned the façade's top three apartments' windows into double doors with a slightly projecting balcony and parapet which he topped with a dark green canvas canopy. On this third level of the building and on its right corner was Wade's apartment.

It had been nearly three weeks since Laney had stopped by to see Wade at the shop. On his return to Jacksonville from his meeting in Atlanta, he called Les to tell him how Wade was getting along. Having this conversation with Laney, Les realized he needed to get up to Georgia to see his friend face to face. He had put off calling Wade because he thought it would be too impersonal. Looking at his itinerary, however, Les could see no way of getting off from work long enough for even a day's visit. He confided in his wife his agony. Louisa thought she had the solution. She would visit him herself.

With all of the commotion and excitement of getting their church back on its feet and with so many problems to solve, it was hard for either one of them to get away. Even so, they both were ashamed that they had not made the sacrifice to go see their dear friend. It was as if two forces were pulling them: helping those in need or re-establishing a loving friendship. As in most cases, it's not should a person do one good thing versus doing another good thing. The human part always comes into play. The question becomes is it more about feeling the power of doing good things and feeding that power by fulfilling the expectations of others versus simply giving one's love to another?

It was Friday morning when Louisa pulled away from her parents' driveway in Meigs. She and Mike had spent Thursday night on their three-day visit with her mom and dad, and now she was on her way to see Wade. She left Mike with her mother and was expecting to make it back by mid-afternoon or at least before dark. She and Mike would then have to leave Meigs by lunch Saturday to get back to Bradford so they could help Les prepare for the next day's worship service. Everything was happening so fast, Louisa thought. She took a deep breath and sighed as she drove into the countryside of Highway 111. In South America, nothing happened quickly, and as hard as she tried to acclimate herself to this new high-speed paradigm, she still couldn't make herself like it. As she drove past fields where cows were grazing and where peanuts or corn had been combined, she wondered where all the time had gone. No longer was Louisa that young girl sitting in her dad's pickup truck as he drove down this road so many years before. Back then, her world had been just what she could see through the windows of that small vehicle. Now, almost thirty-three, she had spent nearly a third of her life living in a foreign land. She'd seen life from all sorts of perspectives and had seen people with every form of need.

At Bradford with Les where the church and its people constantly beckoned her to do this or that, she had no place to retreat, no place to go to get away from it all. She had not been alone or felt the freedom of being by herself in years. Even in the most impenetrable forests on earth along the Amazon, someone was always there with her, someone she usually had to care for. The responsibility to provide for others was unending. Now, all she had to do was drive. She thought that if she had a cigarette right now she'd probably smoke it. She laughed at the wicked thought. Of course, she wouldn't do that, but she could if she wanted to. It had been years since she'd seen Wade. She wondered if he'd changed much since they'd been apart. A smile parted her lips as she thought back to the days they had practiced dancing for the Governor's Ball. How crazy she must have been in feeling the way she did about him back then. But maybe not, she thought as she tried to make herself laugh. Pulling down and gazing into the rearview mirror, she pushed back and patted down some of her hair which was pulled back and neatly tied into a bun on the back of her head. As she did so, she caught her reflection in the mirror and said out loud, "No," then more assertively, "No, it's not like that." Pensively pushing her tongue into her cheek, she fumbled with her purse until she extracted a Lifesaver mint. Popping it into her mouth, she switched on the radio.

In Moultrie, Georgia, she turned onto Highway 319. It would be only a twenty-minute drive to Wade's from this point. She turned the dial on the radio to different stations. Finally, she found a good one coming from Valdosta. An oldie-goldie from Diana Ross swept across the airwaves with a familiar and haunting melody.

"Touch me in the morning then just walk away. We don't have tomorrow, but we had yesterday . . ."

Painfully, Louisa's mind flashed back once more to Athens and Wade and their time together. She was shocked and confused by the disturbing emotions she felt as the song played.

"Hey, wasn't it me who said that nothing good's gonna last forever? And wasn't it me who said let's just be glad for the time together . . ."

At this point, Louisa reached over and changed the radio to a different channel. *Why on earth am I feeling like this,* she thought perplexed. *That was something from years ago. How silly and childish. I'm a grown woman with a husband and child,* she chided herself . . . *a missionary.* These thoughts and feelings for Wade caught her by surprise. The fact that they had surfaced at all and that she could not suppress them troubled her even more. Shaken and unnerved by these very real feelings, she turned the radio off as she came to a stop in the small town of Omega. When the city's one streetlight turned green, she slowly drove onward.

II

Ben gave Wade the day off after hearing about the surprise visit he would be getting from his friend sometime Friday morning. Wade had no idea what was going on but thought he would make the most of this free time by working on his most recent and most critical picture. He had been working painstakingly on this piece for several weeks and uncharacteristically had not painted his original thought, a theme involving a father and his son. Rather than following his intuition, he had chosen a subject drawn from a piece he had done for hire—a man and his dog.

Standing at his easel in the early hours on this Friday morning, Wade kept staring at his work in total frustration. He had started correcting parts of the painting the afternoon before and hyper-focusing, as he could, worked through the night on coffee, sodas, and cheese toast with no sleep at all. He was, by 3:00 a.m. on this particular Friday morning, a dead man painting. His olive complexion smudged in patches of multicolored paint. His jet-black hair speckled with the stuff. His penetrating brown eyes were now bloodshot with dark circles surrounding them. Physically and emotionally, he was a mess—pissed off and angry. Even so, he wouldn't allow himself the luxury of resting. No, Wade had to get it perfect. A painting shouldn't be started if you couldn't capture its essence. Seldom if ever had he encountered the problems he was having in getting a work done right.

Had he not been in such good shape from working with lumber, building furniture at the shop, and running several times a week, he would have long since crashed. And that positive attribute of conditioning had ironically led him down this path of destructive behavior and poor decision-making. He had even stopped taking his anxiety medicine as he thought it might be interfering with his creativity.

This was the work, the oil painting, that he would be entering into the Capital City Art Show held in Atlanta which promoted artists especially from the Southeast and often gave those who placed national recognition.

Wade felt that he could produce good work, but he desperately wanted the recognition and acceptance of his peers and various art associations attesting to the quality of his work. He was aware of the local infatuation with his paintings, but he felt that they were only comparing what he did to other local artists. That he happened to be the best of only a handful of artists in his small area of the country gave him little consolation.

His ability to paint was both a sin and a gift, he often thought. *How can I be both a humble Christian and a well-known talent at the same time? Is it un-Christian to desire to be well known for what I do? How can I know if what I do is good without the adulation of others?* This paradox troubled him often, but he was intent to know and knowing, he thought, meant he had to strive for that sort of praise and recognition.

Standing there tired, worn out, and depressed, he viewed the canvas before him. Every portion, every aspect of the picture had to meld, but unlike other paintings he had created, this one was not coming together. Portraits he had done of individuals or families and pictures of houses, or for that matter, anything he'd done for pay didn't have to possess this quality. He could paint those types of pictures quite realistically, and in some cases, he could even embellish the characteristics of a woman's face, her nose maybe, to make it "look better." But those commissioned paintings weren't really his creations. No, his creations possessed an extra characteristic, an additional quality, an intangible essence, a riveting or sublime poignancy that would evoke an immediate response from the viewer. But such a thing could not be found in this picture.

What is it that's missing? he asked himself.

He closely viewed his work. The central cast of the picture consisted of a man and his dog on the steps of an old wood frame farmhouse in the early evening around sunset. The subject matter, the man and dog, were seen resting on the wooden porch steps at an angle to the viewer. The background sky seen behind the subjects and through the porch needed to be a shade darker, but not more than a shade. It had to be the right hue.

He contemplated a color change in that area of the painting and what color combinations he would have to try this time to make it right. He'd already darkened the sky's color once and knew that doing so again it would involve the tedious sanding and repainting of the sky's peripheral aspects. Would that color bring the picture to fruition, or was it something else that was missing?

Wade went as far as meeting with a veterinarian to watch a dog autopsy to understand the anatomy and texture of the muscles under the animal's fur. The dog's features were splendid as were the man's. He had painted hundreds of people, so the realism was right. It had to be the interplay of light and the way it contrasted his subjects. He dreaded the thought of changing this viewpoint of the work as it entailed tweaking almost everything else in the painting.

"Son of bitch," he muttered under his breath. He left his easel and headed for the kitchen. He had changed the colors so many times he couldn't remember what combinations he'd tried. Wade momentarily entertained the thought of stopping for the night. As he poured a cup of coffee from his coffee maker and drank the first sip, with his mind still racing, he had a thought—permanent blue, white, cobalt violet.

Rapidly, with his cup of coffee in hand, he rushed back to his canvas. Putting the almost full cup on his cluttered worktable, he quickly fumbled about until he extracted a clean pallet. Observing the dozens of full and partially filled tubes of paint located all over the large table, he started to sort. Besides the paint resting before him he had a plethora of other art supplies to go through as well. There were jars crammed with every kind and size of paintbrush one could imagine, linseed and poppy seed oil, gesso bottles, jam jars, drying mediums, old newspapers, paper towels, you name it; it was on that table. He found the three tubes of paint he desired: permanent blue, white, cobalt violet. Squeezing some of each paint feverishly onto the pallet, he thought, *I found it.*

With a pallet knife, he gently mixed his colors while adding a drop of refined linseed oil to modify the paint film. Looking down—there it was, the mood he'd been searching for. The missing link to solving the riddle of his picture. With the corner of his Filbert brush, he placed a point of paint on the canvas where he wanted to darken the late afternoon sky. Then he stood back and observed.

III

Louisa had made her way to the downtown area and parked her car across the street from the elegant brick building Wade called home. For several long minutes, she sat in her car gazing through her driver's side window at his third-floor canopied balcony. By this time, she had regained control over what she had told herself were silly schoolgirl emotions.

Once again, she looked into the car's rearview mirror, but by now with stoic purposefulness. Placing a little Vaseline lip balm on her lips, she turned the mirror back up to its proper position, stepped out of the car, and crossed the street.

In order to get to Wade's apartment, Laney had told her that she had to use the side entrance coming off Eighth Street. She entered the dimly lit stoop and was amazed to see a gorgeous mahogany baluster staircase leading up to spacious landings on the second and third floors. Focused, composed, and with her eyes adjusted to the dull glow of the hallway lights, she couldn't help but be impressed by the workmanship. Finding herself on the third floor, Louisa turned from the stairwell and headed down the hallway toward Wade's apartment. She felt as if her heart was starting to skip beats.

As she walked, thoughts and feelings poured uncontrollably through her mind. The last time she had seen Wade had been at his trailer in Athens. She knew back then that she had fallen in love with Les' best friend. That's why she had to leave without telling him goodbye. Had she seen him even one more time, she didn't think she would ever be able to leave him again. She knew back then that what she was feeling for Wade was misdirected; she had already promised herself to Les.

I pray, God, that I made the right decision. Could there have been another way? She agonized over the thought.

Almost breathless, her mind racing, she stood in front of his door trying to compose herself and wondered if she should turn around and leave. She took several deep breaths, regained her poise, and with a determination to put these feelings behind her, she gently knocked on the door. She waited for Wade to respond, but she didn't hear a sound coming from inside. Looking down at her watch, it read 10:30. Certainly he was awake, she thought. Again, she knocked but a little bit harder this time, and much to her surprise the force of her third strike knocked the door slightly ajar.

Entering the darkened flat, she called Wade's name softly but received no response. She could see all the way through the apartment from the small kitchenette at the entrance to the opened balcony doors facing the building's front street. Outside on the balcony the ting and tinkling of a set of wind chimes could be heard as a strong breeze blew freely through the veranda's opened doorways. Peering around the unlit apartment, there was still enough light to see that someone was lying in a recliner across the room. Between Louisa and the lounge, there was a huge disastrous mess spread all across the beautiful hardwood floor. It appeared to be a wild assortment of things all muddled together. Broken glass, paintbrushes, liquids, paper towels, paint tubes—scattered about as if being knocked to the floor.

Louisa reached back behind her and quietly closed the door to the apartment. She tiptoed around the mess on the floor and stood next to the chair. The ambient light from the opened balcony doorways shown down on Wade who was fast asleep. Louisa looked him over as he lay there. It was amazing, she thought as she gazed down at his face, he appeared almost as he had back in college, except for some slight little wrinkles at the corners of his eyes. He had paint all over him, even in his hair. She couldn't help but smile. There was a small paintbrush that he'd been using still tucked behind his ear.

"Wade," she whispered trying to wake but not startle him. He didn't move. With the catastrophe on the floor and paint all over him, Louisa surmised that Wade had probably been up painting all night and finally crashed. Reaching down, she gently pulled the paintbrush from behind his ear and feared she had woken him. All he did, however, was to turn over on his side. Then he was dead to the world again.

It was cold in the apartment, Louisa thought as she stood next to Wade. She quietly went over to the balcony doors and gently closed them. She walked softly across the room and into Wade's bedroom where she found a blanket. Returning to the recliner, she tenderly covered him. He didn't move. Realizing that she probably wouldn't wake him easily if she were careful, she found a small fluorescent light just under the top cabinets above the kitchen sink and turned it on. This gave her enough light to get a good view of the mess on the floor, and after rolling up the sleeves of her black sweater and white long sleeve shirt, she went to work cleaning the place up.

She picked up the easel and canvas lying next to the floor's jumbled mess and reset it in an empty corner of the room. She picked the broken and shattered pieces of glass from the clutter and put them safely away in a trashcan. Finding a large plastic bowl, she collected the remaining items from the floor and Wade's worktable and carried them to the sink. As quietly as she could, she washed and rinsed off the sticky mess that covered most of the objects. Placing the tubes of paint in one bowl and the paintbrushes in a pan, she kept organizing each set of products and utensils until all were finished. Setting these containers on the freshly cleaned worktable, she tackled the wet floor with a hand full of paper towels and a mop she found in a closet.

In Wade's zeal to get his picture right, he had left coffee brewing in his coffee maker, a loaf of bread and a package of cheese opened where he'd made cheese toast, and an assortment of cups, half-empty plastic soda bottles, cooking utensils, and toast crumbs spread all over the kitchen. While cleaning his entire apartment and sliding things around and rattling dish pans, Louisa found it unbelievable that Wade was not awakened by all the commotion. More calm than confident that he was out cold, she went about doing what all women do best in another person's home—inquisitively observe their surroundings. Louisa wasn't trying to pry. However, she did accidentally come across a card on the kitchen table that read, "Thinking of You." On its inside, it was signed, "Love, Angie." Even with her curiosity piqued at the find, she was much more interested in Wade's artwork. From the kitchen area where she was standing, she noticed the volume of work surrounding her.

The first thing she observed were pads of paper clumsily stacked on a large countertop in the kitchen's bar. In actuality, they were canvas painting pads, gesso boards, and sketchbooks all of which were stacked and organized by type, though not neatly. She saw two additional easels with partial paintings held onto backboards by large clips. The rest of the room had a few completed paintings hanging on the wall. Some paintings were in various stages of development; others were resting on shelves. Some paintings were done on canvas and if done on paper they had backing on them. A host of larger canvases were stacked standing up in little dividers where the paintings' sides faced the wall and could be easily pulled out and replaced. There were a dozen or so various sized blank canvases ready to use.

Walking around the room, she saw that the two easels holding the paper were unfinished watercolors. The third painting on the easel she had picked up off the floor and reset in the room's corner was gorgeous. The painting looked almost like a photograph. *What on earth could make Wade so upset with this picture that he would knock it to the floor?*

Louisa went to the large table filled with sketchpads and started thumbing through them. She couldn't believe her eyes at the detail of the sketches. Even the drawings of the dog autopsy were done with refined perfection. The muscles and ligaments were all drawn out exquisitely, and if that weren't enough, he had pictures of living dogs sketched in almost every posture from running to sitting to lying down and even jumping. The anatomy of each pose was done to complete perfection. It was amazing that he could see all of those details, especially the postures of the animals during movement. Captured by the drawings, Louisa lost any sense of time. Finding herself mesmerized, she had to tear herself away in an effort to find a special painting before Wade awoke. She remembered from back when they were in Athens a painting Wade had done of a woman looking out the front door of her house. There was a child in it somewhere, but it was the desperate look of the woman that was so tantalizing and so telling.

Maybe the picture was on the rack by the wall. She had to hurry, she thought as he would soon be waking up and probably wouldn't want her going through his stuff. He had always been modest, and she knew that part of him would never change.

Finding herself in front of the canvases, she slowly started lifting them out one by one to examine them. They were all fantastic and she could have admired each one for quite a while. She knew she didn't have the time. There must have been forty paintings, all varying in size, but most were at least 20x24 inches. Carefully she slid them out then slowly returned them. Suddenly, she gasped. Dropping to her knees, she finished removing a large 24x36-inch canvas so she could really absorb it.

Setting it on the floor in front of her, a lump grew in her throat as tears started welling in her eyes. In the painting before her was a picture of what seemed to be the

Amazon River. On the riverbank, the scene depicted a small native woman holding her young son in her lap. Both were weeping as a small crowd of natives and white people surrounded the woman along the river's edge. At the center of the painting was an empty canoe which had been pulled to the side of the woman and which contained a broken paddle and a leather necklace holding a cross. "Mico, Mico," Louisa whispered through tears while not being able to take her eyes off of the picture. Overcome by emotion, she composed herself, closed her eyes, and said a short prayer.

Standing, she gently slid the artwork back into its setting. Viewing the work had frayed her nerves even more. She was tired. She pushed a rocking chair close to where Wade was sleeping. As she took a seat watching him, she couldn't help but wonder how he could have come up with such an idea for a picture. Though the woman and child didn't exactly resemble Mico's wife and son, Louisa couldn't help but know it was them.

Who was this person sleeping before her? The troubling thought kept entering her mind as she pleaded with God. *Why? What is the purpose of our lives intersecting like this? Why do you keep allowing this to happen? Have I done something wrong? Are you angry with me?*

The thoughts of Athens and the trailer were becoming more and more poignant as she looked down at Wade as he slept. She hated herself for surrendering to those hidden thoughts where reluctantly she allowed herself to remember how it really was back then. How dutiful he had been to Les by watching after her. What kindness and compassion he had displayed when she needed it. It was that quality of goodness in him that kept him from betraying his friend when he was with her. That same quality of goodness that came from his heart and made his art so special. She knew it all along. The distance to South America didn't matter. Being pious and a missionary couldn't break its hold. Having a husband and a child didn't make a difference.

Tortured, Louisa closed her eyes . . . her heart pounding from the emotions. *Oh, please God*, she prayed. *Is this the cup from which I must drink? Forgive me for these feelings. I didn't even know that they were still there. Please protect me, my Dear Father. Please protect me. I can bear this no longer.* With that thought, she sank down into her chair and fell into a deep sleep. It was noon.

It wasn't until 1:00 in the afternoon that Wade rolled over and started coming out of his stupor. Opening his eyes, he could see through the balcony windows that it was still daylight. *Good*, he thought. *I haven't wasted the whole day.* Suddenly, he realized that a blanket was covering him. He didn't remember getting a blanket this morning. Confused he shifted his eyes to the front of his apartment. There sitting with her head down was a woman sleeping in his rocking chair. Except for her white shirt, the woman wore all black. Black slacks, black sweater, black hair. With her feet tucked under her, even the empty untied sneakers in front of her chair were black.

Though she had pulled the rocker close in front of him, he still could not recognize her with her head down. Seeing past her, he noticed that the apartment was clean. Even after throwing a temper-exploding tantrum when he couldn't get the colors right and knocking everything off the table and knocking the canvas to the floor, all of that looked as if it hadn't happened. *Who is this person?* he asked himself scrutinizing her now more cautiously and curiously than ever. Finally, for some reason she stirred. Maybe it was because of the feeling people get when they feel someone is staring at them. She opened her eyes and lifted her head. Stunned, Wade broke the silence of the room.

"Louisa? Is that you?"

"Yes," she said as she stretched then slowly stood up, smiling.

"How did you get in here?"

"The door was open. I just came on in."

"Hmmm," Wade responded puzzled at how that could have happened. He could have sworn that he locked it.

Louisa walked to the side of the recliner where Wade had brought himself up into a sitting position. Once there she got down on her knees eye level with Wade and, placing her hands on the armrest of his chair, beamed deeply into the face of her still-astonished friend. She joked, "How ya' been doing, Rembrandt?"

Wade gave a little laugh as he smiled in utter delight seeing this most wonderful sight sitting before him.

"More like van Gogh. Wasn't he the tormented one?" His eyes scanned the room then back to her. "Thanks for cleaning the place up. I owe you one," he said. He reached from under the blanket and held her hand. She wrapped both of her hands around his.

Louisa's eyes had grown moist and teary. It was the first time that she'd touched Wade in years. And in that one moment, it felt as if she had traveled back in time. She had hoped and prayed that those sparks from the past would have long since died, but they hadn't. It was wonderful to feel his warm touch and closeness again. At the same time, it was awful to feel this way about him and she was so ashamed. She tried choosing her words carefully. "Wade, we've missed you so much while we've been gone," she said almost weeping.

"I've missed y'all too, Louisa," Wade said with a jovial smile.

Louisa looked down pensively at her hands wrapped in Wade's. Her eyes darted about as she gathered her thoughts about what she should say.

Wade watched her every nuance as only an artist could, knowing that she was struggling in trying to tell him something very important.

Louisa raised her beautiful eyes. Tears streamed down her cheeks as she gazed into his warm, compassionate face.

"I need to tell you something, Wade."

Wade stared back at her questioningly.

"You know those times we had in Athens were really very special for me."

"We had a lot of fun didn't we, Louisa?" Wade was trying to give her a way out of this unnecessary display of honesty, but she wasn't accepting it.

Louisa continued. "Yes, but at least for me, it might have been more than just fun. I left without telling you goodbye. You remember that?"

"Yes," Wade smiled warmly.

"Well, I think I need to tell you why." Solemnly she searched his eyes hoping he understood what she meant. "The problem was . . ." she paused. "That I was in—" Before she could finish her sentence, Wade reached up with his index finger and gently pressed it against her lips.

"I know, Louisa," he whispered. "You did the right thing." Louisa burst into tears as Wade leaned forward and held her.

CHAPTER 20

The Conscience Within

Angie Returns

With the balcony doors open, Wade sat outside his apartment under the awning of his third-floor veranda. A lit finger-width Cuban cigar that Ben had given him rested between his fingers as he read the morning paper. It was Sunday, and he felt a hint of coolness in the fall air. Below him, on the street, everything was relatively quiet. Almost all the businesses were closed, and most of the town's people were either at church or home. Wade could see the spread of the city. The community's water towers loomed large in the distance. Radio and communication towers rode high over the rooftops of the businesses below. On the horizon, he could see almost every structural aspect west of town: from the high school and its large football stadium all the way out to the mall and the interstate highway just behind it. He could have seen further, but the forests of pines and hardwoods masked the homes and other buildings.

A knock on the door broke his trance, then it opened. Searching tentatively, a young woman walked into the kitchen area and sat a large brown paper grocery bag on the bar. Seeing Wade on the balcony watching her every move, she spoke. "There you are," she exclaimed with a smile as she walked toward him.

Wade flipped the ashes of his cigar into a clamshell sitting on the table in front of him then rested the cigar on it. Smiling back, he responded, "What are you up to today, Angie?"

"Well," she said kissing him on the forehead then sitting down in an adjacent chair. "I brought you over a few things that I thought you might be out of." Wade glanced at her questioningly. She responded with a grin, "Cokes, cheese, bread … You know, what you survive on. Last time I looked into that refrigerator of yours, I think it had bottled water and some bologna," she laughed. "Oh, yeah it had some mustard and mayonnaise. I wouldn't have touched that mayo with a ten-foot pole. It looked like it was over a year old."

"Thanks for getting that stuff for me, but you didn't have to do that."

"But I wanted to," Angie smiled seductively. "Somebody needs to take care of you."

Wade responded bluntly, "You know I'm quite capable."

Angie was disarmed by this display of self-confidence. "I know you are," she acquiesced. "I guess I just wanted a reason to come by and see you." She hung her head and lowered her eyes. Wade reached over and took hold of her hand.

"I'm glad you did," he said warmly.

Contemplating his handsome face and compassionate eyes, she realized that he was indeed a changed person. Gone was the pudgy self-effacing mass of a man who whiled away most of his off time either studying accounting or watching television. Gone was the man who came home most nights in a depressed funk and never had the wherewithal to draw even a stick figure. In his place was a man with strong hardened features: the athlete she had married. The poor soul whose eyes had once become pale and frail now returned an aura that was burning and piercing with passion. It was a miraculous transformation that she saw sitting before her and she realized poignantly that this had all occurred without any help from her. His descent into the abyss of anxiety and despair happened while they were a couple living together. If she looked at the situation objectively, she had to take at least part of the blame for what happened to him.

Wade spoke up. "You won't believe in a million years who came by to see me Friday morning."

Angie had no idea who it might be. She thought of Karl, but didn't dare bring him up.

Seeing that Angie was stumped, Wade blurted out, "Louisa Wess. I mean Louisa Ellis."

Startled wasn't the word to describe Angie's feelings hearing him say that name. Here was the one person who knew Angie's deepest, darkest secret. The last person on earth she thought that she would ever have to deal with again would be her old roommate especially not now, as Angie was trying so hard to get back with Wade. Stammering, she tried sounding glad that Louisa had dropped by to visit. "Oh. My gosh. They're back in town?"

"Oh, no," Wade countered. "She came over from Meigs where she and her son were visiting her parents. Les and Louisa are living in Bradford, Florida. It's a small town close to Lake Seminole just across the Georgia line."

"Isn't that town north of Quincey?"

"Sort of, but more west, I think. In any event, she told me it was a good two to two-and-a-half hour drive from here."

Relieved that they weren't living too close by, Angie continued to sound interested in what they were up to. "So, are they still doing the missionary thing or are they back in the country for good now?"

"I don't know how long they plan on staying there, but for the time being, they've taken on this church where Les will be preaching. They're living down there in the church's parsonage, and from what Laney James tells me, they're doing great things. Says that in the two months since they've taken over they've already doubled the size of its congregation. Now that's really something, isn't it?"

Wade related all that Louisa had told him concerning their mission work along the Amazon. He told her about how their little boy got his name and finished by telling her what Laney had said concerning Les' surprising ability to preach a sermon.

As Wade described the missionaries' odyssey, Angie's feelings went from total dismay and fear to a more calming sense of awe of what the duo had been through in South America. She was amazed at what they had accomplished with their lives. She was ashamed of her own life and wanted a second chance. A chance to make amends for past mistakes and a chance to do things right in the future. After teaching one more year in Atlanta, she had followed Wade back to his hometown.

He had become her obsession. She could not and would not, if at all possible, live the rest of her life with this sense of conflict and remorse overshadowing her. If she was lucky enough to regain Wade and their marriage, she did not want to be troubled by what she saw as her unworthy past. Sitting there on the balcony, she listened to everything Wade said about Les and Louisa. When he finished talking about them, she abruptly stood up, leaned over, and kissed Wade on the cheek. Telling him goodbye, she left the apartment. Puzzled by her rapid departure, Wade watched as she closed the door behind her.

II

Wednesdays are busy days at Baptist churches. Preparations had to be made for serving both midday and evening meals at Les and Louisa's church. The R.A.s and G.A.s met each week on this day for teenage boys and girls to be with their friends and to have some good clean fun. The Sunbeams for children met earlier in the afternoon so they could get home in time for their earlier bedtimes. Of course, the grand finale of this midweek Baptist ritual culminated with the Wednesday evening service.

Les and Louisa oversaw the various functions and activities to make sure everything ran smoothly and any and all problems were quickly solved. They would meet back at their house to change clothes for the evening service about forty-five minutes before it started. Normally, Louisa would return to the church and sit in one of the pews at the front of the sanctuary to hear her husband's sermon. This night, however, little Mike started running a fever, and they decided it would be better if she stayed home with him. She could get him to bed earlier and give him some medicine if he needed it.

Les sat at the kitchen table as he watched his son paw at his supper of toast, tea, and a bowl of soup. Louisa had taken the youngster's temperature earlier, and it was already 100 degrees Fahrenheit and appeared to be climbing. "You'll need to take him to the doctor in the morning, hon'," Les told his wife. Looking down at his son concerned but still smiling, he asked, "Your throat sore or anything, buddy?"

Mike nodded affirming that it was. He pushed the plate containing his food back and away.

Louisa chimed in, "Okay, let's go get your pajamas on and get in the bed. We'll skip our bath tonight, okay, sweet boy?"

Slowly the little boy rose and quietly slid his chair back under the table. Reaching over, he gave his father a big hug. "I love you, Dad," he said quietly without complaining about how bad he felt.

"I love you too, Mike," Les beamed as he picked up the little fellow and carried him to his room. Helping him put on his PJs, Les tucked the five-year-old into his bed where his son then said his prayers.

"Now I lay me down to sleep. I pray the Lord my soul to keep. If I should die before I wake, I pray the Lord my soul to take. If I should live for other days, I pray the Lord to guide my ways. Bless Mamma and Daddy, and Mema and Daddy Jim and Papa and Grandma and bless all of our friends back down on the river. Amen."

Normally he would take forever blessing everyone that he could think of, but he was too worn out to say any more this night. Tenderly Les reached over and kissed him on the forehead. Louisa stood in the doorway watching. She followed her husband into their bedroom as he changed from a pullover sports shirt to a white short sleeve dress shirt. He had taken a shower earlier in the afternoon, but he still sprayed on a little extra deodorant as he swapped shirts.

As he stood looking in the mirror brushing his hair with a hand brush, Louisa came up from behind him and wrapped her arms around his chest. Resting her chin on his shoulder, they observed each other in the full-length cheval glass mirror before them.

"I love you so much," Louisa cooed into her husband's ear.

Les smiled warmly back at her and said, "I love you too."

They kept staring into each other's eyes in the mirror, and he went on to say in a more serious tone, "I love you more than you'll ever know. No matter whatever has transpired in the past or whatever could happen in the future, I'll always love you. You understand that, don't you Louisa?" His words were direct and piercing like being fired from a gun. It was as if he'd suddenly become omniscient and could see right into her mind and heart. How could he possibly know what had been troubling her? Yet it seemed that he did.

Louisa glanced down and away as her husband continued to speak.

"Let not your heart be troubled as I forgive you of all your transgressions."

Startled by what he was saying, Louisa turned and faced him.

Radiantly smiling back, he said, "That's going to be the theme of my sermon tonight. I've noticed some sad faces out in the congregation. You think I'll hit my mark?"

Tearing up, she said, "Yes. I think you're right on target." She reached over and kissed him on the mouth. With a smile, she said, "By the way, I'll always love you too."

"I know you will," he responded as he pulled on a zip-up jacket.

An unusual cold front was making its way from Birmingham. As it headed for Bradford, the night air had become crisper. Straightening his collar and kissing him again, Louisa sent her husband on his way.

III

When Les made it into the chapel, he hung his jacket on a coat rack standing in the building's rear atrium and entered the sanctuary. He was running a little late because of Mike being sick, so the room was almost packed by the time he made his entrance. After he walked up the few steps leading to the pulpit, he quickly took a seat next to the assistant pastor. As Les did this, the minister of music addressed the congregation and announced the song they and the choir would jointly sing.

When the singing was done, the assistant pastor got up and discussed the activities the church would be performing over the next several weeks. He also said a short prayer mentioning those who were sick or who had recently died. When he finished his part of the proceedings, he turned the rest of the service over to Les.

Les stood as the assistant pastor returned to his seat. Wearing a pair of tan khaki pants, a white short sleeve dress shirt without a tie, and saddle-soaped scuff-cleaned brogan boots, Les didn't look like an ordinary Baptist preacher. Smiling as always, the unpretentious young man stepped up to the podium.

Though thin and standing only five-feet-seven-inches tall, he was built angular and tough. Constantly paddling dugouts through river sloughs and chopping his way through thick jungle foliage had chiseled fat away from his entire body. This lean look was amplified even more by his constant bouts of hypoglycemia. Each day this condition required that he often eat, sometimes five to six times, to take in enough calories to maintain a healthy glucose level.

The reddish-blonde thirty-three-year-old reached over to the top of the pulpit and pulled the microphone down to a comfortable speaking level. He tapped the mouthpiece a couple of times to make sure it worked.

"Bill over there loves to leave this thing bent way up where my voice won't reach it, so he'll sound better than me."

The audience joined in his laughter momentarily then fell silent. Looking out over the congregation, Les heard the back door of the sanctuary open and close as a young woman slipped into the rear pew of the church. It was the only pew that still had a couple of unoccupied seats.

Les began to speak. "We've been here now for three months and we are so pleased with the participation that the church is enjoying at this time. I hope the little sermon that I'm about to give will warrant your presence here tonight." Les paused for a moment in reflection as he pressed the palms of his hands together then folded his fingers.

"Let me go back in time for a moment," he continued, "and let me clear up some misconceptions that you may have about me. You know Louisa and I have told you many stories concerning our mission trip along the Amazon River. I must confess, that when I started on that trip way back in the seventies and just having graduated from seminary, my ideas concerning one's life were rather unrealistic and naïve."

"There are many traps people can fall into in life. You can get your mindset that things should be a certain way. Believing if you follow this path, these good intentions, then you'll be successful, and everything will work out just fine for you and for those that you've sent down that path. I never remember this being a problem for my wife, but it certainly was for me. I could feel this in myself. And it was the desire of self. But I didn't think of it as something bad at the time."

Hesitating, he scanned the crowd as he collected his thoughts. "When I graduated from college and got involved in the mission's program I couldn't wait to get out into the field and get started. At the time, I didn't have the experience or the realization of knowing who I was or what on earth I was doing. I guess who I was at that time in my life was one very overzealous Christian do-gooder bent on saving as many souls as I possibly could, wherever I would end up. Great intentions, but misguided as hell. Trust me. I did not go down there and come back being the same person that you see standing before you today. I did not attain the stature of a Billy Graham for those people living along the river in Columbia, Peru, and Brazil."

As Les smiled chuckling at the thought, the congregation gave him a short nervous laugh. Les became more serious. "It took me longer, much longer than it should have, for me to get things figured out. My original idea was to bring in food, medicine, and American ingenuity to the uneducated peoples of those regions. Winning trust among the people, I would then share my Christian religion with them. Winning souls for the Lord was my goal and ambition—still sounds like what I'm doing is not so bad doesn't it?" Les paused as he surveyed the audience seated before him for their reaction. Every eye in the room was on him as he spoke.

Lowering his head, Les continued, "I was ecstatic when I found out that our destination would be the mighty Amazon River, a place that contained so many varied and unsaved souls, a situation with so much potential for converting the lost that I could not fathom the thought of failure in any way, shape, or form. I saw myself as the leader of this great mission, the authority on what needed to be done and on how to get things done in the best possible way. I saw myself, the seminary graduate, as being our group's master of the Bible. After the inordinate amount of time and work that I had put into studying the scriptures, I felt, therefore, that I was the one who understood its meaning and application the best. I was the one that everyone came to for spiritual advice. Many of the other missionaries even sought out my council. I didn't feel that I was demanding or even wanting this role of leader. I just felt that the Lord had put me at this place in time for this purpose."

"At first, and I hate to admit this, but I loved the power of what I was doing. I thought to myself, this can't be wrong, after all, I'm just helping these people. I was God's right-hand man down here. He depended on me to get the job done, and that's what I was trying to do. Surely, He would be pleased that I was bringing Christ and salvation to the unsaved of the world. I prayed every night for God to give me the ability to do good things for Him through our mission's work. We now had several sites up and running independently. I was proud of that fact. Everything seemed to be going according to plan. Plenty of money was coming in to fund our Christian program. And this meant we had plenty of medical supplies and volunteer medical professionals coming in to help the people. Plenty of food, clothing, and all sorts of other supplies were coming in by boat. Sometimes special shipments were dropped from planes via parachute. Everything was running smoothly."

"Then just like that," Les snapped his finger. "Everything turned asunder." Somberly, he began to recall what happened next.

"The wet season came a little late toward the end of the second year we were down there, but when it got going it came at us with a vengeance. A rogue flash flood completely took out all the buildings at one mission almost drowning everyone there. This particular mission was situated too close to a tributary that fed the larger Amazon River. It was too close because that's where I insisted it be built. Logistically, in my mind, it matched up well for deep water vessels, and it was a supply route for nearby villagers as well as several Indian tribes that used the area. There had been no real high water there in over nine years. But the native elders kept telling me that the bad floods occurred in cycles of about ten, with the really bad ones happening about every twenty to twenty-five. From their calculations, it was time for the next big one to hit. In fact, it was overdue. And we should be building this mission that I was planning further back up the river on higher ground."

Les paused. "But I was the authority, the chief architect of the mission. I didn't believe in those old wives' tales. I researched it and it hadn't flooded there seriously in over twenty years according to some scientific data that I had found. The land in this area was higher than most and, as far as I was concerned, it could be another twenty years if ever there were to be a flood capable of reaching this particular region again."

Les stopped as he broke into a warm smile. "Yutca was my little Indian friend at that mission. The Mission of Olives we called it because we could get delicious cured 'Mission olives' from some of the large cargo boats that stopped there. Yutca was about ten or eleven years old when we established our base camp there along this particular tributary. He was a congenial little fellow having big brown eyes and always wearing a big bright smile."

"When we first got to this site, we found that no one there had ever been treated by a medical doctor or nurse before. A village elder had provided medicine for the community from a variety of sources, all of which came from the forest or its inhabitants. Many of his treatments were quite effective, by the way. But the village's medicine man was a little wary of us, and if what we wanted to do didn't meet with his approval then it wasn't going to happen. At least that's what we were beginning to find out. So, when it came time to give out vaccinations for such things as tetanus, diphtheria, polio, and host of other diseases their medicine chieftain said no. He didn't like his people being stuck with needles by outsiders."

"We demonstrated that these shots were safe by injecting them into ourselves, so the villagers could see that they wouldn't be harmed. But this was to no avail until little Yutca came forward and held out his arm for a vaccination. After he received his and showed that it was no big deal, then everyone else lined up for theirs."

Les smiled. "That was my first encounter with the unique abilities of this beaming little sprite. As we laid the groundwork for this mission's development, Yutca was always by my side. At first, he helped us gather the area's children to play at our playgrounds. Of course, the children's curious parents followed their children and Yutca to the mission to see what was going on. This worked out exactly as we had expected, and we fed them all fish and beans much to their delight. As time went by, nearby villagers and natives alike would come to the mission for medical treatment. Sometimes they would be running a fever. Sometimes they were involved in an accident or had been bitten by a poisonous snake or insect. Or their children had worms. Most of the time, we were able to solve their problem. Now and then, we'd lose a patient, but such occasions were very rare. As we fed and took care of these people's needs, they began to trust us more and more. Soon we had a following at our Mission of Olives Church and began teaching them our Christian religion and customs."

Les paused. "Take note of that comment. We were instructing them in our religious ways and by this method were able to save many souls. And for me . . . that was the whole objective of this endeavor." Pausing once more, he looked out over the audience. "As this process of trust took hold, the villagers grew less cautious of what they had been taught by their elders concerning the river and its ways. They had seen at the mission that there were new and different ways of doing things. They had heard radio and seen television broadcasts for the first time in their lives. They had seen their pictures made with Polaroid cameras right before their eyes. When we started hearing rumors that many people were planning to abandon their villages to live at the mission, we were not surprised. We built many huts knowing that they would eventually come. And soon they did."

"Yutca's family was the first to move from their home on the heights down to the mission below, and soon, many other families joined them. By the time we moved to our next base camp over thirty families had prospered at the Mission of Olives site. At the small deep-water port, they had easy access for trading their goods for supplies and materials coming in from the outside world. Little Yutca had been a large part of the success of our first established mission. What we learned from him on dealing with those who feared us proved invaluable during our stay in South America. Besides helping us gain the support of the local communities, Yutca and his family taught us many skills useful for our survival. He, his brothers, and father taught us how to build dugouts. How to catch all sorts of river creatures and fish including piranha. They also showed us how and where to find the best drinking water. What fruits and vegetation were safe to eat and which were not. How to prepare and cook the various foods taken from the jungle. Yutca's family was very kind to all the missionaries, but especially to Louisa and myself. I think they thought we were special, not because we provided them with medical and religious care so much as they looked on us as being vulnerable: two soft-skinned whites in the bug-infested inhospitable jungles of the Amazon's rainforest. They must have wondered why on earth we had come down there. But if the truth were known, I imagine they were probably watching over us much more than we were watching over them."

"Before we were hit by the devastating flood of the third year, we received a few new missionaries. Every year or two, some volunteers would leave us and some fresh, enthusiastic new faces would show up." Les paused frowning. "Well . . . that's how it usually happened, but not in this particular case. A beautiful and charming twenty-one-year-old Brazilian student named Catalina was being replaced by a fifty-year-old battle-ax of a nun named Angelina Argueo from Panama. I thought to myself when I first saw Angelina stepping off the riverboat all suited up in her habit—her Sunday best it appeared—that she'd last about a week out here in this climate before giving it up. But-Boy-Was-I-Wrong. As tough and rugged as she appeared, she was."

As Les shook his head in disbelief, the congregation burst into laughter. "I'm telling you," Les said. "This woman would have been more than a match even for the likes of General George S. Patton. I've never met anyone—in my life—to this day—who could take charge of a situation and resolve a difficult circumstance as quickly and efficiently as she could. But the best part about her, other than her ability to command and control almost anything, was that every villager, every native Indian, every boat captain and crew member that stopped by and met her—within fifteen minutes, they all fell in love with her. They'd do anything for Angelina." Shaking his head, Les glanced down at the podium in amazement. As he looked back up at his audience with an exaggerated grin, he said, "And they'd do it with a smile on their face for heaven's sake."

The congregation roared with laughter as Les told them this.

Laughing with them for several moments, he waited until they grew calm before continuing. "On one such occasion, about forty barrels of kerosene were mistakenly unloaded next to our mission's dock. The load should have been carried further west and dropped off at Iquitos, but somehow the paperwork had it coming to us. For several months we tried to get some of the larger vessels docking nearby to get these containers off our property and to their proper destination. We had long since discovered which fuel depot at Iquitos they were supposed to be shipped to. But no one was willing to take this cargo off our hands. Not even when we tried to pay them a small sum of money just to get it off our landing site."

"Then Angelina arrives, and one week later, when the first big vessel comes by, she has it flagged down. She mans a small motor-powered boat driven by some villagers and heads to the middle of the river to board the larger vessel so she can talk to the ship's captain. Within an hour the huge boat has docked. The forty containers have been placed on board and the Captain comes out to the landing and gives Angelina a big hug just before he and his vessel depart. In total dismay, Louisa, myself and all the other people of the mission stood at the other end of the dock with our mouths agape. We could not believe what we'd just seen. And though I asked and asked her often as to how she got the Captain to do it, she would only look at me and smile. To this day I don't know how she got that Captain to gleefully load those forty fifty-gallon barrels of kerosene on to his boat for delivery at Iquitos."

The congregation burst into laughter as Les grinned. As he regained everyone's attention, his countenance grew much more solemn.

"But it was a fortuitous event that she came when she did . . . at least for me. Because it changed my entire outlook on life." Les' words became more impassioned as he started telling of the tragedy that happened at The Mission of Olives. "As I had mentioned earlier, shortly after Angelina arrived, the terrible flood at our first mission occurred. We had established two more mission sites before this event at about twenty to thirty-mile intervals going west. So, by the time this happened, we were a good way away from our Mission of Olives location."

"Like I said earlier the wet season had come a little late that year, but it had come upon us with a vengeance. Two of the Amazon's major tributaries, the Javary and the Putumayo rivers intersected the Amazon at a town called Leticia, which was just west of where our third mission had been built and where we were now staying. We could tell from the continuous downpours and heavy flooding at this site, which was located on some high hills overlooking one of the Amazon's northern feeder rivers that things were beginning to look a little dicey. The river was climbing our banks rapidly, alarming even our mission's most senior villagers who were used to seeing the river flood year after year. Allaying their fears, I told them that we were high enough up on these hills that the water would have to rise many more meters before it would even be considered a threat to us. Thinking this to be true, I also felt comfortable with our second mission's position. It was also situated on some high ground north of the Amazon's main channel."

"As for our Mission of Olives site, I realized that though I had chosen to go against the elders' advice to move it to higher ground, I had not chosen the lowest point either. We had situated it in an area just below the highest hills. So, we felt confident that since we had built the majority of the buildings and all the huts high up on poles that everyone staying there would be safe."

"It took over a week for the news of the disaster to reach us. The flooding had disrupted our normal radio contact with all of the other villages located along the river. The storm knocked out any communications we had with the outside world as well. Finally, after considerable time, we were able to reconnect our equipment and make contact with one of our two other mission sites further down river. It was a relief to hear that they were okay. They were wet but doing fine. However, we could get no response on our radio relays down to Site One, the Mission of Olives, though we tried and tried and tried. It didn't take long, however, for someone monitoring our channel to claim that wooden structures as well as some bodies had been seen floating in the river's torrents east of the mission's location. Hopefully it was only a rumor, I prayed, and hopefully this was not coming from our village if it were true. I knew that we would have to find out soon, so if there were any survivors in peril, we could go to their aid. But to find this out, we would have to take on the challenge of a wildly flooding river which seemed to be running boundless and out of control."

"Louisa and I talked it over as far as trying to make such a rescue attempt. At present and from watching the river's currents blasting past, we knew that taking such a risk would be inadvisable. That more people would probably perish if the boats were to capsize. For over a week we had to sit tight until the river's onslaught subsided. All attempts to make radio contact with the mission had continued to fail."

"I can tell you right now that it was one torturous week of not knowing. Not only did I wonder if our mission had survived, but the thought of its location. My adamant desire that it be built there for all the right reasons. These thoughts kept pouring through my mind."

"As the river finally calmed down enough for us to man our boats, I took three motorized vessels to survey the damage if there was any. Sister Angelina insisted on going and was in one of these boats. The ride down the river was swift and perilous. One moment we'd be on top of a swell, and the next we'd be nosing downward at an almost forty-five-degree angle as we rode it down its other side. It called for some skillful steering to keep the bow of the boat from burying into the next surging wave where we would have certainly swamped or been flipped over. Thank goodness we had three villagers who were well experienced in handling boats in such rough water."

"Everything was moving fast by now. Huge trees and limbs came zinging by us if we tried to slow our boat down. And to make things worse, if that were possible, a thick heavy fog started settling down on us making everything in our path impervious to our sight. It was like trying to work your way through a maze and a minefield at the same time as the boat's drivers would veer one way then the other to miss an obstacle they suddenly found in from them."

"There was a sharp turn, almost an oxbow in the river's tributary just west of the Mission's site. Nervously I pointed this out to my boat's driver as he led the three crafts around the bend. Then my heart sank into the pit of my stomach. Only one building on stilts remained. Everything else, including the dock and small port, the church, all the rest of the huts, the infirmary, and dining hall . . . not a shred of evidence that they had ever even been there or existed. Even the trees and vegetation had been swept away."

"As we pulled our boats ashore and looked around, a very small stream of villagers poured down from the heights to meet us. These were the people that had continued to live on the higher hills and did not come to the mission to live. A few stragglers from the mission did manage to make it back up to where they were, but for the rest of them, they all drowned in the flood." Les stopped at this point of the sermon and pulled a handkerchief out of his back pocket to wipe the tears from his eyes. When he regained his composure, he continued to speak. "So here I was. This great leader for Christ. Who had done all of these wonderful things for these people. Who had saved all of these souls for God. And I was the reason they were no more. I was the reason for their deaths! My path to God! My religious belief on what was best for them!" With sadness, he faced his congregation, many of whom were teary-eyed too, as they shared in his agony.

"My good intentions on saving souls for God and building His great church on the Amazon River killed thirty families. As I looked into the eyes of the grief-stricken relatives standing there wanting to hear me pray. Wanting to hear me talk. To say something—anything. But I couldn't. My grief—My remorse—My guilt of what I had done by not listening to the older leaders of the villages—of the flood that they knew was coming. My thoughts ran in circles, but no words came from my mouth."

"Angelina, who was standing by my side at this point, spoke up. She communicated, as we all did, in Spanish because that was the language that almost everyone could understand. 'Let us all kneel and give thanks,' she said. *Give thanks?* I thought to myself. *Almost all of their relatives. Their children. Had been swept away in this terrible flood because of me. And she wants to give thanks.* I hung my head in shame as she started to speak. 'Father,' she prayed, and I'll never forget what she said, 'You are a merciful Lord. You have spared us our lives to live for another day. As You have taken away our loved ones to be with You in Heaven. We will miss them so badly. We will cry and grieve that they aren't with us now. But on this wonderful river of Yours, You let them play in the sunshine, and fish, and hunt, and laugh, and we thank You for those wonderful, joyful times. We know that You have made us a place in Heaven next to them where we will all meet again one day in our future. And that's for certain. Help us to get all of these people and their families who have survived, the food, and shelter, and medicine that they will need for these difficult weeks and months to come. Until they can stand on their own two feet again. Watch over all of us and meet all of our needs. Amen.'"

"I wept openly when she got through with the prayer. But the villagers, though still stunned by the catastrophe, seemed more resolute as they dispersed and made their way back up to their huts on the heights."

"As they did so, I went off alone walking down the eroded mud washed shoreline. I was inconsolable that first night and did not sleep a wink. The next day Sister Angelina had a fire going and food cooking in a large pot for the remaining villagers. She had a group of men to help her write down all the names of those who were lost. Afterward, as she noticed these men and boys grieving silently and sitting around with no purpose, she had them carve and make small wooden crosses for all who had perished. Then, with what was left of the remaining women and girls, she asked them if they would be kind enough to write each name on a cross. Gladly the girls and ladies, young and old, took to the task of doing something constructive for those who died."

"When all of this work was finished, they carried these crosses far back from the river's shore. On a small hill, they planted them in groups according to who was in each family. They decorated each site with ferns or flowers or pretty pieces of colorful artwork. As they did so, I could see a small hint of peace start to overcome them. Someone would smile or laugh. The process of healing among the villagers was beginning."

"But as we stayed there for several more days, Angelina was the one in charge. I was merely a shell of my former self. The guilt—the remorse—the 'what if I had done it this way or that.' All of these things crushed my soul. The light of my life grew darker and darker until finally any vestige of life that I had ever possessed seemed gone."

"If there's one thing that you cannot fake, it's being alive. I was dead, and I knew it. I walked dead. I talked dead. I ate dead. And I slept dead. My missionary cohorts knew it, as did the villagers who came to comfort me. But their attempts to care for me felt like steel daggers going through what was left of my pitiful heart. As each day passed, for the most part, I did little to help out. I purposefully and shamefully kept to myself as I desperately tried staying away from all the others. If there had been a way to end my life at that point, I would have. One morning before breakfast as I came down the slight hill which overlooked the river and where Yutca and his family's crosses were and where I had been praying over them, I noticed Angelina was sitting on the edge of a large fallen tree watching me. 'Come,' she said motioning to me with her hand. 'Come, sit here next to me.' As I did so, she looked me in the eyes, and asked, 'Les, did you not love little Yutca more than did all the other missionaries?'"

"I found this appalling that she would ask me such a question at this point knowing of my closeness to the boy, but I answered her, 'Yes, Angelina, you know that I did.'"

"She said, 'Then help me feed these children today.'"

"I knew that it was getting close to breakfast and, up until now, I hadn't helped feed anyone. I'd been too depressed. But before I could respond, she asked me again, 'Are you sure that you really loved Yutca?'"

"Frustrated, I said, 'Yes, you know how much I loved him. I just told you. Why are you tormenting me with this question?' I asked her."

"She said, 'Then help me feed their parents too.'"

"I stammered back, 'I will.'"

"Then she asked me one last time, 'Les, tell me this time how much did you really love little Yutca?'"

"Then I knew what she was saying. I was Peter. I fell on my knees crying out from the bottom of my heart, 'I said that I loved him with all my heart and soul! Dear Jesus, I love you!' I screamed out sobbing in tears."

"Angelina knelt down by my side and tenderly put her hand on my wet cheek. Then she compassionately said to me, 'Then help me feed all the people. All the people up and down the river. All the people everywhere.'"

Les stopped preaching for several long quiet seconds.

Then he said, "My grief did not stop at that moment, but that moment is when my healing began. I found that God could make things right in ways my mind and heart could not understand. Not only could he do that, but he could make something wonderful come out of something so terrible. God realizes and understands that we are of this world. We're not saints. We've made mistakes in the past. We make mistakes in the present, and no matter how hard we try not to, we'll make mistakes in the future. But if we love God, we can be forgiven no matter what. Love God first. *Thou shalt love the Lord thy God with all thy heart, and with all thy soul, and with all thy mind—then thou shall love thy neighbor as you love yourself.* That's the only two commandments Christ left for us to do. All the rest will take care of themselves if you do those two things."

Les walked to the side of the podium with his hands folded prayer-like over his nose, his thumbs resting just under his chin. Gazing over his audience, he brought his hands to a full clasp at his heart and again began to speak.

"Most of you in attendance know that my method of operation is not for people to come down after a sermon to be saved or join the church or whatever. After that story, you now know why. Rather than do that, I prefer that the person alone or with a friend or family member make an appointment with me to talk about your relationship with God. You can call my office or call me at home anytime to make an appointment to talk about this most all-important matter of your life. You see, I don't believe in cheap grace where we act as we want and are not sincere in our contrition. I believe in 'costly grace.' Christ taught us how to live our lives with His 'Sermon On The Mount.' Love your enemies? Pray for those who persecute you? God suffered on the cross because He loved us. Dietrich Bonhoeffer was the great German theologian who resisted the evilness of the Nazis in Germany and was thus executed. He said 'to be a Christian is to share in the sufferings of God at the hands of a godless world. To share in God's suffering for humanity.' That's what grace is."

Les paused for a moment as he looked over the congregation with a warm smile. "I hope some of you gained some insight into your lives from my mistakes. I encourage you to stay close to Christ and He'll stay close to you. Don't get too upset that you're just a plain ol' mortal human being that can mess things up at times. Just remember," he paused, "that life is full of choices. Try to make good ones." Les gave a short prayer and the service was over.

Afterward, many people came down to the front of the church to shake his hand and to offer him their heartfelt thanks for giving such a marvelous sermon. Soon the jostling talkative crowd started to thin out as the churchgoers headed home for the evening. As they did so, Les noticed that the young woman who had come into the sanctuary late and had taken a seat on the back pew was still there. Finally, as the last of the Wednesday night crowd made it out the doors of the sanctuary, the young lady dressed in a simple white blouse and a knee length black skirt stood up and, with her coat in hand, walked toward the front of the sanctuary to where Les stood. Les realized a strange familiarity about her. When she got halfway down the aisle, he called out to her with a wide grin. "Angie. I can't believe it's you. I'm so glad to see you."

Tentatively, Angie lowered her gaze as she approached. "I'm glad to see you too, Les," she said nervously.

Seeing her anxiety, Les instantly reached over and gave her a big hug. Jovially trying to make her feel comfortable and sensing why she probably wasn't, he asked her to have a seat next to him. "So, what brings my wife's college roommate way down to Bradford, Florida, to hear your old friend preach?"

Angie glimpsed at Les' shining face. "That was a wonderful sermon you gave tonight, Les."

"Thank you," Les smiled back warmly. "I'm so glad you came."

"The fact of the matter is . . . it hit at the very heart of why I've come to see you."

Les noticed Angie glancing about the room nervously. Whether it was that she didn't want someone hearing what she had to say or maybe it had something to do with Louisa, Les figured that their conversation would probably be best held in private. Standing up, he looked down at Angie and said, "Come, follow me."

CHAPTER 21

B.S.U. Reunion 1985

It was 10:00 Saturday morning when Wade got back to the shop from delivering a bedroom set that he and Ben had made for a client. As he entered, he saw Ben sitting in his swivel chair his feet kicked up on his desk reading the morning paper. Wade headed across the room to his own desk to see what was next on his itinerary. From behind his newspaper, Ben mumbled something about Wade having a female visitor stop by to see him earlier.

"Say what?" Wade asked. He was irked that Ben was purposefully muttering and giving him so little information concerning who the young woman might be.

"Well," Ben said as he continued to read, "she had on some rather form-fitting blue jeans and a red University of Georgia T-shirt. Pretty good looking if you ask me."

"That tells me a lot, Ben," Wade frowned. "You didn't recognize her?"

Wanda, who had been standing and listening at the entrance to the back room, chuckled. Wade glanced at her. Rolling her eyes and shaking her head, she smiled while observing Ben who was still reading his paper. "It was Angie, Wade. She came by to remind you of that party at the college tonight. Remember the party she came in here telling you about a week or so ago? The one that she didn't want to go to alone? That one. She asked me to tell you that she'd stop by and pick you up at your apartment at around six tonight." Wanda eyed Wade sternly. "Now I've given you the message, so I don't want it blamed on me if you're not where you're supposed to be."

"What would make you say a thing like that, Wanda?" Wade acted upset.

"Because you and Mr. Ben over there can get so engrossed in what you're doing down here that you lose track of time. That's why. And I've seen both of you forget things like this before, now haven't I?"

"Okay. Okay," Wade exclaimed surrendering. "I just needed you to explain it to me where I could understand it."

Wanda, her head bent slightly downward, raised one eyebrow and gave Wade a threatening look. She thought Wade might be trying to make fun of her helpfulness.

"Peace," Wade proclaimed giving her the two-fingered "V" sign with both hands raised. "If I don't make it home on time—It-Will-Not-Be-Your-Fault-Wanda. It will be Ben's," Wade cackled.

"Don't get me involved in all of this female u-baw-da—daw-goo-baw-da! I get enough of that from my own wife and sisters. Keep me out of it," the older man said solemnly.

Chuckling, Wanda asked, "U-baw-da—daw-goo-baw-da, what's that supposed to mean, Mr. Ben?"

With a deadpan look, the older gentleman peered up from his paper at Wanda. "You know, it's all that female stuff that us guys are supposed to know, that you want us to know before you even know that you want us to know it. That's the best way I can explain it. It's a no-win situation for us. We lose every time no matter what."

Wanda and Wade studied each other for a moment confused about what Ben had just said. They both burst out laughing as Wanda asked Wade while giggling, "U-baw-da—daw-goo-baw-da?" Ben never cracked a smile as his two cohorts snickered about the word and its meaning for the rest of the day.

II

By 5:15 that afternoon, Wade had made it home. He showered, shaved, dressed, and was ready for the BSU reunion, which would be, of all things, a fish fry. *Surprise, surprise*, Wade thought cynically. At least he could wear jeans and a flannel shirt to the event if he wanted. Thank goodness it wasn't going to be a formal affair. He hated the pretentious nature of stiff-shirt events. After grooming himself in the bathroom mirror, he made his way into his den studio and perched on a stool facing the almost-finished canvas of his latest work. He was now working on his original idea for the picture he would enter in the Capital City Art Show after giving up on the portrait of the man and his dog.

Unlike the other painting he worked on, this one had the paint flowing off of his brushes almost magically and without interruption. The conflicts of color, light, and composition had practically vanished as he, virtually in a state of unconsciousness, had rapidly put the piece together.

As he sat observing his workmanship, the phone rang. It was 5:45 and when he answered it, he was surprised to hear Angie's voice. He was expecting her to walk through the doorway at any moment. "So, you want me to meet you at the Baptist Student Union? Oh, the shelter. Isn't this kind of like—*déjà vu*? Like, haven't we done this before?" he kidded.

On the other end of the line, Angie laughed and promised she wouldn't leave him this time.

Hanging up the phone, Wade left his apartment and made the ten-minute drive to the backside of the college where the lake and a newly improved open-air shelter were located. A single line of cars, maybe thirty in all, were already parked there. Exiting his vehicle, Wade stepped over a single-chain barrier fence that separated the parking lot from the green metal roofed structure. He noticed around sixty adults and students mingling.

Approaching the shelter, memories from those many years ago flooded his mind. He saw students doing what he had done back then as they put the finishing touches on the table decorations. He watched the boys surrounding the fish cookers as they jawed and poked fun at one another. He noticed that they were wearing cowboy hats, boots, and lots of denim. A far cry from what his group had worn.

Wade grinned as he noted the unspoken excitement going on between the young men and women in attendance. He got a nudge on his shoulder from behind. Glancing back, he saw the sparkling green eyes and seductive smile of his former wife. She too had been watching the students who were cooking and preparing the food and drinks. Noticing that the boys and girls were staying mostly in cliques among themselves, she couldn't help but be amused. "Doesn't look like things have changed much, does it?" she noted.

Wade nodded. "Not a whole lot it appears. But one thing I don't see out here this time are all those damn longhaired hippies we had. Where do you reckon they got off to?"

Angie shrugged her shoulders then said facetiously, "Who knows? They're probably our congressmen and senators by now."

Wade grinned, "You think? Even that goof you stood me up for way back when at our B.S.U. cookout?"

"I didn't stand you up for some guy at that cookout," Angie said faking a frown.

"Then what do you call leaving me out there to finish doing all those candles and torches by myself. Remember you went off to chat with that dude and his freaky friends."

Pretending to be miffed, but still smiling at his allegation, Angie responded, "Wow. I didn't know you had such a good memory, Wade. If you were so upset with me back then you should have just asked who that guy was?"

Wade's expression grew inquisitive. "All right then, who was he? I think you'd feel much better if you got that off your chest, now wouldn't you?"

"Got it off my chest? Oh, if I'd only known that this was what was tormenting you so and for all these years," Angie feigned remorse. "Well, if you really want to know that young fellow just happened to be my cousin from back home. I thought maybe—just maybe you could handle things by yourself for at least a few minutes while I asked him how he was doing." Wade grimaced and wanted to respond, but Angie intervened. "Now I know that I may have stayed gone a little longer than I should have, but when I looked back over at you, the next thing I saw was this gorgeous girl straightening your collar and patting down your hair. Then forget me—you and her start doing the candles and everything else. I didn't want to interfere or anything, so I just went off and found something else to do."

Wade, shaking his head, gave his ex a quick grin. "Cousin Ann, I presume?"

"I didn't know who cousin Ann was back then," Angie responded still feigning incredulity.

"Well, all I got to say about that is u-baw-da—daw-goo-baw-da," Wade said stoically.

"What?" Angie laughed.

"U-baw-da—daw-goobaw-da," he repeated.

"What's that supposed to mean?" Angie asked puzzled but enchanted.

"Just means that you're right and I'm wrong. No getting around it." Impulsively, Wade took the bemused Angie by the hand and started leading her through the shelter.

"Where are you taking me?" she asked excitedly.

"Don't worry. I want to show you something." As he led her out from under the shed, he noticed she was wearing gloves. Holding up one of her hands so they both could see the fashion accessory, he grinned. "You reckon' it's cold enough out here to be wearing these?"

"Don't make fun of me," the green-eyed beauty demurred. "You never know what the weather's going to do at night around here. I didn't want to be cold."

As he got close to his destination, he walked her out onto the wood-planked dock. There suddenly, he stopped as he leaned in close to her at one of the railings. It was of little consequence to Angie why he had brought her there. It felt good to be so close to him again. After all the time that they had been separated, just touching him in this way made chills run down her neck. It was the same feeling she had when she'd first started dating him.

Nodding his head upward, Wade spoke quietly, "This is what I wanted you to see." Facing west, they could see the sunset was now ablaze. Streaks of orange and red mixed subtly with the soft hues of pastel purples and pinks caused the distant tree line to be cast silhouette-like across the horizon. Wade stood mesmerized by the constant changing of shapes and tones as the sunset headed toward darkness.

Noting his trance-like state, Angie spoke almost in a whisper, "What do you see as an artist when you see something like that, Wade?"

Slowly turning away from the blazing sky, Wade searched his ex-wife's eyes. "I see the same thing you do, Angie." He paused as she studied him curiously. "Inspiration. Isn't that what you see?"

Angie's heart was pounding as his face was almost touching hers. How badly she wanted to kiss his lips and for him to hold her closer.

Just as he was about to do this, a young college coed came out to where they stood and started loudly ringing a large triangular dinner bell. The student yelled, "Dinner's ready! Come on and get it while it's hot!"

For a few long moments, Wade and Angie stood frozen in time. Their eyes locked in an impassioned gaze even through this untimely distraction. Pulling her away by the hand once more, he remarked, "Well, I guess we better head in that direction. Seems like there's a lot of people out here tonight that they've got to feed. We better get in line."

Disappointed by the intrusion, but gleeful from the experience of being so close to him once more, Angie held Wade's hand tightly as they headed for the long line which was forming under the outdoor shelter. Getting their drinks and plates of food, they saw the only place left for them to sit was with a group of B.S.U. students. "Mind if we have a seat here with you guys?" Wade asked unabashedly.

"Not at all," a tall blond-headed young man called back.

Wade noted that the student wore one of the college's basketball letterman jackets, so he asked the undergraduate if they expected to have a good season this year.

"Yes, sir," the young man responded as the rest of the young people surrounding him stopped eating and looked at Wade and Angie.

"Please don't call me 'sir'. It wasn't that long ago that we were out here doing this very same stuff."

Angie chimed in, "Matter of fact, it was at one of these fish fries where we first met each other."

The girls sitting at the table all beamed when Angie said this. The boys, however, could only manage to act pleasant as they tried hard not to wince. The thought of marriage and commitment at their young age was a dreadful one. Wade, appreciatively, caught the boys' look. *If they only knew the whole story*, he thought.

Eating their meal, Wade and Angie found chatting with the young people pleasurable. The students were eager and ambitious when they talked about what they were doing now and what they wanted to do with their lives in the future. None of them were negative except when the discussion touched on the topic of a difficult class they had to take like organic chemistry or physics. It was refreshing to see such positive attitudes, smiles, and jokes coming from the group. It brought back fond memories for both Wade and Angie of how things had been so exciting when they too had been that age.

The evening of eating and talking with such energetic and interesting people seemed to rejuvenate the couple. As Wade and Angie finished their meals, they told their new acquaintances goodbye then got up from their seats and strolled back toward the lake.

"Gosh," Angie said. "It really takes you back talking to those kids and being back out here, doesn't it?"

"Yes, it sure does," Wade responded. "Doesn't seem that long ago that we rode our pizza pans down that hill there." He pointed through the darkness toward the torch-lit east end of the lake.

"Look, Wade. They've placed torches all the way around the lake tonight. Look at the reflections that they're making in the lake's ripples. Isn't that pretty?"

"It really is," Wade said as he looked across the shimmering water. "The breeze that's doing that is making it a little chilly though. I think you were right about having those gloves with you after all." He smiled at her.

"Yeah, I'm glad I'm wearing them too, now. This cold air reminds me of that day we were out here sledding in the snow. It still sends shivers down my spine thinking about Les nearly dying out there on that hill," she winced.

"Yeah," Wade reflected. "That was a scary day all right going out to the hospital and everything. On a lighter note, you remember going over to the Holiday Inn Bar and waiting on Laney to get there during the snowstorm? Now that was one hoot of a night, wasn't it?"

"Yes, it was. That old drunk salesman trying to get us girls to dance with him. And you playing the spoons. Remember that Wade?" Angie laughed.

"Yeah, that fellow that taught me how to play them was really good, wasn't he?" Wade chuckled at the thought. Smiling, he stared into Angie's eyes, "You know, we really had a lot of fun back then, didn't we?"

"We did indeed!" Angie beamed back. "Say, do you remember it ever snowing up in Athens when we were there? I can't recall if it did or it didn't."

"Yeah, I remember it snowing all right," Wade exclaimed. "It was right before the Governor's Ball. It had to have snowed at least a good two to three inches because of the big mess it made out around the trailer park. The reason that I say that is because the roads iced over out there, after a dancing class, and Louisa had to spend the night at the trailer. You don't remember that happening?"

"No. Not really."

"Then you must have gone back home that weekend or something."

"Maybe I did. I must have."

"Yeah, you'd have remembered that for sure. As I recall, all up and down the Atlanta Highway trees and limbs had fallen and taken down the phone and power lines. Louisa couldn't call anyone to let them know what was going on. It took work crews well into the next day before they got traffic back up and running to where we could get Louisa over to y'all's apartment. All I can remember about it was that it was freezing cold and Louisa being a nervous wreck."

Angie hung her head as Wade kept referring to Louisa. She gazed up into his eyes more seriously. "Tell me something, Wade." Abruptly she paused not knowing if she should ask this question or not, but in her heart, she felt she had to know. It troubled her back then, and though she thought it would never be a problem again, it was something she wanted to find out.

Wade eyed her curiously. "What is it, Angie?"

"Well, this happened so long ago, and it really doesn't matter that much anyway. So just forget it . . . you might take it the wrong way."

"Take what wrong? You've got my curiosity peaked now."

Still hesitant, Angie finally spoke up, "Okay, I'll ask you this question, but don't be mad at me, all right?"

"What could make me mad?" Wade asked puzzled.

Peering into Wade's questioning eyes, Angie slowly began to speak. "Wade, were you ever . . ." she wrestled with the words for a second then blurted it out. "Were you ever in love with Louisa?"

"Sure, I was. Wasn't everybody?" Wade smiled back.

"No. I don't mean like that . . . I mean—"

"I know what you mean, Angie," Wade's voice grew more solemn as he continued. "You mean was I romantically involved in an intimate way with Louisa? Isn't that what you want to know?"

"I shouldn't have asked you that, Wade," Angie apologized as she hung her head in shame. "You don't have to answer that question or anything else about it."

Wade continued anyway despite Angie's pleas to stop. Just as she had feared, she could see a burning look in his eyes, a terseness coming from his voice that she had never heard coming out of him before.

"So, like you want to know if I had sex with Louisa? Isn't that what you're really talking about here?"

"No, Wade! Just forget I asked! I'm sorry. Please—don't," Angie cried out anguished that she'd even brought up the subject.

"Well, for your information, I wouldn't have had sex with my best friend's girlfriend, and I certainly wouldn't have done that with his fiancé. Would you have done something like that?"

Angie hung her head in humbled silence. "It was a stupid question. I know you would never have done anything like that, Wade. I'm so ashamed I asked you."

Wade did not respond to Angie's display of remorse. Silently, he reflected on his relationship with Louisa and realized that no one had ever questioned him about this before. Even when Louisa had come back to visit him and tried to tell him about her feelings, he was able to suppress his. She had done the same with him when she left early for Texas and for Les at seminary school. Maybe it was time to open up and tell someone what had happened back then. Maybe it would help release him from the false sense of guilt that kept bubbling up inside him concerning what their relationship was . . . confused, he couldn't even describe it. Regaining his composure, he caught Angie's gaze. In a less agitated tone, he said, "I didn't mean to tear into you like that. It was a legitimate question."

"No, it wasn't, Wade. I had no—"

"Hear me out," he pleaded.

Acquiescing, Angie grew quiet. "The fact of the matter was that Les had asked me to watch out for Louisa when he left for Texas. He wasn't worried about other guys. He was worried that she would be depressed and lonesome. So, I did and Les was right. She was depressed and lonesome, and after you dumped me, I was too. So we took care of each other as really good friends do. Could we have become romantically involved with one another? Yes, we probably could have and very easily, but we both guarded against ever letting that happen."

Wade continued with his revelation. "This wouldn't have happened in a million years, but what if Louisa hadn't gone out to Texas to be with Les and had stayed with me instead? Would Les have given up on becoming a missionary? Would all of those people that they brought food, medicine, and Christianity to on the Amazon have been helped by someone else? Maybe--maybe not. Would a precious little boy named Mike, who's sleeping in his bed this very night at his parents' house down in Bradford, been born? Maybe not. And what about me? Had I taken another man's wife like that what else would I have been capable of doing wrong, huh? I imagine doing the wrong thing would have gotten easier and easier for me to do. And there would have been consequences to all that, wouldn't you think?"

"Yes," Angie responded meekly. She mumbled, "More than you'll ever know." Angie pondered her own misdeeds. As if longing for reassurance, she asked, "But you do believe people can be forgiven for the mistakes they make, don't you?"

Wade studied Angie's eyes puzzled by her response. "You know I'm a Christian, Angie, so sure I do." Still curious about why she was asking him this, he said, "If we ask God from our heart and we really mean it—we all can be forgiven for the mistakes we've made."

Angie paused after he said that. It was the same thing Les had told her down in Bradford. Glancing down, she asked, "You've spent a lot of time thinking about your life, haven't you, Wade?"

"Yes, I have, and I've had a lot of help in trying to get it straightened out too."

"Well, you're doing a good job of it. I really mean that, Wade." Pausing, she continued staring downward as she said, "That's what I'm trying to do too."

Wade nodded. "I know you are, Angie." By now, almost all of the others from the party had left. As they stood there in the darkness next to one of the wind-blown, flickering torches, Wade reached over and took hold of Angie's hands. Slowly, she gazed up into his eyes.

CHAPTER 22

Bradford

The Wednesday afternoon following the B.S.U. party, an irritated Wade found himself going through his closet and digging through his dresser drawers. Intensely, he searched trying to round up as much gear and appropriate clothing as he could find for a fishing trip he was about to take. Most of these items like blue jeans, underwear, socks, and undershirts were stacked all over his bed. Tennis shoes and rubber boots rested at the foot of the bed along with a tackle box, a knife, and a Gore-Tex rain suit.

It was amazing, he thought, that he had any fishing equipment left at all. He almost never went fishing when he was married. Studying the piles of clothes and gear laying before him, he wondered what he really needed. He knew that the space in the car and on the boat would be limited.

The trip was planned for four days and three nights. Spending the first night on Thursday at Les' house, he would then travel on down to Keaton Beach with his old buddy. There, the two friends would meet up with Karl, the organizer of this trip, where they would spend the second and third nights at Karl's cabin on the canal.

Still planning in his mind what would be necessary for him to have each day, Wade walked back across the room and reentered his closet. As he did so, he heard several knocks coming from his hallway door followed by the soft voice of a female calling his name. "Hello? Wade? It's me."

Instantly recognizing who it was, Wade called out from his bedroom. "I'm back here, Angie! Come on back!"

Entering the room, Angie couldn't believe the scattered mess she saw. Piles of clothes, shoes and fishing gear were stacked all over the room in a confusing jumble. She winced at the sight. "You carrying all of this stuff with you?" she asked.

"No, I've got to consolidate it," Wade said as he thumbed through the clothes in his closet. Pausing a moment, he contemplated her question. "How did you know I was going somewhere?"

Standing at the foot of his bed, Angie said, "Oh, I just stopped by the shop and Wanda told me that Les, you, and Karl were going fishing."

"Let me tell ya'," Wade responded disparagingly. "That Wanda knows everything I'm doing, now doesn't she?" Wade kept up this cynical attitude toward his coworker as he dug through his closet. "Did she tell you that I'd be stopping by to see Les and Louisa?"

"Yes," Angie replied, bemused by his agitation. "She said you'd be staying with them Thursday night and that you'd be spending the next two nights down at Karl's cabin at some beach."

"Wow, my full itinerary," Wade shot back. "For your information, she's correct. By the way, that beach you're talking about is called Keaton Beach."

"Well, I hope you're not mad that I found all this out?" Angie asked poking her head into the small room where Wade was still searching. "I just dropped by the shop after school to see if you wanted to do something this weekend and Wanda filled me in on all that. I didn't ask or anything."

"I know you didn't, Angie," Wade countered as he exited his closet. "Wanda just needs to get a life or a boyfriend or something. She's too wrapped up in what Ben and I are doing."

Angie thoughtfully remarked, "In her defense, she does take very good care of you two guys. And whether you want to be or not, you're probably the only real family she's got. Didn't you say that she moved down here from South Carolina a few years back to get away from her family?"

"Yeah, that's where she came from, and you're right. I shouldn't be so hard on her, but I just don't like someone meddling in my business so much even if she's just trying to be helpful. It can get on your nerves if you know what I mean."

"I can imagine," Angie said trying to pacify him. "So tell me about this trip? Who called you about it? Les?" Angie really wanted to know if it was Karl who had called him. It was still hard for her to get past what she had done years ago. It was even harder for her to believe that Karl had the gall to take Wade fishing after what he had done behind his good friend's back.

"Yeah, it was Les. He called me at work, but I didn't get to talk to him for very long."

"Why not?" Angie asked.

"Well, we had an irate customer to deal with and I had to get off the phone."

"I'm so sorry you had to deal with something like that on your first call from him, but when you get down there, you'll have a whole day and night to get caught up on things."

"Yeah, it'll be good to see him all right."

Wade stopped organizing and packing. After all of the digging he had done, he had the things he wanted to take with him crammed into three small containers. A shoulder bag, a clothes hang-up bag, and his tackle box. Glancing at Angie, he said, "I'm glad you came by. I was planning on calling you to see if you wanted to grab a quick bite to eat tonight and to let you know what all was going on." He paused. "Look's like you've already been filled in on my whole trip. Still interested in getting something to eat?"

Smiling, Angie nodded that she was.

II

Early the next morning Wade got up and loaded his car. He had decided to make sure that no matter what else he carried with him he had warm clothes and a rain suit. He would be prepared for either of those two unpleasant contingencies if they were to occur. Swinging by the shop, he checked with Ben and Wanda one last time to make sure everything was okay and there were no problems he needed to attend to before he left town.

In Bradford, Les was doing much the same thing with his associates. Meeting with the assistant pastor, the minister of music, and Louisa, he went over with them all that needed to be done while he was away.

The church's organization was running like clockwork. Everyone knew what to do, how to do it, and who to contact in the event of a problem. A list which excluded Les; they had voted that he would not call back to check on anything while he was gone. With all the hard work he had put into the successful reestablishment of their church, he deserved at least a weekend sabbatical.

By mid-morning, Les and Louisa made it back to their house where Les had to decide what to carry on this trip. As he finished packing, the doorbell rang. Les could hear Louisa calling out happily, "Wade! It's so good to see you! Come on in!"

Hurrying, Les zipped his suitcase and, almost at a run, headed down the hallway into the living room. There he saw his old pal standing next to his wife. After all these years, the two friends charged into each other's arms, Les almost in tears. Stepping back, he exclaimed, "Man, oh man! It's so good to see you, Wade, ol' buddy! I hope you haven't been too upset with me for not getting up to visit you yet?"

"No, no, Les," Wade said absolving his friend of any guilt. "Laney's kept me posted on all you guys have been doing down here. Besides, I feel a little guilty myself for not getting down sooner to see y'all." Pausing as he surveyed his friends, Wade shook his head dismayed. "I can't believe how young y'all still look. You guys haven't aged a bit. Not one little bit. Both of you appear like you've just graduated college."

Les and Louisa grinned at one another, both embarrassed and skeptical regarding Wade's compliment.

"No!" Wade continued. "I'm being serious now! I'm not just trying to patronize you. It looks like you guys found the fountain of youth while you were roaming around down there. Maybe a witch doctor gave y'all some secret potion or something, huh?" Wade chuckled as he scrutinized the pair.

Les laughed, "Your kindness is greatly appreciated, ol' buddy, but I think all those years in the rainforest probably aged us a little bit more than you're letting on. Louisa mentioned to me earlier when she got back from visiting you what great shape you were in. I see she was right. You been hitting the weights—working out some?"

Wade snickered at Les' suggestion. "Not hardly. If you'd seen me about two years ago, you definitely wouldn't have said that. Believe it or not, I'd gotten up to over two-hundred pounds, and it was all fat. I looked awful. But going through a divorce, it'll take the weight right off ya'. Anyway," he continued, "besides dealing with that situation when I got back from Atlanta, I started working for this older guy who refinishes and builds furniture. Most of what he does involves working with wood. Initially, he hired me to do his books, but I'm more into helping him build furniture now. You know sawing, lathing, sanding, the whole bit. I guess doing it has kept me in pretty decent shape."

As Wade and Les continued to talk, Louisa quietly slipped out of the room. In a few minutes, she reappeared with their little son. Interrupting the two friends' gregarious reunion, she interjected, "Wade, I've got someone here that I want you to meet."

Turning around and seeing the boy, Wade knelt so he would be at eye level with the little fellow. With a wide-eyed expression, he exclaimed, "You must be Mike."

"Yes, sir!" the five-year-old belted out. "And you must be Mr. Wade!"

"That's right," Wade acknowledged to the sparkling blue-eyed youngster. "Wow," Wade declared grinning at Louisa. "He's got your eyes all right. And there's no doubting that big voice and personality comes from you, Les," Wade laughed out loud.

With a big smile, Les gazed down at his son. "He's my best buddy for sure."

Letting go of his mother's hand, the small boy charged over to hug his father's leg. Peering up into his dad's shining face, he announced, "We're bestest pals aren't we, Dad?"

"You better believe we are!" Les responded as he picked his son up and kissed him on the cheek.

Standing back up, Wade asked, "Hey, you know what, Mike?"

"What, Mr. Wade?"

"I think there's something out in my car that I forgot to bring in. Something I brought just for you."

"For me?" Mike's eyes grew wide.

"Yep, just for you. Let me go get it. Okay?"

Facing Les, Mike wondered if his dad knew what it was.

Raising his shoulders, Les replied, "I don't have any idea, Mike."

Both watched from the doorway as Wade headed to his car. Soon he returned holding a large box. "This is for you, pal," Wade announced following Les and his family to their kitchen. Setting the package on the breakfast table directly in front of the eager little tyke, Les pulled out his pocketknife and cut the tape from the end of the box. Splitting some of the cardboard to loosen the container's hold, he slid the package partially out, so Mike could get at it.

"All right, bud. I think you can pull it out now," he told his son.

When the child got the go-ahead, he tore into the carton as only an excited little kid could do. Yanking the contents from its paper wrapping, he raked the brown cardboard container to the floor and out of his way. Noticing the box had come out upside down, he quickly flipped it over revealing a picture of what was inside.

"Wow!" Mike said elatedly but puzzled. "What is it, Dad?"

"Well, let's see," Les reflected as he took his pocketknife back out and cut the tape holding the box closed. "Careful," Les urged his son as the boy started tearing the box's top off.

Working more slowly, Mike soon had the carton open and the contents revealed. "A paint set, Dad!" His eyes gleamed with joy as he pulled out each colorful jar of paint.

"You know what these are, Mike?" Wade asked holding up some long thin round pieces of wood that he had removed from the package.

Mike pondered for a moment. With a matter of fact voice, he said, "Tent poles, Mr. Wade."

Les chuckled then whispered to Wade so his son couldn't hear, "He associates everything with what he's seen down in South America along the river."

Wade smiled at Les' comment. "That's a good guess, Mike. They sure do look like tent poles, don't they? But watch this." Wade put the poles together forming a tripod on which he rested a thin, stiff, piece of cardboard. "These little poles here are what you call an easel. It's something you can set," he held up the paint set's cardboard canvas, "your picture on when you're painting it."

"Wow! That's neat, Mr. Wade," the small boy said as he viewed the stand.

Les interjected, "Okay, Mike. What do we tell Mr. Wade, now?"

"Thank you for the paint set, Mr. Wade."

"You bet, buddy."

Beaming with excitement, Mike asked, "Can we get started painting now? I'm ready."

Wade started to answer, but Louisa interrupted him, "I think we need to eat first. It's about lunchtime. Okay?"

"Okay, Mom, but when we get done can we paint then?"

"We'll see about doing that later, okay? But guess where we're going to take Mr. Wade to eat lunch today?"

Mike thought hard his mouth slightly open and his tongue licking his lower lip.

"It's your favorite place," his mother coaxed.

Mike whispered up to his mother unsure, "Pauly's Pizza?"

"You guessed right, Mike," his mom said with praise.

"All right!" the youngster shouted while spinning around in his chair and giving his Dad a high five. "Pauly's Pizza, Dad!"

Les grinned as Louisa turned toward Wade. "I hope Mr. Wade likes pizza?" she asked smiling.

"You better believe I do. Pizza's my favorite."

"Mine too," Mike echoed.

Before leaving the house to eat, Les offered to help Wade bring in the rest of his luggage. After doing this, Wade, along with Les and his family, piled into Les' car for the ride to the restaurant. For Wade, this meal was a real treat. It had been a long time since he'd eaten with a little kid. The fact of the matter was that such a situation hadn't occurred since he used to eat at his parents' house with his much younger sister Kelli when he was back in school. How enjoyable it was for him to tease the little boy with tall tales about the things he and his dad had done when they were Mike's age.

Throughout the meal, Wade couldn't help but be impressed, but not surprised by the large number of people who had come by to speak to Les while they were there. To him, Les' magnetic personality had not changed much over the years. Wherever this small man went, there was almost always a remarkable sense of affection and enthusiasm displayed toward him.

As they arrived back at the house, it was time for Mike to take a nap. Without much commotion, Louisa and her five-year-old son disappeared into her bedroom for a half-hour rest. As his wife and son did this, Les motioned for Wade to follow him outside. "I need to do one more thing at the church before we leave. You mind riding with me?"

"Not at all," Wade responded. "Maybe you can give me the grand tour of the place."

"I'd love to," Les smiled back as the two headed to his car.

As they rode along, Wade couldn't help but note the familiar grid pattern of city blocks resembling their old hometown. The only difference was the large steep hills and deep troughs of the paved road course-way.

Pulling into the parking lot, Wade could see the simple elegance of this house of worship. It was comprised of solid, dark red brick, and it had a steep-pitched roof. The church contained five, moderate-sized, stained glass windows on each of its sides with two more on the building's edifice. Those in the front were symmetrically located on each side of the building's entranceway.

Getting out of the car, they walked down the sidewalk then up the brick steps that were bordered by two intricately designed wrought iron handrails. At the landing, on the top of these stairs, was a handsomely built wooden alcove where two prominent front doors stood. Opening one of the heavy oak stained portals, Les led Wade over the black slate floors of the foyer and into the church's sanctuary which was quiet and dimly lit.

"Wait here," he said. "I'll be right back."

As Les walked away, Wade's eyes became more acclimated to the darker interior of the building. Gazing down the descending aisle, he viewed row after row of gorgeously finished oak pews culminating at the pulpit area where Les preached. Looking further back, he noticed the sanctuary's perfectly arched choir loft and a baptismal pool just above this upper level where it was centered for easy viewings of church baptisms.

Wade was awestruck by the sanctuary's stained-glass windows that composed most of the eastern and western walls of the room. As the early afternoon sun penetrated the colorful glass, a stunning array of colors shone brightly from each motif. Each window depicted a different story or stage of Jesus' life in bright sublime hues.

Waiting for Les, Wade walked down the burgundy-carpeted aisle to the midway point of the room and took a seat in one of the pews. Marveling at the high, wood-laced cathedral ceilings, and the magnificent scenery, he soon realized that it wasn't just the beauty of the place he found so compelling; it was the silence of the room and its stillness.

Wade reflected on the tranquility surrounding him. It reminded him of one night when he had been studying in a cubicle at the college library. The janitors that night tried their best to work quietly as they cleaned and dust-mopped around him and the other students who were reading and reviewing their coursework. For him, this unique sensation of solitude had always been an elusive and fleeting occurrence, one that seemed to happen at the most inexplicable places and times. There were points in Wade's life when this sudden sense of awareness was powerful and enlightening. Sometimes though, it would subtly creep up on him like a cat coming from nowhere then suddenly be at his side. It was something he couldn't make happen, and it was something he couldn't make last. But when it came, he relished every moment of it, though it was mysterious and beyond his comprehension. There was no term he could use to describe the encounter even though he had never confided in anyone about it. But it almost always happened in seclusion. Blissfully, he sat as still and serene as possible. In this moment everything seemed to connect. Everything had a place and purpose, and he was just a part of it all. Just as abruptly as it arose, the event was over. Wade smiled thoughtfully having enjoyed the experience. Tacitly, he patiently waited for Les to return.

Ten minutes passed before the loud echoing sound of a large wooden door being opened and closed from the rear of the sanctuary broke the stillness of the room. Making his way down the aisle and walking up to where Wade was sitting, Les said, "Sorry for the delay. I had to write a check for the custodian who gets paid every Thursday, and I almost forgot about it. While I was back there, the secretaries got onto me and demanded I leave the building pronto."

Wade looked puzzled as he stood up.

Les explained. "I'm supposed to be on a four-day vacation and I've already been back up here twice today. They're demanding that I get out of here and start my vacation."

Wade laughed. "What a tough spot to be in. Maybe you can get them to write a letter to my boss and tell him that I need to get out of the shop for a while. He's dying for me to get back as soon as I can."

Les' eyes sparkled at Wade's remark. Sounding disappointed, he said, "Well, I guess that kind of kills our little tour, doesn't it?"

"We'll do the tour when we get back Sunday night. How about that?" Wade suggested.

Les nodded and turned to face the front of the church. Pausing, he viewed the room of empty seats as he rubbed the back of his head. "This is some sanctuary, isn't it, Wade?"

"Yes, it sure is," Wade responded reverently.

As an artist, Wade was sensitive in nature, but the unusual event he had just experienced had heightened his perceptions even more. Strangely for Wade, there seemed to be an almost prescient feeling of angst emanating from his friend's voice.

Gazing toward the front of the sanctuary and facing opposite Wade, Les reticently stared upward at one of the stained-glass windows frozen deep in thought.

Intently and respectfully, Wade watched his friend from behind. It was odd, he thought, how long Les was silent.

Les, lowering his head, scanned the sanctuary then began to speak, but in a much more subdued tone. "Sometimes, Wade, I come in here alone to meditate and pray."

Wade listened patiently. He could tell by the tenor of his voice that Les had something on his mind that was causing him great pain. If it was something he wanted to share with Wade, for some reason he did not. Taking his handkerchief out of his back pocket, Les wiped his teary eyes and blew his nose then poked the cloth back into its hold. Slowly, with his head bowed, he turned to face Wade. As Les looked up, Wade noticed that Les' eyes were still tearing. With a quick smile, he said, "As much as I'd like to stay here, Wade—I have to leave. We better get going, hadn't we?"

Wade followed his friend as they headed for the exit. Leaving the church, Les cheered up. He never gave Wade even a hint that there had ever been a problem. Still, Wade could sense that something wasn't right.

For the next few hours, Les gave Wade a tour of the town. Bradford was small-town America. Only one major road ran through the city of about eight thousand. The town's economy in 1985 was built primarily around agriculture, especially cattle farming, small independently owned businesses, and some large governmental agencies and hospitals. Grocery, hardware, and clothing stores flourished here along with a couple of independent pharmacies.

After touring the countryside and talking, Les and Wade made it back to the parsonage. They found Mike hard at work on his painting with his mother hovering over him as the paint by numbers picture set required that she keep him on track concerning which color he would use next and where. Seeing his father and Wade walk into the room, Mike exclaimed, "Look a here, Mr. Wade. Look at my picture."

"Wow. You did this by yourself?" Wade acted astonished. The picture was nearly halfway complete.

"Yes, sir," the little boy said. He proudly stepped back to observe his work.

Louisa's eye sparkled at her son's delight. Glancing at Wade and Les, she asked, "What have you two guys been up to today?"

Les caught Wade's eye just as Wade was about to answer. Les interjected, "Well, I wanted to show Wade our little town down here. After we finished driving through the area, which didn't take long at all, I drove him out to see some of the big ranches and farms we have. You know, the big plantations out around River Junction and Starling Heights. Other than that, not much. We've just been talking and catching up on things."

Louisa eyed her husband with scrutiny. "Not much, huh? Did you happen to go by the church?"

Les had told Louisa that he wouldn't be going back there until after the trip, but he couldn't lie to his wife. "Well, I had to go pay the custodian."

Louisa glared back as she surmised the word game he was trying to play on her. "So, I suppose you just paid him outside—back at the tool shed, right?"

Les continued stuttering, "Well, I had to go to my office and write him a check."

"You mean you went back inside the building again, right?"

"Dadgummit, Louisa," he said in exasperation. "You know I did." He sighed. "I did have to pay the custodian though, and I did want to show Wade a little of the church, too."

Amicably put out with her husband, she turned her attention to Wade, "What did you think?"

"He did have to pay that fellow, Louisa," Wade said trying to take up for his friend.

"I know he did, Wade," she concurred.

"Oh, I only got as far as the sanctuary and we were only there for a minute or two."

"Wade," Louisa said dryly. "You don't have to defend him. We're just trying to get him away from there for a while." Concerned, she gave her husband an upset look. "He needs a break, and he just won't take one."

Amid all of the adult conversation, Mike was left to paint by himself. With his mother ignoring what he was doing, Mike started making his own decisions about what colors he would use. Glimpsing back down in his direction, Louisa quickly noticed that her son had painted several numbered areas the wrong colors.

"Oh, Mike," she asserted pointing to two of the problem spots. "I think you missed on a couple of those."

Mike's enthusiasm for painting the picture immediately ebbed. Confusion and hurt came across his innocent little face. "I didn't ruin it, did I?" he asked as tears started welling up in his big blue eyes.

"No way, Buddy." His dad came to his rescue. "You see these paints that Mr. Wade gave you are what they call watercolors. That means that if you mess up, you can just use water and wash the spot off and paint right over it. It'll look brand new like the wrong color wasn't even there. How about that?"

Unsure, the little fellow didn't know if this was the way it would work out or not. For him, seeing was believing. Louisa left the room, and when she returned, she had a small bowl of water and a little rag that she handed to her husband.

"This is so simple," Les told Mike, "that I'm going to even let Mr. Wade do it to show you how easy it is to clean up these mistakes."

Smiling, Wade took the bowl and rag and started washing the paint gently off the cardboard. "Mike, ol' Pal," Wade said as he worked, "you've got the greatest dad in the whole wide world helping you out with problems like this. You're one lucky boy. Did you know that?"

Mike grinned up at his father.

"Look a there," Les said. "Look at how that paint's coming off just like I said it would."

"Sure is," Mike exclaimed.

"Okay, Mama," Les said as he peeked at Louisa. "Let's get that canvas dried off and let's let Mike put the right colors on it. Then we can see what we got."

Louisa took a dry dishrag and gently tapped the hardened cardboard canvas dry. Taking his paintbrush and with his mother's help, Mike slowly and meticulously as a boy his age could repainted the two messed-up spots.

"Very good," his dad declared when Mike finished. "Now let's ask an expert like Mr. Wade, who is a professional artist, what he thinks about these repairs."

Mike stared up at Wade with anticipation. After purposely giving the boy a serious look for effect, Wade carefully observed the picture. "Can't tell that there's ever even been a mistake made," he said. "It's perfect."

Hearing this, the little fellow cast a big smile up at his father.

Knowing full well what Les was trying to teach him, Wade spoke up, "Mike, I've made lots of mistakes painting my pictures, and I'll bet you money that I'll make lots more. But don't you ever be afraid of making a mistake. I've learned a lot about painting by making and fixing my mistakes. Sometimes, just like you, I've even needed a little help fixing them. Remember, anything can be fixed if you do it the right way. Sometimes that even means starting over with a brand-new picture. There's nothing wrong with doing that either."

When Wade finished talking, Les gave him a wink. It was truly a pleasure for Les to find out that his best friend also understood and could share with others one of life's most important lessons.

As the late afternoon progressed into the early evening, Louisa got Mike to stop painting so she could finish fixing supper. She already had meatloaf in the oven, and some potatoes and green beans were cooking on the stove. As the timer went off in the kitchen indicating that the meatloaf was ready, she called for the guys to "Come and get it!"

Smelling the inviting aroma of the food, the foursome didn't take long to devour their meal. When they were done, everyone carried his dish to the kitchen sink where Les and Louisa quickly washed and dried them.

Keeping to their routine, it was time for Mike's bath, and it was Les' turn to have the honor.

"You got some clean pajamas for us, Mama?" Les asked Louisa.

"They're already on his bed," she answered as she stood at the sink.

He looked down at Mike and said, "It's time, little buddy."

"Dad, can't we skip tonight since Mr. Wade is here?"

"What on earth are you talking about?" Les grinned as he reached down and threw Mike over his shoulder. Holding Mike's hands out like an airplane, Les sang, "Off to the tub we go! With a hidey, hidey, hidey, hidey, ho! We'll wash our big ol' toe with a hidey, hidey, hidey, hidey, ho!" Les kept singing all the way into the bathroom where his voice was finally muffled by the door closing and the bath water running. Wade and Louisa stood in the kitchen as all of this commotion was going on. "Does Les do that every night?" Wade asked.

"Well, not every night because we take turns giving him a bath. But when it's Les' turn, it's a big ordeal," she snickered. "Come on, we'll go sit in the living room until they're finished."

In about fifteen minutes, Mike's bath was over, and he felt clean and frisky. Like a shot fired from a cannon, he charged up the hallway into the living area in his pajamas. Jumping up into his mother's lap, he asked if he could stay up later this night since Mr. Wade was here.

"Nope, not tonight," she said. "You've had some real fun today, but you'll need your rest to finish that painting tomorrow. Don't you think?"

Disappointed, he said, "Yes, ma'am."

From the back of the house, Les called out, "Okay, Rooster! It's time to hit the sack!"

"Coming, Dad!" Mike called back.

Kissing his mother and giving her a big hug, he jumped off her lap onto the carpeted floor like a cat. With a skip and a jump, he bounded up into Wade's lap catching the artist off guard. Giving Wade a hug, he whispered into his ear, "Thanks for the paint set, Mr. Wade."

Whispering back, Wade said, "You're welcome, ol' Pal. I'll see you in the morning, okay?"

Mike jumped to the floor and disappeared down the hallway headed for his mother and father's bedroom. Wade was sleeping in his bed, so Mike had to sleep with his mom and dad tonight.

Coming into the room, he found his dad lying on the bed waiting for him. Quickly, the little rascal climbed up the sideboards and mattresses and snuggled up beside his father.

"You ready to say your prayers?" Les asked.

"Yep."

"Okay then."

Mike closed his eyes tightly as he began to pray.

"Now I lay me down to sleep. I pray the Lord my soul to keep . . ."

This night Mike excitedly blessed everyone and everything he could imagine. When he finished, he looked at his Father and said, "I love you, Dad."

Les smiled at his sleepy little boy. "I love you too, Mike, and I always will, no matter what."

"Dad?"

"Yeah, Mike?"

"Why do you always say 'and I always will, no matter what?'"

"Well, because it's true. No matter what happens to you or to me. If you become a rich man or if you become a poor man or even if we got separated for a while and we couldn't see each other. I'd still love you. And you'd still love me too, wouldn't you?"

"Yep, I would," the little boy yawned. "Dad, I'm getting sleepy."

"Okay, go on to sleep now. I'll see you in the morning."

"Good night, Dad."

"Good night, Son."

As Mike closed his eyes, Les left the room and shut the door behind him. Walking to the front of the house, he found Louisa and Wade talking about the fishing trip the guys were about to take.

Louisa wasn't particularly crazy about Les going off anywhere with Karl, but she was being a trooper about this little excursion.

Unsmiling, she asked, "Are you two guys sure you really want to go out fishing with your old friend?"

Louisa didn't know it, but Les knew a lot more about Karl than she realized. Besides, concerning this trip, he knew something else: When Karl found out Les had returned to the States, this trip had been planned for he and Les. Wade had not been invited. It was only on Les' overt insistence that he was even allowed to come. In any event, Les never let on what he knew. "Karl's always a treat, isn't he?" Les grinned at his wife.

Hearing him say this, Wade chimed in, "Unless he's changed, I think if you looked in the dictionary next to the words jackass and control freak you'd probably find a picture of him."

They chuckled at Wade's remark, even Louisa.

Wade continued, "It's like I was telling Angie. I'll bet he'll have the finest boat that money can buy, and he'll have all the latest equipment to go with it."

Les smiled at the thought. "Yeah, you're probably going to be right about all that, but speaking of equipment, Karl wanted to know if either one of us was certified to scuba dive."

"Scuba dive?" Wade questioned. "I've never done that before, have you?"

"Yeah, we use to travel over to the Peruvian coast once or twice a year where we'd dive the beaches at El Nuro and Mancora. Not Louisa. Just me and some of the other male missionaries who could dive would take these trips. I learned how to dive on the fly. Wasn't certified when I first did it, as I should have been. But I did take the course and got my certification card later on."

"So, if you decide to dive, do you think you'd have much trouble diving here in the Gulf?" Wade asked.

"I wouldn't think so. I imagine the only difference in diving Peru versus the Gulf of Mexico would be the water temperature. Like our Gulf Stream here, they have what they call down there the Humboldt Current. Unlike our warm current, the Humboldt is extremely cold and you have to be fully suited to be able to stand it."

"Hmph," Wade remarked. "I would never have thought that being so close to the equator and all. I bet the water there is a lot clearer though."

"Not really. The visibility is pretty poor all along Peru's coastline. What makes the diving so special down there are its fabulous sea creatures. Turtles, sea lions, massive schools of fish—it's really something to behold. But if you want to talk about really clear water—where I found that was on a couple of dive trips we took up into the Caribbean at a place called San Andres."

"San Andres? Can't say I've ever heard of it."

"Yeah, probably not. It's a Colombian island off the coast of Nicaragua. Beautiful warm water. Crystal clear with visibility up to about thirty or forty meters. Lots of coral and different species of fish and tons of huge lobsters. But anyway, getting back to Karl and our scuba diving trip here, I don't know if the card I got down there will be valid here in the States or not." Les paused thinking for a moment. "But you know with Karl having his, and all the gear, I guess it really won't matter."

"Why not?" Louisa asked concerned.

"Because the restriction comes when getting your air. You have to be certified to get your tanks filled. Karl will already have that done. All I'll have to do is dive."

Louisa continued to be cynical concerning this aspect of the trip. "I can't believe you would trust him to be your dive partner. He's likely as not to go off and leave you to fend for yourself down there."

"Now, Louisa, you know I'm a good enough diver and swimmer to take care of myself even if that were to happen. I would guess that Karl's never come close to diving the rough conditions I've experienced in Peru. So, there's no need for you to even worry.

Listening to Les, Wade asked, "Why do you think he wants to go diving in the first place?"

"I'm sure it's to spearfish, Wade. I imagine he wants to bring some big fish home one way or the other."

"Have you done that, Les? I mean, have you spearfished?"

"Yeah. We speared a lot of them on those dives I was telling you about down in Peru. We'd camp right on the beach we'd dive from, and after shooting a stringer full, we'd come in, clean our fish, and cook them over an open fire. Fresh fish cooked like that are really tasty. The only problem I had when I did all that was my hypoglycemia."

"I thought what you had was diabetes," Wade responded, "and you had to use insulin or take pills or something."

"No, you use insulin if you have hyperglycemia, too much sugar. My problem is that I don't have enough sugar in my bloodstream at times. So I have to eat lots of little meals throughout the day. Matter of fact, when I was diving off those two beaches, the problem for me was that I was burning more calories diving and spearfishing than I was gaining by eating the fish that I speared. That's why I had to supplement my diet with carbohydrates and lots of other foods to keep my sugar level up. But getting back to diving in the Gulf, I'm sure Karl knows where the big fish hang out. So, if we have to spear a few to make our limits that shouldn't be too much of a problem."

"What about sharks?" Wade laughed. "You ever had any problems with them when you were spearing fish?"

"Once or twice with some hammerheads. I just gave them my stringer of fish and got away from them as fast as I could. Where we'll be going this weekend, I think the bull sharks are what you have to watch out for. Ordinarily, unless there's a lot of blood in the water from a hit fish, I wouldn't expect any problems. Sharks are usually just curious. They typically don't bother you when you're down there."

"Well," Wade raised his eyebrows. "We'll just hope you guys don't come across any hungry sharks when you dive."

Louisa quickly spoke up, "Y'all just better hope that boat of Karl's stays afloat."

Both the guys looked at each other and laughed.

"Now, Louisa," Les replied sarcastically. "You know that we'll all have life jackets out there with us."

Louisa rolled her eyes, not in the least bit amused at them having a life jacket with them on a boat forty miles offshore in the Gulf of Mexico. "You can act like everything is going to be all downhill, Les, but you ought to know Karl better than that by now."

Les smiled back at his wife giving her an unappreciated little wink.

Snapping his fingers, Wade remembered something. He mumbled the word, "downhill." In an instant, he stood and headed down the hallway leaving his two cohorts confused as to where he was going. Momentarily, he was back carrying a wrapped present with him. "Almost forgot this," he said. He handed the package to Louisa. "Go ahead. Open it," he told the puzzled pair. "It's for both of you."

Removing its wrapping paper, Louisa paused for a moment as she uncovered what was inside. Gazing back at Wade, she said, "Boy does that bring back memories." Leaning over to see what it was, Les also took a long look.

"You're right about that. It really does."

Pulling the rest of the wrapping off of the present revealed a framed picture. It was a 12x16-inch acrylic of Les having pushed Louisa down the snow-covered hill at the college's lake back when they went to school there. In the picture, Les was at the top of the hill laughing and waving. Louisa, who was riding a pan, was about three-fourths of the way down the slope. The illusion that Wade had created was that the viewer was transfixed on the smiling Louisa as if they were fixing to catch her at the bottom of the hill. It was a fantastic piece so realistic that the snow even appeared cold and the features of both Les and Louisa, down to their expressions, were right on cue.

"How you can paint a picture like that, I have no idea," Les said admiringly. "You certainly haven't lost any of your ability over the years. If anything, which seems to be virtually impossible, you appear to have gotten even better.

Louisa nodded in agreement, "I told Les about all of those pictures you had stored in your studio. They really are remarkable, Wade. It's so good to see you taking your artwork seriously now." Having given Wade that compliment, Louisa stood up and, holding the picture, thanked him for the gift. "I'm a little tired, fellows. I think I'm going to turn in for the night. Hope you guys can get some sleep knowing Karl's going to be your captain down there."

"Still on Karl's case, I see," Les chuckled.

Louisa feigned frustration then turned down the hallway. "Good night, guys," she called out heading for her bedroom.

"Good night," the two friends responded.

As they heard the door to the room close, Wade asked, "What time are we supposed to get down there tomorrow?"

"I told him we'd be at his place by ten a.m."

"So what time do you think we need to hit the road?"

"I think if we get up around six that should give us enough time to have a good breakfast and a cup of coffee. If we can be on the road by seven or so, we should be able to get down there with plenty of time to spare."

"How far is Keaton from here, Les?"

"I'd say a hundred and twenty to thirty miles, give or take a few. I figure going through Tallahassee it'll probably take us around two and a half hours or so. Maybe a little longer if we stop along the way. Besides, if we get there a little late, we'll just get there a little late."

"No, Les. It won't be like that at all. We get there a little late, and Karl will be beside himself. You haven't forgotten that much about him, now have you?"

"Well, let's give Karl a break. After all these years of being married and being a doctor, maybe he's a changed man. Who knows?"

Reluctantly Wade agreed, "Maybe so."

As their conversation ended, the two men stood and bid each other good night. Les walked down the hallway to his bedroom while Wade headed to Mike's room. Closing his door, he picked up his bag and tossed it on the bed. Unzipping it, he pulled out a pair of pajamas that he hadn't worn in years. He wouldn't have worn them even now, but if something came up and he had to go outside of the bedroom during the night, he didn't want to get caught in his usual attire, his underwear.

Taking his shaving case from his duffel bag, he went into the bathroom to brush his teeth. Once done, he took a leak and noticed a soreness in his bladder. He had urinated a lot over the last few days and he felt sure it was from the caffeine he'd been drinking. Too many diet sodas and too much coffee. As he thought back to the wonderful meatloaf supper that Louisa had cooked, he had drunk a barrel of sweet tea. *Oh well, this might make for a long night*, he thought as he stood there. He flushed the toilet then made it back into the bedroom. Clearing the bed of his luggage, he turned the covers back and climbed in.

The digital clock on his bedside dresser read 10:00 p.m. when he closed his eyes. At 1:15 a.m., he awoke. His fully stretched bladder, just as he expected, was killing him. Staggering sleepily through the darkness with his arms outstretched, he found his way back into the bathroom. Holding his urine for as long as he had, he now felt as though he was trying to hold back the water to Niagara Falls. When he released it and let it flow, it came out in a torrent of relief. Finishing up and about to flush the toilet, he heard a car door close and Les' car crank up. Making his way to the bedroom's window, he pulled the curtain back just in time to see Les backing his car down the driveway.

Going to the bedroom door, Wade cracked it to see if anyone else was up. From there, he could see a light coming from the kitchen where Louisa was standing in her bathrobe. Wade wanted to go out to see what was the matter, but he was afraid he might scare her. Watching as she turned off the light, he saw her walk down the hallway toward her bedroom. She suddenly stopped. There was just enough ambient light from the hall's night light for him to see that she was rubbing her forehead deep in thought. A troubled expression covered her face as she paused in the doorway. Looking up and stretching her neck back and forth, she sighed then disappeared into her room.

Quietly, Wade closed the door and made his way back into bed. For a long time, he lay on his back staring at the ceiling. *What was going on?* he thought. *Had Les had a church member fall ill or die? Maybe he was going somewhere for himself.* With Louisa seeing him off, it was obvious his friend couldn't be doing something out of character. As Wade contemplated the day's events, the episode at the church, and now this, something felt wrong. Still, he had no idea what it could be.

In the commotion of the night going on and with Wade having to get up at least two more times to relieve himself, he had forgotten to set his alarm. In a deep sleep and wrapped up in his covers which protected him from October's inevitable morning chill, he felt someone shake him.

"Wade," the loud whisper sounded. "Wade," it sounded again as someone shook him harder. "Wake up, boy."

Rolling onto his side, Wade peeked out from beneath his covers.

"Damn, Les," Wade whispered back trying not to wake Louisa and Mike. "It feels like I just closed my eyes."

"Come on, bud. Louisa's got us some breakfast cooked up and it's getting cold."

Les left the room as Wade crawled out of the warm bed. As his bare feet hit the cold wooden floor, he winced. Grabbing the blue jeans he'd worn the previous day, Wade changed clothes and headed to the bathroom. Relieving himself once more, he combed his hair and went to the kitchen. He found Louisa and a single place setting of grits, toast, fried eggs, and bacon. A simmering cup of black coffee and a glass of orange juice sat next to this overflowing platter of food.

As she watched Wade enter the room, Louisa smiled. "You look sleepy, Wade. Did you not sleep well last night?"

"No. I felt like I'd just closed my eyes good when Les woke me up."

"Was the bed uncomfortable?" Louisa asked apologetically.

"Oh, no. Nothing like that," Wade quickly answered. "I've got a little bladder issue going on, I think. Too much caffeine maybe."

Louisa looked down at Wade's coffee. "Do you want some decaf?"

"Oh, no. Full strength coffee is fine this morning. It's just that I need to watch what I drink this afternoon and evening. Has Les already eaten?"

"Yep. He just left to put some gas in your car."

"He did what?" Wade asked frustrated as he felt for the keys in his pocket.

Louisa's eyes sparkled. "Well, he said that y'all had decided on taking your car since Mike and I would need ours. Besides, he knew you wouldn't let him pay for it."

"That little sneak," Wade exclaimed. "He stole the keys right out of my pockets. A preacher who's a thief! I can't believe that, Louisa."

Grinning back at him, she walked to the kitchen door leading into the hallway and closed it. Putting her finger to her lips, she indicated they were trying not to wake Mike.

"Sorry," Wade whispered.

"It's okay. He's still asleep for now."

Returning to the table, she sat across from Wade as he ate. Soon he was finished. "That sure was a good meal, Louisa," he remarked. "If I ate like this every day, I'd be as big as a cow."

"Well, I'm glad you enjoyed it," she said staring back at him. Catching herself, she glanced down. Seeing Wade's empty orange juice glass, she asked, "You need some more juice?"

"No, but thanks anyway." Peering inquisitively into Louisa's eyes as he thought about the strange episode that had occurred in the middle of the night, he asked, "Did one of your church members get sick or something last night?"

"No?" Louisa responded questioningly.

Wade didn't know if he should continue down this path or not, but curiosity got the best of him. "Well, I told you I was up all night in the bathroom. And on one trip I heard y'all's car crank up, so I peeked out the curtains and saw Les backing down the driveway." He stopped to see Louisa's reaction.

She began to squeeze at the collar of her robe. Her other hand was tightly clenched around her waist. She sat silently for a long moment gazing down at the table. Raising her eyes up at her friend, she slowly began to speak. "I don't know what's going on, Wade." She paused. "I know where he's going. He's going to the church."

"Does he do this often?" Wade queried.

"Oh, he's always going off by himself from time to time to be alone and pray, but never like this."

"What do you mean 'never like this'?" Wade asked confused.

"I mean—he's going to the church almost every night and staying there longer and longer—at least two or three hours. I'm talking from twelve to two or three in the morning before he gets home sometimes. He's never done anything like that before, Wade, even when we were down on the Amazon and we went through some especially hard times." Her eyes grew dark as those memories ran through her mind. She continued, "I can remember a time in Brazil that was particularly bad. Les would go off once or twice a week to be alone and pray. But over these last two weeks, he hasn't missed a night and he seems to be staying longer each time he goes. When he gets back, he seems totally exhausted."

"Louisa, I know this is none of my business, but are you guys having any kind of problems, financial or health related maybe?"

"Not that I know of, Wade. Les and I both had physicals when we got back to the States, and except for his sugar problem, both of us got a clean bill of health as far as I know. As far as money is concerned, you know us. We don't need much to get by." Louisa was obviously disturbed. "For once, Wade, I just have no idea what could be on his mind. When I ask him, he just downplays it. Says he's just doing some soul searching."

Wade gave her a more serious look. "Don't be offended by my asking but could there be another person involved."

Louisa smiled back. "No. He wakes me up every time he leaves, and lets me know every time he gets back." Embarrassed, she said, "I did follow him to the church one night though. Mike was spending the night with a friend and I had borrowed one of the church's cars that day like I often have to do to run Mike and myself around." She bowed her head. "I'm ashamed to say it, but I tiptoed inside the building just long enough to see him from behind. He was sitting in a pew with his head bowed and he was alone."

Wade remembered how he too had sought isolation when he was going through his own emotional nightmare. "You reckon he's suffering from depression or something like that, Louisa?"

"You've seen him around here. Does he act depressed to you?" she retorted still bewildered.

"No, not really," Wade answered. Wade thought it prudent not to tell her about Les crying in the sanctuary the day before. It would only worry her more. Reaching over, he put his hand on her shoulder and peered deep into her eyes. "I'll tell you what, Louisa. I'll keep a close watch on him during our trip. And I'll see if he'll open up to his ol' pal about what's going on. How about that?"

Louisa placed her hand on top of Wade's and through her worried eyes which were starting to tear up, she said, "Thank you, Wade. You're such a good friend."

Smiling back and with a wink, Wade said, "There's nothing I wouldn't do for you two. You know that, don't you?"

CHAPTER 23

Arriving at Keaton

Wade and Louisa sat in the living room waiting for Les to return. Wade had shaved, showered, and gone to the bathroom once more.

As the clock on the mantle read 7:00 a.m., Louisa and Wade heard Mike bounce from his parent's bed to the floor. Soon the five-year-old came into the room through the hallway door.

"What's everybody doing?" he asked as he climbed into his mother's lap.

"Don't you remember?" Louisa answered. "Your dad and Mr. Wade are going fishing today."

"Can I go, Mom?"

"No. You know we've already talked about that, now haven't we? We decided that they were going way too far out and were going to be gone for way too long for little boys like you to be going with them."

Mike, his eyes half glazed from sleep, stared at Wade for several long moments. He asked groggily, "You gonna catch a big fish, Mr. Wade?"

"I hope so, Mike," Wade exclaimed smiling back at the sleepy little fellow.

They heard a car door slam. Les, bright-eyed and jubilant, came bounding into the house.

"You about ready to go?" he beamed at Wade.

"Got all my stuff sitting right here. Ready when you are," Wade answered in high spirits.

"Okay," Les declared. "I've already got my things in the car."

His eyes shifted from Wade to Louisa.

Realizing Les wanted to be alone with his family, Wade gathered his gear and headed for the door. Turning around with a quick grin, he called out, "Guess I'll see y'all when we get back. I appreciate you giving me a place to stay and feeding me, Louisa."

"You're quite welcome, Wade," she said graciously her eyes gleaming.

The dark-haired young man waved goodbye and made his way to his vehicle. Getting there, he tossed his luggage into the back seat and climbed into the front seat of the car.

Waiting patiently, he watched Les along with his family make their way to the front stoop. Looking through his windshield, he saw Les give his wife a long passionate kiss. Playfully, he picked up his son and put the little fellow on his shoulders. Riding him across the yard to Wade's vehicle, he shifted Mike back down into his arms where he gave his son a big hug and kissed him on each cheek. "You do whatever your mother tells you to do while I'm gone. Okay?"

Meekly, Mike replied, "Okay, Dad. I wish I could go with you."

"I know you do, Son," he said rubbing and patting the boy's head.

"Now you remember what I always like to tell you?"

Mike looked into his father's eyes questioningly as Les coaxed him. "That I'll always…"At this point, they both said together, "love you no matter what!"

"That's right, Mike. That's our deal," Les exclaimed as they both laughed. Kissing his son on the cheek again, Les placed the boy on the ground. Giving him a pat on the butt, he sent the little fellow heading back to his mother atop the steps.

"I love you, Dad!" Mike sang out as he ran back across the yard to Louisa.

"I love you too, Mike!" Les called back.

As the preacher climbed into the car and shut the door, he grinned at Wade and said, "All right, Pal. What you say let's get going?"

It was 7:15 a.m. as the two men headed out onto Highway 90 southeast. Through Mt. Pleasant and Gretna and on past Quincy, the two soon rolled into the western outskirts of Tallahassee, Florida. Passing Florida State University and arriving at the intersection of the Apalachee Parkway, Wade and Les could see the greenish patina reflecting from the coppered dome of Florida's stately old capitol building. The Apalachee Parkway merged into Highway 27/20. This would be the road that would carry them to Perry, Florida, a small town situated just northeast of Keaton Beach.

Once outside the city proper and out into the countryside of eastern Leon County, Wade took note of the differences between the northern district they had just traveled and the area that they were now passing through. The rolling clay hills, deep ravines, and large lakes of the state's northern Red Hill Region leveled off into grass-pastured flatlands. They appeared to completely flatten out around twenty miles outside of Perry as the highway turned south. At this location, the Cody Scarp, an ancient shoreline, separated the northern rolling Red Hill Region of the state from a geological area filled with dissolving limestone and other porous bedrock, which formed the springs and sinkholes of the Woodville Karst Plains. The area they were now traveling made up the primary geography of the Floridian peninsula.

"You know Les, you'd expect all of Florida to be as flat as a pancake like it is going over toward Fernandina. I was surprised to see all those steep hills back there between Bradford and Tallahassee. How about you?"

"Yeah, I was expecting the big lakes like Jackson to be there, but it was a lot hillier than I thought it would be. It almost looks like the foothills just past the Oconee National Forest from Monticello to Madison going back up to Athens, doesn't it? Remember where they had all those hay fields and dairy farms?"

"Yeah, right down to even the giant live oak trees you'd see growing in the middle of those fields."

Wade paused thinking as he spotted a few of these majestic older trees shading huge sections of the roadside Their massive limbs spreading outward with soft gray Spanish moss draping them like tinsel made him think of the antebellum South and a much slower pace of life.

Interspersed between the long lines of hardwoods, one could see giant fields of Bahia or Bermuda grass where Wade and Les had expected to see large herds of cattle grazing. Whether it was the time of day or year, or maybe even the market for beef, few were seen.

What was notable to the guys was the absence of all but a few homes located on each side of this highway. Making this observation, they figured that ranchers or paper mill companies probably owned most of this land or at least that was their mutual opinion.

For several miles, neither of the friends talked as they took in the sights of the pastures and forests surrounding them. In a spell of melancholia, Les lowered his eyes pensively. Noticing this after a time, Wade spoke up, "Something bothering you, Les? You seem a little down today."

Les countered with a snicker. "Oh, it's nothing. Just something that happened a few days ago. It can wait until I get back."

Wade thought about what Louisa had said concerning Les going to the church almost every night for weeks. Whatever it was having happened so recently couldn't possibly have anything to do with that. Still, Wade thought it might be something worthwhile to dig into."Say, why don't you let me in on what happened, Les? I might not be able to give you any advice on the matter, but I'll give you my opinion."

Les' smile dimmed. "I don't mind telling you, Wade, if you really want to know."

Nodding, Wade glanced over at him, "Go ahead. Hit me with it."

"All right then," he said. "This past Wednesday, we had a unique couple want to join our church."

"Unique?" Wade was perplexed by Les' choice of words.

"Yeah, Wade. They were gay."

"Whoa. You mean they came down to the front of the church together as a pair?" Wade was astonished.

"Nooo," Les frowned back at his friend disappointed by his attitude. "In the first place, I don't have people come down to the front of the church to join after one of my services. They come to my office later on. I made that clear when I first got to Bradford." Saying this and still disturbed by Wade's reaction, Les eyed his old pal. "But let's say they had come down to the front as a couple like you're talking about. Tell me, would they have been doing something wrong if they had done that?"

"It would have been pretty peculiar, Les. That's for sure," Wade chuckled back.

Irritated, Les continued. "So, you're telling me that God loves only straight people and he doesn't love homosexuals. Is that what you're trying to say?"

"I didn't say that, Les," Wade retorted. "I just said it would have been odd."

Les gave Wade a disgusted look. "In whose eyes?"

"In your congregation's," Wade said trying to make light of the situation.

"And where does that go on God's big scorecard, huh?"

Wade was humbled by Les' questioning. "I see what you're saying, Les, and it doesn't. And you're absolutely right. It shouldn't be like that."

"Yeah, but it is, my friend."

Disappointed, Les continued. "Christ comes to earth and the masses see Him befriending the tax collectors, the prostitutes, and the lepers and the downtrodden, but they just don't get it."

"Get what, Les?" Wade asked curiously.

"That everybody's included. He loves everybody just the same, Wade."

Contemplating what his friend was saying, Wade responded. "There's no doubt that what you're telling me is the truth, Les. But I think Louisa was right in saying that you need a break from the church. You know you can't be nailed to the cross every single day, Pal."

"You think it's that bad, huh?" Les smiled back.

Wade nodded as he glanced back at his friend.

They had passed over the small bridges of two of the area's most notable rivers, the Aucilla and Econfina. They were now within miles of Perry's city limits. For the last ten or fifteen minutes of their trip, both men had noticed the increase in homes lining both sides of the road. Many were mobile homes. Some were shiny new doublewides with well-kept yards. Some were nice singlewides, but many of these smaller trailers were in ill repair showing both their age and neglect.

Getting closer to town, they passed more wood-framed and brick houses with only a smattering of mobile homes in the mix. On the city's outskirts but still out in the countryside, they came across the empty shells of buildings where gas stations, stores, and motels once stood verifying the boom and bust nature of this remote region's economy.

"You need to turn left, right here!" Les suddenly called out.

"Where?" Wade asked alarmed.

"Right there! Where it says, 'Wilson's Bait and Tackle.' See it?"

Wade struggled as his eyes darted up and down the road's left perimeter.

Excitedly Les pointed. "The black sign with white writing right out in front of that building. You see it now?"

Finally, Wade's eyes focused on the store's signage.

Miffed, he said, "Yeah I see it now. Thanks for the head's up there, Les."

Grinning, Les looked at his irate friend. "Well, I didn't see it either until just then!"

The sign read: BAIT. WILSON'S BAIT AND TACKLE. At last, it dawned on Wade where they were. Back when they were young boys, they'd always stopped at this bait shop before heading out to the flats to fish with Karl's dad.

"Good gosh," Wade exclaimed, as he quickly made his turn through darting traffic.

Heading down a side street, he made his way into the back end of a small dirt parking lot adjacent to a faded aqua-colored single-story building. As he tried to find a place to park, he saw several pickup trucks, some hauling boats on trailers, parked in his way. So many vehicles surrounded the area that the store's front entrance was completely blocked off.

After a few moments of meandering through the quagmire of cars, trucks, and boats on trailers, Wade finally found a parking place under a large moss-covered live oak tree a good distance from the building. Coming to a stop, the two men got out and stretched.

"Wow. This is just the way I remembered it, Les."

"Yeah, hasn't changed much," Les said excitedly. "I'd thought all these people would have cleared out of here earlier this morning, though. I guess the tide must be too low to get out in some areas."

"Must be," Wade replied as the two of them walked through the maze of vehicles surrounding the place. At the middle of the parking lot, they heard the booming voice of a barrel-chested young man shout, "Sir! You in the yellow hat there! You're going to have to move that truck of yours. You're blocking these guys from getting out of here." The worker yelled this from his perch on the store's icehouse dock. The man down below waved back understanding what he needed to do as the employee handed down two white five-gallon buckets of crushed ice to another fisherman standing on the ground below.

Les and Wade watched as another customer approached the loading dock and handed the brawny store's employee a ticket. Reading the piece of paper, he moved an aluminum shovel that he'd been using to shovel crushed ice into buckets and reached down under it where he picked up a set of ice hooks. Disappearing through a metal doorway, he entered the icehouse. He clambered back outside pulling a twenty-five-pound block of ice across the deck.

"You think you can pick this thing up or will you need some help, sir," he called down to the elderly man below.

"I'll get it for him," said another fisherman standing next to the man buying the ice block.

Les looked at Wade as they walked toward the bait shop.

"That's what we're coming for too, block ice. Karl said that the ice would be all that we were responsible for as far as fishing was concerned. He has all the rods and reels, tackle, and all that other sort of stuff taken care of."

"How much did he say to get?"

"Oh, about fifty to seventy-five pounds or so. He made sure to tell me to get the block, though. Said the crushed melts too quickly."

Wade questioned him. "So about three of those blocks?"

"Yeah, that's what I'm thinking."

The pair made their way inside the building. To them, the place looked outdated, a relic from the past. In the midst of the old wooden walls, the pegboard shelves, scattered counters, and concrete floor, however, were some of the latest and finest tackle for fishing the flats anyone could find anywhere. They had every kind and size of hook, weight, leader, and plug a fisherman could possibly desire. There were fish gigs, dip nets, throw nets, spear guns, gaffs, floats, rods and reels, and a complete assortment of safety gear so the boater could be in full compliance if he was unfortunate enough to be checked by the marine patrol.

Along with all of this fishing and boating gear, the owners kept in mind what these fellows would want to eat and drink when they were out on the water as well. Things like Vienna sausages, sardines, crackers, chips, nuts, and every other kind of storable or dry food were kept in stands by the cash register. Items that needed cooling such as cold beverages like sodas and beer, along with pre-made sandwiches were held in several large refrigerated coolers at the front of the place. For extra stock and for fishermen who had time to ice down their drinks, they kept bulk displays containing twelve packs and cases of beer, along with sodas stacked around the shop's cement floors.

"You got your Florida fishing license?" Les asked Wade.

"You know that's the one thing I hadn't even thought about," Wade exclaimed in disbelief.

After paying for their ice, they gave the clerk, an attractive young woman in her mid-thirties, their driver's licenses to obtain their fishing licenses. Finding such a lovely beauty behind the counter in a place filled with scraggly old fishermen was like finding a pearl in an ugly oyster.

"You guys mind moving down here and filling out the rest of this information for me?" the woman cheerfully asked as she handed them each a form to fill out.

A small line had developed behind Wade and Les, so they gladly did as she asked. When they finished, they got back in line and waited their turn again to pay for their permits.

While standing there, Wade asked Les, "Where do you plan on putting all this ice?"

"I got that covered, bud," Les asserted.

"Well, I hope so. Those ice blocks look pretty big to me."

Once again, they found themselves in front of the pretty, brown-eyed young woman. She had chestnut colored hair and dark tanned good looks. Every man in the place couldn't help but take notice of her.

"Back again, I see," she winked at the two friends.

Les grinned. "You must be one of the owner's wives. Is that what you're doing down here?"

"Almost," she said, her bright eyes crinkling. "My dad's the owner."

"Aha. I knew there had to be a good reason for someone as lovely as you to be down here selling bait."

Again she chuckled. "I've been doing this my entire life since I was a little girl. There's no place I'd rather be."

Les gave her a warm smile when she said this.

She quickly finished ringing them up and completing their licenses. Tearing off the part of the form she needed to keep, she smiled and handed them their portion of the permit.

"Okay you two, here's where you need to sign." She pointed to the bottom of the license. "And here's the ticket for your ice. Just give it to the young man outside there."

"Oh, wait. I want to buy this too," Les said as he almost forgot to pay for the ice pick he'd been holding.

With that done, the two friends walked back outside where they found the powerfully built young fellow that they had previously seen now taking a break.

"Looks like some of the fishermen have started to clear out of here," Les said handing the ticket up to him.

"Yes, sir. The tide will soon be high enough where they can get their boats out. They'll all be pretty much gone from here in about another hour or so." The burly twenty-year-old grabbed his ice hooks and went into the freezer. With its thick metal door slamming hard behind him on each trip inside, he slid three blocks of ice onto the dock. Freezing smoke poured off each one as they rested there.

Wade noticed Les walk to the car and unlock the trunk. He watched him open one of two large ice chests sitting inside. Walking over to where his buddy was, Wade asked puzzled, "Do you think you can get those big blocks down into those little things?"

"No. That's why I got this ice pick, goober. You mind bringing us one over here and let's see what we can do with it?"

"Goober?"

Les grinned devilishly. "Yeah, goober. Now go get us one."

Walking back over to the icehouse, Wade grabbed one of the glistening frozen blocks. It was heavy, awkward, and freezing, but he easily carried it over to the open ice chest where he rested the smoking cube onto the mouth of the box. Just as they both had thought, it was too wide to fit.

"Slide the corner down in there, Wade, and let me try cutting it with this pick."

Wade glanced at Les confounded. "I thought the whole point of getting these things was because crushed ice melted too quickly."

"It does, but we're not going to crush it. We're just going to cut 'em down to size so they'll fit. You know, in chunks. They still won't melt fast like that." As soon as he said this, Les started chiseling the ice into smaller pieces. In no time he had the whole block broken apart enough so it would fit inside the chest. Wade walked back and retrieved another large block which he rested in the mouth of the other cooler. As he held it there in place, he used the ice pick Les handed him to finish chopping it up. Swiftly doing this, Wade arranged the chunks of ice in the cooler where more could be put into it. Turning around to see what Les was doing, he saw his friend struggling toward him with the last large block. Going down on one knee, Wade quickly came to his aid.

"Here, let me get that for you," he exclaimed warmly.

"No, I've got it!" Les said defiantly as he battled to stand back up on both feet again. Shakily, he made it to the last cooler where he was barely able to lift the block high enough to set it into the container's opened top.

For the first time since they were reunited, Wade noticed the frailness of his smaller friend. Taking over, Wade handled the ice pick on this last block as Les went back into the shop where he said he had to get something else. When he returned, he had with him a brown paper sack containing two soft drinks and two candy bars.

"Here, you want some of this?" he asked Wade as he opened the bag for him.

Wade took note of how sluggish Les appeared. "I'll let you keep the candy bars, but wouldn't mind a cola," Wade replied reaching for the drink.

Both men got into Wade's car. Sipping his beverage, Les spilled it down his shirt. Oddly, he seemed unable to swallow the cola and eat the candy bar at the same time. "Are you all right, Les?" Wade gave him a concerned look. "Here, let me help you." Taking the paper bag that held the candy bars, Wade tried to dry the spilled drink from Les' shirt.

"Stop it!" Les called out angrily pushing Wade's hand away. "I can do it myself!"

Mystified by his pal's sudden change in behavior, Wade let Les try to clean himself up. Keeping a close eye on his friend, he started the car and drove around to the curb of the highway. He turned onto the road heading northwest back in the direction from where they'd come.

"You're going the wrong way, Wade!" Les yelled slurring his words.

"No, I'm not. You can't cross here. There's a concrete median over there, Les. I'll have to drive back up there to where we can cross then turn back around."

Wade watched Les more concerned, as his friend seemed to be growing even more agitated and out of it by the minute. To Wade, Les appeared almost drunk. "Are you okay, buddy?" Wade asked his pal as he noticed that Les' shirt was becoming wet with sweat.

Trying his best to respond to what Wade was asking, Les' speech had become as thick as molasses. Even so, he gave his best effort in telling Wade what was happening to him. "Yeah, I … okay," he stammered.

Alarmed, Wade watched as it looked as if his friend was about to pass out. Trying to collect himself, Les drank some more of his soft drink, then said, "I just … went … low, my sugar." Beads of sweat dripping down his forehead, Les struggled to concentrate and try to make sense. "Had … to get … sugar, back, in me." Again, he took another couple of deep breaths, then he said still stammering, "I'll be … fine … just give … me a minute."

Wade was driving very slowly as he pondered whether to continue the trip or try and head to the local hospital. "Is there anything I can do for you, Les?"

"No—go—to Keaton. I'll be … fine," he told Wade as he took another deep breath. Noticing Wade's worried look, he reiterated, "Promise you—Wade … Go on."

Wade decided to trust his friend. Continuing onward, he knew better than to ask Les, who had originally been the trip's navigator, for directions. He didn't know what, if anything, he could get out of him coherently.

Driving down the highway and into Perry, Wade felt more than likely he was on the right road to Keaton. One reason he thought this was because some of the old motels he was passing seemed vaguely familiar. He was relieved to see that he was traveling down U.S. Highway 19/27A. Seeing this sign, he remembered Les telling him that this would be the road that would get them to their turn off for Keaton Beach.

Thinking back to the last time he'd been down here as a boy, there were certain things he didn't remember about this part of the trip. One thing he did recall, however, was that this road crossed over a small stream called the Fenholloway River because, for some unknown reason, Karl's dad always made such a big deal about it. Sure enough, the bridge over the river appeared just where Wade thought it would be and from this point on he remembered it being only a short distance until he would make his final turn.

Within a few more minutes of driving, Wade came upon a sign with an arrow pointing to the right that read "Keaton Beach." Underneath the name in smaller letters it read "17 miles". Turning southwest off the major highway, Wade started traveling down a county-maintained road numbered 361. Smiling at how easily he had found his way after all these years, he looked over to where his pal was now sleeping. Lightly punching him in the shoulder, he wanted to make sure his buddy was all right.

More coherent, Les opened his eyes and mumbled, "I'm okay, now. Let me sleep, Wade."

Wade noted that Les' breathing had returned to normal. Glad that the trip to the hospital had been unnecessary, Wade sighed as he made his way to the Gulf.

CHAPTER 24

Karl At Keaton

(The Numbers Game)

The morning sun had risen high enough in the eastern sky to start peeping through the forested horizon of Keaton's tidal basin. It had been a relatively quiet morning with the early risers of the small coastal town going about their business of either fishing or tending to those who did.

A glimmer of sunlight crept through the shaded windows of Karl's cabin illuminating everything inside. As it did, a hidden soul, covered snuggly with sheets and blankets, began to stir. Like the dead coming back to life, the person concealed beneath these covers finally slipped one foot out onto the cold wooden floor and then the other. Pushing herself up into a standing position, she ambled over to the doorway and gently leaned her long nude body sensuously against it.

Karl, who was drinking a cup of coffee and reading the morning paper, noted her presence from his chair in the adjoining room. He admiringly studied the willowy twenty-two-year-old blonde from head to toe. *What a set of legs*, he thought as her hips gently and seductively nudged the side of the doorway molding. Looking up past her firm, supple breasts with their tight brown nipples, he saw the beautiful complexion of a young woman peering back into his face with an inviting smile and a sparkling set of blue eyes.

"Good morning, sweetheart," he said in an almost fatherly tone.

In a soft cooing voice, she responded, "Good morning to you, too. Do you have some more of that coffee over there? It's a little cold in here to me."

"Yes, dear. It's on the stove. Help yourself." Karl watched her lean sculptured body as she strolled over to the stove and poured herself a cup. Aroused by her lack of modesty, as any man would have been, Karl asked, "Don't you worry that someone out there could see you in here naked like that?"

"Not at all," she said as she walked over to the glass sliding door overlooking the busy boat canal below. Stretching her arms over her head and arching her back, she blatantly exposed herself to anyone outside who could see her. She giggled. "Let them have a good look. What do I care?"

Karl stood up as Brittany sipped from her cup of coffee. Several boats had passed by on the canal where at least one fisherman had spotted her. As the young man leered at her nakedness, the sensuous beauty raised her cup toward him as if giving him a small toast. Smiling back while tipping his hat, he almost ran into another boat. Regaining his focus after receiving her voyeuristic gift, he continued down the canal heading for the open waters of the Gulf.

What a great ass, Karl thought as he saw her standing there shamelessly. "All right, quit giving those guys a heart attack out there," he exclaimed with a grin as he walked over to her. Grinning, she turned around and rested her arms on both of his strong shoulders. As he held her lithe hips in his strong hands, she planted a long tongue-probing kiss into his mouth. When her lips broke free, she stared up into Karl's eyes seductively. "You want to climb back in the sack with me this morning?"

Karl chuckled. "I think we had enough fun last night for a while. You aren't still horny, are you?"

"Not really," Brittany said. "But I'll do it for you."

"I thought you told me you had a twelve o'clock class this morning, Sweetheart?"

"I do, but I can miss it if you want me to?"

Karl grinned as he removed her arms from around his neck. "No," he replied affectionately. "You don't need to miss any classes if you plan on getting into medical school."

Brittany playfully pouted as Karl reached over and took her chin between his thumb and index finger, pulling her lips close to his. He gave her a little kiss, then gently turned her around and popped her bottom with his bare hand.

"Oooh—I like it when you spank me like that," she giggled.

"Get going," Karl called out. "Or you'll be late for class. Besides, I've got a couple of buddies coming down here this morning I'm carrying out fishing."

Picking up her pace, Brittany took a quick shower and was soon dressed. After putting on the final touches of her makeup, she came into the kitchen carrying a small overnight bag and started to sit down at the table next to Karl who was still reading the morning paper.

Observing her as she took a seat, Karl said, "I liked what you had on when you greeted me earlier, but you do look very nice today, kid."

"Thank you," she beamed.

Reaching into a white cardboard bakery box, she pulled out a fresh sugarcoated cinnamon bun. As she did this, Karl spoke, "I hate to rush you, honey, but my friends will be here shortly and one of them is a Baptist preacher. Might not look too good if they find an attractive young woman eating breakfast with me with her suitcase sitting next to her."

Brittany laughed. "Probably not. How about pouring me a cup of coffee in one of those paper cups while I go to the little girl's room?"

Karl did as she asked and when she returned, he had her cinnamon bun sitting on a paper plate next to a steaming cup of hot coffee.

"Thanks," she said. Picking up her luggage with Karl following her, they headed outside to her candy apple red Volvo.

As she started the car, Karl leaned in and kissed her. He told her he'd call later when he got back to Tallahassee. With that, the long-legged, blue-eyed beauty backed out of the drive and left.

II

Letting Les sleep, Wade made his way through the oak-pine forests and poor sandy soil of coastal Taylor County. The only distractions he saw as he traveled were sporadic but increasing numbers of low-roofed, single-story, brick and wood framed houses. An occasional fenced-in pasture dotted with small scrub oaks might hold a few cows. Nothing he saw was out of the ordinary until he came across a well-kept farm with much better maintained fences and fields containing, of all things, giant bison.

When Wade saw these massive animals grazing about the place, he was tempted to wake up his hypoglycemic friend and show them to him. In retrospect, however, he thought better of it. After the fit his pal had just endured, all Les needed to see when he opened his eyes was a huge buffalo staring him in the face as the animal slobbered while chewing its cud. *How improbable*, Wade thought, *for these massive cold-climate animals to be down here on the tropical coast of Florida.*

Wade shook his head realizing that Les would never believe what he had seen until he saw them for himself on their way back. Still traveling around sixty miles per hour in his small white sedan, Wade started to slow down as he noticed a yellow road sign indicating a dangerous bend up ahead.

Vaguely, Wade remembered this sharp turn. Years before Karl's dad had almost missed making the near ninety-degree angle. As usual, the doctor was going too fast and had to fishtail sideways just to stay on the pavement. Wade recalled some of the locals referring to it as "Dead Man's Curve" because of the number of people who had lost their lives at the spot.

As Wade approached the corner of the turn, he slowed down even more, and as luck would have it, just in time. Heading into the hairpin curve coming from the opposite direction in what seemed like a blur was a red Volvo traveling at high speed. It was heading straight for him. Instantly, Wade veered off to the right-hand side as the car, driven by a young blonde, came barreling past. Straddling the road's centerline, the young woman never even slowed down to see whether Wade was okay as she continued onward.

Trying mightily to maintain control of his car, Wade suddenly stopped. Shaken by how close he had come to colliding with the other vehicle, he found his heart pounding and his hands trembling. Amazing to him as he had careened down the bumpy roadside into a shallow ditch, he noted that Les had not even stirred. The young preacher had slept right through the whole ordeal. Gazing over at him, Wade shook his head. Slowly, he drove back onto the road and traveled onward.

In just a few minutes, Wade pulled up to the Keaton Beach Marina. As the car came to a stop, Les stretched his arms, seeming to come back to life.

"So here we are, huh?" he yawned.

"Yeah, no thanks to my chief navigator. You feeling all right now?" Wade smiled at him.

Les took a deep breath of air through his nose, "Ah, yes. The salty, muddy smell of Keaton's marshes. The tide must still be pretty close to low, I guess. Continuing to stretch, he glanced back at Wade. "Oh, yeah—I'm doing just fine. Never felt better."

Les surveyed the area once he stood up outside the car. "Seen any sign of Karl, yet?"

"Nope. None whatsoever. Why don't we go inside the Marina? Maybe they've seen him. You need another drink or candy bar? I don't want you passing out on me again."

"Yeah, another coke probably wouldn't hurt."

Walking up the steps to the entrance, Wade noticed that there weren't many boat trailers or vehicles surrounding the place. There were only a couple of boats moored down below the giant boatlift north of the Marina. Waiting for Les to catch up, he kept scanning his surroundings. Wade couldn't remember a time he'd been down here that he'd seen such little activity.

Entering the building, they found a slightly more refined selection of merchandise than what they had seen back at Wilson's. Being on the water, the Marina seemed to cater more to the needs of those having boats, but it did maintain a small selection of tackle for the fisherman who had forgotten theirs.

Reaching into a cooler at the back of the store, Wade pulled out a grape soda for himself and a coke for Les. Walking toward the cash register, each one of them picked up a pack of peanut butter crackers. At the checkout counter, they placed their items on the store's glass-covered countertop.

"Hey there," came the deep, gravelly, but sweet voice of a woman in her early fifties. Having a tinge of gray in her black hair, she wore a white, beach-looking, buttoned-down, short-sleeved shirt imprinted with little orange and blue fish. She was neatly dressed, but had the look of a smoker: slightly puffy eyes, with a face full of premature wrinkles.

Les was the first to speak. "How are you doing today?" he asked watching as she rested a cigarette on a nearby ashtray.

"Oh, we're doing pretty good. Will there be anything else?" she smiled back.

"Yeah, I'm looking for a fellow named Karl..."

Before he could finish his sentence, she asked, "Karl Jackson? You guys with Doc?"

Wade and Les eyed each other at her quick response, then Les said, "We're supposed to be meeting him down here to go fishing today."

Instantly, she pulled out a large flip top notebook from under the counter and said, "He told me to be on the lookout for you two guys."

She wrote down what each one of them had gotten to eat and drink, and said, "He told me to keep a tab. Said that he'd pay for whatever you guys needed."

Wade looked at Les. "Is this the same Karl we know and love?" he asked in disbelief.

Les mirrored Wade's expression and turned to the woman. "That's awfully nice of him to be doing that, but tell us something."

"Okay. What is it you'd like to know?" She cut her eyes at the two men.

"Well, for starters let's get acquainted. What's your name?" Les asked.

Suddenly, the clerk appeared distressed as she put her hand to her throat. With a rasping voice, she said, "Betty." She began hacking and wheezing violently. Turning away from Les and Wade, she patted her chest as the coughing subsided. Swiveling back to face the pair, she said, "Please excuse me. I've had a little allergy problem going on for the last couple of days." She continued, "So, I'm Betty, and you are?"

"Well, this is Wade," Les pointed to his friend, "and my name's Les."

"Glad to meet you, Les and Wade." She began coughing again, but this time much deeper and harder. Reaching over, she took a long sip from a steaming cup of coffee resting on the nearby counter. This seemed to remedy her wheezing momentarily. Her eyes still watering slightly from the discomfort the coughing had produced, she said in a deep whisper, "Excuse me again, fellows." Taking another sip of coffee and wiping her mouth with a napkin, she said, "I think that took care of it that time." Looking over at the two friends inquisitively, she asked more stoically, "So exactly what is it that you want to know, fellows?"

"Well, ma'am—" Les started to ask, but the woman immediately cut him off.

"Please don't call me ma'am, Les. It makes me feel like an old woman. I know I'm one. But I don't want to go around feeling that way all day. You know what I mean?"

"Yes ma—I mean I certainly do, Betty." Les grinned back as she rolled her eyes. "You see, me and Wade here and Karl all grew up together. Right across the street from one another back in our hometown. It's been years since we've seen each other. Maybe nine or ten at least. So, we'd like to find out a little bit about our old friend before we see him again."

Betty thought for a moment before saying anything. "Well, him being a surgeon and all, we call your friend Karl 'Doc' around here. He has a cabin right down on the canal and a nice boat. I think it's maybe a Contender that he's added a few things to. If you don't know much about boats that's one of the nicer models that they make for fishing. Has two big 200 Yamaha outboards on it so it can really skedaddle. He comes down here a pretty good bit, especially on the weekends and he usually has someone with him—if you know what I mean?"

Les gave her a curious look after which she said plainly, "Well, we won't go down that little path, okay?"

"All right," Les responded. Wade shook his head disgusted because he knew what she meant.

"Anyway," Betty continued. "He's very well-known around here and quite the character. Think they broke the mold when the Good Lord created him, I'd say." Saying this, she couldn't help but chuckle.

"What do you mean by that, Betty?" Wade spoke up with an inquiring smirk.

The Marina manager peered into his eyes. "Well, he's pissed just about everybody you can piss off around here at least once. But even so, and for whatever reason, most of the folks around here still love him to death. And those that don't . . ." She paused and took another deep drag from her cigarette then exhaled the smoke up toward the ceiling. "Well, those people pretty much just stay out of his way."

"As in fear him?" Les queried surprised as he looked at Wade bemused.

"Yeah, if you grew up with him, you ought to know he's an in-your-face sort of guy. Right? Especially if you disagree with him. I imagine he hasn't changed that much in ten years. Do you?"

Les did not answer as he kept listening.

"Don't think I've ever seen anyone back him down around here either," she remarked taking another drag of smoke. Noticing the stares Les and Wade gave her, she changed her tune. "But don't get me wrong, fellows. He's a nice guy and all. He just wants what he wants, and it doesn't pay to cross him."

Wade chuckled sarcastically. "Well, sounds like Karl hasn't changed that much after all, Les."

Betty laughed and said, "Probably not."

Les asked, "Does he bring his wife and kids down here with him very much?"

Betty suddenly quit laughing and grew somber. Eyeing Les, she said, "In all the years I've seen him down here, I've seen his family only once or twice."

She paused reflectively smiling at the thought of Karl's cute little boy and girl. "Let me tell you, Les. The most beautiful little, blonde, blue-eyed children you ever laid your eyes on. The oldest one's a little girl probably seven or eight I'd think by now." She took a draw from her cigarette then exhaled it as she calculated in her mind the last time she'd seen them. "I think it's been about two and a half years since they've been down. That'd make it about right," she said thinking to herself. "And the little boy, I'd say he's about five or so by now."

Les winced at the thought of Karl not bringing his family with him. "Boy, that's pretty odd, Betty. Isn't it?" Les queried.

Betty became serious. "You're telling me. But hey," she shrugged, "that's none of my business. You know what I mean?"

Both Wade and Les caught a certain semblance of fear in the older woman's face as she said this. Puzzled, Wade tried giving the lady an escape from her preoccupation with Karl. "So," Wade exclaimed cheerily, "tell us how the fishing's been doing around here lately? People been having much luck?"

"Not much," she complained as she pulled out her lighter and lit up another cigarette. Taking a deep drag and holding it for a moment seemed to relax her from their previous conversation. Turning her head and exhaling the smoke away from Wade, she asked, "You've heard what's been going on down here, haven't you?" By the look on Wade and Les' faces, she could immediately tell that neither of the two men had a clue as to what she was referring to.

"Heard what?" Wade asked.

"Well, about six to eight weeks ago, we had a red tide come through this area and we had a huge, I mean huge fish kill. All the way from up around the Aucilla, all the way down past Steinhatchee, some saying as far down as Pepperfish Keys. Stunk the place up for weeks on end. Everyone around here, not just me, was coughing and having breathing problems from it. You know it produces something that gets in the air and does something to your lungs or whatever. I really think that's what my problem is today. Anyway, it was a disaster. It's been gone now for weeks, but most of the fisherman still haven't come back yet."

Les glanced past Betty through the large picture window behind her. From where he stood, he had a good view of the Marina's boatlift and the small cove's launch site. As he peered out, he noticed a truck pulling a boat drive up.

Seeing that something had caught Les' eye, Betty spun around and exclaimed happily, "Well, speak of the devil and look who shows up, boys. Ol' Doc's finally made it."

Karl drove up in a brand-new four-wheel drive, black, Chevrolet Silverado pickup. Attached to his vehicle was a trailer, which carried a twenty-eight-foot center-console fishing boat. It was a thing of beauty with a twin set of two-hundred horse outboards jutting out from its stern just like Betty had said. Above the boat's console was a royal blue T-top whose color perfectly matched the name painted on the vessel's sides: *Doc's Out!*

With the truck's dark-tinted windows, it was hard to see Karl. He pulled the large vessel to the exact spot needed for the cable-operated boatlift to place his craft in the water. Climbing out of his vehicle, the lean, tan, and still muscular thirty-five-year-old walked back to the stern. He reached his six-foot-four-inch frame under the boat's tandem set of motors to insert the plug in the rear. Crawling from underneath, Les and Wade had their first good look at Karl in over a decade.

Aside from noticing that he hadn't become fat, flabby, or bald, they took note of his fishing attire. Wearing a Marquesas short sleeve fishing shirt, which had a mesh back panel for breathability, white boat shorts, and a pair of Orvis boat sandals, Karl gave the appearance of a well-heeled mariner and fisherman. Complimenting this image, he wore a corded pair of Oakley sunglasses along with a khaki colored Bone-fisher's hat, the kind that has the long bill sticking out front with a shorter bill projecting out the back, to keep the sun off of his neck.

Wearing faded blue jeans, tennis shoes, and colored pullover t-shirts, Wade and Les watched their spiffy counterpart walk up the steps and enter the Marina. He shifted his sunglasses from his eyes to the top of his hat's bill to see better.

Les watched Betty nervously smile as Karl came toward her. "Hey, Doc. Got some friends here to see you."

A stoic Karl, still displaying a full head of sandy blonde hair, considered his two old friends. Walking over, he shook hands with Les and Wade. "Glad to see you guys could make it."

"Glad to be here," Les responded cheerfully.

Karl looked at Betty with disgust. Agitated, he said, "That guy Benny you told me who could fix anything electronic? Well, he doesn't know crap about radars. Hope you hadn't told anyone else to use that dumb ass."

"Hey, Doc. I'm sorry. I was just suggesting him because Tony said he used him to fix the radar out on his shrimp boat. He said he did a good job."

"Well, maybe that's why Tony stays broke. How the hell can he find shrimp when his radar's broken and he doesn't even know where the hell he's at out there?"

Wade and Les watched Betty sympathetically. Her fearful, submissive nature had resurfaced once more with Karl's condescending remarks. "I'm sorry he didn't get it fixed, Doc. You want me to see if I can find someone else to work on it for you?"

"No. I think I'll take my chances over at Steinhatchee where someone knows what the hell they're doing." Looking around the place, Karl asked in a more civil tone, "Where's Yank this morning by the way?"

Betty glanced out the window. "He's out there somewhere, probably around back. He was working on re-bolting the back-dock's aluminum ramp back there the last time I saw him."

"Come on, guys." Karl motioned to his friends, still displaying his irritation with Betty. As they walked outside, Karl, ever the man in charge, took long fast strides as the three headed for the dock. Les and Wade had trouble keeping up as Karl walked and talked. "Yank's the fellow that runs the lift for the Marina. He's an indolent drunk and if he's not out here where Betty said he should be, he's probably somewhere sleeping off another hangover." Karl said this without ever breaking his pace.

They made it to the aluminum ramp Betty had told them about in short order. Sure enough, a tanned leathery looking man of about fifty-five wearing no shirt and no shoes was there wrestling a frozen bolt with a wrench and a can of WD-40. A cigarette hung from his lips as he strained to break the grip of the rusted bolt.

"Hey, Yank!" Karl called out. "I need you to help me get my boat in the water."

Yank was one of the few people in the area who was not intimidated by Karl or anyone else.

"Give me a minute. I've got to replace this one last bolt."

"I haven't got a minute, Yank. I'm a paying customer now. So, you going to play with that damn bolt or come put my boat in the water like I pay you to do?"

The cigarette between Yank's lips started rapidly going up and down as the older man spoke. "You don't pay me nothing, Doc. Keaton Beach Marina pays me and right now they're paying me to replace this son of a bitch'n bent bolt."

Karl appeared pissed as Yank glanced at him casually. "You can get over it anytime you want to, hotshot," Yank said as calm as a cucumber. Spraying more lubricant on the metal pin that was not cooperating, he again strained with all of his might to break the bolt loose from its hold. Once more to no avail.

Seeing a metal pipe laying on the ground where Yank was working, Karl called out for Yank to stop. Picking up the cylinder, he took the wrench from Yank's hand

and, placing the pipe over the wrench's handle for leverage, Karl tightened the wrench onto the nut. With a couple of hard jerks along with help from the lubricant, he instantly cracked loose the stubborn piece of metal. Asking Yank for the new bolt and its set of nuts and washers, he quickly forced the metal screw through its two openings and tightened it back down with the wrench. "All right, Yank. You owe me one. Now let's go get my boat in the water."

"Be my pleasure, Doc," Yank countered unhurriedly.

As the four men got to Karl's truck and the boat, they carefully lined the lift over the trailered vessel then strapped its heavy-duty canvas belts underneath it. Yank operated the electronic switch where he would lift the boat up from the trailer, swing it across the landing, and place it down into the water. Karl, as always, was in complete command and control of the entire operation. "Don't let that frame up there hit my antennas, you fool!" he yelled at Yank who was operating the controls to the lift.

Yank shot back, "The only fool you'll see around here is you in your rearview mirror, Doc."

As the electrical zap of the winch's motor sounded as Yank pressed one of the buttons to make the lift move in one direction or another, Karl would immediately yell for Yank to stop. Everything had to line up just right before Karl would allow Yank to make the next move.

"You're like an ol' woman who can't make up her mind, Doc. Either you want it in or you want it to stay out which is going to be?"

"Shut the hell up, you moron, and just do as I say. This is my boat you're screwing with dammit, and you're not going to tear it up by getting in a hurry and being an idiot."

"So you're telling me that you're letting a moron and an idiot run the winch to put your big badass boat in the water? That'd be pretty stupid of you, wouldn't it, Doc?" Yank grinned and laughed as he said this.

"Just pick the boat up higher, will you?" Karl asked exasperatedly.

"Your wish is my command, Doc," Yank shot back as he never quit smiling. Yank was obstinate, but he did as he was told as the electrical device crackled, and the machine's motor strained. Moaning, the weight of the vessel rose with the ever-tightening grip of the straps as Yank had the outboard completely lifted off the boat trailer.

"All right!" Karl yelled. "Swing it on around. Slowly."

Again, Yank hit the buzzing buttons which guided the lift's massive arm out over the open water of the landing. Without Karl's permission, Yank gently lowered the center console down into the murky water of the canal below.

"Good. Stop it right there," Karl commanded. Swiftly, Karl, Les, and Wade made it down to where the boat had been placed and tied it up to two of the dock's galvanized metal cleats. After getting the boat unhooked from the lift's belts, Yank gently swung the crane back over the drive-through where he parked the machine.

As Karl moved his truck and boat trailer across the street from the Marina, Les and Wade got the coolers of ice that they had brought with them from Perry. Placing the frozen chunks into two of the boat's 96-quart floor coolers, they returned their empty chests to Wade's trunk. From there, they walked across the street to where Karl had parked.

Seeing Les and Wade walking up, Karl called out for Les to unhitch his trailer from his truck. Les went to the back of the four-wheel drive and noticing that the electrical supply for the trailer lights was still attached, unplugged it. Wrapping the loose electrical wire from the boat trailer around the galvanized steel bracing that secured the trailer's tongue, Les unhooked the two safety chains connecting the trailer to the truck's steel bumper. All Les had to do was to release the latch that locked the trailer to the truck's hitch then lift the trailer off the hitch via a jack located on the trailer's tongue, but he was having trouble. He couldn't get the fastener pried upward to release the hitch.

After Les worked with the stuck latch for several minutes, Karl impatiently got out of his truck to see what was the matter. Butting Les out of his way and raising the trailer jack higher, he tried to lift the clamp himself, but couldn't. Taking a step backward, he stepped forward and kicked the latch with his heel as hard as he could. The clamp popped open immediately. Karl spun the jack handle quickly and lifted the trailer off the hitch completely disengaging it. He did all of this in under a minute. Calling out to Les who was standing on the other side of the trailer, he said, "All right. Let's get going. We got to get over to Steinhatchee to get our Scuba tanks filled." Jumping back into the truck with Les and Wade, Karl hit the gas and they were off, heading down Beach Road toward Steinhatchee.

Russell, a friend Karl had met while diving, had a dive shop at the mouth of one of the creeks leading into the Steinhatchee River. A quick fill up with air at Russell's shop and they'd be back at Keaton in time to set out some pinfish traps and maybe do a little trout fishing before dark.

As they drove along taking in the prairie-like marshes of grass and muddy, brackish tidal creeks, Karl began to discuss his diving plans with Les who sat directly across from him. "You did bring your scuba gear with you like I told you to, didn't you?"

"Yeah, I've got my mask, fins, booties, and all that stuff in Wade's back seat."

Karl interrupted, "I'm not hearing that you brought your spear gun down. You did bring it with you, didn't you?"

"No. I told you on the phone that I didn't have one. I gave mine away to one of my friends in Peru before we left South America for the States. Remember, I told you that in our conversation?"

"No, I don't," Karl countered.

Puzzled, Les couldn't believe that Karl didn't remember discussing this. He had made such a big deal about giving away his favorite spear gun.

"It's no problem, Karl," Les responded.

"Well, it is if you're planning on using mine," Karl said giving Les a goading grin.

"Karl, I don't care one thing about spearing a fish on this trip if that makes you feel any better. I am willing to bet you though, that before this fishing trip is over, ol' Pal, you'll spear something special just for me. How about that?" Les gazed at his older friend.

"Don't count on it," Karl retorted.

"We'll see," Les said stoically. Lightening up the conversation a bit, he continued, "Say, what size tanks will we be diving with this weekend?"

"Eighty cubic foot. I brought four down for this trip."

Les grew concerned and asked, "Are they steel or aluminum?"

"Aluminum alloy. Why?" Karl asked puzzled looking in Les' direction.

"Well, to be truthful I prefer the steel tanks. I dove with the aluminum ones before. But for someone my size, diving from the surf, those things were a little too big and bulky. You know I had to use a heavier weight belt and all that sort of stuff. Don't get me wrong. I'm not trying to bash your tanks or anything, Karl. I appreciate you bringing them down here for me to use."

Hearing Les say this, Karl appeared dismayed. "You've never been diving from a boat, Les?"

"No. Never had to. We always just camped out on the beaches down at El Nuro and over at San Andres. Down there you were pretty much where you wanted to be as soon as you got past the waves. Tons of sea life at El Nuro: green sea turtles, sea lions, and thousands upon thousands of schooling fish. Over at San Andres, up in the Caribbean, the reef fish over there were right offshore. And there were plenty of tasty lobsters over in that area too. But to answer your question about a boat, I guess I'd have to say no. There was no real need for us to ever have to use one."

Karl was jealous of Les' diving experience since he'd never dove in such extraordinary places, but he tried hard not to show it. "Well, it's a lot easier diving off the side of a boat than walking in from a wave-battered beach, Les. I don't think you'll have too much trouble suiting up and falling over the side, do you?"

Les laughed at the way Karl said this. "Yeah, but getting back in might be another story."

Karl snickered. "Maybe your muscled-up pal back there can help pull your wimpy little butt up the dive ladder before you drown. How 'bout that?" Karl sarcastically said trying to aggravate Les a little more.

Quickly interceding on Les' behalf, Wade said, "It'd probably be easier if he just took his tank off in the water and handed that up first. Wouldn't you think?"

Les answered, "Yeah, that'd probably be the best way to do it."

"Well, don't worry about getting back in, Les. You know I've got your back, boy."

Wade caught Karl's glare in the truck's rearview mirror. Their older friend wasn't too pleased with Wade coming to Les' defense. Intent on getting under Wade's skin, he decided to turn things up a notch.

"Say, Wade. Didn't I hear that you split the sheets with the old lady and that you've recently moved back in with your mom and dad?"

Wade smiled back at Karl in the mirror appearing unfazed by the doctor's rudeness.

"Well, you got part of that right, Karl. I'm divorced. But hey, didn't I hear you were too and that you moved shortly afterward to Tallahassee to escape Augusta?"

Karl wasn't expecting this kind of response coming from Wade, and it pissed him off. He shot back. "Yep. My first wife and I did divorce. Irrevocable differences. How about you?" Karl glared back at Wade in the mirror.

"Something like that, Karl. But the part about living with my parents, who I love dearly, by the way, that part's wrong. I live in a studio apartment downtown. You might remember the old Dorminey building. They renovated the building just across the street from it into some really nice flats, and that's where I live now."

Karl seemed to pay little attention as Wade shared where he now lived. This little exchange between him and Wade had become more about dominance than a friendly little rift as far as he was concerned. Riled up, Karl wanted to show that, even after all of these years, he was still an indomitable force to be reckoned with. "Say, Wade. Les tells me that you just up and quit your job in Atlanta and that you moved back home to become an artist. Was it because you couldn't hold down a job that your wife left you or was it that you couldn't hold down a job, so you decided to become an artist, then she left you?" Karl chuckled as he looked at Wade in the rearview mirror.

Protesting Les spoke up, "Now, Karl. Why would you say something like that to Wade about his marriage? Don't you suppose that might be a rather sore subject for him?"

"Well, I just wanted to know why he did what he did. The only way to find out the truth is to ask and get it straight from the horse's mouth, right?"

Wade replied, "You don't need to defend me, Les. Karl's right about being open about things and telling the truth. So, tell me, Karl. Why did you leave Augusta? Did you get run out of town, or did you leave on your own?"

Karl did not offer a response. He cut his eyes at Wade in the mirror and gave his smaller friend a sinister sneer.

Les was ticked at the way Karl was talking to his friend but was proud of Wade for standing up for himself. It appeared that Betty was right. Karl indeed was still an "in your face" sort of guy— maybe even worse now than back when they were younger.

Karl's reaction to confrontation remained the same. It was not to get mad, but to get even. As a calculated comeback to what had just occurred with Wade, he'd just isolate his old friend, pretending he wasn't even there. Knowing Wade's sensitive nature, Karl knew that this would probably bother him most. In one way or another, Karl was going to put Wade in his place, and how long this might take was of little consequence to the doctor. "So, Les," Karl asked enthusiastically, "what say you about South America?" As Karl had planned, the rest of the conversation on the way to Steinhatchee centered on what Les and Louisa had done for the past ten years along the Amazon River. Les had no idea that this was the game plan Karl had conjured up to exclude Wade and, since the opportunity arose, decided to enlighten Karl on some of the more spiritual aspects that he and Louisa had gleaned on their remarkable journey.

As Les recounted he and his wife's experiences, many of which were painful to talk about, he became increasingly troubled and disheartened by Karl's reaction and indifference to what he was saying. Concerned, Les stopped talking and looked over at his older friend whose eyes never left the road as he silently drove. *Who was this person*, Les thought. He knew Karl had always been a self-centered soul, but did he have no feelings for others at all? Contemplating these disturbing thoughts, Les leaned back in his seat.

Soon, they entered the city limits of Steinhatchee. At the intersection of 1st Avenue, they took a right and drove about a block and a half until the pavement ran out. From there they rode down a short sand road to a small oyster-shelled parking lot. At the base of this lot, a long-corrugated tin building rested on pilings jutting out into one of the creeks feeding the Steinhatchee River.

As Karl's tires crunched over the oyster shells, Les noted a large sign over the entrance that read SCUBA. On each side of it, red flags were painted with a single diagonal white stripe angled across them. This striped red flag was known universally as the symbol denoting a dive shop or, when held up by a floating buoy in the water or as a boat's flag, marked the place where divers were swimming underwater.

Karl's truck came to a sliding halt as he hit the brakes at the building's entrance. As the guys got out, Karl called for his friends to reach in the back of the truck and retrieve the four cylinders to be filled with air. The truck being a bit higher off the ground than most, Les unlatched and lowered the tailgate to climb into the bed. In a front corner near the cab, he found the tanks placed upright into a tied down holding rack. Sliding each one upward and out, he handed them down to Wade. As Les passed the last one to him, he jumped off the back of the truck and went around to help Wade carry two of the tanks inside. Entering the building, they found Karl with the shop's owner Russell and his wife Jen talking at the checkout counter in the center of the room.

Seeing Les struggle with the tanks, the tanned, six-foot tall shop owner quickly came to his rescue. Taking the empty cylinders from Les with a grin, Russell said, "Think these tanks are heavy now, wait till you get some air in 'em and try carrying 'em around with all the gear attached."

"You're not telling me anything I don't know," Les responded, relieved to relinquish the weighty objects. "I've dove with tanks this size before from a beach in heavy seas, believe it or not."

Wade walked his two tanks back to the far right-hand corner of the building where Russell had carried the other two. He set them down in front of a small electric compressor as Russell called out to Karl, "Hey, Karl. Where will y'all be diving this trip?"

Thumbing through a rack of colorful t-shirts, Karl responded, "I've found some good hard bottom about thirty miles offshore going out about two-hundred-thirty from Keaton. Caught some nice grouper out there a couple of weeks ago with a different set of friends, so I kept the numbers. If we don't have any luck fishing there, I'll start rock hunting with my depth finder and we'll see if we can maybe spear a fish or two."

"So, these are just in case tanks," Russell laughed out loud. "Just in case the fish don't bite you guys can have some fun diving." He smiled at Wade not knowing that Wade would not be participating should such a contingency occur.

Karl spoke up, "Yeah, that's a pretty good way to look at it, at least for tomorrow. But these guys are going to be down through Sunday, so if we don't get a dive in tomorrow, we'll certainly get one in on Sunday."

As Karl bantered with the owner, Les started wandering around the shop pawing at the various scuba gear. It was not a large dive shop. It was equipped with only fifteen or so tanks. Of these air cylinders, the majority of them were used and kept for teaching classes. Only two or three of these vessels were brand new. Still looking, Les found other complimentary diving equipment. There were tank backpacks, buoyancy compensators, breathing regulators, masks, fins, snorkels, booties, and gloves. Hanging from racks projecting out from one wall, he noticed an assortment of men and women's wetsuits. Though small in size, the shop seemed to have it all, Les thought as he inspected the place.

Making his way from one side of the store to the other, Les ended up back by Russell who was starting to fill Karl's first tank with air. Wade, who had been discussing knives and spear gun paraphernalia with Russell's wife Jen, walked over next to Karl, who was standing at the back door. Looking out, both men could see what was going on down at the river as well as Russell's dock. Noticing a medium-sized cabin cruiser motoring inland from Deadman's Bay, Karl called back over his shoulder to the rest of the group, "Now there's a mighty fine-looking boat for you."

Russell stopped what he was doing and walked over to the doorway to get a better look at the passing vessel. Big and fit but not really muscular and with eyes that were a little too close together, Russell looked like he might not be the sharpest knife in the drawer. Such observed conclusions, however, would be entirely wrong. Graduating as salutatorian of his class back in high school, he was fanatical when it came to details. With a photographic memory, he knew the make and model of just about every boat around the area and had almost total recall of not only who owned each one but could even estimate each vessel's true value within a few hundred dollars. "Looks like a Rampage," Russell said stoically. "I'd say a thirty-eight-foot Express. Don't see any outboards sticking out from behind its dive platform so I'd say it's probably powered by a twin set of diesels. My guess, as quiet as it's running would be Yanmar 315's."

Karl asked curiously, having heard vaunted stories of Russell's amazing memory, "Who owns that boat, Russell?"

Without expression, Russell cut his eyes at Karl, "Wouldn't have a clue. Never seen that boat around here before."

Karl paused staring at the shop's owner. "Tell me something, Russell. What kind of speed do you think he can get off those set of twins?"

Russell pondered a moment as he watched the purring vessel slowly glide by. "Probably cruises at, um… twenty-five to twenty-six knots if they're not in a hurry. And I'd say it tops out WOT at around thirty-two. Shouldn't push it over 3900 RPMs if I'm right about the specs on that setup."

"That's balling the jack for inboard diesels for that size boat, wouldn't you say?"

Nonchalantly, Russell swung his gaze from the boat to Karl. "Yeah, that's pretty fast. Last year I went out on one with close to that same set up over at Port St. Joe on a dive trip. It won't jump out of the water like a 'deep vee' when you hit the throttle, but once it gets going, it can really move. A boat like that'll surprise you. Trust me." Russell held a small, dark-blue towel and used the cloth to wipe some grime off his hands as he talked. Turning, he made his way back to the air compressor where Les stood by one of the tanks being filled as it sat in a container of cold water.

Karl and Wade remained at the doorway watching the Rampage as it traveled by. The boat captain had shifted the vessel's transmission into neutral then suddenly used the boat's forward momentum to turn into the landing of the fish house next door. Karl found it odd for such a nice large boat to dock way up here instead of further in at one of the large Marinas at Steinhatchee.

Watching as the boat headed for the dock, Wade asked Karl, "How fast would you think your boat is compared to that one?"

Keeping a close eye on what the boat was doing, Karl answered, "What I have is a twenty-eight-foot Contender with a twin set of Yamaha 200s pushing it. That's a thirty-eight-footer with twin diesel inboards. In flat water, I can max out at about fifty miles per hour WOT or roughly forty-five knots, but I don't usually do that because it puts too much stress on the engines. Besides that, you don't know what's floating out there in front of you when hitting that kind of speed." Still observing the large cruiser, Karl said pensively, "From a dead start, I could probably get a pretty good jump on that dude over there in that Express in a light chop, but he might have the advantage on me over the long haul in heavier seas. There are many variables you have to consider concerning boat speeds, Wade." Karl turned slightly toward his smaller friend as he explained, "The size of your boat. It's hull's configuration. How much weight you're carrying. Wave heights and intervals. That sort of thing."

"WOT, what's that stand for?"

"Wide open throttle. Each engine has a full throttle operating range charted as horsepower to RPMs. At a certain RPM, you've reached the maximum horsepower that you're going to get out of the engine. Exceeding that range can injure your motor. Basically, it involves having the right prop and pitch. Each new motor comes with specs telling you what your WOT is so you won't damage the engine by trying to get more out of it than its capable of producing."

"I see," Wade responded impressed. There was no doubting that Karl was still as sharp as ever, especially when it came to technical matters. Unfortunately, Wade could also see from their trip over that there had been little change in his disposition. He could still be a jackass. Even with Karl's behavior as a downside, Wade felt more assured that at least his older friend would know how to handle his boat when they got offshore.

Karl and Wade eased their way out through the shed's back door to the railing of the porch deck. They intently watched as the captain of the attractive black and gray vessel pulled the throttle in reverse to break the boat's speed. Gently, it drifted toward the dock next door.

There were two other men on the boat. One was a very tanned Caucasian and the other was much darker but did not appear to be black. Quickly they started flipping out bumpers, which were tied to the boat's cleats. This was done so the hull of the vessel wouldn't take the blow when they docked. Finally making contact with the pier, the white guy who appeared to be in his mid-twenties and who wore a faded pair of jeans, a burgundy colored t-shirt, and no shoes, scampered over the boat's side and began tying the vessel to the dock's large galvanized steel cleats. The owner of the fish house came out of his corrugated tin building and from his back-porch deck watched as the crew moored their black and gray cruiser.

An aluminum ramp ran at a steep angle from the top of the porch where the owner stood down to a thirty-foot long mid-level dock. At the end of this walkway, another gangway led down to the floating dock. It was to this final portion of the pier that the impressive vessel was secured.

There was quite a disparity between this boat and the fish house owner's trawler, which was parked up at the pier's midlevel dock on the wharf's other side. In contrast to the old, corroded, rust-stained, forty-foot shrimp boat with its many booms and grimy green netting all piled up unkempt in the stern, here was a meticulously kept cabin cruiser. Its hull was painted a shimmering black. The rest of the boat, from the top of its gunnels, to its decking, all the way to the top of its cabin and cockpit, was colored in a misty shade of gray, a serene almost mauve color that was so understated it could virtually meld into a late afternoon sky.

"Señor Heeks," the boat's captain waved and called out to the fish house owner on the dock above.

"Raphael," the owner called back down. "I've been waiting on you. Where are my fish?"

Wade and Karl watched as the boat's captain, having the dark, handsome features of someone of Spanish descent, stepped over the vessel's gunnels and onto the sun-bleached wooden planks of the floating dock. Gliding his lanky, muscular frame up the two ramps of the pier, Rafael effortlessly made his way up to the building's back porch to shake hands with the fish house owner.

Like his boat, the fishery's owner was not as dark, handsome, and lanky as was the captain of the yacht. On the contrary, this fellow was a wild-looking man of medium height. With a thick, stocky build and weighing two hundred and twenty pounds or so, he was partially bald and, unlike his counterpart, he did not appear to be in his thirties but rather closer to fifty.

The dissimilarities between the two didn't end there. The boat captain wore a pair of clean white shorts, sandals, and an expensive light blue short-sleeved Caribbean-styled shirt. As for the owner of the fish house, it appeared that being well-dressed and dapper wasn't his main concern. His wardrobe consisted of a dark plaid shirt with the sleeves cut off and a pair of well-worn khaki pants that had the hems let out. He also wore grungy old tennis shoes.

When the two men finished greeting each other, they looked back toward the dock where the Rampage's two remaining shipmates had finished docking their vessel. With the boat secured, the cohorts tramped barefoot up the ramps of the pier, and soon the crew stood face to face with the fish house owner. After shaking hands, the strangest one of these two new arrivals, someone who Karl whispered to Wade was probably a Guatemalan, swiftly ran back down to the boat.

Rough and rugged, this fellow was short, maybe five-feet-five-inches tall and shirtless. Sporting long straight black hair that hung almost to the top of his calf high cut off tight-fitting pants, he didn't have a single ounce of fat on his ripped muscular body. Easily pitching himself over the side of the boat with one hand, he opened a large cooler resting in the back corner of the boat. Reaching into it, he pulled out a huge gag grouper. Grinning, he held it up over his head so the owner of the fish house could see it. Setting it over the side of the boat onto the floating dock, he reached back into the cooler and pulled out another one. With these two large fish in hand, he dashed back up the pier toward the waiting men.

Eyeing the two sizeable fish, the fishery owner said "Very nice. Very nice. But what else do you have for me besides, 'mero'?"

The captain of the yacht nodded for his shipmates to unload the rest of the vessel. Hastily they did as they were told.

Watching the two men unloading the fish from Russell's dock, and seeing at least six more of the same size grouper, Karl called over to Wade in amazement, "Look at the size of those son of bitchin' fish. Damn, I bet some of those gags over there are over thirty-six inches long. Hot damn. I wonder where the hell they caught those big bastards."

"You reckon' they're commercial fishermen, Karl? That's a lot of fish they're piling up over there."

Watching intently, Karl replied, "Yeah, it is. Way over the limit for recreational fishermen, or even charter boats for that matter. But if they are commercial, I've never seen them use a boat set up like that before. My guess is that catch is questionable. Might be why they've stopped way out here instead of going on into Steinhatchee." Karl observed the grizzled-looking character standing on the back-porch deck of the building next door. "Probably selling the fish to that creature over there. Grinning bastard sure looks happy with what they're unloading, doesn't he?"

Karl started walking down Russell's pier to see the other kind of fish they were throwing over to the dock from their boat. Impulsively, Wade followed him. Almost immediately, he had second thoughts concerning Karl's intentions. "You're not heading over there are you?" Wade called up to Karl.

Not responding, his taller buddy was thoroughly engrossed in what was going on next door. As the two went down Russell's second ramp, they came to a crossroad. They could go straight out and onto Russell' floating dock where his thirty-foot dive boat was moored, or they could turn left and walk down a seemingly well-worn sand path that cut through the tall marsh grass growing between Russell's and his neighbor's dock.

Stealthily, Karl turned left down the path heading to the boardwalk where the Rampage was docked. By now, the longhaired Guatemalan-looking guy had climbed back over the port gunwale of the vessel and was heading back up the neighbor's ramp. Karl and Wade stopped to avoid being seen as they watched the dark-skinned man carry two of the massive fish by their mouths, one in each hand. Rapidly the fellow headed back up the walkway toward the three other men standing on the upper deck of the fish house. Furtively, Karl leaned toward Wade and whispered, "Follow him up to the porch and see if you can make some small talk. Try distracting them while I get inside the boat. I want to see if I can find some of their LORAN numbers."

"Their what?" Wade asked in disbelief.

"Shhh," Karl placed his index finger to his lips as he countered Wade's outburst. "If we can get those numbers, they'll give us the coordinates to exactly where they caught those huge grouper."

"Are you crazy, Karl?" Wade whispered back incredulous. "Why not just ask them for the numbers?"

Karl gave Wade an exasperated look. Still whispering, but more seriously, he said, "Guys like those would cut your throat before they'd give up those numbers." Glancing up as he said this, he saw the longhaired fellow making his way up the last ramp. "All right, Wade. Get going. We haven't got time to argue about this now. As soon as you get their attention, I'll make my move. See if you can get them back inside the building or at least get them as far back on the porch as possible. Keep them distracted."

Karl lowered himself behind the cordgrass as he crept closer to their floating dock. Wade stood upright and stepped onto the dock to head up to where the other men were. He apprehensively turned back around and gave Karl one last look.

Aggravated at Wade's tentativeness, Karl motioned for him to go on. "Get going. We've only got a minute to do this. Hurry."

Wade no more wanted to be a part of this ridiculous scheme than he wanted to be shot—which he felt might happen. Whether he wanted to or not, like the fish themselves, he was in this right up to his gills. As Karl watched, Wade finally made it to the top deck where Karl noted, just as he had expected, Wade became the deprecated focus of the four men standing there.

Noticing the uninvited intruder's presence, the stubble-bearded owner of the fish house became incensed. Agitated and angry, he snapped at Wade in the deep hoarse voice of a drill sergeant. "Where the hell did you come from, pal?"

"Well, I—" Wade was cut off.

"Who the hell gave you permission to come out here onto my dock? You didn't see that 'no trespassing' sign I got posted out front, son?"

"Well, I didn't come in from the front, sir."

"What the hell you talkin' about, boy? You telling me you came swimming in here from up the river there?"

Hearing him say this, the other three men who were all facing Wade began to laugh.

Meanwhile, Karl smiled as he heard the pugnacious brute hurling insults at his friend. He knew that all of the men standing there would be focused on Wade. This was Karl's chance. He swiftly headed down the dock and slipped onto the large vessel unnoticed. Quickly, he made it to the boat's cockpit and the captain's swivel chair where he took a seat and started fumbling with any papers he could find. Looking around the dashboard behind the stainless-steel steering wheel, he found plenty. But much to his angst, he discovered that every piece of paper he found was written in Spanish and not one single number had shown up on any of them. Hurriedly, Karl kept going through every crack and crevice of the console desperately trying to find the captain's LORAN numbers, but to no avail. As he hunted, he couldn't help but notice how well equipped the vessel was for fishing. It had chart plotters, radar, depth finders, fish finders, an autopilot, two Vhf radios, and a LORAN.

Not being able to find any papers or notebooks showing the numbers he sought, he turned his attention to the LORAN device itself. Swiftly, he found out that the software program it used was too different from the one he was used to using. Though he was able to obtain a few waypoints from the machine, he noticed that the locations they pointed to denoted places from Tampa Bay south, which were of no use to him. Sitting at the console, he was frustrated at not being able to find a notepad, a notebook, or even a single piece of paper with a number he could use. He swiveled the chair around facing the stern of the boat. Mounted in the front and middle of the transom, he saw a rack holding six scuba tanks. In the left-hand corner of the vessel mounted atop the starboard gunnel, he could see a seated yacht's deck crane, its rotating arm projecting back over the boat's transom. That was an odd sight on such a small vessel, Karl thought. Must have had something to do with them diving or maybe even pulling up fish traps even though he knew that such traps had been banned. As he continued to scan the area, he couldn't help but notice the piles of spotted redfish lying scattered across the causeway of the dock. He surmised that breaking the law for these guys must have been customary because the law banning the catch of redfish had been enacted this very year, and everyone who fished knew of its existence. Fines up to one thousand dollars per fish had already been reported.

Karl knew time was of the essence, so he redirected his search. He knew it wouldn't be long before the crew would head back to the boat to gather up more fish.

Meanwhile, on the back porch of the fish house, Wade was getting an unrelenting scolding. That was until the pugnacious owner demanded he know who permitted Wade to come onto his property. After stalling for as long as he could, Wade's answer was quick, "Your brother."

The owner became quiet and gave Wade a loathsome stare. "How do you know my brother?"

Realizing he had hit a nerve, Wade continued. "He fishes, doesn't he?"

Eyeing Wade curiously, the owner shot back, "What's his name?"

Without blinking, Wade said matter of factly, "Russell."

"Russell?" the man gave Wade a questioning grin. Looking back at his cohorts, he exclaimed, "I ain't got no brother named Russell."

Wade immediately confessed, "Russell next door's not your brother?"

Grimacing, the owner called out loudly, "Hell no!"

Trying to keep his wits, Wade shot back, "Well, I thought he was because he gave me permission to come over here."

"Bullshit!" the man yelled back. "Russell ain't my brother, and he ain't my friend. Russell keeps his ass over at his dock, and I keep mine over here. You got that, son?"

"Yes, sir. My mistake." Wade acquiesced.

"You damn right it's your mistake! But since you've made it over here to my dock and seen these fish—if you know what I mean." The man glared at Wade when he said this not realizing that Wade had no idea what he was talking about. "That means you're fixing to become a willing participant in helping us load all those fish from down there into the back of my truck up here. You got that, son?"

"Be glad to." Wade responded still oblivious to the owner's reasoning. "Say, what all do you sell in your building here?" Wade headed for the back-door entrance in an attempt to keep the men's eyes in his direction and away from Karl down at the boat.

"You're a real dumbass, aren't you, son?" The grizzly owner exclaimed, agitated as he moved to stop Wade from entering the building. Placing one of his big paws on Wade's shoulder, he said, "Do you want us to whip your ass right here and now, or do you want to start loading fish?"

Wade raised his hands high in the air as he pulled away from the man's grip. "Load fish for sure." Wade grinned back. "Do you have some buckets or something to put them in?" he asked still trying to keep the focus on him and not the boat.

"Get him some buckets, boys. And y'all get a move on. The least amount of time we got the fish on the dock, the better."

"Y'all got any gloves I can use?" Wade asked still attempting to slow things down.

Laughing loudly with the rest of the men on the porch, the owner called back glaring directly into Wade's face, "Hell no, you little prick! Now get your ass down there and start loading those damn fish. You hear?"

Hearing the laughter, Karl, peeped through the boat's windshield to see what was going on. Noticing that the owner and crew were still distracted, he decided to use this window of opportunity to open the cabin's doors and go below deck. Just as he was about to go through the opened doorway, he saw a mounted horizontal tube of PVC pipe sitting above its entrance. Each end of the pipe, he noticed, was plugged with large rubber stoppers. As he pulled one of the plugs out of the tube to see what it contained, Karl was surprised to find what he was hunting. In a nice neat roll was a set of Nautical Charts, which included all areas of the Gulf's west Florida coast. Leafing through the laminated charts, he found the one he wanted to see. It was an NOAA marine map, which read UNITED STATES GULF COAST FLORIDA, TAMPA BAY TO CAPE SAN BLAS. On the side of the map, it read LORAN-C OVERPRINTED SOUNDINGS IN FATHOMS.

Looking back up through the cruiser's windshield, Karl could see that the vociferous owner was no longer laughing but was once again getting back into Wade's face. Hastily, Karl scanned the map to see if he could glean any information. There were several asterisk marks five miles out between Steinhatchee and the Aucilla River, but Karl knew that those locations were too close in to catch grouper. As he heard a loud commotion coming from the porch, he found what he was searching for. It was a red star with two circles around it about twenty miles or so out from the Fenholloway River showing a drop off in depth from three to four fathoms to somewhere closer to six. A perfect underwater terrain for grouper. The LORAN numbers at this spot read 14426.30/46265.10. These numbers located next to the circled red star had been written in with a blue marker. Adjacent to these numbers still written in blue was the word "Descenso," which Karl assumed was Spanish. With his photographic memory, Karl banked the coordinates and word and peeped back through the windshield to see what was going on with Wade back up on the fish house deck.

To Karl's dismay, he saw Wade, followed by the other two crew members, heading down the ramp toward the boat with buckets. Seeing the precariousness of his situation, he ducked then eased his way into the deck's cabin below and quietly shut the door behind him. Hunting for a hiding place, he suddenly noticed he was still holding the laminated nautical chart. He had put the rest of the maps back in the tube, but the large rubber stopper was still out and sitting on the boat's console. Karl shook his head as he realized this mistake but knew there was nothing he could do about it.

Glancing around the cabin, he saw a small door on his left, which he assumed contained the boat's head. A small refrigerator, stove, some cabinets, and a built-in table were situated to his right just across and back from this door. Looking up toward the bow of the boat, he saw a U-shaped set of cushions where the three men could comfortably sleep. In between these thick pads, he saw two enormous orange, ball-shaped anchor floats and a rack holding a set of numerous short lines and hooks. Overall, he didn't see much of a chance of hiding in this place or escaping if they found him here. His only hope would be that Wade would keep them off the boat and away from the cabin. At this point, Karl didn't even know if Wade knew that he was still on the boat.

In less than a minute after he had entered the boat's cabin, Karl heard the voices of the men coming from the dock just outside the vessel's port side. "Here they are, bud," came the voice Karl figured to be that of the Caucasian. "I guess this is what you came over here to see. Now you're going to have the pleasure of helping us carry 'em back up to the top of that ramp. So, let's get going."

Hiding in the boat's cabin, Karl couldn't see that each of the men carried an empty white five-gallon plastic bucket in each hand. Karl heard Wade's voice next.

"These are mighty nice grouper, fellows. Haven't seen any this big in a long time. Where'd you guys catch these things?"

Karl winced when he heard Wade ask this question.

"In de fuckin' mout, A-hole!" the longhaired foreigner shot back.

"Hey. Listen, pal. I'm just trying to give you guys a friendly hand here. Doing you fellows a favor. No need to..."

Bitterly the shirtless man began to rant, "We no need no frikkin favos from you! You white skeened muther!" With a menacing grin, the muscular Latin native locked eyes with Wade.

"Pacón! shut the hell up!" the Caucasian fired back at his crewmate angrily. "You want me and you to have to move all these fish by ourselves?"

"Besar mi culo!"

"No. You kiss my ass, Pacón! Mr. Hicks wants these fish off his dock as in right now. You catching on to what I'm telling you, you longhaired bastard?"

Pacón snatched his long, sharp, white handled filet knife from its holder on his belt. "I tale you wat I cach onto. I cach onto your balls in my hand an cut dem off. Sneep! Sneep! You cry like el bébé, To-mas!"

Thomas laughed as Pacón said this. "Mr. Hicks will cut your head off, Pacón, and you won't be around to see me cry if we don't get this done and fast."

Wade was already filling his buckets with fish. He was well aware that Karl had not made it off the cruiser. Trying to pace himself where he would be close to the other two men when they were around the boat, he filled his buckets accordingly.

Back and forth, the men made their way from the boat, six buckets of fish at the time. At the top of the ramp, they poured them into several number-two washtubs Mr. Hicks and Rafael would carry and place in the back of the owner's long-bed dually pickup truck.

After numerous trips, Wade finally walked back down the ramp for the last haul. As he did so, he noticed that Rafael was with them. When they got to the boat, there were only two buckets of fish left to pick up and Thomas quickly gathered those up. Wade swallowed hard not knowing how to extricate Karl from this situation, as it appeared that Pacón and Rafael were there to stay.

Rafael looked at Wade, "You are wan lucky hombre, mi amigo. Meestor Heeks is not someone you play wid. It wood be very wise for you to say nutting about what you see today wid dees fish. No?"

Impassively, Wade gazed back into the captain's eyes, and asked, "What fish?"

Rafael gave Wade a wide smile. "Like I tol Meestor Heeks, you are a queek one to learn."

Nodding his head in affirmation, Rafael was still acting friendly as Wade turned and slowly began walking back down the dock headed for Russell's shop. All Wade could think about was how Karl was going to get past Pacón and his razor-edged knife when the longhaired wild man made his way back inside the cabin.

Watching Wade step off the dock's walkway, Rafael jumped over his boat's gunwale and onto the deck. He sent Pacón back up the ramp to the top deck to retrieve the long fuel hose they would use to refuel their boat with diesel. As Rafael walked over to the cruiser's console, he immediately saw the PVC pipe's rubber plug resting on the LORAN by the steering wheel. Searching, he reached inside the open end of the tube and thumbed rapidly through his charts to see if any were missing. Finding one of his most important maps gone, he became alarmed. Someone had come onto his boat and he knew it. Walking straight for the closed cabin door, he slid his filet knife from its sheath. Carefully, with his free hand, he reached for the door's handle. In one quick motion, he slung it open expecting to find the culprit hiding there. There was no one. Frantically, he searched the area, angrily throwing back blankets and cushions, but it seemed as if the intruder had disappeared.

Questioning himself for his stupidity, he thought of one more place to check. Quietly reaching under a cabinet sitting above his small refrigerator, he pulled out a well-concealed .38 revolver. Ever so slowly, he grasped the door handle to the boat's small one-man head. With the gun cocked and his adrenaline pumping, he yanked the door open and shoved the barrel of the gun inside the bathroom ready to fire. To his dismay, however, the only thing he found was his missing nautical map neatly rolled and sticking out of the toilet's flush hole.

Swiftly he went back outside onto the deck where he saw no sign of the guy who had just helped them unload their fish. Finding Pacón fueling the boat, Rafael quizzed him concerning the unknown man having access to their boat. Thomas walked up and joined in the conversation, but they both told Rafael that there was no way the stranger could have entered their vessel. They had been with him at all times. Rafael looked over at the dock where Wade had disappeared. Standing on his porch, the dive shop's owner gave him a cold hard stare. For a few moments, the two men locked eyes, then Russell turned around and went back inside.

CHAPTER 25

The Flats

Despondent, Wade made his way back across the sandy path, up the pier, and across the porch to Russell's dive shop. He had no idea how to rescue his friend from the cabin of the boat next door. Russell was sitting on a stool by his wife at the shop's counter, and he appeared sullen and irritated. Leaning forward in his seat, the unsmiling scuba instructor pointed to the door implying that Wade's friends had already gone outside to their truck.

Giving a deep sigh of relief realizing Karl had escaped, Wade decided it best not to stop and explain what had just happened. Thanking Russell and his wife with a nod, Wade promptly exited the building where he found Karl's truck with its motor running in the bleached oyster shell parking lot just outside. "Holy crap!" Wade furiously called out in Karl's direction as he climbed into the truck's back bench seat. "You almost got us killed by those wacko's over there! Thank you very much!"

Karl chuckled as he spun the truck's tires in reverse slinging oyster shells in all directions. Then, turning hard to the left, he bolted back up the incline of the parking lot and onto the two-rut sand road that they'd come down only an hour or so earlier. "Those goons we were dealing with back there were black marketing fish, Wade. From what I saw, they'd broken just about every law in the book. Species, size limits, quantities of catch … I think the only thing that was legit over there were some black sea bass. If the marine patrol had caught them with all I saw laying across that dock, they probably would've been put under the jail. I kid you not, fellas. You're talking about a fine of thirty to forty thousand dollars—minimum."

Irate, Wade snapped back at his bigger friend, "Then why the hell did you want to go over there in the first place—knowing all of that? That's about the dumbest thing I've ever been involved with in my life!"

Karl grinned back at Wade in the truck's rearview mirror. "Hey, fool! I got the numbers we wanted, didn't I?"

"I sure hope you did, Karl, because you almost got my butt skewered in the process."

"Damn, Wade. For a minute back there, I was almost proud of you. That's until you let those little pecker heads off that porch. You almost got my ass caught when you let that happen, you little shit."

Angrily, Wade shook his head and rolled his eyes. More curious than mad, he asked, "So tell me, how did you get out of there anyway?"

"Well … no thanks to you of course. When you and your two new little pals were carrying that first load of fish back up the ramp to the building, I was able to make a break for it."

Wade tersely shot back, "Karl, if I hadn't had your back, back there, that longhaired maniac would have gutted you like a mullet, and he wouldn't have thought twice about doing it. You can say what you want to."

Les, who had sat quietly by until this point, finally spoke up. "Well, I pretty much missed out on everything until Karl came back into the shop. When Russell found out that y'all had gone over there, he gave Karl a pretty good tongue lashing for what y'all did."

Astonished, Wade asked, "You mean he found out that Karl was over there on those guy's boat?"

"No," Les said. "All he knew was y'all went over there to see their fish. Said he knew from time to time this guy next door had some unsavory characters over there unloading fish that weren't exactly kosher. He was afraid that you two guys would somehow get him all mixed up in that mess if either one of you ever told anybody about it."

Karl laughed, "He was really pissed off, wasn't he, Les? But what the hell, he'll get over it. Besides, they know he won't say a word to anyone; it was just his way of warning us to keep our fat mouths shut too."

Wade said, "Yeah, that's what Rafael the boat's captain told me. Told me not to talk to anybody about anything I'd seen over there."

"Well, boys," Karl smirked at his friends. "Nothing like a little excitement to get our trip started off on the right foot."

Sitting in the back seat, Wade couldn't believe what Karl had just said. More than somber, he asked, "So what's the odds of us meeting those characters out on the water, Karl?"

"Zero to none, my friend. But I knew you'd find something to fret about before this trip was over, you little worrywart. Seems like you haven't changed one little bit, even after all these years. Always worried and scared about something, aren't you, Wade?"

With a steely stare, Wade countered, "I've probably changed a little more than you might think, old friend."

Trying to calm the conversation, Les looked at Karl. "What's the game plan for the rest of the day?"

By now, Karl was heading north on county road 361, the road that had brought them to Steinhatchee. "Well, as soon as we get back to Keaton, we'll stop over at the Hot Dog Stand for a quick lunch, then we'll take the boat out. This wind that they've been experiencing down here over the last several days seems to have laid down, for now, so I don't think it'll be too rough to give the boat a good run."

"Are we going to try going offshore this afternoon or will we be fishing the flats?" Les asked.

"The first thing we're going to do is to set our pinfish traps out for tomorrow … out around the tripod. Then, I thought I'd take you guys on a short run south to a bird rack just out from Dallus Creek. We'll see if we can pick up a trout or two out in that area. If we don't catch anything there, we'll swing back north toward Bonita Beach. There're some pretty good oyster bars and rocks over in that area where I've caught some big reds recently."

Wade chimed in, "Isn't that area a little too shallow for a boat your size?"

"Actually, it is. But after all the fishing I've done down here, I think I know where just about every rock and oyster bar is located along that shoreline. Besides, the tide should be high enough by the time we get over there this afternoon that we can get in and out without too much trouble."

II

The drive back to Keaton finally took a more relaxed tone as Karl's mood became less vengeful, and as the three old friends started recalling fond memories of their former neighborhood days. The creek, their dogs, the rock alley squirrel hunts. Bantering back and forth, it didn't take long before they found themselves pulling into the small sandy parking lot at the Keaton Beach Hot Dog Stand, a little restaurant that served sandwiches and seafood.

After devouring a meal of fried shrimp, grouper sandwiches, and soft drinks, the three men headed back down to Karl's boat.

As they stepped out of the truck, Les called over to Karl, "You want us to get these tanks?"

"Not yet, Les. I'm a little leery of leaving anything of value in the boat overnight down here. You never know if you'll find it there in the morning."

Les smiled curiously at the remark as he followed Karl and Wade down the ramp to Karl's center console.

"*Doc's Out!* Now that's a clever name for your boat," Les grinned at his taller friend. "For some reason, I didn't notice it while we were putting it in earlier."

"Yeah, I came up with that name because in my line of work sometimes you need to get away from all those Gomers out there that never seem to want to leave you alone. When I get on this boat, I just leave everything behind—forget it all."

"Yep," Les cheerily said as he climbed aboard, "it's a good thing to have a relaxing hobby. Good for the spirit."

Karl, who had enlisted Wade to help him carry some of his electronic gear down to the vessel, asked Wade to go out and untie the boat. Having done this, Wade gripped the bow's starboard gunwale to steady the outboard as Karl placed and tightened the remaining electronics into their settings. When he finished locking them in place, he switched the key on to the motors and they immediately started to purr. While still in neutral, he revved the engines with a couple of solid roars. Glancing at Wade with a nod, he signaled for him to climb aboard.

By 3:30 p.m. the three men all stood under the boat's blue canvas T-top. Karl had backed the boat away from the dock and was steering the craft slowly down the canal's center as he headed for the Gulf. Wade noticed that on their right and just behind the Marina was a long set of floating docks. It was the same docks where Yank had been working on the ramp earlier in the day. Only a couple of large boats, a thirty-two-foot Pro-Line and little larger Privateer, were docked there. Up from the dock, Wade could see several camper trailers parked there by their owners. The fisherman that owned these units had much cheaper monthly rates than they would have if they had paid for rooms at the adjacent Marina's motel. It was also much more convenient than staying seventeen miles away in Perry where they would have had to travel back and forth to fish and eat.

As they motored past this area, but still scanning northward, Wade could see the uppermost part of a seawall consisting of 2x10-inch treated boards stacked maybe three to four board widths high and held in place, fencelike, by large creosoted wood pilings. This structure was used to prevent the sand from the land above from eroding down and into the canal below. Just across the waterway from this spot and standing about four-feet off the ground on pilings was what Karl pointed out as his single-story three-bedroom cabin. Wade noticed its wide sliding glass door which led out onto a small balcony overlooking the waterway.

Still traveling westward, Wade noted that only cabins or small homes lined the left side of the canal. On its right side, he saw mostly rusty tin fish houses or weathered wood buildings whose businesses primarily catered to the fish, crab, and shrimp industries. Only a smattering of cabins and homes could be seen facing starboard.

They passed by Fisherman's Marina, which was a small place in comparison to Keaton Beach Marina, but a location Karl enjoyed using because he liked the owner. From this point, they then passed a small fleet of fishing vessels. Two of these rusted-hull boats were trawlers rigged with dark green shrimp nets. The other two, having no towing booms or nets, were probably used for commercial fishing far offshore in places like the Gulf of Mexico's Middle Grounds.

None of these vessels in the fleet, however, resembled those on Florida's east coast. The Atlantic boats were at least two to three times larger. The freeboard of the bow's hull of a commercial fishing or shrimp boat over there cleared the water at about ten to fifteen feet at its peak. The small boats coming in and out of the shallower waters surrounding Keaton cleared only a span of maybe six to eight feet at most.

As they passed these boats, Wade noted the same rough looking characters standing on the decks that he had encountered back at Steinhatchee. The exception was that all seemed to be white. Most of the deck hands here wore dark-colored rubberized aprons over their blue jeans and t-shirts to help keep their clothes clean while handling their catch and culling their by-catch. Along with this dark colored attire, they all wore a pair of white rubber boots that stood out noticeably in contrast.

Les waved at one of the deckhands as those on board paused to look up at Karl's boat as it passed. Though not five yards away from Les, Wade, and Karl, the crew stared coldly back without a hint of friendliness.

Taking note of the poor attitude coming from these guys after Les' friendly gesture, Karl called out with a menacing smile, "Hey, boys! How are y'all doing today?"

All on deck immediately paid homage to Karl with a small wave and a slight smile except for one, the boat's captain. In his early forties, he was a big man standing over six-feet tall and weighing around two hundred and fifty pounds. With his size and the authority he possessed as the captain and probably the owner, he was not an easily intimidated person. Chewing on a parched peanut and scowling, he spat the hull out at Karl's craft as it passed. Karl, however, didn't see him do this as he had already turned back around.

Just ahead, they could see the back side of a sign which read NO WAKE ZONE. At this point, the channel ran next to a small set of jetty rocks which jutted out south and easterly into the shallow waters of the Gulf of Mexico. This limestone rock barrier had been placed there years before to protect the inlet's waterway from high seas and storms providing a relatively safe haven for boats moored at Keaton.

As Wade and Les casually observed the calm light chop of the Gulf occurring on the other side of this barrier, Karl suddenly and without warning slammed the boat's throttle forward gunning the engines full bore. With a thunderous roar, the bow of his boat immediately jumped upward out of the water.

Les and Wade were thrown off balance and looked for anything they could grab to steady themselves. It appeared that Karl was going to drive the vessel straight into the jetty's boulders. At the last moment, he spun his stainless-steel steering wheel hard left and missed the rocks by mere feet.

As Karl gained speed by trimming the boat's engines and lowering the bow, Les and Wade were able to climb up and grab hold of the aluminum pipe bracing that supported Karl's customized T-top. Glancing back at the area they had just left, Wade noticed a massive wake battering the jetty rocks. Had anyone been standing on them as Karl's vessel roared past, they would have been knocked off by the large waves produced. If not, they certainly would have been soaked to the bone.

Barreling southeast with his hull trimmed low, Karl took a hard-right turn as he passed the first square green channel marker. The angle of his cut was so sharp that for a moment Wade thought the Gulf waters might even spill over the gunwales and into the boat's stern.

Karl trimmed his engines once more as the boat's bow had risen slightly from this first turn. Regaining his speed, he blasted his way across the water some forty or so more yards. He passed a post on his port side containing a red triangular day beacon where he then took another right at the next green marker swinging his vessel in a more west-north-westerly direction. With the boat still trimmed and the Gulf waters at only a mild chop, he was able to shower down on his engines taking them to their max. Ever mindful, however, as a good practitioner should be, he kept a close eye on his gauge indicating the RPMs he was running.

Two small rooster tails shot upward in back of the engines as a foaming and growing V-shaped wake spread laterally behind the vessel. Wade took note as Karl made a slow continuous turn steering his Contender to a heading of about 250 degrees. Within minutes and just as impulsively as he had started out on this wild rampage, Karl flipped the throttle into neutral. Tapping the transmission into reverse for several seconds, he then flipped the throttle back into neutral once more. Except for a mild breeze and the cool Gulf's currents pushing it slightly eastward, the boat came almost to a standstill.

"Are we putting the fish traps out here?" Les asked confused. "I thought we were putting them out by a tripod."

"The tripod's over there," Wade pointed toward the Keaton Beach marker which was about a hundred and fifty yards north and behind them looking from the boat's starboard side.

Karl glanced at his questioning friend, "Didn't want to be right on top of it. Someone could easily steal our bait if they found these things before we did." As Karl baited the first of three traps with frozen Spanish sardines that he had pulled out of his bait cooler, Les noticed the odd appearance of the cage's markers. Tethered to each trap by a short black strand of rope was a white cannon ball float which had been cut in half.

Les, puzzled by the setup, asked, "Won't these be hard to find tomorrow morning when we come back by to pick them up?"

Karl listened but did not respond as he placed the bait in each trap. Throwing the cork and line in first, he then threw in the first two-foot by three-foot mesh wire trap. A frothing explosion of tiny bubbles gushed to the surface as the trap sank rapidly to the Gulf of Mexico's shallow grassy bottom. Waiting several moments as the boat drifted away from the first trap, he then threw in the second and likewise the third. He looked at Les as he reached over and hit a button on his electronic LORAN causing the device to beep. "Just put in the waypoint coordinates for these traps. We'll find them easy enough."

Taking a deck brush, he poked it over the boat's side and brought it back up wet. There were a few places on the gunwales and stern's decking where the bait had bled and stuck. Karl, ever the perfectionist, wanted it cleaned immediately. Scrubbing these areas with the hard-bristled broom, he had the bait stains washed off and the boat back clean as a whistle within a few short strokes. Dipping the brush back into the water to get it clean, he placed the broom bristle-side up in one of his stern's hollow rod holders. Glancing at Les, he said, "Come here and I'll show you how this machine operates."

Les stepped forward and stood beside Karl as he started explaining the device. "The short version of how this thing works is using triangulation. There are towers all around the Gulf's coast here that send and receive signals. If you know the exact location of any two given points on a fixed baseline, you can derive a third point by measuring the angles to it. Basic trigonometry. So I'm going to punch in my waypoint to my favorite bird rack. From where we are right here, you can see it says that we're seven-point-eight miles away with a bearing of 165 degrees southeast. As we travel, it will tell us our updated distance and arrival time. It also corrects for currents, waves, wind, or anything else that pushes us off course."

Les marveled at the device. "Wow. Now, that's really something. All we had along the Amazon was a compass and a prayer book, and I think the prayer book came in handier than the compass most of the time."

Gazing at Les, Karl let out a suppressed snort then asked, "What say we go to the Bird Rack, boys?" Turning his wheel, he pointed his vessel in the direction that the LORAN indicated which was 165 degrees southeast from their present position.

Traveling slowly at first as he got his bearing and making sure that everything important in the boat was tied down and in place, he once again pushed the throttle full bore.

For the rest of the afternoon, the three old friends tried catching fish at various spots. First casting rubbery grubs around the gray weatherworn rack which was stained with white bird feces, they were only able to catch a couple of speckled trout of legal size. Without much luck there, they headed back north, past Keaton, and closer toward shore. In this area near a place called Bonita Beach, which was shallow and filled with oyster bars and hidden rocks, they fished for reds but with little success.

After trying to fish out in deeper water but with the same result, Karl decided to take Les and Wade on a boat ride along the coastline in the direction of the Rock Islands. Driving slowly for a change, he pointed out areas of interest. The doctor showed them that they were just now passing a stream that opened into the Gulf called Yate's Creek. Traveling further north, he showed them Little Spring Creek then Spring Warrior where he said it was almost impossible to come in or go out at low tide. He also noted he had friends at Spring Warrior with whom he would play cards and go fishing from time to time.

Picking up speed, he pointed out a good place to fish called Eagles Nest Creek. He told them at this spot, he'd caught numerous big red drum over the years, and he thought this was the best spot in the area to find such fish. Next came Big Spring Creek followed by a large set of oyster bars just off the entrance to the Fenholloway River. Karl could have carried them further north but stopped short of taking them to the barren Rock Islands. He thought that unless you were a marine biologist, there was nothing there of any real interest.

Looking at the coastline with the V formations of ducks and other sea foul flying overhead, Les remarked, "Man, it really is beautiful out here, isn't it? After living in South America for so long, it's hard to believe such vast areas of undisturbed wilderness still exist here in the good ol' U.S. of A."

Karl viewed the rugged shoreline to their east as Les said this. "It may appear calm and isolated around here, ol' Buddy, but even in the most remote place you can find a quarrel or two going on."

"A quarrel? What kind of quarrel would you be talking about?" Les asked intrigued.

Hearing Karl's remarks, Wade also wanted to know what he meant.

"Nothing that you two guys need to be getting involved with, that's for sure."

Puzzled, Les gave Wade a quick glance then peered back at his older friend. "If we don't know what you're talking about, how will we know how to avoid getting involved?" Les asked curiously.

Karl smiled down at his missionary pal. "You know, opinions are kind of like tail holes, Les. Everybody's got one. Just don't be giving yours out about anything that might seem controversial while you're down here. That's all."

Karl paused momentarily, then gave both of his friends a more serious look. "There's some bad blood going on between certain people around here concerning certain issues. We don't want to be starting any trouble for ourselves while we're on this trip. The less you know about all of this, the better off we'll be. All I'll tell you is that it has to do with the disposal of certain materials along the coast in this area. Just in case you hear someone arguing about this, don't take sides. Get away from the situation as fast as you can. You guys understand what I'm telling you?"

Puzzled, both men tentatively nodded in agreement.

For a few silent minutes, Karl let his boat drift as they all stood watching the sun starting to set in the west. Behind them, one of the most uninhabited coastlines in the continental United States endured. It was a literal maze of forested marsh grass, tidal creeks, rocks, and oyster bars which only a handful of people could navigate.

III

Heading back to Keaton, the three landed their boat at the dock located on the canal across from Karl's cabin. As they disembarked onto the floating boardwalk, Karl gave Les the key to his bungalow telling him how to drive around to it, so they could unload their things.

Heading in two different directions as they got to the top of the walkway ramp, Karl strode over to one of the parked campers residing on the sand camping and parking lot and knocked on its door. Les watched the door open and then Karl disappeared inside.

Taking the key Karl had given them, Les and Wade drove around to Karl's house where they carried their luggage and gear inside. It was an unbelievably neat place, Wade thought. Walking through the cabin and placing his luggage at the foot of the bed in which he would be sleeping, he noticed there wasn't a wrinkle in the bedspread. When he went to use the bathroom, it was so clean it appeared as if no one had used it in months. With Karl coming down here so much, this seemed rather odd to Wade as he surveyed the place. Making his way back to the kitchen living room area, he heard Les beckoning him to come out onto the balcony.

"Take a look at that, Wade," Les said pointing to the purplish-red sunset as the giant orange ball had just dipped below the horizon. "That'd make for a good picture, now wouldn't it?"

"Yeah, it really would. Has a lot of beautiful colors in there. Would probably make for a better photograph, though. Wouldn't you think?"

Les nodded in agreement as the two men watched the magnificent sight eventually start to fade. Hearing the groaning engine of Karl's truck as it came to a stop in front of the house, they headed in that direction. Making it into the kitchen, they met Karl at the front door.

Holding it open for him to enter, they saw that their tall, lanky friend had both of his arms filled with electronics.

"Decided to bring these inside tonight," he remarked. "Heard that someone's truck got broke into over at the docks last night and they made off with about fourteen hundred dollars' worth of equipment."

"Got anything else you need to bring inside?" Wade asked.

"I don't think so. I padlocked my air tank rack. If they can get past that, they deserve 'em," he said. "Say, are you two guys about ready to go get something to eat?"

Les spoke, "Yeah, but don't we need to clean up a little first."

"Just change shirts and wash the fish off your hands. I've got a friend meeting us over at The Old Pavilion Restaurant in about ten minutes."

"Is that a restaurant back in Perry?" Les asked.

"Nooo," Karl groaned from his room where he was changing shirts and putting on deodorant. "You know it takes more than ten minutes to get to Perry from here, Les. What were you doing—sleeping the whole way down here today?"

Les responded with a laugh. "Something like that."

Puzzled by his comment, Karl carried on, "It's across the street from the Marina. You guys didn't see it when we unhitched my trailer earlier? It's right next door."

"Well, now that you mention it . . ." Les called over his shoulder as he headed for his room.

"Well, y'all hurry up and let's get going. We don't want to be late," Karl prompted them.

CHAPTER 26

260 West South West

In ten minutes, the three men had cleaned themselves up and were entering the lobby of the eating establishment. For Keaton Beach in 1985, this was a rather large place comparable in size and refinement to the seafood restaurants found in Perry such as Pouncey's which could easily seat fifty to sixty people. Though it had as much room, The Old Pavilion, unlike Pouncey's, never came close to filling the place.

Scanning the room full of sparsely filled tables, they saw a lone man quietly sitting and reading the local weekly newspaper. Approaching him as they followed Karl, Wade noticed that the gentlemen appeared to be in his mid-sixties. Wearing khaki pants, a white short-sleeve buttoned-down dress shirt, and black horn-rimmed glasses, he possessed a head full of silvery gray hair which was conservatively cut.

Standing up and grinning as the three friends drew near, he called out to Karl and shook his friend's hand.

Kindly greeting him, Karl pointed to Les and Wade, "These two guys are my buds from back home that I told you about. The ones I told you I would be carrying out fishing tomorrow."

The man with the bright brown eyes cordially offered his hand to Les.

"Buck. Buck Anderson," he said shaking Les' then Wade's hand as they introduced themselves in turn. "So good to meet you guys," Buck exclaimed. "Any friend of Karl's is a friend of mine." He paused. "Maybe I shouldn't go quite that far—what say you, Les?" Chuckling, he winked at Karl's smaller buddy.

Les furrowed his brow bemused as they took a seat. "Hey, that accent of yours, Buck, you're not from around here are you?"

"Well, not exactly. For most of the last twenty years or so, I've lived in Tallahassee, if that counts. What I imagine you're probably detecting is my Illinois, Midwestern accent. I haven't been able to shirk that blasted thing either, Les," he cackled happily. "Now you good ol' boys from southern Georgia, y'all don't carry around such noticeable accents, now do ya'?"

Smiling along with Wade at Buck's parody, Les asked, "So, being from Illinois and Tallahassee, how on earth did you end up meeting ol' Karl down here at Keaton Beach?"

"I'll give you the short version, Les. You see I use to work for the Florida Division of Law Enforcement. That was until I retired about two years ago. I'd done a little flats fishing from time to time with some of the other agents down here over the years, but I usually stayed too busy chasing bad guys to do it very often. Thought when I retired, I'd try coming down here a little more, but my wife wasn't really into the fishing thing. You know how it goes. Too hot. Too many bugs. No convenient bathrooms. So, you get the picture."

Both Les and Wade nodded acknowledging that they understood.

"So, unfortunately and unexpectedly for me, my wife died. She had an aortic aneurysm. And well . . . suddenly she was gone, and I was by myself."

"I'm so sorry," Les responded compassionately.

Pausing to regain his composure, Buck once again flashed his friendly smile. "So, rather than me being all alone in Tallahassee, I decided that I'd have a setup down here at Keaton where I could go fishing whenever I wanted. I have a camper over behind the Marina there where I pay an inexpensive lot rent. To keep myself occupied and active, I go back and forth between here and my home in Tallahassee. That's probably a little more of an answer to your question of how I met your friend here than you wanted. But the bottom line simply is that we just kept bumping into each other until we finally introduced ourselves."

A waitress came up and served them all ice water, and took their orders. When she left, Karl spoke up as he looked at his companions.

"Boys, Buck here and I've been offshore fishing many times, and if there's one person around these parts who knows where to go and how to catch fish, it's him. I'd say only a few commercial fishermen know this area as well as Buck does."

Buck was quick to reply to Karl's assertion. "I'm humbled by your praise, Doc, but it's awfully hard to figure out just what these commercial boat captains down here really know."

"Why is that?" Wade asked curiously.

"For starters," Buck said with incredulity, "they won't talk to you."

"That seems strange. Why wouldn't they?" Les asked confused.

Pausing, Buck eyed the pair. "Besides not wanting you to know where their fishing hotspots are," he stopped again, "I'll give you my opinion."

Buck glanced around the room. Seeing that no one was within earshot, he began to open up.

"Fellows, I'm not talking in regard to all the fishermen and crabbers down here. I'm not even talking about most of them. But a few bad apples have seemed to shut the mouths of the rest of these guys pretty tight."

"What do you mean by bad apples, Buck?" Les asked inquisitively.

Peering at Karl's two friends, Buck could see that neither one of them had any idea of the crime wave that had recently swept through the area.

"Some of these boys we're discussing here have been in trouble with the law."

"You mean like for selling illegal fish?" Wade asked.

Buck grinned at his new acquaintance's guess. "How about selling illegal drugs, Wade?"

Both men raised their eyebrows when they heard Buck say this.

"You see, the department I used to work for before I retired was the Drug Strike Force. Not living around here, you may not have heard of this case, but I was one of the agents involved in the big drug bust up at the Aucilla River several years back.

Karl gazed at his two friends, "You guys haven't heard about this, have you?"

Both men indicated that they hadn't.

"Well, Buck," Karl continued, "why don't you fill them in on what happened over there. It's an interesting story."

Taking note of the two men's interest, Buck began to talk. "As usual in such big cases like the one I'm referring to involving drugs and large amounts of money, you can bet your last dollar that the mob was somehow involved. Remember now, this was the time when the really big money being made was coming from marijuana. Other recreational drugs were out there for sure, but marijuana, at this point, was the big cash cow."

"I'll get to how they did this in just a minute. But first, I want you to know that wherever these plants can be grown, wherever they have little interference coming from the government, and wherever this stuff can be mass produced cheaply, places like Mexico and South America, well, that's the route it will take."

"Now, the money they made doing this came easily at first. Only token measures were put in place to slow down its usage. But then, as the drug became more and more prevalent and made its way from the poverty-stricken inner city out to the more affluent suburbs—shockingly and miraculously the government wanted it stopped." Buck sneered shaking his head. "Too close to home, right? So law enforcement shifted its focus from the drugs usage to its trafficking."

"As for how they got it into the country, South Florida at this time was its major point of entry. More specifically, the Miami, Dade County area. So, this was the region the state and federal law enforcement agencies put the pressure on first. But like any good chess player, these thugs made a move in order to evade their adversary. You see, the guys involved in this criminal enterprise weren't exactly stupid, by no means."

Buck's eyes sparkled as he recalled the case. "So, guys, where do you think they moved to next?" Awaiting their response, he could tell they were eager to know. "You've probably already guessed it. Right around here, boys."

"At Keaton Beach?" Les asked amazed.

"No. Not just here, Les, but around this whole area that they call The Big Bend." Glancing at Karl, Buck said, "He can tell you how isolated and porous this coastline is around here."

Les spoke up, "Yeah, I saw that this afternoon for myself up around the Fenholloway River. But tell me, how were they doing it?"

Buck sighed. "It was a pretty simple operation, really. All they had to do was load a large shrimp or fishing boat from South America with their drugs, cross the Gulf, and rendezvous with a group of smaller boats off the coast." He paused. "Really not just off the coast. Actually, where they met was in a place called the 'Middle Grounds' which is an area about a hundred or so miles southwest from here."

Buck continued, "Now remember, the people doing this weren't some hoods that had just moved to town. These were some of your local folks living right around here who were going out to meet these vessels. Of course, all of this was done clandestinely and mostly at night, but anyway, when they'd get to the bigger boats out there, they'd split the cargo up into smaller lots. That's when the next phase of the operation went into effect occurring in closer at various spots along the coast. They'd offload these bales of marijuana onto smaller boats like airboats or whatnot where they could get the stuff through that rugged coastline, like what you saw today, and on into shore."

"Now, this operation worked out very well for everyone involved at first. But you know how it goes. It didn't take long for the big boys behind the scenes to want a bigger slice of the pie. So, one of these big Kahuna's decided it would be a great idea if they were to purchase most of the land surrounding the mouth of the Aucilla River where it spills into the Gulf. Doing this and using a little friendly intimidation, so to speak, on the local landowners and others living in that area, they gained control of its entrance. Now, rather than having to offload their cargo for a second time closer to shore, they just drove their boats straight to the dock they'd just bought, cutting out the middleman. Nobody using the river to fish or crab was going to squeal because they knew somebody named Bull or Moose would come deal with them. That kind of cockiness and greed is what finally did them in just like it does every crook. When they made the audacious mistake of taking their product straight into that dock on the Aucilla, the takedown from our unit, much to their surprise, came quickly and easily." Buck leaned back in his booth smiling as he thought of the repercussions which occurred from the bust.

"When all was said and done, we'd arrested local citizens, fishermen, law enforcement agents, county commissioners, and, I think, even a judge. It seemed like everybody was in on the action," saying this Buck shook his head.

Les acknowledged, "Yeah, it was a lot like that down on the Amazon river except it was the cocaine trade. The communist rebels would sell it to buy arms. The only difference between it and your story, Buck, is that the people down there seemed to be much more ruthless. They'd kill you just as soon as look at you if you happened to cross their path."

Buck seemed impressed concerning the missionary's experience. "So, you know what I'm talking about firsthand, Les?"

"Unfortunately, I do, Buck. I lost my best friend down there to such people."

"I'm sorry to hear that," the former agent responded sympathetically. "Karl told me that you had recently been a missionary along the Amazon, so I'm not surprised that you encountered such problems."

"Yeah, it was an affliction all right. The drug had started filtering its way down the river by the time we left." Les peered at the former agent curiously. "So tell me, where was this marijuana coming from? Columbia as well?"

"You name the country, Les. Peru, Ecuador, Brazil, Mexico—it was coming from all over the place. But you're right, Columbia overall was probably the worst offender."

Wade interjected, "So, Buck, getting back to the commercial fishermen, what you're telling us is some of these guys were on the take. Is that right?"

"Not just fishermen, Wade. Like I told you there were a lot of people involved.

"Why so many? Weren't they afraid of getting caught and going to jail?"

Buck sighed. "Wade, what you've got to understand is that not everybody around here is making a good living. Those that were and got involved, well, they were just plain greedy. But some did it to support their families. Money can talk when you're trying to provide for your wife and kids. Know what I mean?"

Wade nodded solemnly.

As Buck finished his story, he grew pensive. With Les' disclosure concerning the problems he'd seen in South America, Buck was trying to decide whether he should let them in on some new information he'd recently gleaned. Thinking Karl a doctor, Les a missionary, and Wade probably a harmless friend, he finally spoke up. "I don't know if I should be telling you what's going on with this or not, fellows," he said pausing as he intently observed the three men, "But I might have come across some news that you guys and particularly Les might find especially interesting."

Noticing their intrigue, Buck leaned in toward the table to keep his comments even more guarded than before. As the other three men leaned forward also, he quietly began to speak. "Now I want you guys to remember, even as I'm about to tell you this information, I'm no longer privy to the intelligence coming out of the department anymore. So, you might want to take what I'm going to say with a grain of salt." More seriously, he said, "And then again, you might not." Surveying the room cautiously, he spoke just above a whisper. "Guys, I think we've just seen the tip of the iceberg. There could be even worse trouble brewing down here right now. At least that's what I'm hearing."

The retired agent grew quiet as he noticed that their waitress was approaching their table. She had some of their food with her. Making several trips back and forth to the kitchen, she at last had the four men served. Les had a seafood platter; Wade had a meal of broiled mahi-mahi; Karl had a fried grouper sandwich; and Buck had a large bowl of oyster stew and a shrimp cocktail.

After getting their plates and drinks situated, Les blessed their food. As they began eating and enjoying their meal, Karl quietly asked Buck, "Exactly what kind of trouble would you be referring to?"

Popping a cocktail sauce-covered boiled shrimp into his mouth, Buck took a sip of sweet tea, wiped his lips with his napkin, and looked around at a now almost empty room. Cautiously and in a low voice he began to talk. "Well, the problem Les was referring to down in Columbia? Unfortunately, it seems to have made its way here to the U.S."

"You're talking about cocaine, right?" Karl asked.

Buck's look turned very somber for the first time. "Yes. And from what I'm hearing it's coming into the country like there's no end in sight. The demand for this drug is nothing like any of us in law enforcement have ever seen before, Karl." He stopped to take another sip of tea.

"You know, fellas," he continued quietly, "I never really saw marijuana as being that addictive a drug. Sure, there are problems with it. Mainly it can lead to the use of stronger substances, but you never hear of someone having to go to a rehab clinic to get off the stuff." He paused pensively, "But this cocaine, well now this is a whole different story. Wouldn't you say, Les?"

Les stopped eating as he had been carefully listening to what Buck was telling them. In a serious tone, the preacher said, "In more ways than you can imagine, Buck."

"How so?" Karl inquired.

Les directed his attention toward his older friend. "This has been a problem since the time we got to South America, and it's been growing at an accelerated rate. We saw this especially over the last several years we were there. I'd say now it's gained a foothold and is making its way through the towns and villages we visited with devastating results. During the last year we were there, we had a doctor from Virginia come down to join us at Iquitos for a six-month stay. He wrote in the final entry of his journal that he'd never seen anything as addictive as this drug other than heroin. He was so surprised by what he was seeing, he told me he was going to send reports of his findings to both the Department of Justice and to the DEA warning them that this drug was probably on the way, meaning heading to the U.S."

Listening to Les' story, Karl responded, "This may be pretty startling news to you guys, but the addictive property of cocaine is a well-established fact in the medical community. So, I guess the real question I'd like to ask you, Buck, is why you'd say you see it as a problem just now? Are you talking about this happening here in Florida or about it hitting the U.S. in general?"

"Both things are happening simultaneously as I speak," Buck said staring into Karl's eyes. "As I told you with respect to marijuana, it follows the path of least resistance. As far as your first question of why now? Here's why."

Leaning back in his seat, Karl, still unimpressed, crossed his arms as Buck began to explain.

"Basically, there are two reasons for this occurring at this time. One is that the heat's on in Miami again. Just as it happened with marijuana, this drug is following the same old routes. Secondly, the amount of money they've found they can make—makes the marijuana trade pale in comparison. The differentiation of the two besides cocaine's more addictive property revolves around logistics and sales. The selling structure of cocaine versus marijuana is vastly more complicated. Marijuana is sold in bulk bales around twenty-five pounds at twenty thousand dollars wholesale here in the U.S. The government has calculated that after the initial sale, it's sold three more times. By the time it's sold on the street that twenty-five-pound bale will have yielded sixty-five thousand dollars in tax-free revenue. We're talking right now in 1985 at today's prices. Now let's take a single two-pound brick of pure cocaine, roughly a kilo. That cheap-to-produce little brick will sell on average in the U.S. for around forty-five thousand dollars wholesale. After it's sold three more times where it's cut and diluted with stimulants and such, it brings in approximately three hundred thousand dollars when you include its price when sold on the street. Consider this fact also; the big boys are usually involved in more than the initial sale. They control or get a take at several different levels. But for argument's sake, let's say they got only money on the initial sale. Would you rather handle a twenty-five-pound bale of marijuana for twenty thousand dollars or a two-pound brick of cocaine for forty-five thousand dollars? Like Les said, the user's appetite for this stuff is insatiable. Once they use it, they're hooked. And it's spreading throughout the country like wildfire."

Karl glowered at the agent. "You're talking about some mighty big money there, Buck. Who in their right mind would trust these yokels around here with handling that kind of cash or transporting such a valuable asset, huh?"

Buck grinned back. "Wouldn't be like the good old weed days where everybody and their brother was in on the action, now would it?"

The doctor, far from being convinced by what Buck was telling him, played along. "So, you're telling me that they might be doing this right around here? And if so, precisely where would they be bringing it in, Buck? Looks like wherever that place would be, it would be buzzing once the word got out."

"Can't tell you where they're doing this because it stays a well-kept secret. And big money doesn't talk, Doc. People keep their mouths shut, or they just disappear. These guys, as Les said, are a hundred times more violent than the people who were doing this during the marijuana days."

Karl was intrigued by what Buck was telling him. But, even knowing that the former agent probably still had some connections inside the agency, he was still quite skeptical. "So, someone, maybe an informant, is releasing or giving the FDLE this information," Karl suggested.

Buck shrugged. "I already told you that I'm no longer in that loop. Let's just say this is my conjecture."

Dispassionately, Karl nodded in agreement.

"This is strictly my story so take it as such. Wouldn't want you guys to divulge this information to anyone else for sure. First, it may be totally worthless, and second, it may give someone the heads up. But if you're interested, just as I told you about the Aucilla River story, I'll give you my take on the workings of this deal too."

All at the table nodded that they wanted to hear more.

"Okay then, this is what I think is happening. Being a bit of an obsessive-compulsive personality, I haven't really been able to stop myself from being an investigative sleuth. Considering that and this being my hobby, I guess, I've followed the news and reports coming out of Bogotá. That's Columbia, Wade, if you didn't know where I was talking about. This is the home of Pablo Escobar, the ruthless drug lord of the Medellín Cartel down there. The word is that he's getting tired of his transports being given the shakedown by the Mexican government. It's costing him millions of dollars to ship his drugs across Mexico's borders. So now, he's rerouted his supply chain through Cuba. Also, many of the communist guerillas, rebel fighters from South America like M-19, the Shining Path Guerillas, and some say FARC, but I'm not so sure about them, are training in Cuba where they're probably, like Les said earlier, running drugs for the cartels in exchange for weapons. With his partnership with Castro, Pablo is taking Mexico out of the equation and is gaining another channel partner so to speak to help distribute his drugs. Impoverished Cubans are getting some much-needed cash while Castro delights in sticking it to his most hated enemy—America. Doesn't get much better for him than this, now does it?"

Buck looked at each member of the group. "So, one thing you're probably asking yourselves now is with our Navy, our Coast Guard, and our Air Force out there watching for all of this sort of illegal activity, just how capable are these guys of doing this?" Buck paused dispirited then grumbled, "Supposedly, from what I'm hearing—they're doing it pretty darn well."

Karl let out a deep unbelieving sigh, "So, pray tell, Buck. Just how are they doing this? After the Aucilla bust, I doubt there's a boat crossing the Gulf from South America that's not being trailed via satellite."

Noting that the doctor had become skeptical, the former agent responded to his question with a slight smile "They're doing it with planes, zinc strips, and flotation devices. How about that for a combination, Doc?"

Karl was put out by the absurdity of Buck's response, "Planes, zinc strips, and flotation devices? Can't wait to hear how this deal might work, Buck."

The retired agent didn't flinch at Karl's disparaging jab as he began to tell the group how the drugs were being logistically processed. "I know for a fact from some aerial photos I've seen that the Russians are modifying Cuban planes for speed and stealth. They've done this primarily for military purposes, but they'll work just as well for operations such as the one I'm referring to. I also know for a fact that they've already made drug drops successfully offshore along the coast of South Florida. They've developed a scheme using the dissolving properties zinc has when mixed with saltwater as a timing mechanism. Using varying strips to wrap around the ropes connected to the dropped container and its floats, they can regulate the time when these buoys will pop to the surface. They can make this occur over long or short periods of time depending on the wire's thickness. All of this has been prearranged, so they won't give away their hiding place until the pickup boat gets there. This last point also concerns the use of lead shot to keep the package located in one stationary spot, so they can find it electronically using coordinates. Pretty clever operation, huh?"

"Wow!" Karl scoffed cynically. "Pretty elaborate setup you've got figured out there, secret agent Anderson," Karl said, mocking his friend as if he was an actor in one of the spy movies made popular in the 1960s and 70s.

"Yep. About as elaborate a setup as that winch and bow pulpit you had put on your perfectly sculptured Contender. Why on earth would you ever have let one of your buddy's put one of those things on such a magnificent boat?"

Karl gritted his teeth in a menacing grin and quickly shot back, "I guess it's because I just wanted to, Buck. How about that for an answer, huh?"

The former agent delighted in getting under Karl's skin. "Say, is the anchor rope rolling through that pulpit still catching on the roller and giving you trouble, Doc?"

"I bet anything coming from a pulpit would give Karl trouble, Buck," Wade interjected as both he and Buck began to cackle.

Karl paid no attention to either the remark or its response. Glaring at Buck, he said, "Are you about finished with your little story there, Chief Intelligence Officer Double Naught Seven?"

"Yeah, so let's get on to the real reason that you wanted me to eat with you tonight, Karl. Where's your map? I saw the tube you had it in when you walked up to the table."

By this time, most of the customers had left the building and the employees seemed to be all in the back. Taking note of this, Karl reached under his seat and pulled out a small hollow cylinder about a yard long. Standing up, he walked over to an adjacent table and cleared off its dining utensils. Unscrewing one end of the tube, he pulled out an NOAA nautical map of the area that read Tampa Bay to Cape San Blas. It was an exact duplicate to the one he'd seen while prowling the cabin cruiser back in Steinhatchee.

Re-rolling it backward first, he then flattened it out on the empty tabletop. Examining a bearing of 230 degrees southwest and twenty-seven miles out of Keaton, he pointed to an area that he had recently fished and where he had some success.

Buck inspected the map as Karl showed him the spot. "That's pretty good hard bottom right in there," the retired agent said eyeing the territory. "I've fished it before, but if you take a heading of two hundred and twenty-six degrees and run another ten miles farther on out, you'll find a line of rock outcrops right here." He marked the spot with a pen he had in his hand. He took into account the chart's Loran number coordinates. "I recently discovered those rocks with a pal of mine when we fished that area three weekends ago. Caught some very nice grouper out there along with some big amberjacks. Your pals here would have a blast hauling up some of those things."

Taking note of what Buck was showing him, Karl goaded his friend, "Did you happen to catch any thirty-six-inch gags while you were out there, ol' man?"

"A three-foot-long gag? Not hardly. I think the biggest grouper we caught was a twenty-five-inch red weighing maybe fourteen to fifteen pounds or so. We limited out on them and caught a lot just under the eighteen-inch limit that we threw back." Buck paused, staring at Karl. "Where have you seen a gag that big that's been caught around here?"

"Saw some at one of those real remote fish houses in the marsh over at Steinhatchee earlier today. They had to have been at least that big. Some maybe bigger."

"Commercial fisherman or charter?"

"Neither. You wouldn't have believed how many fish those guys had piled up on that dock, Buck. Not just the huge gag grouper like the ones I'm telling you about but lots of undersized red grouper and red snapper. They had some of the largest bull redfish I've ever seen over there too. From what I could make out, almost their entire catch was illegal. If they'd been caught, like I was telling these guys earlier, they'd probably be sitting in jail tonight." Karl paused reflecting on this thought.

"My first take, Buck, was that these guys were using traps, but when I looked around their boat cabin, I saw some clip-on trace sets and some large ball anchor floats."

"You got over on these guys' boat?" Buck laughed out loud.

Glancing at Wade with a wide smile, Karl said, "I have my ways, you know."

Frowning after hearing him say this, Wade shook his head.

"Trace sets? What are those?" Les asked.

Buck glimpsed at Karl first, then angled his head toward Les. "They're a short shank of line and hook assemblage that longliners use to hook onto their main lines. They hook them close to two meters apart between what they call stoppers."

"Oh yeah," Les responded now aware of what they were. "I've seen them do that over on the Peruvian coast. They'd have those giant spools set up in the back of their boats."

"Yeah," Buck said. "Those are the big operators that can run their lines for miles. What Karl saw over at Steinhatchee was small time almost recreational stuff compared to that."

Leaning over the map, Karl cut his eyes at Buck and pointed to the location that the Rampage's captain had marked on his map with a star and the Spanish word "*Descenso*."

"Hey, Les," Karl asked, "What's *Descenso* mean in English?"

"Could mean several things, Karl—like a fall—a drop. Usually something like that."

Karl became excited when Les told him this. "Buck, it looks like that captain's marked off a ledge or a big drop off. Maybe some big holes in there. That's got to be where those guys caught those grouper. You know some of my friends fishing out of Panacea fish over in this area." Karl pointed to a place on the map that was west-south-west ten to fifteen miles from the starred point that he was referencing. "They've run into some monster gags over there from time to time."

"Yeah, but your map shows it's a lot deeper water over there too."

"I can see that, but we're talking drop-offs here. What do you think about that starred spot, Buck? You ever fished that vicinity before?"

Buck gave Karl a serious look. "You don't want to go up into that area right now, Karl."

"I didn't ask you if I should go there. I'm asking you if you've ever fished around *Descenso*," Karl stoically gazed at the older man as he said the word he'd written on his map. "Seems like there are some pretty good gradients down there, according to this chart."

Buck, stroking his chin, eyeballed the spot and its surrounding depths meticulously. "Can't say that I've fished that section of the Gulf before, Karl. But it looks pretty shallow. The spot you're pointing to is roughly five fathoms. You know as well as I do that the deeper the water where there's live bottom or rocks, that's where you want to be fishing. It's only thirty-feet deep right there where you've got it marked."

Irritated, Karl rammed his index finger repeatedly onto the starred spot on the map, "Well, I have it from a very reliable source that there are some massive fish right here!"

Concerned, Buck spoke almost pleadingly, "Listen to me, Doc. You want to stay two hundred and forty-five degrees southwest from Keaton or further south if you're going offshore fishing right now. I can't give you any more information than that. Do you understand what I'm telling you?"

"No. What I understand is that you've concocted this wild drug smuggling scheme in your mind to such an extent that you're now even starting to believe it yourself. Listen up, if you're still depressed about your wife, I'll bring you some drug samples I've got back at the office on my next trip down. I'll get you to feeling better and back on track in no time."

With a light-hearted snort, Buck chuckled at Karl's quick psychological assessment of him. "No, I don't think I'll be needing any of your anti-depressants anytime soon, but thanks for the thought. All I can tell you is if you fellows head north up into that area offshore that you'd better be careful. You guys can take my advice or leave it."

Karl chuckled. "I think we'll leave it. As far as I can see, the only thing going on out there right now is some illegal fishing. And no one's going to shoot your damn boat out from under you over that—not even if you caught 'em doing it red-handed."

Buck shook his head smiling as he watched Karl roll up the map and place it back into its canister.

CHAPTER 27

Fishing the Rocks

The next morning came early with Karl up at 5:00 a.m. rousing his friends with a cup of coffee. "There's milk in the refrigerator and cereal, peanut butter, and bread in the cabinet to the left of the sink. Jelly's in the fridge too if you want it."

Both men entered the kitchen quietly. Les made a cup of coffee and a peanut butter sandwich while Wade took a bowl of cereal to go along with his coffee.

Coming inside and going back out to his truck, Karl had already loaded the electronics and an ice chest that he would keep clean ice in for food and canned drinks. "Neither one of you boys gets seasick, now do you?" he called out from the bathroom.

Les glanced at Wade who shook his head, then Les called back, "No. Neither one of us do."

"Well, I'll carry some Dramamine out there with us just in case one of you guys wuss out on me. Don't want puke on my boat, you know."

Wade thought, *Karl always thinking about the other guy, uh huh.*

Heading for the front door, Karl called back, "All right, fellows. We'll be leaving the house in five minutes. I've got all the fishing tackle you'll need. We'll stop at the Marina to get us something to eat on the boat and some drinks. If there's anything else that you want to carry with you out there make sure and get it now."

Wade considered carrying his tackle box, but knew it would probably just be in the way. The only things he would be taking with him were a sharp knife that he carried in a holder on his belt, some sunscreen, and his rain suit.

Les went back to his bedroom and retrieved a small, insulated box. It seemed just big enough to carry a can of soda. Getting the container, he re-entered the kitchen where he found Wade. "You ready to go, sport?" Les asked.

Wade nodded; then out the front door and into the darkness they went. Karl was already seated in his truck. The only light they could see at this early hour was the penetrating high beam headlights coming from his vehicle as it cut two separate hazy paths through the moist black air surrounding them.

It took only a couple of minutes for the three to drive from Karl's cabin over to the sand parking lot located just behind the two-story Keaton Beach Marina. Wade and Les noticed the glow of lights coming from the place indicating it was open as they passed the entrance.

The three men slid out of the truck and into the eerie quietness of the early morning. Going inside, they purchased a few pre-made sandwiches, some chips, and a couple of six packs of soft drinks from Betty. They didn't buy any beer because Karl thought they might be scuba diving at some point during the day, and alcohol wasn't something that went well with this sport. Tossing all of this stuff inside Karl's clean ice cooler, Les and Wade grabbed the handles on each side of the chest and carefully walked it out the door through the pre-dawn darkness and down to Karl's twenty-eight-foot center console.

Getting the cooler situated in the stern of the vessel to Karl's liking, they went back to the truck to retrieve the rest of his electronics. While ferrying these items back to the craft, they also carried with them some rod and reels that Karl had earlier put in the bed of his truck.

Helping Karl with his equipment, Wade handed the electronic devices he had carried down to the dock across to Karl one at a time. Karl was now standing in the boat at its console. With precision from plenty of practice, the doctor quickly set each device into its brackets and locked each one securely into its proper setting.

After making one last trip to the bed of Karl's pickup, the three friends had everything including their scuba gear properly placed and fastened down for their trip offshore. Karl switched on the powerful motors which quietly garbled the waters at the boat's stern. Reaching over his steering wheel to the dashboard, he punched the WX button to his VHF radio to get the latest update on the day's Marine Weather Forecast. Climbing aboard, Wade heard the loud robotic-sounding weather report as it started to broadcast.

APALACHEE BAY

WATERS FROM SUWANNEE RIVER TO APALACHICOLA FLORIDA FROM TWENTY TO SIXTY NAUTICAL MILES

FIVE-TWENTY-FIVE AM EASTERN DAYLIGHT TIME SATURDAY, OCTOBER TWELTH, NINETEEN-EIGHTY-FIVE

SOUTHWEST WIND FIVE TO TEN KNOTS. SEAS ONE TO TWO FEET. PROTECTED WATERS SMOOTH TO A LIGHT CHOP. PATCHY DENSE FOG NEAR THE COAST.

SOUTHWEST WIND FIVE TO TEN KNOTS INCREASING TO TEN TO FIFTEEN KNOTS IN EARLY AFTERNOON. SEAS ONE TO TWO FEET BUILDING TO TWO TO THREE FEET. A CHANCE OF ISOLATED THUNDER SHOWERS THROUGH THE AFTERNOON PERIOD . . .

As the robotic broadcast started to repeat itself, Les asked, "Hey, Karl. You think we'll be in for some rough weather out there today? I didn't bring any rain gear with me."

"Nah, this is pretty typical for this time of year and we should be heading back in long before any inclement weather hits. If it were to catch us though, I've got some extra ponchos down in the cuddy we can put on."

Turning away from Les, Karl switched his loud echoing radio off and his red, white, and green navigation lights on as he pulled away from the side of the floating dock. It was hard to see as they made their way slowly down the canal. Many of the businesses' and homeowners' piers jutting out into the run were obscured by a thin veil of mist that enveloped almost everything.

Little activity could be seen coming from anywhere except one or two of the fish houses where boats were just coming in or were being prepped to go back out. After a few minutes run, the boat entered the area where they had abruptly encountered the jetties on the previous day. Seeing and remembering this spot, both Les and Wade firmly grabbed hold of the aluminum pipes which braced the T-top's roof. But on this early morning outing, Karl did not gun his motors. Instead, he smoothly turned his vessel to port and headed southward to the first square green channel marker.

Looking sternward, Wade noticed the northeastern horizon silhouetted the shoreline of Keaton like a slender black mask against a misty gray background. Only a light or two could be seen from a streetlamp, house, or business. This dark border along with the early dawn haze obscured the town almost completely. As they continued onward, one by one, the rooftops of buildings gave away their hiding places. The lightest first, then the rest.

The boat glided through the path of red and green markers of the channel with Karl slowly picking up speed as he headed out toward the Keaton tripod. An ever-growing hourglass of foam blasted out from the dual set of Yamaha 200s. Its trail of gaseous bubbles expanding laterally into a giant V as the craft made its way from the inlet into the great expanse of the Gulf of Mexico.

As the water grew choppier the farther they progressed, Les could see a thick, foreboding fog bank confronting them. Until now, the moisture in the air had produced no more than an airy vapor. Noticing the almost impenetrable denseness of this cloud hovering to their front, Karl spun his wheel southward giving them a course that Les noted as 265 degrees southwest.

"Look to your right, Les," Wade called out as they passed the red flashing light of the tripod that stood about fifteen yards off their starboard side.

"That why you made that turn back there?" Les asked probing his older friend.

"Pretty good reason, wouldn't you say?" Karl winked back.

Holding onto the metal post of the roof's frame with one hand, Karl's smaller friend grinned as he dug his other hand deep into his jacket pocket. Shivering, Les had become unaccustomed to this kind of weather. It was a drastic change from the weather he'd experienced in South America.

A series of beeps erupted from Karl's LORAN device.

"What's that mean?" Les asked.

"Means we're right on top of our pinfish traps," Karl retorted as he pulled the throttle back into neutral. "Get the gaff, Wade."

While Wade rushed to do this, Karl flipped the switch to fill the boat's bait well with seawater.

"Y'all see anything yet?" Karl asked eagerly.

"Here's one," Wade excitedly said as he hooked the rope under the buoy with the gaff. Pulling the line into his hand, he hurriedly hauled the trap out of the water and saw that it contained maybe fourteen to fifteen little wriggling pinfish. Included in this group were a small grunt and a couple of spot tails. Most all of them were big enough to use as bait.

"Hurry up. Get 'em in the water back here, Wade," Karl commanded as he lifted the live well's floor door.

As Karl made it back to the wheel and drove onward, Les found the next float and started pulling it in.

"Hey Karl," Wade asked. "Where do these empty traps go?"

"What?" Karl shot back irritated. "Back in the water of course! We don't want to have all that crap out there in our way when we're trying to fish. Come on, man. Use your head, Wade."

"Just asking, Karl. Never hurts to ask, now does it?" Wade was miffed by Karl's attitude. He figured that if his older friend was going to start acting like this, it was going to make for a very long day of fishing indeed.

"Coming through," Les gleefully proclaimed as he hauled his pinfish trap containing ten or so fish toward the live well.

"This isn't looking too good to me," Karl mumbled under his breath. "If this last one's not loaded, we'll have to go out to the 'Twenty' marker and fish for some more bait there."

Within minutes of driving and searching, Wade finally spotted the last float. Reaching it with the gaff, he pulled the line up for Les to catch the cord. In a moment's time the young preacher had the trap pulled inside.

Seeing that it contained only four baitfish, Karl lashed out, "This sucks, boys!"

Eager to goad his tall friend, especially after the way Karl had talked to him earlier, Wade loudly responded with a grin, "Looks like a trip out to the twenty marker to me, Karl."

Glaring at Wade, Karl shouted with an angry sneer, "Yes, it does, doesn't it, Wade!"

As Les was attempting to throw the last empty trap back over the stern, Karl swung the boat to a heading of 267 degrees. Just as Les let go of the cage, the doctor slammed the throttle down as far as it would go causing the craft to almost leap from the water. With its bow riding high, he quickly trimmed the motors bringing the fore hull downward as he sped across the Gulf at close to forty knots. Pissed or not, he was taking his pals' lives into his own hands as they were now completely enveloped in the fog bank. It allowed for a field of vision of only ten yards gazing in any direction. Any boat crossing their path or just sitting in front of them in this blinding cloud could certainly be hit or run over in a millisecond.

Ticked by his older friend's recklessness, Wade was nervous, but he was too mad to give Karl the pleasure of knowing it. Les, who had been temporarily thrown to the deck as Karl gunned the motors, eventually achieved enough balance to stand partially. Struggling to overcome the boat's rapid forward movement, he finally made the four to five steps it took to get back to where he could grip the T-top's bracing. Steadying himself, he stared at Wade and shook his head in disbelief.

From where they were, it was roughly a five and a half mile run out to the twenty marker, and it didn't take long to get there. Within ten minutes, the LORAN's beeper once again sounded signaling a spot just south of the beacon where Karl wanted to start slowing down.

"All right, Wade," Karl demanded. "How about reaching down there in the sidewall and getting us all one of those spinners."

Pointing to where the small rods were, Wade reached down and retrieved three of them from their indented holders.

Karl peered through the heavy haze surrounding them. "Okay. We should be just about there, now."

"There it is," Les declared as he saw the tall structure's flashing red light through the mist.

Aptly, the marker was called the twenty as the red triangular lighted beacon had this number written in the center of two concentric reflective triangles. In actuality, this was one of several navigational guideposts for boats making their way up and down Florida's west coast. The twenty marker was located just out from Keaton Beach, and going south from there came the eighteen marker out from Steinhatchee, then the sixteen marker out from the Pepperfish Keys, and so on down the coast. On a nautical chart, the "Twenty" signpost was denoted by an exclamation point with Fl R 6s 19ft 5M "20" which meant this was a lighted beacon flashing its red light at six-second intervals. The light was at an elevation of nineteen feet and had a range of five nautical miles at night.

As Karl pulled his vessel close to the beacon, Wade noticed that the tall center steel post holding the sign was supported lower down by a tepee-looking set of steel girders. Affixed to the top of the structure was a red flashing light powered by a solar panel and an accompanying power pack.

Karl wanted Wade to tie off to one of the leaning metal supports at the base of the framework, but the boat was moving up and down too much for Wade to get a rope around it. As Karl backed the craft away, Wade noticed like the bird rack the day before, the structure was covered with white stains from bird droppings except where the wave action had washed it clean.

Disgusted by Wade's failure to secure the boat to the girders, Karl was beside himself. "I give you one little job, Wade, and you fail miserably getting it done. I guess only you two can fish for bait now. I'll have to try driving right next to this thing, which, by the way, is no small chore." Karl's sullen face reflected his obvious frustration.

Glancing back at Karl with a little smile, Wade shrugged at his older friend's outburst.

Les was checking one of the small spinner outfits Wade had just given him. The rigging hanging down from the rod tip was an odd-looking contraption consisting of a set of small gold hooks with red beads residing below each hook's eye. A small piece of plastic covered the upper portion of each hook's shank. Separated at six-inch intervals, these were anchored by a one-ounce weight. "What do you bait these things with?" Wade asked.

"You've never seen a Sabiki Rig?" Karl asked in disbelief.

"Nope."

"Just drop it over the side. That's all you've got to do," Karl said.

Wade and Les dropped their weighted rigs over the boat's side just as Karl told them to do and almost instantaneously both of their rods bent double.

"Holy cow," Les shouted. "I think I've got one."

"You've got more than one by the way that pole's bent," Karl laughed out loud.

As Les reeled the fish in closer, Karl quickly stepped from behind the boat's wheel and, grabbing the Sabiki Rig leader, pulled the catch onto the deck. There was a wriggling fish on each hook and just as soon as they landed, flopping across the floor, Wade pulled his fully loaded rig into the boat too. Unbelievably each of these un-baited hooks had caught a six to eight-inch minnow.

"All righttttt!" Wade sang out as he high-fived both Les and Karl. "That's what I'm talking about," he said energetically as the fish wriggled and flapped across the deck.

Beaming, Karl said with excitement, "Bring 'em on back here to the live well, boys. We do this a few more times and we'll have enough for today and tomorrow."

Wade studied the fish as he unhooked them then put them in the well's aerated water.

"What kind of fish are these, Karl? They look like baby amberjacks."

"They're Blue Runners, Wade. Great bait. I'm going to get us back up to that spot where y'all caught them and we'll hit 'em again."

The craft had drifted away from the marker, so Karl once again revved his motors to bring his vessel back next to the signpost.

"Drop 'em over, boys," he hollered as he held the boat on what he thought was the right spot. But this time nothing struck.

"Reel 'em in halfway. I've found a pod on my depth finder that we're fixing to drift over."

Both did as he said and just as Karl predicted, both poles bent double again.

"Whoo-hoo! We're on 'em again, Karl," Les sang out.

"Me too!" Wade called back ecstatically.

"All right. Get 'em in, boys. Get 'em in," Karl encouraged them. "That makes thirty-two we've gotten here. Let's do it twice more, then we'll go."

"Go hell," Wade exclaimed. "I could do this all day long."

Karl roared with laughter. "You ain't seen nothing yet, Wade. But catching these little bastards is addicting, isn't it?"

"It sure is," Les declared pulling in another rig full of fish.

It took only a few more pulls, and the bait well was more than full of teaming baitfish. All three friends high-fived one another as Karl floated away from the steel girders of the wave-splashed tower.

"Okay, Wade. How about putting those rods back up and Les, would you mind taking that white bucket back in the stern and throwing some water across the deck to wash off where those fish landed?"

As Wade and Les did this, Karl started pressing buttons on his LORAN.

"All right, fellows. From where we are now, it's going to take somewhere around an hour and fifteen minutes to get us there. That's if these seas don't build on us too much this morning."

Scanning the horizon at a heading of 225 degrees, he said, "We're facing a south-southwest wind out there today which is not good, but at least the tide's going out and we're going into it at an angle. All in all, it shouldn't be too rough of a ride." Stepping across to the side of the boat facing north, he called to his companions. "If you guys got to take a leak, now's the time to do it. Once we get underway, it's going to be balls to the wall, boys. I'll try to get us there as fast as I can."

As Les peed over the starboard gunwale facing northward, he asked Karl if he was heading to the spot Buck had suggested.

"Absolutely," Karl responded. "I wasn't kidding last night when I told y'all he was probably the best offshore fisherman around here. He's never led me wrong on where to find fish. As far as all that mumbo jumbo about planes dropping cocaine way up here, well, that's about as much bullshit as I've ever heard coming from him. Frankly, I was shocked when he came up with all that nonsense."

"What makes you think that he doesn't know something?" Les asked curiously.

"Well, and this is just my opinion, but I think that he's still pretty depressed over losing his wife. Studying up on what some drug cartel 'might' be doing probably keeps his mind distracted from thinking about her would be my guess. I mean, who in their right mind would keep up with news coming out of Bogota, Columbia? That's when it started getting a little too deep for me." Karl stopped talking for a moment as he punched a few more waypoints into his machine. "Okay, boys! Everything tied down?"

Les scanned the stern. "Looks like we've battened down the hatches, Cap'n."

Karl smiled as he saw Les and Wade on each side of him holding onto the T-top's aluminum posts. "Then let's do it!" he exclaimed as he showered down on his boat's powerful engines. Turning his hat backward so it wouldn't blow off his head, he poked each of his pals in the shoulder showing them to do the same. Without shouting into each other's ears, they couldn't hear much of anything over the roaring set of Yamahas rocketing them forward.

The waves had grown from one to approximately two-and-a-half feet in height since earlier in the morning. Across the Florida peninsula on the deeper Atlantic side, such seas would appear as long swells where they would go almost unnoticed by east coast boaters. In the shallow waters of the Gulf, however, these waves would pop up in short chopping intervals through which a vessel had to batter its way. If their height got to three or more feet, this trip could instantly become one hell of a ride even for a fantastic craft such as Karl's Contender.

In a hectic environment, it's strange how sometimes a person can see the relative calmness of the world surrounding him. For several long minutes and much to their surprise, a small school of bottlenose dolphins came up and took turns surfing the boat's bow. They swam so close to the craft at times that Wade and Les felt they could reach over and touch them. Just as serendipitously as the school had appeared, they disappeared into the aquamarine haze below.

The sun continued to burn off the once thick fog. Somewhere during their trip almost unnoticed, the air was rid of it. There was no land, no markers, and no boats in sight, but life did abound. It was the migratory season, and rafts of ducks floating and others flying could be seen in almost every direction.

Karl's boat's deep vee hull had to take on the much taller oncoming waves in more of a pounding fashion as he swung his vessel more to the south. "Sorry about this, boys," he called out apologizing for the bumpier ride. "I've got to get us back on course. We veered off of it a little as I tried to make the ride out here a little more bearable." In reality, Karl had quartered the crests to go faster, but now he had to take the water head on to get back in line with Buck's rocks. Unlike the weather forecast predicted, the swells had grown more than three feet, and with their short beating intervals, Karl had to slow down as the bow would top a ridge then slam nose first down into the next incoming chop.

Wave after wave, they punched their way through the close incoming surge of the Gulf of Mexico. Each crash downward made by their boat into the next trough would send water spraying out from under its bow like spumes of crushed glass as far away as ten to twenty feet from the vessel's sides. There was no rhythm to this up and down motion, and certainly no predictability. One moment, Les and Wade would feel the deck falling out from under them. The next they would find their feet landing hard on it once more. It paid to keep your knees bent and to ride it like a surfboard. Wade figured this out but only after being pummeled for the majority of the trip. Suddenly, Karl slowed the craft almost to a stop.

"Is this the spot?" Les asked as the boat rode up and down each short swell that passed under them.

Karl, who was studying the display on his depth finder, caught Les' eye then pointed back to the monitor. "That's a sand bottom beneath us right here. See how that line is so straight there on the bottom?"

"Yeah," Les acknowledged as he studied the display. "Buck didn't give you the exact coordinates?"

"Not exactly. He just gave me a spot on the map, but we're in the general area all right. What I'll have to do now is start going in circles right here until we run across those rocks he told us about or at least until we find some good hard bottom." Karl stepped to the back of the boat and retrieved a beach ball-sized float wrapped with nylon line and anchored by a small weight. Dropping it over the side of the boat, he slowly began driving in giant concentric circles around the spot Buck had shown him at the restaurant.

"Here're some small rock formations right here, Les," he called out for his smaller friend to come see. "That looks like some pretty good hard bottom right in here. See how the color is different?" he said pointing to the device's screen.

Reaching up to the keypad on his LORAN device, Karl punched the site in as a waypoint. The machine beeped indicating that it had accepted the coordinates. Continuing, Karl kept finding larger rocks that he would input into his device followed by vast areas of lifeless sand bottom.

Karl circumnavigated the area four or five times and was within one-hundred yards of the float when suddenly he shouted, "Here they are, boys! Look at the size of those things!"

All three men gathered under the T-top to view the screen. What they saw was an awesome sight for this area of the Gulf.

Rocks in this number jutting up eight to ten feet off the bottom in some places were a remarkable find, Karl thought. He promptly punched the site into his LORAN. Continuing onward, he wanted to see what else he could find. "Whoa, whoa, whoa! Look at this, fellows!" he yelled throwing his boat into neutral. The display on his depth finder showed green elevations coming up from the bottom that were covered in blotches of hot red. "Those are fish right there," he said excitedly. "Wade, go open that door under the bow and pull out that big float and anchor weight. Quick now."

Going up front as Karl tried steadying the boat above this spot, Wade reached into the storage compartment and retrieved the marker. A white plastic spool-like float was attached to a twenty-pound weight by a thin rope.

"All right. When I tell you—drop it over the side," Karl called to Wade as his smaller friend climbed onto the front of the boat's bow. With bent knees, Wade rode the bow up and down as each wave passed under the vessel.

Driving the craft in various directions to get back on the spot, Karl finally shouted, "Now! Drop it!"

Hurriedly, Wade flung the float with its weight overboard as all three friends watched. With the spool rapidly spinning, the weight went straight to the bottom.

"Does it have enough rope to make it all the way down?" Les asked concerned.

"Yeah," Karl responded. "We're in sixty feet of water here and there's around seventy-five feet of line on that spool."

Karl paused staring at the float as its line became taut. He looked at Les, "What we're going to do now is anchor upwind from our marker and drift back over the rocks. The position of the float in the waves will give us the direction we should anchor in." Once again, Karl called back to his dark-haired friend, "Okay, Wade. While you're up front there, loosen the anchor rope and be ready to drop it when I tell you to."

Wade, who was still standing on the bow, reached down and unlaced the rope from a large cleat on the starboard gunwale. Holding the rope in his hand, he yanked it up and down several times to free the anchor from the jammed position it had obtained on the ride out. With the constant beating from their trip, the upper portion of the anchor had become wedged between the anchor rope's roller and Karl's transplanted teakwood pulpit that projected from the front end of the bow. Jerking the rope several times, Wade, at last, had it loose and ready to fall.

"Okay, Wade. I'm going to carry us thirty or so yards in front of where we want to be. When I tell you to drop the anchor, we'll let enough rope out for it to catch. It's a sand anchor, so we're going to have to let a good bit of line out. Okay?"

"Got you," Wade called back. "Just tell me when to drop it and when to tie it off."

Karl gave Wade the thumbs up sign from the console as he drove the boat in a southward direction. Driving slowly and keeping an eye back on his float, he painstakingly obtained the alignment he wanted. "Toss it over, Wade," he yelled.

Pitching the anchor from above the bow with a splash, Wade let the rope slip through his hands simultaneously. In doing this, he could guide the line atop the pulpit's rubber roller as was intended and not allow it to slip off the pulley to one side and become jammed. Without a hitch, the anchor secured itself to the sandy bottom as Karl let the vessel drift on back above the rocks where he'd found the fish.

"All right. Tie it off right there, Wade," he called back.

Yanking the rope quickly back down to the side gunwales cleat for leverage, Wade momentarily held the craft in check. Crisscrossing the line back and forth across the cleat in a series of figure eights, he lastly pulled a tightening loop around one side of the cleat securing the anchor's line once and for all.

Les, watching his athletic friend at work, called over to Wade impressed, "Nice job there, ol' buddy. Hadn't seen anyone handle a rope that well since I was down on the Amazon." Peering at Wade curiously, he asked loudly, "I didn't think you'd been out on the water that much. Where'd you learn how to do that?"

Wade smiled at Les and Karl as he made his way to where they both stood at the boat's console. "You probably won't believe this, but Karl's dad taught me that trick way back in the day when we fished the flats as boys."

Karl chuckled. "That was a long time ago, Wade."

"Yeah, it was, wasn't it? I guess you remember things better when you're young and having fun, I suppose."

Karl perked up. "Well, get ready to have some real fun now, ol' pal." Reaching up to the back of the boat's T-top roof, Karl pulled down three rods from his rack of stainless-steel rod holders. The setup was the same for each: a sixty-pound rated rod with a four-ought Penn Reel carrying forty-pound monofilament line. Each one of these poles had the end strand of line tied off on the last eyelet of the rod located closest to the reel. Carrying the rods back to the console, Karl clipped each line free from its eyelet with a pair of fingernail clippers. From a sliding drawer, he extracted three clear, quart-sized, plastic bags each containing a single pre-made grouper rig. Each rig consisted of a five-foot one-hundred-pound monofilament leader with an eight-ought circle hook tied on one end and a four-hundred-pound barrel swivel tied to the other. Another swivel and short leader tied to this contained a sliding eight-ounce egg sinker. Karl tied the reel's line to the leader's barrel swivel with a Trilene knot. Checking the drag on the first completed rig to make sure it was good and tight, Karl handed the pole to Les.

"Okay, Les, this is how you—"

Les interrupted him. "No need to tell me about fishing. I've used rigs just like this one more times than you can count down on the Amazon and over on the Pacific coast."

Karl queried, "You used circle hooks?"

"Yep. They may be new to this area, but they use them down there all the time.

Wade spoke up confused, "What's the deal with circle hooks?"

Les answered, "You don't have to set the hook. When the fish hits it, just start reeling. Besides that, they don't swallow the hook as much. Usually, it catches them in the side of the mouth."

Karl remarked in Les' direction as he rigged the other two poles. "Okay, Mr. Know-it-all. Get a bait on and get to fishing."

Les took the small floating dip net located inside the live well and proceeded to snag a pinfish. Hooking it just below its back dorsal fin, he dangled it over the boat's side by his rod's tip and flipped the spool's release sending the weighted rig downward. When he felt the line go slack as the weight hit the Gulf's bottom, he wound his line back up until it was taut.

It didn't take long for both Wade and Karl to have their rigs tied on and their baits in the water next to his, one on each side of Les.

Karl, seeing his screen light up earlier with fish, expected a bite almost immediately. As they waited for several long minutes, a period he thought that was taking too long, he glanced back at his depth finder to see if they had drifted off the rocks.

Just as he did this, Wade called out, "I've got one!

His stiff, heavy rod bent hard toward the water as he struggled to reel in the fish.

Karl laughed, "Come on! Pull him in, Muscles!"

Wade strained, pulling with all his might as Karl had tightened down their drags to keep the fish from taking almost any line out at all. With grouper, he wanted to keep them from getting back down into the rocks where they'd puff out their gills and be nearly impossible to move. Wade wrestled turning the handle of his reel as the fish pulled him to the rear of the boat.

"Haul him in, Wade. Quit pussy-footing around with him," Karl said laughing.

As Wade struggled, the fish slowly started taking more line and was on the other side of the boat and going pretty much anywhere it wanted. Meanwhile, Les, who was shaking his head and laughing with Karl, had a bite. Les reeled hard as his rod bent, but nothing like what Wade was experiencing.

Struggling as he cranked the gear's handle, Les eventually pulled in an eight-pound red grouper which Karl, reaching over and grabbing Les' long monofilament leader, helped him land. As Wade continued his fight from the vessel's stern, Karl unhooked Les' fish and threw it back in.

"Not big enough, Les. Get another bait on."

Turning to Wade, Karl called over to him, "Hadn't got that little fish in yet, Mr. Biceps."

Wade responded weakly, "It's big. I can see it down there swimming."

Karl and Les looked at each other laughing under their breaths as Wade kept tugging. Finally, he had the monster in sight.

"Damn, it's a shark! Son of a gun."

Karl and Les cackled at the effort that Wade had put into pulling the fish to the surface. From the way the fish had behaved and from their own experience at catching them, they both knew what Wade had on his line almost from the get-go.

Handing Les his pole, Karl went over to help Wade retrieve his line. Putting on a glove and carrying a pair of pliers in his other hand, he reached down and grabbed the long monofilament leader, which he couldn't believe hadn't been cut by the shark's teeth. As he did this, the seven-foot hammerhead saw him and immediately dove taking more line once again.

"Why don't we just cut the line off here, Karl?" Wade asked exhausted.

"Because I want to save as much of that leader as I can. Bring him on back up."

Wade continued his fight as Les called to Karl that he had a fish on each pole. Dashing across the deck, Karl grabbed his rod, and each man pulled in two nice gags.

Wade, who was still struggling to get the shark back up, heard his pals laughing and high-fiving each other as they each got a fish on board.

Karl held up two fish and yelled to Wade, "Hey. Take a look at these bad boys."

Seeing the two keepers, one weighing maybe ten pounds and the other closer to twelve, Wade beamed at his friends, "Nice fish there, fellows."

"Damn better believe it," Karl called back. Happily he started to sing, "You're going on ice, boys. You're going on ice. Oh, get ready cause you're going on ice." Lifting the cooler lid with his sandaled foot, he tossed the two fish down onto the broken-up block ice that Les and Wade had brought down with them. As he slowly let the door back down, he talked to the fish as if they were little kids. "Bye-bye now. We'll be bringing you some more of your buddies over for a little visit in just a minute." Wiping his hands with a towel he kept in a small bucket by his console, he hollered back to Wade, "You about got that shark in yet?"

Wade stood up and walked his pole back where Karl was standing. "Yeah, I got his head out of the water just enough to cut the line off above the hook. Here's your pliers . . . where do you keep your extra hooks?"

Karl was a little shocked that worrywart Wade had enough guts to get that close to the chomping teeth of an angry shark. He was even more surprised that Wade didn't act like it was that big of a deal after he'd done it. "That was a pretty nice size shark, Wade. It didn't lunge at you or anything?"

"Hell, I think he was as tired as I was, but he did try to snap at me as I tried to flick the hook out of his mouth with my knife."

Karl, still amazed at Wade's nonchalant attitude, retrieved a hook from one of his console drawers.

"You want me to tie it on for you?"

"Nah, go on back and catch another big one. I'll tie it on myself."

As Wade got his line back in the water alongside Les', the fish below were growing more and more attracted to the scent of blood and bait now surrounding them down on the bottom.

"Got one!" Les sang out as he started reeling hard. Before he could get his fish halfway up, Wade also started cranking aggressively.

"Nice one here too!"

As they strained to pull their fish in, Karl waited transfixed on feeling a bite, but nothing hit.

Reaching down for his leader line, Les pulled in a ten-pound red snapper. Wade a twenty-three-inch red grouper. Swiftly they put them on ice and had another bait on that they quickly had heading back to the bottom.

Again they both hooked up. This time Wade reeled in a thirty-pound amberjack that he had to fight almost as hard as he fought the shark and which Karl had to come over and gaff. Les, in the meantime, brought in another large red snapper.

The fish coming aboard excited Karl, but he was getting pissed off that he wasn't the one catching them. With Wade and Les hauling in another set of keepers, Karl pulled in a small pink-mouth grunt, one he was going to throw back until Les asked him if he could use it as bait. "This is bullshit," Karl growled. "Hell, I'm fishing the same spot y'all are—with the same bait—and I'm not catching anything."

Les winked at Wade then, looking back at Karl, said, "You fish here in my place, and I'll go fish this grunt you gave me off the other side of the boat."

Karl hurriedly reeled in his line and put on a fresh live bait taking over Les' spot. A smile did not part his lips as he did this. At this new position, he instantly hung a small snapper that was a non-keeper. As he tossed it back into the water, he watched Wade reel in another nice red grouper which made him even madder. Dropping a fresh bait back to the bottom, Karl heard Les let out a holler, "Whoa!!!"

All of a sudden, line started singing from Les' reel as he rapidly loosened the drag to accommodate the fish.

"Whatcha got over there?" Karl called over to him.

"It's either a King or a Wahoo, and it's big! I hope it doesn't cut this mono we're using for a leader."

Karl was thinking just the opposite. Still angry, he was hoping that the fish would cut Les' line. Indifferent to what Les was doing, he continued to bottom fish. Wade, in the meantime, reeled his bait in and retrieved the gaff from where Karl had put it in an inserted rod holder in the gunwale. As he made his way back to where Les was fighting the fish, the King Mackerel leaped out of the water about thirty yards off the portside of the boat. Les bowed his rod to the fish as it did this while at the same time trying hard to keep his line reeled up tight.

"Hot damn that's a huge fish!" Wade enthusiastically proclaimed. "How much do you think he weighs, Les?"

"I'd say fifty pounds easy, Wade." His voice was straining as were his muscles.

The fish had made its way from the portside of the vessel to the stern. Les, fighting hard, would reel it in about twenty yards or so then the fish would bolt taking another twenty to twenty-five yards of line back in a matter of seconds with the drag screaming. After two more good runs, the fish was done and Les had it coming up to the boat worn out and swimming on its side.

As Wade was telling Les to get the fish in a little closer so he could gaff it, Karl, having reeled in his bait, came charging toward the pair. He grabbed the gaff from Wade's hands and butted him out of the way. "You don't know what the hell you're doing with this thing, Wade. Let me show you how it's done." Leering at Les, Karl commanded him to pull the fish in closer. As the fish lay on its side exhausted and prime for an easy gaff, Karl purposefully missed it spooking the fish into another short run.

Les glanced up at Karl as he brought the fish back toward the boat. "You sure you don't want Wade to do it, Karl? That was a pretty poor attempt."

Karl glared at Les. "Bring that bastard back over here. I'm trying to gaff him in the mouth so we won't mess up the meat." Once more, Les swam the fish on its side next to the boat for another easy gaffing. Again, Karl tried hooking the gaff in the fish's mouth. This time, however, he caught only the line yanking the hook free from the fish's bottom lip. Slowly, the fish swam away into the aquamarine sea. Karl stared coolly at Les and without a bit of guilt or remorse said, "Sorry. Shit happens." Karl went back to his rod and reel, placed a fresh bait on it, and started fishing again at the spot Les had been earlier.

Les checked his line for cuts and scrapes. Glancing at Wade, he noticed his friend was not smiling. "Hey. At least I got my leader back in one piece, and my hooks not bent," Les grinned.

Fuming, Wade couldn't stand what Karl had just done. "He did that on purpose, you know."

Les, who was now sitting on the portside gunwale, smiled warmly back at Wade. "'Vengeance is Mine, says the Lord.' Always remember that, Wade."

Wade shook his head in disgust at Karl's wickedness as he looked back into Les' eyes.

Trying to diffuse his friend's anger, Les distracted him. "How about let's getting something to eat, pal. I'm feeling the need to get a little sugar back in my bloodstream. How about you?"

Wade, still mad, nodded in agreement then headed for the ice chest.

Gazing at Karl as Wade did this, then back to the sea surrounding them, Les loudly remarked, "One exciting thing on a trip like this is ya' never know out here what you might bring aboard, and well, what you might lose. You know what I mean?"

Neither man seemed to pay attention to what Les was saying as Wade called back over his shoulder, "What would you like to eat, Les?"

The former missionary paused momentarily to observe his friend. "Why don't you go ask Karl what he'd like to eat?"

Hearing him say this, Wade eyed Les exasperated.

"Go ahead," Les nodded in Karl's direction.

Reluctantly, Wade walked a few steps toward Karl. Coldly he asked, "Hey. You want something to eat?"

"Yeah," Karl said giving Wade a surly expression. "I'll take one of those turkey sandwiches and a Dr. Pepper."

Turning around, Wade pursed his lips then obstinately dug through the crushed ice of the cooler until he found the two items Karl had requested. Catching Karl's eye, Wade tossed the sandwich and drink across the deck to him.

Snagging them, Karl snorted angrily, "Thanks for shaking up my drink, you little shit."

"You're quite welcome, Karl. I did it just for you."

Karl eyed Wade unfazed by his comments. He popped open the cold drink which did not spew. Unwrapping his pre-made sandwich, he began eating it as he sat on the starboard gunwale in the shadow of his T-top.

Turning to his smaller buddy, Wade asked kindly, "What would you like, Les?"

"I'll take a coke and any kind of sandwich that's in there, please."

Wade dug through the ice quickly and retrieved a sandwich and beverage for his pal. After serving Les, he went back to the cooler to get himself something to eat and drink.

Les rose and went over to sit in the shade of the console on the captain's bench across from Karl. From this perch, he opened his drink and began to eat his sandwich.

"So, preacher man!" Karl sang out as he watched Les sit near him. "Have you been saving any souls lately?"

Les smiled back at his older friend who he knew was being cynical. "Saving one's soul is not up to me, Karl ol' pal. That's something between God and the individual. In that respect, I'm just a facilitator."

"A facilitator!" Karl laughed with a sneer. "I've heard saving souls put a lot of different ways, Les, but I've never heard it put quite like that. But I'm sure no matter what you call it, you still have all those weak and sinful brothers and sisters coming down the aisle at the end of every Sunday's service to have all their sins cleansed and washed away, right?" Laughing, Karl began mocking the voice of a Bible-thumping evangelist. "Cle-a-nsed and forgiven! Forgiven by the be-lud of Jeee-sssus!" Excited, he exaggerated the Lord's name for effect.

Les cackled at Karl's theatrics and said, "With a voice like that, and with the way you can ring out the name Jeee-ssssus, you should have been one of those televangelists. You'd probably have made a good one."

Karl glared at Les disgusted. "Please. Don't tell me that you believe any of that bullshit those guys dish out from T.V. land. They're in it for the money. Both you and I know they are."

Les never lost eye contact with his friend's bright blue eyes as Karl griped about what he saw as religious hypocrisy. Les said, "You know, Karl, Christ said, 'every good tree bringeth forth good fruit; but a corrupt tree brings forth evil fruit. By their fruits ye shall know them.' Am I not right?"

"They're all the same, Les. In it for the money, the power, the recognition. Sometimes they're even in it just for the sex."

"So, do you believe this is just a problem with television evangelist or is this your opinion of small church pastors, missionaries, and all the rest?"

Karl answered dispassionately, "Six of one, half dozen of the other. They're all the same."

"Do you not go to church at all anymore, Karl?"

"I haven't been in a church since high school, Les. I see no need for religion. It disgusts me. Look what religion's done for the world throughout its history. Ahhh . . . let's see. Well, it gave us the Crusades where millions of innocent people were killed—got to be proud of that one. The Spanish Inquisition. Either you believe what I tell you to believe or we'll kill you—that's a pretty fair deal I'd say. And oh yeah, let's not forget the Roman Catholic Church being run by men with a propensity for pedophilia. All those poor young boys who had their lives ruined—Need I say more, Les?"

Les listened patiently to all that Karl was telling him. Replying pensively, he said, "I tend to agree with you about the part concerning religion, Karl. I'm not too much a believer in all that either. Faith and following that path is what it's all about for me."

"Faith!" Karl exclaimed laughing. "Hmmmph—Christian Faith. Your religion. I'm sorry to be the one bringing this bad news to you, Les—but Christianity is the religion for losers."

Calmly Les reacted, "What do you mean by that, Karl?"

Half smiling, Karl said, "It's a theology of hope for those who are unsuccessful. An excuse for those who are failures in life. They believe that this superhuman being is going to come down out of the clouds and solve all of their problems. Save them from their ignorance and lack of motivation." Grimacing, Karl continued. "I see it in the hospital all the time. The family members gathering around the patient when nothing else can be done for the poor sap. They're praying to this make-believe persona you call Christ to come down and give them a miracle. To save their loved one." Karl started shaking his head. "But you know what, Les? He never shows up—And if the patient happens to live, it's because of what we've done for him, and if he dies, the family members cry and tell me pitifully that their loved one is in a much better place now. Up in this make-believe heaven where there is no suffering. It's a sickening thing to watch. Because, Les—it's all a lie."

As Les listened to Karl's remarks, he was not shocked by what he heard.

"So, you don't believe in God then? Is that right, Karl?"

"Not really. I don't believe in a God sitting up there on a cloud in the sky watching my every move, ready to strike me down because someone else believes that I'm doing something wrong in their eyes. And I don't believe that when I die, I'll go to some grand place, heaven, where there is no pain and only peace. When I'm gone, I'm just going to be gone, and that's going to be the end of it." Karl took a sip from his drink then looked at Les intrigued by how his missionary friend was going to respond to what he'd just said.

Les could sense that Karl was eager to hear his reply, but he lingered, which he could tell agitated his older friend. Finally, he spoke up as he now knew he had Karl's full attention. "You seem to be preoccupied with death, which you seem to be telling me is where you'll find your ending."

Karl cut his eyes at Les as he heard him say this.

Continuing, Les said, "But I don't know how you can contemplate this absolute ending you speak of without finding your beginning. You'd probably tell me that you came from your mother's womb—would that not be right, Karl?"

"I don't know about you, Les, but that's where I came from."

Les smiled back. "And your ancestors would go all the way back through evolution to the Big Bang, I suppose?"

"Yep. That would be correct too." Saying this indifferently, Karl wondered how Les was going to get past this point.

"So, tell me, Karl. Can you reason what was—before the Big Bang?"

Retorting cynically, Karl frowned back. "Does it really matter, Les?"

"Probably not. Thinking and logical reasoning won't get you there will it?" Les paused. "Personally, I believe in an infinite and timeless form of love I call God. I think we and It have always been together. I don't think a person finds God only at death but rather he finds God always at the center of his or her life. In the right here and now of the present. You know," Les continued, "life is full of fun and joy like we're having on this fishing trip. But it's also filled with pain and suffering and struggle like we all also have witnessed and experienced in our own lives. Often times we humans don't want to share in these things with God. We don't include Him in our joy, and we don't share in His pain when we see others suffer. Many have turned their backs on Him altogether as they seek to chase after their own desires." Les paused, then said, "You know, Karl, there's only one thing that really matters here . . ."

Intrigued by what Les had just told him, Karl cut his eyes back at his younger friend waiting to hear what this might be. But Les, still looking into Karl's eyes, said nothing. Gathering up his napkin and empty coke can, he stood up and walked to the back of the boat.

CHAPTER 28

Hooks and Gaffs

After they finished eating, the friends fished for a couple more hours with Les and Wade catching their limit of both grouper and snapper while poor Karl caught nothing else of any real consequence. Not happy but unbroken, Karl kept searching the bottom with his depth finder for better structure to fish. They were unanchored and slowly running back and forth across Buck's area once more.

"Looks like some dark clouds coming toward us from the west, Karl," Les called out from the stern. "You think we ought to start heading on back in?"

Glancing away from the screen, the doctor shot back. "The forecast called for some isolated showers out here today. Nothing major. That squall should head north of us anyway. Nothing to worry about, Les." Once again, he refocused his attention on the monitor.

As Wade finished storing the boat anchor rope in the bow, he went back to the stern where he found Les and asked, "Y'all see those clouds over there, don't you?"

"Yeah. Karl thinks they're going to swing north of us."

Wade frowned and shook his head in disbelief at his pal's gullibility. Walking to the front of the console, he opened the door to the cuddy and pulled out his Gore-Tex rain suit. Bringing it back to where Les was, he threw these clothes under the backside of Karl's captain's seat. Karl had covered its aluminum legs three-quarters of the way around with a white canvas apron leaving the back portion facing the stern open for storage purposes.

"Did you bring any rain gear out here with you, Les?"

"No. Karl told me earlier he had some ponchos in here somewhere and that if we got caught in a rainstorm, he'd get me one."

"Expect to get caught," Wade said dryly. Wade prepared for the approaching severe weather by securing anything of value he thought could be blown overboard. Karl leisurely drove a serpentine course through the water. He had no intention of leaving the area. Come hell or high water, he was going to find some way to catch the biggest or most fish of the day.

As Les and Wade continued to watch, the black clouds rapidly approached them, not only from the west but the south as well. They could hardly believe Karl's nonchalant attitude.

Oblivious to all else as he hyper-focused on his machine's screen, Karl stared at every gradation his depth finder was showing him. For ten minutes he did this until Wade finally notified him that he could see the dark streaky downpour of rain coming from the clouds just behind them. Karl looked away from his monitor momentarily as a white bolt of lightning streaked down through the ominous thunderhead. "Well, boys," Karl exclaimed as he heard the bolt's accompanying boom. "I think y'all were right after all. That thing's definitely going to hit us." Reaching into one of his console's compartments, he gave Les a cheap, made-in-

China, plastic disposable poncho. Shifting his boat into neutral, he went around to the cuddy and pulled out an expensive Cabella's all-weather hooded rain suit. Climbing into it and a pair of white rubber boots, he then walked back around to the stainless-steel steering wheel and shifted his craft back into drive.

"Ya' think we can outrun that thing?" Les asked as he peered at the oncoming weather.

Monitoring the thunderstorm himself and seeing the racing clouds bearing down on them, Karl exclaimed, "Don't think so, Les. It's moving in here mighty fast. A lot faster than I think this boat can go."

A cold wind was beginning to build as the downdrafts from the approaching rainstorm were forcing air out into its lead. Karl felt it blow and started having second thoughts about sitting there and taking a direct hit. Telling his friends to hang on, he got his boat moving east and slammed the throttle down full bore. With a roar from the stern, the powerful motors propelled the V-hull forward. Lunging and plunging from one tall crest to the next, the *Doc's Out!* cut through the waves of the Gulf of Mexico.

Pushing his craft as fast as conditions would allow, he seemed to temporarily keep the squall at bay as he monitored its approach. After several minutes of running and without any warning, he suddenly threw the boat into neutral tossing his two friends off balance. "All right, boys! Here it comes!" he called out feeling the blasting wind and seeing the driving rain plastering the water just behind them.

Wade, standing behind the bench from where Karl was seated, reached down under it and picked up the coat and jacket to his rain suit. An almost gale force wind was howling through the raised console of the T-top blowing overboard anything light and not secured. Empty aluminum drink cans, plastic food wrappers, cloth hand rags, any and all such items were being whirled skyward as the intensity of the gusts seemed to be increasing. Wade hollered to Les who was standing next to him, "Here, put these on quick."

"No. This poncho here will be fine," Les shouted back.

"Dammit, Les! I insist. There's no time to argue about it." Shoving his hooded rain suit into Les' hands, Wade ripped through the flimsy plastic baggie containing Les' poncho. As he unfurled and opened it out into the raging currents of air, the orange plastic rain sheet began to jerk and flail as he struggled to get it over his head, shoulders, and finally over the rest of his body. In this violent setting, the hooded garment, reeking its plastic stench, wasn't much protection, but it was better than nothing.

Instantly, just to the starboard side of their vessel, all three men saw the blinding white camera-like flash of a bolt of lightning as it simultaneously ripped out a supersonic ear-piercing B-O-O-M!! Then the rain began pouring down on them in sheets. "Holy crap!" Wade shouted above the roaring wind. "That son of a bitch was right on top of us!"

"Hey, Wade," Karl called out trying to get his attention over the raging deluge. "We've got to get those two antennas down from up top. I've already got the last rod down from our rod holders up there."

Stunned by what he was about to have to do, Wade knew there was no need to protest. He knew as well as Karl that those poles swaying high above the boat were acting like lightning rods begging to be hit.

Taking a deep breath, Wade and Karl jumped out from under the protection of the T-top into the driving rainstorm. Each climbed onto the gunwale of their side of the craft and tried reaching over the canvas to where the fiberglass antennas were securely locked into their mounts.

Unlike Karl, who was much taller, Wade was having difficulty as he had to stand partially elevated on the side bracing of the console where he was still only barely able to reach the VHF radio antenna. Struggling to pull the clamped latch located at the base of his antenna down which would allow its pole to release, he noticed that Karl had already gotten the LORAN's antenna down and had stepped safely back under the Contender's roof.

As if to spite Wade, another blinding flash of lightning accompanied by a terrifying "BOOM" hit nearby. This one was closer to the boat than the last. Paralyzed with fear and with his heart pounding out of his chest, Wade cursed, jerked, and yanked at the stubborn unmoving latch. Enraged, he threw himself up and over onto the top of the canvassed roof so he could get both of his hands on the obstinate mount's handle. With the leverage he gained by using both hands, he loosened the clamp and, in an instant, had the pole down and secured. As he swung himself back down to the deck from above and stepped back under the relative safeness of the console, Karl gave his younger friend a stern look and shouted, "It's about damn time, son!"

"You can kiss my ass, Karl!" Wade yelled as another bolt of lightning blasted right next to them.

Laughing into Wade's sullen face, Karl bellowed, "Hee! Hi! All right, boys. We're heading 'er on back in! Batten down the hatches!" With no time for rebuttal, Karl pushed the throttle all the way forward once again then swiftly eased back on the gas. Even with his free spirit mentality, Karl well knew what was confronting him on this dangerous trip back to Keaton. The tide had turned and was heading back inland, and with the wind coming hard out of the southwest, Karl found himself in a difficult spot. Large waves were heading inshore from behind him. Wind gusts he figured were hitting close to twenty to twenty-five knots. Whitecaps could be seen in almost every direction. Knowing the wind usually outpaced accompanying waves, Karl realized it was only a matter of time before the heavier seas would overtake him. This was especially true considering the amount of open sea or fetch residing behind the storm.

Aware of this circumstance, Karl knew that even with the surging heights he was encountering now, he couldn't go straight back in the northeast direction as he desired. Steering an outboard over a following sea was difficult. A boat travelling too fast would often veer sharply off to one side as it surfed down into the deep trough of a wave and would have to be immediately pulled back on course. Broaching or capsizing was a real possibility if this occurred. Choosing to angle the waves slightly on the trip back in would enhance his craft's speed somewhat but with the chance of overturning. Deciding on speed over caution, Karl slashed through the precarious whitecaps of the late afternoon. At last, he arrived back at Keaton's channel where he soon rounded the jetties to the canal. Not only had the ride at times been jolting, but on two occasions the *Doc's Out!* almost broached waves where Les nearly fell overboard.

It was 5:00 p.m., and all three men were exhausted. Wade flipped off his orange plastic poncho as they made it to the landing. He jumped over to the dock and tied off the boat. Karl and Les came out of their rain suits likewise.

As Wade finished securing the vessel to the landing, he noticed a lone older man carrying lightweight fishing tackle over toward a much smaller bass boat moored nearby. Stopping along the way, he greeted Karl's crew curiously.

"You guys have any luck today?"

"We caught a few," Les responded quietly and with a smile.

By the time Wade and Les had finished talking to the elderly fellow, Karl had extricated all the electronics from their mounts.

"Okay, boys," he said in a subdued manner, but only due to fatigue. "Let's get all of this equipment back up to the truck then we can tend to the fish."

Making three shuttles, they transferred almost everything including the three rod and reels sets that they didn't use. These rods held very expensive big Gold Penn International reels that Karl used in trolling for big game fish like Wahoo and Tarpon.

As Wade, who was standing in the boat's stern once more, surveyed the area he saw Karl's scuba tanks laying in their racks. "You want these out of here too?"

Karl pondered that thought a second. "Hell, we'll just leave them down here tonight. If they get stolen, they get stolen." Pointing, Karl said, "Up at that shed at the end of the dock over there, there's some buckets that we can put our fish in." Above the dock on the sand parking lot overlooking the canal there was a screened-in fish cleaning shelter. "Les, you mind going and getting them for us while Wade and I throw these things on the dock?"

"Seems like I've done this before." Wade laughed alluding to his experience down at Steinhatchee. Reaching into the floor cooler, he and Karl started tossing their ice-cold fish across the boat's port side onto the wood planked platform.

Responding to Wade's remark, Karl called over to his dark-haired friend, "Those were some big fish those bastards had. The biggest ones we've got here are small in comparison by far."

"Yeah, but ours are legal, and they sure were fun to catch!" Wade grinned.

"I wouldn't know," Karl said soberly. He was still pouting from being out-fished.

Les made his way back down to the dock ramp with four five-gallon buckets just as Karl and Wade were tossing the last big Amberjack onto the pier. By anyone's standards, they had a nice pile of fish. They had a two-person limit on grouper and snapper and had caught two large Amberjacks along with a smaller twenty-pound King. For Les and Wade, it had been a fabulous day. For Karl, it sucked.

As they hauled the fish up the ramp to the shelter, Karl noticed Les wasn't wearing a knife. Handing him his white-handled filet knife, Karl leered at his smaller friend, "You do know how to clean a fish, now don't you, preacher man?"

"Nah, Karl. There aren't any fish down on the Amazon River, you know," Les grinned.

Karl didn't crack a smile as he started walking away from the shed.

"Hey," Wade called out after him. "You're not going to help us clean these things?"

Karl kept walking as he shouted over his shoulder, "You guys had the pleasure of catching them. You can now have the pleasure of cleaning them."

Wade shook his head as he watched Karl walk over and turn on a water spigot attached to a hose that was used for rinsing off boats when they were pulled out from the water. Finding a bar of soap nearby, Karl washed his hands, rinsed them off, and then shook them in the air to dry.

Glancing from Karl back to Les, who was already skinning and filleting a grouper, Wade remarked, "That guy's something else, isn't he? Hasn't changed one damn bit from what I've seen."

Les eyed Wade as he worked. "If he has, Wade, it hasn't been by much." He pushed the filleted backbone, head, and guts down a hole cut into the wooden table, and could hear a splash as it hit the water below.

"Well, one thing's for sure," Wade continued. "He's been riding both our tails pretty hard ever since we got down here."

"Yeah, he's especially been on your case for some reason," Les said looking at his pal.

"Yeah," Wade chuckled. "That's the understatement of the year. You know it's never taken very much to get his little panties in a wad, now has it?"

"That much certainly hasn't changed. But I do think he's become a bit more malicious than he used to be, wouldn't you say?" Les asked.

"Hey. I don't let all of that B.S. of his bother me one bit, Les. He can have the black tail every day we're down here if he wants to. I couldn't care less. I'm far from being that timid little guy that he still thinks I am." Stopping, Wade stared directly into Les' eyes.

"I can tell, Wade," Les said looking back at his friend.

"So, the bottom line for me," Wade remarked, "is that we don't have to continue this little trip if he keeps this crap of his up. I'm like Delta Airlines. I'm ready when you are. We can leave this little shindig any time we want to. Don't think for a skinny minute that we're stuck down here with that butthole by any means."

Pondering as he continued to work, Les remarked, "Well, I'd say excluding all of Karl just being Karl, as for me, that was a pretty rough day out there on the water. I don't know what he has planned for us tomorrow. But I guess—"

Impetuously Wade blurted out, "Hell! I'll tell you what he's got planned for us tomorrow, Les. It ain't rocket science. He wants to head up to that spot on that Latino's map. That's his big plan. And if you ask me, that's just asking for trouble. Those guys we ran into back at Steinhatchee were bad, bad folks I'm telling you, Les. Those guys were some real sure enough thugs."

"Yeah, I gathered that." Les paused from his work to reflect. "Say, how about this for a plan, Wade. I think I'm going to give Louisa a call tonight. If she wants me to come on back, then that'll give us an excuse to leave. If not, well, we'll just play it by ear. That all right with you?"

Wade could tell that Les was a far more forgiving soul and wanted to give his old buddy another chance. As for himself, in his mind, they couldn't get away from the asshole fast enough. Reluctantly, Wade agreed to his best friend's wishes. "Yeah, that suits me, I guess." He paused and turned back to Les, "If that's really what you want to do?"

With the slight nod of his head, but showing no sign of a smile, Les indicated that this would be the plan.

Wade and Les placed the cleaned fish into gallon-sized plastic bags, which they carried back down to the boat. After putting them into the iced cooler, they washed the grime off their hands at the spigot Karl had used earlier.

This done, they walked around to the other side of the Marina to see if Karl's truck was still there. It was nowhere in sight, so they went inside the building, and each bought a sandwich and a cold drink. Sitting at one the few tables, the two men began to eat.

Over the course of the day, Wade had grown worried about Les being out on the water for so long. After cleaning their fish, he began to notice that waxy, pale look overcoming his friend. It was the same look he had seen on their trip from Perry. Watching him as they ate, Wade could see color coming back into Les' face. "You feeling all right?" Wade asked concerned.

"I'm feeling fine. Why do you ask?" Les responded puzzled by his question.

"Well, you were looking a little puny out there from time to time. You seem to kind of get that way if you haven't eaten in a while."

Les chuckled, "You can't hide something like that from a professional observer, I suppose."

"Don't think you'd have to be a professional at anything to notice that, Les."

"That obvious, huh?"

"'Fraid so." Wade nodded back.

"You're right. That was a pretty long afternoon without much to eat. We sure weren't going to stop for a snack on the way back in, now were we?" Les laughed out loud.

Wade grinned back and said, "Hell, I'm just glad we made it back in period. A couple of times I thought we'd bought the farm on that last trip. Thought we were going to just roll right on over and capsize." Both men chuckled and cackled as they recounted their rugged journey back to Keaton with their gung-ho friend at the helm. Regaining their energy from the little snack and feeling much better, they walked over to the store's main counter where Betty had just come in for her late evening shift. She greeted them once again with that same gravelly voice. Her eyes sparkled.

"Hey, fellows. Did y'all make it out today?"

"Yep, we did," Les beamed.

"Catch anything?"

"Yeah," Wade said. "We caught pretty much all of that storm that passed through here."

Betty laughed. "Yeah, that was a pretty bad one. But did y'all catch any fish? That's the real question."

Modestly Les replied, "Yep. We caught our limit of grouper and snapper, and we caught a couple of nice Amberjacks too."

"Sounds to me like y'all had a really good day out there, guys."

"Yeah, I thought we did pretty good too," Les exclaimed cheerily.

"So," Betty said as she cautiously scanned the store and out its windows, "where's your pal, Doc?"

Wade interjected, "That's a good question. He kind of left us hanging—cleaning fish."

Betty laughed out loud. "I'm not surprised by that—and you aren't either are you?"

Wade glanced back as he shook his head in disgust, "No. Not really."

Betty peered out the windows overlooking the lift area. Pointing across the road and marsh, she mumbled, "I bet he's gone over to Bubba's."

"Bubba's?" Wade questioned.

"Yeah. Bubba's place is over there at Ezell Beach." Again pointing through the window, she said, "You see that house out there on that point on stilts. Well, you go back up." She paused and squinted. "You really can't see it from here because of those palm trees. But if you go across that inlet where the water goes back toward that side road, his house is right in there. It's kind of an isolated spot over there where he lives."

Wade gazed at Betty questioningly. "Ezell Beach you say? I don't think I've ever heard of Ezell Beach, Betty."

"Yeah, honey. Nobody who's not from around here—well, most folks have never heard of the place. Just a few houses and vacation homes. On the other hand, everybody's heard of Dekle just above it though."

"So, this Bubba fellow," Wade asked. "What would Karl be doing over there? Just friends?"

"Oh yeah. They're good pals. Real good friends. And uhh—" Betty grimaced shaking her head. "Like you guys would know this. I mean, what am I thinking?" she chastised herself as she faced the two friends who now appeared confused. "Well, fellows, Bubba's having his big annual party over there tonight. He calls it Bubba's Fall Festival. Has it over there at his place every year. Only has one party each year, mind you, and that's probably one party too many if you ask me." Betty shook her head disparagingly.

Hearing her response, Wade became irritated. "So you think he's over there at this party right now?"

"Oh. No," Betty quickly replied noticing Wade's anger. "He's probably just over there helping set things up. That party won't get started good until around nine or ten tonight, fellas." She grinned at Wade and Les, "And some people probably won't leave there until nine or ten tomorrow morning."

Considering her age, Les asked, "Have you been over to Bubba's party before, Betty?"

"One time, Les." She paused then said, "And that was enough for me."

Thinking on the matter momentarily and pulling out a cigarette, she told them, "And being friends of Karl's, I'm sure you'll get a chance to go tonight and see for yourselves. Everyone from around here, even some from as far away as Perry will be there. It's an open invitation according to Bubba. Whoever wants to show up is invited, if you know what I mean." In a more serious tone, she said, "Just be careful if you guys do go, though."

"What do you mean by that?" Wade asked.

"I mean you might end up doing something you might regret. Like I said, a lot of crazy stuff goes on over there at that thing—you'll see."

Wade, wanting her to explain herself, delved further. "You know my friend here's a preacher?"

Betty fired back, "Why do you think I'm telling you all this, Wade?"

Wade was amazed that she remembered his name since they had been introduced only once, but knowing Les' occupation without them telling her—that he found perplexing.

Almost intuitively, she read Wade's thoughts. "Doc mentioned the smaller of you two was a pastor."

"You've got a pretty good memory there, Betty. Being able to keep up with all the people coming and going around this place is pretty impressive," Wade said smiling.

"Thank you. The old gray mare ain't what she used to be, but she doesn't forget too much." Continuing she said, "You guys know that your friend Karl likes to hold court wherever there's a gathering around here. Like I told you fellows before, people down here love, hate, or fear him, but they all defer to him. Men and women alike. He's pretty good at closing a party down too. One of the last ones to leave, if you know what I mean. So you boys don't get shanghaied over there all night if you go, you hear?" Betty kept glancing out the window behind her as she was telling them all of this. Finally, she saw what she was expecting, Karl's shiny, black four-wheel drive pickup truck barreling down the road toward the Marina. "Here he comes, boys. Now I've given you the warning. You can take it or leave it. Just do me one little favor, guys."

"What's that, Betty?" Wade asked intrigued.

"Just don't tell him I've told you about any of this. Okay?"

"Don't worry. We won't say a word," Wade said trying to alleviate her fear.

"Thanks, guys."

"No. Thank you, Betty," Wade reiterated.

Telling her goodbye, the two men headed out the front door of the Marina so she wouldn't have to confront Karl at all. As they walked outside and approached his truck, Karl buzzed down his electric passenger window, "You boys got the fish cleaned and put up, I suppose?"

Les answered, "Yep. Cleaned, bagged, and put on ice, Cap'n."

"All right, get in," Karl commanded. "We'll go to the house and get cleaned up. I'm still dripping wet with sweat. I don't know how you guys fared, but I got a little hot out there today."

As they drove back to the cabin, Wade asked Karl where he'd gone, and just as Betty had said, Karl told them that he had gone over to his friend Bubba's place. But other than telling them that, he offered no further information concerning Bubba or what he was doing there.

Parking in the driveway in the front of his cabin, Karl got out with his two buddies. "Hey, Les," he called out. "We need to get those reels washed off with that water hose over by the side of the house. When you're done, put them in that shed over there and lock it. Wade," Karl continued. "You can help me get these electronics inside."

When they had put everything in its proper place and went back inside the cabin, it was 6:45 p.m. Karl was heading to his room, but stopped momentarily and turned around to face his friends sitting at the kitchen table.

"I don't know about you guys, but I'm ready for a shit, shave, and a shower. There's plenty of hot water so take as long a shower as you'd like." Karl disappeared into his room as the other two men headed for the back where there was another shower.

When they were through getting washed and dressed, each one reappeared in the den area one at the time. Refreshed, they lounged as Karl switched on the TV to catch up on the news.

As Les entered the room, he asked Karl if he would mind letting him borrow the telephone to call home.

Karl nodded okay and pointed to the phone on a table next to the sofa. Sitting down on the cushioned couch adjacent to this table, Les lifted the handle and punched his number into the keypad. He heard it ring. It rang again, and again.

Maybe Louisa and Mike had gone out to eat with some friends. Finally, the soft feminine voice of his wife answered, "Hello?"

"Hey, Louis'."

"Hey there. Y'all doing okay?" she asked.

"Yeah. Karl took us offshore today, and we really caught the fish. Some really nice ones too."

"That's great. I don't think we've had any delicious fresh fish to eat since we've gotten back home," Louisa lamented.

"I know," Les exclaimed. "And these are some of the tastiest: Grouper, Red Snapper, Amberjack.

"Y'all did do good, didn't you, honey? Oh, here comes Mike. He wants to speak to you."

"Put him on," Les said as he smiled at Wade and Karl who had been listening to his conversation.

"Hey, Dad!" came the small voice of Les' son.

"Hey, ol' buddy! What you been up to?"

Les listened as his excited son began to talk rapidly.

Les spoke intermittently trying to get a word in edgewise. "Playing with Pepper?" Les said confused but excited. "Oh, your pal Jason's dog? What kind of dog is he? Uh-hu—a little weenie dog? I see." Les glanced across the room at Karl and Wade who were both chuckling. "You want a dog like Pepper too? Well, we'll have to see about that, okay?"

Mike on the other end of the line pleaded his case on why he needed such a dog.

"Okay, we'll see, but guess what I've been doing? Yep, fishing. That's right. Mr. Karl, my good friend, took us way far out into the Gulf of Mexico in his big boat. Yep, that's the place I showed you on the map. We went so far out that you couldn't even see land. How about that? Yes, Mr. Wade went with us too. Mr. Karl? He's one of my good friends that I grew up and played with when I was your age. Let me tell you about these great big fish we caught. As big as a whale? No, but Mr. Wade caught a big shark. Yeah really. Oh, he was longer than I am tall. Okay, I'll see you too."

Louisa came back to the phone. "He just took off back outside with his two friends. So, I guess you now know how you stack up against Jason and Pepper." Louisa laughed.

"I guess so," Les declared. "Man, that boy can talk a mile a minute. And was that twenty questions or what?"

"You always said that he was an inquisitive little fellow."

Les laughed out loud, "Yeah, I was certainly right about that. Don't know if one day he's going to be a lawyer or an auctioneer."

Charmed by her husband's remarks, Louisa asked, "So, what time will you be making it back home?"

"Depends on if or how far out we go tomorrow," Les said as Karl eyed the preacher surprised.

Delighted, Louisa said, "Hey, another day like y'all had today, and we could fill our freezer with fish."

"That's for sure, and I bet they could use some over there at the Bradford Halfway House too. That might be a good idea, Louis'."

Louisa's voice grew thoughtful, "Well, you know how much I love and miss you. So y'all be really careful out there, and I'll see you when you get home."

"We will, and I love you, Louis'. Give Mike a real big hug for me." Les smiled warmly.

"Love you too, honey. Let me run out back and see what the boys and Pepper are up to."

"Okay. Bye now," Les spoke lovingly.

As Les put down the receiver, Karl glared at him and asked defiantly, "*If* we go out? We're definitely going out tomorrow morning, Les."

Thinking of Wade, Les countered, "You sure you want to, Karl? We've got a pile of fish already and that was a pretty rough trip out there especially—"

Karl cut him of in protest, "Yeah, but we haven't even been diving yet."

Les continued, "Well, Wade doesn't even dive, and I think he's kind of beat too. But I tell you what we'll do, Karl—"

Beside himself, Karl rudely butted in, "That's bullshit! I invite you guys to come down here to fish and dive, and you two assholes bail out on me. Screw you SOBs! Hell, I'll find someone else to go out with me tomorrow."

Les looked at his enraged friend surprised by Karl's outburst. With a placid shrug of his shoulders, he peered deeply into Karl's eyes, "Well, if that's the way you want it."

Karl could get irate about something that offended him in a millisecond, but his philosophy, as it always had been, was not to get mad but to get even. For a moment, he thought he might have blown his chance at doing this with such a tear of anger. But if there was a way he could get even with Les not only for being so virtuous, but now for bailing on him as well, by the end of the night, Karl was going to try his best to do so. Thinking quickly and always calculating, he figured that if he was going to catch his pious little friend off guard, he was going to have to act remorseful for what he had just said and without delay. Sounding repentant, he meekly said, "Say, Les. I hope you'll forgive me for blowing off steam like that. I've been under a lot of pressure at work, and well, sounding off like that, that was just uncalled for." Karl paused for a second. "I got you two guys to come down here more or less for a reunion. I've just been looking forward to this trip for such a long time, I hope you'll forgive me for venting on you like that?"

Wade viewed Karl's show of remorse with suspicion, but Les forgave him instantly telling Karl that they were all just out of sorts from the long, hard trip that they'd endured coming back in. To Wade's displeasure, Les had just let Karl off the hook.

The doctor smiled and acted relieved that Les had accepted his apology. Then he asked, "Whatcha say we go over to the Old Pavillion for a bite to eat?" Eagerly and more relaxed, the three headed for Karl's truck and struck out for the restaurant. As they were walking in, they ran straight into Buck, who had just finished eating and was getting ready to leave.

"Hey, guys," Buck greeted them as Karl and his crew entered the lobby.

"You doing all right, Buck?" Karl asked.

"Doing fine, Doc. Did you find those rocks I showed you?"

"Hit 'em just like you showed us out two twenty-six."

"Did you have any trouble locating them?"

"Not really. Your spot on the map was around seventy five to one-hundred yards off from where they actually were, so I was really pleased about that."

"Good. So, I know you guys limited out on most everything then. Did you put the guys on some of those big amberjacks I was talking about?"

"Oh yeah," Karl exclaimed. "They had a big time pulling in a couple of those bad boys."

Wade chimed in, "Yeah. We even got a huge maybe fifty-pound King Mackerel right up to the boat, but we couldn't get him in."

"A fifty-pounder. For god's sake, that's a huge Kingfish, guys. What happened?"

"You'd have to ask Karl. He was the one in charge of that deal," Wade responded.

Embarrassed, Karl said, "Hey, I couldn't get him gaffed. What can I say?"

"Ouch. That hurts, boys. Missing a King of that size—a fifty-pounder?" Buck pondered the thought, "That's more like an east coast smoker." Facing his doctor friend, Buck chortled. "Say, Karl, that might have been a first. I can't say that I've ever seen you miss gaff a fish before."

Karl shrugged trying to suppress the irritation caused by Buck's comments. With a sneer, he retorted, "By the way, Mr. Double Naught Agent Man, you haven't seen any planes loaded with cocaine flying overhead today, now have you?"

Buck grinned back at his sometimes fishing partner. "No. Can't say that I have, Doc." Buck knew this was his cue to leave. Knowing Karl well, he knew that if he didn't leave now, he would receive more of Karl's baneful jabs, which were sure to follow. "See you guys later," Buck said as he turned for the door. Calling back over his shoulder as he opened it, he questioned them, "You guys going out tomorrow?"

Karl bit his tongue as he glanced at Les, "We're deciding."

"Well, if you do, good luck."

Karl nodded at Buck as he left the building.

Finding a table near the spot where they had eaten the night before, the three childhood friends sat down in a booth. It didn't take too long before an attractive, long-legged woman in her mid-thirties wearing a pair of short black shorts came to wait on them. When she took their orders and left, Karl said, "Stacey. That's her name. Her husband's Slade."

"Slade?" Wade queried. "Now that's an interesting name. Don't think that I've ever heard that name before."

"Yeah," Karl said speaking quietly where no one could overhear what he was saying. "But what's more interesting is that while Slade's working the night shift over at the mill . . ." Karl suddenly paused. "I did tell you guys that there's a large wood processing plant over on the Fenholloway river when we stopped and drifted around that area yesterday, didn't I?"

Both of his friends shook their heads indicating that he hadn't.

"Well, while Slade's over there working his ass off, ol' Stacey over there . . ."

Wade and Les both turned their heads to where Karl was watching the brown-eyed beauty wait on another table.

"Well, she's been working her ass off too. Just in a different way," Karl chuckled.

As they watched her, Stacey disappeared for several minutes into the kitchen. She reappeared carrying two trays. One contained their salads and tea, the other some appetizers Karl had ordered for them: a bowl of boiled Gulf shrimp and another bowl of fried crab claws. When she left their table after having served them, Karl shook his head. "Poor bloke. He's out there working his tail off for her and their two kids, and she's running around behind his back with anyone who's wearing a pair of pants."

Wade, realizing the true nature of his older friend, winked at him and with a wry grin asked, "Karl, you haven't been with her, now have you?"

"Heavens no!" he shot back as if insulted. "I don't believe in running around on my wife or with the wife of another man. Trust me."

Les gave Karl an inquisitive look. "So tell me. How long has this woman been doing this?"

"I have no idea. I just have it from a reliable source that it's going on."

Les kept his eyes on Karl. "A sad situation when stuff like that happens. Hurts everybody involved, doesn't it?"

"Les, I don't think her husband Slade will ever find out. He's not exactly the brightest bulb in the box, if you know what I mean. As for Stacey, I don't think she really gives a damn."

"Well, nobody has to find out for something bad like that to do harm, Karl. You know it can be more the way she reacts to her husband and kids. The way they react back to her. Ultimately it gets back to the way she thinks about herself. What goes around seems to come back around at some point in a person's life."

Karl snickered back at his missionary friend, "That sounds like you're telling me that the adulterous woman in the Bible story that Jesus saved should have been stoned to death. If what goes around comes around."

"No. That's not true at all. Those who accused her didn't stone her because Jesus made them realize that they were just as sinful as she was. God can forgive our waitress there if she truly seeks forgiveness. And she and the members of her family can be made whole again."

"So, you're telling me, Les, that if her husband were to find out about all of her little dalliances, he would want to stay married to her?"

"Would you, Karl?"

"Hell no."

"Come on, Karl. You can actually tell me that you, or let's say even for the sake of argument, your wife couldn't stay married to you if she found herself in Slade's shoes?"

Pensively, Karl lowered his eyes.

Les continued. "Now, I'm not saying that they would have to stay together for her family to be healed, but there's nothing impossible for God. Nothing that He can't fix."

The conversation was getting way too close to home for Karl's liking. Changing the subject quickly, he said, "Well, enough about that. I'm ready to eat. How about you guys?"

Les smiled at him exuberantly, "You know, Karl. Food is just food until you're really hungry."

"Yeah, and I'm starving to death, Les. I see Stacey heading our way with three platters of seafood."

Grinning Les responded, "Nothing is more satisfying to a hungry soul than the nourishment from a good meal, now is there?"

CHAPTER 29

The Party

"Quo Vadis, Domine?"

As Stacey made her way to their booth, she set down three platters of food on an empty adjacent table. When she finished serving the men, she smiled at Karl.

"Hey, Doc. What you been up to?" she asked with a glint in her eye.

"Oh, nothing much," he muttered attempting to ignore her.

"You going to Bubba's tonight, I suppose?" she questioned him.

Acting indifferent, Karl said, "You know, I'm not really sure what we're going to do, but if we make it, it'll probably be pretty late. Say, are you and Slade going to be there?"

"You know Slade works the late shift, Doc, but I'll probably stop by after work. Hope I'll find you when I get there." Crinkling her eyes as she said this, she gave him a seductive little smile. Then the lovely young woman turned and sashayed her way back toward the kitchen.

Wade gave Karl a questioning look to which his older pal immediately replied, "Anything wearing pants, my friend."

Stacey had staked her claim for the night. Karl's earlier conversation with Les concerning adultery seemed even more embarrassing. Pissed off, but not to be outdone, Karl wanted to prove to his pious little missionary friend that the preacher's soul was no purer than his own. Seeking not to spook Les into wanting to go back to the cabin, the doctor tried to avoid any controversy during the rest of their meal. By 8:30 p.m., they were through with supper and had made their way back outside to Karl's truck. Entering it, he informed his friends that he needed to put some more gas into his boat. Driving the short distance to where the craft was parked, all three men got out and drove Karl's vessel back around to the docks which were situated below the Marina's boatlift.

After stretching the long gas hose from the Marina's pump down to the *Doc's Out!*, Karl unscrewed the boat's stainless-steel gas cap. Sticking the nozzle into the tank, he began the process of refueling. It had been a long rough day's ride on the water. The concomitant strain of wind and waves on the engines had caused them to use more gas than normal. As the number of gallons rolled higher and higher, the nozzle finally clicked to a stop. The guys noticed that they had burned through almost two-thirds of the gas they'd been carrying on board. Seeing how expensive it was, Les insisted that he and Wade should pay their share of the tab. Disarmed by this suggestion, Karl called back to his friend, "You know, Les. Out of all the people I've taken offshore fishing, there's only been a few who've ever offered to pay for anything."

Reticent until now, Wade remarked, "It's the only fair way to do it, Karl."

"We'll see," the doctor said as he placed the nozzle back in its holder.

Signaling Betty, who was standing on the Marina's porch, to put the fuel bill on his tab, Karl and his two friends climbed back into the Contender. With Karl pushing them away from the dock, they rode the vessel back around to where it had been previously moored. Calling out, Karl said, "All right, boys. I think we've got everything done down here that needs doing. It's about time to head on over to my friend Bubba's place. There's some people over there that I'd like to talk to about fishing tomorrow."

As the men headed back up the boat ramp for the truck, Les and Wade knew what to expect next. Getting back into the vehicle, Karl spun his tires into reverse. Wheeling around, he proceeded down the road in front of the Marina. Les and Wade could see bright lights shining from across the inlet in the direction they were heading. Veering north off the main thoroughfare onto Ezell Beach Road, they found themselves adjacent to what appeared through the darkness to be a forested pasture. Interspersed with groupings of trees, shrubs, and palmettos was an area of grass filled with pickup trucks and cars parked in almost every direction and manner. The locale was about three and a half acres with Bubba's house sitting a hundred yards away from the open waters of the Gulf. The isolated spot was just as Betty had described it. Wade could see no other homes or buildings nearby.

On this dark, moonless October night, the three exited Karl's truck to a slight but building breeze. The wind was just strong enough to make the fronds of nearby palms rattle and cause the pines overhead to sway. As they walked through this shadowy maze of trees and vehicles, they were eventually able to see the brightly lit backyard of Bubba's house. Throngs of happy partygoers immersed in an atmosphere of bright lights and blaring music surrounded the place. Entering the noisy area of mayhem, Karl heard someone calling his name.

"Hey, Doc! Over here! Come on over and tell us if you caught any fish today."

Peering through the crowd of people, Karl spotted his buddy Billy standing next to another one of his friends, Jack. A large 96-quart cooler of iced-down beer rested on the ground between the two men. Like most attendees, Jack and Billy had been looking forward to this party for a long time. Coming all the way down from Spring Warrior where both of them lived, they were ready to "so-sal-ize," as they called it, and eager to enjoy the festivities. Reaching down into the large ice cooler as the newcomers walked up, Billy, in his mid-forties, retrieved all three of them an ice-cold can of Milwaukee's finest.

"Thanks, Billy," Karl exclaimed, "but only Wade here can drink tonight. Les here's a preacher. I'm going diving tomorrow, so I'm on the wagon myself." Introducing Billy, who was a retired naval mechanic, Karl called over to Les and Wade, "Fellas, this Rhodes Scholar here's named Billy Blue."

"How is it going, Billy?" Les asked as he and Wade each shook Billy's leathery hand.

Having introduced themselves, Billy said, "My name's not really Billy Blue. It's just the name these yokels around here gave me because they think my girlfriend never gives me any."

Jack quickly spoke up in his high-pitched nasally voice, "Well, she don't! At least that's what she tells us."

Karl busted out laughing as Jack gave his new acquaintances a wry grin. "Billy Blue Balls!" Karl roared. "He's the man! And this old fart standing next to him is ol' Jack. Jack is old as dirt, isn't he, Billy?"

"He's older than dirt. Try bituminous coal," Billy responded dryly.

Weathered old Jack, who had snow-white hair and a set of the palest blue eyes one could imagine, took a sip from his beer can. In his high-toned southern drawl, he said, "You know, Doc. I just had a birthday."

"How old are you, Jack? A hundred?" Karl goaded as he and Billy roared with laughter.

Jack eyed the two bewildered as the alcohol he'd been drinking for most of the afternoon temporarily befuddled his mind. Then, with a slur, he asked, "Well, how old are you, Doc?"

"I'm thirty-five years old, old man."

Jack paused calculating. Then, with that same slurring drawl, he said, "Well, Doc. That makes me thirty-one years smarter, wiser and handsomer than you." All the guys standing nearby got a good laugh from the older man's wit.

"Handsomer? Is there such a word?" Karl questioned.

"You dang right there is. And I'm that," Jack said grinning and taking another sip from his can.

Karl chuckled at his older friend as he scanned the grounds. "Hey, fellows," he said glancing back at Jack and Billy. "We're going to go check on ol' Bubba. Y'all seen him around here anywhere?" They both shrugged indicating that they hadn't. Motioning for Les and Wade to follow him, Karl walked through the crowd in search of his friend. "Fellows," Karl said as they walked along. "I don't know who half these people are. Can't believe this many people actually showed up for this thing."

It was 9:30 p.m. Well over a hundred people were milling around Bubba's backyard. Karl spoke to various people who knew him. Looking around, Les and Wade could see that four huge Pioneer speakers had been set up and were booming the music of Jimmy Buffet, the Doobie Brothers, and George Strait. The party was loud and rambunctious. Following Karl, Wade was as nervous and out of place as a lost puppy. Les, on the other hand, smiled at anyone looking in his direction and took great delight in seeing all the happy partygoers. After circling the place for a time, Karl found his gregarious friend Bubba talking to a voluptuous group of young women.

At forty-five years old, two-hundred-and-twenty pounds, and slightly handsome, Bubba wore a gold chain necklace and a mustache. The darkly tanned Bubba was the life of the party. Slightly drunk, a lit cigarette dangling from his lips, he gave Karl a high five when he saw him and his friends walk up. "Hey, Doc! Bay-beee!" he roared with delight. "Where the hell have you been, man? I've been waitin' half the night for you to get here. You got him with you?" he asked peeping over Karl's shoulder.

Karl swiftly leaned over and whispered into Bubba's ear, "Shut up, you dumbass. He's standing right behind me, and I don't want him to know what's going on."

Bubba gave Karl an exaggerated grimace of repentance, then a quick smile, "Sorry. Sorry. My bad," he tried whispering back. Eager to get things started, Bubba called for someone to bring him the microphone. The music was turned down and the lights were dimmed low.

The mic in his hand, Bubba began to speak into it as if he were a ring announcer at a prestigious boxing match, "All right! Ladies and gentlemen, gather around and LET'S GET READY TO STUMBLE!—I mean, RUMBLE!" Bubba howled as he exaggerated stumbling after taking a huge hit from a bottle of Crown Royal that he held in his left hand. Everyone began chanting, "Bubba! Bubba! Bubba!" until he finally regained control of the crowd.

"Okay, okay," he shouted. Then he boomed, "Ladies and gentlemen! Tonight, we have chosen five contestants for your viewing enjoyment. Whoa! Wait a minute! I see another beauty wanting to get into the contest right over there." He pointed into a dark area behind a truck. "Make that six lovely ladies that you'll be introduced to tonight!" He paused as the girls were readying themselves just out of view of everyone else. "They're a modest group, you know."

Hearing him say this, the crowd all began to laugh and whistle in wild anticipation.

Realizing what was about to happen, Wade poked Les and said, "We need to get the heck out of here."

Amused by the circumstance, Les shot back, "It's too late, Wade. Look behind you."

Swarms of people had gathered all around them. Standing shoulder to shoulder and completely encircling them along with Bubba, there was no escape.

Spotlights were fired off from across the yard illuminating a line of six attractive females wearing only bikini bathing suit bottoms and t-shirts for tops. These girls were standing five steps away from Bubba, Les, and Wade. Bubba sang out, "Here they are, ladies and gentlemen! The contestants for this year's wet t-shirt contest!"

As the words left his mouth, a huge roar erupted from the crowd with wolf calls, whistles, yells, and hollers. A wave of electricity and excitement filled the night air. Not only was the crowd hot and bothered with the expectation of what was about to occur, but the contestants themselves were enjoying the attention they were getting.

"Okay," Bubba proclaimed. "We're going to spray them down one at the time and find out just who has the best set of Hooters! Boozoobies! Milk Jugs! Or Titties! Call 'em what you want! There's gonna be a whole lot of shakin' going on around here in just a minute."

The partygoers went even wilder as they anticipated the start of the spectacle. "But wait a minute!" Bubba continued as a few boos followed his proclamation. "An event this big and exciting has to have some judges, and we've found two of the very best around. Michael C.—Lights please." All of the sudden, Les and Wade found themselves in the blinding beam of a spotlight.

"Let's hear it for these two fellas! This year's judges. Les and Wade, folks. Here they are!" As a large cacophonous cheer arose from the crowd, Wade scowled at Les. "He's set you up, Les. That son of bitch."

Les countered quickly, "Calm down, Wade. I can handle this. Don't worry."

Bubba walked into the spotlight holding up a stack of bills. "We've raised three hundred and fifty dollars which will go to our lucky winner tonight. So, ladies, we want a good show!" He held the money up for everyone to see then handed it to Les.

The multitude, in pandemonium, chanted, "Spray 'em! Spray 'em! Spray 'em!"

Bubba motioned for the water to be turned on.

In wild anticipation and with the music turned back up, the crowd became a creature of lust and salaciousness. It was mankind displaying his true nature of self-centeredness and self-gratification. Seeing all this mayhem surrounding them, Wade leaned over to Les and said, "Nothing like being right in the middle of Sodom and Gomorrah, eh?"

Trying to respond over the roar, Les snickered as he witnessed the crowd's riotousness too. "Sometimes, Wade, we're just like a bunch of pigs wearing masks," he spoke loudly so Wade could hear him. "Sometimes our dignified masks come off and reveal what's just beneath the surface. It's in us all. Every one of us. Remember that."

Bubba exclaimed, "Okay, everyone. Our first contestant is Amy from—well, we won't say—step out into the line of fire, AMY!"

Amy stepped out from the line of girls and was immediately hosed down. With the music turned back up, she did a little dance, sensually grasping at her breasts through her t-shirt as the hose soaked them. The crowd whistled and applauded, yelling with delight as Amy stepped back into the lineup. The women knew what they had to do to win the prize. With the introduction of each new contestant, they provocatively put a little more into their act in order to beat the previous performer. The frenzied roar of the crowd had grown constant as the last contestant got her chance.

"All right, ladies and gentlemen," Bubba yelled. "Our sixth and final young lady—Stacey! Show us something special, Stacey!" Wade and Les realized she was the same Stacey from the restaurant, Slade's wife. As she stepped forward, it was obvious that the attractive young woman was either drunk or high on something as she could hardly stand. The water hose sprayed her as she began to dance sexually to the music and smile seductively at someone in the audience. Continuing to look in the same direction as before, she pulled out a bar of soap and started washing herself off to the pleasure of the crowd. Declaring, "this is for you, Doc!" she pulled off her top. Twirling it around several times, she slung it in Karl's direction. In an even more erotic manner, she began to lather her bare breasts with the soap once more.

Shamed and humiliated by what she was doing, especially in front of his two friends, Karl immediately called over to Bubba to have the water cut off and to stop the show. Unfortunately for him, this didn't stop the performance as Stacey, spying

Karl once more, ran and jumped into his arms. With her legs wrapped around his waist, she then tried kissing him on the mouth.

Karl, who was mortified by this scandalous display, immediately attempted pulling her off of him. Finally, she fell sprawling to the ground. Barely able to get back to her feet but still gleefully exposing herself, the married woman staggered back and re-entered the line of contestants. There was no way, she thought, that she could lose either the money or Karl this night.

Bubba made his way back to Wade and Les who were once again in the spotlight. With the microphone in his hand, Bubba sang out, "Ladies and gentlemen! What do you say? How 'bout let's giving 'em all a big hand for all that shaking, jiggling, and *bathing* they did for us tonight?" Laughing, Bubba rolled his eyes as a raucous cheer and ovation immediately rang out for the six soaking wet performers. Looking at Les and Wade, Bubba asked, "Have our judges made their final decision? It's got to be a tough one the way all these beauties performed out here tonight."

As Les took the microphone, the crowd began to chant, "Stacey! Stacey! Stacey!"

Bringing the mic to his mouth, Les said calmly, "Yes. We've made our final decision."

The cheering spectators quickly grew quiet hearing him say this.

Continuing as the crowd noise leveled off, Les exclaimed, "I've just recently returned from spending some time along the Amazon River." Even the chattering of the crowd hushed when they heard him say this. "Nudity was a way of life for many of the native people down there, but here in America we're ashamed of ourselves, so we hide our nakedness behind clothes."

"Hell yeah!" A small cheer went up from a few people believing Les was condoning nudity.

"And we use nudity here in America only as something sensual and erotic."

"Tell 'em about it!" the same group of people proclaimed patronizing him.

Les paused as he surveyed the pitiful throng of humanity that surrounded him. Intently they had become one, en masse in order to have their way. There would be no appeasing them, and Les knew it. But the truth would have to be told, whether they liked it or not. Slowly and more softly, he continued to speak, "I am standing here tonight, not to judge these young women, for they're human beings just like you and me. Rather than give this money to any of these individuals for such a display, I would rather see this money go to the benefit of the poor and sick of this area especially to the neglected children who live around here."

Les handed the microphone and the money back to a stunned Bubba as someone in the crowd called out, "A freakin' preacher!"

Another irritated spectator yelled, "Who brought his sorry ass down here anyway? Throw that wet-blanket son of a bitch outta here! He's ruining the whole damn thing for everybody!"

As the crowd moaned, groaned, and heckled Les and Wade, Karl hurriedly disappeared as a trapped Bubba tried denying that he even knew who the judges were.

"We picked those guys at random," Bubba kept telling everyone as he struggled to defend himself. "We didn't know who they were or where the hell they even came from."

Away from the line of fire, Karl found Jack and Billy. He directed them around to the dark north side of Bubba's house. There, he hoped to escape the fury of the crowd for what he had done.

In his nasally high-pitched drawl, Jack spoke first. "What'd you bring us over here for? Wasn't that your pals that was judging that contest?"

"Yeah," Karl whispered embarrassed, "but I didn't tell anybody to pick them to do that."

Concerned for their safety, Jack said, "Well, you better get their tails out of here and fast. Somebody's liable to hurt those fellas. That crowd got pretty ticked off the way that thing ended. You know a preacher don't have no business being down here at a party like this, Doc. You ought to have known better than to have brought them down here in the first place."

Karl rubbed his chin nervously as he spoke, "Yeah, I know. It was my bad for bringing them over here. But first, before I leave to go get them, I want you guys to give me your opinion on something I discovered."

"What's that?" Billy asked curiously.

"I've found some numbers for a spot where some of the biggest grouper I've ever seen have been caught. You guys interested?"

Both men perked up when Karl said this.

"Where's it at?" Jack asked.

"It's about twenty some odd miles out around 260 degrees."

"260? Hell no!" Jack said, his face turning pale. "Stay away from that area, Doc."

Karl shot back. "What's wrong with that spot?"

Jack grew noticeably nervous. His eyes darted across the crowded backyard then back at Karl. "Something's going on out that way, Doc. Trouble," he said shaking his head.

"What kind of trouble?" Karl asked intrigued.

Billy chimed in, "Fishing the flats in that direction a few miles out is okay, but some of the boats going offshore where you're talking about have come back telling us they've been harassed."

"Harassed," Karl said. "What the hell do you mean by harassed?"

Jack cut his eyes at Karl. In his nasally twang, he said, "Hell! They pulled guns on 'em!"

"Guns?" Karl asked amused.

"Drug boys would be my guess, Doc."

Billy interceded, "Nahhh. Some illegal fishermen using traps is what I think's going on. They're just trying to scare people away from seeing what they're doing."

"Trappers you say, Billy?"

"Yeah."

Jack kept shaking his head as he gave Karl a cautious look. "You don't plan on going up that way, now do you?"

"No—I'm sticking southwest. I've had a lot of luck in that area lately. Matter of fact, we loaded the boat today on some good locations Buck showed me."

Billy scrutinized Karl and became serious. "Stay away from anything above 250 degrees offshore, Doc. At least until we figure out who it is we're dealing with up there. From Spring Warrior and Fenholloway north, we're warning all the recreational fisherman to stay in close so they won't have to deal with those folks."

Karl asked surprised, "They haven't been bothering the commercial boys any?"

Billy countered, "No, those guys aren't fishing that area right now. They claim there's nothing's much over there because it's been overfished. From what I'm hearing, they're pretty much sticking to the Middle Grounds southwest." He paused reflectively. "It would just be my guess that whoever it is out there doing this wouldn't want to tangle with our commercial friends."

II

While Karl had concealed himself from the view of the throng at the northwest side of Bubba's house with Jack and Billy, Wade and Les found themselves in the midst of a belligerent mob. Either a drunk was hurling an insult at them, or the revelers would roll their eyes in abhorrence as they walked past. As the crowd dispersed, the wet t-shirt contest unceremoniously came to an end.

Glancing at Les, Wade cautiously spoke as he eyed the people surrounding them. "Bubba calling us out by name and the spotlight shining straight down on us? Any doubts of who was behind that, Les?"

"No. I don't think so. That was carrying things a little too far, wasn't it?"

"A little, hell," Wade exclaimed in disgust as he kept a close eye on the partiers nearby. "He threw us under the bus. Especially you being a preacher and all. Son of a you-know-what." Wade stopped watching the crowd and turned his attention back to Les. "Are you about ready to call it a trip now?"

Les paused as he caught a glimpse of another passerby who was staring at them with a smirk and shaking his head. "Yeah, I think so. Enough is enough, isn't it?"

"Heck yeah," Wade replied as he searched the crowd for Karl. "Where is that jerk anyway?"

"I don't know. I haven't seen him anywhere since this all ended."

"Well, I tell you what we do," Wade said cautiously. "Let's walk to the front yard. It's dark on that side of the house. If we don't find him on the way, you can stay over there until I find him." Wade paused worried. "These people aren't after me, Les. It's you and what you represent—that's what they want out of here."

As Wade and Les made their way through the partygoers to the darkened south side of Bubba's house, they still saw no sign of Karl. "All right," Wade said. "You hang out over here while I go hunt for that sorry butthole. I'll be back as soon as I find him."

Standing there a moment, Les' eyes became more adjusted to the dimmer light surrounding him. As both of them had figured, no one had ventured over to this side of the house, making it a much safer place for Les to be. Turning around, Les could see from where he was standing in the darkness, the brightly lit festival going on before him. The atmosphere was still electric as the partygoers, standing in clustered groups, were still in high spirits as the party rocked on. For the revelers, the disappointment of the wet t-shirt contest seemed to be only a brief interlude in the grander scheme of their night's fun. Les smiled as he watched the people enjoying themselves. Tiring of this after a while, he walked over to Bubba's front porch steps and took a seat as he waited for Wade to return.

It was 10:45 p.m. and after another ten minutes of waiting, Les grew weary of just sitting there. Observing his surroundings, he saw a path running from Bubba's front steps across the yard to what appeared to be a marshy estuary. Between him and what he perceived as the Gulf stood a small grassy yard followed by an extremely sparse wooded area. It had a few small stands of skinny pines and a scattering of isolated palms with a slightly denser undercarriage of short saw palmetto bushes. His curiosity getting the best of him, Les rose and ambled down the rambling sand path, through the slight forest, and on to where the trail ended. The trek, close to a hundred yards, left the chattering and din of the ongoing party muffled, but not too far off in the distance.

Standing at the shoreline of the estuary and gazing beyond a half-acre or so of marsh cordgrass, he saw the broad expanse of the continuously moving Gulf of Mexico. Above him on this cloudless, moonless night, he scanned a spectacular view of the Milky Way and the star-laden heavens shining down on him. Taking a deep breath of the Gulf's fresh air, he felt the east wind had begun to build just as the weather forecast had predicted. Dressed lightly wearing a thin long sleeve shirt and jeans, Les shoved his hands deep into the pockets of his pants for warmth.

With the madding crowd so close, it was amazing to Les that he could find himself in such a spiritual setting. Time seemed momentarily frozen as all he could see were the billions of stars shining above him. All he could feel was the wind whipping and tugging at his clothes. Awareness of what he was experiencing ran through him like someone alone in the presence of a great work of art for the first time. Like the initial viewing of a sculpture done by Michelangelo or listening to the music of Mozart. Those comparisons were only a fraction of what he was realizing. An inner glow filled his soul as he closed his eyes relishing the moment.

He held this refrain for as long as he could, several minutes. Realizing that one cannot freeze time and that he must move on, he slowly began to open his eyes once more. Startling him at first as his vision began to adjust, he noticed a presence. A young dark-haired teenage boy was standing in the shadows of the shoreline some eight paces away from where he stood. Not wanting to spook the lad, Les said, "It's a nice night out here tonight, isn't it?"

The boy said nothing; he just stood there gazing up into the brilliant night sky.

Noticing his shyness, Les pointed out Cassiopeia overhead and then the Big Dipper constellation which was one of his favorites, Ursa Major. Speaking toward the youngster, he said, "Look there." He pointed to where the stars of the cup portion of the Big Dipper were located. "You line up those last two stars of that cup, and it points over to that really bright star. That's Polaris, the North Star. That's what sailors used to use to guide them at sea. On a clear night like this one, you can really see it shining, can't you?"

The boy slowly nodded in silence indicating that he could. Turning, he started to walk away.

"Where are you going?" Les called after him.

The young boy called back over his shoulder, *Volver al rio.*

Stunned by the sound of Yutca's voice, Les stood frozen as the presence disappeared into the darkness. Immediately Les fell to his knees. With his arms outstretched toward the heavens, he cried pleadingly, *Quo vadis, domine*? "Where are you going, Master? Are You telling me as You told Peter that You are going to Rome to be crucified again? Must I do this Lord? Must I be Your apostle?" he called out in anguish.

CHAPTER 30

October 12, 1985

After searching, Wade found Karl sitting in his truck with the driver's side door open. When he saw Wade approach, he angrily asked, "Where the hell have y'all been?"

"Looking for your sorry ass!" Wade fired back. "Real nice job you pulled on us out there tonight. I really want to thank you for that."

"Hey. That wasn't my fault, man. Bubba just asked who I was with and he just picked y'all."

"Riiiight," Wade exclaimed cynically. "I was born, but it wasn't yesterday, Karl. You know, Les might fall for that bullshit, but not me."

"Think what you want to," Karl said shrugging.

Disgusted by Karl's indifference, Wade turned to leave.

"Where you going now?" Karl inquired.

"I'm going to get our friend from where I've got him hid," Wade retorted sharply as he turned to face his adversary. "You know, some of your drunk pals running around out there would probably like to get their grimy little hands on his ass. So, I don't suppose you'd like to come with me, huh?"

Karl dismissed Wade's concern with a detached stare. "No. I'm sure you're quite capable."

Wade grimaced as he stared directly into Karl's eyes, then he left. Taking a few taunts along the way for being one of the judges, Wade made it through the loud, lively party where he eventually found himself in Bubba's darkened front yard. Searching the area where Les was supposed to be, Wade became alarmed when he couldn't find him. *Where on earth is he,* Wade wondered. He entered Bubba's house to see if Les had found his way inside. But after a thorough search and noticing only a few people sitting around in the den area, Wade exited the back door.

Once again, he found himself in the midst of the celebrating crowd where he happened to come across Jack. Seeing the older man, Wade asked him if he'd seen Les anywhere. Jack told Wade that he hadn't, but he'd be on the lookout for him. He also cautioned Wade that he should get his preacher friend away from here as soon as possible.

Hoping that Les had returned to Karl's pickup without Wade having seen him, Wade headed in that direction again. Still sitting with his truck door opened, Karl noticed Wade as he approached alone.

"Where's Les?" he asked, showing some concern for the first time.

"I don't know. He's not where I left him on the other side of Bubba's house. I was hoping he'd made it back here."

"Did you check inside?"

"Yeah. He wasn't there either. I walked all around the party trying to find him and ran into your friends Jack and Billy, but neither one of them said they'd seen him either."

"You left him in the front yard over there, huh?" Karl asked exiting his Silverado and shutting the door behind him.

"Yeah. That's the last time I saw him," Wade replied as they both headed in that direction.

As the two made their way across the backyard still filled with partygoers and blaring music, a couple of locals who were still perturbed by Doc and Bubba picking a preacher to judge the contest needled him. However, a more somber Karl was in no mood for their antics.

"Y'all haven't seen that little guy that judged the contest around here, have you?" Karl's demeanor had turned serious, and they knew it.

"No," they both responded soberly.

Karl was starting to worry. Some of the drunken rednecks were pissed off about how the contest had ended. Lit and already half crazy, they would have no problem taking Les off to some desolate place where they'd abandon him to find his way back. More worrisome to Karl than this was that if they happened to be mad and drunk enough, their anger could easily result in Les getting hurt. Entering Bubba's house, Karl told Wade to circle the dwelling and he would meet him at the home's front porch steps if he didn't find Les inside. It was 11:40 p.m. when they met in Bubba's front yard their friend still nowhere in sight. As they became more frantic, they went to the side yard and scanned the large group of remaining revelers.

"He seems to have vanished into thin air," Wade said.

"Yeah, that's what I'm afraid of," the doctor acknowledged. "I think we'll have to go through the crowd there and find out who saw him last."

Karl suddenly glanced at Wade. "Did you hear that?"

Wade shook his head.

Puzzled by Karl's intense look, Wade listened too. Both men heard the sound. Like a call from afar, it emanated from the other side of the yard behind them. Turning around, they saw to their amazement Les coming toward them from the wooded sand path that he had taken to get down to the Gulf marsh.

"Hey! Y'all looking for me!" he declared with a grin still a good distance away.

"Hell yes!" Karl retorted with an uncharacteristic smile of relief. "Where on earth have you been?"

"I've been down to the inlet there." He pointed behind him. "Beautiful view down there tonight overlooking the Gulf and sky."

Karl kept peering at Les as he walked closer. "Man, you had us worried as hell. Thought something bad might have happened to your little butt," Karl divulged with total sincerity.

"Glad to hear that you were concerned about my well-being, old buddy. That's what friends are for, isn't it?"

Wade bit his tongue knowing full well Karl's complicity in getting Les into this mess in the first place. Now, unbelievable to Wade, Les was praising his smug older friend for watching out for him.

II

The ride back to Karl's cabin was a quiet one for the most part. Not wanting to admit it was he who had committed the treachery of making Les a judge, Karl was almost too embarrassed to talk. *How has everything backfired? Why am I always the victim?* he thought.

Les asked, "Did you find anyone at the party tonight to go fishing and diving with you tomorrow?"

"No, I didn't," Karl said disappointed.

Les, who was seated in the front passenger side of the truck, gazed across at his older friend through the darkness. "Well, if the offer's still good, I'll go with you."

"Great!" Karl exclaimed surprised. "I'd love for you to go with me."

"What time do we need to leave?" Les asked.

"Not too early. Eight-ish maybe," Karl answered taken aback. Reflecting on what had transpired earlier in the evening, Karl thought for a moment. Certainly, Les knew, as did Wade, it was he who had put Les in that bad spot back at Bubba's. Why on earth would Les still want to go fishing with him after being treated like that? Glancing back at his friend pensively, Karl could only wonder.

Wade had been sitting in the back seat quietly listening to this conversation and was utterly dumbfounded by what Les had just said. What in the world could have made Les change his mind so suddenly?

When the truck stopped in Karl's driveway, they exited the vehicle and headed for the cabin. A rumbling vibrating noise rapidly approached them from the southeast. Instantly, they heard a terrifying blast right over them.

BUROOM!!!

The sonic boom of fighter jet engines near tree-top level made all three panic and duck. Caught off guard, their legs turned to jelly.

BUR*OOM!!!*

A second jet followed behind the first; its blast was so close and disorienting that it made the three fall to the ground.

Recovering his balance and getting to his feet, Wade hollered, "Where the hell did those things come from?"

The other two men, now standing beside him, marveled at what they'd just witnessed. Just as rapidly as the supersonic fighters had appeared, the roar from their engines faded off into the distance.

"Hell, boys," Karl exclaimed astonished. "I've never seen anything like that down here before. My god, they seemed like they were rooftop high."

"They were getting it, that's for sure," Les cackled. "That might be as swift as I've ever seen you two guys move. Quicker than even back when you fellas played football."

"Hey!" Karl said with a grin. "You were ducking down there pretty fast yourself, ol' pal."

They made their way to the side yard to get a better view and to see what direction the aircraft were traveling.

Wade, who was always the observer, spoke first, "Looks like they're heading northwest. What's up that way, Karl?"

"Carrabelle, Panacea, Panama City. They could be heading toward any of those spots. They're probably just on a training mission."

Wade interjected, "A training mission? If that's what it was, then the local Air Force, wherever that is, will get an earful tomorrow morning. Hell, it's past twelve a.m. and they're blasting their way just above these people's houses on a training mission?"

Karl countered, "I'm sure those guys could care less about a little place like Keaton Beach, Wade. They're probably just practicing flying under radar. That would be my guess."

As they watched, it didn't take long for the aircrafts red and green flashing lights to disappear over the darkened horizon. And just like that, they were gone. Lights, noise, and all.

When the excitement of the jets ended, the three men drifted toward the entrance to Karl's cabin. Inside, Karl was the first one of them to bail. "This was about as much of a day as I think I can handle, boys. I'm hitting the hay." With that comment, Karl walked into his bedroom shutting the door behind him.

Les followed suit and called to Wade, "I think I'm heading that way myself." As Les disappeared into his bedroom, Wade found the bathroom. Brushing his teeth and washing his hands, he headed for his own bed down the hall. As he passed Les' doorway, he noticed it was open.

Poking his head inside, he saw his smaller buddy with his back propped on a couple of pillows reading from his Bible in the dimness of a table lamp. Glancing up, Les caught Wade's eye and knew exactly why he was there. Speaking first and with a smile, he said, "Listen, Wade. You don't have to go fishing with us tomorrow if you don't want to. I can catch a ride back to Tallahassee with Karl. It won't be too much of a trip for Louisa to come down and get me from there. So, if you want to, you can leave in the morning if that's what you'd like to do." Wade sighed still confused by Les' intentions, especially considering what had happened to them earlier in the evening. "No. If you're going fishing, I am too, Les," Wade said disheartened. He paused in contemplation. "I suppose you're not going to tell me what made you change your mind about leaving though."

Les gave Wade a disarming smile. "You know, Wade, you've been a great and wonderful friend of mine for all these many years. You've always been there when I needed you, too. Like when I passed out down at the bottom of that snowy hill, you were there. When I needed a trusted friend to take care of Louisa when I was way down in Texas, you watched over her. Tonight, when we found ourselves in that very compromising situation," Les chuckled, "you stuck with me and got me away from that angry mob."

"I'm not that great a guy, Les," Wade said embarrassed by Les' patronage. "I did nothing that you wouldn't have done for me."

Les beamed in response, "That might be true, Wade, but the fact is that you did do it for me. I've appreciated all those things that you've done. I've appreciated your constant and loyal friendship very, very much." Les gave Wade a wide grin. "You know I love you, man."

Smirking, Wade shook his head. "I knew you wouldn't give me a straight answer, Les."

CHAPTER 31

Out at Keaton

The next morning Karl woke at 6:00 a.m. It was still very dark outside as he made his way quietly down the bungalow's hallway. He noticed a light coming from under the door to Les' room. Gently knocking on it, he murmured, "Hey, Les. You awake in there?" Waiting for a response, he got none. "Les?" he called again softly. Still hearing nothing coming from inside, he opened the door only to find the bedroom empty.

Confused about where Les might be, Karl noticed that resting on the made-up bed was an opened, flip-top notebook. On it, he saw a series of paragraph size notes trailing a header written in heavier ink entitled SERMON. Karl didn't stop to read what was there, but instead went down the hallway to Wade's room and cracked the door to see if he too was awake and gone. Peeking inside, he saw Wade bundled under a pile of covers. The morning was brisker than usual. Karl closed the door, got dressed, and walked into his living room. Opening the curtains to his balcony, he thought surely he'd find Les meditating there. It too was empty. This was odd, he thought, but gathered that Les must have grown hungry and walked around the canal to the glowing lights of the Marina. Karl got into his truck and drove that way.

Still early morning, Betty was at the register where she was waiting on groups of early-rising fisherman. Hearing the jangling bells of the Marina's front door ringing, she glanced across the room and noticed Karl walk into the building. "Morning, Doc," she exclaimed as she saw the unshaven thirty-five-year-old approach. Rasping, she chuckled as she took another draw of smoke from her cigarette. "Didn't think I'd see you up so early this morning."

Glaring back at her, Karl asked, "What would make you say something like that, Betty?"

Realizing she'd overstepped her bounds, Betty timidly said, "Just heard that they had a real blow out over at Bubba's last night, and you being Bubba's friend and all I…"

Karl cut her off mid-sentence. "We stopped by there last night, my buddies and me. But I'll have you know that I was back in bed and asleep by twelve o'clock, for your information." Karl said this braggingly as if he'd done something remarkably good.

Betty couldn't help but grin as she just finished ringing up the last group of fishermen. "Miracles never cease, I guess, huh?" She chuckled. "That preacher friend of yours must have given you a little religion since he's been down here, eh?"

Not missing a beat, Karl responded, "I've always been a religious person, Betty. What would make you think otherwise?"

Betty couldn't help smiling as she looked back at him. Blowing a stream of smoke from the corner of her mouth, she wondered if Karl really believed that.

Changing the subject, she said, "Say, Doc. Those jets flying over last night—didn't knock you off your mattress, now did they?"

Karl searched the place for Les but saw no sign of him. Glancing back at Betty, he replied, "Yeah, they were flying pretty low all right. You see them doing that very much down here?"

"No, Doc. Can't say that I've ever seen them do that before. Not ever. I hope they aren't gonna make a habit of it either. Don't you?"

"Nah, I doubt they will. Probably on some sort of evasive military exercise or something like that would be my guess." Karl paused as he made direct eye contact with Betty. "Say, have you seen Les, my shorter friend, the preacher? Has he been by this morning?"

"Can't say that I've seen him today, Doc," Betty said concerned. "He did make it back with you guys from Bubba's last night, I hope?"

Karl rolled his eyes. "Yes, Betty. He made it back with us last night." Disgusted with her remark, he sighed. "Maybe he's down at the beach. I think I'll go down there and check around." Leaving the store, Karl drove the short distance down to the spit of sandy beach at the far end of the small fishing village's peninsula. Parking his truck, he could see someone silhouetted against the glowing horizon. The individual sat perched on a set of jetties separating the rippling Gulf's waters from the calmness of Keaton's canal. Karl, walking through the cool breeze of this early morning, recognized the figure as he drew nearer. With an unfamiliar sense of relief, he saw that it indeed was his pal. Making his way agilely onto the limestone boulders stacked there, he observed that Les had not noticed him approaching.

As Karl closed the distance between himself and his friend, Les turned toward him. Over the slight gusting wind and the small waves lapping against the rocks, Les exclaimed, "So, you finally found me, I see."

Karl stopped next to his seated companion as they both looked seaward. "How long you been down here?" Karl asked curiously.

"I don't know, a while I guess."

"I saw where you'd been working on your sermon in the notebook lying on your bed," Karl said as he too took a seat on one of the jetties smoother rocks.

"Yeah, I worked on it a little last night and a little more this morning."

As they sat there, Karl became unusually quiet. Gone was the brashness he had displayed during the previous two days.

Knowing his friend was embarrassed by what had transpired the preceding night, Les broke the silence, "So, tell me, Karl. How's life been treating you?"

"Oh, pretty good, I guess."

"What do you mean—you guess?"

Karl grew pensive for a moment. "I guess I pretty much have everything that I'd ever wanted in life. I mean, I'm a surgeon, something I've always wanted to be. I've got two homes, one down here. A boat, a couple of kids running around the house, and a wife. What more could I ask for, Les?"

"I don't know," Les remarked making no suggestions.

"How about you, Les? Has life been all it's cracked up to be being a missionary and a preacher?" As he asked this question, he did so without expressing his usual sarcasm.

"I don't think I really look at myself or life like that, Karl."

"What do you mean? Either you're having a great life, a mediocre life, or you wish you were doing something entirely different. What other way is there to look at it?"

"What I mean is that I don't view it from that perspective."

Karl sneered, "So, I guess you're now going to tell me that you see it from God's perspective. Right?"

Les gave Karl a serious look. "Who knows the mind of God, Karl? Certainly not me." Momentarily, he paused eyeing him. A little smile parted his lips. "You aren't telling me that you do, now are you?"

Karl chuckled at Les' quick wit, but even so, his cynical smirk remained. "Now, Les. You know from our conversation fishing yesterday that that's your territory and not mine."

"I would think that this would be everybody's territory, Karl. From my perspective life is all just about one thing."

Karl was perplexed as he remembered Les alluding to this point in their previous discussion.

Noting Karl's intrigue, Les said, "It's what each individual has to find for himself. I can't take you there, but are you interested in knowing what I am talking about?"

Karl considered his friend carefully. "No. Not really, Les. I think I'll just let you keep that little secret all to yourself." Karl stood having had enough of the bothersome subject. Dusting off the back of his pants, he said, "Hey, a little breakfast is starting to sound pretty good to me. What do you say to that?"

"Sure, why not?" Les shrugged as he slowly rose to his feet. Watching Karl walk away and realizing how uncharacteristic it was for his older buddy to come and check on anybody much less him, he called out, "Hey, Karl."

Turning to see what his friend wanted, Karl stopped.

"Thanks for coming down here to find me."

"Sure. Now come on."

Pivoting, Karl backtracked hopping rocks as he made his way easily across the jetties and down toward the beach and his vehicle. Les, with his shorter legs, moved more slowly through the cumbersome boulders as he followed. When he got off the rocks and onto the sandy beach, he made his way to Karl's truck.

II

Arriving back at the cabin, the two men found Wade dressed, packed, and ready to go. He was still angry with Karl for his deceit the night before. Even so, he had no intention of leaving Les there to endure Karl's obnoxious behavior all by himself.

As Karl walked through the doorway, his eyes met Wade's and the two men gave each other a cold stare. After he'd seen Wade's fishing gear packed by the front door, Karl said, "I take it you're going fishing today too, huh?"

"Yeah. I thought it might be best if I were out there to give Les some backup."

Karl smirked when Wade said this, then he barked, "All right, boys. Let's get something to eat. We need to get this show on the road."

Hurriedly the three scrambled through the kitchen cabinets and refrigerator throwing together a meal. Scarfing his down first, Karl stood up from the table and declared, "Okay, if there's something you need to take with you today, you better hustle and get it. We should've been over at the dock loading our boat thirty minutes ago."

"There's something I've got to get. Hang on a minute," Les said as he got up and hastily walked to his bedroom.

Calling from the doorway of the cabin, Karl goaded his virtuous friend to get a move on. "We'll be waiting for you out in the truck. Hustle up!"

Wade was smoldering mad at the way Karl was conducting himself. "Give him a break. A few minutes aren't going to matter that much one way or the other, Karl."

The doctor tauntingly shot back. "Why don't you just lighten up, loser? You don't know what the hell matters down here and what doesn't, now do you, hotshot?"

As Wade bit his tongue, Les came from the cabin carrying what appeared to be a duffel bag with part of his wetsuit hanging out of it and the same container he had taken on the boat during the previous day's trip. Placing the two articles in the bed of Karl's truck, he hurriedly climbed into the passenger side front seat.

Karl laughed as he watched him. "So I see you brought a wetsuit with you after all?"

"Yeah, I bought an old rental from Russell when we were in Steinhatchee on Friday. You two guys were too busy making good your escape to even notice."

"Well," Karl retorted, "The water this time of year can be a little chilly, but with the mild weather we've been having lately, I doubt you'll really need it."

"It's better I have it with me than realize too late that I needed one, wouldn't you think?"

"Probably so," Karl agreed as he drove down the road to Keaton Beach Marina. Fearful that they might run out of live bait, he wanted to stop by the place and buy some frozen Spanish sardines just in case. Karl pulled in behind the shop and parked where he would be closer to his boat. He went inside and soon returned with four boxes of the frozen minnows. "Here!" he said coarsely. He aggressively shoved the boxes into Wade's arms. "Put these down there where you guys had our fish stored yesterday. Then come on back up here and help us get these rods and reels and my electronics in the boat."

Chafed by his attitude, Wade glared at Karl sarcastically, "I'll be more than glad to, Doc."

Snickering as Wade walked away, Karl yelled, "And hurry your sweet little ass up every chance you get!"

Peeved at having to tolerate all of his crap, Wade carried the frozen bait down to the cooler. Soon, he was back at the truck where, only for Les' sake, he quietly helped them get the rest of the gear loaded and on board.

When they had finished, Karl drove his boat around to the landing by the Marina's lift where the three got out. Climbing up the metal boat ramp, they headed to a large outside icebox and began loading twenty-pound bags of crushed ice into two medium-sized coolers. Les and Wade carried the two ice chests down to the boat and unloaded them into the Contender's floor coolers. Meanwhile, Karl finished seating his electronics into each of their respective frames. With everything in the boat situated, he signaled Les and asked him if there was anything else that he thought they needed.

Looking around and seeing the air tanks in their holders along with their rod and reels and ice chests in place, Les queried, "We've got something to eat and drink in here, don't we?"

"Got all of that covered," Karl confirmed as he punched a few waypoints into his LORAN.

"Well, I guess we're good to go," Les called from the stern.

Hearing this, Wade, who was perched on the dock holding the boat in place, pushed it off and nimbly jumped onboard. Karl, who had kept the boat idling, backed the vessel away from the landing until he'd cleared the structure. Shifting his throttle into forward, he slowly swung his boat around headed for the channel.

Down the canal, the boat made its way passing the dock where they had moored the previous night. Past the Fisherman's Marina. Past some docked fishing yachts, and Keaton's small fleet of fishing and shrimp boats. Keeping the pace slow to avoid throwing up a wake, Karl rounded the jetties where, in an explosion of water, he gunned the motors wide open with a roar. Rapidly, they got on plane as the center console cut through the serpentine path of day beacons lining the channel. Observing from the stern, Wade noticed that cormorants seemed to like perching on these tall, signed pilings. Drying their wings in the morning sun, the birds were making ready for yet another day of fishing.

Out past the tripod, unexpectedly and just as suddenly as it had occurred on the previous day, Karl slammed his engines into neutral causing the craft to float drunkenly forward. Its following huge wake lifted the vessel upward momentarily as the massive wave went speeding just beneath the vessel's hull.

"How 'bout getting the gaff, Wade, and let's check these traps one more time."

Wade did as he was told, but showed little enthusiasm. Only one trap contained more than five fish. With these in the bait well and the gaff placed in an empty rod holder, Karl began the process of again setting the coordinates on his LORAN.

Looking back at the other two men, he spun his hat around. Wade and Les followed suit and firmly gripped the aluminum bracing of the boat's T-top. Karl thrust the throttle handle full bore and adjusted the power trim as he spun his wheel hard right. Wade from behind took note of his heading via the cockpits large floating compass. Lunging through the one to two-foot chop on this temperate, slightly overcast day, the boat raced offshore.

Karl, just as Wade had figured, wasn't returning southwest to their excellent fishing spot of the previous day. Instead, Wade saw the compass was pointing due west. They were heading right for the area Buck had told them to stay clear of. Wade gritted his teeth thinking of Karl's obstinacy. Hopefully, Wade thought, this day would somehow go smoothly. There was no need to cross that bridge of concern yet.

Scoping the shoreline as the craft's powerful twin engines pushed its deep "V" hull through the waves of the Gulf, Wade could see the boats of the flats' inshore fisherman dotting the seascape. He wished they too were fishing that area today. Then they could run down as far as the Fenholloway River or the Rock Islands and be heading home by 1:00 or 2:00 in the afternoon at the latest. Sighing, he realized he would have to endure at least two long boat rides on this trip. One out, and one back. But at least there were no storm clouds on the horizon or at least none so far, he thought. Wade was desperate for any kind of silver lining regarding their journey.

As they traveled into the endless horizon of the Gulf of Mexico, the water changed from a murky brownish green near shore to a more transparent green the farther along they went. When they truly found themselves offshore, the Gulf transformed itself once again into a brilliant clear display of aquamarine.

Making it to the half-way point of their trip, Karl abruptly shouted, "Look over there, guys!"

Peering in the direction he was pointing, Wade and Les could see a school of large fish cutting through a teeming bait pod as they ripped the water's surface in a frenzy.

"What do you think it is?" Les asked as he surveyed the churning spectacle.

"Could be Spanish. Possibly Kings," Karl asserted as he had slowed his boat to get a better view. Walking around and reaching above him for the rods resting in the rod holders on the backside of his T-top, he quickly said, "Les, look in that tackle box next to the transom over there and get us a couple of those giant Rapalas and a couple of Clark Spoons."

As Les did this, Karl handed Wade two of the poles he had gotten down and gave him two pre-made steel leaders that he had retrieved from under the cushioned seat of his captain's chair. Both had a swivel tied on one end and a swivel clip on the other for hooking the lure.

"Here. Tie these to the two big rods and put a Rapala on each."

As he handed Wade the wire leaders, Karl reached into the recess of the boat's starboard gunwale and pulled out two lightweight casting rods. Tying on heavy-duty monofilament leaders to these, he rigged the rods with Clark Spoons. Bumping the throttle slightly, he put the boat into a slow gear as he spun the vessel's wheel toward the continuously moving bait pod. Soon, he had the boat traveling in an area adjacent to the frothing school of fish.

"Hey, Wade," Karl called aloud. "You got those poles ready?"

"Yeah," Wade answered more excitedly.

"Okay, put one of them on each side of the stern in those inset rod holders. Let one of them out around forty yards. The other—thirty or so."

"All right," Wade said feeding line from one of the larger Penn reels holding a large minnow-like Rapala.

Karl handed Les one of the smaller rod and reel sets telling him to let his lure ride around twenty yards behind the boat and to try to make sure it didn't get tangled with the other lines Wade was letting out. He stressed for them to check the drags. "Loosen them up some. We've had to tighten them down for the grouper, so those big Penns need to be loosened a bit. Not yours, Les. Those spinners are set just right."

Karl cast the last Clark Spoon rig out of the boat on the opposite side from Les. With his other hand, he steered trying to quietly run the lures along the edge of the teaming school of baitfish without spooking them. From time to time he, Les, and Wade could see a streaking wake and a ripping splash as one of the massive predator fish would hit the shoal. At times it appeared that the whole bait pod was under attack, as the Kings or Spanish would rifle their way through the school en masse. Zips and zings of shooting, splashing fish hit the bait from almost every direction.

"Fish on!" Les shouted as one of the heavier rods bent double with the line singing and spinning from its reel.

"Get him, Wade!" Karl bellowed.

"Got another one!" Les yelled as the line from his reel started crying.

"All right, you two morons! You better not lose those fish!" Karl taunted them laughing.

Noticing Wade reeling too fast, Karl immediately chastised him. "Slow down, Wade! Don't try to horse him in. Play him, fool. Play him."

With the fish taking more line on yet another run, Wade rolled his eyes as he grinned at Karl.

Les had his fish almost reeled in and it was resting on its side in the water next to the boat. Karl leaned over the side, and with one swift jerk, had the fish gaffed and landed aboard. It was a good-sized Spanish Mackerel close to twenty-eight inches long.

Karl held the fish up as it dangled from his gaff, "Nice Spanish, Les, ol' man. Hey, Wade! Take a look at this thing."

Turning to see as he made his way to the front of the boat fighting his fish, Wade nodded excitedly, "Nice one, Les. Way to go there."

Karl cackled, "Hey, Wade? What do you think you got on there, sport? It's not another shark, is it?"

"I don't think so," Wade yelled back. "Whatever it is, it's got me walking all over this boat." Wade was heading down the other side of the center console where Les and Karl were standing. Just as Wade would reel in more line and seem to make progress, the sizeable fish would strain and pull making another line-letting run.

Having put the boat in neutral after their first hook up, Karl reached for the throttle once more to press the trim button to raise the props as close to being out of the water as possible. His move to do this couldn't have been timelier as the fish made another run, this time taking the line right under the stern. "It's got to be a cobia, Wade," Karl remarked. "They'll circle the boat over and over until you get them in. Can you see him yet?"

"Yeah, I see a huge dark shadow down there," Wade spoke grimacing as the strain of the battle was starting to take a toll on him.

Noticing Wade's fatigue, Karl laughed aloud. "Not going to throw in the towel on us, now are you, Mr. Muscles?"

Wade glanced back at Karl and Les as they stood nearby grinning from ear to ear. "This bad boy can pull! I'm telling you, fellows. This thing's a horse." He started reeling harder as the fish seemed to be giving in just a bit.

"All right," Karl exclaimed. "Keep reeling him, now. Keep him coming."

Turning to Les, he said, "In that compartment in the bow, you'll see a billy stick just inside. Bring it back here. We're going to need it." Wade gave Karl a questioning look. "We've got to hit him in the head, Wade. When we get that fish in the boat, that's when the real fight will begin. He'll be thrashing around all over the place." He asked Les, "You guys caught cobia down in South America, didn't you?"

"Yep and you're right. That fish will own this boat if we don't crack his noggin."

"Okay, boys!" Wade announced. "He's coming up!" Wade began to reel harder as the fish made it almost to the surface. With Karl hanging across the port side gunwale with the gaff in his hand, the fish, seeing him, made another short run making the reel sing one last time. As Wade reeled him back up, he tried guiding the powerful fish where Karl could easily gaff it. Back and forth the fish swam under the boat as Wade struggled to get him closer to the surface.

Arduously working for two or three more minutes, Wade had the cobia under control and coming in Karl's direction perfectly. With one quick jerk of the gaff, the large hook hit its mark just underneath the fish behind its head. With a strenuous heave, Karl pulled the fish over the side and into to the vessel flipping and thrashing in all directions at once. It was raging out of control just as Wade's two cohorts had told him it would.

Reaching over, Les tried to pound the fish with the heavy stick, but this proved difficult as he carefully tried to avoid getting snared by the treble hooks still rattling and dangling from its mouth. Each time the fifty-pound monster would jerk and twist, Les would have to yank his club away to avoid getting hooked. Finally, Les got one good lick to the top of the fish's head, which slowed him down. With another harder knock, the cobia grew still.

Shaking hands and high fiving each other on their fantastic catch and teamwork, the three men stared down marveling at the enormous fish they had just landed. Karl was the first to speak up. "That's one hell of a catch, Wade! You probably don't realize it because you don't fish much. But that's a hell of huge cobia. Wouldn't you say so, Les?"

"Heck yeah! I've caught a lot of big fish off Peru on the Pacific that were different species, but as far as cobia go—that's a monster."

Wade peered down at the fish then at the now distant bait pod. "I thought that was King Mackerel attacking that school. I was surprised to see this thing when I got it to the surface."

Karl spoke up. "What was hitting that bait pod was large Spanish mackerel like the one Les caught. I don't recall seeing cobia attacking a school like that. Usually, they run in groups of three or four and love to hide under or around things like a buoy or a large clump of sargassum—sea grass. I imagine this big fella was just in the area when the school was hit by the Spanish and saw our lure."

"His bad luck, our good fortune, wouldn't you say, guys?" Les exclaimed beaming.

"I'd say so," Karl said smiling. "What say you two get him into the cooler while I get us pointed in the right direction."

Wade started to relax as the fun he was having with his friends mollified his anger and distrust of Karl.

"Where're we heading?" Les asked as he went to the cockpit where his older companion was sitting at the wheel.

"Going after those big grouper I showed you guys on the map at the restaurant with Buck, remember?"

"Yeah. Didn't I recall him saying that there might be problems in that area, though?"

Karl winced sarcastically. "What's going on, Les, is that those guys, like the bums we ran into over at Russell's place, are taking fish illegally. All they're trying to do is to scare off anyone getting in their way." Staring directly into Les' eyes, he continued. "You think those fellows would be dumb enough to really hurt someone out here and get the Coast Guard and Marine Patrol chasing them down? No way, Jose."

"Sometimes," Les said, "it might pay to listen to some of the locals, Karl. After all, they're the ones who live down here and keep up with what all's going on, you know?"

Ignoring him, Karl slowly wheeled the boat back to a heading of 260 degrees. Turning the bill of his hat backward once more, he told Les to hang on. It would be only another thirty minutes or so before he got them to their destination. Slamming the throttle forward, Karl showered down on his twin 200 Yamahas. Within seconds, he had the boat trimmed and barreling across the light chop of a mild following sea.

Wade, noticing Karl's heading from where he was standing, kept his eyes peeled for any other boats in the area. So far, none could be seen, much to his relief.

The air above was growing clearer as they rocketed across the waves. The clouds that had been present earlier were disappearing as the sun made the waters glisten all around them. As the ride became smoother and without the hull pounding over the Gulf's persistent chop, Wade made his way to the stern and took a seat on the transom. Almost falling asleep as they traveled, he was only kept awake by the chin of his nodding head hitting his chest.

By 10:30 a.m. and less than three miles from their destination, Karl slowed the boat. He then stood up and lifted the cushioned bench seat of his captain's chair. Retrieving a powerful pair of binoculars, he scanned the horizon in front of them.

Watching him, Wade asked, "You see something up there?"

Karl said nothing in response as he slipped the binoculars' strap around his neck and let them dangle to his chest. Bumping the throttle handle forward to gain a little more speed, but still staying slow, he kept heading the boat in the same direction.

Wade shifted his position to one of the support beams at the front of the console where he could also view what was going on ahead of them. Squinting, he could see a dark dot growing larger on the horizon as they traveled in its direction. Continuing onward, Wade could see that it was a boat and not some navigational device like a buoy. Other than that, he couldn't tell much else.

Karl once again reduced his speed and the boat almost came to a stop. Placing the binoculars to his eyes, he took another look. "Son of a bitch," he said in disgust as he held the lenses to his eyes.

"What do you see?" Wade asked in earnest.

"It's those assholes we ran into at Steinhatchee, and they're sitting right on top of our spot."

"Maybe we ought to get the hell out of here." Wade suggested strongly. "Those guys, especially that scar-faced Indian, are crazier than hell, Karl."

"Hey, this water doesn't belong to them," Karl scoffed. He continued surveilling their boat. "Strange though, it looks like they're trolling the way they're circling that area. I'd have thought that they'd been bottom fishing over there or running their long lines."

Les' interest piqued, "Yeah, if they were bottom fishing they'd be using electric reels and it wouldn't take long for them to yank in a boatload. I saw that done on the Pacific quite a bit. It's amazing how fast they can catch them."

Karl lowered his binoculars and considered Les' comment. "Over where you're talking about, there are more fish and they're much more concentrated. In the Gulf in this area, it might take stopping at five or six spots to load a boat. You'd spend most of your time hunting them."

"So, what are we going to do now?" Wade interjected realizing that these weren't the kind of people to be messing with.

Karl sat on his bench seat. "Well, right now they don't know who the hell we are. As far as they're concerned, we're just another boat offshore fishing and we aren't close enough to disturb them yet."

Les spoke up. "You think they've spotted us?"

"Oh, yeah. With the radar I saw in that boat, they've been watching us for quite some time."

"Boy, that makes me feel really good," Wade said as he watched the cruiser in the distance.

"Damn, Wade. You're still the worrier, aren't you?" Karl frowned at his dark-haired friend.

"Nah, I just have a better sense of danger than you do, Karl."

The doctor shook his head as he heard Wade say this. "If it makes you feel any better, in this slight chop, with this much distance between us, there's no way he can catch us."

Wade grinned and said, "That's what I've been counting on, Karl. If there's something I've learned on this trip—it's that this boat can fly. And that you know only two speeds, wide open and stop."

Karl and Les chuckled at Wade's accurate assessment of Karl's driving style.

Karl exited his seat and again took aim at the other boat through his binoculars. "Strange, strange, strange, fellows," he murmured as he tried to figure out what the other vessel was doing. "They still seem to be going back and forth around that area. Each pass a little farther out than the last for some reason." Pushing his throttle to the fore, Karl again slowly started moving toward the other boat.

Les took stock of what Karl was doing from behind the captain's bench seat. Wade also watched while hanging on to the T-top's starboard support beam. He wondered why on earth his older friend would want to get any closer to these creeps. Agitated by Karl's display of carelessness, Wade knew he had no control over what was going to happen next.

Wade could see the other vessel. It was the black and gray Rampage Express that had been docked next to the dive shop in Steinhatchee. On board, he could just barely make out two people, but Karl, examining it through his field glasses, could see much more.

Les, still standing behind Karl, inquired, "What do you see, Karl?"

Holding the glasses to his eyes as he spoke, Karl said, "Well, they sure aren't trolling. Apparently, they're just searching the bottom. I'd guess they've raped most of that area of fish and are trying to squeeze a few more out from whatever else is left over there."

Still curious, Les asked, "Do you see any floats in the area?"

Karl scanned the vicinity of the boat and the surrounding seascape. "No. Nothing." He paused reflecting as he lowered his binoculars and declared, "I'm like you on that, Les. I thought we'd at least see one large orange ball marking the beginning of their long line. But nothing's around there." Returning his field glasses to his eyes, Karl again began taking stock of the situation.

"How many people do you see onboard?" Wade asked squinting as he watched the boat.

"Well, I see our Indian, the captain . . ." Karl suddenly stopped in mid-sentence. From the cabin underneath the Rampage's deck appeared someone disturbing.

Wade called out, "I see three people on deck now. Who's the third one, Karl?"

Karl glanced at the third man knowing exactly who he was. "I don't know. I don't think I've ever seen him before." Karl saw that the boat's captain had captured the *Doc's Out!* with his own set of binoculars. Karl watched as the captain gave the glasses to the other man that had just come from below deck. Giving Karl's boat a good look, he lowered the binoculars then seemed to be in an animated argument with the captain. "Well, we've been spotted, boys. Might be a good time to make our exit," Karl said.

Wade thought, *Just great. Karl gets the picture that it's time to leave now that he's driven right up on 'em.*

"All right, boys! Hang on," Karl commanded. "We're going to take a course south-east then circle back around to a spot close to the one we fished yesterday."

As Karl spun the boat to 160 degrees and punched the waypoints into the LORAN, Wade made it to the rear of the vessel's console where Les was still standing. Scanning behind them toward the Rampage, Wade informed Karl, "Looks like they're heading our way now."

Hearing that, Karl whirled around to see the other boat. Sneering at Wade and Les as he got his vessel moving, he slammed the throttle all the way forward. Like a rocket being fired from a launch pad, the motors roared as the *Doc's Out!* jumped almost clear out of the water. The twin 200 Yamahas blasted the craft forward with only the bottommost edge of the deep vee's hull touching the small waves below.

Wade watched as the other vessel gave chase. As the distance between the two boats widened however, it finally turned away. After fifteen to twenty minutes of hard running at speeds of thirty-five knots, and with the black-hulled diesel long out of sight and at least ten to twelve miles behind them, Karl began to slowly make his turn.

As he swung his boat southwest to a heading of 200 degrees, he leaned close to Wade and remarked, "Well, I guess those guys didn't want to play after all."

"Oh, yeah," Wade responded with a grin. "They turned back almost from the get-go."

Karl laughed and said, "They knew they couldn't catch us in these light seas. So, they did all they wanted to do. Run us off their little honey hole. But hell, there probably wasn't much reason for us to fish over there anyway. They've probably yanked every living creature with gills off that bottom and then some. Screw 'em! At least we may have made them worry a little about being reported."

Wade sighed with relief glad to be away from that particular area of the Gulf. Leaning over toward Les, he spoke loudly, "Well, I think it's about time for some lunch. What do you think?"

Hearing this from behind the wheel, Karl shouted at his two friends, "Hell yeah. Too much driving and not enough fishing, boys. I'm hungry as hell. One of you guys hand me a sandwich from that cooler with the good ice."

As Karl reduced his speed, Wade went to their clean ice chest. From it, he retrieved one of the pre-made ham sandwiches they had purchased at the Marina.

"What do you want to drink, Karl?"

"A bottle of water will be fine. They're down in the bottom there somewhere."

"How 'bout you, Les?" Wade asked.

"I'll take a cola with mine, thank you, sir."

As the three men ate, Karl slowed his boat to trolling speed. He turned on his depth finder never wanting to lose the opportunity to find a new, good place to fish or dive. As he searched the bottom and ate his sandwich, he looked up and noticed Wade staring across the stern at the northern horizon. "They're not coming, Wade, so quit your worrying," Karl said with confidence. "If my radar was working, I could show you that those bozos back there are nowhere in range. Unfortunately for us, however, that dumb ass Benny that Betty hooked me up with to fix it has it totally messed up. If it had been working yesterday, we could have dodged that thunderstorm completely or at least come back in before it slammed us."

Wade knew Karl was lying. His poor attitude from not catching many fish the previous day, meant he had no intention of returning home until he scored a large catch or somehow caught the most fish. Staying put the day before and flirting with that storm was, for him, like easing up to those maniacs on that other boat or hiding on their boat to get their LORAN numbers back on Friday—Karl enjoyed pushing things to the edge. It was whatever it took for him to win no matter the danger or consequences involved.

Still viewing the seascape as he took another bite of his sandwich, Wade rebutted Karl, "I'm not worrying, but you never know what crazy fools like that'll do."

Karl gave his boat mate a disgusted sneer. "Still ever the scared little chicken shit, aren't you, Wade?"

"Screw yourself, Karl! And the horse you rode in on!"

Karl laughed at his friend's brashness, "Say, when did you become such a little bantam rooster, Wade? You know, since we've been down here, you've been on my ass the whole damn time. I mean right in my face."

"Hell, somebody's got to keep your tail in line, Karl. Take ol' Les there. I bet if you ask him he's probably been praying for your sorry soul every day we've been down here, especially with all the crap you've put him through yesterday."

Shaking his head, Les eyed the two men.

Hearing Wade say this, Karl began evangelizing to Les, "Is that true, *my good brother*? You don't think the *Lo-ward* is disappointed with ol' Doc's behavior, now do you, preacher man?"

As the free-spirited captain was right in the middle of dogging Les, the boat's depth finder started making loud beeping sounds. Standing up, Karl focused his full attention on the machine to see what was appearing beneath them.

"Hey, boys! This might be interesting!"

With a sudden thrust coming from his engines, he almost knocked Wade and Les to the deck from where they had been sitting in the stern. Spinning the boat around in a circle, Karl attempted to go over the same spot once more. With the vessel traveling more slowly, Les and Wade were able to make their way again to the T-top's bracing where they could hold on. Karl switched on his depth finder's graph paper function.

Carefully, he drove his boat on the course where he thought he'd seen something unusual below. Suddenly the machine began to beep once more. This time, however, Karl was able to punch the exact spot into his LORAN as a waypoint. Driving across the place a few more times and from a couple of different angles, he ripped off the graph paper, which was feeding out of his machine and studied it.

"Hey, Les, take a look at this," Karl said showing him the long data-filled paper. Pointing at different areas, he said, "You see there's mostly sand all through this area, then a little live bottom, but no structure showing up. No slopes. A real flat bottom—then *this*."

"How deep is it here?" Les asked.

"Close to fifty feet," Karl replied as he peered at the screen.

"You don't think it's a sunken boat down there, do you?" Les queried.

"I don't know. It could be, or it could be where somebody dropped something off to attract fish. They do that around here sometimes, but it would have to have been pushed off a pretty nice size boat gauging the size of it."

When the other two men quit scrutinizing the paper, Wade picked it up and gave an assessment. "It looks too small to me to be attracting much of anything, guys."

"Give me that!" Karl scolded him as he snatched the graph paper from Wade's hands. "What the hell do you know about attracting fish out here? It doesn't take much at all down there to get them congregated, you dumb ass!" Pointing to the paper as he showed Wade, he exclaimed, "It's flat as a flitter on the bottom for miles and miles in any direction from here."

Not taking offense, Wade said, "Well, considering the structure I saw on the graph of the bottom we were fishing yesterday, there just doesn't appear to be much down there in comparison."

Holding Wade's gaze, Karl retaliated, "You just don't get it, do you?"

"Get what, Karl? That there's a little piece of junk down there not worth fishing around."

"No," Karl erupted. "In an isolated place like this, there's going to be some nice fish around any structure down there, you moron."

"Nice fish?" Wade laughed. "What are you talking about—a two-pound pink mouth grunt?"

"You're so full of shit, Wade," Karl said as he stood up from his chair once more. "I'll tell you what. Why don't you go get the anchor and drop it overboard and I'll dive down there with my spear gun and prove to you that there's big fish down around that thing? You're such a dumbass," Karl exclaimed as he went to retrieve his gear.

"So you want me to go be your anchor boy after talking to me like that?" Wade paused momentarily, "I don't think so, pal."

Karl leered at Wade in exasperation. "Okay, I'll tell you what. I'll go get the anchor and you drive. We'll see if you can park it right on top of that spot, hotshot. Think you can handle that?"

"That suits me, Karl."

"Hell, Wade. You don't know the first damn thing about driving a boat, now do you, sport?"

"All you've got to do is turn the motor on, push the throttle a little, and turn the steering wheel. It ain't exactly rocket science, Karl. If you can do it, hell anybody ought to be able to do it," Wade said with a smirk.

Dismayed by Wade's attitude, Karl became even more agitated. "Listen, Wade. I'll give it to you that you can probably drive this thing. But I've got to set the anchor with respect to the wind and current so we'll be right on top of that structure down there. If I ask real nice, would you mind taking care of the anchor for me?"

"I might."

Incensed, Karl shouted, "Dammit, Wade! What the hell have I got to say—*Please?*'

"That'd be a good start," Wade retorted with a wink at Les as he went to the front of the boat to take care of the kedge.

Grimacing, Karl faced Les who was beaming with a wide grin.

"Karl, he's not the same wimpy little dude that we use to know, now is he?"

The doctor bared his teeth as he gave Les a cold, mean-spirited glare.

"He's fixing to cross me one too many times, Les, and it's not going to be a pretty sight when that happens. I mean it."

Les returned Karl's look solemnly without responding.

Seeing the stare coming from his friend's eyes, Karl's anger abruptly abated. Almost ashamed, he lowered his head. Wincing and trying to change the subject, he said, "You going down with me?'

Still staring at him, Les dispassionately replied, "Yes, Karl. I'm going down with you. It's always good having someone covering your back when you're down, right?"

Karl paused noting the tone in Les' voice, then he retreated to the helm.

With Wade's help, Karl coordinated the setting of the anchor and had the boat situated almost directly above their target.

Cutting off the motor, Karl gazed at Les who was standing in the boat's stern. "I'll bring you a BC and regulator. You got everything else you need?"

Les signaled to Karl that he did as he pulled his duffel bag from beneath the stern side of Karl's bench seat. From the bag, he pulled his mask, fins, snorkel, and booties. Then he retrieved his short-sleeved short-pants Neoprene wetsuit. Pulling off his t-shirt, pants, and tennis shoes, he stepped into his wetsuit and pulled it up to his chest thrusting his arms down each sleeve. Stretching the Neoprene into place over his shoulders, he reached across his back and zipped the suit up.

Karl walked toward Les. He was wearing a full-length black wetsuit, hood, and gloves. His black-framed mask and snorkel hung loosely around his neck. In each hand, he carried a buoyancy compensator and a regulator for each of their tanks. He also brought a spear gun.

As he made it past Les and Wade, he put these items down in the rear of the boat. Unlatching one of his large black eighty cubic foot tanks from its mount in the stern, he slid one of the buoyancy compensators onto the vessel strapping it onto the unit's backpack. Next, he popped the valve open for a second, closed it, and seated the regulator into the tank's valve O-ring where he hand tightened it into place. Attaching the low-pressure inflator into the buoyancy compensator, he opened the tank's air valve completely then screwed it clockwise a quarter turn. Taking note of the unit's dual console with its depth and concomitant pressure gauges, he checked the tank's air pressure and pressed the button to the BC and regulator to make sure that they were working properly.

Satisfied that everything was good with his gear, he inspected Les, who had put on his booties and gloves and was wearing his blue-framed mask and snorkel riding high above his eyes on his forehead.

"Except for your air, looks like you're good to go, sport," Karl called to him. "Let me get this last tank and BC put together and we'll be off."

As Karl worked on the second tank, Les went and sat on the starboard gunwale.

"You got a dive flag, Karl?" he asked.

"A damn dive flag? Are you kidding me, Les? Look around. There's nobody within twenty miles of here."

Les smiled at the busy outspoken skipper.

"Well, if the boat shifted or became unanchored, it might not be a bad idea to have something showing where we went down.'

Karl gazed at Les disgusted. "You're starting to worry me. Starting to sound like your nervous little friend there." Saying this, he nodded at Wade who was standing at the console studying the monitor of Karl's depth finder unaware of what was being said.

"I'm not worried one bit, Karl," Les said flatly. "If that doesn't bother you, it certainly doesn't bother me. Are you sure you got everything ready?"

Karl studied Les curiously as he stood up having finished the second tank. "You ever seen me when I wasn't prepared, Les?"

"I don't know, but I suppose we'll soon find out."

Karl scoffed at Les' remark. Reaching down, he lifted one of the outfitted tanks and with one flip over his head, the unit was positioned perfectly on his back. Wade made it to Les' side and was helping him get his buoyancy compensator and tank put on. When that was done, Karl told Wade to get each of them a weight belt from a latched box that was next to the remaining air tanks. He then instructed Wade to hand him the heavy belt and Les the lighter one. When Wade finished doing this, he noticed Karl sitting on the side of the boat pulling on his fins. Falling backward into the water, the doctor instantly disappeared.

"So much for a dive plan," Les proclaimed.

"How long do you think you'll be down there?" Wade questioned Les who was positioning his mask over his eyes as he had taken a seat on the side gunwale.

"With these tanks and at that depth, we can't stay down much over an hour and I imagine we'll resurface much sooner than that." Surveying the deck, he said, "Throw me my fins when I go in. Do you mind? They're over there by my duffel bag."

As Wade retrieved and brought them to where his pal was sitting, Les pulled his mask up to his forehead and looked at his friend.

"One more thing, Wade. You know you're depending a lot on that anchor down there to hold you in place. But by chance, if it doesn't, you may find yourself adrift. What are you going to do then?"

"I'll check the LORAN coordinates and drive the boat to where y'all are."

"And what if you can't get the thing to work, and that plan fails?"

Wade grew quiet as he pondered this problem.

Seeing his friend's confusion, Les grinned. "Well, I'll tell you what you'll need to do."

Wade stared at him questioningly. "Whenever you find yourself in such a predicament way out in some lonesome place like this, you put your faith in the only captain you can really trust, and you let Him lead you to your destination."

"Is that your sermon for this Sunday's service, preacher?" Wade chuckled.

Les gave him a wink and placed his mask over his eyes. Holding it and the regulator in one hand and his gauges in the other, he fell backward over the side of the boat and down into the water below.

As Wade watched, Les momentarily vanished. From the aquamarine abyss surrounding him, the young minister pressed the button to his buoyancy compensator where air was pumped immediately into its jacket. Almost instantly, Les popped back to the surface.

Wade tossed his partner's dive fins down to him. Never taking his eyes off of his struggling pal, he watched Les as he laboriously wedged each flipper over each of his stubborn booties. This done, he rearranged his mask and placed the regulator mouthpiece into his mouth. He made eye contact with Wade once more. With his fingers circled, he gave his buddy the okay sign. Releasing air from his BC, Les disappeared under the small lapping waves of the Gulf of Mexico as he went in search of his obstinate friend.

CHAPTER 32

Fishing the Bottom

As Les started his descent to the seafloor, he realized that some water had crept into his mask. Letting his fins fall below him and bumping the button to inflate his BC slightly, he agilely slowed his downward progression. Gazing upward and exhaling through his nose as he pressed inward on the top of his mask, he instantly cleared the water.

Unlike the crystal-clear waters of the Caribbean reefs where he had dove before, the environment around him appeared murky green, more like the waters of the Peruvian Pacific. At this upper-level stratum, he found the range of good visibility to be about forty to fifty feet. This distance was hard to discern as he was encompassed in a vista of wavering shades of sunlit green mixed with a more subtle haze of blue.

Holding his nose as he cleared his sinuses once again, he spun back downward headfirst. Using several more kicks from his long black fins, magically and suddenly, he saw the bottom of the Gulf come into focus. Scanning the sand reef biotope beneath him, he quickly realized how fast he was moving. Not seeing Karl, the anchor rope, or any sign of the object for which they were searching, Les calmly looked at the compass he was wearing watch-like on his left wrist. Setting his bearing southeast and straight into the tide's strong current, slowly he began to make his way.

Swimming just above the seafloor with his arms resting motionless along his sides and using slow wide kicks, he headed back in the direction from which he'd come. Making his way along the beds of crushed white shells and sand lying below him, he sporadically began to see evidence of what Karl had described to him as hard bottom. At first, the appearance of this came in the sighting of an occasional limestone rock. As he progressed onward, an abundance of small fish could be seen swimming in and around these slight stony outcrops.

Through the blurring, moving haze in the distance, Les could finally make out Karl swimming around and tugging at what appeared to be a massive rectangular object. As he swam to the location, Karl turned to him and, throwing his palms upward, let Les know that he had no idea what he had found.

The whole thing appeared tightly wrapped in a dark-green colored canvas bound by black poly monofilament rope. The broken end of this cord was frayed and loosely hung as it dangled up and down in the tidal currents. This strange rectangular-looking object they had stumbled across was unlike anything either diver had ever seen. Rising at least five feet from the sea floor, it was maybe six feet long and five feet wide.

Les' first impression was that it was trash or some sizeable unwanted debris that had been dumped overboard by a large vessel here in the middle of nowhere. Exploring its exterior, he remained curious as to why someone would go to so much trouble covering it so tightly. Maybe it was hazardous waste they had under this thing, he thought. Rather than risk a fine or a lawsuit from not handling it properly, they just dumped it in this isolated spot. Considering what Karl had said earlier about the locals arguing over the disposal of some materials, this seemed to be a possibility.

As Les pondered this conundrum, Karl, who had secured his spear gun on top of the object, swam over and grabbed the rope that was wrapped all the way around the encasement. Pulling it as hard as he could, he couldn't budge the thing one bit. He floated in one spot by kicking his fins several times to maintain his position. Reaching down to where his knife was strapped to his leg, he pulled it out. Glancing at Les and indicating what he was about to do and with a couple of quick kicks, he positioned himself at the bottom of the tarp.

Karl poked the canvas, but his knife met with hard resistance. Feeling this, he began probing along the base of this one side of the object. Finding this whole lower level of the structure to be solid, Karl started to methodically poke and pry his way around it in a counterclockwise manner. As he eventually made his way to the rectangle's shorter width side, his knife finally pierced the cloth. Continuing to cut away the sheet from the bottom, Karl soon realized that whatever was inside had been placed on a large pallet. He peeled enough of the covering back to show Les.

In Les' mind and according to his previous assumption of a bigger ship dumping it here, this all made sense. They had taken a forklift, placed this thing on this covering, wrapped it securely, and pushed it overboard. The cover was tight purposefully to keep the contents from creating a debris field or slick which could easily be spotted from the air or by a passing boat.

Karl started carefully cutting the first layer of canvas off the structure. Noting that another layer was just beneath this first one, he was cautious not to probe his knife too far into the object's interior lest he open something undesirable. Like Les, he was also starting to believe that the material inside could be dangerous. Making an L-shaped cut along this corner and up its side, Karl pulled back a section of the first layer of heavy-duty cloth. Doing so again with the second layer as Les swam closer to observe, they both saw numerous similarly wrapped objects positioned tightly inside.

Sliding his knife between a crack where two of these articles were positioned next to each other, Karl pressed the flat of the blade downward to extricate one. Struggling, using his fingers, and with Les' help, they pulled one of them apart from its interlocked fitting.

Inspecting the thing as Karl held it in his gloved hands, each could see that it was around nine to ten inches long, the same length in width, and about four inches thick. Observing it carefully then peering over into the opened container, Karl gave Les the thumbs up signal indicating that they should resurface to see what it was. Nodding and giving Karl the okay sign as he watched him retrieve his gun, both men tapped the inflator buttons to their BCs and slowly ascended toward the boat above. Having been down for less than ten minutes, neither of the divers stopped to decompress as there was no need. More than excited over their find, both men burst to the surface full of chatter.

Wade, who was sitting at the console, hastily spun around to face them, completely caught off guard by their sudden appearance. "Y'all got one already?" he called out excitedly. Unlike Karl, he would rather see a big fish on the end of that spear than to be right about none being down there at all. Walking to the rear of the Contender where the two men had quickly drifted, he asked, "Where's he at?"

Looking up from around the vessel's twin set of motors where he was bobbing in the larger waves, Karl yelled to his dark-haired pal, "Hey! Catch this! It's heavy now!"

Karl slung the canvas-wrapped package over the stern as Wade caught it with a slight grunt.

"So, what's this? I thought y'all had a fish for me," Wade questioned his friends who were hanging onto the dive platform at the back of the boat.

"That's what we want to find out," Karl replied. "How about giving us a hand here?"

Agilely, Wade straddled the transom where a small dive platform jutted out from the stern's starboard side.

"Incoming!" Karl warned Wade as the taller diver threw his large fins over the boat's side. As Wade dodged the flying flippers, Karl handed Wade the empty spear gun and grabbed hold of his boat's small extendable ladder which was connected to the vessel's teak wood platform. Still wearing his tank but with his mask hanging around his neck, Karl placed his booted feet onto the ladder's one metal swiveling rung and pulled himself from the water. Immediately, Wade caught him by the hand and helped pull his weighted friend over to the deck. Karl took a seat on the transom.

"So, no fish, huh?" Wade asked, but not gloatingly as he reached down and collected the canvas-covered object from where he'd placed it earlier.

Noticing Wade do this, Karl called out, "Hey! Give me that."

Les was hanging on to the ladder as he tried hard to keep from losing his grip in the fast-moving current and swells. With his mask and snorkel once again riding high on his forehead, Les looked inquisitively as his older friend took the package from Wade's hands.

Glancing at Wade, Karl said, "Once we found this down there we quit hunting for fish." The object mesmerized the doctor. Examining it carefully, he was particularly interested in its heavy-duty machine stitching. Being a surgeon, this double row of stitches intrigued him as he knew a lot of care had gone into the process of packaging this article.

As Karl observed his find, Wade, who had taken a seat on the stern's starboard gunwale, impetuously blurted out, "Did you guys find what we saw on the depth finder down there? Or is this it?" Cackling, he laughed at his two companions.

Karl, however, was oblivious to anything Wade was saying or doing as he tried prying his way into the package with his dive knife. Unable to do so with this duller, bulky blade, he called to Wade pointing, "Look there on the side of my seat and bring me my filet knife. I'm going to need something with a really sharp point to get into this thing."

Retrieving the knife, Wade too had become curious about the object. Speaking out, he asked, "Why mess with the laces? Why don't you just cut the covering off?"

"I tried to, but all I can do is get my knife point into it," Karl responded. "It won't rip or cut. It's a much tougher material than what we were cutting through down there."

Wade gave Karl a puzzled look.

Les, noticing Wade's confusion from where he was still floating behind the craft, remarked, "We found this giant container down there, Wade, and that's what's packed inside it. There was a tarp down there that covered the whole thing. It must not have been as hard to cut through as what he's trying to go through now. That's what he's talking about."

Wade's expression immediately grew somber as Les told him this. Continuing to watch the doctor slice through the final stitches of the package, Wade agonized knowing what was about to be revealed.

Karl cut through the last strand of stitching. He had one end of the container completely opened. Reaching inside, he carefully removed a flat piece of steel. Observing the weighty object momentarily, he threw it over the boat's side then pulled out what Wade had so dreaded to see. It was a sealed bag of white powder. Not one, but three such brick size containers had been concealed within the large canvas pouch."

"Holy shit!" Wade exclaimed. "It's cocaine! Buck was right after all!"

"Damn, if he wasn't." Karl chuckled with an acknowledging smile.

"What the hell are you grinning about, Karl?" Wade admonished him. "We need to be getting the hell out of here right now! And as fast as we can! You know damn well somebody out here is trying to find that stuff."

"Calm down, bud. Who knows we've found anything?" He surveyed the horizon while sweeping his hand. "Not a boat or anything else out there in sight, worry wart. This is just our little serendipitous discovery. No one, and I mean no one, has a clue about what we've just stumbled on to."

Wade noted that it was true that there were no other vessels that he could see—yet. Still he realized the danger at hand. "They might not know where it is right this minute, Karl, but they're damn sure looking for that stuff. That's one thing you can count on." Wade paused as it dawned on him what was going on. With disgust written across his face and a little apprehension tempering his speech, he continued, "That's probably what those thugs were searching for back over at that spot you wanted to fish."

Karl chuckled, "Took you long enough to figure that one out, Einstein."

Wade gave Karl an incredulous look. "Hey! Wasn't it you who kept telling us that the only thing going on out here was some illegal fishing? Now all of the sudden you act like you knew about this whole scam—right from the start."

Dismissing Wade's angst, Karl scrutinized each brick of cocaine he was holding. "Nope," he countered. "I thought that it was just illegal fish those assholes were after too."

Just as Karl's mannerisms had appeared to be so lighthearted and laid back, suddenly, like the shades of a set of blinds being turned down, his demeanor began to grow dark and menacing. Staring at one of the cocaine bricks he was holding, he stuck his knife through the plastic of the vacuumed sealed bag. He swiped the blade with his finger and tasted the substance. Licking and smacking his lips, he called to his two companions, "No doubt about it, boys . . . it's the real thing." He paused momentarily. "Tastes just like what we used in the lab when I was in medical school."

"Yep," Wade exclaimed even more aroused. "And speaking of things that are real—we need to be getting the hell out of here real fast."

"Bullshit Wade! You little puss-ass coward! You always want to run and hide when the going gets tough, now don't you? Just like you did back at Russell's dive shop. You little dipshit."

"Russell's dive shop?" Wade blurted out enraged. "If I remember right, it was me back there facing down those guys. All you did was hide and sneak around on their boat."

"You damn right it was me out there on that boat! You wouldn't have had the balls to do that in a million years, Wade! You little puss!"

"I wouldn't have been stupid enough to do that, Karl! And now look where that's got us?"

"Damn, Wade," Karl said lifting his palms and shrugging his shoulders as he scanned the horizon once more. "Has it got us into any trouble yet?"

Karl glared at Wade. Chuckling, he looked down toward Les who was still hanging on to the ladder floating in the water.

"Hell, this is the only real fun and adventure we've had this whole damn trip. And all you want to do, Wade, is to run for the hills just when the fun begins?"

Wade, who was fed up with all that his older friend had already put them through, shook his head in disbelief. Smiling at Les, he then scowled at Karl.

"So, we're just now starting to have fun? Is that right, Karl?"

"That's right, Wade. Just like I told you before, there hasn't been any trouble, and there won't be any. At least not for us."

Cynically, Wade asked, "What's that supposed to mean, huh?"

"Well, like the Good Book says . . . you do unto others like they do unto you!"

Wade paused gazing down at Les astonished that Karl would even bring the Bible into such a discussion, but if it suited Karl's needs, anything and everything that would promote his cause was fair game in his mind even if he had to use the passage's meaning backward to justify his point.

Watching Les raise his eyebrows, amused, Wade shot back, "Okay, Karl. I'll bite. What exactly are you trying to tell us here? Is there something you're planning on doing to somebody concerning this coke? Is that what you're trying to say?"

Karl's gritted his teeth. "Those hotshots down at Steinhatchee on that Rampage thought that they were some real bad asses. Thought they could scare and intimidate us, now didn't they?" He paused. With a sinister grin, he said, "Well, now it's going to be our damn turn, boys."

Wade mocked him, "Our turn to do what, Karl?"

"Our turn to put the fear of God into their dumb asses! That's what!"

Wade couldn't imagine why Karl would even entertain such an idea. He scathingly responded, "And just what's your proposal for getting us killed by those psychopaths back there, Karl?"

"None of us are going to get killed, Wade, you little chicken shit. Now listen up and I'll tell you exactly how we're going to get this done."

Wade rolled his eyes and shook his head. He could hardly believe what Karl was saying.

Unfazed by Wade's response, the doctor continued, "You see, what we're going to do is to get all those packs of cocaine up from that pallet down there and onto our boat." He said this as if he were talking to one of the cocaine bricks that he was holding in his hand. He stared at it intently. "And then, when we get them all on board, we're going to take them back to a spot just north of Bonita Beach. I have a deer stand halfway between there and Spring Warrior that nobody knows about and you can only get to it by boat." Karl glared at Wade. "Right there is where we're going to bury this shit. All of it."

Silently pausing for a moment, Karl sorted his plan through his mind. As he did so, Wade smirked at his larger friend's plot disapprovingly while he surveyed the skyline for other vessels that may have wandered into the area.

Watching him, the doctor grew disgusted. "Loosen up, Alice. There's nobody out there coming to get you." He tossed the brick of coke that he was holding into the box where he kept his weight belts. Replacing his dive knife back into his leg sliver, he glanced at Wade and Les. "When we finish burying this stuff, we'll wait two or three weeks. Then we'll call the D.E.A. and the Tallahassee Examiner, anonymously of course, and give them the details on where it is and who put it there." A menacing sneer parted his lips as he told his friends his plan.

Frustrated, Wade still couldn't accept what he was hearing. That Karl could even concoct such a plan was outrageous. And all for what—to satisfy his humiliated ego?

Wade shot back, "Buddy, have you lost your damn mind or what? Don't you realize what will happen if those guys catch us out here with their drugs. It would be hard enough to try explaining this crap to the Coast Guard if we were lucky enough to be caught by them first. And bury it? Are you kidding me?" Wade continued shaking his head. He was outdone with his older friend and couldn't believe he was even arguing with him about such a ridiculous idea in the first place.

Reeling in his emotions, Wade gazed into the cold, menacing stare of his larger companion. "All right, Karl. Let me give you a plan," Wade said pausing to gain his older buddy's full attention. "Why don't we haul tail back to Keaton Beach and call the Coast Guard to come and get this stuff? Then they can round up those fellas back on that other boat and put 'em in jail where they belong. How about that for a plan?"

Glowering at his dark-eyed friend, Karl was infuriated that Wade couldn't comprehend the vengeance he was trying to extract. "Get those assholes for what, Wade? They'd get off scot-free. Maybe a fine for some illegal fish they'd have on board. Then they'd lay low for a while, come back out here, and be right back in business. Is that what you want?" Karl leered threateningly into Wade's cold stare. "That tarp down there is holding a multimillion-dollar payday for some group of fools somewhere! Think of all the lives that'll get screwed over if that stuff hits the street. I'm telling you, Wade. They won't be back in this area if we get rid of it like I'm saying we should."

"Karl, they won't be back if the Coast Guard comes and gets it, and they know that the U.S. Government is patrolling these waters."

"Bullshit! If the Coast Guard gets it, those goobers' handlers will know it was a botched drop. Nothing will happen to those jackasses over on that boat. Doing it my way, it'll look like they stole it for themselves especially if we let it be known to the Feds and the press that they were the ones who buried it there. A contract will be put out on their skinny little asses and in less than twenty-four hours . . . chop, chop. Their little heads will come right off." A wicked grin covered the doctor's face.

Wade replied, "Is that what this is all about, Karl? Getting even with those guys? Is that it?"

Karl scowled defiantly. "You damn right it is! They won't know what the hell hit 'em when I'm finished sticking it to their little asses! It's on now, baby!" he yelled angrily. Still glaring into Wade's eyes, but more subdued, he tried justifying himself. "Sons of bitches like that deserve to die. They're the scum of the earth. They hurt innocent people."

Wade had heard enough. Walking closer to the Contender's stern, he leaned across the transom. Watching intently for a positive signal from Les to pull anchor and leave, Wade called out to his missionary friend, "What do you think?"

Les turned loose of the boat's ladder momentarily as he started floating freely away from Karl's craft.

Impassively, he responded, "You guys have to make that decision for yourselves."

Les' answer momentarily caught his passionate artistic friend off guard. Wade, only a foot from Karl's face, spun around glaring at the surgeon. Through gritted teeth, he sternly said, "I say we leave! The sooner, the better!"

Their eyes never shifted as they stared each other down.

Karl snarled back, "I say we stay. This is my boat and I'm the Captain here, sport."

"Well, Captain! You're an idiot! You know somebody's probably going to get hurt if we do this," Wade said heatedly.

Karl broke into a steely victorious grin knowing that once again he had gotten his way. Shouting over his shoulder, he said, "We're going back down, Les! Hang tight!"

CHAPTER 33

Landing the Catch

Retrieving his fins and repositioning himself on the starboard gunwale, Karl noticed his dive partner had made his way back to the boat's ladder. "Hey, Les. Let's go see what our chances are of bringing that whole thing up. We'll only stay down for a minute. I think it could save us a lot of time unloading if we could get it back up to the surface in one piece. What do you think?"

Les nodded in agreement.

Karl slid his mask and snorkel over his face. Placing the regulator in his mouth, he abruptly flipped backward into the water.

Soon he and Les were once again observing the canvassed object. Taking his knife, Karl cut the cloth away from the forklift openings at the bottom of the pallet but saw no way to connect anything there. Realizing that the black ropes surrounding the object might suffice as something to hook to, he followed them, pulling to see how secure they were. He stopped at the top where all the cords crossed. Motioning with his hands, he showed Les how to run the anchor rope under the cables where they could use the winch to pull it to the surface.

Les gave Karl the okay signal letting him know he understood. The two men then pressed the air button to their BCs and effortlessly rose to the surface. As they emerged and slid their masks up, Karl said, "I'm going back aboard. You stay behind the boat until we get things ready. Okay?"

Les nodded as he paddled his fins to hold his position. Breathlessly, he replied, "Gotcha."

Once more, Karl climbed the ladder to his dive platform. This time, however, Wade was not close by to greet him with a helping hand. Laboring from the swiveling rung of the ladder to the small teak dive deck, he was finally able to pull himself up. As he worked gaining his balance, he removed his tank and set it to the inside of the stern. Free from the heavy cylinder, Karl easily stepped over the transom to the deck, and while pulling his black Neoprene hood away from his head, he made his way to the console. Glancing aft and making sure that Les was clear of the boat's propellers, he cranked the engines.

Calling back to Les, who was trying to maintain his position in the water, Karl yelled over the rumbling motors, "Les. We're going to pull the anchor up enough to drag it over to the pallet then I'm going to give it some slack. What I want you to do is to go back down, and once I give you some loose line, tie it onto those cords like I showed you. Give it a couple of good jerks to let us know that you've got it secured."

Karl paused and studied his depth finder confused. "Hold on a minute, Les!" Stopping, he let the boat drift since he couldn't see the pallet on the screen. Bumping the throttle slightly, he turned his vessel more northeastward. Not finding it in that direction, he spun his wheel reversing course. Driving slowly, he hawked the monitor for what it was showing him below. Finally, he spotted his prize. Punching its position in as a waypoint and taking a compass reading relative to his anchor line for a heading, he put the engines in neutral and let the Contender drift. As the anchor cable grew taut and the boat came to a stop, he noted the current had shifted them fifteen yards from the pallet. Studying his compass once more, he now knew approximately the angle he wanted to slide his anchor to hit his target.

"Okay, Les!" He called out to his younger buddy who was still struggling to remain stationary against the powerful current. "Hold on now. We've got to get the anchor up enough so I can slide it over to you. Okay?"

Les gave Karl the thumbs up that he understood as he continued pumping his fins.

"All right, Wade!" Karl shouted to the bow of the boat where his cohort stood facing the Gulf. Karl jovially bellowed commands as if he and Wade were both excited about attempting his bold plot. Nothing, however, could have been further from the truth. "Wade, I want you to pull that anchor up using the winch until it stops holding us. I'm going to give you some slack now, and after you pull in fifteen or so yards, we'll let the boat drift back to see if it catches or not."

Karl checked on Les and, making sure that he was out of the way of the growling motors, he pressed the throttle forward heading his vessel toward the anchor. As he did this, Wade used his knee to press the "on" button to the winch making it purr as it started reeling in the line.

Wade stopped the machine at what he thought was fifteen yards. Karl, hearing the droning electrical engine stop, shifted into neutral and let the boat drift to see what the anchor would do. Once more, its rope rapidly grew taut as the grapnel caught. Almost instantly with this shorter stretch of line holding them, the craft's hull was pounded by the ensuing waves.

Seeing this happen, Karl drove forward where Wade, for a second time, tried reeling in more rope, but to no avail as the anchor still held firm. After several more attempts with the same result, they gave up. The anchor was hung. It must have found the only rock structure in miles of this seemingly barren place, but regardless, there would be no sliding the anchor back to Les.

Realizing their dilemma, Karl yelled, "Okay, Wade, this ain't working. I'm gonna try pulling us off whatever's down there from the other side. Hang tight."

Wade remained stoic giving Karl no response as he continued to face the front of the boat in the opposite direction. In what seemed an instant, Karl showered down on the motors causing Wade to stagger until he regained his balance. Almost as quickly as Karl had shifted it forward, he threw the throttle back into neutral as he had swung the vessel due west then south to line the anchor just opposite its previous position. The path of the wide semicircle, to get to the other side, was Karl's attempt at keeping the rope from running under the craft and becoming entangled in his engine's propellers. With the alignment of the cord correct, he bumped the throttle gently forward where the anchor gave way effortlessly. Still giving orders from the console, he asserted, "All right, Wade. It's loose. Pull it on in. You've got plenty of slack now."

Using his knee to start the motor, Wade had the line reeling in, and just as the anchor's chain was about to climb over the pulpit's front pulley, Wade let the machine turn off. The weighted object swung freely just above the waves at the bow of the boat.

Karl shouted over the gurgling of his twin motors, "No need to pull that chain and anchor up. Just hold it there in place."

Spinning his stainless-steel steering wheel starboard and circling back around, he called to Wade once more. "Looks like Les has drifted on back a pretty good ways from us. Might as well pull that anchor on in and tie it off after all. When you finish doing that, check in the cuddy. I've got a black ski rope down there somewhere. We'll throw it out to him and pull him back over to the pallet. That way he won't have to swim so far."

As Wade begrudgingly did this, he opened the door to the cuddy. Peering inside, he could see that it extended well below deck and contained all sorts of marine and emergency equipment. There was also a bevy of fishing tackle and scuba gear. All well organized and precisely secured. In one corner, he saw a couple of spear guns in a stack of five-gallon buckets. One was the gun Karl had gone diving with earlier and that he had just replaced before they attempted retrieving the anchor. Wade shook his head as he saw the guns and realized Karl had lied to Les when he told him that he had brought only one with him. *That was Karl for you*, he thought, *always having to antagonize somebody else for his own pleasure.*

As Wade scanned the darkened area, he saw a .30-06 rifle equipped with a scope harnessed tightly to the pegboard siding of one wall by a series of short, strong rubber bungee cords. Why on earth would he need something like that way out here, Wade couldn't fathom.

Still hunting the rope, he saw another smaller anchor and chain on the cuddy's floor decking. Looking more carefully at it through the darkness, he finally saw what he was searching for: the neatly coiled ski rope that was lying beneath the anchor and its conjoined chain.

Reaching into the cuddy, Wade had to extend his body almost halfway down through the doorway to grab the black cord. Karl, who was not slowing down, was of no help. In fact, he was pounding through the waves more rapidly as he headed in Les' direction. Each time Wade would almost get his fingers on the rope, the boat would crash into another wave jarring him and causing the door to painfully slam into his back. Retrieving the rope, Wade made his way out of the hole. Walking past the console where Karl was driving and heading toward the stern, he declared, "Thanks for slowing down back there, pal. That door only beat half my ass off."

Karl gave Wade a devilish little smile. "Hell, Wade, you're in the best shape of us all. A couple of little love pats from that door shouldn't bother someone built as strong as you are, now," he laughed mockingly.

Paying little attention to Karl's jousting, Wade was shocked to see that Les had drifted more than fifty yards from where they'd left him. As Karl maneuvered the boat closer to his bobbing pal, Wade used the cord like a lasso and threw the handle end of the ski rope out toward Les. Watching to make sure his buddy got hold of it, he shouted, "Hang on, Les. We're going to pull you back over to the—" Wade cut his sentence short. He in no way wanted Karl to think that he was "into" his older friend's ridiculous scheme.

Tying his end of the rope in a looped figure eight around one of the craft's starboard stainless-steel cleats, Wade watched Les slide his mask and snorkel down covering his eyes and mouth. It wasn't a second too soon. Karl kept the boat at its constant rate of speed. The rope quickly tightened causing chopping waves to cascade over Les' face and head. Soon enough, especially for Les, Karl got him to the drop sight. Calling out, he told Les to let go as he threw the engines into neutral. Giving Les directions on how to tie the anchor and rope to the corded pallet below, Karl repeated the instruction to tug at the line to signal them to start winching the thing up. As he put the vessel into drive to maintain his position, he told Les that they were going to give him a minute to get situated before dropping the anchor.

Once again, Les gave a thumbs-up then released the air in his BC and dove to the bottom. With the pallet containing the cocaine right below him, Les wisely moved off to one side to avoid a head-banging encounter with Karl's anchor when his friends released it. He vaguely saw the boat positioning above him through the light reflecting haze. Through a shot of bubbles, he saw the anchor zipping downward, its rope trailing behind. As it grew closer, it suddenly flared sideways landing in a sandy area next to the pallet. Following it came the crackling, jingling sound of the connected metal chain. It fell with a clank partially covering the metal kedge. Seeing that the line to the anchor was slack, Les swam over and lifted it from the sand. He was glad it was made of lightweight metal. As he swam with it to the top of the canvassed pallet, he took stock of what he had to do.

He thought about what Buck had told them earlier. Everything seemed to check out with the former agent's story except that the black poly monofilament rope that he was dealing with had spooled itself around the width of the tightly held bundle. There seemed to be no sign of a float in sight either. Noting the frayed loose end of the line, he surmised that the floatation device must have been ripped off as the pallet hit the water. Passing the anchor, its chain, and a section of rope several times around the width of all of these black cords and pulling it tightly to make sure it would hold, Les signaled Karl to start the lift.

Wade was at the bow silently staring at the line below him. As he saw it tighten, loosen, then tighten again, he reluctantly turned around and looked at Karl. Unenthusiastically, he announced, "Les is giving you the signal."

"All right!" Karl sang out with delight. Swiftly he pulled the throttle back into neutral, no longer needing to keep any slack in his anchor's rope for Les below. "Hit the windless, Wade, and let's see if we can get that thing on up to the surface."

Wrapping the winch's roller with the rope once more, Wade again used his knee to turn on the motor. Stacking the rope, which was temporarily slack as it fed in from beneath the vessel, he watched as the boat was pulled forward toward the load.

Finally, the *Doc's Out!* came to a standstill above Les and the packages of cocaine. Pulling and tugging in the line, the hoist groaned as the front end of the vessel was forced downward into the water by the immovable freight. With the winch moaning pitifully with each subsequent reel of incoming line, the electric motor overheated and ground to a stop. With the boat's bow pulled perilously low in the water, the crest of a massive wave surged over the vessel's front-end soaking Wade, the deck, and everything else in sight with a lathering gush of foaming salt water.

Appalled by what was happening, Karl immediately switched on his two bilge pumps which began spraying water out from two holes located on each side of the stern. As this was occurring and as a load of water was being released from the scuppers located in the transom, another giant wave rushed over the front end. Angered by what he saw as Wade's complete ineptitude, Karl yelled, "Loosen the damn rope, you fool! It's going to swamp us! We're taking on too much water, dammit!"

Unknown to Karl, Wade had already loosened the rope from the motorized pulley, but to no avail. The cord on the second roller in the front part of the pulpit had slipped off to one side between its rubberized guide and the anchor's teakwood platform wedging the rope and jamming the unit's ability to roll in either direction. Yanking and pulling at it as hard as he could, Wade couldn't get the rope to come loose.

Seeing what the situation was, Karl came running to the bow through ankle-deep water. With a short iron pole in his hand, he jumped onto the vessel's fore and with all his might began prying the stuck anchor rope as he tried getting the line back up and onto its roller. After another large wave slammed into the bow causing another rush of water to surge across the deck, Karl set the jammed rope free. Immediately, the bow of the boat shot forcefully upward throwing a wall of water almost a foot high toward the stern, and along with it, Karl, who flew backward into the door of the cuddy.

As the bilge pumps and scuppers worked hard to drain the salt water from the drowning vessel's deck, Wade made his way back onto the bow. There he made sure he let out enough rope over the front roller to keep the front end from becoming stuck again.

Glancing back, he saw Karl grimacing in pain and holding his shoulder as he lay sprawled across the foot of the compartment door. "Hey, are you all right? Do you need some help?"

Defiantly, the doctor stood up stretching and trying to shake off the agony that pulsated throughout his body. "I'm fine," he shot back. "Obviously, that thing didn't budge down there. Now, I guess we'll have to go down and pull those packets up by hand. What a pain in the friggin' ass!"

Sighing heavily, Karl returned to the helm. Grabbing the wheel and hitting the throttle, he headed back toward Les and their contraband. Drawing closer, he saw that Les had resurfaced.

Smiling up at his diving partner, Les tried yelling over the metallic muffling of the motors. "I see y'all couldn't move it!"

"Yeah," Karl responded without telling him about the circumstance that almost got them swamped. "We're going to have to reset the anchor up above it again and rig up a way to bring those packets up over the boat's side."

"Okay," Les uttered breathlessly his mask now riding high on his forehead. "When I saw the slack in the line down there, I figured that you wanted me to untie it. It's loose now. You can bring it on back up."

Looking back from the wheel, Karl saw the ski rope still floating stretched out behind the boat. Calling back to Les, he told him to grab it and hold on.

As Les did so, and with Wade having already pulled in the weight, Karl studied his LORAN. Punching in some data, he slowly headed south, and after allowing a good distance of line to be let out, called for Wade to drop the anchor.

Watching his unhappy friend feeding out the line as the boat drifted back northwest, Karl called for him to tie it off to see if the anchor would hold. It dug into the sandy bottom below and held fast. Karl called for Wade to untie it again to let the craft drift back where they could get it to hover as close to the pallet as possible. Watching his depth finder, Karl had the container in sight and told Wade to finish tying the rope off.

With that done, and with Les already having returned to the bottom, Karl walked around his console and opened the cuddy. Reaching inside, he pulled out a downrigger and a large dip net. Walking back to the boat's stern, he mounted the large rod and reel-looking device into its pre-affixed set plate on top of the starboard gunwale. Fumbling through a wooden box which had held his weighted dive belt, he picked up a hand-sized metal cannonball and hooked it onto the steel wire which made up the line to his downrigger reel.

Without talking to Wade, who was curiously watching what his obstinate friend was doing from near the console, Karl tied three strands of 80-pound monofilament on three sides of the aluminum dip net. Lashing them all together at the top, he ran a double strand of this heavy-duty monofilament binding all the strands into one knot at the crown. Continuing, he ran this through a small circular opening located on the lower side of the ten-pound cannonball weight attached to the downrigger. The metal dip net dangled over the boat's side.

Looking across at the still stoic Wade, Karl started to talk as he took his air tank from its hold and placed it on the deck in front of him. "I'm going back down," he said staring hard into Wade's eyes. Turning the reservoir's air back on in one coordinated movement, he flipped the tank backward over his head and shot his arms through his BC jacket's sleeves. Having not taken his weighted belt off while out of the water, all he needed to do was to slip on his fins, hood, and mask, and he'd be ready to go. As he sat on the top of the starboard gunwale buckling his vest, he said in a mocking voice, "Listen up, Wade. I know you don't want to be out here—you little chicken shit! But since you are, and since you have no choice in the matter, you'll have to play this game my way."

A scowl swept across Wade's face as he heard the doctor say this. "Hasn't it always been that way, Karl? Your way?"

Karl gave Wade a cold disgusted stare but pretended not to be affected. "Now, all you've got to do, nimrod, is to hit that release handle on this downrigger and when you see it jerk you'll know you've got a load. Reel it back up as fast as you can, which won't be hard for a scared little mouse like you, and stack the packets up in here the best you can. Keep the stacks low or down in the floor compartments so nobody will see them when we head back to shore. Okay, Einstein? Think you can handle that?"

Wade was unusually calm as he glared back at Karl. "That's okay with me, genius, but what do you want to do if someone drives up?"

Karl scanned the horizon once more and seeing nothing said, "Worrywart. We're forty damn miles offshore! Nobody's just going to come driving up. Have you seen anybody around here since we got to this spot, huh?"

Wade looked back at Karl showing no intimidation. "Oh, it must have slipped my mind. I forgot. You're never wrong are you, Karl?"

Irritated, Karl shot back, "Listen up, Buckwheat. If we do this right, we'll have this done in less than twenty or thirty minutes. Then we'll all be heading back to shore where you'll be safe and sound, and you can powder up that soft little ass of yours. That sound good to you, sport?"

Wade grinned into Karl's masked face and mockingly said, "Hey. I know you'll figure out some way to screw this thing up. It's just gonna be a matter of time, Karl. Mark my words."

Shaking his head, Karl placed his regulator into his mouth and flipped backward over the side disappearing into a cloud of bubbles as he dropped below the waves.

Watching the water where Karl had just entered, Wade noticed the floating ski rope following his obnoxious friend rapidly toward the bottom. Soon it drew tight, straight down from the cleat where Wade had tied it off earlier. In retrospect, Wade hadn't seen him do it, but Karl must have caught hold of it at some point and carried it down with him. Begrudgingly, Wade had to hand it to the guy. He was an asshole, but Karl was a smart asshole. At least he had enough sense to carry the rope down to tie it off to the pallet so the boat wouldn't keep shifting off-site.

Wade realized he better get going dropping the weighted net contraption over the side. As bad as he hated to admit it, the plan Karl had concocted to get the stuff onto the boat was probably the most efficient method of doing it considering what they had to work with. Reaching over, Wade hit the release lever on the downrigger reel, plunging the weight and net into the water where it headed straight to the Gulf's bottom. It didn't take long once it was down for the net to be filled with dark green packets of cocaine. Within minutes, Wade saw jerks coming from the device's rod. Reeling as hard as he could, Wade realized this was going to be a much more challenging job than he had anticipated. The heavy cannonball in tow made the netted contraption come up even slower. After burning his bicep and forearm muscles from reeling, Wade had five packets of cocaine poured out onto the deck.

Letting the weighted net zip to the bottom again, he immediately started thinking of how to lighten this load. Scrambling to Karl's tackle box, Wade opened it to where he'd seen his older friend store his weights and pulled out two five-ounce sliding egg sinkers. Walking back to where Karl had suited up, he found the spool of heavy-duty mono that his older companion had used to concoct the carrying device out of the dip net. Before Wade could thread the line through the sinkers, the wire leader to the downrigger began to jerk. Reeling hard once more, Wade realized that he couldn't keep this up, especially since the reel's gear ratio wasn't adapted for this much weight. He felt every pound of material coming from the bottom seeming to double in weight as he pulled the load out of the water. Again, Wade dumped the packets out of the net onto the boat's deck floor. This time, instead of sending it straight back down, he unclipped the cannonball from the downrigger and tied the two five-ounce weights to the leader line instead. When Wade hit the release to the reel this time, the lighter weights slipped through the water's surface without making as big of a splash. The setup worked, and it was only moments before the line jerked indicating that he had another full load to land. The retrieval process was much easier with the heavy ten-pound cannonball removed from the rig.

Down below, Karl and Les worked diligently to separate the packets from the pallet. After stripping the canvas away, they found a set of interlaced bags. They were stacked tightly to keep them from shifting on impact when dropped from a fast-moving boat or high-flying plane.

Finding and cutting more binders used to stabilize the load made the process of getting the packets into Karl's makeshift net much easier. The question of how long the two men would have to stay down to complete this task depended on two factors. One was the maximum time they could remain at this depth according to their dive chart. The other was how much air they would consume during the process. With each retrieval of the heavily laden net, Wade's two friends below noted that his subsequent pull to the surface seemed to grow slower.

Onboard, Wade worked hard to get this ordeal over with so they could get out of the area as quickly as possible. Without wearing a watch, however, only Les and Karl knew that his time intervals for pulling up and unloading the net had grown from thirty to sixty seconds. It was becoming obvious that Wade was wearing out. At this rate, and with Les having only about fifteen minutes of air left, there was no doubt that the former missionary would soon have to resurface.

Surveying the deck as he waited for the signal to start reeling once more, Wade realized that he now had around sixty-five packets of cocaine semi stacked in the rear of the craft. Certainly, there couldn't be that much more down there, or at least he hoped.

As he scanned the horizon nervously for any sign of another boat, he noticed the height of the waves becoming significantly taller. A few random four to five-footers were starting to swell past the center console. Some of these even bore small breakers as the wind had noticeably picked up.

Breaking his gaze from the surrounding Gulf, he saw another pull on the line from below. Grappling with the reel the best he could, he tugged the load to the surface. Locking the reel's release in place, he then reached over and pulled the torturously bent aluminum-rimmed dip net over the sidewall. Emptying the contents of the netting onto the floor, he once again tossed Karl's net contraption over the side and hit the release to let it dive back down.

Using only the half minute or so he had between reeling, he started gathering the loose containers from his last load and continued filling the empty holds in the stern with as many as he could. When they were full, he started stacking the remainder across the bottom of the transom with the others he had already stacked there. The short chopping intervals between the Gulf's continuous waves made for a wobbly affair—rising one second, dropping the next. A wave hitting the boat at an odd angle followed by a lone cresting four-footer surging the bow upward and keeping him unbalanced was only adding to his anxiety and churning stomach. As he caught himself on the portside gunwale, he once more saw the yanking of the line from below.

Wade was struggling. The muscles in his tired right arm started cramping as he reeled. He concentrated his effort by focusing on each turn of the large, awkward handle until finally, he pulled the load out of the water. He locked the reel's release once more. Gazing over the sidewall of the *Doc's Out!*—he grew petrified. With a flash of panic overcoming him, he saw through the building seas the top of a cabin cruiser and its dangling antennas as the craft headed straight in his direction. Calculating the distance between himself and the approaching boat at a quarter of a mile, if not less, he became frantic. *Where the hell did they come from?* Wade thought. He hurriedly poured the contents of the beat-up dip net onto the floorboard. Trying to calm himself, he carefully walked across the dancing deck to Karl's console and retrieved the doctor's binoculars from underneath the bench seat. Focusing the lens on the vessel, he became even more disturbed. It was them. The black-hulled boat from Steinhatchee. He could easily make out the long-haired Indian sitting on the port side transom as the Rampage Express crested then plunged into the trough of the next large wave.

What the hell was he going to do now? He couldn't alarm his buddies because they'd surface right in front of these cutthroats. Grabbing Karl's filet knife, he rushed back to the downrigger hitting the reel's lock release button as soon as he got to it. Pulling out extra cable from the reel, he took the knife and with much effort, cut the device's steel line. Tying the loose end to the cannonball weight he'd used earlier, he headed for the gunwale. Without hesitation, he dropped the ball overboard in hopes that the guys below would know to stay put, that something at the surface was amiss. As he kept his gaze focused on the advancing vessel, he started unscrewing the reel's hardware from its metal plastic-covered mount. There was no way they hadn't seen him pull in that last load of packets.

With the rod unattached, he lifted the unit hastily carrying it to the cuddy and dropping the apparatus inside. Noticing that the black and gray cruiser was closing in on him swiftly, he saw it was only about two hundred or so yards off his port side bow.

Below at the pallet, Karl and Les had heard the motor of the other boat long before Wade had seen it. Instantly, they knew what Wade was trying to tell them from up above as they saw the downrigger's weighted cannonball zipping down behind Karl's rigged dip net.

Les had already run out of air and was having to use Karl's octopus-regulator to breath. Les also knew it wouldn't be the lack of oxygen that would get him if he stayed down much longer.

Karl started untying the ski rope from the pallet as Les swam alongside attached to him. Little did Wade know or little would he care to know that almost all of the cocaine had been brought up and was now on board. All that remained on the pallet was three packets and four layers of sacks containing nothing but lead shot. Buck had been right, Karl thought as he noticed the heavier bags.

As Karl finished untying the ski rope, he passed its handle to Les, who was still breathing on the extra regulator from his tank. Releasing his BC buckle, Karl pulled it and its attached cylinder off and motioned for Les to do the same.

As Les did this, Karl took his vest and tank, which still contained air, and placed it on Les like a person helping someone else get into their jacket. Buckling it up for Les, Karl adjusted his straps and tightened them according to Les' smaller size. He finished getting Les situated not a moment too soon. Karl saw the end of his anchor rope come floating down toward them. Wade had cut it off at the end of the pulpit. Almost simultaneously, Karl heard the sound of his engine crank. Reacting immediately to this dilemma, he motioned for Les to stay down.

Taking the ski rope back from Les with one hand while releasing his weight belt with the other, Karl discarded his regulator's mouthpiece. Blowing out a continuous stream of bubbles from his pressed lips, he made his way upward in a desperate ascent. Karl had to make a quick decision. He knew that he was close to having too much nitrogen in his bloodstream. If he had a tank, it would have been prudent for him to take a five-minute stop near the top to decompress. But as was usual with Karl, it was do or die time—full steam ahead.

Karl hit the water's surface just as Wade was starting to throttle the boat into gear. In Wade's haste, he didn't remember to untie the ski rope from the stern cleat. Karl's goal, as he wrapped a shortened length of this rope still connected to the boat around his arm, was to pull himself up to the extended ladder where he could then climb onto his dive platform.

Luckily for Karl, Wade didn't shower down on the motors as he didn't want to look like he was fleeing from the other vessel. As Karl struggled up the rope, Wade started playing with the engine's tilt to see which way he'd have to push it to get the bow to come back down on plane. The motor's propellers swung up to just beneath Karl's legs. Looking underwater through his mask as he was being pulled along, Karl saw to his horror the fast spinning blades coming up toward him at the surface. Terrified, Karl tried to straighten out his legs and fins so he could glide through the water as shallow as possible hoping that these whirling razors wouldn't slice him to pieces. Quickly, Wade figured out that he had pressed the tilt in the wrong direction, and just in time. Karl, to his relief, watched the spiraling props drop back down.

Swinging the boat starboard to angle across the oncoming waves as he'd seen Karl do earlier to gain speed, Wade throttled the motors. This gave Karl just enough slack in his rope to pull himself forward and gain a foothold on the swiveling rung of his boat's ladder. Determined, he dragged his body out of the churning water onto his dive platform. The roaring vibrating noise coming out from his dual set of 200 HP engines seemed overwhelming.

Karl was not in control of the situation, and he didn't like it, not one bit. Crouching forward, he tried balancing himself as he wrapped his arms around the transom. Struggling through the chaos created by the boat lunging through the obstinate waves, he slipped one leg then the other over the fiberglass wall of the stern and made his way inside the vessel where he stood up. Wade glanced back, startled by his friend's sudden appearance. He frantically yelled, "Get down, Karl! Get down! They're shooting at us!"

Karl hit the deck and crawled forward to take Wade's place at the wheel. He could see the bullet holes in his console and windshield made only seconds before by bullets fired from an AK-47. Hunkering down as he steered from the smoke-laden console, he could see bullets hitting the water behind him and to his side as he drove almost wide open in a bow-busting serpentine path.

Soon the boat from behind quit shooting but continued to stalk them. It had only momentarily slowed to more accurately fire on Karl's engines. As the high-speed chase resumed, Karl figured out that he must have gained enough separation from the other boat to put his vessel out of the accurate range of their weapons. Now, with the black-hulled cruiser accelerating its pace once again trying to catch Karl's Contender, he knew that their bumpier ride through these surging, irregular seas would virtually eliminate any more gunfire. That was only if he could maintain this distance.

Calmer, Karl took stock of the situation. He looked over his mangled electronics. His depth finder had been blown to pieces, and with a single bullet hole piercing his VHF radio, any attempt to communicate with Keaton or anyone else was impossible. Frustrated, Karl blurted out, "You didn't happen to get a mayday called out back there, did you?"

As Wade watched the boat trailing from behind, he shouted, "No I didn't, Karl! Everything just happened too fast!"

Karl shook his head then yelled in disgust, "You mean to tell me that you saw these creeps coming for us and you didn't even have enough sense to put out a call for help? Are you kidding me or what, Wade?" The roar of the fully throttled engines was deafening.

Karl's craft was blasting and jerking through the waves as the doctor tightly gripped his steering wheel. Wade, doing the same thing, held firmly onto the mounted stainless-steel handrail attached to the top of the console. Every few seconds they would pierce a wave sending a broad spray of seawater drenching everything on board that was not under the T-top.

Wade angrily responded as he struggled to hold on. "Listen up, Karl!" he shouted over the thunderous roar of the vessel's twin 200s and the blasting sound coming from the bow as it beat the seas. "I'm not the one who wanted to be out here in the first place! Remember, this was all your big idea! These guys weren't supposed to show up—right?" Wade paused a moment as he let his remarks sink into his older friend's mind. Sullenly, Karl focused hard on driving his galloping boat through the rough waters confronting them. Wade continued castigating Karl, who wouldn't even look in Wade's direction, "So tell me, genius! How's this big plan of yours working out for you now, huh?"

Intermittently as he steered, Karl glanced at Wade wild-eyed and outraged at Wade's accusatory tone. "You can just kiss my ass! You little chicken shit asshole! You're scared you're going to die out here, aren't you little prick?" Karl scornfully laughed as he kept the throttle to the boat pressed forward almost at full bore.

"Yeah!" Wade retorted as he looked back at the boat that was trailing them with no let up in sight. "Matter of fact, I am." With biting sarcasm, he shouted, "But I suppose you're not, right?"

Laughing with a menacing sneer, Karl yelled, "No! I've never been afraid of dying, Wade."

"Wouldn't have expected you to say anything else, Karl."

Ignoring Wade, Karl scrutinized his electronics tapping each of them. All but one, his LORAN machine, had been electrically fried by the bullets. Even though it seemed to work, the monitor flickered on for a few seconds then back off. Karl's expression grew dour as he noticed this. Noting that Wade was watching him, he hesitantly said, "This is our only path back to Les." Poking cautiously at the machine, he continued, "If it goes out …" He didn't finish his sentence.

Wade knew that there was no sense in chastising Karl for his actions any further. They'd have to work together now as they'd never done before to get all three of them out of this predicament. Considering this matter, Wade was not naïve. He fully realized that Karl, at his very best, was going to be a reluctant team player. After all, it had always been Karl's way or the highway. But this time, the most important time, Wade knew that things would have to be different. If Karl kept holding on to his old way of thinking, they wouldn't stand a chance. The contest they were in was already one-sided as they were confronting a boatload of murderous drug smugglers armed to the teeth with automatic weapons. Wade observed Karl who seemed more detached than ever. Trying to sound cordial, he asked, "So, what do you think we need to do now?"

Karl pensively clung to the wheel for a moment and then turned the vessel to a southeast heading.

Shouting over the continuous noise, he said, "We're going to have to circle on back to where we can hopefully find Les while my LORAN is still working."

Peering aft, he could see that the black-hulled boat had turned as well, following him in hot pursuit. Karl continued talking as he constantly kept the other vessel in view.

"There's no way we can outrun that thing in these seas. Even if we could," he yelled at Wade, "we still might lose our shot at finding Les."

Wade called back, "So, what you're telling me is that we hopefully find Les on this pass, pick him up, then haul ass out of here and back to Keaton? Am I right?"

"That would be our best-case scenario. My guess is Les came up after we left the area. But the problem is he might have drifted a half mile or more away from the pallet where we left him." Karl eyed the other craft which seemed to be gaining on them. "Our other problem is that when we stop to pick him up, they'll probably have a good chance of overtaking us." When Karl finished saying this, he was surprised to see Wade's calmer demeanor.

"Hey. You know we got some leverage over those guys, Karl. That cocaine back there should be our ace in the hole, wouldn't you think?"

Karl nodded in agreement as the boat twisted and turned as it landed awkwardly, angularly, and hard in the growing seas. Facing Wade and probing his eyes with a cool, icy stare, the doctor called out condescendingly, "So, what do you propose we do with that crap, hot shot?"

Wade thought a moment. "Do you have a gas can on board? Maybe we could threaten to set it on fire if they didn't back off."

"Threaten to pour gas on that shit and burn it?" Karl exclaimed while laughing out loud. "What's that going to accomplish? So, we set the boat on fire and then they shoot us as it sinks?" Karl shook his head in disgust. "No, nimrod! Fortunately, I don't have a gas can on board so you can burn up my damn boat."

"All right, Einstein, as you like to say. What's your idea?"

"I say we cut open a few of those packs and threaten to dump the crap out."

Wade gave Karl a quick smile. "I've got an even better idea." With that, he left the helm and made his way carefully to the front console of the boat. Staggering and being thrown to the deck repeatedly as the boat plowed through the uneven waves, he was able to unlatch the door leading to the cuddy below. Using every sense of balance he possessed as the boat lunged and rocked its way back and forth over the torturous waves, he climbed down into the darkness of this stairless compartment.

Once inside with the door to the console opening then slamming with each lunge and crash of the hull through the shattering waves, Wade's beating continued. Hitting his head and shoulders on the walls as the bottom would suddenly drop out from underneath him, he was finally able to retrieve the three 5-gallon buckets which held the spear guns. Dragging himself from below and onto the deck, he was slammed between the door and its opening more than once. Free and clear and with the cuddy's door latched, he staggered as he made his way back to the center console's T-top.

Once there, Karl noticed a stream of blood pouring from a long, jagged gash deep in Wade's left cheek. It had probably come, Karl surmised, from a bolt sticking through one of the pegboards he had personally mounted on the inner walls of his cuddy for binding things.

As Wade made it to the helm, he reached to the side and took the filet knife strapped to the end of Karl's bench seat. Continuing, he stumbled back to the vessel's stern.

Sitting down in this smoother riding area, Wade started taking the packets apart with Karl's sharp knife and began to unload their powdery contents into each of the large white plastic buckets he had brought to the rear with him. As he did this, Karl glanced back to see what his companion was up to, and after catching Wade's eye, gave his friend little encouragement for what he was doing.

Karl had the waypoints of the cocaine stash stored into his LORAN device. Its monitor, when it was working, read that they were about three miles away from the spot where he hoped he would quickly find Les. Contemplating getting him back on board, Wade worked hard and continuously filling his buckets with packet after packet of the drug runners' powdery contraband. In Wade's mind, the thought of the smugglers losing their precious cargo might just keep these thugs at bay until Wade and Karl could retrieve their pal from the sea.

At eighteen knots, the *Doc's Out!* beat its way up and down the rough, still growing seas in a grinding fashion. Apprehensively, Karl realized that with such wave heights surrounding them, it was going to be particularly difficult to find Les floating in them. With less than a mile to go, Karl called for Wade to head to the front of the boat and to retrieve the rifle from the cuddy. "If those bastards start shooting at us when we slow down for Les, we'll give them something to think about," he said with obvious concern.

Once again, Wade made his way into the cuddy of the speeding boat experiencing the same battering. Soon, he returned to the console with the loaded weapon along with several clips of ammo he'd found strapped tightly to the pegboard next to it.

Karl, looking at Wade, noticed that most of the blood had coagulated around Wade's facial wound. Only the deep gash seemed to ooze a bit. Impressed that Wade was not complaining, he called out to him, "Get those binoculars from behind the seat. Use them and try searching everything in front of us. East to West. We're heading north now. I'll try looking from back here."

Probing the vastness of the aggressive Gulf of Mexico through the set of binoculars in an erratically bouncing high-speed boat proved near impossible for Wade. But no matter what it took, no matter how dangerous it was, Wade was going to find his best and closest friend. Anchoring his thumbs to his cheeks to steady the glasses, he scoured the seas—hoping for a contrast in color or the glinting shine reflecting off the metal of some part of Les' scuba gear.

Karl took note of the discouraging obstacle Wade faced in trying to still the field glasses enough to get a good view of the water. For once, Karl became downhearted, as his expectation of finding Les dimmed with each passing minute. Being chased along with the deteriorating weather conditions made the odds of rescuing their pal minuscule. Karl, unlike Wade, was an experienced seaman and knew the direness of the situation at hand. Coming out of this temporary funk and trying to sound upbeat, Karl called to Wade, "Okay, we're now about one hundred yards from the pallet. Keep your eyes peeled."

With the wind from an unforeseen front turning more toward the northeast, Karl kept Wade focused in that direction. Wade scoured the Gulf where the water met the sky and back, but there was no sign of Les.

The LORAN kept beeping as they crossed over the pallet's location. Karl swung the boat leeward and into the following sea. Manically, he worked the throttle as he powered up the face of each wave then straightway backed off the gas until the wave dissipated. Cutting his course at an angle to let the waves from behind roll under him gave Karl a fighting chance against the twin-engine diesels of the Rampage, which had been riding hard on his tail.

With the change in direction and with a smoother ride going with the waves, Wade was able to move back to the front of the console. Leaning on the cuddy's large door, and holding part of the T-top's frame, he had a much easier time scanning the water where they hoped Les had drifted. Just as Karl was putting some distance between his boat and the drug runners, he pulled his throttle back into neutral. With the waves coming from behind them, the *Doc's Out!* slowed then lunged as it rode partially down the crest of a large wave.

Wade was thrown off balance by Karl's sudden maneuver. Regaining his equilibrium as he struggled to get his footing, he turned back to Karl and the other craft to see what had happened.

Immediately, Karl demanded, "Come here! Give me those glasses, Wade!"

"What are they doing back there?" Wade queried as he went to the helm to hand over the binoculars. He saw that the other boat had made a sharp turn northward and seemed to be idling.

"I don't know," Karl said concerned.

"You think they've found Les?"

"Not hardly. It's too close to the pallet. Matter of fact, that might just be what they've found with their depth finder. You know, with their radar, they already had its coordinates when they found us parked on it back there. As for Les, he should have drifted a good way from that spot. I'd say probably at least a half a mile. Maybe even further."

As Karl said this, Wade now understood the reality of their predicament. He thought that Les would have somehow figured out a way to stay close to the pallet. Thinking back and remembering how far Les had drifted when he was at the surface as they were trying to set the anchor, Wade became downhearted. Feeling the deep troughs of the waves rise and crest under their boat, Wade tried scoping the windblown, white-capped, horizon for their friend. What was up one moment would be down the next. It would be easy to miss Les when he might only be visible for a two to three-second interval. Finding his pal in these conditions was going to be much more difficult than he could have ever imagined.

As Karl looked through the binoculars, he could see that all three men aboard the other vessel were gathered on the portside gunwale positioned opposite from where he could see what they were doing. Aggravated, the doctor declared, "I can't see what they're up to, Wade! I know they didn't just stop over there to take a leak!"

Studying the other boat, Wade asked, "You think they might have found one of those sacks of cocaine floating up from the bottom?"

"Not a chance," Karl shot back. "There were only three packets left down there and they were sealed tight. Besides those, the only thing left on that pallet was loaded bags of lead shot. I guess they used that to sink the load or whatever. But as far as those bags containing the bricks of coke are concerned, each one of them had a shank of flat steel in it. There was no air in 'em. You know how heavy they were. Whoever packed those things was expecting them to stay put."

Karl looked through his binoculars as he tried figuring out what the smugglers were up too. Pensively, he said, "Our stopping, has just shown them our hand, that we've got something out here worth hanging around for too. But good for us, they don't appear to be watching us right now."

Karl handed the glasses to Wade. "All right, hang on and keep hunting. We're going to start hauling ass again like there's no reason for us to be out here. I'm pretty sure that we'll find him along this line I'm taking," Karl said trying to sound confident.

Wade lowered the binoculars when he heard the doctor's plan. Solemnly, he asked, "What if we don't run into Les, Karl? Then what are we going to do?"

Karl stroked his chin as he surveyed the Rampage, which was slowly starting to head in their direction once more. "Well, we can't just go over the horizon and hide from those sons of bitches. They can track us with that damn radar system that jackass has for quite a way. If it wasn't for that, that's what I'd do," Karl said with disgust as he veered his boat away from the intruder and back in the direction from which he'd been running. "I guess what we'll have to do is to carry them back around on a couple of loops until we locate Les."

Karl noticed the sea's terrible conditions. Feeling helpless for the first time in his life, he bumped the throttle slightly to gain a modicum of speed. He scanned the deceptive maze of waves obscuring his view in almost every direction.

Suddenly and without warning, he erupted in rage. Slamming his fist down on his instrument panel, he shouted, "Damn these waves, you sons of bastards!" The whole dashboard shook, throwing what was left of his already destroyed depth finder vibrating from its mounting to where it bounced clanking along the deck below. "If he just had a damn flare or anything he could use to give us a signal. Dammit!" Trying to peer through his water-marked, partially shattered windshield, Karl yelled in frustration, "This is like trying to find a friggin' needle in a haystack out here. This is bullshit! Total bullshit! You hear what I'm saying, Wade?"

Karl gritted his teeth. He began to rub his chin nervously deep in thought. Wade saw the unmistakable signs of indecision pressed painfully across the brow of his older companion. Gone was that air of self-confidence he always wore. It was gone in his look, and it was gone in his voice. His eyes darting back to the other boat and then ahead to the water beyond, Karl had to decide on a different course: a course into an area with which he was unfamiliar—one that he had never encountered or ever even knew existed. He was being challenged to have faith and reliance in something with greater capabilities than those he possessed himself. Anxious and hollow-eyed, he called to Wade, "Keep looking! Keep looking, Wade!"

Karl once again showered down on the motors. In his mind, this was going to be the mother of all bluffs as he hoped to make the other boat think he was heading for the coast. Maybe they'd give up and leave as he could easily outdistance them while running in this leeward direction. If not, he would have to circle the area over and over until he found his pal. Would they take the bait and leave them alone? Karl was sure of only one thing—he'd soon find out.

With this move the ride became calmer allowing Wade to perch on the front door of the cuddy with his field glasses. He scanned the waters from due north all the way down to 180 degrees south.

The larger Express, with its crew of thugs, lazily puttered from behind. Suddenly, it came on in hot pursuit. Noticing the actions of the black-hulled vessel, Karl saw that it was giving chase just as he hoped it would. Outdistancing the bigger boat, Karl hoped it would drop off and let them go. If it didn't, this degree of separation would give Karl enough time to pluck Les out of the water without being caught. Of course, all of this depended on them being lucky enough to find him. "How 'bout it, Wade? You see anything we ought to be taking a look at?"

Lowering his glasses briefly, Wade called back, "Nothing yet!"

As both Karl and Wade searched the waters, Karl realized that somewhere along the way he would have to make his move. He recognized he had probably run past the longest distance that Les could have drifted. Going a little further to fool the vessel behind him into believing that they were leaving, Karl continued. But as he looked back, he could see that the other boat was not giving up.

Understanding he was going to have to show his hand, the doctor started moving north to his port side and running parallel to the waves which were rolling more in an easterly direction. As he turned at this location, he punched in his waypoint so he could keep Les' drift line between this spot and the pallet aligned.

Shocked, he noticed his gas gauge showed that he had already burned through more than half a tank of fuel. Karl quickly began to calculate. He wouldn't be able to continue looping this area for more than a couple of more times. Beyond that, he wouldn't be able to make landfall.

As if the matter couldn't become any more urgent, Karl was going to have to scale down the circumference of the laps he was going to make. After shifting north only moments before, once again, he had to rotate his heading even farther by angling his vessel in more of a northwestward direction to shorten the runs back through where he hoped to find Les. As he glanced back to gauge how close the other boat was trailing him, he was shocked to see that the thirty-eight-foot Express had altered its course entirely. Astonishingly, it had dropped back and was already heading due north, which would cut Karl off midway into his semi-circle.

Seeing them do this, Karl first thought they were backing off from the chase as he had hoped. Immediately, Karl spun his steering wheel hard right curving the boat to its starboard side as he continued his bluff back toward land due east. But then, much to his surprise, he saw that the other boat was turning too, heading straight for *Doc's Out!* once more.

After a hard three minutes of running at almost full bore and gaining little distance on the thugs behind him, Karl realized that with his gas running low he could no longer afford to play. He'd have to swing around and try for another loop immediately. This time, however, he would run south-southwest then cut west and try running in that direction as he circled back.

He boldly maneuvered his craft due south where he came perilously close to having his boat capsize as he angled across a wave too sharply. Wade, being the primary recipient of this unannounced turn, almost went overboard. Regaining his balance, he made it back to the helm where he once again clung tightly to the console's stainless-steel passenger handle. "What in the hell are you doing?" he scolded Karl.

"I thought they were dropping off back there. Whether they knew it or not they had me cut off when I tried circling northwest." Karl paused as he watched the twin-engine diesel behind them. "Look! They're doing it again and heading south now!"

Karl watched them for a few moments as his boat leaped through the water. Yelling to Wade who was standing by his side, he exclaimed, "They're onto us! I don't know how the hell they know what we're trying to do, but they're blocking us again. See?" He pointed at the other boat.

With his diving hood pulled away from his head parka-style, Karl stroked his blonde hair from front to back. Deep in thought, he began slowing his southwestward pace.

"Hey, Karl," Wade said as he noticed the other boat. "Slow down a minute."

Easing off the lever to his gas even more, Karl peered into Wade's eyes puzzled.

"They've got something dark hanging above their boat that wasn't there before. A flag or something. Slow on down and let me take a look."

With the other boat too far out of range for accurate gunfire, Karl drew the throttle upright into neutral giving Wade a chance to see what this thing was.

As Wade placed the binoculars to his eyes, Karl stepped out from under the console's T-top where he sighted the object as well. "It's probably a damn skull and crossbones they've got flying overhead. Sons of bitches!"

Wade said nothing as he held the glasses firmly in place observing the other boat. When he was through looking, he pulled the binoculars down, but without any expression.

"What is it?" Karl questioned him.

"Here, see for yourself," Wade said stoically.

Gazing at his friend curiously, Karl took the field glasses. The first thing he saw was a black short-pant wetsuit hanging above the cruiser like a flag. Scanning down to the deck, he could see that four men were standing at the stern instead of three. One was wearing only his underwear. It was Les.

Karl lowered his glasses as he stared at Wade. "Well," Karl sighed, "it appears they've got him, doesn't it?"

"Yeah," Wade responded. "I don't know how they could've spotted him when we couldn't."

"Doesn't matter now, does it?" Karl said as he viewed the Rampage through the binoculars.

"I suppose not."

Both men paused a long moment as they looked back at the other vessel.

Thinking that Karl was going to be more cooperative, Wade was the first to speak. "Well, I guess we're going to have to make a trade with this cocaine to get Les back."

As he said this and facing Karl, Wade noticed a curious transformation in his taller companion as the doctor peered through his field glasses. Chewing on something he had put in his mouth, Wade could see the blood vessels in Karl's temples starting to flare. The larger man was focused solely on one thing: the thugs on the black-hulled Express.

Karl lowered his binoculars. Wade could see that any semblance of the indecision he had noted earlier was gone from his formidable friend's face. In its place was the icy stare of defiance and an almost gleeful desire for the confrontation that they were about to encounter. Karl knew too well what had to be done in this situation. The components of this circumstance were running tantamount to his unbridled abilities. It was the fight portion of the fear syndrome. The adrenaline rush that he loved so much and for which he lived.

Wade could see that Karl was back to being Karl. Come hell or high water, Wade knew that this was what he'd have to be up against. The metamorphosis of Karl's conversion now complete, the strapping surgeon scowled at Wade with a deprecating grin. Mocking him, Karl spouted, "I suppose you think all we have to do is just pass that cocaine over to those clowns and they'll be all nice and sweet and just hand Les right back to us. Is that the way you see this playing out, Wade?"

Wade didn't crack a smile, as he quickly retorted, "No, that's not the way I see it happening at all, Karl." Pausing, he sullenly asked, "But, pray tell, how do you see it coming down, ace?" Wade turned away heading to the back of the vessel to retrieve the rifle where he had it stored in one of the air tank holders. From the weight box, along with the diving weights and another cannonball for the downrigger, he started picking out the gun's extra ammunition clips. He had stored them there to keep them from sliding around the deck as they plowed through the rough seas.

Incensed by Wade's insults and dismissive action, Karl followed his adversary to the stern intent on setting things straight between himself and his cocky little friend once and for all. Ignoring him, Wade gathered up the gun and its ammunition.

Rankled by Wade's indifference, Karl wanted to teach him a lesson. Scanning the deck, he could see that the buckets of cocaine that had been sitting there were nowhere in sight. Pissed off, he shouted at Wade in disgust, "What the hell did you do, you dumbass? Let our cocaine blow out of the boat while we were running back there? Dammit, Wade! You're such a friggin' moron! Do you know that? Do you know how stupid you are, you idiot?" Yelling this, Karl glared into Wade's face.

Unfettered by Karl's attitude, Wade stuffed the extra rifle clips into the pockets of his pants. "Look under your bench seat. Your tackle box is holding them there where I tied 'em in."

Glancing under his chair, Karl saw that they were there. Wade had even covered them each with black plastic garbage bags to keep the powdery substance from flying overboard. Unimpressed and still belittling the smaller man, Karl questioned him further, "Where'd you find those bags, slick? Steal them from my damn cabin this morning?"

Wade replied unflinchingly, "They were in the bucket with your spear guns. I see that you did have two guns, after all, Karl. What were you going to do—not let Les use one?"

Karl jeered at Wade, "Doesn't look like it makes much difference at this point, now does it?"

Solemnly, Wade eyed Karl shaking his head, reviled by the doctor's pettiness at such a time when their friend's life was at stake.

As ferocious and menacing as he could muster and within inches of Wade's face, Karl asserted, "You asked me how I see this thing going down, Wade. Well, I'll tell you how it's going down, hot shot. As usual, it's all going to be up to me. You're too damn stupid and too damn scared to be of any help. That's the truth. And you know that's the truth. Now isn't that right, Wade?" Pausing as he glowered nose to nose with Wade, Karl roared, "So, what you're going to do, Wade, is to sit your soft little ass down! Keep your big fat mouth shut! And do exactly what the hell I tell you to do! Or your little pal Les over there could die! Do you understand what the hell I'm trying to tell you, buckwheat?"

In a nanosecond, Wade gave his response.

WHACK!

With a jaw-jolting blow from the butt end of the rifle, Wade caught Karl on the chin sending him crashing headfirst to the deck. Just as quickly as Karl hit the floor, Wade was on top of him with the rifle barrel jammed under Karl's chin.

Karl didn't move a muscle as he came to his senses with Wade directly over him, his hot breath right in Karl's face.

Watching Karl open his eyes, Wade bared his teeth and began growling in rage, "Now you listen up, you dumb shit. Our friend is over there on that other boat because of your sorry ass. You arrogant jackass! And now your sorry tail is going to help me get him off that boat." Incensed, he whispered intensely but quietly into Karl's ear, "Do you understand what I'm telling you, Karl?"

"Yeah," Karl mumbled unconvincingly.

Angered by the bigger man's indifference, Wade clicked the gun's safety off as he jammed the barrel even harder under Karl's chin. Shouting, he exhorted, "Do you understand what the hell I'm telling you, Karl?"

"Yes!" Karl cried.

Still raging mad, Wade yelled, "I ought to blow your damn friggin' head off right here, you sorry piece of shit! You've got my best friend stuck over there! I ought to kill your ass right now! You hear me?"

"Listen, Wade. He's my best friend, too. If killing me would save Les' life, I'd say do it now," Karl pleaded. "But you're right. It's going to take both of us to save him."

Karl and Wade's lungs were heaving in and out as their contentious exchange left them both sucking in air as hard as they could. Wade, still peering down at his older companion, saw the grimace of agony resurface in Karl's face and eyes as the doctor considered Les perilous position.

Wade clicked the safety to the rifle back on and crawled off Karl. Standing as he held the rifle in both hands, he gazed back down toward the doctor and gently tossed him the weapon. Turning away, he went and sat on the port side gunwale where he placed each of his hands on its top to steady himself against the rolling seas.

Still smarting from taking the hard shot to the chin, Karl stood up. Carrying the rifle with him, he went over and sat down next to Wade with the weapon laid across his lap. At last and with such a huge obstacle standing before them, both men stared across the churning waters toward the dark vessel where their friend was now imprisoned.

CHAPTER 34

Setting Les Free

Time seemed to unwind in slow motion as the two unyielding foes gazed across the wind-blown, chopping waves of the late afternoon Gulf. Looming in the distance was the dark-hulled boat and Les. Without saying a single word, each fully understood the seriousness of their dilemma. Though it was unspoken, they had united and become a team.

After several long minutes of observing the Rampage, Karl stood up from the port side gunwale and handed the rifle back to Wade. Now more than ever, Karl realized the grit and determination Wade possessed. He knew that Wade would give it his all, even his life, in an attempt to rescue their good friend.

As Karl headed for the console, he called back over his shoulder, "Hey, Wade. We better start making our way over there. We want those sorry bastards to be the ones who have to react to us not the other way around. Come on up here with me and let's talk. We got some critical planning to do."

Wade walked to the helm where Karl had the boat in gear and was driving slowly through the building seas toward the Rampage. Looking at the other craft as they eased along, Wade asserted, "The problem we've got, Karl, is that they not only have Les, but they've got those automatic weapons on board. I might be able to take out one of those guys with this .30-06 of yours, but when the shooting starts, they'll probably kill Les immediately then blow us right out of the water. Might think that they could get to the cocaine before our boat would sink."

Nodding, Karl agreed with Wade's assessment. In a disheartened tone, he added, "But that might be exactly what we have to do, Wade, if it comes right down to it. Try to hit them as hard as we can before they hit us." Having veered off course, Karl spun his wheel toward the other vessel and headed upwind. Pondering the possible ways they could extricate their friend, he glanced at Wade.

"How about this for a plan? We can use my long gaff and tie all three buckets to it." He paused and winced then said, "It'll put you right in their gun sights you know, but if we set those buckets loaded with coke on top of our port sidewall with you holding the gaff to keep them from slipping overboard—they shoot you—they can kiss their drugs goodbye."

Karl watched for Wade's reaction then blurted out, "Listen up. I'll be glad to be the one to hold them there myself, but—"

"No, you're right, Karl. You need to be in charge of the boat. Matter of fact, I want to be the one to do it. They'd be crazy as hell to shoot me holding their multi-million-dollar loot like that. The only thing I'm concerned about here is how we trade this crap for Les."

Karl grew pensive as he crept his vessel across the waves toward the black-hulled boat, which was about a quarter of a mile away. Finally responding to Wade's thinking, he said, "Yeah, that's the whole enchilada because just like you said, once they get their hands on that stuff, there'll be nothing to stop them from killing us and filling this boat full of holes. Somehow, we've got to prevent that from happening. Got any ideas?"

"Not yet," Wade replied still eyeing their opponents up ahead.

"Well, keep thinking. We haven't got much time to figure this out."

Surveying the stern for his long-handled gaff, Karl realized it was probably still above them in a rod holder next to the other poles. Turning to Wade, he remarked, "How about taking the wheel and keeping us on a compass heading of about two-eighty. We want to keep to the southeast of them if at all possible. I'm going up top to get the gaff down and start rigging it up for our buckets."

Turning the steering over to Wade, Karl retrieved the metal pole and made his way to his tackle box. He pulled out three rubbery plastic grubs which were lures normally used for catching trout. With his long-handled hook, the same spool of monofilament Wade had used earlier, and the grubs which each contained an implanted hook, he made it to the transom. Sitting there, he tied the three soft lures to the left, right, and center of his pole. His idea for this design was to keep the fishing line from slipping off the slick anodized aluminum of the gaff's metal shaft once the buckets were tied on. Once he had this done, he went back to the rear of his captain's chair where he extracted the three containers of wrapped cocaine.

"Hey, Wade?" Karl called out in astonishment. "There must be thirty or more packets you got stacked under here."

"Yeah. That's all the powder that I could fit into the buckets. We probably don't need to let 'em see those."

"You're right about that," Karl acknowledged. "We might need those for a backup plan."

"My thoughts exactly," Wade responded as he kept steering.

Karl finished tying the buckets to the gaff. After a trial lift to see how badly the rig's metal pole would bend, he slid the three full containers of cocaine to the safer area of his stern where he secured them. Returning to the helm, he said, "The pole bent a little when I lifted it, so we've got to be careful. Matter of fact, when we get closer, I'll help you set them up on the side so we won't chance spilling any."

Wade nodded and said, "I've come up with a plan for the swap."

Intrigued, Karl looked at his friend. "Okay. Let's hear it."

As they discussed Wade's idea, Karl kept a constant vigil on what was happening on the other boat with his field glasses. When he saw the shirtless Indian with long black hair come up from below deck with an AK-47, Karl, who had control of the wheel, put his boat into neutral.

Seeing the danger they faced, both men decided it was time to get their buckets of cocaine situated. Sliding the containers to the portside gunwale, Karl and Wade carefully lifted the gaff and its holders to the top of the vessel's sidewall. With Karl holding the contraption steady, Wade slipped under the rod where he could keep the gaff and its buckets stable without any help.

Studying the Indian with his binoculars, Karl could see that their Latino boat captain was standing next to this vile, muscular, little man and was staring back at Karl's boat with his own set of field glasses. Karl quickly shouted, "Grab a handful of that coke, Wade, and let it slide back down through your fingers into the bucket so they can see it." Karl continued talking as he watched, "We want to make real sure that those bozos over there know who they're dealing with here and what could happen to their precious little powder if they screw with us." Snickering, he kept peering back at the Rampage. "Yep! That's right, you bunch of morons! It's sitting right here on top of our sidewall just waiting to fall, you sons of bitches. You better hold your damn fire if you don't want us to start dumping your shit overboard, boys."

Karl observed the Rampage's captain in an animated conversation with the Indian. It appeared that he and the shorter man who was throwing his hands up into the air and shaking his head violently were disagreeing. Soon the Indian headed below deck only to return moments later seemingly unarmed and empty handed. Russell, the dive shop owner that Karl had not mentioned seeing to his friends earlier in the day, came into view.

Making it to the helm, Russell hastily yanked the field glasses away from the Latino captain and gave the *Doc's Out!* a good look. Trying to show Karl that they were unarmed, all three men raised their arms in the air as they turned around in a circle. "No guns, my ass!" Karl roared with laughter. "They're three steps away from a gun probably in any direction. You can count on that. Can you see what's going on over there?"

Wade could make out, with some difficulty, what the three men on the Rampage were doing. "Yeah, I can see them turning around and all. But if they think we're stupid enough to think they're unarmed and won't shoot us . . ."

Karl continued to bring his vessel closer to the other boat. Contemplating their circumstance and what needed to be done next, Wade asked, "Hey, Karl?"

Wade's older friend turned back around to face him. "How about taking that scope off your rifle? If one of us has to take a quick shot, that thing's going to be more of a hindrance than a help. Especially with these big waves knocking us around like this."

Karl agreed as he turned and lifted his bench seat. Probing through several items stored inside, he retrieved a Philips head screwdriver. Reaching toward his filet knife, he lifted the rifle from where they had it slung with its shoulder mount hung across the knife's handle. He began dismantling the mounts and rings of the gun's scope. Watching him, Wade asked, "You seen any sign of Les."

"No. None." Karl replied. "They must have him below deck."

When Karl finished removing the scope, he again lifted his seat and placed it with all its components down inside the hold. Gaining Wade's attention, he said, "All right, I'm going to keep this thing . . ." he held the gun low and away from the prying eyes of the thugs, "down here on the floor between us. The last thing we want them to know is that we've got it."

Retrieving his binoculars, Karl once again inspected the black-hulled diesel. It was drifting nearer his vessel with the wind and current. "Okay, Wade, we're coming up on them. Remember, whatever you say to me out here echoes loudly over our motors, so they'll be able to hear anything you say if you don't talk quietly."

The Rampage was some fifty yards away as Karl glanced back once more to check on Wade. "Everything okay back there?"

"Everything's fine, Karl. We're good to go."

"All right then," the doctor responded cautiously. "Be ready for anything coming from these assholes now. I mean anything."

"Don't you worry about that. I'll be ready."

Karl gunned his engines until he was about twenty-five yards away from the other boat. Putting his center console into neutral, the two vessels drifted in tandem quickly heading back toward the east.

From the other boat, Pacón, the dark-skinned Indian, grinned maliciously when he saw Wade sitting on the side of the *Doc's Out!* Shouting, he exclaimed, "If eet eesn't our leetle freend from da Steen Hat Chee! So I see eets more dan de feesh you wanted from us you, fukkeen leetle a-hole!" He yelled while laughing sarcastically at his dark-haired adversary.

Wade shot back unflinching, "What I want from you is my friend! Where do you have him?"

Pacón sneered. "Hee's whar hees spose to be, you yelo skeened peese of sheet!"

It became obvious that big Russell was the overpowering presence and leader of those on the other boat. Placing his big paw on Pacón's shoulder, he hurled him backward as he pulled himself to the forefront of the group.

"Shut the hell up, Pacón!" Russell yelled back at the native. He didn't have much use for the impulsive, unpredictable maniac from Peru. Having him around hadn't been his call. Someone higher up the chain of command had saddled him with the imbecile.

Regaining his composure, Russell turned around and faced Karl on the other vessel. He began to bargain, "Let's cut to the chase here, Doc. You've got what we want, and we've got what you want. So let's say we make a deal here?"

Karl was uninterested in what his rival wanted. He had his own way of doing things, his own timetable. "So, tell me, Russell," Karl lectured his opponent. "How did you get caught up in this filthy little racket here?"

Russell smiled back knowing that he was being played. Nonchalantly, he replied, "At this point—does it really matter, Karl?"

Karl railed, "Yeah, I'd say it matters. Probably more so now than ever."

"Listen, asshole," Russell retaliated. "I'm not out here to gain salvation for my misdeeds. All I want to do is to get back what's ours from your boat. Do you understand what I'm saying, Karl?"

"So, Russell!" Karl paused as he faced the dive shop owner in defiance. "Tell me! Just how do you suppose you're going to do that?"

Wade realized that Karl had done just what he had wanted to do . . . rile up and put the astute dive boat captain on the defensive. Smiling to himself, Wade could see what was coming next.

"Pacón!" Russell yelled angrily. "Show these men our prisoner."

Immediately and with glee, the Indian went below deck. He reappeared pushing Les in front of him. Each of Les' arms were outstretched with his wrists secured by zip ties to a grouper rod. The rod rested on the nape of his neck and bare shoulders cross-like. With a hard shove from Pacón, Les landed face first on the hard deck at Russell's feet.

Struggling to rise, Les made it to his knees. Slowly regaining his balance, he made it up to his feet. Blood from his busted nose ran over his mouth, down his face, and onto his chest. Breathing hard through a bloody smile, he called to Karl, "I've been waiting on you, Karl—I knew you'd find me. Say, pal, you still love your little buddy, now don't you?"

Looking at his pale, blood-smeared friend, and trying not to show any sign that he was infuriated by the way Les was being treated, Karl called back, "Yeah, I still love you, man. But I'd love you a whole lot more if you hadn't let these assholes catch you. Why did you go and do a thing like that, Les?"

With his chest heaving, Les took in deep breaths as he tried answering. "Used the rope from the anchor and the pallet to stay just below the surface. Ran out of air at just the wrong time, I guess." He grinned back in Karl's direction.

As soon as Les got the last word out of his mouth, Pacón punched Les in the stomach dropping him to his knees. Les moaned in anguish. The handle side of the rod Les was strapped to scraping the deck, caused the preacher to topple. His arms outstretched, he lay flat on his back. Scowling at him and laughing wildly, the scar-faced Pacón suddenly had a momentary flash of recognition. Instantly growing quiet, the vile man then leaned over and spat in Les' face.

Seeing this happen from the other boat, Wade snarled, "Give me the gun, Karl."

Whispering back to his friend as he tried remaining calm, Karl said, "No, not yet, Wade."

Seizing this opportunity to get what he wanted, Russell shouted at his adversaries, "You guys want to play some more, Doc?"

Hearing him say this, Karl gazed stoically at Russell. He discretely leaned toward Wade and said, "Do this slowly, but start throwing one handful of cocaine at the time overboard until I tell you to stop."

Already angered to the nth degree, Wade started throwing the cocaine into the water as Russell and his crew watched.

Russell was outraged. Furiously he screamed, "Are you guys fools? What the hell are you doing over there, you dumbasses?"

Defiantly Karl responded, "Say, you want to play games, Russell! We can dump these three buckets of coke overboard before you can take your next breath, hot shot. Just let me know when you want us to stop."

"Stop! Stop now!" Russell pleaded.

Catching his eye, Karl nodded at Wade indicating for him to quit.

As Wade paused, Karl called to Russell, "All right. Now that we have an understanding of where we stand with each other, this is how we want this trade to go down."

Russell bit his tongue as he tried subduing his anger, "Okay, Karl. I'm all ears."

Karl continued, "We're going to drive off and put your cocaine out about a quarter of a mile from here. You drop our friend overboard with his dive suit and a life vest on. We can watch each other do this with our binoculars. Then you come and get your prize, and we'll get ours. This shitty little job that you're into will be our little secret. You'll never see or hear from us again."

Russell shot back, "That'd be a no go, Karl. We couldn't be sure that our coke would be there when we showed up. You could haul ass with your little wimp ass friend here and our coke. I know how fast that boat of yours can run."

Russell paused. "I say you pull over and give us our drugs right here and now. Your little friend here steps straight onto your boat. We part ways, and as you said, that's the end of the story."

Laughing out loud, Karl roared in response, "That way when you get your drugs, you could shoot all three of us with that AK of yours. I don't think so, Russell!"

"Hey. It's your friend's life we're talking about here."

"That's right, Russell. And it's your multi-million-dollar boatload of coke over here. Probably your lives as well—especially if you don't cash in on this crap. Right?"

Russell leaned back and secretly counseled with his two cohorts. Turning around to face Karl, he said, "I guess it's going to be who blinks first, Doc. If that's the way you want to do this."

Karl whispered to Wade, "Keep your eyes peeled. Looks like they've got something terrible up their sleeves now. There's no doubt about it."

From time to time during his discourse with Russell, Karl had to put his vessel in gear to keep his bow pointed at a right angle to the unrelenting wind as they floated east paralleling Russell's craft. Had he not done this, the front end of Karl's boat would have spun around with the bow facing the bandits' vessel. All the Rampage's driver would have had to do then was to hit the throttle to Karl's port side exposing Wade to being shot in the back and falling into the boat instead of overboard. Had such an opportunity arisen, Russell and his gang would have quickly taken advantage of Karl's mistake and opened fire.

Karl watched as Pacón reached across and swung the boom arm of the motorized crane from over the back of the transom to where it hung inside the stern. Hitting the release button on the winch-like device, he pulled out enough of the heavy-duty steel cable for it to hit the deck.

Heading to the mid-deck area behind the helm, Pacón opened a built-in cooler. Pulling out a couple of large bags of frozen Spanish sardines, he placed them on the floor. Retreating to the stern, he retrieved a white five-gallon bucket and filled it halfway with seawater.

Karl tried calculating what Russell and his misfits were doing. The Rampage had fallen back. It was floating more to the north and west of Karl's Contender. Karl saw it as an opportunity for him to gain access to his cuddy without being seen. Retrieving something he thought might prove useful later as he tried out-calculating Russell, he made his way back to his boat's helm where he then secreted the device on the boat's floor next to the rifle.

Just as he made it back to the wheel, he saw that Russell had the Latino captain put their boat in gear and turn it back to a course due west at a slow speed. As Karl watched, he saw Pacón taking bait out of his fish filled bucket and start cutting up the sardines on a rod-mounted cutting board located on the starboard side. Slicing three bait fish, cutting them into thirds with a single draw from his knife, he then flipped these bloodied pieces into the water to set up a chum line which would entice sharks among other fish crossing its path.

Seeing that he had no choice but to play his rival's game, Karl put his boat into gear to stay adjacent to the Express. Still watching curiously, he had a good idea what was going to happen next. Just as he had supposed, he saw to his horror Les was stood up and life vests were threaded down the protruding rod which was secured to each of his arms. When they got two flotation devices jammed up to each side of Les' neck and torso, they lapped several rungs of rope tightly around his chest securely tying these vests together.

Both Karl and Wade could see the confusion on their friend's face as the crew of the black-hulled vessel worked.

"Hey, Karl?" Wade whispered.

"Les' sugar got too low on the way down here, and he had that same look. He hasn't had anything to eat all afternoon. We've got to get him out of there and, I mean fast."

Karl responded, "I've seen him bring a box or something with him both days we've gone out. Do you know where he put it?"

"I think he might have put it in a compartment back there next to the clean ice cooler," Wade nodded toward the stern. "Why?"

Taking quick steps, Karl opened the hold and found a small thermos bottle in a zipped bag. Shaking it, he could hear that something was inside it, but it wasn't liquid.

Karl kept an eye on the other boat and saw that they had lowered Les into the water just behind the Rampage. With his feet bound securely by the steel cable of the winch, Les' bare feet were just inches out of the water. The orange life jackets kept his head and torso floating just above the waves.

Making his way back to his steering wheel, Karl straightened his boat. He quickly unscrewed the cap to the thermos to see what was inside. Wade curiously looked on.

Quietly, he said, "It's the Glucagon shot he uses to raise his blood glucose in an emergency. If I can get this into him soon enough, he'll be fine."

Russell interrupted Karl's conversation. "Hey, Karl! With all this bait and your friend's blood in the water; it won't be long until we start seeing some fins around here, wouldn't you think?"

Placing the powdered and liquid contents of the kit down behind his seat, Karl fired back, "If he's attacked you can kiss all this cocaine of yours goodbye, ol' buddy!"

Russell laughed in response. "Oh, they'll probably just mouth him a bit to start with. It'll give you guys plenty of time to hand those buckets over to us before they actually kill him. I'd hate to know that I was the one responsible for the senseless death of my good friend."

Karl injected the liquid from the prefilled syringe into a vial containing powder. When all the contents had been pressed out, he removed the needle from the vial's rubber stopper and began furtively shaking the mixture out of the view of those on the other boat. He sarcastically shouted back at the Rampage, "Talking about friends, Russell! You call those mullet-heads over there on that boat with you your friends? If that's who you think they are—then hell, you haven't got any friends, son."

Karl paused as he plunged the needle back into the vial stopper. "What does all this money mean if you don't have any friends to enjoy it with, say?"

Russell laughed aloud. "You let me worry about that, Karl. Your almost-naked shivering little pal down there is looking a little sickly already to me. It might not even take a shark to finish him off the way he looks."

Both Wade and Karl winced as he said this. They both realized that unwittingly the ringleader might very well be telling the truth.

Karl drew the vial's contents back into the syringe, recapped its needle, and secretly set it aside. With disgust, he watched Pacón cutting and flicking bait over the Rampage's sidewall. Intermittently, the Indian poured some of the smelly liquid from his bucket overboard. Never stopping, the longhaired savage continued his wicked work with unyielding precision. It wouldn't be long, Karl thought, until a shark was spotted.

As Karl intently watched the native toil, Wade, witnessing the same thing, whispered loudly to him, "All right, Karl. I think it's now or never. We've got to make our move."

Looking back at the Rampage, Karl paused momentarily to take in everything that was happening on the other vessel. He could see where the captain was. He could see where Russell was. He could see Les' head bobbing on the far side of the boat just out of the water. He also noted that the chum line had already attracted a line of seagulls and other smaller seabirds. Screaming and fighting with each other, the birds tried to steal a shiny piece of the cut fish bait from a gull that had been lucky enough to pluck one from the waves below.

Turning to Wade, Karl spoke, "Okay, this is what I think we ought to do." Wade, who was ready to get things going, nodded for Karl to continue. "I'm going to pull the boat forward at an angle to them where they can't see what we're up to. My plan is to take that spear gun I brought up from below to ward of any sharks I might encounter along with this syringe of medicine for Les. I'm going to position the boat pretty close to their course, so when I slip over the side, I won't have that far to swim.

Wade interrupted him, "We're out of air tanks. You can do that all in one breath?"

Karl peered down from where he was driving and spoke quietly, "I'm going to have to. We're out of regulators. We don't have any other choice."

"So, what do I need to do?" Wade intently asked.

"Well, my goal is to get Les cut free from that line they're dragging him with as quick as I can. We're going to put these buckets down between the helm and sidewall where the rifle is, and you're going to have to drive and cover me. Hopefully, at this angle, they won't be able to see us doing this. Like I said, I'm going to try to inject him with this shot as soon as possible."

Wade nodded in agreement. "Let's say we get Les cut free and I take out one of them with the rifle . . ."

Karl interjected, "You're going to have to shoot and drive the best you can to pick us up, Wade—that's about all I can say."

"Do we still have the ski rope out the back?" Wade asked.

"Nope. I pulled it in earlier, but that's a good idea. You can swing by, and I'll grab it. It'll probably be our best shot at getting us out of there."

Karl inspected the other boat seeing nothing much had changed. He stared back into Wade's eyes. The doctor had become very solemn.

"This ain't no sure thing, Wade, not by a long shot." He paused, looking down. "And just for the record . . . I want you to know that no matter what happens out here now, you were right about us leaving. I should have listened to what you were trying to tell me."

"Karl, that's water over the dam. You know where I stand. You know you can count on me totally—right?"

"Yeah. I know I can, Wade."

With a determined smile, Karl's gashed-cheeked, dark-haired buddy declared, "I think it's time, Karl."

"I think so too, partner." Karl's face lit up with a huge grin. "I say LET'S GET IT ON! WADE! BABEE!!!"

Revved up and ready, Karl reached behind the console and slapped Wade's hand giving him a high five. Then he thrust the throttle forward. As the engines growled to life, Wade, balancing himself, slid toward the stern where he found the ski rope.

On the other boat, Russell and Pacón, hearing Karl's engines roar, made their way to their boat's portside gunwale and watched in wonder at Karl and Wade's actions. Calling to his crewmates with bravado, Russell chuckled, "Don't worry about those fools, fellows. They aren't going too far. Not without their little pip squeak friend we've got dangling out the back of our boat." All three men howled with laughter. As the snickering trickled, everyone returned to their work except Russell. Worriedly, he watched the other vessel through his field glasses.

Karl had gotten the Contender to about eight boat lengths in front of the black-hulled craft where he had doubled the distance between the two vessels. Straightening it up, but still at a slight angle to Russell's cruiser, Karl pulled his throttle back to mimic the speed of his trolling opponent.

With the chopping wave heights still growing and Karl's vessel so far ahead of the Express, Russell and his compatriots couldn't see what Karl and Wade were doing. Wade had already slipped the ski rope overboard and, with Karl's help, had moved the cocaine buckets from the boat's siding to the portside console as they had planned. Wade placed the rifle on Karl's bench seat and took over the wheel.

Everything was working like clockwork. Karl, sitting on the deck next to the cocaine, told Wade to slow down to let the Rampage catch back up. This would give him a better chance of getting to the other boat on a single breath. Karl timed his move and closely monitored the oncoming boat. Satisfied that he was in close enough range, he pulled on his fins, placed his snorkel and mask into position, and climbed over the port side gunwale with Les' syringe and the spear gun. Holding the boat's siding with his forearm and letting his legs slide through the water, he took several deep breaths. Giving Wade a thumbs up to which Wade responded with his own, Karl disappeared down into the depths and under the boat.

Wade watched him drop out of sight. He reached back for his gun and chambered a cartridge while simultaneously clicking off the rifle's safety. Wade felt his body start to sweat and his heart beat faster. He knew that this was going to be it. There would be no stopping the show now.

Slowing down even more, Wade waited for Karl to surface. Russell on the other craft knew something was up. Pointing at Wade, he was yelling at his captain and Pacón in an animated and disturbed manner as all three gathered at the port side of their boat's helm. Just as Karl had predicted, they were all suddenly holding a weapon in their hand as their captain took a heading straight for the *Doc's Out!*

Karl surfaced at the Rampage's stern just in time to grab hold of his fast-fading nearly comatose friend. He was shocked to see the severity of Les' condition.

"Karl . . ." Les slurred when he saw his older buddy. "I knew . . . you'd show up."

"I'm here for you, Les," Karl said as he struggled to hang on with his left elbow wrapped around the cable attached to Les' feet. Karl held the barrel of Les' life-saving syringe in his teeth and his spear gun in his left hand as he tried cutting the cable securing Les' ankles with his other hand.

Sawing as hard as he could with the teeth of his dive knife, he saw only a few strands of the strong thick cable were beginning to break free. Not wanting to give up, Karl kept at it as he endured the up and down chops of the Gulf's waves slamming into him.

Vigilantly, he kept an eye on the boat's stern expecting the malicious longhaired Indian to return at any minute. Realizing he was getting nowhere fast in cutting his friend loose, Karl decided it would be best to go ahead and give Les his shot.

Taking the syringe from his mouth, he pulled the cap off with his teeth. As he rode up and down on the oncoming waves, he squirted a few drops out of the needle and plunged it into Les' right quadricep above his knee.

"My . . . shot?" Les garbled trying to speak.

"Yep. I found it for you, Les."

Almost unresponsive, Les smiled weakly.

Wade saw that Raphael, the Latino boat captain, had picked up speed and was quickly cutting the distance between the two vessels. The *Doc's Out!* was just about three boat lengths in front of the Rampage Express, but with Karl having aligned the boats closer for his dive, they were only around fifty to sixty feet apart.

With Wade pressing his throttle forward to make up the difference, Russell saw an opportunity as he commanded the other boat from behind. Not knowing where Karl was, but seeing that the cocaine was no longer on Karl's boat's side, he ordered his crew to exploit this advantage.

As they watched Wade regain the distance between them, Russell ordered Pacón to take out the motors of Karl's center console. With an eruption of gunfire from the Rampage's AK-47, Pacón was able to hit everything but the engines. The seas had become too rough to shoot accurately.

Wade ducked as the rest of the windshield and the back of Karl's bench captain's seat was blown to pieces. Thinking fast, he reached for a bucket of cocaine next to the helm. Pulling it up to the top of the gunwale, he started raking it out overboard as fast as he could.

Seeing Wade do this, the crew started firing shots straight up into the air to gain Wade's attention. Peeking from behind the bullet-ridden console, Wade could see once again that they had stopped their boat and were signaling for Wade to quit dumping the cocaine.

Still holding his bucket, Wade stopped ditching the drugs and put his boat into neutral. He tried with difficulty to open the storage compartment beneath the captain's seat. Finding it jammed from its hinges being blown apart, he was barely able to lift it enough to retrieve the binoculars. Looking back, he could see Russell throwing his hands up in the air seemingly in a disgruntled rage.

From behind the black-hulled vessel, Karl and Les had been given a welcomed reprieve from being pulled rapidly through the water. Hearing the blasts of gunfire and fearing he could soon be caught, Karl worked even harder to saw the cable in two. Even with this monumental effort, he had the twisted wire cut only about a third of the way through.

Keeping his eye on Les as he continuously worked, Karl could tell that the injection he had given him earlier was starting to take effect. His smaller friend was becoming more coherent.

"Karl?" Les called up to his masked friend. Trying hard to be heard above the grumbling noise of the boat's idling engines, he exclaimed, "If you can save yourself, do it."

"I'm not going anywhere without you, Les." Karl responded as he continued sawing as hard as he could. "That you can count on, ol' buddy."

Suddenly, as Karl pushed down hard on the unyielding cable and as he raked the teeth of his knife across it, a thought popped into his mind. The boat's plug.

"Damn, what was I thinking?" he thought to himself, mad for not considering this option earlier.

Glancing at Les, and with no time to elaborate, he said, "Les, I'm going down for the plug. Hang on."

Karl dove below the vessel's dive platform where he found himself at the bottom of the boat's transom between both of its unmoving propellers. There he saw the metal-fingered handle to the boat's plug partially sticking out from the hull. Removing it would possibly sink the craft or at least slow the boat down until the thugs on board realized they had a serious problem.

Reaching his fingers around the handle to the small inserted device, Karl thought he would have it out in an instant, but the metal T used to pull the cap out was bent. Besides that, the thing was jammed. After several knuckle-busting attempts to remove it with his hand and even after trying to pry it free with his knife, the plug held fast. Soon, Karl had to go back up to the surface for air. Immediately after grabbing a quick breath, down he went, hell-bent on removing the stopper.

Beginning to think that this might be the only chance they'd have to rescue Les, and with time running against him, he was not so sure he'd be able to cut through the cable before being caught. The plug, he knew, would have to be removed.

On deck, the three outlaw crewmates were gathered at the helm watching Wade in disgust as he held onto one of the large buckets of their cocaine.

"That little son of a bitch!" Russell spewed. "As long as he has our coke to play with—" He stopped suddenly. "I'd like to know where his pal Karl got off to."

Russell began searching the turbulent waters surrounding each vessel with his binoculars. Trying to find anything out there in the badgering slop, however, was fruitless and he knew it. He also knew that if Karl had tried to board his boat using scuba gear, he had been unsuccessful. There was no way that someone wearing all that gear could be lucky enough to intercept a boat going any speed and especially in these conditions.

"Fellows," Russell announced. "I think we can be pretty sure that we're now down to just one man over on that other boat. I think the bigger one, the one that I was talking to, tried to come after us underwater with a tank. That was a ways back, so he's gotta be a goner now. It appears now that we're down to just this one little prick." Russell paused as he stared at Wade through his binoculars. "This one weak little putz is all that's standing between us and our big payday."

Raphael cautiously reminded him, "He might not be as dumb a mon as you think, señor Russell. He deed make us stop shootin' at him—no?"

Russell gave Raphael a hard look and said, "Watch. I'll show you how we're going to break that little bastard's heart over there, Raphael. He won't be able to handle watching his little putz pal back there being beaten to death right in front of him. That I can guar-own-tee you, señor."

Russell eyed Pacón who was waiting with bated breath to get his hands on Les.

"Pacón! Fish our prisoner out of the water and let's get this day from hell over with."

Pacón gave out a loud fiendish laugh as he gleefully marched his way barefoot to the port sidewall. There was nothing the sadistic native enjoyed more than exacting cruelty on someone who was weak and helpless. This had become his renowned method of operation over the years, something that he prided himself on doing well. More importantly, he had concluded that the torture he inflicted more often than not got the result he wanted.

"Si, Señor Russell. Si." he exclaimed with excitement. "I weel fish de leetle shrimp owt of de see with dees nice long feeshing gaff. Eh?" Pacón reached down and retrieved a six-foot gaff.

Russell couldn't care less how he pulled their prisoner in as he lit a cigarette.

"Yeah, yeah. Whatever, Pacón," he said as he took in a large draw of smoke. He kept his eyes intently peeled for what was happening on the other boat.

Smiling with the long sharp hooked gaff in hand, Pacón tiptoed toward the rear of the vessel. Calling out hideously at Les, he tried sounding like he was calling to a little dog.

"Heere, leetle shreempy! Heere, leetle shreempy-shreempy! I comming to geet you!"

From the other boat, Wade could see Pacón heading to the stern with a gaff. Not knowing if Karl had made it to Les or not, he knew it would be up to him to protect Les from this madman.

Hurriedly, Wade shifted the throttle in reverse to get a shot at the crazed maniac. As he frantically tried making up the distance between the two crafts, and as water from the tops of the larger waves surged across the stern, he saw that he was going to be too far away and too late.

Aboard the Rampage, Pacón had snuck up to the rear of the boat where he crouched and dangled the gaff over the transom door. With the instrument's large sharp hook hovering just above Les' face, he tried tormenting his prisoner by wiggling the pole back and forth making sure Les knew what was going to happen to him next.

"Okay, leetle shreempy. I come for you now."

Pacón flipped open the door to the transom just in time to see Karl partially draped over the dive deck aiming the spear gun straight at and less than a yard away from his face. Smiling, Karl yelled, "Hey there, asshole!"

Luckily, on his last trip up from trying to loosen the plug, Karl saw the gaff sticking over the back end of the boat where he realized something bad was about to happen.

With a whoosh, the expression on Pacón's face was one of shock as the spear from the gun held firm to his head with the back of the projectile sticking out just below his eye, the fore point protruding from the upper back part of his skull. In a frozen moment in time, the squatting longhaired man did not move. Then, in one complete motion, he tumbled over. The point of the spear stuck deep into the fiberglass decking of the stern and pinned the evil man bloodily into place.

Russell and Raphael, the motors drowning out any noise from the back of their boat, didn't know what had just occurred. They had been curiously watching Wade who was rapidly driving toward them with his boat in reverse. Seeing that Pacón had been killed, Wade quickly threw his throttle into neutral as Russell and his Latino captain realized that Wade was not watching them, but Pacón.

Thinking that his plan was working, Russell turned around expecting to see Pacón with their prisoner. Instead, he saw his crewmate shot dead and pinned to the floor by a speargun bolt. Russell, still holding his 9mm, immediately ran to the back of the boat.

Karl had discarded his fins and facemask and lay crouched behind the transom on the dive platform. With his knife in hand, he was hoping luck would be on his side. When Russell leaned over the Rampage's rear with his pistol ready to fire at anything that moved, Karl reached up and grabbed his gun arm with one hand. Still holding his knife, he was able to point Russell's pistol away from him and take a swipe at Russell's throat with his blade.

Karl missed. Russell countered with a hard punch to the doctor's face causing Karl's booted feet to slip on the wet platform deck. Falling backward into the sea as a large wave rolled under the boat saved Karl's life as it temporarily threw Russell off balance. Regaining his position and with nothing but a clear shot down into the water where Karl could not escape, Russell leaned across the stern and took quick aim with his pistol.

Suddenly, a crack sounded from the other boat. Staggering, Russell stood up and awkwardly took aim again. A second blast echoed. His whole body jerking as blood started spurting from his neck, Russell fell over the starboard gunwale into the lathering waves of the rolling Gulf.

Instantly and in retaliation, a blast erupted from an AK-47. Karl watched Wade, who had just saved him and who was still holding his gun, duck down behind the Contender's console which was being shot to pieces. The *Doc's Out!* was now only separated by a mere ten yards from the black-hulled boat that Karl and Les were floating behind.

Strafing the console and severely damaging it, Raphael fired another blast at Karl's engines. Smoke and flames erupted from the starboard motor's hood as most of the bullets hit this engine.

Karl knew that Raphael would not leave the safety of his helm and chance being shot by Wade. He also knew that after observing the Latino in action, the man had no stomach for this sort of confrontation. Standing alone against the three of them and with no one providing him leadership, Raphael would cave.

Karl grew desperate. There was no doubt in his mind that the panicked captain was about to flee. With no knife to finish cutting the cable in two, Karl's last attempt at saving his friend's life would have to be for him to board the Rampage and try overtaking the well-armed Latino.

Karl placed one hand partially on the dive platform as Raphael put the boat in gear. Instantly, Karl's grip was broken. With one last huge effort, he lunged toward Les and was able to grab hold of his friend and pull himself up as far as Les' tied-on feet. At the accelerating speed they were traveling, he could climb no further. Karl was totally dejected. No longer having a knife or any other method of setting his friend free, he knew that there was nothing else he could do to save Les' life.

Les too saw the reality of their situation; he smiled warmly up into Karl's anguished eyes and calmly declared, "It's okay, Karl. You did your best."

Pitifully, Karl gazed down into his smaller friend's eyes which had become lucid and clear.

"No I didn't, Les. I let you down, buddy." Tears started streaming down his face. "This was all my fault, Les! All my fault!"

"No. No. Karl," Les called out compassionately. "It was meant to be this way."

Raphael started to throttle the engines as Karl relentlessly tried to hold on to Les. Both were being pulled faster and faster through the pounding water. Les looked into Karl's crying eyes and with a big grin asked, "Do you still love me, pal?"

"Yes, you know I do, Les," Karl responded.

As Raphael slammed the throttle down sending the boat rocketing forward, Les yelled to his friend one last time, "Hey, Karl! Tell me! How much do you really love me?"

Sobbing uncontrollably, Les' older friend cried out as loud as he could.

"I love you with all my heart, Les!"

As he shouted this into Les' still-smiling face, Karl could hold on no longer. Tumbling off the cable, he fell away from Les and deep into the lap of the mighty Gulf of Mexico.

CHAPTER 35

The Waters Serene

As Karl fell away from the speeding boat, Wade tried to give chase with Karl's Contender and its single working engine. Seeing the fruitlessness of this endeavor, he pulled the throttle into neutral as he watched the other craft swiftly outdistance him. Immediately, he picked up his rifle from the vessel's floor, aimed, and fired several rounds at the captain on the fleeing Rampage. Firing, ejecting, and re-bolting the next of a series of bullets, he realized that it was to no avail. There was no way his shots were going to stop the lunging boat ahead of him.

With his usable motor sputtering and his bullet-ridden engine engulfed in flames billowing black smoke, Wade steered the craft toward Karl. Seizing the opportunity to still save Les, Karl swam hard to get to the ladder and onto the vessel's small dive platform.

Pulling himself over the transom while avoiding the burning engine's flames, Karl hurriedly reached down and lifted a small door to a concealed floor compartment. Feeling inside it, he turned the valve off that sent gas to his boat's burning motor.

"Look down in the cuddy!" Karl yelled at Wade. "There's a fire extinguisher down there on that pegboard! Hurry up and get it and spray that fire out!"

As Wade disappeared below deck to retrieve the canister, Karl rushed to the helm to take over the steering. Seeing what remained of his controls, he noted that the only items left intact were his compass and his stainless-steel steering wheel, which had an enormous ding in it.

Urgently, Karl tried getting his boat up on plane to follow the Rampage, but it became apparent that the craft was too damaged to make any headway. In the meantime, Wade had made it back to the stern where he quickly extinguished the flames coming from the burning engine.

The wounded boat limped across the churning seas of the late afternoon Gulf at speeds of only six to eight knots. As they trekked toward the black-hulled vessel in front of them, they saw the Rampage appeared to stop. It was idling about half a mile away. Wade watched it with squinted eyes as he tried hard to see what was happening on the other craft. Glancing at him, Karl asked, "Where are our binoculars?"

"I think they got knocked overboard when we got shot up. Can you make out what's happening over there?"

Both men looked intently across the Gulf at the other vessel.

Straining his eyes, Karl continued guiding his crippled boat as it made its way over the large frothing waves facing him.

"No. I can't see much, Wade, but it appears the captain's standing in the back of the boat."

Bam! Ba-ba-ba-ba-ba bow! Both men immediately heard the unmistakable crack of an automatic rifle echoing in the distance.

Just after hearing this, Wade saw the craft once again moving and back up on plane. It swiftly gained speed and barreled even faster across the waves heading westward toward the darkening horizon. Wade looked at Karl who stood stunned and bewildered. Turning, Karl stared back through Wade as if he wasn't even there. Trancelike, the doctor staggered to the back of the boat where he despondently took a seat on top of the stern's transom.

In the face of this bleak 13th day of October, Wade took over steering. He intended to at least try retrieving his friend's body. Heading in the direction where he thought the Rampage had stopped, Wade hoped that as he traveled into the wind, he would find Les' remains floating along in the unrelenting current.

Crawling tediously over the oncoming waves, he finally made it into the vicinity of where he thought the shots had been fired. Calling back for Karl to help him look, he saw that his older friend was too shaken to respond.

Circling the area slowly and just before leaving the site, Wade caught a glimpse of something orange floating in the water just off the starboard bow. Driving closer, he realized what it was. Using a small gaff, he held the object in place in the water but decided not to bring it on board.

Unmistakably it was one of the life jackets that had been tied onto Les. Wade could see that it had been ripped apart and riddled with bloodstained bullet holes. If there was any hope left in Wade's mind that his friend may have survived, this morbid piece of evidence proved otherwise.

After shooting Les, Raphael must have cut the jackets off his captive to make Les' body sink to the bottom. Not wanting Karl to see the grotesque article, Wade quickly poked the jacket under the boat's hull with his short-hooked pole. He called back to his older friend who was still sitting stunned and motionless atop the rear of the vessel, "It was nothing. Nothing but some trash, Karl."

Placing the gaff in a sidewall rod mount, Wade headed to the helm hoping the jacket's belts wouldn't become entangled in the propeller of the single running motor. As darkness was catching up with them, Wade tried to determine the craft's heading.

Earlier during their rescue attempt, Wade remembered Karl telling him at one point that he was steering the boat 240 degrees west-southwest. He had told him that this was only about 10 degrees north of where they'd safely been the day before. Karl regretted having not returned to that spot. As the certainty of Les' death sank in, Wade turned the vessel east-northeast which he thought would get them back to shore. Looking back at Karl, he could see distant flashes of lightning coming at them from behind. Dejected but resolved, Wade piloted Karl's Contender for home.

II

Back in Keaton, with all of her clients having made it in but Karl and his crew, Betty was becoming a little concerned. Knowing that Karl had passengers on board, and that it was Sunday, she was accustomed to seeing her sometimes-obstinate friend on this day of the week coming back in much earlier. This was especially the case with such foreboding weather conditions already visible and with reports being repeatedly blared over her radio's weather station cautioning small craft to stay ashore. As worrisome thoughts crossed her mind, the bells on the front door of the Marina began to jingle. Buck, the former Tallahassee agent, walked inside.

"Hey. What's going on, Betty?" He called out to her with a friendly smile. Buck would often walk over from his trailer to share a cup of coffee with Betty while she worked her evening shift.

In her gravelly, but friendly voice, she responded, "Not a whole lot, Buck." Thumping the cigarette that she was smoking into a nearby ashtray, she asked, "You heard from Karl today by chance?"

Puzzled, Buck looked back at her, "No, should I have?"

"Oh, yeah, you didn't go out today did you?"

"No, I've been having some problems with my boat. I don't know whether it's in the wiring and switch going to my tilt, or if it has something to do with the motor's hydraulics, but every now and then the thing wants to stick in place a bit. Thought it might be better if I carried it over to Hull's in Perry and let him check it out before I took it offshore and ran into some real problems." He paused as he glanced at the Marina's clerk. "So, what's up with Doc?"

"That's a good question. All I can tell you is that he carried his two friends out this morning, and he hasn't made it back in yet." Stubbing out the spent cigarette, she caught Buck's eyes. "Which is unusual for him on a Sunday with the weather out there looking like that . . . wouldn't you think?" Betty and the agent peered through the shop's back window at the gusting wind and rain.

"You tried calling him, I suppose?" Buck asked referring to her VHF radio.

"All afternoon and evening," Betty responded. "Not a word."

Puzzled, Buck asked, "Do you know the direction he was heading today?"

"No, when they left he didn't say—which I thought was a little peculiar."

Buck pondered what he had told Karl earlier about not heading into that west-northwest quadrant.

Looking back at the worried woman, he said, "Mind if I have a cup of coffee, Betty? I'll wait with you here until they show up. How about that?"

"I'd appreciate it, Buck." She went to a table behind the counter to her coffee maker as Buck watched.

"Why don't you try giving him another call? He might be in range by now."

After pouring Buck a cup of the black brew and handing it to him, Betty reached down to the side of the counter where her VHF microphone was mounted and pulled it free stretching its flexible cord up to her mouth. Pressing the button to the mic with her thumb, she called out, "Doc's Out. Doc's Out. Doc's Out. This is Keaton Beach Marina KBM40978. Can you read me? Over." Releasing the switch, she and Buck waited for a response. Getting none after a minute or so, she hailed Karl again. "Doc's Out. Doc's Out. Doc's Out. This is Keaton Beach Marina KBM40978. Can you read me? Over."

Hearing only static, Buck asked, "What channel you got it on?"

"Sixty-eight. That's where he usually hangs out, you know, but I've tried 'em all."

"How about Steinhatchee? Have you checked with the guys down there?"

"Yep, I put the word out a little earlier this evening just before you came in. Told everybody all up and down the coast to be on the lookout for 'em. When I called Jack up at Spring Warrior, he told me they must have been crazy staying out this late knowing the wind was going to pick up like it was this afternoon."

"So, none of them have heard from him all day, huh?" Buck questioned her.

"Not a peep, Buck." She cut her eyes at the former agent again. "He usually gets a radio check out there from somebody."

"Yeah," Buck tried sounding reassuring, "but like Jack said . . . probably not too many people were out there today especially knowing that a storm like this would be blowing up."

Shaking another cigarette from an almost empty pack, she placed the smoke into her mouth instantly lighting it with a red plastic lighter that she held in her other hand. Taking a deep drag and blowing the smoke back out, she gazed nervously at her companion. "I'm really worried, Buck. I mean seriously this time."

Betty was fully aware that Karl frequently liked pushing things to the limit. "Without them havin' a serious problem—this just isn't like him to be out there in that sort of stuff. You know what I'm talking about?" Pausing, the two of them once more looked out the window past the Old Pavilion Restaurant, toward the dark, ominous clouds heading their way.

III

In Bradford, Louisa was putting Mike to bed.

"Hey, Mom," the small boy called out excitedly. "You reckon Dad's gonna bring us back a great big ol' fish?"

"Yeah, I bet he will," Louisa said, inspiring her son's enthusiasm. Seeing the clock on the wall, which read 8:30, she was surprised that Les hadn't made it back home already. She expected him to walk through the door at any moment.

Mike said his evening prayers and threw in a little extra request for the big fish that he hoped his dad would bring home for them. He finished praying and drifted off to sleep. Louisa smiled down at her son as she continued to rub his little back for several more minutes. Once she tucked the covers around her small child, she made her way to the front living room and took a seat on the room's large sofa. Opening a paperback novel from her coffee table, she began to read. The tick-tock coming from the clock on their fireplace mantle read 8:40.

Absorbed in the book, Louisa heard the clock chime nine times and then once again at nine-thirty. She started feeling edgy. During their time on the Amazon, she and Les could almost never communicate when they were apart, but this was no longer the norm. It was unlike him to not call her if something had come up and he wasn't going to make it home on time.

As she folded her book shut, thinking of who she could call to find out what was going on, she realized that there weren't too many people involved with this trip who might know. Deciding to call Karl's wife, she dialed zero on the telephone. Instantly an operator came on to assist her. Unfortunately, however, this attempt proved futile as Karl, being a doctor, kept his home phone number private and unlisted. Louisa instead had the operator locate Wade's parents' number.

Responding, Wade's father answered, "Hello?"

"Hello, this is Les' wife, Louisa. I was—"

Wade's dad interrupted, "Oh, hi there, Louisa. Have the boys made it to your house yet?"

Trying to sound upbeat, Louisa replied, "No. Not yet. That's why I'm calling you. I was hoping you might have heard from them. It isn't like Les to not give me a call when he's going to be late, you know."

Wade's father took note of Louisa's apprehensive tone. "Oh, I'm sure it's just that they got caught in that afternoon shower down there. On the weather report tonight, it said they really had a downpour along that part of the Gulf. I imagine getting their boat out of the water and getting their fish cleaned took them longer than usual in all that mess, wouldn't you think?"

"You're probably right," Louisa responded, still uneasy.

Realizing her angst, Wade's father said, "I'll tell you what, Louisa. I'll give the marina down there a call. That's where they put their boat in according to Wade, and if they're still open, I'll find out where they are. Give me your number, and I'll call you right back. Okay?"

Louisa gave him the number and said goodbye. It was close to ten o'clock as she stepped back to Mike's room to make sure he was still asleep. Returning to her seat in the living room, she picked up the book and began to read once more.

Just as the clock began to chime, the phone on the table next to her started ringing. "Hello?" she answered cautiously.

"Well, Louisa," Wade's father spoke more soberly. "This is what I've found out. Looks like they haven't made it back to the marina just yet. That rainstorm I told you about earlier is still going on and is much more severe than I first believed. Betty, the manager of the marina down there, is a little worried. Says she knows Karl well and says it's not like him to get stuck out in a storm like the one they're having. She also said that they could've made it back to one of the smaller landings along the coast. There are many of these around Keaton where they could have gotten out of the weather and be perfectly fine. As a precaution though, she's notified the authorities to be on the lookout for them."

"Authorities?"

"Probably the Marine Patrol and maybe the Coast Guard. They're just playing it safe. I've talked to my wife and she says we probably ought to head on down there to give them a hand when they make it back in. Would you like for us to come get you to go with us?"

"Oh, no. But thanks for asking. I've got to get our five-year-old son situated. I'll head that way as soon as I get that handled."

"Okay, Louisa. Don't worry now. I imagine they've made it back in somewhere else, and I'm sure we'll hear from them soon. Betty said the weather's still pretty rough, so drive carefully going down."

"I will. Thanks for finding all this out for me. I'll see y'all when I get there. Goodbye."

With a trip to the coast a certainty, Louisa threw a few things together in an overnight bag and called the assistant pastor's wife to see if she could come over and stay with Mike. Making light of the situation, she told the woman that Les and a group of his friends had gone fishing and hadn't made it back yet. It was probably something minor like an engine problem, which was usually the case, and they would be back home by early the next morning.

She did tell her friend to tell Mike that she had just gone to help dad get back home and to leave it at that. As Louisa left her house, she was quite angry. Somehow, she knew without any doubt that Karl was behind this little fiasco.

As Louisa headed for the Gulf, a group of Karl's buddies and other concerned citizens living around Keaton were already gathering at the Marina. With a local boat going missing in a squall like this one, it didn't take long for the bad news to spread.

One of Karl's good friends knew the unlisted number to the doctor's home. Giving Karl's wife a call and using little tact, he told her that her husband and his two buddies had been reported as missing because they hadn't made it in from fishing due to the terrible storm. She became panic-stricken. Like Louisa and Wade's family, she rapidly headed for the Gulf Coast.

The Coast Guard, Marine Patrol, and all of the good people living in this region of the Big Bend were doing their part to help out. With the night's colder air and the winds blowing at a minimum of twenty-two knots with gusts up to and well over thirty-five, they knew better than most that the Gulf of Mexico, especially at night, was no place to be. Trying to raise Karl's craft from their docked boat radios and their home base stations, they hoped that someone would luck up and make contact with the three missing men. So far no one had.

IV

On the *Doc's Out!*, Wade steered Karl's crippled boat the best he could as it crawled over the sea's tall windblown waves. Through the blinding rain, in constant darkness, and with the vessel's single engine sputtering badly, the boat slowly made its way.

Looking toward the stern, Wade could barely make out the downcast form of Karl as he sat wearing his wetsuit in the constant rain. Not until a flash of lightning would temporarily light up the darkened sky could Wade see the pale hollow expression and lifeless eyes of his suffering friend.

Fearing that Karl might simply drop off the back of the boat and take his own life, Wade knew that he would have to do something to help save his companion. Over the wind and stammering noise of the motor, Wade yelled, "Hey, Karl! Come on up here by me and get out of that rain! It's freezing cold back there!"

Unresponsive, Karl sat motionless atop the vessel's transom. With his feet on the floor and with his hands barely gripping the transom's top, he only seemed to move with the listing of the *Doc's Out!* as it rose and sank in the indomitable waves pounding them. In despair, he stared downward feeling lost.

Turning back to the wheel, Wade was frustrated. Without Karl's help, Wade had no idea how far out he was or even how fast he might be going; worse yet, he wasn't sure he was traveling in the best direction. As he tried to keep his heading to the northeast, the only thing he could think of which was even remotely positive was that he was going with the wind and waves and thankfully not into them.

Surmising that he couldn't be going more than nine to ten miles per hour and thinking at worst he was maybe twenty miles offshore, he felt it reasonable that he would be making landfall in two to three hours. Little did he know that at 10:00 at night, he was more than thirty miles from his destination and traveling much less than five knots into what would soon be a turning sea. At this rate, it would take all night for them to make landfall, and that was only if the craft's fuel and one stammering motor held out.

V

By 11:45, Jack and Billy walked into Keaton Beach's Marina; the clanging of bells sounded out from atop the front door. Wearing their glimmering wet, yellow, waterproof parkas and pants, they pulled down their hoods and shook themselves off.

Betty called out to them, "So, I see it's starting to rain cats and dogs out there again. That's all we need."

Jack, always looking a little hunched over, glanced back at her through his pale blue eyes and called out in his distinctive nasal drawl, "Yeah. It's really coming down hard out there now. I hope them fellows have some rain suits with 'em. Otherwise, they could freeze to death out there on that boat for sure."

Buck called to Jack and shook his friend's hand, "They've got Karl's cuddy to get down into if it gets too bad. Say, Jack, you don't know where they went today do you?"

Cutting his eyes back at Buck, Jack paused momentarily. "Last night, Doc was talking about going out there where we've been having some problems." He paused again. "You know where I'm talking about, Buck." He gave Buck a disapproving frown. Buck nodded that he knew. He was in disbelief.

The Coast Guard's effort had gone into full swing. They were using every asset they had at their disposal. But even as planes, helicopters, and boats fanned out across the Gulf, the weather confronting them was growing worse by the minute. High winds, low fast-moving clouds, and rough seas were making it impossible for those involved in the search to see anything. By 3:00 a.m. with no sign of Karl's vessel, and without knowing in which direction to magnify their search, the Coast Guard radioed back to the Keaton Beach Marina that they were temporarily calling it off. At sunrise when the visibility would be better, they would resume.

The Marina, which had been previously filled with people, was now primarily holding just the families of the three men along with Betty. With dispiriting news coming in from the Coast Guard, they quickly grew downhearted.

Betty, seeing the sad, worried countenances of those surrounding her, said kindly in her raspy voice, "Don't y'all worry now. Karl is a good boat captain. One of the best around here. They're probably hunkered down out there until this storm blows over, and we'll find them come driving up first thing tomorrow morning."

Looking around at the tired group, she said, "I can get y'all some sleeping bags and pillows rounded up for y'all who want to sleep down here, but if you'd like, I have room for about three or four of you over at my place. Might be a little crowded, though."

Karl's wife Trey, who had been sitting despondently and alone, spoke up. "I can take everyone else over to our cabin, and we can stay the rest of the night there for those who would like."

All the women took up the invitations made by Betty and Karl's wife to sleep in a bed. Only Wade and Les' dads said that they would stay at the Marina to keep an ear on the radio in case their sons either called or made it back before dawn.

"Sure would be nice if Karl's dad was here," Wade's father mentioned to Mr. Ellis as the ladies headed out the door.

"Yeah, it sure would be. From what I've heard, he knows this area of the Gulf as good as anyone. Karl's wife says they won't be making it down here though. They're somewhere out in California visiting friends. She hasn't been able to make contact with them yet," Mr. Ellis said.

As Wade's mother, his sister Kelli, and Les' mom all went to stay with Betty, Louisa caught a ride over to Karl's cabin with Trey. Worn out from the ordeal, the two women's ride was very quiet until loud drops of rain started thumping then pouring down on the roof and hood of their vehicle. Parking in front of the cabin, the two young women tried quickly to get inside without getting drenched by the freezing water.

With the wind whipping overhead and sometimes bringing with it very dark and heavy clouds, sudden downpours like this were starting to occur with more frequency. Just as soon as they would appear, these abrupt bursts of rain would drown everything in sight then off they would go as the wind kept pushing them rapidly eastward.

Inside, Louisa took off her raincoat and placed it and her small carrying case on the kitchen table. "Nice place y'all have here, Trey," she said in trying to remain upbeat for her new acquaintance.

"Thank you. Me and the kids don't come down here very much," she said as she looked away nervously. Halfway smiling, she faced Louisa, "It's more or less Karl's place. You know he needs a place to get away from it all sometimes."

Tears welled up in the young woman's eyes. Moving to her side, Louisa guided her into the small den where they both took a seat on the sofa. "Everything's going to work its way out, Trey," Louisa said consoling her distressed companion. "You know sometimes we just have to turn our problems over to the Lord and have faith. Especially when we, as simple human beings, can't control a situation. As a missionary, I came to accept this long ago—that life's never really in our control in the first place, now is it?" Pausing for a moment, she noticed Karl's wife trying hard to recompose herself by drying her wet eyes with a tissue.

"You know, Trey, all we can really do is work with what we've got. Try not crossing any bridges until they show up. And just plain out do the best we can. God will see to the rest of our needs in His own way. Don't you think?"

Trey tried looking back into Louisa's face a little calmer. "I know you're right, Louisa, but when our husbands are out there in a storm like that . . ." She lifted her hand toward the sliding glass door where they could both see the thundering cloudbursts blasting across the night sky.

Louisa gave Trey a warm smile, "There's nothing we can do about that storm out there, now is there? So, why don't you go on to bed and try to get some sleep? That bad weather will be long gone by tomorrow morning, and by then we'll be able to see things more clearly. Okay?"

Trey thanked Louisa for her kind words of encouragement. Standing up, she left for her room, the one Karl had slept in the night before. Louisa took her things and went searching for the room Les had slept in the previous night. Finding his duffel bag packed neatly on the end of his made-up bed, she saw his Bible resting on top.

Slipping into her nightgown, she placed Les' Bible and his notepad filled with notes, back into his bag. Along with his traveling case, she set hers at the foot of the bed. Turning the covers back and switching off the small lamp that he had used to read the night before, she crawled under the covers. It was remarkable, she thought as she lay there, how his lingering scent made it seem as if he was laying right there next to her. If not in person, in presence. Quietly she fell asleep after talking to God through a short prayer.

VI

Back on the boat, Wade half-dragged Karl from the rear of the craft to a drier area beneath what was left of the captain's seat to get him out of the torrential rain. Untying the tackle box, and removing the green packets of cocaine which had been packed into the spot, Wade got Karl underneath it and for the most part out of the weather. Using the same ropes that he had used to tie in the box, Wade created a belt stretching across Karl's lap to keep him from sliding back to the stern as the vessel precariously rode up then down each huge foaming wave.

It had been a long night for the swollen-eyed young man as he had slipped on his rain suit to combat the cold and wet conditions surrounding him. With giant whitecaps originating from the perpetual gusting wind, some five to six footers, Wade didn't know how long the boat could keep going.

If the boat's one staggering motor were to quit on him, Wade knew that there would be nothing he could do to keep the bow from turning sideways into the waves. The capsizing of the vessel, if this were to occur, would be almost inevitable. Wade tried hard not to focus on "what ifs." In his mind, he had two things to do. First and foremost, the most nerve-wracking was to make sure that Karl didn't go overboard. The second, which would be much easier, was to keep the craft on course if he didn't pass out from fatigue. His heading was still 50 to 60 degrees east-northeast. If he could accomplish these two things, they would have to run into land.

As the hours passed and as Wade kept checking on Karl, who had eventually rolled over and fallen asleep, the dark-haired artist could tell that the wind was subsiding. Gone were the huge breaking whitecaps. Replacing these were much smaller waves no taller than three feet.

He gladly noticed the storm front was starting to leave them. Still, Wade had no idea of how long they'd been traveling or how close they were getting to shore. As another hour slowly passed, out of the darkness up ahead, he thought he saw lights. Then, as soon as they appeared, they suddenly disappeared. With all that he'd been through and no sleep for sixteen to twenty hours, he felt he was probably just hallucinating. Either that or a boat really was up ahead of them. He knew, however, that if the craft wasn't coming straight for the *Doc's Out!* there was no chance of his crippled boat catching it.

As the waves became even more subdued, and the wind precipitously fell away, Wade caught the first glowing hint of dawn low on the eastern horizon. Amid the slight glow of the start of this new day, Wade could make out a cluster of bright whitish-looking lights just off his portside bow. Realizing that they had made it back to somewhere along the coast, he was momentarily overcome with joy. It took only a second, however, for him to remember that Les would not be returning with them. Bowing his head, he gave God a tearful prayer of love in Les' memory and asked the Lord for His help in making all of their lives count. Especially his and Karl's, since He had given them a second chance.

Opening his eyes when he was done, Wade saw that their vessel was traveling through what appeared to be a light chop. The boat hardly even rocked as they more placidly cut their way through the Gulf's shallower waters. Walking back to where Karl was secured under his seat, Wade called out to his sleeping friend. "Karl. Hey Karl!" He tried to roust him as he untied the safety rope. "Wake up, man! We made it back. You got to get up and tell me where we're at now."

Karl rolled over into an upright position but was still unable to concentrate on what was being said.

"Come on, Karl," Wade again called out to him. "You've got to get out from under there and show me the way back into this place."

Sadly, his distressed friend appeared to have no idea what was occurring. Taking him by the arm and pulling him to his feet, Wade called out, "Come on, now. We hadn't got much further to go. You've got to tell me how to get back in, Karl, so we won't run aground."

Wade knew that at low tide and this close to shore, he would encounter shallow water. Oyster bars and limestone rock could pop up out of nowhere a good way out into the Gulf. The last thing that he wanted to do now was to get stuck. He turned Karl to face the lights ahead, but his older friend said nothing at first. With Wade prodding him a little, he peered back into Wade's face.

"It's Keaton, Wade. You know the way back in."

Without speaking another word, and still appearing lost, Karl walked back to the stern where he once more took a seat on the transom. With the same vacant expression as before, he stared transfixed at the flooring of the rear deck.

Wade let out a deep sigh as he agonized over Karl's suffering. He squinted his eyes as he scanned the waters where he thought the Keaton tripod should be. He knew from going offshore in the darkness of the early morning on their first full day trip that the beacon would show up as a red flashing light in contrast. As he slowly made his way northward paralleling the shoreline, he finally spotted the marker. Staying on this course, he knew he would be far enough and deep enough out to avoid the snares jutting up from the bottom.

Ten more minutes passed, and as the eastern horizon glowed with more intensity, Wade made it to the site of the red flashing beacon which also marked the entrance to the unencumbered channel to Keaton. Putting the boat into neutral just as he passed the marker, Wade, noticed how quiet the town appeared.

Wade decided to try talking to Karl one more time before they made it in. Walking back to the boat's rear, he found his friend just as he had left him, still sitting on the stern in a stupor. Trying to break his friend from this spell of remorse, Wade called out, "Karl."

Not moving or even acknowledging Wade's presence, the doctor kept staring forward just as lifeless as before.

"Karl," Wade repeated taking his older friend by the shoulders. Gazing directly into Karl's eyes, he shouted, "You've got to come to grips with what's happened now."

Peering up at Wade with sorrowful eyes, Wade's companion could say nothing.

"Look, Karl. It wasn't all your fault what happened out there."

Karl hung his head as Wade kept speaking to him.

"When I gave Les the chance to leave, he didn't say not to do it. He went right along with your plan. He could have sided with me and said 'let's go. Let's get on out of here.' But he didn't."

Wade paused hoping he was getting through, but it didn't appear that he was. "Listen, it was just as much his fault as it was yours."

Karl looked back up at his friend whose one un-swollen eye had become piercing. He shook his head in grief.

"Karl, you tried as hard as you could to save him. We both did. When you tried rescuing Les from those maniacs over on that other boat, we both knew you could have been killed. Les knew it too. He was proud of you for what you did, Karl. You know he was."

Tears streamed down both men's faces as they thought about what had transpired only hours before. The finality of it all—the realization of the death of their best friend seemed overwhelming.

Seeing that Karl was still speechless, a teary-eyed Wade reached over and held Karl, patting him lovingly on the back. Standing up and only slightly regaining his composure, Wade turned and headed back to what was left of the boat's helm.

CHAPTER 36

Requiem

Wade pressed the throttle forward, and the sputtering motor on the *Doc's Out!* continued to push the vessel onward. As darkness began lifting its veil, Wade could now just barely make out the homes and buildings of Keaton up ahead. Rhythmically, like Mozart's Requiem in D minor, Karl's boat made its way. The diminishing shades of the monochromatic night beginning to fade against the ever-brightening sky gave hope and color to a new existence and a new day.

Slowly, in a forlorn cadence, the silhouetted boat rode down the channel, which was marked by red triangular day beacon on its right side and green rectangular ones on its left. Each symbol riding high atop a faded creosoted telephone-like pole, some carrying cormorants drying their wings outstretched—made the scene surreal—as if the boat were in a processional traveling through a corridor of salt-strewn crucifixes.

Back on shore, a call had been received from someone who thought that a boat similar to Karl's had been spotted just off Keaton. The phones started to ring at Betty's place and Karl's, and soon all the family members began arriving back at the Marina.

Karl's Contender, with Wade steering, finished making its last turn along the inside portion of Keaton's small set of jetties. Continuing wearily in the dimness of the early morning light, the tattered craft could be seen from Keaton's singular adjacent street as it passed between each set of houses and parked boats.

Down the canal, Wade saw the piers with their floating docks running down from houses perched on pilings higher up on shore. He could see the large trawlers and shrimp boats jutting out in his path. With sadness and a heavy heart, he knew that soon he would be at Keaton's dock where those who loved Les would be waiting.

As the families of the three men gathered at the base of the canal's long, floating dock, a small mass of concerned spectators stood cautiously above them on the banks of the waterway. In silence, they waited as word came in that the boat had taken a severe beating and was running on only one engine.

Standing with her friends and hearing this, Trey began to quietly weep as Louisa gazed intently toward the canal's western end in search of Karl's approaching vessel. Finally, it came into view, rounding a large docked thirty-two-foot Privateer. From this distance, the reports of it being severely damaged appeared to be true. As it drew closer, a gasp went up from the crowd. The craft had indeed been buffeted and riddled with bullet holes. Louisa struggled to find Les on board. All she could see was Wade with a wound to his cheek driving and Karl sitting in the stern with his head bowed in a state of despair.

As Wade pulled the throttle back into neutral, the boat hit the floating pier. Its port side bow skidded to a stop as Buck and Billy immediately jumped inside to tie it off. Buck called to Wade asking him what had happened and where his other friend was. Wade could only peer grievingly at Louisa as he saw the tears start to stream down her pale cheeks.

All of the family members looked on despondently as Karl's little son bolted through the masses surrounding the ramp. Moving quickly, he skipped down the incline at a full run and made it to his mother's side where he clung to her leg as she scanned the boat in tears. Through an opening at the top of the ramp, Trey's parents appeared. They followed their grandson to be by their daughter. Buck and Billy took the still-shaken Karl by the arms and helped him onto the dock. His wife and son hurried to his side.

Full of sorrow, Wade never took his eyes off Louisa's. Shaking his head with streaming tears, he indicated that Les was gone. Les' parents stood next to her and saw Wade's expression. The three of them stood frozen in disbelief. Speechless and distraught, they watched as Karl, appearing lost, was led down the dock by his family and friends. Once he had made it along the gangway to just in front of Les' family, he suddenly stopped. Looking at Louisa briefly, he bowed his head and whispered through tears, "I'm sorry. I'm so sorry, Louisa." He tried lifting his eyes to meet hers but couldn't do it. Slowly, with his head hanging and his heart full of guilt, he was led down the dock and up the ramp wanting nothing more than to die.

On the shoreline above and behind the seawall, a crowd was still gathering as the Taylor County Sheriff with red and blue lights flashing on his squad car arrived. Wade made his way from the boat to the dock where he met Les' family. Weeping, they simultaneously gave each other a long, heartfelt hug as Louisa whispered out in grief, "I just knew it, Wade. I just knew it was going to end this way. Oh, God! Oh, God!" she cried out into the sky. "Why have You forsaken me?"

Holding onto each other for support, Wade wanted so badly to comfort them all, to tell them that everything was going to be okay. He knew that Les would want him to, but the words just wouldn't come. He had lost his best friend, but they had lost a son and a husband. Wasn't he the one that Louisa trusted to watch over her husband while they were here?

Tormented, he closed his eyes as Les' compassionate father spoke, "I think we need to get her inside, Wade. We'll talk to you later on and you can tell us what all happened out there, okay?"

Wade, still in tears, nodded at the older man. He stepped aside and watched Les' inconsolable widow as they walked away.

With the crowd looking on, the sheriff and his deputy entered the boat and found the packets of cocaine scattered at the boat's stern. Swiftly, the deputy concluded that this appeared to be a drug swap gone bad. As he curiously lifted Karl's long gaff with the buckets still tied to it, he noticed that each one contained only a little of the powdery drug which was wet and stuck in the bottom of each container. The remainder had washed out when the buckets turned over on the journey back. The pounding rains had drained the coke through the boat's scuppers and overboard.

After inspecting the boat, the sheriff and deputy stepped out of the vessel and back onto the dock. They called out to Wade, who had not even noticed their presence. Consumed with sadness from the death of his friend and even more brokenhearted hearing Louisa grieve, he watched Les' parents walk their distraught daughter-in-law back toward the Marina.

Hearing the sheriff's call, Wade turned to the official. The lawman, a wiry man in his early forties wearing a straw cowboy hat with the sides rolled up, walked up to Wade. Scrutinizing the wounded boater, he asked bluntly, "Is this boat here yours?"

"No, sir," Wade responded.

"Well, does it belong to that fellow who just left here wearing that scuba suit?"

Even though he was trying not to sound too antagonistic, an exhausted Wade shot back tersely, "Yep, it would be his all right."

"Bill," the sheriff called to his deputy. "You better go round that dude up before he high tails it out of here."

"I don't think that'll be necessary, Sheriff," Wade retorted as he grew more agitated.

Sneering at Wade, the lawman asked, "And just what would make you say that? Do you have a driver's license or any kind identification on you that I can see, sir?"

"Because right now," Wade said ignoring the lawman's request, "you can see that he and his wife and children have just pulled up to his cabin." Wade pointed to a long, shiny jet-black Chevrolet Suburban which had just parked in front of Karl's cottage across the canal. With the sheriff watching, he could see that Karl's family was having to help lead the distraught boat owner slowly to the front door of his house.

"Wait up, Bill," the sheriff called over his shoulder to his deputy. "He's definitely not trying to get away over there." Turning back to Wade, he asked sternly, "Why don't we start by you telling me exactly who you are, and what went down out there, bud?"

Unseen by Wade and the sheriff, two dark unmarked government sedans flew into the parking lot behind the swarm of spectators who were still gawking and standing on the landing above the floating dock. The two vehicles skidded to a stop––one in front of and one behind the sheriff's car, its lights still flashing. The drivers and passengers got out. Buck walked over and began talking to one of the drivers as if he had been expecting them. The remaining law enforcement agents, wearing dark glasses, khaki pants, and dark jackets, went and stood by the sheriff's cruiser.

Back on the dock, Wade tried to give details to the sheriff of what had happened on Karl's boat. Two of the agents made their way through the crowd and down the dock's ramp. Picking up their pace, they headed along the landing toward Karl's vessel and the three men standing there.

Their haste caused the sheriff to turn and look at them. Instantly, he knew which agency they represented. Calling out with a wry smile, he said, "Say. What brings you fellows out this way?"

The first agent pulled out his badge. "Special Agent John Stinchcomb, United States Drug Enforcement."

The second agent pulled out a pistol and pointed it straight at the deputy. "Are you Bill Nash?"

The deputy, taken aback, answered with a drawl, "Yes, sir. I am."

"Mr. Nash, place your hands on top of your head and please turn around, sir." The agent confiscated Bill's weapon, gave him a quick pat down, and placed him in handcuffs. The agent turned the deputy around to face him and showed the officer several pages of signed legal documents. "Mr. William Raymond Nash, I have warrants here for your arrest concerning the following charges: Drug smuggling and trafficking, conspiracy to transport cocaine for sale, money laundering, and receipt of a bribe by a public official. Do you understand the charges that have been levied against you, sir?"

The deputy responded sarcastically, "Yes."

"You have the right to remain silent. You have . . ."

As the second agent listed the rest of his legal rights, the first agent glanced into the face of the astonished sheriff and smiled, "Did you have any idea?"

"None," the sheriff replied bewildered. Removing his hat, he held it fidgeting in his hands. "Was I in your crosshairs too?"

"Yes, originally, but ol' Bill over there always had you going off in another direction when he wanted something done. It became evident early on in this case that you weren't a participant."

"So, I imagine there were plenty of others involved, eh?" the sheriff asked. "Any other locals?"

"Yeah, starting last night we've made over fifteen arrests from New York to Miami. Three of these we got this morning over in Steinhatchee: a commercial fisherman, his nephew, and the wife of a dive shop owner over there. Couldn't find the woman's husband though, but we'd like to. He was one of the big ringleaders of this organization, but he seemingly got away."

Wade spoke up, "No—he didn't get away."

Eying Wade, the agent said, "Buck told me that you and I should talk."

"Yeah, I think we should."

Exhausted or not, Wade knew he would have to continue with the ordeal of debriefing until it was finished. Turning to the Drug Enforcement agent, he told the man to wait a minute. There was something he had to do, but he'd be right back.

After seeing that he was all right, Wade's family made their way off the dock to be out of the way of the lawmen surveying Karl's boat. Seeing them, Wade climbed the incline. Reaching the top, he was immediately smothered by their loving hugs.

After holding it together for so long to get to safety, Wade broke down. Sobbing uncontrollably, he wailed, "We lost Les, Dad. They killed him! They killed my friend, Daddy! They killed him!" Falling to his knees, Wade wept as his family mourned with him and never turned him loose. He cried inconsolably. With his father still holding him tightly trying to assuage his son's grief, Wade's sobs finally subsided.

Speaking softly, his dad said, "It's going to be all right, Wade. It's going to be all right. Les wouldn't want you to be upset like this. You know he wouldn't."

With the help of his family, he stood up. Wiping the tears from his face with a handkerchief his father had given him, he looked around at each family member and said, "Thank you. Thank you all for being here for me."

"Wade, we love you so much," his mother responded through tearful eyes. "You know we do." In that moment of love and acceptance, Wade let out a deep sigh of relief. It was what he had wanted to hear all of his life, but now, of all times, he could not relish it. He knew what lay ahead of him. Turning away, he saw that the lawmen were patiently waiting for him. "I've got to go and tell those guys what all happened out there." Sorrowfully, he looked at his dad. "This might take a while."

"Don't be in a hurry, Son. We can wait, Wade."

"I know, Dad. But what I'd really like for you to do is to go and be with Les' family and Louisa. They're the ones who need us now. Let them know that as soon as these fellows are finished with me, I'll come and talk to them. Okay?"

Wade's father and the rest of his family let him know they would.

Watching them head to the Marina to give what comfort they could to the Ellis family, Wade turned and went back down the metal boat ramp. There he found the DEA official talking to Buck as they walked through the boat. When the two men saw Wade walk up, the special agent called over to him, "Must have been one hell of a fight out there you guys had. I'm very sorry for the loss of your friend to those bastards."

Wade lowered his head acknowledging the officer's condolence. Buck glanced at agent Stinchcomb and suggested, "Why don't we go up to my camper where we can go over what happened in private?"

The officer asked, "That all right with you?"

Wade nodded that it was. With swollen eyes and an oozing gash on his cheek, Wade appeared every bit as exhausted as someone who had been up for twenty-seven hours and had endured a horrible ordeal would be. Not wanting to rehash the painful events leading up to Les being killed, he gave the two men a determined look. "Fellows, how about let's get this over with as quickly as possible?"

With that understanding, the three men walked up the ramp and through the parking lot. As they made their way through the gathering crowd of gawking onlookers, Buck noticed Wade's swollen cheek. It had closed the eye above it and was starting to partially close his other eye as well. "That thing looks pretty bad, Wade. I imagine it's going to require some lancing and stitches for sure."

Pausing at the bottom of the stairwell to the former agent's camper, Wade bared his teeth in anger, "This cheek of mine is the last damn thing on my mind right now, Buck. What I want to see is those son of a bitches responsible for killing my—"

Just as the vengeful words poured out of his mouth, he stopped. Remembering what Les had told him on the boat that first day offshore when Karl missed gaffing the huge King Mackerel, Wade bit his tongue. He begrudgingly continued in a more moderate tone. "I'm sorry, Buck. I didn't mean to yell at you like that. Let's get on inside, and I'll tell you everything that I know."

Making it to Buck's small kitchen table, the three men took a seat. Agent Stinchcomb opened a satchel he had been carrying and pulled out materials including pictures of some of the people involved in the case. Looking at these articles spread out across the counter, Wade instantly began to recognize and point out some of the plot's depraved participants.

Noting the agent's earlier reference to those people involved at Steinhatchee, Wade started by telling them about the thirty-eight foot, black-hulled Rampage and the perilous experience that he and his friends had undergone at the dive shop. As he told them about this boat and its occupants, which had seemingly slipped past the surveillance of the drug unit, the agent quickly notified the Coast Guard and Air Force via Buck's phone to be on the lookout for the vessel.

Wade said, "I guess those LORAN numbers at 'Descenso' was where they anticipated their drugs would be dropped."

Stinchcomb replied, "That's right. Buck told me that he let you guys know how their operation worked using the pop-up floats and all."

"Yeah, we finally put together what the Rampage was up to once we got a packet on board and found out what was inside it."

Buck shook his head. "What were the chances of you fellows coming across that coke like you did, in that area, that far from those rats? Add that to those miscreants finding you guys sitting on top of their stash—that's virtually impossible."

Wade responded bluntly, "Well, it happened, and they did. Maybe they followed us with that radar of theirs. Who knows? Anyway, it was Karl's idea not so much Les' to get the drugs back to shore and to you guys and shut down the operation." Wade told the men about Karl's scheme to bury the drugs and call the FBI to make the thugs look like they stole it for themselves.

Buck asked, "I take it you weren't in on this plan?"

Wade grew stoic as he said, "No, not really."

The two men listened to Wade's story and questioned him about it over the next couple of hours; at last, they let him go. Leaving the trailer, the weary young man started searching for Louisa and the rest of Les' family. Not finding them, he came across his own parents and sister who were having a conversation with Betty at the Marina.

Wade found out that Louisa and Les' family had already left. Realizing that their son and husband would not be coming back, they decided that there was nothing else they could do by staying. It would be better, they thought, to get back home as quickly as possible before little Mike got the terrible news from someone else. Wade's sister reassured her brother that Louisa had pulled herself together before she and Les' parents departed.

"Well," Wade said as he heard this, "I guess there's really no need for any of us to be staying down here, is there?" Thinking of his car at Karl's cabin, he asked if they could drop him by there to retrieve his stuff. Agreeing, the four climbed into his dad's sedan and drove around to the other side of the canal.

Wade's mother wanted someone to ride back home with him and for him to make sure that he got his cheek seen about as soon as possible. As Wade exited the vehicle at Karl's driveway, he assured his family that he would be fine driving himself and that he would stop by the Emergency Room in Perry to see if he needed any stitches.

Understanding his son's need to sort through the tragedy, the older man looked past his fretting wife and into his son's eyes. "We're glad you're okay, Wade. I know you've got some really important things that you need to tend to. Remember, we love you very much, Son, and we'll see you when you get back."

"Love y'all too, Dad," he said. He tried smiling, but couldn't.

As Wade's family drove away, he found himself standing next to Trey's vehicle. Taking a deep breath then letting it out slowly, he walked over to the cottage's front door and knocked. As he waited, he heard someone walking around inside. The door opened slightly. Timidly at first, Trey peered out. Seeing Wade, she told him to come in. Entering, Wade noticed that Karl was nowhere to be seen. The door to his room was closed, and the lights were off.

Wade gave Trey a slight smile, "I guess my ol' buddy finally crashed, huh?"

Tears welled in Trey's eyes as she whispered, "No, Wade. He's just been sitting there in a chair… in the dark. He won't come out to talk to me or the kids. Wouldn't even come out when Mr. Ellis came over to get Les' and Louisa's things. Mr. Ellis knocked on the door and went inside." Trey glanced down at the floor then sadly up into Wade's eyes.

"He talked to Karl for a while, but when he came back out, he told me that Karl could hardly talk about it and that he knew it had to have been a terrible experience for all of you."

Wade reached over and put his hand on Trey's shoulder. Looking her in the eyes, he asked, "He hasn't told you anything, has he?"

"Nothing except that he couldn't save Les."

Wade broke into a warm smile, "Let's see if he'll talk to me."

Walking to the door of Karl's room, Wade opened it slowly without knocking then closed it once he was inside. It was dark in the room as Wade made it to his friend's bed and took a seat. Across from him, he could see Karl sitting in an armless cushioned chair staring at Wade with that same expressionless gaze he had maintained throughout most of their ride back into Keaton. "What did Les' dad have to say, Karl?" Wade asked trying to reach his friend.

Karl sat silent for a while as Wade patiently waited for him to answer. With tears, the doctor spoke haltingly, "Said . . . he was sorry . . . sorry the way things turned out."

"Was he angry at you, Karl?" Wade continued purposefully.

"No," Karl said hesitating. "He wasn't angry. Just sad that his son had died."

"Is that all he had to say?"

Karl blinked as he came out of his stupor momentarily. For once, peering back into Wade's eyes clearly, he said, "No, he said that he was going to keep a close check on you and me to make sure that we were okay." Karl paused almost bewildered, "Can you believe that, Wade? He wants to make sure that we're okay." Karl shook his head tearfully.

"Yeah, I can believe it, Karl," Wade said observing his distraught friend. "I'm going to keep telling you this until it gets through that thick skull of yours. Les allowed this to happen. It wasn't just you. You did everything you could to save him. I mean *everything*." Wade watched Karl for a response. Catching his eyes, he asked pointedly, "What else could you have done, Karl? Tell me."

Karl stared into Wade's eyes for a second, then quickly looked away.

Wade realized that Karl was punishing himself in an effort to reconcile his remorse. Changing the subject, he said, "The Coast Guard found their boat a little while ago."

Perking up, Karl glanced at Wade showing a little more curiosity.

Wade continued, "Agent Stinchcomb, the guy from the DEA, told me that after they issued a lookout for the Rampage, this was after I told them about it, a Coast Guard helicopter found it flooded with no one on board."

"Scuttled?" Karl questioned.

"I guess that's what you call it when you try to sink your own boat, huh."

"You think you hit him, Wade?" Karl questioned, referring to the captain.

Seeing that this was what his friend wanted to hear, Wade responded, "I could have, but unless they find his body floating around out there with a bullet hole in it, I guess we'll never really know, will we?"

"I think you hit him, Wade," Karl said starting to sound a little more upbeat.

Wade nodded at his frazzled friend. "Let's hope so." Wade stood to leave. "Got to get back home, Karl, and so do you. So, listen up. I'll be seeing you I'm sure whenever it is that they decide to have the memorial service, okay?"

Karl nodded at the thought and said with his eyes watering, "Yeah, at the memorial."

Wade bent over and gave Karl a long hug and patted his friend's back. "I love you, man."

As Wade broke his embrace and backed away, Karl gave him a little smile. Stammering, he said, "Same back to you, Wade. I really mean it."

"I know you do, Karl. I'll see you later on now. Call me if you need me."

Wade left the darkened room but purposefully left the door open for Karl's wife to go inside. As he walked out, he turned down the hallway heading for the room where he had previously slept. Gathering his luggage, he headed for the front door. Trey stepped out from Karl's bedroom and intercepted him. Noticing a more positive change in her husband's attitude, she walked Wade to the front entrance. Stopping at the doorway, she wrapped her arms tightly around Karl's wounded friend. "Thank you so much, Wade. Thank you so much for bringing him back alive."

Pausing as he gazed warmly back into Trey's face, and with a hint of a smile, he said, "No, Trey. You should be thanking Les for that."

CHAPTER 37

Making it Back

Suddenly, there was a quietness to the rumbling of a busy world. A pervasive silence for those who had known the man. More of a shock, but not one entirely of disbelief. For those who knew Les, for a while or for a lifetime, the specialness of the fellow, of just being around him, they all knew subconsciously that such a rare existence could not last forever.

It was quiet in Les' hometown for those who knew him. It was quiet in Bradford and especially at his church where he had come into their presence for such a short time. And it was quiet along the Amazon, as towns, villages, tribes and missions discovered the tragedy of his untimely death.

But of all the places and of all the people Les had touched, it was quietest with Karl. The doctor sat silently through the memorial service held for Les at the Bradford church the following Saturday. The pain and anguish he felt were hard to hide from those attending.

For the weeks and months following the funeral, Karl made his way through each day's work subdued. In a daze, he went from one appointment, procedure, and surgery to the next. To the office, to the hospital, then back home only to do it again the next day. Karl reveled in nothing life had to offer.

To bring him out of despair, his wife and his medical cohorts tried to encourage him by offering their sympathy and compassion. It was to no avail. He remained distant from all who knew him.

For Wade it had been a difficult time as well, especially the week leading up to Les' funeral. As he headed home from Keaton, he had the difficult task of telling Louisa and Les' parents what had happened to their husband and son resulting in his death.

They sat in Louisa's living room talking where only nights before she had shown her angst concerning this trip. Wade was cautious with his remarks as he tried his best to limit their pain. He did tell them, however, of Les' courage and the bravery shown by Karl as Les' older friend had tried everything he could, including risking his own life, in his effort to save his beloved companion.

When he was done, Louisa, through tears, said bitterly referring to Karl, "He said I would regret the day I ever met him! And he was right!"

Abruptly, Louisa got up and ran to her bedroom in tears. Mrs. Ellis started to stand up and follow her, but Les' dad reached over and grasped his wife's knee. "No, dear. Let her be. She needs to come to grips with this. We just need to be near if she asks for our help."

Wade, who was sitting in a chair across from Louisa and Les' parents, stared sadly back at them. Painfully, he could see that their eyes were still red and puffy from crying over the shock of losing their son. After a long awkward moment of silence, the older man glanced into Wade's face.

"You know, Wade, we'll probably never really know why Les didn't take your advice to leave. I think there must have been something bigger out there that he wanted to accomplish. Don't you think?"

Hearing Les' dad say this, a puzzled Wade bowed his head thinking about all the events leading up to Les' death. Looking back at Mr. and Mrs. Ellis and seeing their pain, he nodded reaffirming the older man's remark. He could say nothing more.

Wade heard a car driving up in the driveway. It was Louisa's parents bringing Mike back from the home of one of Les and Louisa's friends. Heading up the front yard's walkway, Mike had no idea of the terrible news he was about to hear. Mr. Ellis and Wade quickly decided that it would be best if Wade left unseen.

Retreating down the hallway exiting the side door to the driveway, Wade left the house and headed to his car as the small five-year-old boy entered the home's front door. Agonizing, Wade thought of what Louisa was about to face. Momentarily, Wade figured he might not leave. He wanted to be there to help ease their pain, but he thought better of it.

Entering his car, he looked into the mirror at the large bandage covering the stitches he had received at the hospital in Perry. Thankfully, they allowed him to shower and change clothes before he left. Even cleaned up, he knew had he stayed, little Mike still would have asked him questions about his wound and would wonder why he was there without his daddy. As he headed down the highway, Wade hoped the youngster hadn't seen his car. Realizing that these questions would eventually have to be answered, he knew it was going to be a painful thing for Mike, Louisa, and their families to go through.

Following his and Karl's tormented boat ride back into Keaton, the grilling that he received from the DEA agent, and relaying the harrowing details of Les' last day of life to his broken-hearted family, later that night, Wade made it back to his apartment. As he entered, he was surprised to find Angie waiting for him there. Grief-stricken, she rushed forward and fell mournfully into his exhausted arms. Wrapping hers around him as tightly as she could, and with her cheeks flushed and pressed firmly against his shoulder, she moaned loudly, "I just can't believe this has happened, Wade! I just can't believe we've lost Les! And I thought …"

"We did everything we could to save him, Angie."

Wade's weary eyes teared up. Hearing the despair in his voice, Angie paused trying to recompose herself.

Wade held her as she choked back her sobs, but pitifully in a state of anguish, she began to wail, "I thought you had died too! I don't know what I would do if I'd lost you, Wade! I don't know what I would do!"

Wade felt hollow and worn out. He just stood there. He was too tired to think, too despondent to respond. Overwhelmed, the thoughts of what had transpired over the last forty-eight hours seemed like a demented dream. *Could this really have happened?* He kept questioning himself over and over.

Angie settled down realizing Wade was fatigued and anguished from his ordeal. She gently took him by the hand and led him to his bedroom. Sitting him on the side of his bed, she helped him out his clothes. Standing him back up, she got him into a pair of pajamas she had found as she quickly searched his dresser drawers.

As Wade remained standing, Angie quietly stepped forward and pulled back the covers. Still spent and confused, Wade gazed back at her with a swollen, almost closed left eye. In a whisper, he thanked her. Crawling into the bed, as soon as his head touched his pillow, he was out—leaving this world in a millisecond.

All that had happened left him. Into a netherworld of shadows and exhaustion, he fell. Falling as if off a cliff where he had no control over the event or its outcome . . . the somnolence therein taking him away to a place of precious seclusion and revitalization.

II

The boys of summer from those earlier playful clay-rock alley days had matured. After experiencing the beautiful colors of so many springs, summers, and autumns, at this point in their lives, they finally had to try to survive the isolation and bitter cold of an untimely winter. Like the spiraling downward of the last leaves of fall turned brown from an early frost, Karl suffered the barren loneliness of guilt and despair. He knew in his heart that it was he who, in his lust for revenge and selfish recognition, had caused the death of his good friend.

It had been almost three months since the tragedy. Much had gone on in all the lives of those Les had left behind not just in Karl's. People nearby and as far away as Peru, Colombia, and Brazil had come to honor their revered friend. Most had a wonderful story to tell Les' family of things he had done or said that brought meaning or a positive change in their lives.

This outpouring of love from others allowed Louisa and her son Mike to make it through the heartbreaking days that followed. The sense of loss for Louisa was so powerful and overwhelming at times that she would have to take leave of whatever she was doing to find a place of quiet solitude where she could grieve alone.

Back in Tallahassee, Karl worked stoically, going through the motions of life each day. The doctor could do his job professionally. He could cut the malignancy out of a person's colon. He could amputate the gangrenous foot of a person with diabetes. What he couldn't cut out or dismember from himself was what he accused himself of doing. It lived with him every day. Every morning when he woke, it was there. Every night when he fell asleep, it was there. There was no leaving it, no losing it. As soon as he felt the dawn of a new day, it was the same as the last . . . that hollowed-out void of lifelessness coming from deep within.

No one who was close to Les was spared the grief of his loss, but his mother and father were holding up better than most. When caring individuals would approach them telling them how sorry they were to hear of Les' passing, his parents would not dwell on the tragedy. Instead, they would bring up the wonderful and inspiring things their son had done throughout his life. Almost every time someone would come to them, and before they left, they would feel more upbeat and challenged concerning their own lives. It was a remarkable thing to witness what the Ellis's did to associate Les' name now with a smile rather than a tear.

Louisa, on the other hand, was not doing nearly as well. Even though Les' parents had come to stay with her and Mike for the first couple of weeks after Les' death, they could not console her grief. It was expected that the recently widowed young woman would have preferred her own family to be by her side during this heartbreaking time, but she wanted Les' family there because they knew him best. They could talk to her about him in ways others could not.

When Les' parents decided to go home, Les' dad gave Wade a call. He was concerned for Louisa's well-being. He and his wife couldn't get their daughter-in-law to reconcile her ill feelings toward Karl. They knew that keeping such anger in her heart would consume the life right out of Louisa if she didn't come to grips with these feelings soon. Mr. Ellis suggested that Wade, since he had gone through this horrible experience with both Les and Karl, contact her to see if there was any way he could help her to overcome this angst and resentment.

Agreeing to try, Wade hung up the phone. Leaning his head back on his bed's headboard, he sighed heavily, thinking about what he could say or do to help bring Louisa out of her bitterness.

Waded didn't know about Louisa's encounter with Karl at Fernandina Beach years before at the Georgia Florida game or especially of his older friend's dalliance with Wade's fiancée after Terrie's funeral. As far as Louisa was concerned, she knew Karl as a man almost without a conscious, who would do or say anything to get what he wanted. It would be easy for her to say she had no use for him if she so desired.

There would be no easy answers in solving this problem. Wade thought of how and when he would have the time to handle it. He had begun seeing Angie again or at least going out with her on a more regular basis. Even though they weren't living together as she would have preferred, it was still much to her delight that they were dating once more.

In the days following Les' funeral, Wade had begun to regain his strength and his faculties. In a show of contrition, Angie told her former husband of her shame for putting him through such an awful ordeal while they were married. She confessed to him that back then, she had been nothing more than an immature girl who thought only of herself and what she wanted out of life. This young woman, she told him, was long gone.

She claimed that she was now a much more spiritual person and hoped that he would forgive her and give her a second chance. She said that she still loved him and always would. She did not tell Wade about her meeting with Les at his church after the service that night or the reason that compelled her to go there in the first place. The path that she took that day and a decision that she made that night with Les had changed her life forever.

For his part, Wade told Angie that what she was saying about her cruelty toward him back then was very true. He had struggled long and hard as he tried his best to become the man she wanted him to be. As he thought back to that time, he minced no words describing the torment and hell that she had put him through.

Tearfully, Angie bowed her head almost certain that their relationship was at its end.

As she lifted her eyes, he expressed tenderly, "But you did follow me back home, didn't you?"

With quivering lips and an unsure look, Angie tried smiling back.

He stared directly into her eyes and said, "And for some reason, whether it was what happened down at Keaton and us losing Les or something else, you really aren't the same person, Angie. I know without a doubt that what you're telling me is the truth."

Relieved, she peered warmly back into Wade's eyes. She knew that he forgave her for what she had done to him.

III

It was cold, and late December, when the front door bells to Ben's shop began to jangle as someone entered the warmth of the store. Wanda got up from where she had been drinking a cup of coffee with Wade in the back and headed to the front of the building.

"What are you doing back so early?" came the sound of Wanda's voice. "We weren't expecting you until tomorrow."

Instantly realizing who it was, Wade got up and went to the shop's front end. Seeing his two workmates approaching, he noticed that Ben, who had been to Atlanta, was not stopping, but was continuing to walk toward the back room. Passing Wade, he gave his young cohort a wink. He held a rectangular box wrapped in white tissue paper with a wide red silk ribbon strapping its length and width. A large red bow had been decoratively placed on the center. "They were disappointed in ya', Wade, that you didn't show up."

Following the older man into the back room, Wade gave Ben a somber look, "You know why I didn't go up there, Ben."

Peering back at his woodworking companion without expression, the shop's owner retorted, "Well, do you want to know the outcome?"

Shaking his head with an accepting little smile, Wade replied, "At this point, Ben, it just doesn't really matter that much to me one way or the other."

Ben let out a deep sigh as his eyes dropped from watching Wade to staring down at the attractively decorated box lying across the top of his desk. Glancing down to where the sixty-seven-year-old owner had taken a seat behind the table, Wade could see a slight smile and a glint coming from the blue eyes of his friend.

In a voice filled with compassion, Ben said softly, "You know, Wade, after what you've been through, son, I can see where it doesn't." Pausing as he eyed his younger companion, he asked, "Are you going to open it?"

Wade smiled back warmly. "No. Since it's so nicely wrapped and all, I think I'm just going to give it to Louisa and Mike when I go down there this weekend."

An antsy Wanda looked intently at Wade as she made her way to the exquisitely wrapped article. "Wade!" she exclaimed upset. "You can't just leave me hanging here. I've got to see it! Everybody else in the whole world's seen your picture but me. That's not fair." Like a mother hen in charge of her two little working chicks, Wanda couldn't believe Wade wouldn't even consider showing it to her. With a look of dismay, she glared at him.

"Wanda, it's wrapped up all pretty and nice, and I'd hate to have to . . ."

"I can wrap it back up a heck of a lot better than that, and you know I can, Wade."

"Yeah, I know, Wanda. But I'll bring it back to show you later on, okay?"

Wanda gave her workmate a hurtful look of disbelief, then said, "No. No you won't, Wade. I'll never get to see that picture, and you know it." She paused still staring at him, then glibly called out, "That's okay. Don't show it to me. I didn't really want to see it in the first place."

"Come on, Wanda—"

"Nope. Forget it. I don't want to talk about it anymore either."

Wade pleaded, "Hey, listen. I promise. Scout's honor, I'll bring it back just for you to see."

"No. You're talking to the hand now," she said holding the palm of her right hand out in front of his face. Blowing a breath through her nose and acting hurt, in a huff, she left the room.

Wade looked down at Ben.

"U-baw-da—daw-goo-baw-da?"

"No. I don't think that was an u-baw-da—daw-goo-baw-da, Wade. You really owed it to her to show her that picture as much as she's done for you."

Wade's eyes sank then he glanced back up at Ben.

"You're right. But right now, I don't even want to see it myself. I'll bring it back and show it to her like I said I would."

Having seen the work, Ben nodded. "Yeah. I know you will, son."

As the older man sat there contemplatively, Wade scanned the room and saw several unfinished projects that they had been working on. It was Friday afternoon, and both men and Wanda had intended to work late going into the weekend. Ben and Wanda even planned to get things somewhat caught up by working all day Saturday when Wade would be out of town.

With a cautious peek, Wade caught the proprietor's eye, "This probably isn't a good time, Ben, but could I have the rest of the day off?" Immediately, he began to plead his case, "I know we've got a lot to do around here, but besides carrying this picture down to Louisa and Mike, Louisa wanted me to help her go through some of Les' things this weekend."

"You in that big a hurry to get down there, boy?" Ben asked.

"Well, there's a lot for her . . . that she needs to decide on. You know with her being alone now, and . . ."

Ben interrupted with a wry grin, "You aren't falling for your friend's wife, now are you, pal?"

Taken aback, Wade gave the older man a hard look.

"Of course not! I'm just doing for Les what he would have done for me. That's all." Wade didn't hold back as he expressed his anger and insult.

"Hey, calm down, bud," Ben countered. "You're not married anymore. It's your life. You can do what you want, right?"

Disturbed by what Ben was inferring, Wade responded, "My God, Ben! Les just died! You know that's not what's going on here. All I'm doing is—"

Ben interrupted, "Is doing what your friend would have wanted you to do. And there's nothing wrong with that, Wade. Nothing at all. I'm sorry for insinuating such a thing. Sorry I mentioned it." Pausing, he continued looking up at his still red-faced cohort.

"I know that you've been seeing a good bit of Angie lately. Does this, you know, you going down there like you've been doing lately, bother her any?"

"What is this? Twenty questions?" Wade asked cynically. "I don't think I can ever recall you being so nosy, Ben. I mean do you really want to know every little detail going on in my personal life, huh?"

Feeling admonished, Ben looked back at his younger companion. "Forgive me, Wade. It's just that I know how badly you've been burned in the past by women."

Becoming enraged, Wade quickly shot back, "Just one woman, Ben! Angie! But we've hashed all that past stuff out. She's a different person now. I can't even describe how different she's become. And it's all for the good, okay?"

Contrite, Ben spoke in a more subdued tone, "I understand, Wade. It's like you said, it really is none of my business."

Sighing heavily as he rubbed his chin, Wade was embarrassed that he let his anger get the best of him. Countering himself, he began to speak more calmly.

"I see how you could get an impression like that by what all you've seen going on. I'm sure it doesn't look too good from the outside my going down there. But trust me, it's nothing like that at all."

Wade paused pensively as he peered back down at his mentor who was still seated.

"I probably do need to be a little more truthful with you about what's going on here, I suppose."

Ben cackled back surprised, "A little more truthful?"

"Yeah," Wade cracked back with a grin, "I probably need to be a little more upfront with you about all this."

Pausing momentarily, Wade gave Ben a more sober look. Reluctantly, he said, "Okay, so here's the story."

With an uncertain smile anticipating what Wade was about to tell him, the older man leaned back in his chair and cocked his head to one side.

"When I came back to work, you and I talked. You remember what all I told you that happened down at Keaton on that trip, right?"

Ben nodded.

"I'm sure you remember me telling you how bad Karl felt about not being able to save Les' life and how Louisa blamed Les' death all on him. You remember me telling you that?"

Again, Ben nodded.

"Well, neither one of them has really been able to get over this. Karl's still full of guilt and depression, and Louisa, I'm pretty sure, is still blaming him to some extent for Les' death."

Wade looked down at the floor then back up into Ben's patient eyes.

"Trey, Karl's wife, called me about a couple of weeks ago to see if there was anything that I could do to help him out. I mean, according to her, Karl's still very despondent. She says that she can't even imagine how he can continue to do surgery though somehow she says he can. She also said that he stays to himself when he's at home and doesn't interact much with her or his kids. And he swears that he'll never go back to Keaton again. All in all, I think what she's really trying to tell me is that he's suicidal."

Wade paused as he nervously pushed his hair back from his brow. Sighing, he continued, "Then there's Louisa. Louisa's never held a grudge against anybody. I'm not saying that she totally blames Karl for what happened, but regardless, she can't seem to get over Les' death and move on. For some strange reason, she just seems to be waiting. This may sound odd, Ben, but it almost as if she's waiting for Les to come walking back through that door again."

Wade shook his head and said, "I don't know if it's possible . . . putting people's lives back together after something like this." He looked down at his older friend. "What do you think?"

Ben thought for a moment. "From all you've told me about Louisa and her husband from the beginning right on up to his death, it sounds to me like theirs was a match made in heaven."

"It was," Wade marveled, "When I first met her, it was like the most beautiful virtuous woman in the whole world magically appearing and falling in love with my best friend. I don't know if Les would have become the same man had she not come along."

"Well," Ben said. "That explains Louisa, but what about this Karl friend of yours? Do you really give a damn what happens to this guy, Wade? I mean, after all the crap he put you two guys through down there?"

Wade chuckled. "If you'd ask me that question midway through our trip, I wouldn't have just said no, but hell no!" Wade's eyes blazed as he thought about how arrogant and obnoxious Karl had been at first. "But after I saw him try with all of his heart and all of his might to save Les' life when it could have easily cost him his own, and after I saw how remorseful he was following Les' death, well, I've changed my mind." He paused.

"Hell, Ben. He even asked Les if he wanted to leave before we started messing with that cocaine. Les knew the consequences of us staying out there just as well as I did. I don't know why on earth he didn't, but when it came right down to it, he wouldn't take sides with either one of us. All he had to say was let's go and we'd have been gone. So, all the blame can't go just to Karl in this situation."

Wade paused as painful visions of the trip blasted back to him as crisp as the day they happened. Regaining his composure, he continued, "So you know what, Ben? Karl's gotta realize this too. But for some reason, and I don't know why, I think it's going to take Louisa's help to get him there."

Wistfully the older man interjected, "Her anger and his remorse are going to be a hard one to solve, Wade."

Looking around the room at all of the projects that they were behind on for Christmas, Ben said, "I'll tell you what. You go on down. See what you can work out from that end. I'll keep thinking about it up here. Maybe one of us will come up with a solution. But in any regard make sure that you're back here by Monday morning. We've got a lot of work to get done around here before Christmas hits."

Eager to go, Wade gave Ben a grateful smile. "I'll be back by then for sure. And thanks, Ben. You know I appreciate all you're doing for me and I really mean it."

Wade picked up the present and rapidly gathered a few things from his desk.

As Wade walked quickly out of the back door, a still smoldering Wanda entered the room.

"I can't believe that he wouldn't show me that picture, Ben. Did he even place?" Even though she was still very infuriated with him, her curiosity had gotten the best of her.

Without smiling, Ben pushed her a copy of the day's *Atlanta Journal* that was lying on top of his desk. As Wanda picked it up, he said, "Go to the Arts Section."

CHAPTER 38

Rudyard K's Two Imposters

It was bedtime on this cold December night in Bradford. Mike, with his mother's help, finished brushing his teeth after his bath and climbed into bed. Tucking the covers around her young son tenderly, Louisa climbed on the spread next to him waiting for Mike to say his prayers.

"Dear God," he started as usual. "I sure miss my Daddy. I wish you'd let him come down for a visit to see us 'cause Momma cries a lot 'cause he's not here, and I miss him too."

Louisa's eyes started to water. Then, only as a little boy's attention span can shift, Mike began blessing everybody and everything he knew, even his friend Jason's dog. Louisa couldn't help but smile when he got to that part unable to come up with the word Dachshund, he described the pooch as he'd done for his father, "Pepper—You know, that little weenie dog, God."

When he finished his prayers, Mike opened his big blue eyes and looked directly into his mother's. He proclaimed, as would his dad, "And I'll always love you no matter what."

Louisa beamed back at him, "And I'll always love you no matter what, too."

Mike grinned and kissed his mother. Gazing up, he asked, "Mom, will I ever get to see dad again?"

Louisa thought for a moment and said, "When we get to heaven, he'll be there waiting for us."

Frustrated Mike replied, "I know that, Mom, but I'm talking about before we get to heaven, you know, like tomorrow maybe?"

Louisa realized that at his age Mike couldn't fully comprehend the permanence of death. In her son's naïve little mind, you could travel back and forth from earth to heaven on a whim. She affectionately gazed down at him and warmly said, "Sure you can see him."

"I can. Where will he be?"

"Well, he'll be everywhere. He'll be in the sunshine and the blue sky we see. In the big hills we go up and down every day and the tall trees. He'll be there when you play with your friends and when they laugh. And he'll be here with you at night when I tuck you into bed to go to sleep. He'll be in your heart every day, every hour, every minute, and every second of your whole wonderful life. That's what he promised you when he said that he'd always love you no matter what."

Satisfied by her answer, Mike smiled. His eyes started to grow weak and sleepy.

"Love you, Mom," he muttered as he drifted off to sleep.

"Love you too, my sweet boy," she responded as she kissed his forehead.

Lying there with her head next to his, she waited until he was soundly asleep. She left the room, and quietly closed the door behind her.

II

Earlier in the afternoon, Wade had gone by his apartment and gathered up his clothes. Putting them into his duffel bag, he stopped packing long enough to call Angie and let her know of his new itinerary. As he let the phone ring at her house, he didn't know if she would be there or not. School was out for the Christmas holidays, and she was spending a lot of her time in Broxton helping her mom and dad with their business.

Surprisingly, he got an answer.

"Hey, Angie, I didn't know if I'd be able to catch you or not."

"What's going on?" she asked curiously.

"Well, instead of leaving tomorrow morning for Bradford like I'd told you earlier in the week, I've decided to leave this afternoon. Just wanted to let you know where I'd be."

Angie thanked him for his thoughtfulness and asked, "Is there anything that I can help y'all with?"

"I don't think so. Like I told you, Louisa wants me down there to help her go through Les' stuff. I think it's going to make for a pretty rough day, if you know what I mean.

"Yeah, I'm sure it will be. I'm a bit surprised that she hasn't done that already as organized as she is though. Aren't you?"

"Well, to be honest, I am. But maybe she just didn't want to deal with it until now. I don't know. Anyway, I'll be back sometime Sunday afternoon, and I'll give you a call when I get back in, okay?"

"Okay. Drive carefully now. And remember, I love you."

"Love you, too. See you later." Saying this, he hung up the phone.

As Wade made it to his car and headed down the road to Bradford, he couldn't help but think of how improbable it was going to be to get Louisa over the hurdle of blaming Karl for what had happened to Les. Getting her and Karl back together? He just couldn't see that happening either. Thinking up scenarios to solve this puzzle preoccupied his mind for the better part of his trip.

After the two-hour drive to Bradford, on this cold, dark wintry evening, Wade finally found himself parked in front of the parsonage where Louisa and Mike were still living. Knowing that the motel he had been staying at on his previous visits usually had vacancies available, he decided he would first stop at Louisa's in hopes of catching Mike awake. Walking to their front door, he tapped lightly on the metal knocker hoping to gain their attention without scaring them.

At the kitchen sink, Louisa heard the knocks, but not knowing who would be there at this time of night, she was cautious. Walking up to the front entrance, she turned on the porch light and cracked the door to see who it was.

Through an inrush of frigid air, a voice called out, "It's just me, Louisa. Sorry, I hope I didn't frighten y'all. I intended to call you before I came by."

"You know I wasn't expecting you until tomorrow, Wade," Louisa remarked blushing.

"Yeah, I know. I just thought I'd get on down here tonight so we could get an early start tomorrow, maybe? If that's what you wanted?" Pausing uncomfortably, Wade didn't know if she had something else going on this night or if he might be overstepping his bounds trying to help her. "I hope I haven't caught you at a bad time. I can—"

"Oh, no," Louisa exclaimed gratefully. "Come on in and get out of that cold weather. It's freezing out there tonight." She pulled her sweater tightly around her neck.

As Wade stepped inside to the warmth of the small foyer, Louisa smiled and said, "Come on back here with me."

He followed her to the kitchen where she pointed to a chair.

"Have a seat. I just got Mike to bed, and was trying to finish cleaning up in here." She held up a dirty plate to show him what she'd been doing.

Sitting down on Mike's stool, Wade gazed across the small kitchen table toward his strikingly beautiful friend. It had been almost three months since Les' death. Rather than regaining her strength over this period, she looked even more thin and frail than the last time he'd seen her. Only her radiant eyes and enchanting smile seemed to mask the grief that she certainly had to be feeling. Continuing to scrutinize her, he watched as she took a dish towel and began wiping the water from her last cleaned plate.

"Well, shoot," Wade said disappointedly. "I was hoping that Mike would still be up so I could get to see my little pal. That's why I didn't stop by the motel first and call you. I was hoping you'd both be up, and—" Wade started having second thoughts about what he was about to say next. Maybe the timing for doing this was all wrong.

"And?" Louisa asked perplexed.

"I've got a little something out in the car that I wanted to give to the both of you. But maybe you should—" he stopped abruptly. Pondering it further, he thought what he was about to do was going to be a big mistake, but with the genie already halfway out of the bottle, he knew there was no turning back.

Louisa became even more curious. She finished wiping off the counter her eyes never leaving his as he spoke.

"What is this thing you've got for us, Wade? You seem to be hesitating for some reason." Grinning, she slid the last dried plate back up into the cabinet over her sink.

Still indecisive, Wade fidgeted. "Let me go out to the car and get it. I'll be right back."

Intrigued, Louisa watched Wade rise from the table and leave the room. Making his way back outside into the frigid night air, he took only a matter of minutes to retrieve the gift.

When he returned, he found two steaming hot drinks sitting at his and Louisa's place at the table. Louisa was already sipping from hers.

Suddenly, she realized her neglect. Covering her mouth with her hand, she said, "I'm so embarrassed, Wade. I didn't even ask you if you'd eaten supper. Are you hungry?"

"Oh, no. I'm fine. I stopped in Tallahassee and got a hamburger. But I appreciate the, um—"

Seeing that he had no clue what she'd just given him, she gave him a furtive little smile.

"It's hot cocoa, Wade."

Louisa had always been charmed by Wade's politeness. It was something that she was glad to see hadn't changed about him over the years they'd been apart.

Smiling, he took a seat across from her. "Well," he said taking a sip. "With this cold weather and all, this is just what I need. Thank you." He quietly peered into Louisa's eyes and grew solemn. Gently, he slid the package he'd brought back with him across the counter toward her as he presented the gift.

"Is this for me?" Louisa asked giving him an inquisitive glance.

"For you and Mike," Wade responded humbly.

Louisa's eyes danced from the exquisitely wrapped present back to the quiet yet still uncertain look that Wade was giving her. "It's so gorgeously wrapped," she said appreciating the delicateness of the paper and ribbons as only a woman could. "It's so lovely I don't even know if I can bear to open it." She paused, then gazed back into Wade's deep brown eyes with excitement, "Do I have to?"

Trying to steady himself, Wade responded with a quick half-smile. Accepting it, Louisa began unwrapping the gift by untying its silk-like bows and tatters. She carefully unraveled the tissue paper from the package where hidden beneath its wrappings, she exposed a large white rectangular cardboard box.

"I thought it might be one of your pictures at first, but it feels too heavy for that," she said as she lifted the box slightly off the table.

Turning and reaching behind her, she opened a drawer and pulled out a small paring knife to cut the tape holding the lid down on each of its four sides. Lifting the top off, she intently looked at the object inside.

Finding a basswood carrying case, she quickly realized what must be in it. Standing the wooden box upright, she flipped open the two latches located near the top of the holder that held its hinged lid closed. Reaching inside, she slid out one of the two items that it contained.

Gasping aloud, she placed one hand across her chest astonished. Glancing up at Wade through watering eyes and in a hushed tone, she exclaimed, "Oh my God, Wade." She covered her mouth as she stared back down at the award.

With her hands still trembling and with tears streaming down her face, she slowly turned the citation around for Wade to see. Shocked by his response, she could instantly tell that Wade had no idea of what he had done.

Choking back tears, she whispered in disbelief, "You didn't even know—did you?"

Stunned, Wade looked down at the gold-plated plaque. Inscribed on it along with the Atlanta Art Gallery's insignia, it read:

THE CAPITAL CITY ART SHOW
Sixty-First Showing
FIRST PLACE, 1985

As he finished reading it, his eyes crept back up into Louisa's tearful, but smiling face, and speaking in an almost inaudible tone, he haltingly told her, "No—I had no idea. Ben went up to the show yesterday and brought me this package back this morning. When he asked me if I wanted to know how I did, I told him no."

Wade paused as he turned his sad eyes away from his friend, then he admitted, "You know what, Louisa? I really didn't want to know. I was just going to give the picture to you and Mike anyways."

Louisa's cheerful expression turned more somber as she watched him. Collecting her emotions, she wiped the tears from her face with the back of her hands. With a warm and compassionate look, she reached over and softly stroked Wade's hands which he had rested on the table. Probing deeply into the pain and hurt that she saw radiating from his eyes and face, she asked caringly, "Wade, why wouldn't you want to know how well you did? You've lived your whole life for this. What could possibly keep you from enjoying this wonderful moment?" Louisa knew the answer to this question but asked it only to help relieve her friend's suffering.

Wade's eyes filled with tears. Slowly, he began to speak as he tried to look back into hers, but couldn't. "Louisa, a lot of things have changed for me—since that trip. Some things—they just aren't as important to me anymore."

Louisa gently rubbed his hand with hers as she patiently listened.

"I guess what I'm trying to say is that without—" He abruptly stopped speaking and hung his head.

Unable to continue, Louisa softly spoke the words that were so distressing to him. "Without Les, is that what you're trying to tell me, Wade?"

Wade nodded as tears ran down his cheeks. "Yeah, without him, this just doesn't mean that much to me now."

Louisa didn't take her eyes off of Wade as he spoke. Tenderly reaching over with the palms of her hands, she lifted his bowed face upward.

As his eyes met hers, she lovingly told him, "It's all going to be okay, Wade. It's all going to be okay." A radiant glow of warmth surrounded them for a long moment.

Seeing Wade comforted, she pulled herself back and away from him and once again she focused her attention on the box and its contents. Next, she carefully began to pull the painting out of its wooden hold. Taking it out of the encasement completely, she could view the canvas in its entirety.

Wade, subdued, watched every subtle gesture her face yielded as she was captivated by what she was seeing. From excitement, to sadness, then finally to a serene yet smiling sense of peace, she viewed the work. Glancing back at Wade, whose expression remained downcast, she spoke to him with a quiet sense of assertiveness, "I'm so proud of you, Wade, and Les would have been too. You know that he would." She nodded affirming this point.

Once more, she took a long, absorbing look at the painting and with a soft accepting smile, she slid the canvas back down into its wooden case.

Reflecting back to Wade's hesitancy upon letting her see it, she remarked, "Now, I think I know what you were trying to tell me earlier and I agree. It's probably not the right time to show it to Mike just yet. Maybe he'll understand when he gets a little older."

CHAPTER 39

A Quiet Gentle Spirit

The next morning came early. Louisa had convinced Wade to sleep on her living room sofa. At 7:00 a.m. sharp, he awoke with Mike hovering over him.

"Mr. Wade! Mr. Wade! How did you get in here?" Louisa could hear her son's voice booming through the walls of her bedroom.

She arose and quickly threw on her long, silky, light-blue bathrobe. Entering the living room, she found her young son peering down at Wade only inches from her old friend's face.

"Mike," she gently scolded. "Mr. Wade's probably not used to getting up quite this early. You should have let him sleep."

Mike was momentarily downhearted. "I'm sorry, Mr. Wade. I didn't mean to wake you up."

"It's okay, Mike. I was already awake when you came in here. I usually get up a lot earlier than this."

Realizing that he said this only to raise the boy's spirits, Louisa grinned down gratefully, "Well, since you've already been up for so long, Mr. Wade, I guess we can now all go and get ready for some breakfast. How about that?"

"All right!" Mike called out as he headed for the kitchen. "Can I help you make the pancakes, Mom?" he yelled over his shoulder as he ran for the other room.

"Yes, honey. Can you get the mix down from the cabinet for me?"

"Yes, ma'am," came the echo from the kitchen as both she and Wade heard the little munchkin dragging his stool across the floor to the counter.

Louisa flashed a smile at Wade as she took a seat at the other end of the sofa.

Speaking softly, she said, "This is a real treat for Mike, Wade. We almost always fix pancakes on mornings we have guests over." She paused, saddened by the thought. "And well, we haven't had too many guests over in quite some time, you know." Lowering her eyes, she admitted this in a quiet, solemn refrain.

Wade could see the suffering in her face. The thought of her losing Les—it was something she was unable to mask. Not with her kindness. Not with the radiance shining at him from those crystal blue eyes of hers.

Showing compassion, Wade cackled, "I love flapjacks. They're my favorite, Louis'." Saying this gleefully, he tried mocking Mike's enthusiasm.

Instantly, Louisa's gloomy appearance radiated a spark of excitement. Wade's delightfulness was infectious.

"Okay, Mr. IHOP. You can go get a shave and a shower in Mike's room now if you'd like." She glanced down at his duffel bag then over to the neatly folded clothes he'd been wearing the previous day. "Carry your things back there with you. That's where you'll be staying for the rest of the weekend. When you finish getting cleaned up, Mike and I will have a plate full of hot pancakes waiting on ya'."

Wade, pleased, observed Louisa as she stood. Taking a few steps in his direction, she leaned down and gave him a quick kiss on the forehead. Wrapping her arms around his broad shoulders in a warm hug, she whispered into his ear, "I'm so glad you made it down here, Wade. You just don't know."

As she pulled herself back up, Wade studied her carefully. Peering into her glowing face, he cheerfully said, "You know there's no place that I'd rather be than down here with you and Mike today." Smiling lovingly back down at him, Louisa turned and left the room.

When they finished eating their breakfast, Louisa told Wade that she and Mike would be going to the church where they were to meet Jason and his mother Jane Cavenaugh. This family, she explained, were members of their congregation, and it had already been arranged that they would be taking care of Mike for the day.

Jason lived way out in the country on a cattle farm, and his parents didn't want Louisa to make the long drive just to drop off Mike. After all, Jason's mother had told Louisa there were things in town she needed to take care of, so the trip would not be out of her way.

Wade volunteered to ride to the church with the two. As the three of them piled into Les' car with Louisa driving, they made their way. The area surrounding Bradford was unusually hilly for a mostly flat Florida. Not only were the hills prevalent in this part of the state, but they were particularly steep as well. Little Mike, much to his merriment, enjoyed going up and down each one immensely.

Wade recognized the church's steeple as it appeared through the massive limbs and flittering green leaves of the area's large sprawling live oaks. Like déjà vu, they had come into the area using the same route that he and Les had driven. To Wade, it seemed as if their trip to Keaton had occurred only yesterday.

Louisa drove to the front parking lot where Mike could see Jason and Pepper chasing each other around the churchyard. As the car came to a stop, the back door flung open. Mike flew out and ran as fast as he could toward his friends to play.

Wade chuckled watching all of this unfold as Louisa smiled at him saying, "I guess you can see where his priorities lay?"

"Okay, Mama. Don't get your feelings hurt." Wade grinned back. "We were all like that when we were his age."

Louisa sighed as she watched the two boys and the little dog run behind the brick building. With a reluctant smile, she replied, "I suppose you're right."

As she and Wade stepped out of the vehicle into the frigid morning air, a heavy-framed, kindly-looking woman exited the front doors of the church. Seeing Louisa, she headed in her friend's direction. "Louisa!" the woman called out as she walked up. Compassionately, she held Louisa in a smothering hug. "How have you been doing, honey?"

"Fine," Louisa responded graciously. "We've been doing fine, and I'm so glad you can keep Mike for me today."

"Oh, it's really nothing; you know how much we love to have him come out to play with Jason."

Standing away from Louisa, Mrs. Cavenaugh gave Wade a smiling, but discerning once over. "And haven't I seen you before?"

"Yes, ma'am. I was—am one of Les' friends." Wade immediately felt terrible for referring to Les in the past tense in front of Louisa.

"Oh yes—" the woman began to say, but recognizing the scar on Wade's face and knowing of his and Les' relationship, she too was caught off-guard and embarrassed. Tightening her lips, she was at a loss for words as she attempted to spare Louisa's feelings.

Louisa gave Jane a warm look. "Yes. You remembered Wade from Les' memorial service. He was one of the men out there on the boat with Les on the last day." Glimpsing at Wade, then back at the kindhearted woman, Louisa said with pride, "I'd say without a doubt, Wade here was probably Les' best friend growing up. Matter of fact, he came over this weekend to help me sort through some of Les' things."

Stepping toward Wade, Jane wrapped her strong arms around him. "Let me give you a big hug too, Wade. My thoughts and prayers will be with the both of you." Still holding onto Wade, the woman slightly turned to Louisa and whispered, "Mike can stay out with us for as long as you need."

"Thank you. Thank you so much," Louisa responded appreciatively.

Being released from the warmth of her embrace, Wade was taken aback by how nonjudgmental Mrs. Cavenaugh appeared to be. Seeing him there with Louisa could easily be viewed, he thought to himself, as inappropriate. After all, Les had been gone for only a few months. But Wade detected no hidden feelings of awkwardness in this woman's display of kindness at all.

Leaving them to gather up Jason, Mike, and Pepper, Mrs. Cavenaugh quickly had her three passengers aboard her king cab pickup truck. Mike gave his mom a wave and a grin as they drove from the parking area. Smiling, Louisa waved back. She was grateful that, with all that had happened, Mike could still be a happy boy.

Alone on this crisp December morning, the two old friends bundled in warm coats took stock of the church and grounds. Staring up at the handsomely built sanctuary, Louisa thoughtfully began to open up, a frosty breath appearing with each word she spoke. "You know, Wade, Les really loved this place," she said, gazing at the building where she and her husband had worked so hard to help others. "I'm sure this was where he was supposed to be."

She paused for a second to reflect on that thought, then said, "You know, if you ever really thought about it, Les was always where he was supposed to be. Whether he was up in Athens, out in Texas, all up and down the Amazon River, or even out on that boat with you and Karl, he was always at the right place."

Glancing up, she studied Wade as he nodded in silent agreement. With an uncertain smile, he turned and scanned the stately, old, red brick building. *Why would she include the part about Les being out on the boat that day*, he wondered.

Without saying a word, Louisa started walking down the sidewalk toward the church's front entrance with Wade quietly following. Politely, he stepped forward and opened one of the large, oak-wood doors for her. They went inside the dimly lit building just as Wade and Les had done.

Making her way through the foyer, she entered the sanctuary. A thin burgundy strip of carpet covered the hardwood floor with the downward sloping walkway ending at the elevated pulpit and choir loft. About midway down, close to where Wade had sat before, she stopped, slid into one of the pews, and took a seat.

At this time of the morning, the stained-glass windows on the eastern wall took on a glistening surreal appearance. The theme of those windows where the light was brightest was not of Jesus being crucified but of the risen Christ. The glow cast down a rich aura of holiness throughout the sanctuary.

Sitting down next to the silent Louisa, Wade sat quietly for several long minutes. In a soft tone of reverence, he said, "I guess, we'll never really know why Les kept coming down here in the middle of the night, will we?" Wade paused. His mind aware of the spirit cast by such a blissful, ethereal site. His senses were heightened, especially considering his previous experience at this place. In a hushed voice, he continued, "But being here . . ." he scanned the sanctuary, "this would be reason enough."

Louisa turned and peered into his eyes, "Do you really mean that, Wade? Can you really understand the sacredness here? Even that first time you sat in these pews?"

That question and the direct manner in which she asked astonished Wade. Perplexed, his mind became jumbled. *Sacredness? How could she know how I felt that first time I was in here?*

Seeing that he was unable to explain what he was experiencing, she smiled.

"This is a beautiful place, Wade," she spoke as she gazed mesmerized by her surroundings. Silently, for several moments, she reflected on the experience. Catching the still pondering Wade off guard, she said, "I think we should go now."

Hearing her request, Wade rose. Stepping out into the aisle, he stood far enough back so she could pass in front of him. Soon, they had made their way back onto the sidewalk where they saw the nearby live oaks filled with chattering, winter-chased, redwing blackbirds. As they neared Louisa's car, the birds took flight in waves of hundreds. In perfect unison, they rushed back and forth through the sky above them.

The two friends spent the rest of the day going through Les' things which Wade thought would predominantly be clothing. As was usual for the austere missionary, his attire had been primary and simple. Only a few fancy clothes and suits that had been given to him by his friends and members of the church hung in his closet. His own family, knowing that he would rarely wear exclusive and expensive garments, gave him more practical items. The duo quickly dispensed with this portion of their workload. Almost all of the items were placed in boxes and dropped off at the local Goodwill store on their way to grab lunch.

After getting a bite to eat at a place called Billy's, whose specialty was sub sandwiches, they made their way back home through the community's downtown area. Wade had bypassed this part of the city altogether the night before. Dressed decoratively in its green and red holiday splendor, the town reminded Wade of being behind on their work at Ben's shop. Christmas was just a little more than a week away.

Louisa pointed as she drove. "You see what we've got to get over there, don't you?"

Wade noticed she was referring to a Winn Dixie grocery store. On its sidewalk entrance, there remained only a sparse assemblage of Frazier firs already well picked over.

"A Christmas tree?"

"Yes," Louisa exclaimed happily. "A Christmas tree."

Wade wondered, "You know, I didn't notice it last night, or even today until you just mentioned it, but you haven't put up any Christmas decorations at all at your house, now have ya'?"

Louisa's lips tightened then broke into a grin, "Yeah. I guess I'm a bad mama, Wade. Les would have had all that up weeks ago. He loved Christmas."

Trying to give her a pass on her negligence, Wade countered, "Don't be so hard on yourself, Louis'. You know, you've been through a lot lately." Hesitating, he was enchanted by his sublime friend. "And that's putting it mildly."

Louisa smiled back at him, "Yes—but it's no excuse! We'll have to make amends for my lack of spirit won't we?"

"We can do it," Wade asserted merrily. "When do you want to get started?"

"Tonight. Without a doubt. But we still have a few more things to go through before we can get going with all that, okay?"

Wade nodded as they continued their drive. Traversing the town, they found themselves back at the parsonage. As Louisa emerged from her car and started to her house, she heard the incessant ringing of her telephone. Hurrying inside to her kitchen, she picked up the receiver and answered with a soft, "Hello?"

Strolling in behind her, Wade listened as she continued her conversation.

"He doesn't have any clothes or pajamas with him. Well, okay. It'll be fine if it's no imposition. All right. We'll see y'all sometime tomorrow—after church. That will be fine. I'll be looking for y'all then. Okay. Bye-bye now."

"What was that all about?" Wade asked.

"Mike's spending the night at Jason's," Louisa said stoically. For some reason this news made her appear somewhat downhearted.

Feeling awkward at this circumstance, Wade wondered, self-consciously, if it was the fact of him staying there with her alone. Maybe she had misgivings about that.

"Do I need to go check into the motel, maybe?"

Louisa grinned at him laughing at the thought.

"No, it's not that, your craziness. It's that I was hoping we could all go out tonight and get that tree. You know, let Mike see and enjoy the lights and everything that's downtown." Smiling to herself, she shook her head. Looking up into Wade's face, she said, "You're still the same ol' Wade that I've always adored. Always trying to watch out and protect me, aren't you?" She paused as she eyed him, incapable of hiding her joy. "You think these people around here, my neighbors and church members, will think bad of me if they find out you're staying here with me alone, right?"

Raising his eyebrows as he shrugged, Wade responded, "I mean—I don't know. Will they?"

"I don't think so, Wade," she shot back crinkling her eyes with an engaging little smile. "I hope my friends here think better of me than that."

"I hope so too. I wouldn't want them to kick you out of this place for being immoral or unethical, you know." His smile turned quickly into a grin.

"You'd take us in though if that happened, wouldn't you?" Louisa laughed as she went to the home's side door which exited the kitchen into her driveway. Grabbing the doorknob, she stopped suddenly. Turning back, she glanced at her now silent friend for his answer.

"Of course, I would," Wade chuckled. Acting wary, he asked, "What would make you think I wouldn't?"

Louisa's eyes flashed with delight. "Come on, there are some things we need to get out of the carport before it gets too dark."

Making it back outside where it had become only a degree or two warmer, Louisa made her way to the garage's heavy, wood-framed doors protecting the building's contents. Taking a key from her pocket, she wrestled with the lock until it unbolted. Standing back, she let Wade pull one of these large doorways open.

Going inside first, Louisa went to one of the building's front sidewalls. Switching on a a single, dim, 60-watt bulb that hung overhead showed the place to be filled with an assortment of Amazonian artifacts.

"Holy cow!" Wade exclaimed. "I didn't think y'all brought hardly anything back with you."

"We didn't," Louisa remarked surprised herself. "About all we brought back with us were the clothes on our backs. All of these things were sent to us from our friends down there through the missions we set up."

Gazing around the dark musty room, Wade could see a plethora of interesting gems. There were all sorts of drums and musical instruments. Dart guns, spears, shields, bows and arrows, and all kinds of artwork from ceremonial masks and primitive paintings to hand-carved smoking pipes and ornate wooden carved poles filled the area. Wade wondered aloud, "There's some fabulous stuff in here." He picked up and examined a colorfully painted wooden shield. "Are we going to go through all of this, this afternoon?"

Louisa stared back at him knowing that the artist in Wade would find these novel creative designs compelling. "Some fascinating artifacts, wouldn't you say?" Grinning, she watched her excited friend.

"Very," Wade replied as his eyes devoured each piece of artwork he picked up.

Not wanting to interrupt his enthusiasm, Louisa reluctantly told him, "As bad as I hate to tell you this, Wade, this isn't what we came in here to go through." Wade gave Louisa a puzzled look. Responding, she said, "What I want to get out of here is back over in this corner." She stood in the emptier back section of the garage.

Standing with his palms outstretched in disbelief, Wade shrugged, "What about all these things? What are you going to do with them?"

"A curator from a museum down in Tallahassee came by last week. I called her. I'm sure Les would have wanted all of these things displayed somehow so the public could see them. Don't you think that's what he would have liked?"

Taking stock of all the intriguing items surrounding him, Wade sighed. "Yeah. You're right. He would have wanted that for sure."

Seeing his disappointment at not being able to continue looking, she said, "Listen, you can come back in here any time you want. I'm sure there are a lot of things you'd find interesting. They might even give you some new ideas or whatnot. Anyway, it will be a week or two before they come and get all of this stuff."

Wade dejectedly nodded as he told her thanks and that he might take her up on that offer.

"I hope you're able to," Louisa smiled back.

Slowly, through the dimness, Wade walked to where she stood. Looking down on the floor, he saw two sets of boxes, one of which was wooden crates while the others was made of cardboard. There were four or five boxes in each stack.

"We just want the cardboard ones," Louisa said.

"What's in those wooden ones?" Wade asked.

"That's just more of Les' things—things like his compass and his binoculars. Stuff Mike will probably like to have someday and his writings." Louisa grew quiet when she spoke of these items.

Noticing her sudden change in mood, Wade sympathetically did not respond. He didn't want to bring to mind any more painful memories. At least, no more than she was already experiencing.

Feeling as if she had to explain the reason for the awkwardness of this moment, she softly said, "I got the chance to go through all those things over there the last couple of weeks between doing my work at the church and running Mike around. So, it's just these boxes here that I want to take back inside. Okay?"

"Sure, Louis'," Wade answered kindly. "Are they heavy? Can I take more than one box in at a time or . . ."

"Most of these are pretty light. There are only a couple in there that I'd say were heavy."

"Well, let me get the bigger ones," Wade urged.

Louisa glanced warmly at her still handsome friend. "Hey. I'm no weakling. I can still handle a heavy box, Wade." she exclaimed in mock disgust. "Remember, I'm the one who's lived the hard life down on the Amazon River."

"Yeah, yeah, yeah," Wade shot back. "A real Amazonian muscle woman. That's what you are, all right." He snickered as he looked at her.

Smiling back at him, she picked up one of the smaller boxes. "Under these clothes, I might just be."

As Wade lifted a couple of the boxes himself and headed for the door in front of her, he called back over his shoulder with a cackle, "Well, since I'm probably not going to get to see you naked any time soon, I'm probably just going to have to take you at your word on that one, Louis'."

Louisa grinned to herself at his response then watched as her charming counterpart walked through the maze of artifacts, out of the garage, and toward the warmth of her house.

CHAPTER 40

Reconciliation

Once the two had finished carrying in the last two boxes from the carport, they ended up back in the parsonage's living room. They had neatly stacked all of Louisa's containers at the foot of the sofa where Wade had slept the night before. Louisa began sequentially taking down and opening each box. Peering inside each container momentarily, she placed the box on the rug. Finally, she had them all arranged in order.

Having watched her place the boxes so meticulously, Wade couldn't help but chuckle. "I guess you got 'em lined up just right, now?"

"I do," Louisa asserted with a smile as she sat by the first one. "You guys, like Les and my brothers, just kill me. You never seem to get the importance of doing things the right way the first time. Y'all just start jumping in at any old place until you mess up then you try to fix it."

"Maybe so. Or maybe it's just that you girls probably care more about what you're doing than we do. Wouldn't that be more the case?"

"Most of the time—I think that's pretty obvious, don't you?" Glancing up at Wade, she patted the floor next to her and said, "Come on. Sit down here by me."

Squatting as he sat closely next to her, Wade gazed at Louisa.

"Let's see what we've got in this first box," she said excitedly. She pulled out their junior college 1973-74 annual. "Hmm . . . Let's see who we might find in here." Sitting even closer to one another, so they both could see as they flipped through the pages, the first picture they came across was of Lester Ellis. "Look how young and skinny he was back then," Louisa remarked as her eyes fed upon his image with the warmth of a glowing smile.

Wade studied the picture with a lump in his throat. "Yeah, he was a little bit thinner than I remembered him being, but he was bigger than life in just about every other way, wouldn't you say?'

Louisa graciously nodded at Wade. "Yes," she said, staring down at the page. "Indeed he was." Studying his image for a little longer, she continued turning the pages. "And here's Miss Angie," she noted but in more subdued manner. She had no idea what kind of relationship Wade had with his ex-wife, so she didn't push it.

Wade gave Louisa a half smile as she observed him. "Yep, I can still remember the first time I met her at that BSU fish fry," Wade smiled as he looked down at her picture. "She's changed a lot over the years, you know, and for the better," he said warmly as he eyed the photograph.

Realizing Wade had nothing else to say about his former wife, Louisa continued.

Suddenly, Wade stopped her from flipping through the pages of the book, "Hold up. Go back to that last page there." He reached down sadly and gently touched the picture he had glanced. "That's Terrie, the girl who was my friend—the one that committed suicide." Wade paused as thoughts from the past sprang into his mind. Gazing at Louisa, he asked, "Did you ever meet her?"

Solemnly, Louisa shook her head.

Wade continued. "She was Karl's girlfriend for a time. She was very tender-hearted and very attractive."

Louisa nodded thoughtfully, then said, "Yes. She was very beautiful."

Wade wondered as Karl's name had been brought up if this would elicit a response from Louisa. For some reason, it didn't. For a long moment, Wade scanned the picture of the girl but said nothing of her tragic life. Louisa knew more about Terrie than he was aware.

Wade started to turn the pages. "Uh oh. Who's this little punk?" he laughed out loud.

"You mean that handsome dark-haired fellow there?" Louisa asked as she leaned into him.

"I'm not seeing that picture," Wade laughed back.

"Well, ya' better look harder," Louisa beamed. "Cause he's right there." She pointed at the picture of Wade shining back up from the page at the two of them.

Embarrassed, Wade turned the pages until he got to the picture of Louisa Wess. It was his turn to do the pointing. "Now here's the picture of the most beautiful girl on campus that year, the one that every man there wanted to date. And the one Lester Ellis was lucky enough to entice."

Louisa laughed smiling back at Wade's devilish grin. "It was I who enticed him, Wade, not the other way around."

"Whatever you say, Louisa," Wade chuckled as he seemed to deny what she was telling him.

Louisa paused as she stared directly into her artistic friend's eyes. "No. I'm being serious."

Perplexed, Wade tried reading her face for the truth as she continued gazing at him.

"Really, Wade. It was me that was after him. I was the one who got him to go to seminary too. And believe it or not, it was me who got him interested in doing mission work along the Amazon. Les would never admit that he had second thoughts about going down there, but I was able to persuade him." Louisa gave Wade a furtive little smile which quickly turned into a grin.

"Really? The whole time I had it all backwards?"

Smiling, Louisa gave him a slight nod. Turning back to the book, she began looking at pictures of campus life when they were both at the community college during the early seventies. The two friends refocused their attention to the contents of each page.

"Whoa," Wade called out as Louisa flipped a page showing members of the school's honor society. "There y'all are, you and Angie." He chuckled, "You won't find me and Les in that shot."

"Hey," Louisa replied. "Y'all got your grades up before we got out of there."

"Well, yeah. We didn't have much choice. Our dads—well mine for sure, especially back then, would have killed me if I hadn't."

Louisa peered up at Wade, "Speaking of your father, I hear he's a different man these days. Is that right?"

"Yeah. He really is," Wade said warmly. "You might not know it, but he pretty much saved my life when I was down and out. That all happened a few years back when you guys were still down in South America." Pausing, Wade became more serious. "And I'd say now, especially now …" Wade instantly thought better of brining Les' name into the conversation. "He's probably my most trusted friend. I love him very, very much."

Reaching over, Louisa warmly patted and rubbed Wade's back. "I'm so glad for you two guys, Wade. A father and son should always have a special place in each other's heart, you know."

Another familiar sight came into view as they flipped the page.

"Look," Louisa said pointing in amazement. "I never really noticed this before."

Glancing down at the page, Wade could see that someone had taken a picture of Ann and him at the BSU fish fry.

"How 'bout that," Wade exclaimed. "Ann sure was an attractive thing back in those days, wasn't she?"

"You don't think she looks so good now?" Louisa interjected with a grin.

Wade sighed. "You women can always turn things back around on us guys, can't you? I told Wanda at work the other day, just trying to give her a compliment, that it looked like she'd lost some weight. You know what she says back to me? 'You trying to say I'm fat?'"

"Us gals are just a little sensitive about certain things."

"No, it's more like you gals are just impossible to comprehend," Wade said in mock disgust.

"No, that's not true, it's just that we like to remain a little mysterious. You know, to keep you guys wondering and in line."

"Oh, is that what it is? Thanks for the head's up."

"You're welcome," Louisa said as she gave him a wink. Turning her attention back to the box, she pulled out a large green scrapbook. On the front, written in cursive with shining gold sprinkles, it read: College Life.

"What's this?" Wade asked.

"It's just a hodgepodge of things and pictures from when I was back in school."

Opening the book to its first page, it showed a picture of Les, Wade, Laney, and the girls along with Wade's little sister playing in the snow on the lawn in front of the girls' dormitory.

"Who took those pictures? I don't remember any of us having a camera that day."

"Oh, it was just some friends of Les and mine who were out there. They took them and gave them to us. I tried taking all the pictures from back in those days with our other items of interest and kind of stuck them in here."

Flipping the pages, Wade saw several pictures of the snow-covered Holiday Inn on the interstate with references under them recording who was there and what they were doing.

"I took those," Louisa said. "That was a fun night," she said, glancing cheerfully at Wade.

"Yes, it was. I'm still surprised that Laney even made it considering all the ice and snow he had to drive through that night."

As she continued turning each page, the scrapbook showed Wade the sentimental side of what Louisa thought was important. She had kept tickets from concerts, pictures of classmates, all kinds of University of Georgia Bulldog paraphernalia and game tickets, and photos of her apartment in Athens and her roommates and Les.

Nearing the back of the booklet, Wade sang out with delight, "My old Athens' trailer and my car. Did you take that one?"

Grinning up at him, she indicated that she did as Wade pointed to the far end of the mobile home lot.

"There's Les' old black grill. Right there. We had a lot of good times cooking out on that heavy old iron thing, now didn't we?"

"We did, didn't we?" Louisa responded jovially.

Viewing the pictures for a moment more, Louisa turned the page to see the letter of invitation for Louisa and her date to attend the Georgia Governor's Ball. Both Louisa and Wade grew quiet as precious thoughts of the past arose in their minds.

As they flipped the page, there was the letter from Kelinivitra Staline telling Louisa when and where to meet for her preparatory dance classes.

Wade cackled. "The Bolshevik Headmistress, Mrs. K.! Can't forget her, now can we?" Lowering his voice, he asked Louisa with a grin, "Do you remember when I asked her if she was kin to 'The Stalin'?"

Both friends burst out laughing.

"Yes, I remember that," Louisa laughed as she leaned back onto Wade's shoulder. "I remember her cutting her eyes and glaring at you. I thought she was going to kick us both out of that studio on our very first day there."

"Nyet! Nyet! Nyet! How many times did we hear that?" Wade's eyes were watering from laughing so hard.

"Enough. Every time she said it, she would stop that blasted recorder and we had to start the whole dance routine over again. I can't believe we got suckered into doing that, Wade."

"We?" Wade exclaimed. "It was me. I was the one who got suckered."

"By who?" Louisa asked acting confused.

"By you! You little—fairy princess."

"I did that to you, did I?" Giggling, Louisa gazed up into his eyes from where her head rested on his shoulder once more.

"Yes, you did. You little bugger."

"But aren't you glad I did, though?"

"Turn the page," Wade said acting angry.

Smiling, Louisa righted herself as she flipped the page.

As they both focused on the book, the next page showed a picture of them decked out for the Governor's Ball. Wade was handsomely fitted in his white bowtie and black tails and the modelesque Louisa appeared ravishing in her black fur coat.

Enthralled by what she was seeing, Louisa spoke first. "Do you remember how cold it was that night, Wade? Not a cloud in the sky and I remember it looked like a million stars were shining down on us from heaven."

"Yes, I remember," Wade said fondly as he slowly turned to the next page.

Suddenly his demeanor uncharacteristically changed. He was astonished to see photograph after photograph of them at the Ball. He and Louisa in pictures each by themselves. He with Louisa as her coat was being removed and with the spotlight shining down on her as she was being introduced. Louisa and him dancing to the Waltz to the applause of the crowd. For him, the most damning set of pictures was Wade dancing cheek to cheek with Louisa, their bodies close and their arms wrapped tightly around each other seductively. Wade could hardly believe what he was seeing.

Glaring at these as if he'd been betrayed, Wade asked noticeably angry, "Who took all these pictures of us?" He was appalled as if someone had been spying on them and caught them doing something that they shouldn't have done. To this cruel accusation, Louisa responded meekly, "I think a University of Georgia journalism student." Louisa was truly hurt by the harsh tone of Wade's voice. In her mind and counter to what Wade had implied earlier at his hometown's apartment, it seemed apparent that Wade was suddenly ashamed of what they had done.

As they viewed the images, a flood of memories poured through their minds. Feelings they had tried hard to suppress resurfaced as raw and poignant as if this event had been held only the night before. Ashamed for the feelings he at the time had for Louisa, Wade had nothing to say, lest these guilt-laden passions be set loose once more.

Sensing the depth of his rebuke, Louisa hung her head heartbroken. Distraught by this unspoken revelation, she gently closed the book even though there were many pages left unseen.

"Why are you stopping now?" Wade asked quietly. But secretly in his heart, he knew the truth. It was his anger and his shame that were the cause.

"I think I can probably get the rest of this work done by myself. It's not much," Louisa said sadly as she glanced at the remainder of her boxes. Still looking away, she spoke timidly, "You're a busy man, Wade. Mike and I can deal with all of this stuff tomorrow. You can leave tonight if you need to."

Stunned, Wade was almost speechless. For a long awkward moment, neither of them said a word to one another as they looked everywhere but into each other's eyes.

Finally, a dispirited Wade, softly spoke up, "If you want me to leave, Louisa—I will."

Not making eye contact with him, she sat silently.

Wade didn't know what to say or do. How could the wonderful celebration of reviewing their lives turn into such agony with just a whisper from the past? Confounded, he did not know. Finally, and with Louisa never turning or raising her bowed head, he stood up and walked to the back bedroom. There, broken and downhearted, he gathered his clothes and shaving utensils. Doing this as slowly as he possibly could, he hoped deep down inside that she would come to him. Even with his bags packed and even after sitting on the side of the bed for what he thought to be a long time, she did not come.

Despondently, he headed for the bedroom door. His heart was torn. It was as if he'd just been punched in the gut. How could this be happening? How could he have been so stupid? She had always been the love of his life. He had always known it. Now, when nothing was barring him from reaching her, he blew it and lost her. Suffering hopelessly, he opened the door to the hallway. As he walked toward the front door to leave, he heard something—something that brought the past back to the present. Stopping momentarily, he listened intently.

It was their favorite music that they had danced to at the Governor's Ball. The music to the black and white movie with Humphrey Bogart and Ingrid Bergman, *Casablanca,* "As Time Goes By."

You must remember this

A kiss is just a kiss, a sigh is just a sigh

The fundamental things apply

As time goes by . . .

Hearing this, Wade made it into the living room with his duffel bag hanging over his shoulder. There she stood. Elegantly put together. She wore a simple white knee-length dress with white matching slippers. Without a word or even a smile as the music kept playing, she delicately offered Wade her right hand.

And when two lovers woo

They still say, I love you

On that you can rely

No matter what the future brings

As time goes by . . .

Sliding his bag off his shoulder and dropping it to the floor, Wade gently took her hand. He placed his right hand on Louisa's upper back as Mrs. K would have been proud to see, but Louisa said, "No, not the Waltz, Wade."

Loosening her hand from his as she peered deep into his dark brown eyes, she slid her arms around his neck as she crossed her wrists delicately behind his head.

Mesmerized, Wade couldn't help but stare back into those gorgeous eyes with their alluring little crinkles just beneath. Rhythmically, he swayed back and forth to the beautiful melody as he held her body close to his.

"Why did you stop me?" Wade whispered in her ear as they danced warmly cheek to cheek.

"I think the better question is—why did you stop?"

The music kept romantically playing as Wade pondered this most blissful conundrum. "I don't know why I did, Louisa," he said confused.

Louisa smiled though he couldn't see her do this. "You stopped because I asked you to, isn't that right?"

"You are—irresistible, Louisa."

"As are you, Wade," she said as she momentarily pulled back and looked him in the eyes before once again pressing her cheek tightly against his.

"Louisa, I don't know."

"What do you mean?"

"I mean, what would Les think about all of this?"

"Les would be happy that it was you, Wade. He let you guard me once before. Remember? He wouldn't have trusted just anybody with me."

"You think not?"

"I know he wouldn't have. You've always been the special one, and he knew it."

"You sure it wasn't Karl?" Wade joked.

"Don't worry about him."

Wade contemplated that for a moment.

"He's been having a lot of trouble since all this happened, Louisa."

"I know he has. I went over recently to visit him, and he's fine now. We got everything settled. I can assure you; he's okay."

"What did you tell him?"

"Never mind him, Wade—What about me?"

It's still the same old story
A fight for love and glory
A case of do or die
The world will always welcome lovers
As time goes by . . .

CHAPTER 41

Going Home

The next morning found Wade sitting across the kitchen table from Louisa as they both quietly ate the scrambled eggs, toast, and bacon that Louisa had prepared.

"Would you like some more coffee?" Louisa asked with a seductive little smile.

The handsome artist graciously replied, "No thanks." Pausing, he asked, "Say. When did you tell me Mike was coming home?"

"Sometime after lunch," Louisa responded. "Why?"

"I'm just trying to figure out when I need to leave."

Louisa glanced across the table at him as she knew only too well that Wade wanted to be long gone before Jane made it back to drop off Mike.

"You're not planning on leaving right away, now are you?" she asked alarmed.

"Oh no. It'll be later on."

Louisa grew quiet as she continued dabbling with her food.

Noticing her silence, Wade spoke, "You said last night that you've been down to see Karl."

Looking up from her half-eaten plate of food, Louisa said, "Yeah, I went by after Trey gave me a call a while back."

Wade said nothing as he listened to her intently.

Seeing he was eager to hear more, Louisa slowly opened up about her meeting with Karl. "You know how I felt, Wade. I told both you and Les what I thought about Karl before that trip."

Wade, wishing that they had heeded her advice, begrudgingly nodded his head.

"Well, I prayed over this matter for a long time, a very long time." She gazed down, then back up at Wade. "I finally realized that he couldn't or shouldn't have to carry this burden around with him for the rest of his life. So, I called Trey while Karl was at work one day, and we arranged when I would come down to meet with him."

Momentarily reflecting, she said, "We decided on a Sunday morning when she and her children would be going to Sunday school and church. It seems like none of them had ever gone to church until Karl started suffering this depression. So, I guess there's somewhat of a silver lining in that." She paused at the thought, then continued, "But as for Karl, she told me that he still didn't go. I don't think it was that he didn't want to go, but the truth about Karl was that he was too depressed. The only time Trey said that he'd even come out of their house was to go to or from work."

Wade couldn't help but remember what Karl told Les out on the boat concerning God, that Christianity and believing in God were a religion for losers. Lost in that thought for the moment, Wade quickly refocused on Louisa.

"Anyway, I drove down there that Sunday morning and arrived at their house just after Trey and their children had left. Trey had told Karl a little white lie, that one of her friends would be stopping by with a present for their daughter. Their little girl was about to turn nine, and she asked him to make sure that he answered the door to receive the gift. Sad to say, but this was the best way she could come up with to get him to answer the door."

Wade responded, "Hard to believe after this much time that he's still this despondent."

Louisa somberly agreed, returning his remark with a slight grimace. "So, when I walked up the steps to the front door, I rang the doorbell. I had to ring it several times before I heard him rustling around inside. Finally, he came to the door and opened it!" Her eyes grew watery as she recalled the event. "I couldn't believe what I was seeing. He was so fragile looking, so thin and gaunt. I bet he's lost almost thirty pounds."

Wade winced. "At first, we just stood there looking at each other. All the time, I couldn't help but notice how hollow and dark his eyes were and how pale and waxy his skin had become. He looked unhealthy, very unhealthy. I bet you he hadn't been out in the sun since the fishing trip. Besides that, I could see that he was utterly shocked upon seeing me. Of all the people who could be standing there, I was probably the last person in the world he thought would ever show up on his doorstep."

"Did he invite you in?" Wade asked.

He painfully watched as Louisa grappled with her emotions. Composing herself, she recounted what happened next. "Yes. He motioned for me to come inside." Louisa had taken a tissue from the pocket of her bathrobe as she tried dabbing the tears flowing from her eyes.

"I followed him into their living room, and I thought he was going to show me where to sit down, instead; he turned around and faced me. He was crying uncontrollably by then. Tears were pouring down his face."

"Then like something being dropped, I really can't describe it, Wade." Louisa closed her eyes tightly. "He fell to his knees and he bowed down in front of me burying his face into my feet and began sobbing for my forgiveness. 'It was all my fault,' he kept saying over and over. 'My stupidity caused Les to die. My arrogance.'"

Covering her face with her hands, Louisa cried, "It was awful, Wade! The pain he was experiencing was so unbearable. I don't know how on earth he held up to it. But somehow, he did, and his suffering touched me. It touched my heart."

Wade reached over and gently held the arms of his distraught friend. Catching her eyes through her tears, he asked, "What did you tell him, Louisa?"

"I told him that I forgave him, Wade, and for him to please stand back up, but he just couldn't seem to do it. Finally, I just knelt down beside him and I held him in my arms and rocked him back and forth like I would have done a hurting little child."

"After a very long time of us both crying, he leaned back and looked me in the eyes. Stammering and so pitiful," she said, shaking her head. "he told me that he was nothing more than a worthless human being. He deserved no mercy and no forgiveness from me for what he had done."

Louisa paused as she reflected on the awful ordeal.

"Before I was able to tell him no, that wasn't true, he started spitting out why he was such a terrible person. He told me of all sorts of bad things that he'd done in his life. And there were lots of things he told me about, Wade. Things that he'd kept hidden—but he said he was done. He was finished with all the secrets and all the lies. When he finished getting all of that out, he told me how sorry he was that I had ever laid eyes on him. He couldn't tell me enough times how sorry he was that Les and I had gotten so tangled up in his sorry life."

As Louisa regained her composure, she peered back at her friend.

"He was so full of remorse, Wade, that I finally had to take him by the shoulders and shake him until he grew quiet. He then looked me in the eyes. I told him, 'Listen to me, Karl! You are forgiven for all those things that you have done. They no longer belong to you. You can let them go now—all of them. Today you are a free man.'"

"When I said this, he closed his eyes and breathed a deep sigh of relief. Then I told him, 'Karl, today you've met Christ, and all that you need to do now is to follow. Do you understand?'"

"At first he seemed confused. So, I told him that sometimes Les liked using riddles to make a point. I asked him, 'Did he ever quiz you with riddles?'"

"He told me 'yes,' that Les kept telling him there was only one thing that mattered."

"When Karl told me this," I said, "do you remember what Les kept asking you when you were holding onto him behind the other boat that last day?' When he told me that he did remember, I asked him if he now understood what Les had been trying to tell him."

Suddenly, Louisa's eyes began to sparkle. "Wade, when he nodded that he did, it was the first time I had seen Karl smile in a long time. You remember how shaken and upset he was at the funeral."

Wiping the tears from her eyes, Louisa finally put the tissue she had been holding back into her pocket. Sighing deeply, she said, "Trey called me up a couple of days ago. She said she, Karl, and their kids all went down to Keaton Beach the past weekend to clean the place up, and they all had a ball. She also told me that Karl and another doctor were making plans to open a clinic to help care for some of Tallahassee's poor and homeless people."

Wade shook his head in disbelief.

Louisa beamed. "Simply amazing, isn't it?"

Astounded by this sudden turn of events, Wade replied, "Yes, it certainly is."

Growing quiet, he gazed back at Louisa puzzled. *How could she have known of such a conversation between Les and Karl behind that boat on that last day when he didn't even know about it himself?* Curiously, he watched as she reached into the pocket of her bathrobe and pulled out a piece of paper. With a warm look, she gave it to Wade to read.

"This is something that I copied from Les' last sermon. The one he was writing down at Keaton. I gave a copy of it to Karl."

As Wade unfolded the paper, it read: *The debt owed life is suffering. One can internalize it into self-pity or externalize it into inspiration. The benefit of the latter is significant.*

"Wow. Could Les have written anything more perfect for Karl than that?"

Louisa grinned. "I don't think so. And here's another one."

"Did you give Karl two of these?"

"No. I see this one pertaining more to you."

Wade stared at Louisa curiously as he took the second note from her hand. Unlike Karl, he had already come to grips with the death of his best friend. So, what had Les written that she thought was so compelling for him to read? Wade unfolded the paper and silently read what Les had written.

Some say to follow one's passion is to follow one's talents. A person should certainly pursue his God-given talents. But to follow one's true passion, and it's different for everyone, must be done through faith. Because this gift from God is unknown to us and is constantly unfolding.

Wade peered back at Louisa perplexed. "I'm not exactly sure what this might mean, but I'll keep it with me always—and study it."

Louisa gave Wade a warm smile. To their surprise, they heard a car door slam right in front of her house. Wade had purposefully parked his car further down the road so his presence would look less obvious to someone passing by.

"Who do you think that is?" Wade asked Louisa as she rose to see.

"I don't know," she called back as she headed to the front door. "Mike's not supposed to get back until around lunchtime."

Opening the door, she found her son standing there on the front porch stoop. As she looked toward the street, she saw a car with Jason and Jane waving at her, Jason a little half-heartedly.

Mike spoke up, "Jason got sick, and he's got to go to the doctor. His mama said to tell you about being sorry or something …"

"It's okay, Mike," Louisa spoke lovingly to her son as she waved back at their departing friends. "What was the matter with him?"

"His mama said he got a fever, and he just started throwing up everywhere and all."

"Well, I'm sorry your friend doesn't feel good."

"Me too, Mom. We had a bunch of neat things we were gonna do."

Louisa led Mike into the kitchen by his hand as he talked. He was glad to see Wade.

"Hey, Mr. Wade, watcha doing?" the little boy asked.

"Eating my breakfast. Have you eaten yours today?"

"Yes, sir. Jason's mama fixed oatmeal with raisins in it. And it was good!"

Solemnly, Louisa interjected, "Seems like Jason got sick last night and his mom is carrying him to see the doctor this morning."

Wade gave Mike a consoling look, "I'm sorry, Mike. I bet y'all had a lot of fun stuff planned for today, huh?"

"Yeah, Mr. Wade, we were gonna get up early this morning and go arrowhead hunting before church."

Wade grinned at Louisa, then called to Mike, "Wow. Arrowhead hunting. Man, I'm so sorry your friend got sick and y'all didn't get to do that. Maybe y'all can hunt for arrowheads on another day?"

Mike shrugged, "I don't think so, Mr. Wade. I don't think I'll get to go out there again."

Wade looked at Louisa perplexed, then back at the boy.

"Why not, Mike?" In the back of his mind, Wade was wondering if Mike had done something to make his friend's parents mad.

"Because me and mom are moving over there to Googanda. Isn't that right, Mom?"

"It's Uganda, Mike. It doesn't start with a G. Remember, it's like me and YOU. Uganda."

"Hey! That's a neat trick, Mom. YOU ganda!"

Wade looked at Louisa incredulously. "Y'all are kidding me, right?"

Glancing at Wade, embarrassed because she hadn't told him this yet, Louisa declared, "No. It's true, Wade. We're leaving Thursday, supposedly to a mission in Masaka which is about seventy or so miles south of Kampala, Uganda's capital."

With this sudden blast of news, Wade was stunned into silence. Stammering, he asked, "Thursday? As in, this Thursday?"

Louisa studied Wade's face carefully before answering. When she finally spoke, there was no smile parting her lips. "Yes, Wade. This Thursday."

"What? Why so soon?"

Louisa's look became even more earnest. "There was a nun we met down on the Amazon who helped Les and me out when we really needed it. She's now in Uganda, and says that because of all the turmoil in the country, there's a civil war going on. They just can't seem to keep enough missionaries over there. When she found out about Les' death, she asked for my help."

Rubbing his chin deep in thought concerning all of the events leading up to this moment, and especially after last night, he asked, "When did you find out about this, Louisa?"

"A couple of weeks ago."

Wade sighed, "I can't believe you're doing this. You know if you go I'll probably never get to see you again. Do you realize that?"

As Louisa peered deep into his eyes, hers grew sad and misty. "Wade, I wasn't expecting a pair of little ears to be here when we talked about all of this." She knelt beside her son and asked, "Hey, Mike. Can I get you to go play in your room for a little while so I can talk to Mr. Wade alone?"

Puzzled by this request, the little boy responded, "Is everything okay, Mom?"

"Sure, hon', everything's fine."

"Well, okay then. Can I play on dad's typewriter?"

"Yes. Do you know where the paper is?"

"Yes, ma'am."

In the blink of an eye, the small tyke disappeared into his room. Louisa asked Wade to follow her to the front of her house. Soon, they were seated next to each other on the sofa where Wade had slept only two nights before.

Distressed, Wade was the first to speak. "So, this is what you were up to with the museum curator and with me helping you go through Les' things? That's what all that was about?"

Silently and in pain, Louisa nodded then acknowledged, "I needed you down here with me."

For a long moment they sat there until Louisa finally whispered, "Wade, I don't know where you and Angie are in your relationship."

When Wade heard this, he thought of his lovely ex who had followed him all the way back home and who he knew was patiently awaiting his return. He knew that unlike their first go around, this time she was truly in love with him.

Staring into Louisa's tear-filled eyes, all the memories of this dark-haired beauty, his loving friend and confidant, were starting to overwhelm him. Her warm look, her sparkling blue eyes, the way he felt when he touched and held her, the goodness and virtue that poured out from her as if she were some spectrum of glowing light—he had never experienced this kind of intimacy with anyone, not as he had with her, not with his parents, his sister, or Angie and not even with his most cherished friend Les. Confused, he tried to speak, "Louisa, to be honest, I don't really know where I stand with her when I'm with you. You are and always have been . . ." Wade couldn't say the words.

"The love of your life?" Louisa volunteered with a teary grin.

Wade nodded as his eyes too grew misty.

"And you, Wade, have been mine as well." Louisa again smiled as she gazed back into his warm brown eyes. Continuing, she said, "Over these last weeks and months since Les' death, with all the help you've been giving me, you've been on my mind and in my heart. You and Mike and no one else. I knew it would be you, Wade, when I first met you with Les back in college. I knew it was always going to be you."

Wade was astonished to hear her confession. It was troubling to him as if her love and affection for Les had suddenly evaporated.

"What about Les?" Wade asked as he sought the truth.

"Les, too, was the love of my life. He will be in my heart forever. I love him no less because I love you, Wade. And I love you with all of my heart and all of my soul." Placing her soft hands on each of his cheeks, Louisa caressed Wade pulling him toward her. She kissed him. Wade returned her kiss as he wrapped his strong arms around her.

"You can't leave me, Louisa," Wade muttered between kisses.

"I won't have to if you follow me." Wade stopped kissing her and pulled back as he thought about what she had just said.

"You mean—leave everything that I've got and follow you and Mike to Uganda?"

"Yes, that's what I'd like you to do," she said smiling as she gave him another tender kiss.

"You mean, like, marry you, Louisa?"

"We could and probably should do that," she glowingly replied.

Troubled, Wade sat staring into her enchanting eyes.

"Does that frighten you—marrying me, Wade?"

"No, Louisa. That doesn't frighten me at all. It's just that this is all happening so fast." Wade paused. "I just need more time to think about it. This all is just too overwhelming."

"Is it losing me that you're worried about or losing all that you have?"

"I need to think, Louisa. You've got to give me time to think."

"Wade, there is no time. You have to decide."

"Let me go home and sleep on it, Louisa."

"Wade, the reality is that I may not be here when you get back. My phone line goes out tomorrow. We may even have to leave before Thursday. They said be ready on a moment's notice. When they get the plane tickets lined up, we're gone. Do you understand what I'm telling you?"

"I'll come and find you, Louisa. I promise."

Louisa's eyes brimmed with tears. "I don't think so, Wade," she said, shaking her head. "I don't think you'll be able to."

In a sorrowful voice, she asked, "Wade, we've been together for so long. Do you not know who I am?" Through a window, a glistening shaft of sunlight beamed down illuminating the stunning young woman.

Hearing her say this, Wade stared back at Louisa confused. Noticing a noise coming from the back of the house, he heard Mike skipping down the hallway. When the boy entered the living room and saw his mother crying, he became afraid. Running into her arms, he called out, "Are you okay, Mama? Are you okay?"

Wade, whose eyes had also been watery, observed Les' little son.

"Are you crying too, Mr. Wade?"

"Oh, just a little bit, Mike, but everything's all right. Just a little sad that y'all will be leaving me."

"Oh," Mike said as if that was all this was about.

Wade continued as he tried sounding upbeat, "So, what are you up to now, hot shot?"

"Oh, I was just gonna ask Mom if I could go feed the squirrels."

Wade thought about that for a moment. "How do you do that?"

"Well, Dad got this nut cracker thing."

Louisa, wiping her tears, chimed in, "For pecans."

"And you stick the nut down in there and push down on the handle deal and it cracks open the pecan for ya'." Mike grinned.

"That's all you gotta do?" Wade asked trying to sound intrigued.

"No, not really. When the shell cracks you have to take it out of the cracker thing and peel the nut on out where the squirrels can eat it."

"Oh, I see. So they won't eat the nuts if they're in the shells."

"Oh no, Mr. Wade. It's just that they won't come down the tree. You know, if they don't see the nut a shining."

"Oh … so, I guess these squirrels walk right up to you, huh?"

Mike laughed. "Heck no, Mr. Wade. My dad called 'em, what did he call 'em, Mom?"

Cheerily, Louisa said, "Skittish. You know, kind of scared to get too close because they're afraid of being hurt."

"Yeah, that's right, Mom—skittersh. Dad said there were lots of people skittersh."

Louisa smiled at Mike's pronunciation of the word.

"All right. Put on your coat and toboggan before you go outside."

"Okay, Mom." Mike dashed into his room to find his coat and hat.

Wade and Louisa stood up.

Downhearted, Wade mused, "I guess I better start gathering up my things too, eh?"

Tears streamed down Louisa's face once more.

Methodically, as if on a mission, Wade went to the back of the house and began folding his clothes and collecting his items. Having them all placed neatly in his carrying case, he took his hang up clothes from Mike's closet and put everything in the foyer by the front door.

Louisa appeared from her room. Wearing a pullover black sweater and jeans, she followed him. Seeing her standing there as he turned around, Wade almost fainted at the thought of having to leave her.

Reaching up, Louisa wrapped her arms tightly around him, "Where do you think you're going? You can't leave me like this, Wade. You just can't. We need each other, and you know we do."

Wade was speechless. He didn't want to go. He wanted to stay and be with her, but to do so, he would have to leave behind almost everything he had ever known. How could he leave Angie after she'd become such a loving person? How could he leave work where he was finally successful, and content, and making a good living? How could he give it all up? Everything he had worked so hard for—How could he leave all of that to follow Louisa to a strange unknown place a world away? As much as he hated to and didn't want to, he felt he had to leave her. He would have to reason and make sense of it all before he could change his mind.

Firmly, she held him as he stood shaken.

"Louisa, I just need some time to think all of this through."

Crying back, Louisa told him, "This has nothing to do with thinking, Wade, and there is no time. Please come with me! Please!"

In frustration and pain, Wade gently broke her grip on him. Slinging the strap of the duffel bag over his shoulder and picking up his hanging clothes, he opened the front door.

On his first step outside, he thought that the confusion in his mind would ease, but he was wrong. With each step, it only grew worse.

Glancing to his left as he walked down the sidewalk, he saw little Mike cracking pecans on a redwood picnic table and flipping the nuts out toward a small dogwood tree. Wade watched a squirrel on the ground next to the tree scurry up it. Sitting on the dogwood's lowest limb with its tail curled upward, it adjusted the pecan in its jaw. Hopping up this small sapling, it quickly jumped over to the coarse bark of a large adjacent pine. From there it ran up the trunk of this wide tree for several yards and sprang onto a telephone line that crossed the road.

Wade felt a strong breeze blow as he turned off Louisa's walkway heading down the city's sidewalk toward his car. The squirrel he was watching had quietly crept its way onto the telephone line and paused above Wade.

When Wade saw the squirrel stop, he did likewise. Vaguely remembering the rock alley squirrel hunts of his youth, he pondered what the squirrel was thinking as it stood there frozen watching him intently with only its right eye. Wade did not move a muscle for a long second as he looked on. The squirrel turned its head entirely toward him so it could see Wade with both eyes. It was almost as if the squirrel was showing Wade that it had no fear.

Just as soon as the squirrel did this, Wade watched the creature continue its journey. Ambling down the wire, it finally crossed the road and disappeared into a vast thicket of bamboo, ferns, and pines.

With the wind blowing all about, Wade turned completely around to face the haunting portrait of the beautiful young woman as she stood there. Forlorn, she stared back at him from her doorway.

Acknowledgements

Songs

AS TIME GOES BY (from "Casablanca")
Words and Music by HERMAN Hupfeld
© 1931 (Renewed) WB MUSIC CORP.
All Rights Reserved.
Reprinted by Permission of Alfred Music Publishing

BE YOUNG, BE FOOLISH, BE HAPPY
Words and Music by J. Cobb and Ray Whitley
Copyright © 1968 Sony/ATV Music Publishing LLC
Copyright Renewed
All Rights Administered by Sony/ATV Music Publishing LLC, 424 Church Street, Suite 1200, Nashville, TN 37219 International Copyright Secured. All Rights Reserved
Reprinted by Permission of Hal Leonard Corporation

BORN TO BE WILD
Words and Music by Mars Bonfire
Copyright © 1968 UNIVERSAL MUSIC PUBLILSHING, A Division of UNIVERSAL MUSIC CANADA, INC.
Copyright Renewed
All Rights in the United States Controlled and Administered by UNIVERSAL MUSIC CORP.
All Rights Reserved. Used by Permission
Reprinted by Permission of Hal Leonard Corporation

MOON RIVER
From the Paramount Picture BREAKFAST AT TIFFANY'S
Words by Johnny Mercer
Music by Henry Mancini
Copyright © 1961 Sony/ATV Music Publishing LLC
Copyright Renewed
All Rights Administered by Sony/ATV Music Publishing LLC, 424 Church Street, Suite 1200, Nashville, TN 37219
International Copyright Secured All Rights Reserved
Reprinted by Permission of Hal Leonard Corporation

OH GIRL
Words and Music by EUGENE RECORD

TOUCH ME IN THE MORNING
Words and Music by Ronald Miller and Michael Masser

Cited Works

Chapter 20

1. Bonhoeffer, Dietrich. "Costly Grace." *The Cost of Discipleship.* New York: Touchstone, 1995. pp. 45

2. Bonhoeffer, Dietrich. "Holding Out Until the Overthrow. April to July 1944." *Letters and Papers From Prison.* New York: Touchstone, 1997. pp. 361. "Man is summoned to share in God's sufferings at the hands of a godless world."

Chapter 27

1. Bonhoeffer, Dietrich. "Holding Out until the Overthrow. April to July 1944." *Letters and Papers From Prison.* New York: Touchstone, 1997. pp. 337. Redemption myths arise from human boundary-experiences, but Christ takes hold of a man at the centre of his life.

About the Author

Harry Bowen is a registered Pharmacist with a BBA from the University of Georgia. He's had much experience in traveling wilderness areas where he's backpacked, canoed, kayaked and camped for extended periods of time. Along with enjoying scuba diving, and swimming, Harry has taken many offshore fishing trips in the Caribbean, the Atlantic Ocean and Gulf of Mexico. One thing the author has learned through living and taking part in these endeavors is we never know what life has in store for us.